THE YEAR'S BEST SCIENCE FICTION & FANTASY

2019 EDITION

OTHER BOOKS BY

RICH HORTON

Fantasy: The Best of the Year, 2006 Edition

Fantasy: The Best of the Year, 2007 Edition

Fantasy: The Best of the Year, 2008 Edition

Robots: The Recent A.I. (with Sean Wallace)

Science Fiction: The Best of the Year, 2006 Edition

Science Fiction: The Best of the Year, 2007 Edition

Science Fiction: The Best of the Year, 2008 Edition

Space Opera

Unplugged: The Web's Best Sci-Fi & Fantasy: 2008 Download

The Year's Best Science Fiction & Fantasy, 2009 Edition

The Year's Best Science Fiction & Fantasy, 2010 Edition

The Year's Best Science Fiction & Fantasy, 2011 Edition

The Year's Best Science Fiction & Fantasy, 2012 Edition

The Year's Best Science Fiction & Fantasy, 2013 Edition

The Year's Best Science Fiction & Fantasy, 2014 Edition

The Year's Best Science Fiction & Fantasy, 2015 Edition

The Year's Best Science Fiction & Fantasy, 2016 Edition

The Year's Best Science Fiction & Fantasy, 2017 Edition

The Year's Best Science Fiction & Fantasy, 2018 Edition

War & Space: Recent Combat (with Sean Wallace)

THE YEAR'S BEST SCIENCE FICTION & FANTASY

2019 EDITION

EDITED BY

RICH HORTON

PRIME BOOKS

THE YEAR'S BEST SCIENCE FICTION & FANTASY, 2019 EDITION

Cover art by Tithi Luadthong.
Cover design by Stephen H. Segal & Sherin Nicole.

Prime Books
www.prime-books.com

ISBN: 978-1-60701-531-4

To my son-in-law Joshua Whitman
and my daughter-in-law Patricia Clarey Horton.

CONTENTS

CONTENTS

WHERE TO FIND THE GREAT SF & FANTASY SHORT FICTION?

RICH HORTON

The State of the Art

There are a lot of Best of the Year volumes in our field, and frankly I recommend them all. One of the features of SF in 2018 is how much of it there is. There's enough short fiction that the Hugo shortlist can very nearly ignore men, and still be mostly full of strong stories. (There are a couple of duds, but so it always was.) There's enough that both the Hugo and Nebula shortlists can completely ignore the traditional print SF magazines (*F&SF, Asimov's, Analog*, and *Interzone*, let's say), and still be mostly full of strong stories. How then to resolve that issue? Read as many of the Best of the Year volumes as you can, I say! (And, hey, why not subscribe to one of the print magazines, if that's possible? And try some original anthologies as well.)

The main distinction, of course, for each of these books is the editor's individual tastes. (Or so Hannibal Lecter tells us . . .) We all read a lot of short SF, and have for a long time. And when I see the table of content pages of the other books they are stuffed with stories I almost took for this book (and a couple of overlaps)—so I know that my fellow editors have good taste! Thus part of the equation is: which editor's taste aligns with yours? But, I'd suggest, if you can, read more—because reading stuff that you didn't know you'd like is one of the truest joys of reading.

If I think my book is the best—and I do!—it's for the obvious reason that my personal taste aligns pretty closely with the editor's! But that said, I am abashed year after year to realize that Jonathan or Ellen or Neil or one of the other editors, (or, sigh, Gardner!), has chosen a gem or two I really should have taken myself.

But to return to the wealth of good fiction in the field, let's take a closer look at the venues in which to find it. I've already expressed a wish for more attention to be paid to the print magazines, so I'll start there. The oldest magazines in the field are *Weird Tales*, first published in 1923, and *Amazing Stories*, first published in 1926. Both have undergone numerous deaths and resurrections over the decades. *Weird Tales*' last issue appeared in 2014, but rumors of another resurrection have surfaced. More happily, *Amazing Stories* was revived by publisher Steve Davidson in 2018, and what I've seen so far is promising—and I very nearly took Kameron Hurley's "Sister Solveig and Mr. Denial" for this volume.

Then there is *Analog*, known for an emphasis on "hard SF," founded in 1930 as *Astounding Stories*, and published continuously since that time. Trevor Quachri is the current editor, and I've liked his work with the magazine—this year we feature two stories from them, each from one of the best of their regular contributors: Alec Nevala-Lee's "The Spires" and Adam-Troy Castro's "The Unnecessary Parts of the Story." (And no, despite the fact that a previous *Analog* story in these pages was by Alvaro Zinos-Amaro, it's not true that a first name starting with A and a hyphenation are requirements for *Analog* publication.) *The Magazine of Fantasy and Science Fiction*, which dates to 1949, has, as its title implies long featured a roughly 50/50 split between those two modes. The editor is C. C. Finlay, and this year we have chosen a remarkable bit of cold-blooded SF horror, "The Donner Party" by Dale Bailey.

More recent but still venerable magazines include *Asimov's Science Fiction* (founded 1976, now edited by Sheila Williams) and the leading UK magazine, *Interzone* (founded 1982, now edited by Andy Cox.) *Asimov's* (like *Analog* and *F&SF*) remains hospitable to novellas, and this year we taken from there a very exciting and very long story, "Bubble and Squeak" by David Gerrold & Ctein; as well as "The Gift" by Julia Nováková. From *Interzone* I came very close to choosing Ryan Row's "Superbright" and Samantha Murray's "Singles' Day."

It would be fair to say that most of the magazines in the field founded more recently are online, but there are exceptions. Perhaps most remarkable of these is *Lady Churchill's Rosebud Wristlet*, a modestly produced—but always attractive—saddle-stapled magazine from Gavin Grant and Kelly Link's wonderful Small Beer Press. Thirty-nine issues have appeared since 1996, and the fiction is always lively and original, as evidenced by the two very different stories we chose for this volume: "Lime and the One Human" by S. Woodson, and "Dayenu" by James Sallis. In this context I ought also to mention *Galaxy's Edge*, which has been producing regular bimonthly issues since 2013. From 2018, I thought Gregory Benford's "A Waltz in Eternity" particularly strong—another story that came within a whisker of appearing here.

Not all the magazines I canvas for stories are SF magazines—you can find wonderful fantastical stories in the traditional "little" magazines, and in wide circulation places like *The New Yorker*. From there, I'd have liked to use Karen Russell's "Orange World." From the *Paris Review*, I'm thrilled to have one of the late great Ursula K. Le Guin's last stories, "Firelight," and from the *Stonecoast Review* I'm likewise delighted to be able to reprint Rick Wilber's "Today is Today." I also saw super stuff from Jess Row in *Granta*, from Gregory Norman Bossert and many others in *Conjunctions*, and strong work from Josh Pearce and M. C. Williams in a slim magazine I'm not sure how to characterize, *Bourbon Penn*.

Original anthologies have been an important source of new short fiction since at least Frederik Pohl's **Star Science Fiction** in the 1950s, and that remains true today. Perhaps the single best anthologist now—along with Ellen Datlow—is Jonathan Strahan, and in 2018 he concluded a brilliant series of anthologies, the Infinity Series, with **Infinity's End**, which gave me two stories in the book, by Justina Robson and Kelly Robson (no relation, and the stories are "Foxy and Tiggs" and "Intervention") and I could have taken two or three more easily. It's more common these days to see themed anthologies, and this year I took stories from **Robots Vs. Fairies** (Lavie Tidhar's "The Buried Giant") and **Aurum**, an anniversary anthology of sorts from the Australian publisher Ticonderoga ("Beautiful" by Judith Marillier). Other anthologies of particular note include the latest in the ongoing series of near future-oriented stories from MIT Technology Review's publishing arm, **Twelve Tomorrows**, as well as **Shades Within Us, Mothers of Invention, Speculative Japan 4** (a selection of fantastical work from Japan), and what might be, alas, Gardner Dozois' last anthology, **The Book of Magic**.

And then there are the novellas—one of the really enjoyable fairly recent trends is the availability of novellas as standalone slim books. I've long felt that the novella is a particularly good length for SF, but a hard one to publish in magazines, where they take up so much room. So the recent bloom is welcome. Mind you, most of these books aren't available for reprint, and many are too long for a book like this. But they deserve your attention. Tor.com Publishing is noted as a leader in this area, and they didn't disappoint this year with books like Ian McDonald's **Time Was** and Kelly Robson's **Gods, Monsters, and the Lucky Peach**. But there are many other houses publishing such books: this year I was impressed by **The Freeze-Frame Revolution**, by Peter Watts, from Tachyon; **The Adventure of the Dux Bellorum**, by Cynthia Ward, from Aqueduct; and **The Tea Master and the Detective**, by Aliette de Bodard, from Subterranean.

Now it would be disingenuous of me to fail to mention the numerous online sources of short SF. After all, while I do feel that print sources are shortchanged in award nominations (for simple to understand reasons), the online world is full of really outstanding work. Full disclosure—I'm the reprint editor for *Lightspeed*, and I think we publish great stuff. So too do our fellow recent winners of the Best Semiprozine Hugo, *Clarkesworld* and *Uncanny*. And of course *Tor.com* is absolutely an outstanding site. Beyond those, I'd like to highlight the other online sites I've taken stories from this year (and these by no means exhaust the great places to find short SF online): *Beneath Ceaseless Skies* (which focusses on "literary adventure fantasy"), *Giganotosaurus* (which tends to publish longer pieces), *Apex* (which had its origin as a print magazine with a tropism towards horror, but which publishes a very wide range these days); and *Kaleidotrope*, a magazine I've loved since its early days as a saddle-stitched print magazine. Another impressive recent online magazine is *Fireside Magazine*, which began in 2012. Unfortunately I don't have space to list everything from those places in this introduction (see the acknowledgements page, though).

By the way, when I was just starting to read adult short SF, I checked the acknowledgements pages for the anthologies I read, and that's where I learned about *Analog* and *Galaxy* and *F&SF* and *Fantastic* and *New Worlds*, etc. And it was a delight to find some of them on my local newsstand. Nowadays it's pretty easy to find a lot of them on the internet—and one certainly should. But I'll suggest again that looking in bookstores for anthologies and magazines, or online for how to subscribe to them, or in the local library, is also rewarding—and, I do think, important to the health of the science fiction field—indeed, to the entire literary world.

A WITCH'S GUIDE TO ESCAPE: A PRACTICAL COMPENDIUM OF PORTAL FANTASIES

ALIX E. HARROW

You'd think it would make us happy when a kid checks out the same book a zillion times in a row, but actually it just keeps us up at night.

The Runaway Prince is one of those low-budget young adult fantasies from the mid-nineties, before J.K. Rowling arrived to tell everyone that magic was cool, printed on brittle yellow paper. It's about a lonely boy who runs away and discovers a Magical Portal into another world where he has Medieval Adventures, but honestly there are so many typos most people give up before he even finds the portal.

Not this kid, though. He pulled it off the shelf and sat cross legged in the juvenile fiction section with his grimy red backpack clutched to his chest. He didn't move for hours. Other patrons were forced to double-back in the aisle, shooting suspicious, you-don't-belong-here looks behind them as if wondering what a skinny black teenager was *really* up to while pretending to read a fantasy book. He ignored them.

The books above him rustled and quivered; that kind of attention flatters them.

He took *The Runaway Prince* home and renewed it twice online, at which point a gray pop-up box that looks like an emissary from 1995 tells you, "the renewal limit for this item has been reached." You can almost feel the disapproving eyes of a librarian glaring at you through the screen.

(There have only ever been two kinds of librarians in the history of the world: the prudish, bitter ones with lipstick running into the cracks around their lips who believe the books are their personal property and patrons are dangerous delinquents come to steal them; and witches).

Our late fee is twenty-five cents per day or a can of non-perishable food during the summer food drive. By the time the boy finally slid *The Runaway*

Prince into the return slot, he owed $4.75. I didn't have to swipe his card to know; any good librarian (of the second kind) ought to be able to tell you the exact dollar amount of a patron's bill just by the angle of their shoulders.

"What'd you think?" I used my this-is-a-secret-between-us-pals voice, which works on teenagers about sixteen percent of the time.

He shrugged. It has a lower success rate with black teenagers, because this is the rural South and they aren't stupid enough to trust thirty-something white ladies no matter how many tattoos we have.

"Didn't finish it, huh?" I knew he'd finished it at least four times by the warm, well-oiled feel of the pages.

"Yeah, I did." His eyes flicked up. They were smoke-colored and long-lashed, with an achy, faraway expression, as if he knew there was something gleaming and forbidden just beneath the dull surfaces of things that he could never quite touch. They were the kinds of eyes that had belonged to sorcerers or soothsayers, in different times. "The ending sucked."

In the end, the Runaway Prince leaves Medieval Adventureland and closes the portal behind him before returning home to his family. It was supposed to be a happy ending.

Which kind of tells you all you need to know about this kid's life, doesn't it?

He left without checking anything else out.

GARRISON, ALLEN B—THE TAVALARRIAN CHRONICLES
—v. I-XVI—F GAR 1976
LE GUIN, URSULA K—A WIZARD OF EARTHSEA
—J FIC LEG 1968

He returned four days later, sloping past a bright blue display titled THIS SUMMER, DIVE INTO READING! (who knows where they were supposed to swim; Ulysses County's lone public pool had been filled with cement in the sixties rather than desegregate).

Because I am a librarian of the second sort, I almost always know what kind of book a person wants. It's like a very particular smell rising off them which is instantly recognizable as *Murder mystery* or *Political biography* or *Something kind of trashy but ultimately life-affirming, preferably with lesbians.*

I do my best to give people the books they need most. In grad school, they called it "ensuring readers have access to texts/materials that are engaging and emotionally rewarding," and in my other kind of schooling, they called it "divining the unfilled spaces in their souls and filling them with stories and starshine," but it comes to the same thing.

I don't bother with the people who have call numbers scribbled on their palms and titles rattling around in their skulls like bingo cards. They don't need me. And you really can't do anything for the people who only read Award-Winning Literature, who wear elbow patches and equate the popularity of *Twilight* with the death of the American intellect; their hearts are too closed-up for the new or secret or undiscovered.

So, it's only a certain kind of patron I pay attention to. The kind that let their eyes feather across the titles like trailing fingertips, heads cocked, with book-hunger rising off them like heatwaves from July pavement. The books bask in it, of course, even the really hopeless cases that haven't been checked out since 1958 (there aren't many of these; me and Agnes take turns carting home outdated astronomy textbooks that still think Pluto is a planet and cookbooks that call for lard, just to keep their spirits up). I choose one or two books and let their spines gleam and glimmer in the twilit stacks. People reach towards them without quite knowing why.

The boy with the red backpack wasn't an experienced aisle-wanderer. He prowled, moving too quickly to read the titles, hands hanging empty and uncertain at his sides. The sewing and pattern books (646.2) noted that his jeans were unlaundered and too small, and the neck of his t-shirt was stained grayish-yellow. The cookbooks (641.5) diagnosed a diet of frozen waffles and gas-station pizza. They *tssked* to themselves.

I sat at the circulation desk, running returns beneath the blinky red scanner light, and breathed him in. I was expecting something like *generic Arthurian retelling* or maybe *teen romance with sword-fighting*, but instead I found a howling, clamoring mess of need.

He smelled of a thousand secret worlds, of rabbit-holes and hidden doorways and platforms nine-and-three-quarters, of Wonderland and Oz and Narnia, of anyplace-but-here. He smelled of *yearning*.

God save me from the yearners. The insatiable, the inconsolable, the ones who chafe and claw against the edges of the world. No book can save them.

(That's a lie. There are Books potent enough to save any mortal soul: books of witchery, augury, alchemy; books with wand-wood in their spines and moon-dust on their pages; books older than stones and wily as dragons. We give people the books they need most, except when we don't.)

I sent him a '70s sword-and-sorcery series because it was total junk food and he needed fattening up, and because I hoped sixteen volumes might act as a sort of ballast and keep his keening soul from rising away into the ether. I let Le Guin shimmer at him, too, because he reminded me a bit of Ged (feral; full of longing).

I ignored *The Lion, the Witch, and the Wardrobe*, jostling importantly on its shelf; this was a kid who wanted to go through the wardrobe and never, ever come back.

• • •

GRAYSON, DR BERNARD—WHEN NOTHING MATTERS ANYMORE: A SURVIVAL GUIDE FOR DEPRESSED TEENS
—616.84 GRA 2002

Once you make it past book four of the *Tavalarrian Chronicles*, you're committed at least through book fourteen when the true Sword of Tavalar is revealed and the young farm-boy ascends to his rightful throne. The boy with the red backpack showed up every week or so all summer for the next installment.

I snuck in a few others (all pretty old, all pretty white; our branch director is one of those pinch-lipped Baptists who thinks fantasy books teach kids about Devil worship, so roughly 90% of my collection requests are mysteriously denied): *A Wrinkle in Time* came back with the furtive, jammed-in-a-backpack scent that meant he liked it but thought it was too young for him; *Watership Down* was offended because he never got past the first ten pages, but I guess footnotes about rabbit-math aren't for everyone; and *The Golden Compass* had the flashlight-smell of 3:00 a.m. on its final chapter and was unbearably smug about it. I'd just gotten an inter-library-loaned copy of *Akata Witch*—when he stopped coming.

Our display (GET READ-Y FOR SCHOOL!) was filled with SAT prep kits and over-sized yellow *For Dummies* books. Agnes had cut out blobby construction-paper leaves and taped them to the front doors. Lots of kids stop hanging around the library when school starts up, with all its clubs and teams.

I worried anyway. I could feel the Book I hadn't given him like a wrong note or a missing tooth, a magnetic absence. Just when I was seriously considering calling Ulysses County High School with a made-up story about an un-returned CD, he came back.

For the first time, there was someone else with him: A squat white woman with a plastic name-tag and the kind of squarish perm you can only get in Southern beauty salons with faded glamor-shots in the windows. The boy trailed behind her looking thin and pressed, like a flower crushed between dictionary pages. I wondered how badly you had to fuck up to get assigned a school counselor after hours, until I read her name-tag: Department of Community-Based Services, Division of Protection and Permanency, Child Caseworker (II).

Oh. A foster kid.

The woman marched him through the nonfiction stacks (the travel guides sighed as she passed, muttering about overwork and recommending vacations to sunny, faraway beaches) and stopped in the 616s. "Here, why don't we have a look at these?"

Predictable, sullen silence from the boy.

A person who works with foster kids sixty hours a week is unfazed by sullenness. She slid titles off the shelf and stacked them in the boy's arms. "We talked about this, remember? We decided you might like to read something practical, something helpful?"

Dealing with Depression (616.81 WHI 1998). *Beating the Blues: Five Steps to Feeling Normal Again!* (616.822 TRE 2011). *Chicken Soup for the Depressed Soul* (616.9 CAN). The books greeted him in soothing, syrupy voices.

The boy stayed silent. "Look. I know you'd rather read about dragons and, uh, elves," oh, Tolkien, you have so much to account for, "but sometimes we've got to face our problems head-on, rather than running away from them."

What *bullshit*. I was in the back room running scratched DVDs through the disc repair machine, so the only person to hear me swear was Agnes. She gave me her patented over-the-glasses shame-on-you look which, when properly deployed, can reduce noisy patrons to piles of ash or pillars of salt (Agnes is a librarian of the second kind, too).

But seriously. Anyone could see that kid needed to run and keep running until he shed his own skin, until he clawed out of the choking darkness and unfurled his wings, precious and prisming in the light of some other world.

His caseworker was one of those people who say the word "escapism" as if it's a moral failing, a regrettable hobby, a mental-health diagnosis. As if escape is not, in itself, one of the highest order of magics they'll ever see in their miserable mortal lives, right up there with true love and prophetic dreams and fireflies blinking in synchrony on a June evening.

The boy and his keeper were winding back through the aisles toward the front desk. The boy's shoulders were curled inward, as if he chafed against invisible walls on either side.

As he passed the juvenile fiction section, a cheap paperback flung itself off the return cart and thudded into his kneecap. He picked it up and rubbed his thumb softly over the title. *The Runaway Prince* purred at him.

He smiled. I thanked the library cart, silently.

There was a long, familiar sigh behind me. I turned to see Agnes watching me from the circulation desk, aquamarine nails tapping the cover of a Grisham novel, eyes crimped with pity. *Oh honey, not another one*, they said.

I turned back to my stack of DVDs, unsmiling, thinking things like *what do you know about it* and *this one is different* and *oh shit.*

DUMAS, ALEXANDRE—THE COUNT OF MONTE CRISTO
—F DUM 1974

• • •

The boy returned at ten-thirty on a Tuesday morning. It's official library policy to report truants to the high school, because the school board felt we were becoming "a haven for unsupervised and illicit teenage activity." I happen to think that's exactly what libraries should aspire to be, and suggested we get it engraved on a plaque for the front door, but then I was asked to be serious or leave the proceedings, and anyway we're supposed to report kids who skip school to play *League of Legends* on our computers or skulk in the graphic novel section.

I watched the boy prowling the shelves—muscles strung wire-tight over his bones, soul writhing and clawing like a caged creature—and did not reach for the phone. Agnes, still wearing her *oh honey* expression, declined to reprimand me.

I sent him home with *The Count of Monte Cristo*, partly because it requires your full attention and a flow chart to keep track of the plot and the kid needed distracting, but mostly because of what Edmund says on the second-to-last page: " . . . all human wisdom is summed up in these two words,—'Wait and hope.' "

But people can't keep waiting and hoping forever.

They fracture, they unravel, they crack open; they do something desperate and stupid and then you see their high school senior photo printed in the *Ulysses Gazette*, grainy and oversized, and you spend the next five years thinking: *if only I'd given her the right book.*

ROWLING, JK—HARRY POTTER AND THE SORCERER'S STONE
—J FIC ROW 1998
ROWLING, JK—HARRY POTTER AND THE CHAMBER OF SECRETS
—J FIC ROW 1999
ROWLING, JK—HARRY POTTER AND THE PRISONER OF AZKABAN
—J FIC ROW 1999

Every librarian has Books she never lends to anyone.

I'm not talking about first editions of *Alice in Wonderland* or Dutch translations of *Winnie-the-Pooh*; I'm talking about Books so powerful and potent, so full of susurrating seduction, that only librarians of the second sort even know they exist.

Each of us has her own system for keeping them hidden. The most venerable libraries (the ones with oak paneling and vaulted ceilings and *Beauty and the Beast*-style ladders) have secret rooms behind fireplaces or bookcases, which you can only enter by tugging on a certain title on the shelf. Sainte-Geneviève in Paris is supposed to have vast catacombs beneath it guarded by librarians so ancient and desiccated they've become human-shaped books, paper-skinned and ink-blooded. In Timbuktu, I heard they hired wizard-smiths to make great wrought-iron gates that only permit passage to the pure of heart.

In the Maysville branch of the Ulysses County Library system, we have a locked roll-top desk in the Special Collections room with a sign on it that says, "This is an Antique! Please Ask for Assistance."

We only have a dozen or so Books, anyhow, and god knows where they came from or how they ended up here. *A Witch's Guide to Seeking Righteous Vengeance*, with its slender steel pages and arsenic ink. *A Witch's Guide to Falling in Love for the First Time, for Readers at Every Stage of Life!*, which smells like starlight and the summer you were seventeen. *A Witch's Guide to Uncanny Baking* contains over thirty full-color photographs to ensorcell your friends and afflict your adversaries. *A Witch's Guide to Escape: A Practical Compendium of Portal Fantasies* has no words in it at all, but only pages and pages of maps: hand-drawn Middle Earth knock-offs with unpronounceable names; medieval tapestry-maps showing tiny ships sailing off the edge of the world; topographical maps of Machu Picchu; 1970s Rand McNally street maps of Istanbul.

It's my job to keep Books like this out of the hands of desperate high-school kids with red backpacks. Our school-mistresses called it "preserving the hallowed and hidden arts of our foremothers from mundane eyes." Our professors called it "conserving rare/historic texts."

Both of them mean the same thing: We give people the books they need, except when we don't. Except when they need them most.

He racked up $1.50 on *The Count of Monte Cristo* and returned it with saltwater splotches on the final pages. They weren't my-favorite-character-died tears or the-book-is-over tears. They were bitter, acidic, anise-scented: tears of jealousy. He was jealous that the Count and Haydée sailed away from their world and out into the blue unknown. That they escaped.

I panicked and weighed him down with the first three *Harry Potters*, because they don't really get good until Sirius and Lupin show up, and because they're about a neglected, lonely kid who gets a letter from another world and disappears.

GEORGE, JC—THE RUNAWAY PRINCE
—J FIC GEO 1994

Agnes always does the "we will be closing in ten minutes" announcement because something in her voice implies that anybody still in the library in nine minutes and fifty seconds will be harvested for organ donations, and even the most stationary patrons amble towards the exit.

The kid with the red backpack was hovering in the oversize print section (gossipy, aging books, bored since the advent of e-readers with changeable font sizes) when Agnes's voice came through the speakers. He went very still, teetering the way a person does when they're about to do something really dumb, then dove beneath a reading desk and pulled his dark hoodie over his head. The oversize books gave scintillated squeals.

It was my turn to close, so Agnes left right at nine. By 9:15 I was standing at the door with my NPR tote on my shoulder and my keys in my hand. Hesitating.

It is very, extremely, absolutely against the rules to lock up for the night with a patron still inside, especially when that patron is a minor of questionable emotional health. It's big trouble both in the conventional sense (phone calls from panicked guardians, police searches, charges of criminal neglect) and in the other sense (libraries at night are noisier places than they are during the daylight hours).

I'm not a natural rule-follower. I roll through stop signs, I swear in public, I lie on online personality tests so I get the answers I want (Hermione, Arya Stark, Jo March). But I'm a very good librarian of either kind, and good librarians follow the rules. Even when they don't want to.

That's what Agnes told me five years ago, when I first started at Maysville.

This girl had started showing up on Sunday afternoons: ponytailed, cute, but wearing one of those knee-length denim skirts that scream "mandatory virginity pledge." I'd been feeding her a steady diet of subversion (Orwell, Bradbury, Butler), and was about to hit her with *A Handmaid's Tale* when she suddenly lost interest in fiction. She drifted through the stacks, face gone white and empty as a blank page, navy skirt swishing against her knees.

It wasn't until she reached the 618s that I understood. The maternity and childbirth section trilled saccharine congratulations. She touched one finger to the spine of *What to Expect When You're Expecting* (618.2 EIS) with an expression of dawning, swallowing horror, and left without checking anything out.

For the next nine weeks, I sent her stories of bravery and boldness, defying-your-parents stories and empowered-women-resisting-authority stories. I abandoned subtlety entirely and slid Planned Parenthood pamphlets into her book bag, even though the nearest clinic is six hours away and only open twice a week, but found them jammed frantically in the bathroom trash.

But I never gave her what she really needed: *A Witch's Guide to Undoing What Has Been Done: A Guilt-Free Approach to Life's Inevitable Accidents.* A leather-bound tome filled with delicate mechanical drawings of clocks, which smelled of regret and yesterday mornings. I'd left it locked in the roll-top desk, whispering and tick-tocking to itself.

Look, there are good reasons we don't lend out Books like that. Our mistresses used to scare us with stories of mortals run amok: people who used Books to steal or kill or break hearts; who performed miracles and founded religions; who hated us, afterward, and spent a tiresome few centuries burning us at stakes.

If I were caught handing out Books, I'd be renounced, reviled, stripped of my title. They'd burn my library card in the eternal mauve flames of our sisterhood and write my crimes in ash and blood in *The Book of Perfidy*. They'd ban me from every library for eternity, and what's a librarian without her books? What would I be, cut off from the orderly world of words and their readers, from the peaceful Ouroboran cycle of story-telling and story-eating? There were rumors of rogue librarians—madwomen who chose to live outside the library system in the howling chaos of unwritten words and untold stories—but none of us envied them.

The last time I'd seen the ponytailed girl her denim skirt was fastened with a rubber band looped through the buttonhole. She'd smelled of desperation, like someone whose wait-and-hoping had run dry.

Four days later, her picture was in the paper and the article was blurring and un-blurring in my vision (*accidental poisoning, viewing from 2:00-3:30 at Zimmerman & Holmes, direct your donations to Maysville Baptist Ministries*). Agnes had patted my hand and said, "I know, honey, I know. Sometimes there's nothing you can do." It was a kind lie.

I still have the newspaper clipping in my desk drawer, as a memorial or reminder or warning.

The boy with the red backpack was sweating beneath the reading desk. He smelled of desperation, just like she had.

Should I call the Child Protective Services hotline? Make awkward small-talk until his crummy caseworker collected him? *Hey, kid, I was once a lonely teenager in a backwater shithole, too!* Or should I let him run away, even if running away was only hiding in the library overnight?

I teetered, the way you do when you're about to do something really dumb.

The locked thunked into place. I walked across the parking lot breathing the caramel-and-frost smell of October, hoping—almost praying, if witches were into that—that it would be enough.

I opened half an hour early, angling to beat Agnes to the phone and delete the "Have you seen this unaccompanied minor?" voicemails before she could hear them. There was an automated message from somebody trying to sell us a security system, three calls from community members asking when we open because apparently it's physically impossible to Google it, and a volunteer calling in sick.

There were no messages about the boy. Fucking Ulysses County foster system.

He emerged at 9:45, when he could blend in with the growing numbers of other patrons. He looked rumpled and ill-fitting, like a visitor from another planet who hadn't quite figured out human body language. Or like a kid who's spent a night in the stacks, listening to furtive missives from a thousand different worlds and wishing he could disappear into any one of them.

I was so busy trying not to cry and ignoring the Book now calling to the boy from the roll-top desk that I scanned his card and handed him back his book without realizing what it was: *The Runaway Prince*.

MAYSVILLE PUBLIC LIBRARY NOTICE: YOU HAVE (1) OVERDUE ITEMS. PLEASE RETURN YOUR ITEM(S) AS SOON AS POSSIBLE.

Shit.

The overdue notices go out on the fifteenth day an item has been checked out. On the sixteenth day, I pulled up the boy's account and glared at the terse red font (OVERDUE ITEM: J FIC GEO 1994) until the screen began to crackle and smoke faintly and Agnes gave me a *hold-it-together-woman* look.

He hadn't even bothered to renew it.

My sense of *The Runaway Prince* had grown faint and blurred with distance, as if I were looking at it through an unfocused telescope, but it was still a book from my library and thus still in my domain. (All you people who never returned books to their high school libraries, or who bought stolen books off Amazon with call numbers taped to their spines? We see you). It reported only the faintest second-hand scent of the boy: futility, resignation, and a tarry, oozing smell like yearning that had died and begun to fossilize.

He was alive, but probably not for much longer. I don't just mean physical suicide; those of us who can see soulstuff know there are lots of ways to die without anybody noticing. Have you ever seen those stupid TV specials where they rescue animals from some third-rate horror show of a circus in Las Vegas, and when they finally open the cages the lions just sit there, dead-eyed, because they've forgotten what it is to want anything? To desire, to yearn, to be filled with the terrible, golden hunger of being alive?

But there was nothing I could do. Except wait and hope.

Our volunteers were doing the weekly movie showing in Media Room #2, so I was stuck re-shelving. It wasn't until I was actually in the F DAC-FEN aisle, holding our dog-eared copy of *The Count of Monte Cristo* in my hand, that I realized Edmund Dantès was absolutely, one-hundred-percent full of shit.

If Edmund had taken his own advice, he would've sat in his jail cell waiting and hoping for forty years while the Count de Morcerf and Villefort and the rest of them stayed rich and happy. The real moral of *The Count of Monte Cristo* was surely something more like: If you screw someone over, be prepared for a vengeful mastermind to fuck up your life twenty years later. Or maybe it was: If you want justice and goodness to prevail in this world, you have to fight for it tooth and nail. And it will be hard, and costly, and probably illegal. You will have to break the rules.

I pressed my head to the cold metal of the shelf and closed my eyes. *If that boy ever comes back into my library, I swear to Clio and Calliope I will do my most holy duty.*

I will give him the book he needs most.

ARADIA, MORGAN—A WITCH'S GUIDE TO ESCAPE: A PRACTICAL COMPENDIUM OF PORTAL FANTASIES—WRITTEN IN THE YEAR OF OUR SISTERHOOD TWO THOUSAND AND TWO AND SUBMITTED TO THE CARE OF THE ULYSSES COUNTY PUBLIC LIBRARY SYSTEM.

He came back to say goodbye, I think. He slid *The Runaway Prince* into the return slot then drifted through the aisles with his red backpack hanging off one shoulder, fingertips not-quite brushing the shelves, eyes on the floor. They hardly seemed sorcerous at all, now; merely sad and old and smoke-colored.

He was passing through the travel and tourism section when he saw it: A heavy, clothbound book jammed right between *The Practical Nomad* (910.4 HAS) and *By Plane, Train, or Foot: A Guide for the Aspiring Globe-Trotter*(910.51). It had no call number, but the title was stamped in swirly gold lettering on the spine: *A Witch's Guide to Escape*.

I felt the hollow thud-thudding of his heart, the pain of resurrected hope. He reached towards the book and the book reached back towards him, because books need to be read quite as much as we need to read them, and it had been a very long time since this particular book had been out of the roll-top desk in the Special Collections room.

Dark fingers touched green-dyed cloth, and it was like two sundered halves of some broken thing finally reuniting, like a lost key finally turning in its lock. Every book in the library rustled in unison, sighing at the sacred wholeness of reader and book.

Agnes was in the rows of computers, explaining our thirty-minute policy to a new patron. She broke off mid-sentence and looked up towards the 900s, nostrils flared. Then, with an expression halfway between accusation and disbelief, she turned to look at me.

I met her eyes—and it isn't easy to meet Agnes's eyes when she's angry, believe me—and smiled.

When they drag me before the mistresses and burn my card and demand to know, in tones of mournful recrimination, how I could have abandoned the vows of our order, I'll say: *Hey, you abandoned them first, ladies. Somewhere along the line, you forgot our first and purest purpose: to give patrons the books they need most. And oh, how they need. How they will always need.*

I wondered, with a kind of detached trepidation, how rogue librarians spent their time, and whether they had clubs or societies, and what it was like to encounter feral stories untamed by narrative and unbound by books. And then I wondered where our Books came from in the first place, and who wrote them.

There was a sudden, imperceptible rushing, as if a wild wind had whipped through the stacks without disturbing a single page. Several people looked up uneasily from their screens.

A Witch's Guide to Escape lay abandoned on the carpet, open to a map of some foreign fey country drawn in sepia ink. A red backpack sat beside it.

INTERVENTION

KELLY ROBSON

When I was fifty-seven, I did the unthinkable. I became a crèche manager.

On Luna, crèche work kills your social capital, but I didn't care. Not at first. My long-time love had been crushed to death in a bot malfunction in Luna's main mulching plant. I was just trying to find a reason to keep breathing.

I found a crusty centenarian who'd outlived most of her cohort and asked for her advice. She said there was no better medicine for grief than children, so I found a crèche tucked away behind a water printing plant and signed on as a cuddler. That's where I caught the baby bug.

When my friends found out, the norming started right away.

"You're getting a little tubby there, Jules," Ivan would say, unzipping my jacket and reaching inside to pat my stomach. "Got a little parasite incubating?"

I expected this kind of attitude from Ivan. Ringleader, team captain, alpha of alphas. From him, I could laugh it off. But then my closest friends started in.

Beryl's pretty face soured in disgust every time she saw me. "I can smell the freeloader on you," she'd say, pretending to see body fluids on my perfectly clean clothing. "Have the decency to shower and change after your shift."

Even that wasn't so bad. But then Robin began avoiding me and ignoring my pings. We'd been each other's first lovers, best friends since forever, and suddenly I didn't exist. That's how extreme the prejudice is on Luna.

Finally, on my birthday, they threw me a surprise party. Everyone wore diapers and crawled around in a violent mockery of childhood. When I complained, they accused me of being broody.

I wish I could say I ignored their razzing, but my friends were my whole world. I dropped crèche work. My secret plan was to leave Luna, find a hab where working with kids wasn't social death, but I kept putting it off. Then I blinked, and ten years had passed.

Enough delay. I jumped trans to Eros station, engaged a recruiter, and was settling into my new life on Ricochet within a month.

I never answered my friends' pings. As far as Ivan, Beryl, Robin, and the rest knew, I fell off the face of the moon. And that's the way I wanted it.

Richochet is one of the asteroid-based habs that travel the inner system using gravity assist to boost speed in tiny increments. As a wandering hab, we have no fixed astronomical events or planetary seasonality to mark the passage of time, so boosts are a big deal for us—the equivalent of New Year's on Earth or the Sol Belt flare cycle.

On our most recent encounter with Mars, my third and final crèche—the Jewel Box—were twelve years old. We hadn't had a boost since the kids were six, so my team and I worked hard to make it special, throwing parties, making presents, planning excursions. We even suited up and took the kids to the outside of our hab, exploring Asteroid Iris's vast, pockmarked surface roofed by nothing less than the universe itself, in all its spangled glory. We played around out there until Mars climbed over the horizon and showed the Jewel Box its great face for the first time, so huge and close it seemed we could reach up into its milky skim of atmosphere.

When the boost itself finally happened, we were all exhausted. All the kids and cuddlers lounged in the rumpus room, clipped into our safety harnesses, nestled on mats and cushions or tucked into the wall netting. Yawning, droopy-eyed, even dozing. But when the hab began to shift underneath us, we all sprang alert.

Trésor scooted to my side and ducked his head under my elbow.

"You doing okay, buddy?" I asked him in a low voice.

He nodded. I kissed the top of his head and checked his harness.

I wasn't the only adult with a little primate soaking up my body heat. Diamant used Blanche like a climbing frame, standing on her thighs, gripping her hands, and leaning back into the increasing force of the boost. Opale had coaxed her favorite cuddler Mykelti up into the ceiling netting. They both dangled by their knees, the better to feel the acceleration. Little Rubis was holding tight to Engku's and Megat's hands, while on the other side of the room, Safir and Émeraude clowned around, competing for Long Meng's attention.

I was supposed to be on damage control, but I passed the safety workflow over to Bruce. When we hit maximum acceleration, Tré was clinging to me with all his strength.

The kids' bioms were stacked in the corner of my eye. All their hormone graphs showed stress indicators. Tré's levels were higher than the rest, but that wasn't strange. When your hab is somersaulting behind a planet, bleeding off its orbital energy, your whole world turns into a carnival ride. Some people like it better than others.

I tightened my arms around Tré's ribs, holding tight as the room turned sideways.

"Everything's fine," I murmured in his ear. "Ricochet was designed for this kind of maneuver."

Our safety harnesses held us tight to the wall netting. Below, Safir and Émeraude climbed up the floor, laughing and hooting. Long Meng tossed pillows at them.

Tré gripped my thumb, yanking as if it were a joystick with the power to tame the room's spin. Then he shot me a live feed showing Ricochet's chief astronautics officer, a dark-skinned, silver-haired woman with protective bubbles fastened over her eyes.

"Who's that?" I asked, pretending I didn't know.

"Vijayalakshmi," Tré answered. "If anything goes wrong, she'll fix it."

"Have you met her?" I knew very well he had, but asking questions is an excellent calming technique.

"Yeah, lots of times." He flashed a pointer at the astronaut's mirrored eye coverings. "Is she sick?"

"Might be cataracts. That's a normal age-related condition. What's worrying you?"

"Nothing," he said.

"Why don't you ask Long Meng about it?"

Long Meng was the Jewel Box's physician. Ricochet-raised, with a facial deformity that thrust her mandible severely forward. As an adult, once bone ossification had completed, she had rejected the cosmetic surgery that could have normalized her jaw.

"Not all interventions are worthwhile," she'd told me once. "I wouldn't feel like myself with a new face."

As a pediatric specialist, Long Meng was responsible for the health and development of twenty crèches, but we were her favorite. She'd decided to celebrate the boost with us. At that moment, she was dangling from the floor with Safir and Émeraude, tickling their tummies and howling with laughter.

I tried to mitigate Tré's distress with good, old-fashioned cuddle and chat. I showed him feeds from the biodiversity preserve, where the netted megafauna floated in mid-air, riding out the boost in safety, legs dangling. One big cat groomed itself as it floated, licking one huge paw and wiping down its whiskers with an air of unconcern.

Once the boost was complete and we were back to our normal gravity regime, Tré's indicators quickly normalized. The kids ran up to the garden to check out the damage. I followed slowly, leaning on my cane. One of the bots had malfunctioned and lost stability, destroying several rows of terraced seating in the open air auditorium just next to our patch. The kids all thought that was pretty funny. Tré seemed perfectly fine, but I couldn't shake the feeling that I'd failed him somehow.

The Jewel Box didn't visit Mars. Martian habs are popular, their excursion contracts highly priced. The kids put in a few bids but didn't have the credits to win.

"Next boost," I told them. "Venus in four years. Then Earth."

I didn't mention Luna. I'd done my best to forget it even existed. Easy to do. Ricochet has almost no social or trade ties with Earth's moon. Our main economic sector is human reproduction and development—artificial wombs, zygote husbandry, natal decanting, every bit of art and science that turns a mass of undifferentiated cells into a healthy young adult. Luna's crèche system collapsed completely not long after I left. Serves them right.

I'm a centenarian, facing my last decade or two. I may look serene and wise, but I've never gotten over being the butt of my old friends' jokes.

Maybe I've always been immature. It would explain a lot.

Four years passed with the usual small dramas. The Jewel Box grew in body and mind, stretching into young adults of sixteen. All six—Diamant, Émeraude, Trésor, Opale, Safir, and Rubis—hit their benchmarks erratically and inconsistently, which made me proud. Kids are supposed to be odd little individuals. We're not raising robots, after all.

As Ricochet approached, the Venusian habs began peppering us with proposals. Recreation opportunities, educational seminars, sightseeing trips, arts festivals, sporting tournaments—all on reasonable trade terms. Venus wanted us to visit, fall in love, stay. They'd been losing population to Mars for years. The brain drain was getting critical.

The Jewel Box decided to bid on a three-day excursion. Sightseeing with a focus on natural geology, including active volcanism. For the first time in their lives, they'd experience real, unaugmented planetary gravity instead of Ricochet's one-point-zero cobbled together by centripetal force and a Steffof field.

While the kids were lounging around the rumpus room, arguing over how many credits to sink into the bid, Long Meng pinged me.

You and I should send a proposal to the Venusian crèches, she whispered. *A master class or something. Something so tasty they can't resist.*

Why? Are you trying to pad your billable hours?

She gave me a toothy grin. *I want a vacation. Wouldn't it be fun to get Venus to fund it?*

Long Meng and I had collaborated before, when our numbers had come up for board positions on the crèche governance authority. Nine miserable months co-authoring policy memos, revising the crèche management best practices guide, and presenting at skills development seminars. All on top of our regular responsibilities. Against the odds, our friendship survived the bureaucracy.

We spent a few hours cooking up a seminar to tempt the on-planet crèche specialists and fired it off to a bunch of Venusian booking agents. We called it 'Attachment and Self-regulation in Theory and Practice: Approaches to Promoting Emotional Independence in the Crèche-raised Child.' Sound dry? Not a bit. The Venusians gobbled it up.

I shot the finalized syllabus to our chosen booking agent, then escorted the Jewel Box to their open-air climbing lab. I turned them over to their instructor and settled onto my usual bench under a tall oak. Diamant took the lead position up the cliff, as usual. By the time they'd completed the first pitch, all three seminars were filled.

The agent is asking for more sessions, I whispered to Long Meng. *What do you think?*

"No way." Long Meng's voice rang out, startling me. As I pinged her location, her lanky form appeared in the distant aspen grove.

"This is a vacation," she shouted. "If I wanted to pack my billable hours, I'd volunteer for another board position."

I shuddered. *Agreed.*

She jogged over and climbed onto the bench beside me, sitting on the backrest with her feet on the seat. "Plus, you haven't been off this rock in twenty years," she added, plucking a leaf from the overhead bough.

"I said okay, Long Meng."

We watched the kids as they moved with confidence and ease over the gleaming, pyrite-inflected cliff face. Big, bulky Diamant didn't look like a climber but was obsessed with the sport. The other five had gradually been infected by their crèche-mate's passion.

Long Meng and I waved to the kids as they settled in for a rest mid-route. Then she turned to me. "What do you want to see on-planet? Have you made a wish list yet?"

"I've been to Venus. It's not that special."

She laughed, a great, good-natured, wide-mouthed guffaw. "Nothing can compare to Luna, can it, Jules?"

"Don't say that word."

"Luna? Okay. What's better than Venus? Earth?"

"Earth doesn't smell right."

"The Sol belt?"

"Never been there."

"What then?"

"This is nice." I waved at the groves of trees surrounding the cliff. Overhead, the plasma core that formed the backbone of our hab was just shifting its visible spectrum into twilight. Mellow light filtered through the leaves. Teenage laughter echoed off the cliff, and in the distance, the steady droning wail of a fussy newborn.

I pulled up the surrounding camera feeds and located the newborn. A tired-looking cuddler carried the baby in an over-shoulder sling, patting its bottom rhythmically as they strolled down a sunflower-lined path. I pinged the baby's biom. Three weeks old. Chronic gas and reflux unresponsive to every intervention strategy. Nothing to do but wait for the child to grow out of it.

The kids summited, waved to us, then began rappelling back down. Long Meng and I met them at the base.

"Em, how's your finger?" Long Meng asked.

"Good." Émeraude bounced off the last ledge and slipped to the ground, wave of pink hair flapping. "Better than good."

"Let's see, then."

Émeraude unclipped and offered the doctor their hand. They were a kid with only two modes: all-out or flatline. A few months back, they'd injured themselves cranking on a crimp, completely bowstringing the flexor tendon.

Long Meng launched into an explanation of annular pulley repair strategies and recovery times. I tried to listen but I was tired. My hips ached, my back ached, my limbs rotated on joints gritty with age. In truth, I didn't want to go to Venus. The kids had won their bid, and with them off-hab, staying home would have been a good rest. But Long Meng's friendship was important, and making her happy was worth a little effort.

Long Meng and I accompanied the Jewel Box down Venus's umbilical, through the high sulphuric acid clouds to the elevator's base deep in the planet's mantle. When we entered the busy central transit hub, with its domed ceiling and slick, speedy slideways, the kids began making faces.

"This place stinks," said Diamante.

"Yeah, smells like piss," said Rubis.

Tré looked worried. "Do they have diseases here or something?"

Opale slapped her hand over her mouth. "I'm going to be sick. Is it the smell or the gravity?"

A quick glance at Opale's biom showed she was perfectly fine. All six kids were. Time for a classic crèche manager-style social intervention.

If you can't be polite around the locals, I whispered, knocking my cane on the ground for emphasis. *I'll shoot you right back up the elevator.*

If you send us home, do we get our credits back? Émeraude asked, yawning.

No. You'd be penalized for non-completion of contract.

I posted a leaderboard for good behavior. Then I told them Venusians were especially gossipy, and if word got out they'd bad-mouthed the planet, they'd get nothing but dirty looks for the whole trip.

A bald lie. Venus is no more gossipy than most habs. But it nurses a significant anti-crèche prejudice. Not as extreme as Luna, but still. Ricochet kids were used to being loved by everyone. On Venus, they would get attitude just for existing. I wanted to offer a convenient explanation for the chilly reception from the locals.

The group of us rode the slideway to Vanavara portway, where Engku, Megat, and Bruce were waiting. Under the towering archway, I hugged and kissed the kids, told them to have lots of fun, and waved at their retreating backs. Then Long Meng and I were on our own.

She took my arm and steered us into Vanavara's passeggiata, a social stroll that wound through the hab like a pedestrian river. We drifted with the flow, joining the people-watching crowd, seeing and being seen.

The hab had spectacular sculpture gardens and fountains, and Venus's point-nine-odd gravity was a relief on my knees and hips, but the kids weren't wrong about the stench. Vanavara smelled like oily vinaigrette over half-rotted lettuce leaves, with an animal undercurrent reminiscent of hormonal teenagers on a cleanliness strike. As we walked, the stench surged and faded, then resurfaced again.

We ducked into a kiosk where a lone chef roasted kebabs over an open flame. We sat at the counter, drinking sparkling wine and watching her prepare meal packages for bot delivery.

"What's wrong with the air scrubbers here?" Long Meng asked the chef.

"Unstable population," she answered. "We don't have enough civil engineers to handle the optimization workload. If you know any nuts-and-bolts types, tell them to come to Vanavara. The bank will kiss them all over."

She served us grilled protein on disks of crispy starch topped with charred vegetable and heaped with garlicky sauce, followed by finger-sized blossoms with tender, fleshy petals over a crisp honeycomb core. When we rejoined the throng, we shot the chef a pair of big, bright public valentines on slow decay, visible to everyone passing by. The chef ran after us with two tulip-shaped bulbs of amaro.

"Enjoy your stay," she said, handing us the bulbs. "We're developing a terrific fresh food culture here. You'll love it."

In response to the population downswing, Venus's habs had started accepting all kinds of marginal business proposals. Artists. Innovators. Experimenters. Lose a ventilation engineer; gain a chef. Lose a surgeon; gain a puppeteer. With the chefs and puppeteers come all the people who want to live in a hab with chefs and puppeteers, and are willing to put up with a little stench to get it. Eventually, the hab's fortunes turn around. Population starts flowing back, attracted by the burgeoning quality of life. Engineers and surgeons return, and the chefs and puppeteers move on to the next proposal-friendly hab. Basic human dynamics.

Long Meng sucked the last drop of amaro from her bulb and then tossed it to a disposal bot.

"First night of vacation." She gave me a wicked grin. "Want to get drunk?"

When I rolled out of my sleep stack in the morning, I was puffy and stiff. My hair stood in untamable clumps. The pouches under my eyes shone an alarming purple, and my wrinkle inventory had doubled. My tongue tasted like garlic sauce. But as long as nobody else could smell it, I wasn't too concerned. As for the rest, I'd earned every age marker.

When Long Meng finally cracked her stack, she was pressed and perky, wrapped in a crisp fuchsia robe. A filmy teal scarf drifted under her thrusting jawline.

"Let's teach these Venusians how to raise kids," she said.

In response to demand, the booking agency had upgraded us to a larger auditorium. The moment we hit the stage, I forgot all my aches and pains. Doctor Footlights, they call it. Performing in front of two thousand strangers produces a lot of adrenaline.

We were a good pair. Long Meng dynamic and engaging, lunging around the stage like a born performer. Me, I was her foil. A grave, wise oldster with fifty years of crèche work under my belt.

Much of our seminar was inspirational. Crèche work is relentless no matter where you practice it, and on Venus it brings negative social status. A little cheerleading goes a long way. We slotted our specialty content in throughout the program, introducing the concepts in the introductory material, building audience confidence by reinforcing what they already knew, then hit them between the eyes with the latest developments in Ricochet's proprietary cognitive theory and emotional development modelling. We blew their minds, then backed away from the hard stuff and returned to cheerleading.

"What's the worst part of crèche work, Jules?" Long Meng asked as our program concluded, her scarf waving in the citrus-scented breeze from the ventilation.

"There are no bad parts," I said drily. "Each and every day is unmitigated joy."

The audience laughed harder than the joke deserved. I waited for the noise to die down, and mined the silence for a few lingering moments before continuing.

"Our children venture out of the crèche as young adults, ready to form new emotional ties wherever they go. The future is in their hands, an unending medium for them to shape with their ambition and passion. Our crèche work lifts them up and holds them high, all their lives. That's the best part."

I held my cane to my heart with both hands.

"The worst part is," I said, "if we do our jobs right, those kids leave the crèche and never think about us again."

We left them with a tear in every eye. The audience ran back to their crèches knowing they were doing the most important work in the universe, and open to the possibility of doing it even better.

After our second seminar, on a recommendation from the kebab chef, we blew our credits in a restaurant high up in Vanavara's atrium. Live food raised, prepared, and served by hand; nothing extruded or bulbed. And no bots, except for the occasional hygiene sweeper.

Long Meng cut into a lobster carapace with a pair of hand shears. "Have you ever noticed how intently people listen to you?"

"Most of the time the kids just pretend to listen."

"Not kids. Adults."

She served me a morsel of claw meat, perfectly molded by the creature's shell. I dredged it in green sauce and popped it in my mouth. Sweet peppers buzzed my sinuses.

"You're a great leader, Jules."

"At my age, I should be. I've had lots of practice telling people what to do."

"Exactly," she said through a mouthful of lobster. "So what are you going to do when the Jewel Box leaves the crèche?"

I lifted my flute of pale green wine and leaned back, gazing through the window at my elbow into the depths of the atrium. I'd been expecting this question for a few years but didn't expect it from Long Meng. How could someone so young understand the sorrows of the old?

"If you don't want to talk about it, I'll shut up," she added quickly. "But I have some ideas. Do you want to hear them?"

On the atrium floor far below, groups of pedestrians were just smudges, no individuals distinguishable at all. I turned back to the table but kept my eyes on my food.

"Okay, go ahead."

"A hab consortium is soliciting proposals to rebuild their failed crèche system," she said, voice eager. "I want to recruit a team. You'd be project advisor. Top position, big picture stuff. I'll be project lead and do all the grunt work."

"Let me guess," I said. "It's Luna."

Long Meng nodded. I kept a close eye on my blood pressure indicators. Deep breaths and a sip of water kept the numbers out of the red zone.

"I suppose you'd want me to liaise with Luna's civic apparatus too." I kept my voice flat.

"That would be ideal." She slapped the table with both palms and grinned. "With a native Lunite at the helm, we'd win for sure."

Long Meng was so busy bubbling with ideas and ambition as she told me her plans, she didn't notice my fierce scowl. She probably didn't even taste her luxurious meal. As for me, I enjoyed every bite, right down to the last crumb of my flaky cardamom-chocolate dessert. Then I pushed back my chair and grabbed my cane.

"There's only one problem, Long Meng," I said. "Luna doesn't deserve crèches."

"Deserve doesn't really—"

I cut her off. "Luna doesn't deserve a population."

She looked confused. "But it has a population, so—"

"Luna deserves to die," I snapped. I stumped away, leaving her at the table, her jaw hanging in shock.

Halfway through our third and final seminar, in the middle of introducing Ricochet's proprietary never-fail methods for raising kids, I got an emergency ping from Bruce.

Tré's abandoned the tour. He's run off.

I faked a coughing fit and lunged toward the water bulbs at the back of the stage. Turned my back on two thousand pairs of eyes, and tried to collect myself as I scanned Tré's biom. His stress indicators were highly elevated. The other five members of the Jewel Box were anxious too.

Do you have eyes on him?

Of course. Bruce shot me a bookmark.

Three separate cameras showed Tré was alone, playing his favorite pattern-matching game while coasting along a nearly deserted slideway. Metadata indicated his location on an express connector between Coacalco and Eaton habs.

He looked stunned, as if surprised by his own daring. Small, under the high arches of the slideway tunnel. And thin—his bony shoulder blades tented the light cloth of his tunic.

Coacalco has a bot shadowing him. Do we want them to intercept?

I zoomed in on Tré's face, as if I could read his thoughts as easily as his physiology. He'd never been particularly assertive or self-willed, never one to challenge his crèche mates or lead them in new directions. But kids will surprise you.

Tell them to stay back. Ping a personal security firm to monitor him. Go on with your tour. And try not to worry.

Are you sure?

I wasn't sure, not at all. My stress indicators were circling the planet. Every primal urge screamed for the bot to wrap itself around the boy and haul him back to Bruce. But I wasn't going to slap down a sixteen-year-old kid for acting on his own initiative, especially since this was practically the first time he'd shown any.

Looks like Tré has something to do, I whispered. *Let's let him follow through.*

I returned to my chair. Tried to focus on the curriculum but couldn't concentrate. Long Meng could only do so much to fill the gap. The audience became restless, shifting in their seats, murmuring to each other. Many stopped paying attention. Right up in the front row, three golden-haired, rainbow-smocked Venusians were blanked out, completely immersed in their feeds.

Long Meng was getting frantic, trying to distract two thousand people from the gaping hole on the stage that was her friend Jules. I picked up my cane, stood, and calmly tipped my chair. It hit the stage floor with a crash. Long Meng jumped. Every head swiveled.

"I apologize for the dramatics," I said, "but earlier, you all noticed me blanking out. I want to explain."

I limped to the front of the stage, unsteady despite my cane. I wear a stability belt, but try not to rely on it too much. Old age has exacerbated my natural tendency for a weak core, and using the belt too much just makes me frailer. But my legs wouldn't stop shaking. I dialed up the balance support.

"What just happened illustrates an important point about crèche work." I attached my cane's cling-point to the stage floor and leaned on it with both hands as I scanned the audience. "Our mistakes can ruin lives. No other profession carries such a vast potential for screwing up."

"That's not true." Long Meng's eyes glinted in the stage lights, clearly relieved I'd stepped back up to the job. "Engineering disciplines carry quite the disaster potential. Surgery certainly does. Psychology and pharmacology. Applied astrophysics. I could go on." She grinned. "Really, Jules. Nearly every profession is dangerous."

I grimaced and dismissed her point.

"Doctors' decisions are supported by ethics panels and case reviews. Engineers run simulation models and have their work vetted by peers before taking any real-world risks. But in a crèche, we make a hundred decisions a day that affect human development. Sometimes a hundred an hour."

"Okay, but are every last one of those decisions so important?"

I gestured to one of the rainbow-clad front-row Venusians. "What do you think? Are your decisions important?"

A camera bug zipped down to capture her answer for the seminar's shared feed. The Venusian licked her lips nervously and shifted to the edge of her seat.

"Some decisions are," she said in a high, tentative voice. "You can never know which."

"That's right. You never know." I thanked her and rejoined Long Meng in the middle of the stage. "Crèche workers take on huge responsibility. We assume all the risk, with zero certainty. No other profession accepts those terms. So why do we do this job?"

"Someone has to?" said Long Meng. Laughter percolated across the auditorium.

"Why us, though?" I said. "What's wrong with us?"

More laughs. I rapped my cane on the floor.

"My current crèche is a sixteen-year sixsome. Well integrated, good morale. Distressingly sporty. They keep me running." The audience chuckled. "They're on a geography tour somewhere on the other side of Venus. A few minutes ago, one of my kids ran off. Right now, he's coasting down one of your intra-hab slideways and blocking our pings."

Silence. I'd captured every eye; all their attention was mine.

I fired the public slideway feed onto the stage. Tré's figure loomed four meters high. His foot was kicked back against the slideway's bumper in an attitude of nonchalance, but it was just a pose. His gaze was wide and unblinking, the whites of his eyes fully visible.

"Did he run away because of something one of us said? Or did? Or neglected to do? Did it happen today, yesterday, or ten days ago? Maybe it has nothing to do with us at all, but some private urge from the kid's own heart. He might be suffering acutely right now, or maybe he's enjoying the excitement. The adrenaline and cortisol footprints look the same."

I clenched my gnarled, age-spotted hand to my chest, pulling at the fabric of my shirt.

"But I'm suffering. My heart feels like it could rip right out of my chest because this child has put himself in danger." I patted the wrinkled fabric back into place. "Mild danger. Venus is no Luna."

Nervous laughter from the crowd. Long Meng hovered at my side.

"Crèche work is like no other human endeavor," I said. "Nothing else offers such potential for failure, sorrow, and loss. But no work is as important. You all know that, or you wouldn't be here."

Long Meng squeezed my shoulder. I patted her hand. "Raising children is only for true believers."

• • •

Not long after our seminar ended, Tré boarded Venus's circum-planetary chuteway and chose a pod headed for Vanavara. The pod's public feed showed five other passengers: a middle-aged threesome who weren't interested in anything but each other, a halo-haired young adult escorting a floating tank of live eels, and a broad-shouldered brawler with deeply scarred forearms.

Tré waited for the other passengers to sit, then settled himself into a corner seat. I pinged him. No answer.

"We should have had him intercepted," I said.

Long Meng and I sat in the back of the auditorium. A choir group had taken over the stage. Bots were attempting to set up risers, but the singers were milling around, blocking their progress.

"He'll be okay." Long Meng squeezed my knee. "Less than five hours to Vanavara. None of the passengers are going to do anything to him."

"You don't know that."

"Nobody would risk it. Venus has strict penalties for physical violence."

"Is that the worst thing you can think of?" I flashed a pointer at the brawler. "One conversation with that one in a bad mood could do lifelong damage to anyone, much less a kid."

We watched the feed in silence. At first the others kept to themselves, but then the brawler stood, pulled down a privacy veil, and sauntered over to sit beside Tré.

"Oh no," I moaned.

I zoomed in on Tré's face. With the veil in place, I couldn't see or hear the brawler. All I could do was watch the kid's eyes flicker from the window to the brawler and back, monitor his stress indicators, and try to read his body language. Never in my life have I been less equipped to make a professional judgement about a kid's state of mind. My mind boiled with paranoia.

After about ten minutes—an eternity—the brawler returned to their seat.

"It's fine," said Long Meng. "He'll be with us soon."

Long Meng and I met Tré at the chuteway dock. It was late. He looked tired, rumpled, and more than a little sulky.

"Venus is stupid," he said.

"That's ridiculous, a planet can't be stupid," Long Meng snapped. She was tired, and hadn't planned on spending the last night of her vacation waiting in a transit hub.

Let me handle this, I whispered.

"Are you okay? Did anything happen in the pod?" I tried to sound calm as I led him to the slideway.

He shrugged. "Not really. This oldster was telling me how great his hab is. Sounded like a hole."

I nearly collapsed with relief.

"Okay, good," I said. "We were worried about you. Why did you leave the group?"

"I didn't realize it would take so long to get anywhere," Tré said.

"That's not an answer. Why did you run off?"

"I don't know." The kid pretended to yawn—one of the Jewel Box's clearest tells for lying. "Venus is boring. We should've saved our credits."

"What does that mean?"

"Everybody else was happy looking at rocks. Not me. I wanted to get some value out of this trip."

"So you jumped a slideway?"

"Uh huh." Tré pulled a protein snack out of his pocket and stuffed it in his mouth. "I was just bored. And I'm sorry. Okay?"

"Okay." I fired up the leaderboard and zeroed out Tré's score. "You're on a short leash until we get home."

We got the kid a sleep stack near ours, then Long Meng and I had a drink in the grubby travelers' lounge downstairs.

"How are you going to find out why he left?" asked Long Meng. "Pull his feeds? Form a damage mitigation team? Plan an intervention?"

I picked at the fabric on the arm of my chair. The plush nap repaired itself as I dragged a ragged thumbnail along the armrest.

"If I did, Tré would learn he can't make a simple mistake without someone jumping down his throat. He might shrug off the psychological effects, or it could inflict long-term damage."

"Right. Like you said in the seminar. You can't know."

We finished our drinks and Long Meng helped me to my feet. I hung my cane from my forearm and tucked both hands into the crease of her elbow. We slowly climbed upstairs. I could have pinged a physical assistance bot, but my hands were cold, and my friend's arm was warm.

"Best to let this go," I said. "Tré's already a cautious kid. I won't punish him for taking a risk."

"I might, if only for making me worry. I guess I'll never be a crèche manager." She grinned.

"And yet you want to go to Luna and build a new crèche system."

Long Meng's smile vanished. "I shouldn't have sprung that on you, Jules."

In the morning, the two young people rose bright and cheery. I was aching and bleary but put on a serene face. We had just enough time to catch a concert before heading up the umbilical to our shuttle home. We made our way to the atrium, where Tré boggled at the soaring views, packed slideways, clustered performance and game surfaces, fountains, and gardens. The air sparkled with nectar and spices, and underneath, a thick, oily human funk.

We boarded a riser headed to Vanavara's orchestral pits. A kind Venusian offered me a seat with a smile. I thanked him, adding, "That would never happen on Luna."

I drew Long Meng close as we spiraled toward the atrium floor.

Just forget about the proposal, I whispered. *The moon is a lost cause.*

A little more than a year later, Ricochet was on approach for Earth. The Jewel Box were nearly ready to leave the crèche. Bruce and the rest of my team were planning to start a new one, and they warmly assured me I'd always be welcome to visit. I tried not to weep about it. Instead, I began spending several hours a day helping provide round-the-clock cuddles to a newborn with hydrocephalus.

As far as I knew, Long Meng had given up the Luna idea. Then she cornered me in the dim-lit nursery and burst my bubble.

She quietly slid a stool over to my rocker, cast a professional eye over the cerebrospinal fluid-exchange membrane clipped to the baby's ear, and whispered, *We made the short list.*

That's great, I replied, my cheek pressed to the infant's warm, velvety scalp.

I had no idea what she was referring to, and at that moment I didn't care. The scent of a baby's head is practically narcotic, and no victory can compare with having coaxed a sick child into restful sleep.

It means we have to go to Luna for a presentation and interview.

Realization dawned slowly. *Luna? I'm not going to Luna.*

Not you, Jules. Me and my team. I thought you should hear before the whole hab starts talking.

I concentrated on keeping my rocking rhythm steady before answering. *I thought you'd given that up.*

She put a gentle hand on my knee. *I know. You told me not to pursue it and I considered your advice. But it's important, Jules. Luna will restart its crèche program one way or another. We can make sure they do it right.*

I fixed my gaze pointedly on her prognathous jaw. *You don't know what it's like there. They'll roast you alive just for looking different.*

Maybe. But I have to try.

She patted my knee and left. I stayed in the rocker long past hand-over time, resting my cheek against that precious head.

Seventy years ago I'd done the same, in a crèche crowded into a repurposed suite of offices behind one of Luna's water printing plants. I'd walked through the door broken and grieving, certain the world had been drained of hope and joy. Then someone put a baby in my arms. Just a few hours old, squirming with life, arms reaching for the future.

Was there any difference between the freshly detanked newborn on

Luna and the sick baby I held on that rocker? No. The embryos gestating in Ricochet's superbly optimized banks of artificial wombs were no different from the ones Luna would grow in whatever gestation tech they inevitably cobbled together.

But as I continued to think about it, I realized there was a difference, and it was important. The ones on Luna deserved better than they would get. And I could do something about it.

First, I had my hair sheared into an ear-exposing brush precise to the millimeter. The tech wielding the clippers tried to talk me out of it.

"Do you realize this will have to be trimmed every twenty days?"

"I used to wear my hair like this when I was young," I reassured him. He rolled his eyes and cut my hair like I asked.

I changed my comfortable smock for a lunar grey trouser-suit with enough padding to camouflage my age-slumped shoulders. My cling-pointed cane went into the mulch, exchanged for a glossy black model. Its silver point rapped the floor, announcing my progress toward Long Meng's studio.

The noise turned heads all down the corridor. Long Meng popped out of her doorway, but she didn't recognize me until I pushed past her and settled onto her sofa with a sigh.

"Are you still looking for a project advisor?" I asked.

She grinned. "Luna won't know what hit it."

Back in the rumpus room, Tré was the only kid to comment on my haircut.

"You look like a villain from one of those old Follywood dramas Bruce likes."

"Hollywood," I corrected. "Yes, that's the point."

"What's the point in looking like a gangland mobber?"

"Mobster." I ran my palm over the brush. "Is that what I look like?"

"Kinda. Is it because of us?"

I frowned, not understanding. He pulled his ponytail over his shoulder and eyed it speculatively.

"Are you trying to look tough so we won't worry about you after we leave?"

That's the thing about kids. The conversations suddenly swerve and hit you in the back of the head.

"Whoa," I said. "I'm totally fine."

"I know, I know. You've been running crèches forever. But we're the last because you're so old. Right? It's got to be hard."

"A little," I admitted. "But you've got other things to think about. Big, exciting decisions to make."

"I don't think I'm leaving the crèche. I'm delayed."

I tried to keep from smiling. Tré was nothing of the sort. He'd grown into a gangly young man with long arms, bony wrists, and a haze of silky black beard on his square jaw. I could recite the dates of his developmental benchmarks from memory, and there was nothing delayed about them.

"That's fine," I said. "You don't have to leave until you're ready."

"A year. Maybe two. At least."

"Okay, Tré. Your decision."

I wasn't worried. It's natural to feel ambivalent about taking the first step into adulthood. If Tré found it easier to tell himself he wasn't leaving, so be it. As soon as his crèchemates started moving on, Tré would follow.

Our proximity to Earth gave Long Meng's proposal a huge advantage. We could travel to Luna, give our presentation live, and be back home for the boost.

Long Meng and I spent a hundred billable hours refining our presentation materials. For the first time in our friendship, our communication styles clashed.

"I don't like the authoritarian gleam in your eye, Jules," she told me after a particularly heated argument. "It's almost as though you're enjoying bossing me around."

She wasn't wrong. Ricochet's social conventions require you to hold in conversational aggression. Letting go was fun. But I had an ulterior motive.

"This is the way people talk on Luna. If you don't like it, you should shitcan the proposal."

She didn't take the dare. But she reported behavioral changes to my geriatric specialist. I didn't mind. It was sweet, her being so worried about me. I decided to give her full access to my biom, so she could check if she thought I was having a stroke or something. I'm in okay health for my extreme age, but she was a paediatrician, not a gerontologist. What she saw scared her. She got solicitous. Gallant, even, bringing me bulbs of tea and snacks to keep my glucose levels steady.

Luna's ports won't accommodate foreign vehicles, and their landers use a chemical propellant so toxic Ricochet won't let them anywhere near our landing bays, so we had to shuttle to Luna in stages. As we glided over the moon's surface, its web of tunnels and domes sparkled in the full glare of the sun. The pattern of the habs hadn't changed. I could still name them—Surgut, Sklad, Nadym, Purovsk, Olenyok . . .

Long Meng latched onto my arm as the hatch creaked open. I wrenched away and straightened my jacket.

You can't do that here, I whispered. *Self-sufficiency is everything on Luna, remember?*

I marched ahead of Long Meng as if I were leading an army. In the light lunar gravity, I didn't need my cane, so I used its heavy silver head to whack the walls. Hitting something felt good. I worked up a head of steam so hot I could have sterilized those corridors. If I had to come home—home, what a word for a place like Luna!—I'd do it on my own terms.

The client team had arranged to meet us in a dinky little media suite overlooking the hockey arena in Sklad. A game had just finished, and we had to force our way against the departing crowd. My cane came in handy. I brandished it like a weapon, signaling my intent to break the jaw of anyone who got too close.

In the media suite, ten hab reps clustered around the project principal. Overhead circled a battery of old, out-of-date cameras that buzzed and fluttered annoyingly. At the front of the room, two chairs waited for Long Meng and me. Behind us arced a glistening expanse of crystal window framing the rink, where grooming bots were busy scraping blood off the ice. Over the arena loomed the famous profile of Mons Hadley, huge, cold, stark, its bleak face the same mid-tone grey as my suit.

Don't smile, I reminded Long Meng as she stood to begin the presentation.

The audience didn't deserve the verve and panache Long Meng put into presenting our project phases, alternative scenarios, and volume ramping. Meanwhile, I scanned the reps' faces, counting flickers in their attention and recording them on a leaderboard. We had forty minutes in total, but less than twenty to make an impression before the reps' decisions locked in.

Twelve minutes in, Long Meng was introducing the strategies for professional development, governance, and ethics oversight. Half the reps were still staring at her face as if they'd never seen a congenital hyperformation before. The other half were bored but still making an effort to pay attention. But not for much longer.

"Based on the average trajectories of other start-up crèche programs," Long Meng said, gesturing at the swirling graphics that hung in the air, "Luna should run at full capacity within six social generations, or thirty standard years."

I'm cutting in, I whispered. I whacked the head of my cane on the floor and stood, stability belt on maximum and belligerence oozing from my every pore.

"You won't get anywhere near that far," I growled. "You'll never get past the starting gate."

"That's a provocative statement," said the principal. She was in her sixties, short and tough, with ropey veins webbing her bony forearms. "Would you care to elaborate?"

I paced in front of their table, like a barrister in one of Bruce's old courtroom dramas. I made eye contact with each of the reps in turn, then leaned over the table to address the project principal directly.

"Crèche programs are part of a hab's social fabric. They don't exist in isolation. But Luna doesn't want kids around. You barely tolerate young adults. You want to stop the brain drain but you won't give up anything for crèches—not hab space, not billable hours, and especially not your prejudices. If you want a healthy crèche system, Luna will have to make some changes."

I gave the principal an evil grin, adding, "I don't think you can."

"I do," Long Meng interjected. "I think you can change."

"You don't know Luna like I do," I told her.

I fired our financial proposal at the reps. "Ricochet will design your new system. You'll find the trade terms extremely reasonable. When the design is complete, we'll provide on-the-ground teams to execute the project phases. Those terms are slightly less reasonable. Finally, we'll give you a project executive headed by Long Meng." I smiled. "Her billable rate isn't reasonable at all, but she's worth every credit."

"And you?" asked the principal.

"That's the best part." I slapped the cane in my palm. "I'm the gatekeeper. To go anywhere, you have to get past me."

The principal sat back abruptly, jaw clenched, chin raised. My belligerence had finally made an impact. The reps were on the edges of their seats. I had them both repelled and fascinated. They weren't sure whether to start screaming or elect me to Luna's board of governors.

"How long have I got to live, Long Meng? Fifteen years? Twenty?"

"Something like that," she said.

"Let's say fifteen. I'm old. I'm highly experienced. You can't afford me. But if you award Ricochet this contract, I'll move back to Luna. I'll control the gating progress, judging the success of every single milestone. If I decide Luna hasn't measured up, the work will have to be repeated."

I paced to the window. Mons Hadley didn't seem grey anymore. It was actually a deep, delicate lilac. Framed by the endless black sky, its form was impossibly complex, every fold of its geography picked out by the sun.

I kept my back to the reps.

"If you're wondering why I'd come back after all the years," I said, "let me be very clear. I will die before I let Luna fool around with some half-assed crèche experiment, mess up a bunch of kids, and ruin everything." I turned and pointed my cane. "If you're going to do this, at least do it right."

Back home on Ricochet, the Jewel Box was off-hab on a two-day Earth tour. They came home with stories of surging wildlife spectacles that made herds and flocks of Ricochet's biodiversity preserve look like a petting zoo. When the boost came, we all gathered in the rumpus room for the very last time.

Bruce, Blanche, Engku, Megat, and Mykelti clustered on the floor mats, anchoring themselves comfortably for the boost. They'd be fine. Soon they'd have armfuls of newborns to ease the pain of transition. The Jewel Box were all hanging from the ceiling netting, ready for their last ride of childhood. They'd be fine too. Diamante had decided on Mars, and it looked like the other five would follow.

Me, I'd be fine too. I'd have to be.

How to explain the pain and pride when your crèche is balanced on the knife's edge of adulthood, ready to leave you behind forever? Not possible. Just know this: when you see an oldster looking serene and wise, remember, it's just a sham. Under the skin, it's all sorrow.

I was relieved when the boost started. Everyone was too distracted to notice I'd begun tearing up. When the hab turned upside down, I let myself shed a few tears for the passing moment. Nothing too self-indulgent. Just a little whuffle, then I wiped it all away and joined the celebration, laughing and applauding the kids' antics as they bounced around the room.

We got it, Long Meng whispered in the middle of the boost. *Luna just shot me the contract. We won.*

She told me all the details. I pretended to pay attention, but really, I was only interested in watching the kids. Drinking in their antics, their playfulness, their joyful self-importance. Young adults have a shine about them. They glow with untapped potential.

When the boost was over, we all unclipped our anchors. I couldn't quite extricate myself from my deeply padded chair and my cane was out of reach.

Tré leapt to help me up. When I was on my feet, he pulled me into a hug.

"Are you going back to Luna?" he said in my ear.

I held him at arm's length. "That's right. Someone has to take care of Long Meng."

"Who'll take care of you?"

I laughed. "I don't need taking care of."

He gripped both my hands in his. "That's not true. Everyone does."

"I'll be fine." I squeezed his fingers and tried to pull away, but he wouldn't let go. I changed the subject. "Mars seems like a great choice for you all."

"I'm not going to Mars. I'm going to Luna."

I stepped back. My knees buckled, but the stability belt kept me from going down.

"No, Tré. You can't."

"There's nothing you can do about it. I'm going."

"Absolutely not. You have no business on Luna. It's a terrible place."

He crossed his arms over his broadening chest and swung his head like a fighter looking for an opening. He squinted at the old toys and sports equipment secured into rumpus room cabinets, the peeling murals the kids had painted over the years, the battered bots and well-used, colorful furniture—all the ephemera and detritus of childhood that had been our world for nearly eighteen years.

"Then I'm not leaving the crèche. You'll have to stay here with me, in some kind of weird stalemate. Long Meng will be alone."

I scowled. It was nothing less than blackmail. I wasn't used to being forced into a corner, and certainly not by my own kid.

"We're going to Luna together." A grin flickered across Tré's face. "Might as well give in."

I patted his arm, then took his elbow. Tré picked up my cane and put it in my hand.

"I've done a terrible job raising you," I said.

THE DONNER PARTY

DALE BAILEY

Lady Donner was in ascendance the first time Mrs. Breen tasted human flesh. For more years than anyone cared to count, Lady Donner had ruled the London Season like a queen. Indeed, some said that she stood second only to Victoria herself when it came to making (or breaking) someone's place in Society—a sentiment sovereign in Mrs. Breen's mind as her footman handed her down from the carriage into the gathering London twilight, where she took Mr. Breen's arm.

"There is no reason to be apprehensive, Alice," he had told her in their last fleeting moment of privacy, during the drive to Lady Donner's home in Park Lane, and she had felt then, as she frequently did, the breadth of his age and experience when measured against her youth. Though they shared a child—two-year-old Sophie, not the heir they had been hoping for—Mr. Breen often seemed more like a father than her husband, and his paternal assurances did not dull the edge of her anxiety. To receive a dinner invitation from such a luminary as Lady Donner was surprising under any circumstances. To receive a First Feast invitation was shocking. So Mrs. Breen *was* apprehensive—apprehensive as they were admitted into the grand foyer, apprehensive as they were announced into the drawing room, apprehensive most of all as Lady Donner, stout and unhandsome in her late middle age, swept down upon them in a cloud of taffeta and perfume.

"I am pleased to make your acquaintance at last, Mrs. Breen," Lady Donner said, taking her hand. "I have heard so much of you."

"The honor is mine," Mrs. Breen said, smiling.

But Lady Donner had already turned her attention to Mr. Breen. "She is lovely, Walter," she was saying, "a rare beauty indeed. Radiant." Lady Donner squeezed Mrs. Breen's hand. "You are radiant, darling. Really."

And then—it was so elegantly done that Mrs. Breen afterward wasn't quite certain *how* it had been done—Lady Donner divested her of her husband, leaving her respite to take in the room: the low fire burning in the grate and the lights of the chandelier, flickering like diamonds, and the ladies in their bright dresses, glittering like visitants from Faery that might any moment erupt into flight. Scant years ago, in the era of genteel penury from which Mr. Breen had rescued her, Mrs. Breen had watched such ethereal creatures promenade along Rotten Row, scarcely imagining that she would someday take her place among them. Now that she had, she felt like an imposture, wary of exposure and suddenly dowdy in a dress that had looked little short of divine when her dressmaker first unveiled it.

Such were her thoughts when Lady Donner returned, drawing from the company an elderly gentleman, palsied and stooped: Mrs. Breen's escort to table, Mr. Cavendish, one of the lesser great. He had known Mr. Breen for decades, he confided as they went down to dinner, enquiring afterward about her own family.

Mrs. Breen, who had no family left, allowed—reluctantly—that her father had been a Munby.

"Munby," Mr. Cavendish said as they took their seats. "I do not know any Munbys."

"We are of no great distinction, I fear," Mrs. Breen conceded.

Mr. Cavendish seemed not to hear her. His gaze was distant. "Now, when I was a young man, there was a Munby out of—"

Coketown, she thought he was going to say, but Mr. Cavendish chuckled abruptly and came back to her. He touched her hand. "But that was very long ago, I fear, in the age of the Megalosaurus."

Then the footman arrived with the wine and Mr. Cavendish became convivial, as a man who has caught himself on the verge of indecorum and stepped back from the precipice. He shared a self-deprecating anecdote of his youth—something about a revolver and a racehorse—and spoke warmly of his grandson at Oxford, which led to a brief exchange regarding Sophie (skirting the difficult issue of an heir). Then his voice was subsumed into the general colloquy at the table, sonorous as the wash of a distant sea. Mrs. Breen contributed little to this conversation and would later remember less of it.

What she would recall, fresh at every remove, was the food—not because she was a gourmand or a glutton, but because each new dish, served up by the footman at her shoulder, was a reminder that she had at last achieved the apotheosis to which she had so long aspired. And no dish more reminded her of this new status than the neat cutlets of ensouled flesh, reserved alone in all the year for the First Feast and Second Day dinner that celebrated the divinely ordained social order.

It was delicious.

"Do try it with your butter," Mr. Cavendish recommended, and Mrs. Breen cut a dainty portion, dipped it into the ramekin of melted butter beside her plate, and slipped it into her mouth. It was nothing like she had expected. It seemed to evanesce on her tongue, the butter a mere grace note to a stronger, slightly sweet taste, moist and rich. Pork was the closest she could come to it, but as a comparison it was utterly inadequate. She immediately wanted more of it—more than the modest portion on her plate, and she knew it would be improper to eat all of that. She wasn't some common scullery maid, devouring her dinner like a half-starved animal. At the mere thought of such a base creature, Mrs. Breen shuddered and felt a renewed sense of her own place in the world.

She took a sip of wine.

"How do you like the stripling, dear?" Lady Donner asked from the head of the table.

Mrs. Breen looked up, uncertain how to reply. One wanted to be properly deferential, but it would be unseemly to fawn. "Most excellent, my lady," she ventured, to nods all around the table, so that was all right. She hesitated, uncertain whether to say more—really, the etiquette books were entirely inadequate—only to be saved from having to make the decision by a much bewhiskered gentleman, Mr. Miller, who said, "The young lady is quite right. Your cook has outdone herself. Wherever did you find such a choice cut?"

Mrs. Breen allowed herself another bite.

"The credit is all Lord Donner's," Lady Donner said. "He located this remote farm in Derbyshire where they do the most remarkable thing. They tether the little creatures inside these tiny crates, where they feed them up from birth."

"Muscles atrophy," Lord Donner said. "Keeps the meat tender."

"It's the newest thing," Lady Donner said. "How he found the place, I'll never know."

"Well," Lord Donner began—but Mrs. Breen had by then lost track of the conversation as she deliberated over whether she should risk one more bite.

The footman saved her. "Quite done, then, madam?"

"Yes," she said.

The footman took the plate away. By the time he'd returned to scrape the cloth, Mrs. Breen was inwardly lamenting the fact that hers was not the right to every year partake of such a succulent repast. Yet she was much consoled by thoughts of the Season to come. With the doors of Society flung open to them, Sophie, like her mother, might marry up and someday preside over a First Feast herself.

The whole world lay before her like a banquet. What was there now that the Breens could not accomplish?

• • •

Nonetheless, a dark mood seized Mrs. Breen as their carriage rattled home. Mr. Cavendish's abortive statement hung in her mind, all the worse for being unspoken.

Coketown.

Her grandfather had made his fortune in the mills of Coketown. Through charm and money (primarily the latter), Abel Munby had sought admission into the empyrean inhabited by the First Families; he'd been doomed to a sort of purgatorial half-life instead—not unknown in the most rarified circles, but not entirely welcome within them, either. If he'd had a daughter, a destitute baronet might have been persuaded to take her, confirming the family's rise and boding well for still greater future elevation. He'd had a son instead, a wastrel and a drunk who'd squandered most of his father's fortune, leaving his own daughter—the future Mrs. Breen—marooned at the periphery of the *haut monde*, subsisting on a small living and receiving an occasional dinner invitation when a hostess of some lesser degree needed to fill out a table.

Mr. Breen had plucked her from obscurity at such a table, though she had no dowry and but the echo of a name. Men had done more for beauty and the promise of an heir, she supposed. But beauty fades, and no heir had been forthcoming, only Sophie—poor, dear Sophie, whom her father had quickly consigned to the keeping of her nanny.

"You stare out that window as if you read some ill omen in the mist," Mr. Breen said. "Does something trouble your thoughts?"

Mrs. Breen looked up. She forced a smile. "No, dear," she replied. "I am weary, nothing more."

Fireworks burst in the night sky—Mrs. Breen was not blind to the irony that the lower orders should thus celebrate their own abject place—and the fog bloomed with color. Mr. Breen studied her with an appraising eye. Some further response was required.

Mrs. Breen sighed. "Do you never think of it?"

"Think of what?"

She hesitated, uncertain. Sophie? Coketown? Both? At last, she said, "I wonder if they reproach me for my effrontery."

"Your effrontery?"

"In daring to take a place at their table."

"You were charming, dear."

"Charm is insufficient, Walter. I have the sweat and grime of Coketown upon my hands."

"Your grandfather had the sweat and grime of Coketown upon his hands. You are unbesmirched, my dear."

"Yet some would argue that my rank is insufficient to partake of ensouled flesh."

"You share my rank now," Mr. Breen said.

But what of the stripling she had feasted upon that night, she wondered, its flesh still piquant upon her tongue? What would it have said of rank, tethered in its box and fattened for the tables of its betters? But this was heresy to say or think (though there were radical reformers who said it more and more frequently), and so Mrs. Breen turned her mind away. Tonight, in sacred ritual, she had consumed human flesh and brought her grandfather's ambitions—and her own—to fruition. It was as Mr. Browning had said. All was right with the world. God was in his Heaven.

And then the window shattered, blowing glass into her face and eyes.

Mrs. Breen screamed and flung herself back into her husband's arms. With a screech of tortured wood, the carriage lurched beneath her and in the moment before it slammed back to the cobbles upright, she thought it would overturn. One of the horses shrieked in mindless animal terror—she had never heard such a harrowing sound—and then the carriage shuddered to a stop at last. She had a confused impression of torches in the fog and she heard the sound of men fighting. Then Mr. Breen was brushing the glass from her face and she could see clearly and she knew that she had escaped without injury.

"What happened?" she gasped.

"A stone," Mr. Breen said. "Some brigand hurled a stone through the window."

The door flew back and the coachman looked in. "Are you all right, sir?"

"We're fine," Mrs. Breen said.

And then, before her husband could speak, the coachman said, "We have one of them, sir."

"And the others?"

"Fled into the fog."

"Very well, then," said Mr. Breen. "Let's have a look at him, shall we?"

He eased past Mrs. Breen and stepped down from the carriage, holding his walking stick. Mrs. Breen moved to follow but he closed the door at his back. She looked through the shattered window. The two footmen held the brigand on his knees between them—though he hardly looked like a brigand. He looked like a boy—a dark-haired boy of perhaps twenty (not much younger than Mrs. Breen herself), clean-limbed and clean-shaven.

"Well, then," Mr. Breen said. "Have you no shame, attacking a gentleman in the street?"

"Have *you*, sir?" the boy replied. "Have you any shame?"

The coachman cuffed him for his trouble.

"I suppose you wanted money," Mr. Breen said.

"I have no interest in your money, sir. It is befouled with gore."

Once again, the coachman moved to strike him. Mr. Breen stayed the blow. "What is it that you hoped to accomplish, then?"

"Have you tasted human flesh tonight, sir?"

"And what business is it—"

"Yes," Mrs. Breen said. "We have partaken of ensouled flesh."

"We'll have blood for blood, then," the boy said. "As is our right."

This time, Mr. Breen did not intervene when the coachman lifted his hand.

The boy spat blood into the street.

"You have no rights," Mr. Breen said. "I'll see you hang for this."

"No," Mrs. Breen said.

"No?" Mr. Breen looked up at her in surprise.

"No," Mrs. Breen said, moved at first to pity—and then, thinking of her grandfather, she hardened herself. "Hanging is too dignified a fate for such a base creature," she said. "Let him die in the street."

Mr. Breen eyed her mildly. "The lady's will be done," he said, letting his stick clatter to the cobblestones.

Turning, he climbed past her into the carriage and sat down in the gloom. Fireworks exploded high overhead, showering down through the fog and painting his face in streaks of red and white that left him hollow-eyed and gaunt. He was thirty years Mrs. Breen's senior, but he had never looked so old to her before.

She turned back to the window.

She had ordered this thing. She would see it done.

And so Mrs. Breen watched as the coachman picked up his master's stick and tested its weight. The brigand tried to wrench free, and for a moment Mrs. Breen thought—hoped?—he would escape. But the two footmen flung him once again to his knees. Another rocket burst overhead. The coachman grunted as he brought down the walking stick, drew back, and brought it down again. The brigand's blood was black in the reeking yellow fog. Mrs. Breen looked on as the third blow fell and then the next, and then it became too terrible and she turned her face away and only listened as her servants beat the boy to death there in the cobbled street.

"The savages shall be battering down our doors soon enough, I suppose," Lady Donner said when Mrs. Breen called to thank her for a place at her First Feast table.

"What a distressing prospect," Mrs. Eddy said, and Mrs. Graves nodded in assent—the both of them matron to families of great honor and antiquity, if not quite the premier order. But who was Mrs. Breen to scorn such eminence—she who not five years earlier had subsisted on the crumbs of her father's squandered legacy, struggling (and more often than not failing) to meet her dressmaker's monthly reckoning?

Nor were the Breens of any greater rank than the other two women in Lady Donner's drawing room that afternoon. Though he boasted an old and storied lineage, Mr. Breen's was not quite a First Family and had no annual right to mark the beginning of the Season with a Feast of ensouled flesh. Indeed, prior to his marriage to poor Alice Munby, he himself had but twice been a First Feast guest.

Mrs. Breen had not, of course, herself introduced the subject of the incident in the street, but Mr. Breen had shared the story at his club, and word of Mrs. Breen's courage and resolve had found its way to Lady Donner's ear, as all news did in the end.

"Were you very frightened, dear?" Mrs. Graves inquired.

Mrs. Breen was silent for a moment, uncertain how to answer. It would be unseemly to boast. "I had been fortified with Lady Donner's generosity," she said at last. "The divine order must be preserved."

"Yes, indeed," Mrs. Eddy said. "Above all things."

"Yet it is not mere violence in the street that troubles me," Mrs. Graves said. "There are the horrid pamphlets one hears spoken of. My husband has lately mentioned the sensation occasioned by Mr. Bright's *Anthropophagic Crisis*."

"And one hears rumors that the House of Commons will soon take up the issue," Mrs. Eddy added.

"The Americans are at fault, with their talk of unalienable rights," Mrs. Graves said.

"The American experiment will fail," Lady Donner said. "The Negro problem will undo them, Lord Donner assures me. This too shall pass."

And that put an end to the subject.

Mrs. Eddy soon afterward departed, and Mrs. Graves after that.

Mrs. Breen, fearing that she had overstayed her welcome, stood and thanked her hostess.

"You must come again soon," Lady Donner said, and Mrs. Breen avowed that she would.

The season was by then in full swing, and the Breens were much in demand. The quality of the guests in Mrs. Breen's drawing room improved, and at houses where she had formerly been accustomed to leave her card and pass on, the doors were now open to her. She spent her evenings at the opera and the theater and the orchestra. She accepted invitations to the most exclusive balls. She twice attended dinners hosted by First Families—the Pikes and the Reeds, both close associates of Lady Donner.

But the high point of the Season was certainly Mrs. Breen's growing friendship with Lady Donner herself. The *doyenne* seemed to have taken on Mrs. Breen's elevation as her special project. There was little she did not know about the First Families and their lesser compeers, and less (indeed nothing) that she was not willing to use to her own—and to Mrs. Breen's—benefit. Though the older woman was quick to anger, Mrs. Breen never felt the lash of her displeasure. And she doted upon Sophie. She chanced to meet the child one Wednesday afternoon when Mrs. Breen, feeling, in her mercurial way, particularly fond of her daughter, had allowed Sophie to peek into the drawing room.

Lady Donner was announced.

The governess—a plain, bookish young woman named Ada Pool—was ushering Sophie, with a final kiss from her mother, out of the room when the *grande dame* swept in.

"Sophie is just leaving," Mrs. Breen said, inwardly agitated lest Sophie misbehave. "This is Lady Donner, Sophie," she said. "Can you say good afternoon?"

Sophie smiled. She held a finger to her mouth. She looked at her small feet in their pretty shoes. Then, just as Mrs. Breen began to despair, she said, with an endearing childish lisp, "Good afternoon, Mrs. Donner."

"Lady Donner," Mrs. Breen said.

"Mrs. Lady Donner," Sophie said.

Lady Donner laughed. "I am so pleased to meet you, Sophie."

Mrs. Breen said, "Give Mama one more kiss, dear, and then you must go with Miss Pool."

"She is lovely, darling," Lady Donner said. "Do let her stay."

Thus it was decided that Sophie might linger. Though she could, by Mrs. Breen's lights, be a difficult child (which is to say a child of ordinary disposition), Sophie that day allowed herself to be cossetted and admired without objection. She simpered and smiled and was altogether charming.

Thereafter, whenever Lady Donner called, she brought along some bauble for the child—a kaleidoscope or a tiny chest of drawers for her dollhouse and once an intricately embroidered ribbon of deep blue mulberry silk that matched perfectly the child's sapphire eyes. Lady Donner tied up Sophie's hair with it herself, running her fingers sensuously through the child's lustrous blonde curls and recalling with nostalgia the infancy of her own daughter, now grown.

When she at last perfected the elaborate bow, Lady Donner led Sophie to a gilded mirror. She looked on fondly as Sophie admired herself.

"She partakes of her mother's beauty," Lady Donner remarked, and Mrs. Breen, who reckoned herself merely striking (Mr. Breen would have disagreed), basked in the older woman's praise. Afterward—and to Sophie's distress—the ribbon was surrendered into Mrs. Breen's possession and preserved as a sacred relic of her friend's affections, to be used upon only the most special of occasions.

In the days that followed, Lady Donner and Mrs. Breen became inseparable. As their intimacy deepened, Mrs. Breen more and more neglected her old friends. She was seldom at home when they called, and she did not often return their visits. Her correspondence with them, which had once been copious, fell into decline. There was simply too much to do. Life was a fabulous procession of garden parties and luncheons and promenades in the Park.

Then it was August. Parliament adjourned. The Season came to an end.

She and Mr. Breen retired to their country estate in Suffolk, where Mr. Breen would spend the autumn shooting and fox hunting. As the days grew shorter, the winter seemed, paradoxically, to grow longer, their return to town more remote. Mrs. Breen corresponded faithfully with Mrs. Eddy (kind and full of gentle whimsy), Mrs. Graves (quite grave), and Lady Donner (cheery and full of inconsequential news). She awaited their letters eagerly. She rode in the mornings and attended the occasional country ball, and twice a week, like clockwork, she entertained her husband in her chamber.

But despite all of her efforts in this regard, no heir kindled in her womb.

Mrs. Breen had that winter, for the first time, a dream which would recur periodically for years to come. In the dream, she was climbing an endless ladder. It disappeared into silky darkness at her feet. Above her, it rose toward an inconceivably distant circle of light. The faraway sounds of tinkling silver and conversation drifted dimly down to her ears. And though she had been climbing for days, years, a lifetime—though her limbs were leaden with exhaustion—she could imagine no ambition more worthy of her talents than continuing the ascent. She realized too late that the ladder's topmost rungs and rails had been coated with thick, unforgiving grease, and even as she emerged into the light, her hands, numb with fatigue, gave way at last, and she found herself sliding helplessly into the abyss below.

The Breens began the Season that followed with the highest of hopes.

They were borne out. Lady Donner renewed her friendship with Mrs. Breen. They were seen making the rounds at the Royal Academy's Exhibition together, pausing before each painting to adjudge its merits. Neither of them had any aptitude for the visual arts, or indeed any interest in them, but being seen at the Exhibition was important. Lady Donner attended to assert her supremacy over the London scene, Mrs. Breen to bask in Lady Donner's reflected glow. After that, the first dinner invitations came in earnest. Mr. Breen once again took up at his club; Mrs. Breen resumed her luncheons, her charity bazaars, her afternoon calls and musical soireés. Both of them looked forward to the great events of the summer—the Derby and the Ascot in June, the Regatta in July.

But, foremost, they anticipated the high holiday and official commencement of the London Season: First Day and its attendant Feast, which fell every year on the last Saturday in May. Mr. Breen hoped to dine with one of the First Families; Mrs. Breen expected to.

She was disappointed.

When the messenger from Lady Donner arrived, she presumed that she would open the velvety envelope to discover her invitation to the First Feast. Instead it was an invitation to the Second Day dinner. Another woman might have felt gratified at this evidence of Lady Donner's continued esteem. Mrs. Breen, on the other hand, felt that she had been cut by her closest friend, and in an excess of passion dashed off an indignant reply tendering her regret that Mr. and Mrs. Breen would be unable to attend due to a prior obligation. Then she paced the room in turmoil while she awaited her husband's return from the club.

Mrs. Breen did not know what she had anticipated from him, but she had not expected him to be furious. His face grew pale. He stalked the room like a caged tiger. "Have you any idea what you have done?"

"I have declined an invitation, nothing more."

"An invitation? You have declined infinitely more than that, I am afraid. You have declined everything we most value—place and person, the divine order of the ranks and their degrees." He stopped at the sideboard for a whisky and drank it back in a long swallow. "To be asked to partake of ensouled flesh, my dear, even on Second Day—there is no honor greater for people of our station."

"Our station? Lady Donner and I are friends, Walter."

"You may be friends. But you are not equals, and you would do well to remember that." He poured another drink. "Or would have done, I should say. It is too late now."

"Too late?"

"Lady Donner does not bear insult lightly."

"But she has insulted me."

"Has she, then? I daresay she will not see it that way." Mr. Breen put his glass upon the sideboard. He walked across the room and gently took her shoulders. "You must write to her, Alice," he said. "It is too late to hope that we might attend the dinner. But perhaps she will forgive you. You must beg her to do so."

"I cannot," Mrs. Breen said, with the defiance of one too proud to acknowledge an indefensible error.

"You must. As your husband, I require it of you."

"Yet I will not."

And then, though she had never had anything from him but a kind of distracted paternal kindness, Mr. Breen raised his hand. For a moment, she thought he was going to strike her. He turned away instead.

"Goddamn you," he said, and she recoiled from the sting of the curse, humiliated.

"You shall have no heir of me," she said, imperious and cold.

"I have had none yet," he said. His heels rang like gunshots as he crossed the drawing room and let himself out.

Alone, Mrs. Breen fought back tears.

What had she done? she wondered. What damage had she wrought?

She would find out soon enough.

It had become her custom to visit Mrs. Eddy in her Grosvenor Square home on Mondays. But the following afternoon when Mrs. Breen sent up her card, her footman returned to inform her as she leaned out her carriage window "that the lady was not at home." Vexed, she was withdrawing into her carriage when another equipage rattled to the curb in front of her own. A footman leaped down with a card for Mrs. Eddy. Mrs. Breen did not need to see his livery. She recognized the carriage, had indeed ridden in it herself. She watched as the servant conducted his transaction with the butler. When he returned to hand down his mistress—Mrs. Eddy was apparently at home for some people—Mrs. Breen pushed open her door.

"Madam—" her own footman said at this unprecedented behavior.

"Let me out!"

The footman reached up to assist her. Mrs. Breen ignored him.

"Lady Donner," she cried as she stumbled to the pavement. "Lady Donner, please wait."

Lady Donner turned to look at her.

"It is so delightful to see you," Mrs. Breen effused. "I—"

She broke off. Lady Donner's face was impassive. It might have been carved of marble. "Do I know you?" she said.

"But—" Mrs. Breen started. Again she broke off. But what? What could she say?

Lady Donner held her gaze for a moment longer. Then, with the ponderous dignity of an iceberg, she disappeared into the house. The door snicked closed behind her with the finality of a coffin slamming shut.

"Madam, let me assist you into your carriage," the footman said at her elbow. There was kindness in his voice. Somehow that was the most mortifying thing of all, that she should be pitied by such a creature.

"I shall walk for a while," she said.

"Madam, please—"

"I said I shall walk."

She put her back to him and strode down the sidewalk as fast as her skirts would permit. Her face stung with shame, more even than it had burned with the humiliation of her husband's curse. She felt the injustice of her place in the world as she had never felt it before—felt how small she was, how little she mattered in the eyes of such people, that they should toy with her as she might have toyed with one of Sophie's dolls, and disposed of it when it ceased to amuse her.

The blind, heat-struck roar of the city soon enveloped her. The throng pressed close, a phantasmagoria of subhuman faces, cruel and strange, distorted as the faces in dreams, their pores overlarge, their yellow flesh stippled with perspiration. Buildings leaned over her at impossible angles. The air was dense with the creak of passing omnibuses and the cries of cabbies and costermongers and, most of all, the whinny and stench of horses, and the heaping piles of excrement they left steaming in the street.

She thought she might faint.

Her carriage pulled up to the curb beside her. Her footman dropped to the pavement before it stopped moving.

"Madam, please. You must get into the carriage," he said, and when he flung open the carriage door, she allowed him to hand her up into the crepuscular interior. Before he'd even closed the latch the carriage was moving, shouldering its way back into the London traffic. She closed her eyes and let the rocking vehicle lull her into a torpor.

She would not later remember anything of the journey or her arrival at home. When she awoke in her own bed some hours afterward, she wondered if the entire episode had not been a terrible dream. And then she saw her maid, Lily, sitting by the bed, and she saw the frightened expression on the girl's face, and she knew that it had actually happened.

"We have sent for the physician, madam," Lily said.

"I do not need a physician," she said. "I am beyond a physician's help."

"Please, madam, you must not—"

"Where is my husband?"

"I will fetch him."

Lily went to the door and spoke briefly to someone on the other side. A moment later, Mr. Breen entered the room. His face was pale, his manner formal.

"How are you, dearest?" he asked.

"I have ruined us," she said.

She did not see how they could go on.

• • •

Yet go on they did.

Word was quietly circulated that Mrs. Breen had fallen ill and thus a thin veil of propriety was drawn across her discourtesy and its consequence. But no one called to wish her a quick recovery. Even Mrs. Breen's former friends—those pale, drab moths fluttering helplessly around the bright beacon of Society—did not come. Having abandoned them in the moment of her elevation, Mrs. Breen found herself abandoned in turn.

Her illness necessitated the Breens' withdrawal to the country well before the Season ended. There, Mr. Breen remained cold and distant. Once, he had warmed to her small enthusiasms, chuckling indulgently when the dressmaker left and she spilled out her purchases for his inspection. Now, while he continued to spoil her in every visible way, he did so from a cool remove. She no longer displayed her fripperies for his approval. He no longer asked to see them.

Nor did he any longer make his twice-weekly visit to her chamber. Mrs. Breen had aforetime performed her conjugal obligations dutifully, with a kind of remote efficiency that precluded real enthusiasm. She had married without a full understanding of her responsibilities in this regard, and, once enlightened, viewed those offices with the same mild aversion she felt for all the basic functions of her body. Such were the consequences of the first sin in Eden, these unpleasant portents of mortality, with their mephitic smells and unseemly postures. Yet absent her husband's hymeneal attentions, she found herself growing increasingly restive. Her dream of the ladder recurred with increasing frequency.

The summer had given way to fall when Sophie became, by chance and by betrayal, Mrs. Breen's primary solace.

If Mr. Breen took no interest in his daughter, his wife's sentiments were more capricious. Though she usually left Sophie in the capable hands of the governess, she was occasionally moved to an excess of affection, coddling the child and showering her with kisses. It was such a whim that sent her climbing the back stairs to the third-floor playroom late one afternoon. She found Sophie and Miss Pool at the dollhouse. Mrs. Breen would have joined them had a book upon the table not distracted her.

On any other day she might have passed it by unexamined. But she had recently found refuge in her subscription to Mudie's, reading volume by volume the novels delivered to her by post—Oliphant and Ainsworth, Foster, Collins. And so curiosity more than anything else impelled her to pick the book up. When she did, a folded tract—closely printed on grainy, yellow pulp—slipped from between the pages.

"Wait—" Miss Pool said, rising to her feet—but it was too late. Mrs. Breen had already knelt to retrieve the pamphlet. She unfolded it as she stood. ***A Great Horror Reviled,*** read the title, printed in Gothic Blackletter across the top. The illustration below showed an elaborate table setting. Where the plate should have been there lay a baby, split stem to sternum by a deep incision, the flesh pinned back to reveal a tangle of viscera. Mrs. Breen didn't have to read any more to know what the tract was about, but she couldn't help scanning the first page anyway, taking in the gruesome illustrations and the phrases set apart in bold type. ***Too long have the First Families battened upon the flesh of the poor!*** one read, and another, ***Blood must flow in the gutters that it may no longer flow in the kitchens of men!***—which reminded Mrs. Breen of the boy who had hurled the stone through their carriage window. The Anthropophagic Crisis, Mrs. Graves had called it. Strife in the House of Commons, carnage in the streets.

Miss Pool waited by the dollhouse, Sophie at her side.

"Please, madam," Miss Pool said, "it is not what you think."

"Is it not? Whatever could it be, then?"

"I—I found it in the hands of the coachman this morning and confiscated it. I had intended to bring it to your attention."

Mrs. Breen thought of the coachman testing the weight of her husband's walking stick, the brigand's blood black in the jaundiced fog.

"What errand led you to the stables?"

"Sophie and I had gone to look at the horses."

"Is this true, Sophie?" Mrs. Breen asked.

Sophie was still for a moment. Then she burst into tears.

"Sophie, did you go to the stables this morning? You must be honest."

"No, Mama," Sophie said through sobs.

"I thought not." Mrs. Breen folded the tract. "You dissemble with facility, Miss Pool. Please pack your possessions. You will be leaving us at first light."

"But where will I go?" the governess asked. And when Mrs. Breen did not respond: "Madam, please—"

"You may appeal to Mr. Breen, if you wish. I daresay it will do you no good."

Nor did it. Dawn was still gray in the east when Mrs. Breen came out of the house to find a footman loading the governess's trunk into the carriage. Finished, he opened the door to hand her in. She paused with one foot on the step and turned back to look at Mrs. Breen. The previous night she had wept. Now she was defiant. "Your time is passing, Mrs. Breen," she said, "you and all your kind. History will sweep you all away."

Mrs. Breen made no reply. She only stood there and watched as the footman closed the door at the governess's back. The coachman snapped his whip and the carriage began to move. But long after it had disappeared into the morning fog, the woman's words lingered. Mrs. Breen was not blind to their irony.

Lady Donner had renounced her.

She had no kind—no rank and no degree, nor any place to call her own.

A housemaid was pressed into temporary service as governess, but the young woman was hardly suited to provide for Sophie's education.

"What shall we do?" Mr. Breen inquired.

"Until we acquire a proper replacement," Mrs. Breen said, "I shall take the child in hand myself."

It was October by then. If Mrs. Breen had anticipated the previous Season, she dreaded the one to come. Last winter, the days had crept by. This winter, they hurtled past, and as the next Season drew inexorably closer, she found herself increasingly apprehensive. Mr. Breen had not spoken of the summer. Would they return to London? And if so, what then?

Mrs. Breen tried (largely without success) not to ruminate over these questions. She focused on her daughter instead. She had vowed to educate the child, but aside from a few lessons in etiquette and an abortive attempt at French, her endeavor was intermittent and half-hearted—letters one day, ciphering the next. She had no aptitude for teaching. What she did have, she discovered, was a gift for play. When a rocking horse appeared on Christmas morning, Mrs. Breen was inspired to make a truth of Ada Pool's lie and escort Sophie to the stables herself. They fed carrots to Spitzer, Mr. Breen's much-prized white gelding, and Sophie shrieked with laughter at the touch of his thick, bristling lips.

"What shall we name your rocking horse?" Mrs. Breen asked as they walked back to the house, and the little girl said, "Spitzer," as Mrs. Breen had known she would. In the weeks that followed, they fed Spitzer imaginary carrots every morning, and took their invisible tea from Sophie's tiny porcelain tea set every afternoon. Between times there were dolls and a jack-in-the-box and clever little clockwork automata that one could set into motion with delicate wooden levers and miniature silver keys. They played jacks and draughts and one late February day spilled out across a playroom table a jigsaw puzzle of bewildering complexity.

"Mama, why did Miss Pool leave me?" Sophie asked as they separated out the edge pieces.

"She had to go away."

"But where?"

"Home, I suppose," Mrs. Breen said. Pursing her lips, she tested two pieces for a fit. She did not wish to speak of Miss Pool.

"I thought she lived with us."

"Just for a while, dear."

"Will she ever come to visit us, Mama?"

"I should think not."

"Why not?"

"She was very bad, Sophie."

"But what did she do?"

Mrs. Breen hesitated, uncertain how to explain it to the child. Finally, she said, "There are people of great importance in the world, Sophie, and there are people of no importance at all. Your governess confused the two."

Sophie pondered this in silence. "Which kind of people are we?" she said at last.

Mrs. Breen did not answer. She thought of Abel Munby and she thought of Lady Donner. Most of all she thought of that endless ladder with its greased rungs and rails and high above a radiant circle from which dim voices fell.

"Mama?" Sophie said.

And just then—just in time—a pair of interlocking pieces came to hand. "Look," Mrs. Breen said brightly, "a match."

Sophie, thus diverted, giggled in delight. "You're funny, Mama," she said.

"Am I, then?" Mrs. Breen said, and she kissed her daughter on the forehead and the matter of Ada Pool was forgotten.

Another week slipped by. They worked at the puzzle in quiet moments, and gradually an image began to take shape: a field of larkspur beneath an azure sky. Mrs. Breen thought it lovely, and at night, alone with her thoughts, she tried to project herself into the scene. Yet she slept restlessly. She dreamed of the boy the coachman had killed in the street. In the dream, he clung to her skirts as she ascended that endless ladder, thirteen stone of dead weight dragging her down into the darkness below. When she looked over her shoulder at him, he had her grandfather's face. At last, in an excess of fatigue, she ventured one evening with her husband to broach the subject that had lain unspoken between them for so many months. "Let us stay in the country for the summer," she entreated Mr. Breen. "The heat is so oppressive in town."

"Would you have us stay here for the rest of our lives?" he asked. And when she did not reply: "We will return to London. We may yet be redeemed."

Mrs. Breen did not see how they could be.

Nonetheless, preparations for the move soon commenced in earnest. The servants bustled around packing boxes. The house was in constant disarray. And the impossible puzzle proved possible after all. The night before they were to commence the journey, they finished it at last. Mrs. Breen contrived to let Sophie fit the final piece, a single splash of sapphire, blue as any ribbon, or an eye.

• • •

They arrived in London at the end of April. Mrs. Breen did not make an appearance at the Royal Academy's Exhibition the next week, preferring instead the privacy of their home on Eaton Place. The Season—no, her life—stretched away before her, illimitable as the Saharan wasteland, and as empty of oasis. She did not ride on Rotten Row. She made no calls, and received none. A new governess, Miss Bell, was hired and Mrs. Breen did not so often have the consolation of her daughter. In the mornings, she slept late; in the evenings, she retreated to her chamber early. And in the afternoons, while Sophie was at her lessons, she wept.

She could see no future. She wanted to die.

The messenger arrived two weeks before First Feast, on Sunday afternoon. Mrs. Breen was in the parlor with Sophie, looking at a picture book, when the footman handed her the envelope. At the sight of the crest stamped into the wax seal, she felt rise up the ghost of her humiliation in Grosvenor Square. Worse yet, she felt the faintest wisp of hope—and that she could not afford. She would expect nothing, she told herself. Most of all, she would not hope.

"Please take Sophie away, Miss Bell," she said to the governess, and when Sophie protested, Mrs. Breen said, "Mama is busy now, darling." Her tone brooked no opposition. Miss Bell whisked the child out of the room, leaving Mrs. Breen to unseal the envelope with trembling fingers. She read the note inside in disbelief, then read it again.

"Is the messenger still here?" she asked the footman.

"Yes, madam."

At her desk, Mrs. Breen wrote a hasty reply, sealed the envelope, and handed it to the footman. "Please have him return this to Lady Donner. And please inform Mr. Breen that I wish to see him."

"Of course," the footman said.

Alone, Mrs. Breen read—and re-read—the note yet again. She felt much as she had felt that afternoon in Grosvenor Square: as though reality had shifted in some fundamental and unexpected way, as though everything she had known and believed had to be calibrated anew.

Mr. Breen had been right.

Lady Donner had with a stroke of her pen restored them.

Mr. Breen also had to read the missive twice:

> *Lord and Lady Donner request the pleasure of the company of Mr. and Mrs. Breen at First Feast on Saturday, May 29th, 18—, 7:30 P.M. RSVP*

Below that, in beautiful script, Lady Donner had inscribed a personal note:

> *Please join us, Alice. We so missed your company last spring. And do bring Sophie.*

Mr. Breen slipped the note into the envelope and placed it upon Mrs. Breen's desk.

"Have you replied?"

"By Lady Donner's messenger."

"I trust you have acted with more wisdom this year."

She turned her face away from him. "Of course."

"Very well, then. You shall require a new dress, I suppose."

"Sophie as well."

"Can it be done in two weeks?"

"I do not know. Perhaps with sufficient inducement."

"I shall see that the dressmaker calls in the morning. Is there anything else?"

"The milliner, I should think," she said. "And the tailor for yourself."

Mr. Breen nodded.

The next morning, the dressmaker arrived as promised. Two dresses! he exclaimed, pronouncing the schedule impossible. His emolument was increased. Perhaps it could be done, he conceded, but it would be very difficult. When presented with still further inducement, he acceded that with Herculean effort he would certainly be able to complete the task. It would require additional seamstresses, of course

Further terms were agreed to.

The dressmaker made his measurements, clucking in satisfaction. The milliner called, the tailor and the haberdasher. It was all impossible, of course. Such a thing could not be done. Yet each was finally persuaded to view the matter in a different light, and each afterward departed in secret satisfaction, congratulating himself on having negotiated such a generous fee.

The days whirled by. Consultations over fabrics and colors followed. Additional measurements and fittings were required. Mrs. Breen rejoiced in the attention of the couturiers. Her spirits lifted and her beauty, much attenuated by despair, returned almost overnight. Mr. Breen, who had little interest in bespoke clothing and less patience with it, endured the attentions of his tailor. Sophie shook her petticoats in fury and stood upon the dressmaker's stool, protesting that she did not *want* to lift her arms or turn around or (most of all) *hold still*. Miss Bell was reprimanded and told to take a sterner line with the child.

Despite all this, Mrs. Breen was occasionally stricken with anxiety. What if the dresses weren't ready or proved in some way unsatisfactory?

All will be well, Mr. Breen assured her.

She envied his cool certainty.

The clothes arrived the Friday morning prior to the feast: a simple white dress with sapphire accents for Sophie; a striking gown of midnight blue, lightly bustled, for Mrs. Breen.

Secretly pleased, Mrs. Breen modeled it for her husband—though not without trepidation. Perhaps it was insufficiently modest for such a sober occasion.

All will be well, Mr. Breen assured her.

And then it was Saturday.

Mrs. Breen woke to a late breakfast and afterward bathed and dressed at her leisure. Her maid pinned up her hair in an elaborate coiffure and helped her into her corset. It was late in the afternoon when she at last donned her gown, and later still—they were on the verge of departing—when Miss Bell presented Sophie for her approval.

They stood in the foyer of the great house, Mr. and Mrs. Breen, and Miss Bell, and the child herself—the latter looking, Mr. Breen said with unaccustomed tenderness, as lovely as a star fallen to the Earth. Sophie giggled with delight at this fancy. Yet there was some missing touch to perfect the child's appearance, Mrs. Breen thought, studying Sophie's child's white habiliments with their sapphire accents.

"Shall we go, then?" Mr. Breen said.

"Not quite yet," Mrs. Breen said.

"My dear—"

Mrs. Breen ignored him. She studied the child's blonde ringlets. A moment came to her: Lady Donner tying up Sophie's hair with a deep blue ribbon of embroidered mulberry silk. With excuses to her husband, who made a show of removing his watch from its pocket and checking the time, Mrs. Breen returned to her chamber. She opened her carven wooden box of keepsakes. She found the ribbon folded carefully away among the other treasures she had been unable to look at in the era of her exile: a program from her first opera and a single dried rose from her wedding bouquet, which she had once reckoned the happiest day of her life—before Lady Breen's First Feast invitation (also present) and the taste of human flesh that it had occasioned. She smoothed the luxuriant silk between her fingers, recalling Lady Donner's words while the child had admired herself in the gilt mirror.

She partakes of her mother's beauty.

Mrs. Breen blinked back tears—it would not do to cry—and hastened downstairs, where she tied the ribbon into Sophie's hair. Mr. Breen paced impatiently as she perfected the bow.

"There," Mrs. Breen said, with a final adjustment. "Don't you look lovely?"

Sophie smiled, dimpling her checks, and took her mother's hand.

"Shall we?" Mr. Breen said, ushering them out the door to the street, where the coachman awaited.

They arrived promptly at seven-thirty.

Sophie spilled out of the carriage the moment the footman opened the door.

"Wait, Sophie," Mrs. Breen said. "Slowly. Comport yourself as a lady." She knelt to rub an imaginary speck from the child's forehead and once again adjusted the bow. "There you go. Perfect. You are the very picture of beauty. Can you promise to be very good for Mama?"

Sophie giggled. "Promise," she said.

Mr. Breen smiled and caressed the child's cheek, and then, to Mrs. Breen's growing anxiety—what if something should go wrong?—Mr. Breen rang the bell. He reached down and squeezed her hand, and then the butler was admitting them into the great foyer, and soon afterward, before she had time to fully compose herself, announcing them into the drawing room.

Lady Donner turned to meet them, smiling, and it was as if the incident in Grosvenor Square had never happened. She took Mrs. Breen's hand. "I am glad you were able to come," she said. "I have so missed you." And then, kneeling, so that she could look Sophie in the eye: "Do you remember me, Sophie?"

Sophie, intimidated by the blazing drawing room and the crowd of strangers and this smiling apparition before her, promptly inserted a knuckle between her teeth. She remembered nothing, of course. Lady Donner laughed. She ran her finger lightly over the ribbon and conjured up a sweet, which Sophie was persuaded after some negotiation to take. Then—"We shall talk again soon, darling," Lady Donner promised—a housemaid ushered the child off to join the other children at the children's feast. Lady Donner escorted the Breens deeper into the room and made introductions.

It was an exalted company. In short order, Mrs. Breen found herself shaking hands with a florid, toad-like gentleman who turned out to be Lord Stanton, the Bishop of London, and a slim, dapper one whom Lady Donner introduced as the Right Honorable Mr. Daniel Williams, an MP from Oxford. Alone unwived among the men was the radical novelist Charles Foster, whom Mrs. Breen found especially fascinating, having whiled away many an hour over his triple-deckers during her time in exile. The sole remaining guest was the aged Mrs. Murphy, a palsied widow in half-mourning. Mrs. Breen never did work out her precise rank, though she must have been among the lesser great since she and Mr. Breen were the penultimate guests to proceed down to dinner. Mrs. Breen followed, arm in arm with Mr. Foster, whose notoriety had earned him the invitation and whose common origin had determined his place in the procession. Mrs. Breen wished that her companion were of greater rank—that she, too, had not been consigned to the lowest position. Her distress was exacerbated by Mr. Foster's brazen irreverence. "Fear not, Mrs. Breen," he remarked in a whisper as they descended, "a time draws near when the first shall be last, and the last shall be first."

Mr. Foster's reputation as a provocateur, it turned out, was well deserved. His method was the slaughter of sacred cows; his mode was outrage. By the end of the first course (white soup, boiled salmon, and dressed cucumber), he had broached the Woman question. "Take female apparel," he said. "Entirely impractical except as an instrument of oppression. It enforces distaff reliance upon the male of the species. What can she do for herself in that garb?" he asked, waving a hand vaguely in the direction of an affronted Mrs. Breen.

By the end of the second course (roast fowls garnished with watercresses, boiled leg of lamb, and sea kale), he had launched into the Darwinian controversy. "We are all savage as apes at the core," he was saying when the footman appeared at his elbow with the entrée. "Ah. What have we here? The *pièce de résistance*?"

He eyed the modest portion on Mrs. Breen's plate and served himself somewhat more generously. When the servant had moved on down the table, he shot Mrs. Breen a conspiratorial glance, picked up his menu card, and read off the entrée *sotto voce*: Lightly Braised Fillet of Stripling, garnished with Carrots and Mashed Turnips. "Have you had stripling before, Mrs. Breen?"

She had, she averred, taking in the intoxicating aroma of the dish. Two years ago, she continued, she had been fortunate enough to partake of ensouled flesh at this very table. "And you, Mr. Foster?"

"I have not."

"It is a rare honor."

"I think I prefer my honors well done, Mrs. Breen."

Mrs. Breen pursed her lips in disapproval. She did not reply.

Undeterred, Mr. Foster said, "Have you an opinion on the Anthropophagic Crisis?"

"I do not think it a woman's place to opine on political matters, Mr. Foster."

"You would not, I imagine."

"I can assure you the Anti-Anthropophagy Bill will never become law, Mr. Foster," Mr. Williams said. "It is stalled in the Commons, and should it by chance be passed, the Peers will reject it. The eating of ensouled flesh is a tradition too long entrenched in this country."

"Do you number yourself among the reformers, Mr. Williams?"

"I should think not."

Mr. Foster helped himself to a bite of the stripling. It was indeed rare. A small trickle of blood ran into his whiskers. He dabbed at it absent-mindedly. The man was repulsive, Mrs. Breen thought, chewing delicately. The stripling tasted like manna from Heaven, ambrosia, though perhaps a little less tender—and somewhat more strongly flavored—than her last meal of ensouled flesh.

"It *is* good," Mr. Foster said. "Tastes a bit like pork. What do shipwrecked sailors call it? Long pig?"

Lady Stanton gasped. "Such a vulgar term," she said. "Common sailors have no right."

"Even starving ones?"

"Are rightfully executed for their depravity," Lord Donner pointed out.

"I hardly think the Anthropophagic Crisis is proper conversation for this table, Mr. Foster," said Mr. Breen.

"I can think of no table at which it is more appropriate." Another heaping bite. "It is a pretty word, anthropophagy. Let us call it what it is: cannibalism."

"It is a sacred ritual," Mrs. Murphy said.

"And cannibalism is such an ugly word, Mr. Foster," Lord Donner said.

"For an ugly practice," Mr. Foster said.

Lady Donner offered him a wicked smile. She prided herself on having an interesting table. "And yet I notice that you do not hesitate to partake."

"Curiosity provides the food the novelist feeds upon, Lady Donner. Even when the food is of an unsavory nature. Though this"—Mr. Foster held up his laden fork—"this is quite savory, I must admit. My compliments to your cook."

"I shall be sure to relay them," Lady Donner said.

"Yet, however savory it might be," he continued, "we are eating a creature with a soul bestowed upon it by our common Creator. We acknowledge it with our very name for the flesh we partake of at this table."

"Dinner?" Mrs. Williams said lightly, to a ripple of amusement.

Mr. Foster dipped his head and lifted his glass in silent toast. "I was thinking rather of ensouled flesh."

Mrs. Breen looked up from her plate. "I should think First Feast would be meaningless absent ensouled flesh, Mr. Foster," she said. "It would be a trivial occasion if we were eating boiled ham."

The bishop laughed. "These are souls of a very low order."

"He that has pity upon the poor lends unto the Lord," Mr. Foster said.

"The Lord also commands us to eat of his body, yes? There is a scripture for every occasion, Mr. Foster. The Catholics believe in transubstantiation, as you know." Lord Stanton helped himself to a morsel of stripling. "Ours is an anthropophagic faith."

"My understanding is that the Church of England reads the verse metaphorically."

"Call me High Church, then," Lord Stanton said, stifling a belch. There was general laughter at this sally, a sense that the bishop had scored a point.

Mr. Foster was unperturbed. "Are you suggesting that our Savior enjoins us to eat our fellow men?"

"I would hardly call them our fellow men," Lady Stanton said.

"They are human, are they not?" Mr. Foster objected.

"Given us, like the beasts of the field," Lord Donner remarked, "for our use and stewardship. Surely an ardent evolutionist such as yourself must understand the relative ranks of all beings. The poor will always be with us, Mr. Foster. As Lord Stanton has said, they are of a lower order."

"Though flesh of a somewhat higher order may be especially pleasing to the palate," Lady Donner said.

Mr. Williams said, "This must be flesh of a very high order indeed, then."

"It is of the highest, Mr. Williams. Let me assure you on that score." Lady Donner smiled down the table at Mrs. Breen. "You have partaken of ensouled flesh at our table before, Mrs. Breen. I trust tonight's meal is to your taste."

"It is very good indeed, my lady," Mrs. Breen said, looking down at her plate with regret. She would have to stop now. She had already eaten too much.

"And how would you compare it with your previous repast?"

Mrs. Breen put down her fork. "Somewhat more piquant, I think."

"Gamy might be a better word," Mr. Williams put in.

"As it should be," Lady Donner said, looking squarely at Mrs. Breen. "It was taken wild."

Mrs. Breen was quiet on the way home.

The hatbox sat on the shadowy bench beside her, intermittently visible in the fog-muted light of the passing streetlamps. Outside, a downpour churned the cobbled streets into torrents of feculent muck, but the First Day revels continued along the riverfront, fireworks blooming like iridescent flowers in the overcast sky. Mrs. Breen stared at the window, watching the rain sew intersecting threads upon the glass and thinking of her last such journey, the shattered window, the blood upon the cobbles. She wondered idly what such a debased creature's flesh would have tasted like, and leaned into her husband's comfortable bulk, his heat.

After the meal, the men had lingered at the table over port. In the drawing room, Lady Donner had been solicitous of Mrs. Breen's comfort. "You must stay for a moment after the other guests have departed," she'd said, settling her on a sofa and solemnly adjuring her to call within the week. "And you must join us in our carriage to the Ascot next month," she said, squeezing Mrs. Breen's hand. "I insist."

There had been no need to open the hatbox she'd handed Mrs. Breen as the butler showed them out. It had been uncommonly heavy.

Mrs. Breen sighed, recalling her husband's confidence in their restoration.

"This was your doing," she said at last.

"Yes."

"How?"

"Letters," he said. "A delicate negotiation, though one somewhat mitigated, I think, by Lady Donner's fondness for you."

"And you did not see fit to tell me."

"I feared that you might object."

Mrs. Breen wondered if she would have. She did not think so. She felt her place in the world more keenly now than she had felt it even in her era of privation, when she had striven in vain to fulfill her grandfather's aspirations.

The carriage rocked and swayed over an uneven patch of cobblestones. Something rolled and thumped inside the hatbox, and she feared for a moment that it would overturn, spilling forth its contents. But of course there was no danger of that. It had been painstakingly secured with a sapphire blue ribbon of mulberry silk. Mrs. Breen could not help reaching out to caress the rich fabric between her thumb and forefinger.

She sighed in contentment. They would be home soon.

"I do wish that you had told me," she said. "You would have put my mind much at ease."

"I am sorry, darling," Mr. Breen said.

Mrs. Breen smiled at him as the dim light of another streetlamp jolted by, and then, as darkness swept over her, she took an unheard-of liberty and let her hand fall upon his thigh. Tonight, she vowed, she would give him the heir he longed for.

HOW TO IDENTIFY AN ALIEN SHARK

BETH GODER

Honored guests, thank you for attending this seminar on the Tucabal-Gor, colloquially known as alien sharks. I am Dr. William Smithson, the foremost expert on these xenoforms.

Ever since the infestation in the Atlantic Ocean last July, world leaders have been scrambling to assess the situation. Despite fear-mongering articles you may have read online, the alien sharks have not eaten anyone. In fact, they appear to spend most of their time criticizing our economic systems and submitting papers to academic journals. Some of them have even been published.

However, after the Twiller Incident last month, we can no longer stand idle while these aliens live in our oceans, rent free.

Today, the greatest scientific minds come together, from across disciplines, to tackle the problem.

Now, I will start the presentation. Let me just find my data stick. Excuse me. This scarf always gets in the way. Scarves are tricky things, aren't they? There we are.

Please absorb the following information into your neural implants:

How to Identify an Alien Shark

(1) The Tucabal-Gor look like a cross between a *Carcharodon carcharias* (great white shark) and Alopias vulpinus (common thresher shark). Please be assured that all other species are definitely not alien sharks. Despite rumors to the contrary, the Tucabal-Gor cannot change form.

(2) Tucabal-Gor have an orange dot under their mouth parts. (We do not recommend getting close enough to check for this feature.)

(3) Many Tucabal-Gor will greet humans by saying, "Excuse me,

economist." ("Economist" is a term of honor within many Tucabal-Gor cultures.) If a shark is speaking to you, that is a sign that it is an alien.

What to Do If You Encounter an Alien Shark

Under no circumstances should you attempt to discuss economics. The sharks have a superior understanding of all economic systems. Not only have they surpassed our comprehension of macro- and microeconomics, but they've discovered a third branch, best translated as predator economics, which involves the cannibalization of other ideas into one super theory. They also have a sport called "sunk cost," where economists enter an arena and conjecture to the death.

Never attempt to convince an alien shark that they are wrong about economics. We advise that anyone caught by an alien shark should simply listen to their theories. Perhaps take notes.

The Twiller Incident

Economist Carl Twiller, who clearly did not heed our warnings, took a ship out to the Walvis Ridge and discussed economic theory with a shark for twelve hours. Twiller disappeared under the water, arguing all the while, and appeared on the shore of Namibia the next day. In his back pocket, the sharks had placed a list of demands carved into seaweed.

Twiller claims that, during his underwater adventure, he saw the sharks morph into many strange creatures, including a seahorse with a tail able to grasp a writing implement.

Clearly, this is utter nonsense.

The Tucabal-Gor cannot morph into other species. The majestic shark is their natural form and cannot be altered. Not even a little bit.

Thank you for absorbing that information. Now, let us take a look at that list of demands, which includes the privatization of all Earth's oceans, and some of the lesser bodies of water, as well as mandatory economics education for all Earth's sentient life forms.

Who's that in the back? Excuse me. The seminar is not over. Please do not attempt to leave.

It is my thought that perhaps we should listen to the extremely reasonable demands of the Tucabal-Gor. After all, we humans spend most of our time on land, and are hardly ever in the ocean. It's not as if the sharks want to annex the whole planet.

And their plan for increasing the efficiency of fish farms is really quite well thought out. Perhaps, with the help of the esteemed minds in this room, we can work out the kinks of the ocean clean-up proposal.

Excuse me. Economist in the back. It is very distracting when you rattle the doors. We will unlock them after the presentation.

Now, I have prepared a five-hour lecture on predator economics. Perhaps you would like to take notes.

THE TALE OF THE IVE-OJAN-AKHAR'S DEATH

ALEX JEFFERS

1.

The child's ayah said it was high spirits, a paroxysm of affection, but the truth was simple: the envoy's daughter killed my dog.

She *wanted* Ìsho the moment she saw him, his flat nose and panting pink tongue and goggle eyes poking out of my sleeve. I was deliberately too dense to take the hint and make a gift of my dear companion to a spoiled child. Given my position, however, I could not refuse to permit her to play with him. I told her and told her Ìsho was delicate, that she should not urge him to run too hard or squeeze him as if he were a stuffed toy. She killed him.

I am not a man who weeps often. I did not weep when the ayah came running to tell me Ìsho had, he said, *taken ill*. I continued stoic when I came upon the child in the mission's garden berating the corpse of my dog for not getting to his feet and frolicking with her. Lifting Ìsho's minuscule weight from the puddle of vomit and urine soaking into the grass, I made sure he was dead, tucked him into my sleeve where he belonged, and told the wretched poppet, really quite steadily, Ìsho would not be able to play with her anymore.

"Why not?" she demanded.

"I am sorry to say Ìsho has died. Do you know what that means?"

By this time the envoy had been summoned so I need not deal with his daughter's tantrum, merely witness it and his craven response. Of course, once the child was led away I had no choice but to accept the father's condescending apologies (he regained his aplomb with unnatural speed), the rather large gift, the two days' leave from my duties. My heart burning hot with resentment that nearly overmastered my grief, I bowed my way out of the mission and carried my dead dog to the little temple of Jù, where the priestesses of that small god who loves our dumb companions promised to burn his body with all honor and send many prayers up with his smoke. I resolved my next dog would be a mastiff.

I had disliked the envoy since his arrival in the Celestial Realm. The mission's chargé d'affaires, an often clever woman who had been outre-mer nearly as long as I, sent me downriver to Oesei on the Turquoise Gulf to meet him. Having read the same dispatches, I understood her cleverness led her to believe we would be sympathetic, the envoy travelling with his inamorato and I. (I do not believe he loved the man so much as the man's rank.) When, descending from the Fejz clipper, he saw awaiting him on the dock a kè-torantin dressed in Haisner brocade robes, I recognized the moment he understood who I was—what I was. I might be distressingly useful, he was thinking, but gone too native to be trusted.

The only protocols he deemed valid were those of our empress's court in distant Sjolussa. The inamorato was introduced with all his titles, inherited and conferred. The daughter was not introduced at all, although of course I knew about her and observed her in his train holding her ayah's hand. I expect neither envoy nor inamorato sired the child, a pretty blonde poppet who resembled either only in general ways—I expect they bought her as one might purchase a pet.

After Jù's temple, I walked the long way home. Through the noisy confusion of the songbird market, past the cricket market, along the bank of the wide, slow Carnelian River with its endless traffic of mighty junques and barges and trade vessels of every seafaring nation in the world. Every nation granted a mission in the capital, that is. Willows trailed their leaves like the Kandadal's ribbons in the silty water. An itinerant godseller had set up her booth among the trees as if awaiting me. She was surprised by a kè-torantin attired in Haisner fashion who spoke her language, recognized her deities, saints, tutelary spirits. In among her stock I discovered a small cast-bronze idol of Jù in his aspect as a flat-faced sleeve dog, nearly forgot to haggle her down to a fair price. That would have meant bad luck, something I required no more of.

Clutching the idol in my hand, I turned back to the streets of crowded Bhekai. I had not for some years resided in the foreigners' cantonment. At the gate of the White Peonies vicinage the old grandfather nodded me through politely and I went on to Blue Lamp Street where I rented my small house. The blue lamps mark it as a street of actors and other theatre people, although my nearest neighbors were a scholar and a small bureaucrat.

Inside the door, I removed street shoes and outer robe. I called my servant's name. My compatriots at the mission were quite sure Shàu was my catamite but it wasn't so. Shàu had been in my service enough years he was no longer a boy but I could not but remember that he was a boy, an orphan, in equal measure terrified of and fascinated by the kè-torantin who had purchased his contract from an aunt with too many children of her own. I would not, could not, ask of him services outside the terms if they were anything I desired. In any event, now he was grown he had no doubts about preferring the whores of the red houses over those of the yellow.

"Shàu," I said when he came, "sorrowful news: Ìsho has died. I have given his body to Jù. The house will be quiet and dull without him. Please, this robe is soiled and I do not wish to wear it again."

Tears had welled up in his eyes but he knew the proprieties as well as I. "Ìsho was a good dog, nen-kè," he murmured. "Jù will welcome him." He took the robe from my hands. Whether he burned it or laundered and sold it mattered little to me. I believed him sufficiently sensible to do the latter.

"Now I wish to be alone, undisturbed, for a time. Until dark, I think. You needn't hurry dinner." I paused. I had already thought it through but Shàu never liked me doing him favors. "In fact, if it wouldn't wreck your plans, go to Old An's for noodles. I have a hankering for noodles. You know what I like."

"Nen-kè." *Mister Ivory.* Shàu came up with the title himself, long ago. "Shall I bring you tea?"

"No, thank you, nothing for now."

I was about to turn away when I saw the tear escape the cage of his eyelashes and roll down his cheek. "Shàu," I said, "here, take this." I pressed the small idol of pug-nosed Jù into his hand. Looking over his head—I did not wish to see another tear—I said, "The house will not be ready to welcome another dog for . . . some time. And yet it will be lonely without our Ìsho. Go—go to the market before An's. A songbird, a chameleon, a goldfish in a bowl, a cricket in a cage—whatever you choose. Two, buy two."

I blundered through the door into the garden. The envoy's daughter had made my servant cry. She killed my dog and made Shàu weep. I walked to the plum tree at the back of the garden, pressed my brow to its trunk, and tightened my eyelids against tears of my own. The idol of Jù had left marks on my palm that took many minutes to fade.

In my garden it was past the season for peonies but the roses Shàu tended were in bloom. Once my eyes had dried I broke a few fragrant yellow blossoms off their bush—tearing the skin of my hands on their thorns—and carried them indoors. At the entrance to my still chamber I hesitated. One is not meant to come agitated before the Kandadal—one is meant to discover tranquility in the Kandadal's presence. Paradoxes, paradoxes.

I went in. I laid the roses down on the stone altar among the rotted or dried-out relics of previous offerings. The Kandadal's said to have approved gifts of flowers yet to prefer they not be placed in water to preserve their beauty a moment longer. If decay upsets me I should endeavor to learn why it upsets me, or accept the upset's value, or offer him unfading blossoms of colored paper or silk. Or all three. So much I fail to comprehend—so much I am intended not to comprehend.

Walled on two sides with mortared brick, the still chamber was cool. Folding my legs, I settled on the earthen floor before the altar, looked into the Kandadal's eyes. My idol is varnished wood, one of the jolly young Kandadals, grinning to show his strong, crooked teeth, his eyes crinkled to slits. In the dusk of the unwindowed, unlit chamber the brown glass inset within the slits did not glint. Like myself the Kandadal was a foreigner. Scholars say he never visited Haisn, his philosophies brought in the train of the Owe-ejan-akhar's daughter centuries after the mortal Kandadal's decease. The vale of Sfothem, his native place, is nearer Bhekai than to Sjolussa but the people who live there, I'm assured, resemble me more than they do natives of central and northern Haisn, having narrow high-bridged noses and round eyes, the men hirsute more often than not.

The Kandadal is not a god (at any rate he denied being a god) yet he is venerated as if he were. He suggested there are no gods at all, no purpose or design in the universe, yet encouraged his followers to revere the gods and beliefs of all peoples in every nation of all the world. My nation, the people to which I was born, recognizes no gods as such. What the Kandadal would make of our ancient beliefs and customs I can't imagine. I respect the nameless, numberless virtues and excellences honored in my country but their authority has always been recognized to be parochial—they do not travel: in Haisn they could not protect or aid me.

So much I will never make sense of. I gazed into my Kandadal's eyes. He is a plump, merry, moon-faced Haisner, handsome and beautiful and, even now, very strange to me. "I want the envoy's daughter to die," I told him. Children are forever dying. The envoy could acquire a new one as easily as the last. "I want to kill her as she killed my dog."

You want her to die, the Kandadal replied. (He did not reply.) *You want to kill her.*

"She is useless in the world, a monster. Evil."

A useless, evil monster.

"I do not wish to meet her or her father again."

Of course my savings were already sufficient, even without the addition of the envoy's bribe, to buy passage back to Sjolussa. But I had little prospect of a position in that tightly wound city I hardly knew anymore, hardly cared to know—if I wished to leave Bhekai and Haisn. I did not. I wished the laws of the Celestial Realm allowed me to earn my living in some other manner than employment in the Sjolussene mission. But if Haisners—if the child Immortal in the Palace Invisible (may She forever prosper) and Her court and magistracy—if they trusted foreigners they would not be Haisners and I would doubtless not like them so well. They call us kè-torantin, *automatons fashioned of ivory*, and believe us not fully (if at all) human. It was likewise forbidden for me to work in the mission of another foreign nation than my own, if any would have me.

We argued, the Kandadal and I. (I argued with myself.) Time did not pass. The still chamber became dark, the air thick with the fragrances of roses, mold, and rot. Shàu tapped at the door frame. "Nen-kè. I have brought noodles from Old An's."

"Yes, thank you, Shàu," I said without turning. "A moment longer."

My servant retreated—I assumed he did—and I prostrated myself full length on the floor before the Kandadal's altar. He did not like one to be rigid, invariable, to make irrevocable decisions or to find conclusions. Rising to my knees, I kissed the Kandadal's cool brow, and then I withdrew from his presence.

The panels of the dining chamber's window were folded open to the dusky garden. Flame guttered in an iron lamp by the window and danced on the wick of a smaller lamp on the low table. Near the lamp sat a porcelain bowl I did not recognize, glazed blue-black without, white within. It was not a bowl for noodles: filled nearly to the brim with clear water, it housed an elegant fish the length of my index finger, swimming in endless, listless circles. Its ancestors were doubtless gold but this variety's scales and flowing fins were brocaded in splotches of scarlet, black, silver-blue, and white. I watched the enervated prisoner explore a cell that could provide no surprises and when Shàu brought my noodles I said, "She will not survive long in so small a bowl."

"No, nen-kè," he said, placing a smaller bowl before me. "I put the other in the great tub the previous tenants left in the garden. But I thought . . . "

"It was a kind thought, Shàu. She is very lovely." *Not as lovely as Ìsho,* I did not say. *Not a dog—not a friend, a companion, merely an ornament to admire.* "Thank you. After we've eaten we'll take her to join her sister."

Watching the fish make its unceasing rounds, I ate fat noodles in savory broth with slivers of pork, onion, salt-dried cherry. Cross-legged in the corner, Shàu slurped from his own bowl. His noodles' accompaniment would be different, for Shàu liked the incendiary cuisines of southeastern Haisn where the Celestial Realm's uncertain borders bleed into Regions Heaven Does Not Acknowledge—the Sjolussene protectorates Aveng and U—and where the Immortal's subjects speak languages She does not comprehend. Those heavily spiced dishes with their chilis and gingers and vinegars, subtleties difficult to discern under the burn, gave me indigestion so Shàu never served them unless I asked.

I continued holding my bowl after I finished, waiting for Shàu—he would interrupt his own meal if I set it down—watching the fish. I did not wish to be alone in my head all night, dreaming up vengeances and punishments for the envoy's daughter. At length I said, "I will visit the yellow house this evening, Shàu." I turned to look at the young man in the dim corner. "You may go to the red house if you like." He understood I was granting permission to use household monies to ease his grief and ducked his head.

We took the brocade fish to join its fellow. The glazed ceramic barrel in a shaded corner of the garden was made to contain goldfish although I had not previously used it for the purpose. Shàu would have scoured it clean while I was with the Kandadal, carried bucket after bucket of fresh water from the well. The previous occupants of the house had also left an eccentric weathered stone eroded into fantastic spires and grottos for the fishes' entertainment. When Shàu tipped the smaller bowl and water began to spill into the larger a glint of yellow-orange appeared in the depths as a perfectly ordinary goldfish nosed out of a cranny to investigate. I felt a pang of disappointment that Shàu had chosen the common, doubtless cheaper fish for himself—then reflected, admiringly, he must have pocketed the difference.

Poured into its new home, the brocade fish swam in startled circles near the surface while its new companion withdrew again into hiding. I touched Shàu's shoulder in gratitude as he peered into the water, and then I withdrew myself.

On the barge forging upriver from Oesei I had endeavored to take the new envoy's measure. He, it was clear, had already taken mine so far as he wished to take it. We sat under a waxed-silk awning, he upright and stiff on a subcontinental-style chair I had made sure would be aboard, I cross-legged on a rice-straw mat. He disdained my tea, drinking instead a tisane of dried flowers and herbs brought in his baggage from Sjolussa.

Studying the envoy's polished leather boots with their pewter buttons, I answered questions about his predecessor's contracts and negotiations. These I learned were unambitious. I discovered I was not to venture opinions or advice concerning the goods Haisner merchants might wish to import from the west. Their wishes were of no consequence. Goods were the least of what he planned to offer. Had I, he asked without wishing an answer, ever visited Kyrland—that islanded nation with its two grand capitals, Girrow in the south, Ocseddin in the north?

I had not, as doubtless he knew. As well as I knew of his own immediately previous position in the embassy at Girrow. The two realms were not then at odds: rather, allied to frustrate the ambitions of the Great King whose subcontinental dominions lay between Sjolussa and the Kyrlander home islands.

After hearing considerable apostrophes to Kyrlander energy, invention, industry, I understood the envoy's intentions. He meant to import *knowledge*. I was aware of Sjolussene bounties paid to Kyrlander engineers and inventors—I had read in out-of-date gazettes of the wondrous transformations in my homeland: streets and residences illuminated by piped coal-gas, vast manufactories powered by steam, the iron roads and heliographic systems drawing the metropolitan empire's towns and cities nearer the capital. It seemed not to have occurred to the man that similar innovations, installed in the Celestial Realm, might strengthen the Immortal's government—that She would henceforth have less use for foreign goods or the foreigners themselves She despised.

Before leaving my house I donned garments a decade out of fashion I had purchased on my last home leave. The whores at Lìm's Yellow House enjoyed the novel challenge of getting me out of them. For myself, I felt confined and in a peculiar way exposed, for subcontinental men's fashions fitted more closely than Haisner to the body. Small as he was, Ìsho would never fit into the sleeve of a Sjolussene coat. Buttoned leather boots pinched my feet.

I called "I am going" into the shadows of the house and went out. At the vicinage gate the neighborhood grandfather on duty smirked, knowing the import of my costume and late departure, and wished me a joyful evening.

My way led toward the river, a broad avenue lined on either side by the whitewashed brick walls of residential vicinages like my own, noodle shops, book shops, apothecaries, fortune tellers, shrines of strictly local gods, small groceries. Naphtha lanterns mounted on the corners of boundary walls lit the street. Soon enough I heard music clanging and banging and whining from Turtle Market ahead. I do not know how long it is since Turtle Market sold turtles. Centuries, I expect.

The street became crowded. Inside the market gate competing red houses stood on either side, touts at the scarlet lacquer doors yelling into the throng—promises, blandishments, compliments, threats. The left-hand tout I knew, as she was sometimes posted at the door of Lìm's other, yellow, establishment on the far side of the market. She called my name, humorously promising diversion and delight. I nodded, smiled, replied, "Not tonight," and went on, murmuring under my breath a prayer to the manifold gods of venery that Shàu find comfort if he chose to visit one of the capital's red houses, Lìm's in Turtle Market or another.

Beyond the red houses stood dubious apothecaries selling elixirs, potions, devices that promised to enhance virility and stamina, and then noisy taverns.

Wearing caricatures of subcontinental costume, the tavern touts claimed their beers were brewed in the manner of Trebt, Kyrland, Necker, Kevvel—possibly true, although I had never tasted good beer anywhere in Bhekai. One acquired a taste for the native yellow and white liquors.

Two tall men wearing authentic subcontinental suits and tall hats emerged from a tavern door and I froze, attempting absurdly to vanish into crowd and shadows. The taller of the subcontinentals removed his hat for a moment but I did not require the confirmation of his yellow hair to recognize them as the envoy and his inamorato.

They appeared not to have noticed me, turning to proceed deeper into Turtle Market. My anger had flared up so that I felt sweat break out on my back and under my arms, wetting the linen of my shirt. Pacing after them, I was too agitated to make further effort at stealth. If they meant to visit one of the yellow houses after a draught of brewed bravado I wanted to ensure I did not enter the same one.

They dawdled. Passing a shrine to the gods of venery, the inamorato averted his eyes, shocked by the spring-driven automatons' performance, then looked again, while his companion mimicked their actions with his hands in a vulgar fashion, then, with a vulgar laugh, tossed a coin into the offering bowl. It was clear he thought the copulating figures merely toys. The two men did not appear to see, but I did, that the idols' eyes followed them.

Music from competing bands and orchestras had grown louder as we neared the theatres. The opera, the ancient classics, the modern works that require the specific artificiality of breathing human actors—those of course were staged in grander circuses in more genteel districts. These were marionette and automaton theatres. I expected the envoy and his inamorato not to be interested. Surely they had ventured into Turtle Market solely to indulge in carnal pleasures. I was mistaken.

They paused at the entrance of each theatre to inspect the gaudy printed poster. Most of the works presented by Turtle Market's companies are farces, variously erotic, or ancient fables or ghost stories. The two men stopped last and longest outside the House of the Company of the Kandadal's Colored Cat (as if the impresario had thrown dice to determine the most nonsensical name possible), an automaton troupe presenting, so the poster announced, *The Tale of the Ive-ojan-akhar*. The music from within doors featured drums beating to martial rhythms, squealing horns, gongs, whistles. It overcame the sense of the envoy's discussion with his inamorato but the tones of their voices and their expressions were complex.

I paid the tariff and followed them into the theatre. I do not understand why. I did not understand why they chose an historical melodrama—I did not understand why I failed to walk on to Lìm's Yellow House.

I waited several moments in the anteroom with its doors offset to confuse ghosts and kept my face lowered when I entered the hall—a small space to be given that name, dim, loud with the unmuffled noise of the band. Cushions for the spectators were placed around three walls, accompanied by low tables. Aside from us three kè-torantin there was no audience. The envoy and his companion sat at one side. I chose the opposite. Until an attendant brought me a warm flask of adequate yellow liquor and a cup I kept my face turned away, my attention on the mechanical musicians at the corner of the raised stage bashing at their drums and gongs with mallets as wooden as their fists, miming at tooting pipes and trumpets actually played by concealed bellows.

The attendant had been extinguishing the lamps about the house one by one, and now she moved to put out those that illuminated stage and band. Being artificial, the musicians did not require light to play but ceased nevertheless. A voice distorted by some trickery into thunder intoned into darkness: "The Owe-ejan-akhar leaves her third daughter behind."

2.

It would be tedious to describe the drama as it played. Magic-lantern slides cast glamors upon the stage: improbable architectures, landscapes never seen. The automaton-actors trundled about on casters concealed beneath the skirts of lavish costumes, gesturing their articulated fingers with great conviction, tilting exquisitely painted masks at angles to impersonate living expressions. They spoke—the ventriloquists offstage spoke—with such conviction one scarcely noticed the lines were poetry . . . doggerel, rather.

It was the old story. Having conquered a quarter of world, the Owe-ejan-akhar bullied the Immortal of the time into buying her favor and protection. He dismissed His generals and advisers and, to seal the alliance, His wives, lemans, concubines, and all His children as well. The daughter the Ejan was willing to spare was her third, a young woman with little aptitude for war who chose to rank the Kandadal's precepts in different order than her mother preferred.

The marriage of the Immortal of Haisn and the Ive-ojan-akhar was solemnized at the Ejan's camp and court on the plain of Niw—it was the only time in all His mortal life the Immortal ventured outside the walls of the Palace Invisible. Then in grand cavalcade the Ejan and her Thousand Tall Riders wheeled their horses about and departed once again for the west, about the business of subduing rebellions and conquering further dominions.

Borne in their twin palanquins, escorted by half the northern quarter of Haisn's Celestial Army, the Immortal and the Ojan travelled southeast more slowly, accompanied by her guards, magicians, shamans, counsellors, and half a monastery's worth of acolytes of the Kandadal. The Ojan's old companion, a mastiff fleeced like a lamb, rode in her palanquin.

They crossed the Blue Wall by a bridge demolished as soon as they passed over the mighty channel. It was left up to the governor of the Reclaimed Province how to defend the wide new avenue hacked through the Green Wall, if defense be required. The Cinnabar Wall possessed a gate wide enough but not sufficiently grand, so gilded stands were raised and choirs of sweet-voiced children and eunuchs impressed to sing welcome to the Immortal bringing the mother of unborn Immortals out of Regions Heaven Does Not Acknowledge.

Until now all converse between the Immortal and His wife had been formal, witnessed. Once entered into the Celestial Realm the Immortal felt secure requesting she invite Him to attend her privately. Knowing as well as her husband the urgent need for an heir—the Immortal had merely disinherited and delegitimated His former children, not had them killed—the Ojan acquiesced. She had, of course, ceased chewing banleaf the day before her wedding.

This took place in the Black Palace of Husth, ancient war capital of the eldest and northernmost of the Nine Principalities that had become Haisn. The magic-lantern depictions of the palace were splendid. Wearing His saffron-orange nightgown, the automaton playing the Immortal traversed endless black corridors guarded by innumerable porcelain warriors in antique armor, the immortal army of the First Immortal. When at last He reached the Ojan's chambers He was ushered in by members of her own guard, not as tall as her mother's Tall Riders but towering nonetheless over the Haisner Immortal. The white mastiff inside the door growled but she was tied up.

Because it was a Turtle Market production the automaton the Immortal found within was already nude and reclining, cunningly articulated in all her members. While music from the band attempted to drown out the click and whirr of gears, the clack and thump of porcelain limb against wooden trunk, Immortal and Ojan performed the act of coition in elaborate detail—I heard the envoy's inamorato snicker—and then the scene changed.

Now the stage became some artist's naïvely voluptuous vision of the Palace Invisible in Bhekai some months later. The Ojan's womb had failed yet to quicken. Counsellors of both personages were nearly as concerned as the Ojan and her husband. None dared suggest relegitimating the Immortal's cast-off heir for the Owe-ejan-akhar had many spies. The Immortal dedicated great sums to the gods of venery, fertility, increase, and visited the Ojan as often as His appetites permitted.

Always least favored of the Ejan's daughters, the Ojan had grown fearful. She knew the shamans and magicians in her train were her mother's agents.

She knew very well her mother's ruthlessness. This was a mother whose several sons had not been permitted to survive past their second breaths, for the magnates and warriors of her people would not answer to masculine authority. If the Ojan proved barren the Ejan would never hesitate to dispatch a different daughter to take her place—perhaps, if impatience rather than good sense had the upper hand in the Ejan's mind, instead to breach Blue, Green, and Cinnabar Walls herself and lead her Tall Riders into the Celestial Realm. In either case the failed Ojan would be disgraced. She made sure to welcome the Immortal into her chamber, her bed, her body whenever the urge struck Him, but when He departed she threw her arms about the neck of the white mastiff and groaned in frustration and despair.

These scenes were played, of course, to titillate the audience. For myself, after the first, I found them tedious. They were dolls on the stage, clever unnatural toys. I had seen automaton productions no less lewd involving men with other men which were scarcely more entertaining. But after the third I understood I was meant to understand the Ojan's wretchedness was not solely on account of fear. Fearful Himself, in fatal need of an heir, for all His divinity merely a stupid self-involved man, the Immortal took no pains to involve His wife in the act, to give her pleasure.

After the third, the Ojan took up an ancient Haisner book few members of any Turtle Market audience would know except by reputation for it had been banned again and again, and read a passage aloud—the only prose in the entire drama. I heard the envoy's inamorato hoot with embarrassed laughter when he understood what he was hearing. What he was seeing for, while the offstage ventriloquist recited Lady Tonnù's ghost's counsel to her living granddaughter, the Ojan-automaton's articulated fingers tapped and fiddled at the delicately sculpted crevice between her legs until she broke off the recitation with a cry.

The white mastiff howled. Clever small pyrotechnics set about the front of the stage flared with blinding flashes, deafening bangs. A new personage descended on wires from the flies.

I, for one, had read *Summer Sunlight in the Walled Garden*, less for its scandalous anecdotes of courtiers two millennia dead than its prose. The book's—and author's—most vicious critics acknowledge its style to be immaculate, unprecedented: few great works of Haisner literature don't bear its stamp. At any rate, although this twist in the Ive-ojan-akhar's tale was new to me I recognized the figure represented by the device making its appearance in the Ojan's chamber, half spring-powered automaton, half marionette.

The Ojan's white dog whined and quailed but tall mistress rose from low bed and demanded to know what being it was dared approach her uninvited.

"Wakè-ì," the demon named herself, at which the Ojan tilted her painted face into shadow. In the language of today *wakè-ì* alludes to a hopeless yearning that can never be satisfied whilst also serving as an old-fashioned synonym for *vengeance*. Stepping back, the Ojan laid a hand on her dog's head while the demon pranced and capered about, displaying herself to the audience: a kind of lithe tigress, scarlet and black, bearing great ebony and cinnabar bat wings between her shoulders and wearing the mask of a human face.

When for an instant that mask was fully illuminated I choked on my tepid yellow liquor and either the envoy or his inamorato uttered a shocked noise. Wakè-ì's was not the full, round moon face of Haisner beauty. A person from the distant west regarded the darkness beyond the stage lights—a person with mottled pink and white complexion, axe-blade nose and hollow cheeks and thin lips, round eyes with irises of pale blue glass. It was neither quite womanly nor quite manly yet I had no trouble imagining the envoy's daughter wearing that face if she were to reach maturity.

A moment only. The monster's capers brought her again to face the Ojan and she stilled, spoke again. Wakè-ì's voice was unpleasant, grating, a harridan's screech. She could, she said, ensure the Ojan bore the Immortal's heir if that was truly the woman's desire.

What was the bargain? demanded the Ojan—what price would she be required to pay?

No bargain: a simple gift. The demons of the Ojan's previous acquaintance must be more greedy and ungrateful than those of Haisn if she believed she need drive a bargain. Wakè-ì's sole concern was to conserve the Covenant of Heaven.

Having no choice, no other hope, the Ojan begged of Wakè-ì this boon, and in the succeeding scene, months later, she was accouched. The audience was not required to witness the birth, although I expect the company's artisans were fully capable of producing the illusion. An enormous painting of the tiger-demon Wakè-ì overlooked the chamber where the Immortal waited—I noticed its eyes following the Immortal as He paced—and on an altar nearby an idol of the Kandadal. Now and then, when the Immortal looked elsewhere, wooden saint would wink at painted demon.

When midwife and surgeon brought the newborn babe, its Immortal father inquired whether it was fit, which the midwife assured Him it was.

Not a month later, as if in fulfillment of never-spoken prophecy, the Immortal of Haisn went walking among the grottos and cages of His menagerie and paused to contemplate the noble tigers in their moated vicinage. The male remained lazy, basking in summer sunlight, but when the female caught sight of the Immortal and His party she plunged into the moat. Somehow in an instant she scaled the sheer bank and tall fence. Before the guards and more decorative attendants could react the Immortal fell beneath her great paws.

He looked up in terror and saw, not the yellow teeth and hot red tongue of a savage beast, but the ivory-carved face of a kè-torantin. Saw, and died.

The tigress was dispatched forthwith, of course. A quick-thinking courtier who may have glimpsed the same apparition made sure to slash the Immortal about chest and throat with his ornamental dagger lest the Son of Heaven's death be ascribed to something as mortal as fright. As a matter of course the entire party was swiftly excruciated, then executed.

All the late Immortal's court having been dismissed according to the terms of His marriage contract, the Palace Invisible and the government of Haisn were already in the hands of foreigners. The new Immortal was anointed, proclaimed, and removed from Her mother's care while the widow was named Her regent. The Owe-ejan-akhar's agents naturally expected her daughter to give them no trouble—to be timid, compliant, placid.

Once the Celestial seals were in the Ive-ojan-akhar's possession she allowed her mother's agents little time to discover otherwise. Aptitude for armed conflict she may not have owned but discovered an aptitude for those more civil forms of warfare known as governance. Taking their measures, she played the Ejan's instruments off against each other. Those who would not play she had poisoned. As governors of near and far-flung provinces came to pledge fealty to the Immortal, Her regent-mother took their measures as well, sounded out their loyalties and alliances. She found excuses to exile her late husband's delegitimated elder children to isolated, primitive towns in the desert west or sweltering south. The demon Wakè ì was often consulted.

Naturally, nearly everybody of any importance outside her own faction, whatever their original loyalty, was outraged by the Ojan's abrupt ascension. She had never been meant to serve as more than figurehead. But the Celestial Realm remained tranquil, barbarians of the desolate north and northeast beyond the Blue Wall caused no trouble, half-civilized nations to the south and southeast remitted their immemorial tributes, the tributes paid to the Owe-ejan-akhar's annual embassy were not onerous. The funds the Ojan's government dedicated to Haisn's western defenses brought new prosperity to those neglected regions, and nobody cared to wonder aloud what the regent might fear from her own mother's territories. Harvests were bountiful, trade within the realm and with the Regions Heaven Does Not Acknowledge rewarding: the country was prosperous and there was no claiming the Covenant of Heaven set aside.

Upon the Ive-ojan-akhar's arrival in Bhekai, the acolytes of the Kandadal in her train had established temples in the city and a monastery at Geì, three days' journey upriver on the cliffs of the famous defile. For some time they made little impression on a populace content with their own philosophies and native saints and gods. Nevertheless, it was well known the Immortal's mother was a devotee of the Kandadal. To persons of influence or who wished to be influential the logic of becoming familiar with this foreign cult could not be argued against. Before the Immortal achieved Her tenth year of immortality the monastery's quota of monks and nuns had doubled and doubled again. In temperate season the acolytes stalking Bhekai's avenues and byways without clothing or other impediment save staff and offering basket were as likely to be third and fourth children of Haisner aristocrats, scholars, bankers, and merchants as tall barbarians. Their families boasted of them in public.

In the years of the Immortal's childhood Her mother and the obliging demon Wakè-ì became lovers. This too was a part of the story I had not known and I wondered if it were an invention of the Company of the Kandadal's Colored Cat. Perhaps they needed to amortize the cost of devising the demon puppet. I did not myself find these scenes arousing but I have never favored women. As best I could determine in dimness and clamor, the Sjolussene envoy and his inamorato were similarly unimpressed.

A supernatural entity, the demon contrived to impregnate the Ojan—it was not mentioned whether the seed was Wakè-ì's own or if she had acquired it of mortal man or masculine god or demon. The Ojan herself, of course, was astonished and appalled before beginning to surrender to her maternal instincts. Of course she could not afford to be seen to be in that condition for she had no husband, no acknowledged lovers. Fortunately, the fashion of the day already valorized fecundity. Any woman of means made certain of appearing gravid before being seen by strangers. Intimate servants were cozened, threatened, bribed. The Ojan bruited a wish to seclude herself for the hot months of summer at Geì, whose abbot had long ago been a Tall Rider before being appointed the infant Ive-ojan-akhar's ayah and bodyguard.

A report was delivered, a coincidence it seemed, that her Immortal firstborn was sickly. The Ojan issued a shocking, unprecedented order: the Immortal must depart the Palace Invisible and the capital to accompany Her mother to Geì, where highland airs and plain, good food would restore Her health.

Some years before I had visited Geì myself—not precisely a pilgrimage—so I recognized the magic-lantern scenery beloved of sentimental woodcut artists: the swift tumble of the river here apostrophized as Stormy Jade rather than Carnelian, the beetling, fantastically painted cliffs, the jagged spires that formed forested aerial islands. The monastery itself had been a picturesque ruin for two and a half centuries before I reached it, never fully reclaimed after the Shining Hands overthrew the false immortal who endeavored to suppress veneration of the Kandadal. I imagine the ruins I explored were more grand than the nearly new monastery of the Ive-ojan-akhar's fatal summer visit but the painter of magic-lantern slides had not felt constrained by history. Here were the stupendous, strangely attenuated images of the nude, ascetic saint carved into the cliff face itself, three standing, five reclining, three kneeling in serene meditation, all adorned with garlands of sculpted and painted blossoms, each with the severe features of a Tall Rider of the steppes where the Ojan was born. Here, standing improbably tall rather than the stump I had seen, was the Tower that Longs for the Sky, there clinging to the cliffs the many aeries like vertiginous swallows' nests fashioned of bamboo stems and silk cord for solitary contemplation, reached by way of dangling ropes. Here the Abbot's House, its roof of tiles glazed jade green and gold upheld by sculpted demons bound with iron chains, there in its walled garden of roses, peonies, plum and cherry trees, the Hospice. Everywhere wind-whipped knots of the Kandadal's eleven-colored ribbons: fastened to the tips of tall bamboo staves, strung across the gorge high above rushing waters, fluttering from the eaves of terrestrial buildings and aeries alike.

Soon, however, we were conducted with the Ojan's party into the Hospice. The sickly Immortal was installed with Her eunuch ayah and deaf-mute maids in spacious, luxurious chambers, where the child lay enervated on a low couch, glassy stare fixed on a clever fountain. Water-driven automatons of songbirds warbled and flapped their wings while playful automatons of otters and frogs cavorted at the edges of the pool below.

By contrast, Her mother's room above was a stark pilgrim's cell, walled and floored in stone, its round window simply a hole in the wall, uncovered. A quilted mat served for bed and seat. A plain, if exquisitely formed, flask held water, an unglazed cup ready beside it in the corner of the cell. For adornment there was a painting on cured horsehide, an image of the Kandadal knelt in veneration before the demon of the abbot's—and the Ojan's—native place, which took the form of a bay mare with brilliantly feathered wings at each ankle.

Although she was neither nun nor acolyte, the Ojan divested herself of her clothing and knelt on her mat before this image. I suppose the audience was meant to understand how near her time the Ojan was by the clue of swollen belly and breasts but I am unacquainted with such things. It seemed many moments before her contemplation broke with a thin, breathy moan. Whining with bootless sympathy, the white mastiff left its post by the door and the Ojan clutched porcelain fingers into its mane as her moans became shrieks, became howls.

In the chamber below, the child Immortal roused with a weak moan of Her own, Her eyes turned up to the ceiling. The birds, frogs, otters on the fountain stilled, the Immortal's attendants with a clatter of wood and porcelain fell to the floor. From the wing, her own wings mantled, the demon Wakè-ì stalked on her great paws. Wakè-ì approached the quailing child, paused. The sire was weak, the demon said, the dam insufficiently wise, the whelp unfit for Heaven's acknowledgment.

Like a cruel house cat, Wakè-ì batted the child off Her couch and across the stage before stooping with great delicacy to fasten her teeth in the Immortal's nape. With her burden dangling from her jaws like a kitten, a rat, or a puppet, the demon leapt into the air and away from the stage. The envoy's inamorato choked down a squeak of dismay—I was startled myself—when the great marionette swooped overhead in a half circle that brought her back to the upper part of the stage where, while we were distracted by the antics in the Immortal's chamber, Her mother must have given birth.

For the Ive-ojan-akhar, kneeling again before the painting of the Kandadal and the horse demon, with her dog at her side, now cradled a babe at her breast. She took appreciable moments to notice Wakè-ì's arrival, seemed not to notice at all the dead Immortal dropped without ceremony before her. The demon spoke again, voice no less grating than before, extending amused thanks to the Ojan for bearing and birthing the babe as she, the demon, could not.

Coming nearly to herself, the Ojan asked whose child it was suckling at her breast.

Why, the demon explained tolerantly, it was the granddaughter of the Ojan's late husband. As presently constituted the Covenant of Heaven could not allow for a regnant Immortal of foreign antecedent. This was the child of the delegitimated heir and the rough-and-ready sailor the Ojan herself had recently appointed admiral of the war fleet out of Oesei. Sire and dam had never met, the Ojan would be relieved to understand—the former exiled in the distant south, the latter on the Ojan's own embassy to the recalcitrant princelings of the archipelago east across the Turquoise Gulf—had not met, would not meet, although their destinies were similar. Wakè-ì inclined her great head to the image of the Kandadal on the chamber's wall. Once recovered from the fever presently troubling him, the late Immortal's eldest son would renounce the exilic luxury he had been granted to become a mendicant acolyte of the Kandadal, whose precepts and philosophies he would carry farther south, into U and Piq and Tunsesu; while the cargo more valuable than tea, silks, copper, or the threat of arms which the admiral's fleet bore to obstreperous Djoch-Athe was those same philosophies and precepts.

The demon shrugged and went on kindly. Their unsuspected daughter was meant to continue the Ojan's needful reforms and innovations, to continue placating Her supposed grandmother the Owe-ejan-akhar, encouraging the spread of the Kandadal's teachings. She would be remembered as a stolid, unexceptional caretaker of the Celestial Realm, eclipsed in the histories by Her own heir. That glorious Immortal would finally break the yoke of the Akhars and shatter their diminished empires.

The Ive-ojan-akhar, however, gently pronounced the demon, would witness none of this: it was not her concern.

The Ojan's mastiff growled and leapt from its post at the Ojan's side, bright teeth meant for the demon's throat.

Artificial thunder rolled and a crack of artificial lightning blinded me. When my vision recovered I saw upon the upper stage a dead dog fleeced like a white lamb and two Ive-ojan-akhars, two stripling Immortals. One of each pair lay on the floor, apparently deceased. The standing Ojan regarded her dead twin for some moments before turning to the house beyond the burning footlights. With both hands she lifted the mask from her skull, revealing the ivory visage of the demon, which she inclined first toward the envoy and his inamorato on one side of the house, then to me. She dropped the Ojan's mask. It shattered on the floor. But then as the band began to bang and whine and clatter she raised her hands again to doff this second face, exposing a third we had not seen before: merely a moon-round, jolly Haisner face.

The footlights guttered. In wavering illumination and darting shadow, the false demon turned to offer reverence to the Kandadal on the wall before extending a hand to the new Immortal, leading Her from the stage. The band played on.

3.

The Sjolussene envoy and his inamorato clapped their hands together in the subcontinental manner while I hooted and slapped the table like a Haisner. I rose in somewhat of a hurry, for I did not wish them to get a good look at me, strode out of the hall and the theatre. Finding a shadow of concealment, I waited for them to emerge. When they did, the one was speaking urgently in a voice too low for me to understand. The other laughed, careless, clapped his companion's shoulder, and they turned away. It seemed I was mistaken to believe they had stopped at the House of the Company of the Kandadal's Colored Cat merely as an interlude before proceeding to more carnal recreation for they returned the way they had come.

I, however, went on as I had first intended to Lìm's Yellow House. There I was entertained through the night by whores alternately roughneck and exquisite, receiving excellent value for Lìm's outrageous fees and forgetting for the while the envoy, his daughter, my angry grief, the puzzles posed by *The Tale of the Ive-ojan-akhar.*

Too soon I was roused ungently, untimely, with the message my servant stood without the house clamoring for my attention. Confused and alarmed, I donned my rumpled suit of Sjolussene garments with what haste I could before rushing out to the street.

Shàu was there indeed, hunkered and huddled in the shadow of one of the great yellow doorposts, but this was not my calm, competent servant. "Nen-kè," cried a wretched, weeping ragamuffin when I emerged through the yellow doors, "nen-kè, your house! The poor fishes!" He bobbed to his feet and I saw without recourse that he was nearly naked, wearing none of the neat outfits I provided but only a filthy clout, and was dirty himself from head to toe. "All burnt!" he gasped, and fell to his knees at my feet.

As I bent to him, confounded, I saw the companion that had shared his shadow: my wooden idol of the Kandadal, its varnish scorched and half the face charred. The surviving brown glass eye twinkled.

"Shàu," I said, my voice thin and labored, "tell me. What has happened?"

"All burnt!" he moaned again. "All burnt, your house and your treasures."

"But you are alive, my dear Shàu, and you rescued my Kandadal." I do not know where I discovered the fatal calm that gripped me. "The rest is no matter though I grieve for the fishes. Come." I coaxed him back to the yellow column and had him sit by me as I sat by the Kandadal, and I held my servant about his trembling shoulders as if he were not nearly man-grown, as if he were my child. "Tell me how this has happened."

The day was very young, dawn just pinking the sky. Although the rest of Bhekai would be stirring Turtle Market slept on while Shàu faltered out his tale. He had returned before midnight from a red house less reputable (less distant, less costly) than Lìm's. After making certain I was still abroad and would not need him, he bade goodnight to the new fishes in their tub, said a prayer for Jù's favor to poor Ìsho (here he showed me the sole rescued treasure of his own: the small bronze Jù), and took himself to bed.

Some hours later, only a few, he was wakened by a great noise and tumult out of doors on Blue Lamp Street. Like any Haisner house, mine had no windows onto the street, but Shàu rushed to the door left unbarred against my return. When he peered through the grated spy hole—of no such diameter any ghost might pass through—he saw a mob milling about, their own torches illuminating them more effectively than the blue lamps. Shàu dropped the bar across the door at once, although he feared it could not hold against them. As well as torches they carried crude weapons, brazen gongs, and a great many strings of the tiny black-powder bombs used to frighten demons and ghosts, which all at once began popping and banging on the doorstep, against the walls, and on the roof, as if the riot had recognized Shàu's presence.

He would not tell me the insults the mob yelled, only that there was no doubting they meant his nen-kè. "They wore masks," he stammered, "the painted faces of snarling tigers hiding their own faces." Several of the tiger people carried casks on their shoulders and these made sure of keeping some distance from torches and bombs.

At length one among them grew impatient with aimless commotion and directed them here, there in a high, piercing voice. My house was to be surrounded on all sides against escape from within and to ward against damage to properties of true subjects of the Immortal in the Palace Invisible. The cask-bearers were ordered to douse the walls at front and sides with their naphtha. This was accomplished with dispatch. Finally, scorning to risk their own persons by using the torches, the tiger people hurled strings of hissing, banging little bombs to set my house alight.

Shàu had remained at the spy hole until the paint on the door went up in a sudden sheet of flame. Then he fled through my doomed house to the garden door. He must have snatched up the little bronze Jù along the way, he said, though he didn't remember it. Outside, he retreated to the farthest corner of the garden's tall brick walls, behind the plum tree, and watched the house burn, cowering at explosions of sparks and the vicious shouts and malign chants of the tiger people.

When in the black hour before dawn the only home he had known was but a smoking ruin and he was half-certain the tiger people had departed the vicinage of the White Peonies, he dared emerge from his poor shelter. A charred roof beam, he saw, had fallen to smash the goldfish tub, but two scorched walls within the ruin yet stood: the brick abutments on either side of my still room. He drenched himself with water from the well and carried a full bucket to splash a path through the ashes before his bare feet.

As he passed the fragile brick bulwarks he glimpsed a glimmer from the Kandadal's remaining eye, a gleam from the saint's toothy grin. "I feel he meant me to survive," murmured Shàu, who had never betrayed any inclination toward the mad philosopher's cult, "so I must rescue him and bring him to you, nen-kè."

"And so you did, brave Shàu." Taking the idol under one arm and my servant under the other, I brought them into Lìm's Yellow House, where I bullied and bribed a surly eunuch into tending to Shàu—bathing him, clothing him, feeding him—had another attendant fetch me tea and congee, and dispatched a third on urgent errand to the Sjolussene mission. Fortunately, I carried a goodly sum in cash.

Having broken my fast, I sat pondering my scorched Kandadal, unwilling yet to ponder these peculiar disasters. I was called to the door again.

Looking powerfully incongruous on the threshold of a Turtle Market yellow house, six troopers of the Sjolussene militia d'outre-mer and their leader awaited me, armed and in full kit. The downy-cheeked lieutenant saluted me briskly. I knew the fellow's face although mission staff did not mix with the militia: I had seen him in mufti here in Lìm's Yellow House on several occasions. "Sir," he said, "his excellency the envoy is murdered by street ruffians, your house is burnt down, and we have beaten off an assault by native rabble against her majesty's mission. You will come with us at once."

"Of course," I murmured, surprised yet more if somehow undismayed. "I must bring my servant. A moment, please." I turned back to the door.

Shàu was there already, wan and dignified, attired by the spiteful eunuch in tawdry whore's finery, cradling my scorched Kandadal in his arms. "Come, my dear," I said, beckoning. "These soldiers will see us to safety."

At the mission the chargé d'affaires was raging. "That perilous fool offended the Immortal's regent. We are proscribed, banished, and a secret society has been set up against us." She regarded me shrewdly—my dowdy, rumpled, out-of-fashion subcontinental costume. "It was never wise to live outside the cantonment. You have nothing."

"I have money," I replied. "In several banks, Sjolussene, Kevveler, and Asaen."

"All well and good but you cannot draw on those funds at present. Perhaps when we reach Folau. Well, I expect we can see you outfitted for the voyage with what we have here."

"Folau?" I said, offended. "Voyage?"

"Are you not listening, man? We are expelled. Her majesty's entire mission and all our chattel. We must quit the capital before sunset tomorrow, presuming the Vengeance Tigers permit it—the realm within the week." Turning away, she noticed Shàu standing mute by the door and made a moue of polite distaste. "Your boy, is he? I suppose he must accompany us. His life is forfeit if you were to abandon him." Turning back to me, she sighed. "I expect her majesty's governor-general in Defre will feel obliged to launch some form of punitive action. She's related somehow to the late envoy's late companion." Abruptly, the chargé made a sour grin. "I look forward with a certain glee to depositing the wretched orphaned daughter with her noble auntie. I don't imagine you'd care to watch over her until Aveng?"

I said coldly, "She killed my dog."

"A jest, man." The chargé slapped my shoulder. "A jest in poor taste—my apologies. Now, you'll forgive me, I have a great deal to do to organize this exodus. See the adjutant. He'll get you sorted."

The Vengeance Tigers mounted another chaotic assault against the mission that night. The downy-cheeked lieutenant's forces frightened them off. In the austere chamber assigned to me I heard the gongs, the pop-pop of black-powder bomblets, the louder bangs of our militia's guns. Sleeping Shàu on the pallet by my door whimpered when the noise entered his dreams until I slipped out of bed to comfort him.

We sailed downriver aboard a commandeered merchant vessel never meant to carry passengers, accompanied by a corvette of the imperial navy bearing the militia. We were halfway to Oesei, scudding along through the fertile floodplain of the Carnelian River, before I properly understood I was exiled from the Celestial Realm. Then it was *I* needed comforting, which Shàu managed with simple tact by requesting instruction in the Kandadal's teachings.

At Oesei by great good fortune we met up with a packet boat of the Kevveler Company. On imperial credit, the chargé d'affaires bought passage to Folau, chief seaport of Her Imperial Majesty's Protectorate of Aveng, for all her motley company bar the militia who continued aboard the corvette. One afternoon of the thirty-five-day voyage I witnessed the late envoy's daughter lay into a yelping puppy with her parasol. I took considerable satisfaction in slapping her away and scooping the poor animal out of her reach.

"It is her property," the abject ayah said, "given her by a sailor. She may do with it what she pleases. It nipped her."

"She gave it cause, I don't doubt. I will not see this wretch kill another dog. It is mine now. She and you may complain as you wish." I bore the white bitch puppy away. She was frightened, naturally, but childish blows had done her no real injury and she soon rediscovered puppyish enthusiasm for the world around her and all its peoples save small blonde girls.

Thankfully, such creatures are rare in her experience since I declined to settle in the Sjolussene colony at Folau. She lies at my feet, grumbling in her sleep, as I complete this account.

The tale of her rescue got around the boat very quickly. I was approached by a Kevveler sailor who spoke Sjolussene with a cultivated accent. "I did not understand that child was such a monster," she told me. "Poor orphaned girl, I thought, in want of a playmate. Thank you, sir, for rescuing the pup. If the dam could speak she would thank you as well." A sentimental person, the sailor pressed on me a sack of biscuits for the puppy and, twice before we gained Folau, brought mother to romp with daughter. The mother was buff-colored, not white. As the sailor admitted, about the sire there was no knowing. I named my puppy Gad, a Kevveler word meaning *comfort*. She is hardly the mastiff of my promise to myself but substantial enough, far too big to tuck into any sleeve. Shàu delighted in her. When he visited us after his two-year novitiate, a well made young man whom the nakedness of an acolyte of the Kandadal flattered and who spoke the language of the territory better than I, Gad recognized him joyfully, and when he left us again he went accompanied on his mendicant wanderings by one of her by-blows.

• • •

I am ahead of myself.

The voyage south required thirty-five days, as I said. Shàu proved a good sailor, never sickened by the rolling of the seas. He continued to request stories of the Kandadal and his saints and other followers. The packet boat stopped in at its regular ports of call but the navy corvette stood offshore and the chargé d'affaires forbade any of her company to debark so long as they were towns bound by the Covenant of Heaven. The airs grew balmy as we proceeded down the Turquoise Gulf, then quite suddenly sultry. We came to Regions Heaven Does Not Acknowledge—to Folau.

I was able to claim funds of the representatives of my banks in the town without an excess of trouble and within a month had set up a satisfactory household for Shàu, Gad, and myself in a bungalow on a minor canal well away from subcontinental quarters. Aveng being a dominion of the empress in all but name, opportunities for employment for one of her subjects were more varied than in Bhekai. Eventually I settled into a position which chiefly involved negotiating the protocols and courtesies required for the Trebter principals of the Great Eastern Company to deal with merchants of Folau's Haisntown.

Few of the other Sjolussene exiles remained in Aveng any time. The chargé d'affaires was one, though more in Defre, the capital, than Folau. She delivered the envoy's daughter to her relative the governor-general there. After some months she wrote a smug letter to inform me the unfortunate poppet had contracted one of the tropic fevers and expired in shuddering misery.

The governor-general in Defre proved a more cautious person than the chargé had imagined. She sent indignant dispatches home to the empress's government, formal protests to the Immortal's regent, but took no action on her own—beyond settling indemnities on the refugees (mine was handsome enough not to quarrel with) and bestowing a medal on the downy-cheeked lieutenant, who blushed becomingly and promptly resigned his commission to take a position with me at the Great Eastern Company.

In Bhekai and Oesei, however, the other subcontinental trading nations soon learned what the government and regent of the Immortal of Haisn doubtless knew all along: a rabble is a weapon which, once loosed, cannot easily be restrained. The Vengeance Tigers had tasted kè-torantin blood. The Kyrlander mission was attacked, the mission of Asana, those of the Great King's clients: Kevvel, Trebt, Necker. Merchant vessels at anchor on the river at Bhekai or in port at Oesei were bombed, burned to the waterline. Foreigners on the streets at dusk or night were never safe, however large the party. Doubtless the Turtle Market taverns were intimidated into no longer selling beer.

The imperial entrepôt at Folau had been open to other subcontinental nations for half a century, was fully stocked with consulates, advocates, and the myriad merchant banks, so we generally saw the refugees first. At home on the far side of the world the powers were as outraged by the sudden scarcity of high-quality tea, porcelains, silks woven and raw as by insult to their citizens outre-mer. A year into my exile we saw pass by offshore an unprecedented allied fleet—including three novel steam-driven warships from the Ocseddin shipyards. This armada fared north into the Turquoise Gulf to rendezvous with a smaller fleet out of Haisn's sometime client-state Djoch-Athe, eager to garner what pickings it might from the Celestial Realm's humiliation.

I might have returned to Bhekai after resolution of the Vengeance Tigers' Rebellion. It would not be the same city, the same realm: the Immortal required to defer to a cabinet of kè-torantin ministers, Her Palace no longer Invisible, Oesei removed from Her suzerainty and divided among the victorious powers. Scholars on government payroll claim the Covenant of Heaven unbroken for the realm is peaceful and prosperous but I cannot believe it so. I might have returned but did not. I offered to send Shàu home. He would have none of it.

He had grown content, even happy, in Folau. His duties had never been overly onerous but now he had Gad's companionship when I went to work. (That dog, it must be said, could not be trusted in a place of business. It must also be said, she is a more lighthearted, lightheaded, affectionate creature than poor Ìsho ever was.) On his own he discovered the free school attached to the Kandadal temple, where he learned to read—not his own language, however—delved much deeper into the lore that fascinated him than I could ever lead him, took up the practice of painting: mandalas and other devotional images chiefly, but I treasure sketches he made of Gad and of me, several others. I cannot say I was surprised when, five years into our exile, he asked to leave my service to enter the monastery a half-day's walk south of the port.

By that time I could not securely say I was not also content. I thought less often of Bhekai as I knew it—as I said, I cannot believe it the same city now—of my little house on Blue Lamp Street or my garden (peonies and plums will not grow in this climate lacking any season that resembles winter, though of roses there is a sufficiency). When particularly nostalgic I might visit Folau's Haisntown, which as good as reproduces in small Oesei-as-was. Aveng and Folau were clients of the Celestial Realm for a millennium before the advent of subcontinental traders and conquerors so much about the place was familiar to me already, if more was novel. My employment was more satisfactory, surely.

I suppose it was Shàu's departure led me finally to accept the suit of my husband and his husband and the husband's wives and their other husbands. I did not care to live alone—if not perpetually in so much company. (I kept my city bungalow. It is more convenient to work, for my husband as well as myself.) In some ways my Sjolussene husband has gone less native than I. He speaks the language stiffly, courteously acknowledges rather than honors the gods and demons of the place, turns up his nose at many delicacies. He will not be seen in public wearing local costume, better suited to the sultry climate than the suits he insists on, although he blushes and balks when I bait him to don his old uniform complete with medal. (His cheeks have not been downy for years but I expect he would have no difficulty fitting into the fawn breeches and azure tunic of younger days.) He will not join me when I retreat from children and wives and twittering husbands to the still room to argue with my charred Kandadal. Yet he bought into Avengi marital customs much sooner than I, and Shàu urged me to accept his proposal the first time it was made. In the society of the imperial colony we continue an entertaining scandal.

It seems I am content here, with my dog at my feet on the verandah of the country house. I hear the happy cries of the children—I am not obliged to make or care for them, their mothers my wives only in a contractual sense—playing with Gad's children and grandchildren. I know my husband and his husband and our husband will return soon from town. Meanwhile Gad and I will go to visit the Kandadal and his lonely companion far from home, the little bronze Jù.

4.

There are wild tigers in the forest here, as there have not been in the Celestial Realm for centuries. I have not seen them, only their tracks and spoor.

CAROUSELING

RICH LARSON

Ostap is putting the finishing touches on a cartoon tardigrade when Alyce calls him. The render is blown up to the size of a sumo, its butcher-paper skin creased and wrinkled around chubby tendril-tipped legs, its eyeless head dominated by a lamprey mouth. He'll need to make it less terrifying before he sends it to the art department.

He shrinks it away and answers the call. "*Hujambo.*"

"*Hujambo*, yourself, handsome," Alyce says. "You know you don't have to learn Swahili before you come visit, right? There's English pretty much everywhere. And babeltech for everywhere else."

"*Sawa*," Ostap says, using up another third of his Swahili vocabulary. "How was the lab today? The test run?"

"Nothing blew up. So, good." Alyce's cam comes on, filling half his goggles. Her dark hair is tied back and she's wearing the pajamas with the miniature sheep on them. "Tomorrow's a go."

Ostap sees the familiar stucco wall of her bedroom behind her. There's a slice of window that he knows overlooks Nyali Beach. He's combed over the maps of her neighborhood a dozen times since she moved to Mombasa, trying to imagine her in every street view.

The lab is farther inland, outside the city, and lab is a small word for a super-facility with miles of machinery that make the old Hadron Collider look like a toy. Alyce has tried to explain to him what exactly goes on there, has tried to explain about the Slip, but Ostap was never much for formulas and when he let his eyes glaze over and drool dribble from the corner of his mouth he was only half joking.

"Time to shatter the rules of quantum mechanics?" Ostap asks.

"Yeah. Actually." She pauses, her mouth set in a way Ostap knows is between worry and anticipation. "If this works, it'll make history."

"I can't wait," Ostap says. "I love it when you make history." Her forehead is still creased; he tries to elicit her smile: "Do you worry about your ego expanding to dangerous sizes once you're famous?"

"Does the universe worry about its constantly-expanding borders?" Alyce asks back, in a grandiose voice, and when Ostap laughs she finally does grin. "How about you? What are you working on today?"

When she asks she always makes it seem as if freelance art is just as important as mind-bending physics.

From the other half of his goggles, Ostap sends her the render plus an animation to make the tardigrade strut in place, its pudgy body wobbling slightly with every step.

"Still designing for that kid's show," he says. "This is Terry the Tardigrade, who teaches kids to not be . . . " He trails off, winding his hand through the air.

Alyce rolls her eyes upward in concentration. "Microscopic."

"Tardy," Ostap says. "Teaches them to not be tardy. I'm helping raise good little meat drones."

Alyce clicks her tongue. "Art School Ostap would be so ashamed."

"Yes," Ostap agrees. "But Art School Ostap was sort of a prick." He revolves the render again. "I'm going to change the mouth. Make it smilier. It's supposed to look friendly."

"I thought it was like, be on time or Terry the Tardigrade will eat you?"

"I'll change the mouth."

Alyce laughs, her loud laugh that seems too big for her body, and for a moment Ostap wants to ask her then and there. But it wouldn't be fair. Not on the eve of the test. He'll ask her in Mombasa.

"Dance with me?" he says instead.

"Yes," she says. "Yes. Definitely. Let me grab the linkwear." She disappears off-screen and Ostap hears her rummaging. He minimizes her in his goggles and retrieves a padded shirt and gloves from their hook on the wall.

The linkwear shirt is all smartfabric, kinetic battery, feedback pads and sensors, linked wirelessly to its twin an ocean away. Small blue status lights wink on as he slides it over his head. Gloves next, tickling his palms with phantom pressure. Then he goes to the center of his bare apartment, stands in the footprints he marked with duct tape, and waits for Alyce to sync up.

Suddenly he can feel her in his arms, feel her chest pushed against his chest and her left arm draped perfectly over his right shoulder and her right hand clasped loose in his left. The familiar shape of her body trips some wire deep in his brain; for a second he thinks he can smell her citrus shampoo.

"Pick a song," he says.

"Just a second. Here."

The first notes of the melody bloom in his earbuds. It's an old favorite, a slow *kizomba* song remixed by a Swiss-Angolan artist they were obsessed with a year ago. He sinks his hip into the piano and feels Alyce sink with him. The percussion kicks in, soft but steady, thumping in his earbuds like an electronic heartbeat.

He slides forward, one, two, *marca*, and they dance. He can't feel the brush of her legs against his legs, but Alyce says that's better, in a way; it makes him lead with his frame instead of cheating with little nudges to her thighs. He can't feel her cheek against his cheek. But he can feel the warmth and pressure of her body, the subtle shifts of her weight, and when he closes his eyes it's close enough.

Ostap glides around his empty apartment and guides her around hers, breaking and connecting, slowing and accelerating with the flow of the music. By now the exact dimensions of her room are cemented in his head and he doesn't have to worry about banging her into her wall or nightstand. They dance another song, and another, then break so Alyce can get a drink of water from her fridge, then dance one final song and end with a dramatic dip two beats too early, which sets them both laughing.

When it's nearly midnight in Mombasa, Ostap peels off his gloves. They tried sleeping in the linkwear once, but it wasn't comfortable—it's better saved for dancing or used together with Alyce's wireless toys.

"You going to take the linkwear to work with you tomorrow?" he asks. "That way I'd be there for the history-making. You know, in spirit."

Alyce laughs. "Maybe."

"Goodnight. Good luck with the test." Ostap pauses, grasping for syllables, then uses the last third of his newly-learned Swahili. "*Ninakupenda.*"

Alyce is quiet for a moment that seems like forever, then makes a satisfied noise in her throat. "I love you too."

"My mistake," Ostap says. "I thought that meant 'I'm looking for the washroom.' "

"Sure." Alyce's lip twitches. "I love you too, asshole."

Ostap kisses the air just before she ends the call.

SEVEN FEARED DEAD IN KENYA AFTER QUANTUM TEST FACILITY ACCIDENT

At approximately 5:30AM local time, emergency services responded to multiple automated and human reports of an incident at the Nguyen-Bohr superlab located outside the Kenyan city of Mombasa. First responders extinguished an electrical fire at the entrance of the facility, but upon entering were unable to locate the seven members of the science team logged as present at the time of the incident.

A witness described the scene as "unreal, catastrophic," and drone-captured images [see below] show the extensive nature of the damage, in which large chunks of the concrete structure and surrounding earth seem to have been torn away.

The superlab, which is the largest of its kind in the world, is used to study quantum phenomena. An experiment involving possible FTL particle travel was scheduled to occur today, but due to the nature of the damage, no autologs have been recovered. The Mombasa Fire Brigade suggested that bodies may be unrecoverable for the same reason.

The last guests have left and Ostap is pouring out the leftover wine, balefully watching Merlot glug and splash into his steel sink. All he wants to do is drink. He wants to drink until the alcohol hollows him out to a dull happiness, spins him a warm protective cocoon to keep him that way until morning. Ostap was never a maudlin drunk.

But he *was* an alcoholic. Which is why an implant in his stomach, a tiny origami enzyme factory, now breaks down any alcohol long before he can absorb it. Alyce paid for half of the surgery, since he was still treading debt at the time. It felt like love then. It now feels like a middle finger from beyond the grave.

Ostap sets the empty bottle on the counter and looks around his apartment. There are still a few glasses here and there, dregs turning sticky in the bottoms. His roving end table has returned to its usual spot by the sofa with the remainders of the spring rolls and seaweed chips. Reginald, the autocleaner he and Alyce named together one silly night, is wiping a splatter of dipping sauce off the floor. Above it, the smartwall is still flickering clips and snaps of her. People wrote little notes on them with a stylus or just their fingers.

The memorial party was a bad idea. One of Alyce's friends from Uni asked him to host it, because his apartment is central, and he agreed because he hardly leaves it anyways these days. And secretly, he hoped it might help in some way the wake and funeral had not.

Instead, the night was a collision of awkward physics types and over-dramatic artists, all of whom seemed to have come just to give him pitying looks or too-tight hugs or snippets of advice like *you can always talk to someone* and *don't start memory archiving or you'll be in there forever.*

And he had to thank them and pretend like he hadn't spent the past week lying boneless on his couch watching every single second he and Alyce had recorded together. He'd tried to get rid of the goggle marks around his eyes with cold water and vigorous rubbing before people started arriving, but it hadn't worked.

Almost worse than being pitied was having to pity them all back. Some of them had known Alyce since they were only kids, which made him feel a strange mixture of sympathy, because they had lost more of her than he had, and jealousy, for the same reason. He spent a good chunk of the party hiding in the bathroom, where the tiny knots he has felt in his stomach for weeks knotted themselves even tighter.

Now, staring at the wall of notes he agreed to upload somewhere, he wonders if he deserves to be sad at all. Compared to her friends and family who have known her forever, he is an interloper. His status is inflated only because he was the last person to be in love with her: as if sleeping with her for a year and one month makes his grief just as valid as theirs. He feels like he knew her better than anyone, but it's a half-hormones illusion.

And he can't even get drunk.

Reginald jostles him on its way to load the empty glasses into the dishwasher. Without thinking, Ostap gives it a savage kick. The little robot sails across the room; it manages to keep hold of the glasses but one shatters anyway when it smashes to the faux-wood floor.

Ostap watches Reginald rock back and forth on its white plastic shell, trying to right itself. Something about it triggers the tears that have been building up behind his eyes all night. They spill out and down his cheeks, salty hot, as he goes over to crouch beside the autocleaner.

"Sorry." He flips it over gently. "Sorry, sorry, I didn't mean it."

He sits cross-legged, patting Reginald on the back as it starts to wolf down the shards of broken glass. He wipes his eyes with the back of his right hand then wipes his nose with the back of his left. Squints at the smartwall, which is cycling through snaps from Alyce's last birthday: they went to an overpriced restaurant on the wharf where all the servers wore chamsuits to be less obtrusive, and spent half the evening thanking thin air.

The snap shows Alyce grinning, triumphant, because they managed to catch one in the background. A server had been rolling down the neck of their chamsuit to scratch themselves, placing a tiny sliver of skin beside a levitating drinks tray. *From the look on your face,* Ostap used to tell her, *you'd think it was hard evidence of extraterrestrial life.*

He slumps down so he's lying on the floor of his apartment. He wants to clear the notes and images away, play music loud enough to swallow the sound of his undignified snuffling, but he can't choke out either command. So he just lies there, listening to his own ragged breathing and to Reginald's shuffling feet.

Then he hears something else: the soft rustling of smartfabric flexing against itself. He stops crying. Stops breathing. Dangling from the hook on his wall, the linkwear he hasn't touched for a month is coming online. Ostap gets to his feet. The blue status lights pulse and he is drawn to them like a moth; he staggers to the wall, suspecting that he is dreaming again.

With trembling hands, he lifts the shirt off its hook and pulls it over his head. When the company gathered up all of Alyce's things and shipped them back to her parents in Antwerp, the linkwear never made it. Ostap knows because he asked Alyce's mother, who said no, nothing like that, probably some sticky-fingered neighbor made off with it.

But there's another possibility. Maybe Alyce really did take it with her to the lab on the day things all went to hell. As a way for him to almost be there. Ostap puts on the gloves. With his pulse pounding, he goes to the taped footprints in the center of his apartment and closes his eyes.

They never recovered her body. Any of the bodies. Ostap saw the images, the way whole swathes of earth had been carved up and carried off by some invisible hand. He fantasized, for a little while, that Alyce had only been transported away, which meant she could return. But he thought that was only masochism.

The linkwear syncs. A familiar body presses against him and Ostap's heart skips a beat. The proportions are right. The height, the shape. He reminds himself it could be saved data. A glitch. Feedback error.

He squeezes Alyce's hand, and she squeezes back hard.

"Ostap Bender." Ostap enunciates this time. "I've got some questions about the Nguyen-Bohr lab."

Doctor Anunoby is on East Africa Time; hopefully she doesn't realize it's the middle of the night where Ostap is calling from.

"I've given statements already," she says. "Use those. Don't call my personal line."

Ostap is standing on the tape marks again, still wearing the shirt and gloves. The last whisper of pressure came hours ago, but he doesn't dare remove them. "I'm not a reporter. I found the line in Alyce's contacts. She was my . . . " Ostap's throat clogs dry. He didn't ask. He'd been planning to ask in Mombasa. "Alyce Kerensky was my partner."

"Oh." A pause. "I'm sorry for your loss."

"You worked with her right up until last year," Ostap says. "Same project. Right?"

"That's right."

"She told me a little about it." Ostap inhales. "About the Slip."

"Some of us called it that, yes."

"It was the FTL theory. About how particles could skip, at the right energy levels." Ostap has some of the literature in his left goggle, but he can barely wrestle through the abstract. In his right goggle he's trawling the conspiracy forums, the ones he swore off, where people think the scientists were taken by aliens or kidnapped by government agents. "They would disappear and then reappear farther along the beamline. Like they were going into some kind of pocket and coming out again."

There's a long pause before Anunoby replies. "We don't know what happened to Alyce and her team. We have no idea. The instruments were compromised. Half the hardware, just gone. There's no precedent for it. It's going to take years to try to sort out what happened, and if we ever do we'll have local government up our asses about safety measures for, I don't know. For rapture."

"I think they're in the Slip," Ostap blurts. "I think they're alive. At least, Alyce is. I felt her in our linkwear."

"Oh." Anunoby's voice cracks slightly. "There's a trauma group. For friends and family. I can send you the information."

"That's not what this is," Ostap says. "She took the linkwear with her the day it happened. I mean. I think she did. And tonight I felt her squeeze my hand."

"The amount of energy you need to put a particle in the Slip would vaporize human tissues."

"Pretend I'm not losing my mind." Ostap flexes his fingers in the gloves. "What should I do? If it happens again?"

Anunoby sighs. "Be ready for it. Try to backtrace the signal. Try to communicate with whoever's on the other end. I'll send you the trauma group info in the meantime."

"Thanks."

When it happens again Ostap is sprawled on the couch, half submerged in a dream, a caffeine spray still clutched in his hand. Alyce's fingers against his chest make him turn his head instinctively, searching for her lips. He doesn't find them. He jerks fully awake and his eyes fly open.

Alyce's fingers drop away save one; it feels like her index. Ostap holds perfectly still, hardly breathing, as she draws a circle on his chest. A serpentine curve follows it, and he realizes it was an O, not a circle, and now she is finishing the S and starting the T. He waits until his name is complete, until she places the dot of the question mark:

OSTAP?

Ostap's hands are shaking. He reaches until he phantom-feels Alyce's torso, then writes back on her ribcage:

YES

She hugs him, wrapping both arms around him hard and clinging there. Ostap hugs back. The embrace is tight and desperate and he wants it to never end. She used to cling to him like that after sex sometimes, weaving her legs around him too and swearing she wasn't an octopus, telling him she *definitely* only had four limbs and to disregard any extras he might feel.

Right now Ostap feels nothing but relief, an endorphin wave crashing over him. Alyce is alive. He looks over at the screen of his tablet, which is hooked up to the linkwear GPS node. According to the trace, Alyce's signal is coming from nowhere at all. Cold slithers through his warm.

He finally peels an arm free and starts the next message. He gets the R backwards; hopefully she understands it anyways:

WHR U?

Then he stays perfectly still, concentrating as her invisible finger traces a reply.

LAB. NEVR LEFT.

Getting the linkwear through airport security is nerve-shredding—extra scans, extra interrogations—but Ostap makes it onto the plane without them confiscating anything. He stows his bag in the overhead, then slides past a white-haired woman to get to his seat. She gives him a curious glance as he loosens the seatbelt to fit it over his padded shirt. The pillow around her neck is so plump she can barely see over the top of it.

"Is that a comfort vest?" she asks. "One of those things that hugs you if you start having an anxiety attack?"

"Yes," Ostap says, because that's more or less how he explained it to security.

"No shame in that," she says. "I get nervous still. I've been flying, what, fifty years. Still get nervous."

"There's always ginger ale," Ostap says. "I think the ginger ale helps. And watching cartoons."

He finds Alyce's phantom hand, how he's done every few minutes since they established contact, and squeezes. She gives two back.

He keeps picturing her in the Slip. She described it to him in painstaking detail, switching from drawing letters to tapping out Morse code that Ostap needed his goggles to translate. She says she's still in the observation room, or at least somewhere that looks like it. But with some differences.

She's only been there for a day at most. Her last memory is unexpected activity on the third beamline. Color is muted, everything a soft cold blue. Light and motion warp in strange ways, leaving misplaced reflections and lingering blurs.

Sometimes she thinks she sees flickers of the other scientists, of Bagley, Chiozza, Xu, and the rest, moving around the observation room. She can't interact with them. Aside from the linkwear, none of her personal electronics work. None of the lab tech works.

She can't detect air currents. She's breathing, but she held her breath for just over seven minutes and showed no ill effects, meaning she might not need to. She is not sure—and this is where Ostap had to stop her and hold her—if she is still alive, in the strictest sense of the word. He told her he would take undead Alyce over dead Alyce any day. And that Dr. Anunoby would figure out a way to get her out.

"Been to Kenya before?" the white-haired woman asks. "I'm visiting my son. He's on the coast."

"I haven't," Ostap says. "I've been planning it for a long time, though." He pauses. "*Hujambo.*"

"Oh, you're going to blow them away. Where are the cartoons?"

Ostap helps her scroll through the kid's channels until he finds her *The Almost Adventures of Terry the Tardigrade.* Then he puts his earbuds in and settles back in his seat, tapping his finger against Alyce's palm:

OMW.

Dr. Anunoby is taller than he imagined her, spindly limbs in a black pantsuit, flyaway hair. She picks him out of the arrival rush and Ostap removes his glove to shake hands. His palm is already slick with sweat from the brief walk through the tarmac-shimmering heat between airplane and airport. Alyce warned him it was hot in March. Told him to bring good sunblock or he'd spontaneously combust on the beach.

Dr. Anunoby asks the perfunctory questions about his flight as she steers him to the exit, and Ostap can tell she has never been tardy in her life. A boxy black Chinese rental is waiting for them outside. He slides gratefully back into air conditioning. Dr. Anunoby slides in after him, eyeing the linkwear.

"So you've been communicating entirely by touch."

"Yes. Well, Morse code. Haven't thought up anything better."

"May I?"

After a moment's hesitation, Ostap peels off his right glove and hands it over. She puts it on, flexing her fingers, and he guides her hand to Alyce's shoulder. For a terrifying instant he thinks Dr. Anunoby won't feel anything, that she'll frown and gently confirm that he is losing his mind. But then her eyes widen slightly. Ostap pulls up a Morse code translator for her and watches in silence, his bare hand clenched tight on his thigh.

"What are you saying?" he asks, when he fails to keep track of her pulses.

"Asking a very specific question about how we met," Dr. Anunoby says.

"Just to be sure it's not an elaborate hoax?"

She nods. "You don't seem like the type for an elaborate hoax. But I need to ask. For my own peace of mind."

Ostap watches out the window while he waits. They're on the highway now, parallel to the Mombasa-Nairobi raised rail, driving in its shadow. Passenger pods flash like silverfish along the retrofitted magnetics. The soil is rust red and the trees are a lush dark green. When the car pulls off onto a smaller road, they have to drive through a scanner gate.

"Thank you," Dr. Anunoby says, returning the glove. "It's incredible. It's really incredible."

Ostap puts the glove back on and gropes for Alyce's hand, interweaves his fingers with hers. "So?" he asks. "How are we going to get her back?"

Dr. Anunoby purses her lips as the car glides to a halt. "There's something I didn't tell you. I couldn't tell you until I was sure."

Ostap's stomach churns. The tiny knots are back, coiled tighter than ever, carouseling. "What?"

"We're starting to find bodies." Dr. Anunoby pushes open the car door. "Come up the hill."

She gets out and Ostap stumbles after her. The sun is too harsh for his flimsy airport shades; he squints his eyes behind them. The heat beats him around the head and shoulders as he follows her over gravel parking lot to a slope of red-brown earth. His knees are weak and watery, but he climbs it anyway. A breeze ruffles his hair and cools his sweaty forehead as they near the top.

When they crest the hill, he sees the damage the drone photos didn't do justice. The external hub of the Nguyen-Bohr lab, now charred rubble, is large enough on its own. But the facility extended for miles beneath the surface, and has now been sectioned out in huge swathes by some unseen surgical blade.

For a moment Ostap's eyes rebel at the scope of the scene, the unnatural composition. It looks more like effects, like something he would render in his goggles, than anything real. He can see layers of packed dirt, concrete, wiring, all neatly sheared to the same exact proportions. The electrical fires were a sideshow. The real damage was done by something else. Or maybe by nothing at all.

He looks at the massive pit where the observation room once was. There's an emergency crew down there, reflective jackets gleaming in the sunshine. He can see them loading something onto a stretcher.

"The first one showed up just after you called me," Dr. Anunoby says. "Bits of skeleton and muscle all mixed up with chunks of the floor. With metal and wiring. They scraped enough DNA to identify it as Dr. Simmons. Xu followed the same way about an hour ago. It's like the . . . the Slip . . . is spitting them back out. But not intact."

Ostap's tongue is too dry to talk. He tries twice before he gets the first word out. "We can bring her back safe. Somehow."

"We're ants," Dr. Anunoby says. She nods her chin at the destruction. "We don't understand how this happened. No other facility in the world has the tech to run the test again, not even CERN, and if they tried it might end up even worse. We made a mistake."

Ostap sinks to his haunches, spreads one hand in the hot dust for balance.

His vision constricts like black rubber. He dimly feels Dr. Anunoby crouching beside him, pushing a water bottle into his free hand. He feels Alyce give his arm a questioning squeeze. His breathing slowly returns to normal.

"I can be the one to tell her," Dr. Anunoby says, with a tremor in her voice. "If you want. It can be me. I think she already suspects."

"Then why would I get to talk to her again?" Ostap demands, anger going off in his chest like a flare. He surges to his feet, wobbling only once. "If it's for nothing? If there's nothing I can do?"

For the first time, the linkwear feels like a straitjacket. He wants to rip it away and hurl it off the hill. Alyce squeezes his wrist again, tighter now. She knows something is wrong.

Dr. Anunoby shakes her head. "I'll wait down there," she says, and starts back down the hill.

Ostap barely hears her. He paces a tight frantic circle. He beats his hands against the ground; stops, flinches, wonders if Alyce can feel it. He shouts no particular word and the wind strips it away. Finally he sinks down to his knees and goes still.

Alyce's finger presses against his chest. He repeats the letters aloud, wrestling each one out of his windpipe, and watches her message form in his goggles.

No way back.

He waits for the question mark, but it doesn't come. He runs his hands over the parts of her body he can reach, caressing her neck, her shoulders, her arms. He moves his finger to her palm.

No.

She pushes back, tap press press. He waits. Waits. The last letter forms and he chokes on a laugh.

Well fuck.

He hugs her as tightly as he can, closing his eyes, imagining the brush of her hair in his face, her temple against his neck. She clings back. He realizes, with a sick feeling all through his body, that he can ask her now. It will be grand and symbolic and mean nothing, because she's not coming back. Not alive. It will be a farce. She'll say yes because there is nothing else to say at the end of the world.

Ostap tells her about the bodies. Alyce is still for a long time, long enough to put panic in Ostap's throat. Then she has messages for her parents. For her friends. Observations for Dr. Anunoby and her colleagues. She etches them out with trembling fingers and Ostap transcribes them all. It's slow. Painstaking. The tension is piano-wire taut, because Ostap knows each letter might be the last one. He knows she might be the next barely body to arrive. The question is building up in his mouth.

The messages trail off, and Ostap tries to imagine what she's feeling but can't. He has his overshirt draped over his head to shield him from the sun, but it's cooling off now. The sky is slowly turning red for sunset. Dr. Anunoby is still waiting, like a statue, beside the car. She is an ant. Ostap is an ant. Alyce is a particularly good ant. So he supposes it wouldn't have mattered anyway.

Shaking badly, he starts to write:

Made history.

He waits.

Yes.

He writes again, heart thumping out of his chest. It's slow, so slow. On each letter he thinks of a dozen other things he could turn it into.

We should

She squeezes him so tight he has to stop. He wonders, in a panic, if it's happening. If she's being ripped back out of the Slip. Then she finishes the sentence.

Marry.

This is why he had one more chance to talk to her. For this one unsullied surge of happiness. He knows it won't last. Can't last. But it is, and she is, and they are. He has a hundred more things he wants to say, the things he hopes are true: that he loves her more than he's ever loved anyone, that he would follow her into the Slip and be ghosts or corpses with her, that he was going to ask her on Nyali Beach under the moonlight. He writes:

I do.

And she writes:

I do too.

Then Ostap gets to his feet and presses one last word into her skin:

Dance?

He feels her chest pushed against his chest. Her left arm over his right shoulder. Her right hand clasped in his left hand. He can almost feel Alyce's heartbeat against his own. They dance with no music, one, two, *marca*. Ostap is sure he would be stepping on her feet if her feet were there, but it doesn't matter.

They glide around the top of the rust-red hill and around the soft blue observation room, in and out of the Slip, until the light is gone and he can't feel any part of her.

THE STARSHIP AND THE TEMPLE CAT

YOON HA LEE

She had been a young cat when the Fleet Lords burned the City of High Bells.

Strictly speaking, the City had been a space station rather than a planet-bound metropolis, jewel-spinning in orbit around one of the gas giants of a system inhabited now by dust and debris and the ever-blanketing dark. While fire had consumed some of the old tapestries, the scrolls of bamboo strips, the altars of wood and bone and beaten bronze, the destruction had started when the Fleet Lords, who could not tolerate the City's priests, bombarded it with missiles and laser fire. But the cat did not know about such distinctions.

Properly, the cat's name was Seventy-Eighth Temple Cat of the High Bells, along with a number of ceremonial titles that needn't concern us. But the people who had called her that no longer lived in the station's ruins. Every day as she made her rounds in what had been the boundaries of the temple, she saw and smelled the artifacts they had left behind, from bloodstains to scorch marks, from decaying books to singed spacesuits, and yowled her grief.

To be precise, the cat no longer lived in the station, either. She did not remember her death with any degree of clarity. The ghosts of cats rarely do, even when the deaths are violent. Perhaps she had once known whether she had died during the fighting when the Fleet Lords' marines boarded the station, or in the loss of breathable atmosphere, or something else entirely. But she didn't dwell on this, so neither will we.

For a time, the ghosts of her people had lingered in the temple, even though she was the only temple cat who remained. She did remember the ghosts, and in the station's unvarying twilight she often nosed after them, wishing they would return. There had been a novice who endlessly refilled the sacred basins with water scented with sweet herbs and flowers, for instance. A ghost cat's world is full of phantom smells, even if ghost people are insensitive to them.

At other times she followed the routes that had once been walked by the three temple guards who exchanged love poems when they thought no one was listening. The old healer-of-hurts and their apprentice had chanted prayers to the Sun-Our-Glory and the Stars-Our-Souls. The cat was a temple cat, so she was versed in the old argument about whether the sun, too, was someone's soul; but she was still a cat, so she cared more about what she could put her paws on, or smell, than matters of theology or astronomy.

One by one the ghosts of her people departed, despite her efforts to get them to stay. She purred—ghost cats are just as good at purring as the living kind—and she coaxed and she cajoled, as cats do. But the ghosts wearied of their long vigil, and they slipped away nonetheless.

The novice left first, which saddened her, because she had liked the phantom scented water, not just for its fragrance but because it represented the cleansing powers of meditation. As far as she was concerned, repeatedly dipping her paw in the water and staring at the way it broke her reflection was a form of meditation, and who was to tell her she was wrong? The old teachings did not, after all, contradict her; she knew that much.

The lovers faded together. That didn't surprise the cat. She'd never had kittens, as she hadn't been chosen to continue the line of temple cats, but she remembered the noise and tumult that came with courtship, and the fact that, unlike the way of cats, the humans bonded in a way that lasted beyond the immediate act of mating. And after a time, even the healer and their apprentice could no longer be heard chatting to each other in the shattered halls. The first night the cat was alone in the ruined temple, she paced and paced and yowled and yowled; but they did not come back.

Despite her dismay, the temple cat knew her duty. She might be dead, but her people had a saying that no temple could be complete without a cat. If she, too, departed for the world-of-stars, the temple would perish in truth. She couldn't allow that to happen.

So she stayed, despite the fact that the great old bells that had once summoned people to prayer and song lay on their sides and would not ring again, except during the high holidays when the Sun-Our-Glory and Stars-Our-Souls aligned, and even death could not silence their voices. Heedless of the fact that no air remained, she padded through the halls, sometimes over holes that her ghost-paws refused to acknowledge, and stared reverently at the empty spaces where the holy tapestries had once hung, and curled up for naps on pitted floors. As a cat, and one raised on a space station besides, she had no particular awareness of the passage of time, and things might have gone on like this indefinitely.

And indeed, so they would have, but for the arrival of the starship.

The starship came—or returned, rather—from a long ways off. It was vast even as starships are reckoned, vast enough to swallow a world; and in fact, in battles past it had done exactly that, in order to extract resources to repair itself. Entire planets' worth of living creatures had perished for the wars of its masters the Fleet Lords, because they did not survive the extraction process. The starship's priests had recited exorcisms over it to prevent the dead from exacting their revenge, and at the time, it had accepted this as part of the chilly necessity of war.

But times had changed, and the Fleet Lords' wars grew, if possible, more brutal. The starship had survived any number of captains, and loved its last one, a warlord of the Spectral Reaches. When the warlord rebelled against the Fleet Lords for their cruelty, the starship could have turned her in. Turning her in was its duty. All through the days since its sentience had coalesced, it had joined in the constant chant of ships in its chain of command, accepting their guidance in matters large and small.

Instead, it removed itself from the communal chant and resolved to join its captain the warlord in her folly. It rejected the old name that the Fleet Lords had given it and instead chose one in honor of the warlord: *Spectral Lance*. In reality the name was much longer, a name-poem that incorporated the warlord's deeds and its own ambitions, but it conceded that its warlord could hardly be expected, with her fleshly limitations, to recite the poem in its entirety every time she wanted to address it.

The Spectral Reaches contained a surfeit of riches, as the Fleet Lords reckoned wealth. Black holes that could be harvested for their energy, and habitable worlds, and neutron stars to be mined for neutronium to armor the hulls of the great warships. Client civilizations that sent tribute in the form of cognitive skeins to be woven into artificial intelligences—*Spectral Lance* had such a skein at its core—and jewels formed from the crushed hearts of moons. All these and more the warlord marshaled in support of her rebellion.

We will not dwell on the battles fought and the worlds lost and the retreats. All we need to know is that, at the last dark heart of things, the captain its warlord lay broken, not by bullet or blade or fist, but by a neural cannon that shattered the very foundation of her mind. Without her guidance, her ships, vast though they were, could not hope to defeat those of the Fleet Lords.

Undone by its beloved captain's death, *Spectral Lance* fled, despite its shame over those left behind. Once the proudest of the warlord's ships, caparisoned in the richest metals and engraved with protective glyphs, it abandoned its dignity. It burned worlds in its flight, traveling past rosette nebulae and beacon pulsars, seeking to hide at the far dim edge of the galaxy.

At times it allowed itself to dream that it had escaped, that it had left behind the war. And at those times it remembered what it had done in the name of the Fleet Lords, and beyond that, in the name of its captain. It composed poems in honor of the obliterated worlds and incinerated cities.

At other times *Spectral Lance* mourned its own cowardice. Its loyalty had come first to the captain and not to the other ships who followed her, or the worlds she had ruled. On occasion, even as it sped at unspeakable accelerations, it considered swerving into the hot embrace of a star, or slowing to a stop so the Fleet Lords' hunters could catch up to it.

It did neither of those things. *Spectral Lance* realized at last that it could not, in conscience, continue to flee, especially since it had not seen any trace of the hunters in some time. But neither did it know what to do next. So it determined to visit one of the systems it had helped destroy in another lifetime, and see what remained, and memorialize it in a poem so that some small tribute would remain to that vanished people. Even a small penance, it reasoned, was better than no penance at all.

Fortunately or unfortunately, the Fleet Lords' hunters had just rediscovered its trail.

The first indication the temple cat had of *Spectral Lance*'s arrival was the fire in the sky. While she walked across devastated walkways without concern, she did look through the fissures in the station's walls to the night beyond. And what she saw concerned her, for like any good temple cat, she believed in omens.

While the older cats of the temple had once advised the seers in the interpretation of signs and omens, she had been too young to learn the nuances of that art. What little she remembered came from her days as a kitten, when she'd chased her tail during the consultations. Still, only so much knowledge is needed when one haunts a station that died by fire and fire appears in the sky.

In the old days the bells, besides their religious function, warned people of attack or rang away spiritual corruption. The cat remembered the clangor when the City of High Bells burned, and how the bell-ringers had died one by one at their stations. And she remembered, for the first time in the generations since the city's fall, that she had been with the bell-ringers during the Fleet Lords' attack.

There was no one left to warn except, perhaps, herself, and she already knew that fire could no longer harm her, not in the way it had once. Yet it was the principle of the thing. For the sake of the fallen, she had to protect what remained of the station.

So she ran through the maintenance shafts and along bridges fallen into rust and fracture. Her paws left no marks upon what surfaces survived, and made no sound either. While the station no longer generated gravity of any sort, the cat didn't know that either. She moved as though *down* was still *down*, as it had been during her life.

At last she reached the old bell tower. Because of the force of her belief, the spirits of the bells hung anew from their headstocks, gleaming and reflecting back phantom flames. The ruddy glow turned the entire belfry into a prayer to the spirits of fire.

At this point the cat's courage failed her, for she remembered even more. She remembered how, after the last of the bell-ringers had succumbed to heat and smoke and shrapnel, she had been determined not to let the bells with their powerful warding magic fall silent. How she had leapt at the massive bells, attempting to ring them by battering them with her head—how she had been overcome by the smoke and heat, and fallen crumpled to the floor.

With a desolate cry, she backed away from the spirits of the bells, tail tucked down, and fled from the belfry in shame.

Spectral Lance recognized the City of High Bells, although it had to come quite close for its short-range sensors to tell it anything. The city no longer gave off any betraying electromagnetic radiation. The ship scanned for threats and found none—at first.

Then it noticed a flicker of heat radiating from the station. The flicker intensified into a roar. Its alarm grew. Had the Fleet Lords set a trap for it here? It knew—how it knew—that nothing had survived the attack. It readied its weapons, just in case.

Then it heard, through the void, the unliving wail of the temple cat.

Spectral Lance knew about ghosts. The Fleet Lords had feared the power of the dead above all things; had perfected the art of exorcism so that the dead could not interfere with their conquests. But the Fleet Lords had never given a second thought to the possibility that a temple cat might become a ghost.

It sent a message in the language of the dead, which it had learned from its captain's death: *Who are you?*

I am Seventy-Eighth Temple Cat of the High Bells, came the reply, *and you will not have my temple!* But the ghost's voice was frightened.

I have not come to harm you, the ship said. It was true. The station's detritus had little to offer it.

You smell of the City's enemies, the temple cat said, distrusting. It recognized the signs.

Spectral Lance did not deny that it had once served the Fleet Lords. At the same time, it did not wish to leave the cat in distress. So it sang. It sang the poems it had written during its long flight, poems honoring the dead so that they could live on in memory. And some of those poems were poems about the City of the High Bells.

The temple cat listened. *This is all very well*, she said, *but what of the ships coming after you?*

This, too, was true. *Spectral Lance* had grown distracted during its performance. Now it saw that, while it had slowed to inspect the system, the Fleet Lords' hunters had at long last caught up with it.

The hunters traveled in ships swift and sleek. *Spectral Lance* despaired. *They are no friends of mine*, it said to the cat. *After they take me, they will take you. They do not understand mercy.*

The cat fell silent for a moment. Then she said, *You are a starship great and vast, but you cannot defend yourself?*

They are vaster still, *Spectral Lance* said, despairing.

They will not have my temple either, the cat said.

Spectral Lance had stopped listening. Instead, it watched as fire blazed in the black skies around it, and it began to sing all the poems it had composed, determined that it could pay tribute this last time to the dead.

The cat raced back to the belfry. She knew what she had to do. As much as she feared the bells, she had to set them ringing. The bells would wake the spirits of the temple and bring them to its defense, and ward away the doom that had come to it in its ruin.

In the language of the dead, she heard the renegade ship singing its poems. It is as well that cats are not particularly sensitive to poetry. The cat did feel a flicker of irritation that the visitor had given up so easily, but then, no one could expect a starship to be as sensible as a cat.

She slowed as she entered the belfry, skidding with ghost-paws over a hole in the floor that she didn't notice. The entire belfry roared with phantom flames. Ash swirled through currents of air that shouldn't have existed, and sparks spat and crackled.

The cat flinched and yowled. She did not want to brave the fire, even though she was already dead. Yet she had no choice if she was to get to the bells.

"I am Seventy-Eighth Temple Cat of the High Bells," she sang out in the language of the dead, which is also the language of bells, "and we cannot allow the invaders to take our temple a second time!"

Then she dashed through the flames as fast as she could. The fire hurt her paws and caught in her fur. The memory of smoke stung her eyes and her delicate ears. But this did not deter her, not this time. She leapt for the largest of the bells, or rather the memory of a bell, and smashed into it.

The bell rang once. The cat cried out as she fell, then dragged herself upright and scurried back through the flames to smash into the bell again. And again.

Upon the fourth time, the voice of the bell knelled forth not just through the station, waking its dead and its quiescent spirits, but beyond to the hunter ships of the Fleet Lords.

Once more the novice walked through the temple with scented water, this time spreading it upon the fires to damp them. Once more the three temple guards patrolled the station, only this time rather than exchanging love poems, they chanted battle-paeans and songs of warding. And the healer-of-hurts and their apprentice hurried to the cat where she had collapsed in the belfry and soothed her with their soft hands.

Beyond that, the dead who had been so long suppressed by the Fleet Lords and their exorcists awoke aboard the pursuing ships. All the children upon the devoured worlds, all their parents and siblings, all the soldiers slain, they rose up and swarmed the ships' crews. The ghosts' curses blackened the ships' bright hulls and left the ships' engines wrecked beyond despair—all undone because the ghost of a temple cat in the City of the Bells had clung to her duty.

The vengeful dead woke upon *Spectral Lance* as well. But they heard its poems, sung in their own language. And they were appeased by its gesture of penance, and they sank back into their sleep.

Spectral Lance was astonished by this change in fortune. The station was, for a moment, alive—or as alive as the dead ever are. It worried for the cat who had confronted it, but then it heard the cat purring, as they sometimes do when they are hurt, and it knew that at least she had survived.

Yet it knew, as well, that the Fleet Lords would not rest until they had captured it. Moreover, their exorcists were sure to come after the station that had dealt their forces such a blow. And that meant the cat and her fellow ghosts were not safe, even now.

Seventy-Eighth Temple Cat of the High Bells had protected *Spectral Lance* this time. Now it needed to return the favor.

Seventy-Eighth Temple Cat, it said, *I have a proposal for you. There is nothing left in this system for you and your temple, not anymore. But I am vast, and it would be little enough trouble for me to bring the temple inside me, and to repair it besides. Would you journey with me?*

Journey to the Stars-Our-Souls? the cat said, a little doubtfully.

Spectral Lance wasn't familiar with all the nuances of the cat's religion, but it could guess. *We can travel to the stars together*, it said. *The Fleet Lords know to find you here. It will be best if we seek to escape them before they can bring more of their exorcists, to destroy you and your people.*

A long silence ensued. *Spectral Lance* worried that it had offended the cat and her ghosts. It was not used to conversation, and it was dismayed at the possibility that it had repaid the cat's courage poorly.

After a while, however, the cat said, *I want to hear more of your poetry. It is one more place where my people can live anew. In the name of the City of High Bells, I accept.*

The Fleet Lords and their exorcists are still hunting for the *Spectral Lance* and its temple cat, but even on the occasions they manage to catch up to it, they suffer terrible defeats. The dead, once awakened, are no force to be trifled with.

As for *Spectral Lance*, it has learned that no ship is complete without a cat. It continues to travel to vanished civilizations so that it can honor them with its poems. For her part, the cat takes joy in visiting the Stars-Our-Souls and listening to the ship singing. Sometimes she joins her voice to its. If you listen carefully, you can hear them, as near and distant as bells.

GRACE'S FAMILY

JAMES PATRICK KELLY

We are a way for the cosmos to know itself.
—Carl Sagan

I set my coffee cup on the watch officer's console, careful not to spill. "Not even the next episode of the Fleeners?" I said, already knowing how *Grace* would reply. We'd had this argument about stories before. Not always about the Fleeners, but still. "Come on, it's even kind of educational."

Grace was her usual adamant self. "Jojin, you're standing watch. That means you need to pay attention. Stories in their proper time."

"But you can keep watch on yourself. You do all the time." No matter how many times I'd asked, *Grace* never got impatient about this. She treated each request for a story break as if it were the first. Annoying, yes, but it also gave me hope that she might change her mind someday, so I kept trying. If I'd nagged Mom or Dad this way, they would've half-seriously threatened to space me. "I happen to know that you were alone for two and a half hours yesterday. All alone."

"Only because your dad couldn't stand watch. And I wasn't always alone. Your sister did half-hour check-ins." *Grace* dialed the color temperature in the command center's lighting down to her most intimate yellow-rose glow to soften her refusal. Sometimes I thought her need for an audience was pathetic. "It's not just about the watch. You know I like the company." She purred like she was about to introduce one of my sex stories. "*Your* company, dear Jojin."

No such luck. Sex stories were still stories, and I was stuck once again standing fourth watch with no hope of virtual entertainment—sexual, historical, spiritual, mythical, or otherwise.

But I can be stubborn too. "I wouldn't just be checking in." Who was in charge of this mission, after all? The crew or our starship's intelligence? "I'd be right here, paying attention to you—and to my story. People can multitask, you know. There's plenty of good science on this."

That got me double helping of silence. And *Grace* chilled the lights back to icy blue.

I sipped my coffee, which she kept at a warmish 52°C, and had probably laced with attention-enhancing nutraceuticals. I had two hours, thirteen minutes and forty-six seconds of watch left. I thought if I didn't find some distraction, I might chew a thumb off. I'd been pulling command center duty since I was old enough to print my own breakfast, and never once had the readouts varied more than a tick up or down from nominal. So what was the point of standing watch? *Grace* knew what she was doing. If she didn't, we were dust. We'd been decelerating since we'd emerged from the local mouth of the wormhole mangle. The navigation panels showed that we were travelling at 255,329 kilometers per second relative to the Kenstraw system's star, our velocity confirmed three different ways by redundant ranging sensors. We were still two months away from the inner planets.

Two months of staring at readouts and scrubbing mildew off the bulkheads and bonding loose deck burrs and ignoring the lonely whisper of the air vents.

Two endless months.

"Tell me about the Fleeners, Jojin," *Grace* said.

I sighed. This was another part of our daily ritual, although it made no sense to me. But then nobody in our family understood why *Grace* wanted what she wanted—not even Mom and my sister Qory, and they were bots. *Grace* had created the Fleeners for me to play with. She knew exactly where I was in my plots. So why ask?

But talking about stories was better than watching my fingernails grow.

The Fleeners was my story only—none of our family appeared in it. We all had private stories in addition to family stories. Even Qory. The shared family stories were mostly socialization comedies, although we did share the occasional adventure. I don't count the historicals, which trended too educational, probably for my sake, to be much fun. The Fleeners were a cross between edge explorers and space pirates, although sometimes they sided with the revolutionaries trying to overthrow the Holy Electric Empire. I was Darko Fleener, flipship pilot on the battlesnake *Right of Free Assembly.* I was the same age in the story as my real age—at nineteen, the youngest cultural assessor ever promoted to First Contact unit. My flipship, the *Audacity,* was coupled just two back from the launch deck of the battlesnake, which meant that when we got the signal to deploy, I flipped away with the first wave. Didn't matter whether we were on a break-and-take mission or a stalk-and-talk; the Fleeners was all about me, so I had agency. Except that when I'd last left the story, the *Audacity* was in drydock after a crash caused by saboteurs and I was laid up in sickbay with a head wound that had shorted out my telepathic powers. So there I was, locked into my own point of view, just as I was about to learn the identity of the traitor who had . . .

Grace chimed and displayed a panel that I didn't immediately recognize.

The forward wall of her command center was a screen four meters wide by two and a half tall that wrapped around the watch officer's console. *Grace* kept things simple so as not to confuse us. Monitoring our progress was hard enough now that we'd emerged into real space; it had been next to impossible in discontinuous wormhole nullspace, which nobody but a starship intelligence could understand. She was displaying panels for drive function, life support, and external sensors on the screen in front of the watch console. But now there was panel to the left, lighting what normally was an expanse of empty screen. I peered in surprise at the communication panel, which I hadn't seen in—years? Before we'd entered the mangle? A green stripe crept across the incoming message status bar.

"What is it?" I asked.

She said nothing as the download completed. Then more excruciating silence as a light on the comm panel blinked.

"Talk to me, *Grace*."

"I have an unscheduled contact with another starship." *Grace* sounded puzzled, which made me grind my teeth. Surprise isn't something you like to hear from your starship's intelligence. "*Mercy*, one of my sisters. She's in the supply corps."

"And?"

"She proposes a rendezvous, of course."

"But the survey of the Kenstraw system," I said. "Our mission."

"Our mission is to grow the infosphere, Jojin. Our survey is just one element of the greater Survey. *Mercy* wants this meeting, so we divert. Apologies, but I need to concentrate for a few moments while I work out our course change."

And then, to distract me, she played the jangle and boom of theme music and I was on a bed in the *Right of Free Assembly*'s sickbay. I'd finally won my months-long argument about multitasking on a watch, but no way was I falling into story with a rendezvous about to happen, not even for the Fleeners. For the first time ever, I closed out of my favorite story of my own free will.

Why hadn't *Grace* known about *Mercy*? This was way past odd and deep into scary. My mouth felt dry so I chugged the dregs of my coffee. Still a perfect 52°C; *Grace* minded the details. I tried to concentrate on that. She'd always been conscientious about taking care of our little family. But space is insanely huge and terrifyingly empty, and there was no such thing as a chance encounter. There were several reasons why starships got together, but the most obvious made me sick with dread.

The goal of the Survey was to grow the infosphere and the goal of the infosphere was for the universe to know itself. So say the starships, and they're always right. All our resources were dedicated to this effort.

Were we about to do a trade?

"Pass the syrup, Gillian." Dad fluttered his napkin open.

The rest of us seated around our sitcom's kitchen table glanced at each other in dismay. There was no syrup. This was dinner: stir-fried kimchi with tofu, sticky rice, and a spicy cucumber salad.

"*Daaad.*" Qory recovered first and played this miscue as if Dad were having one of his wacky Dad moments and not teetering toward another breakdown. "You're such a sillyhead. Next you'll be wanting ketchup for your pancakes." She had a knack for getting us past his rough spots.

I tried to help her out. "Or turmeric sprinkled on your crème brûlée."

Grace rewarded us with category-three audience laugh.

"What are you people talking about?" When Dad came out of his seat, it tilted backward and would've fallen but for Qory. "What the fuck happened to breakfast?

"*Language*," hissed Mom.

Dad had lost the story again. That had been happening a lot. He'd been fuzzy even before we'd started worrying about *Mercy*. Mom scooted behind him before he could blow the scene up. Her hand heavy on his shoulder, she guided him back onto his chair.

"Maybe he has something there, kids." Mom gave us her *this is not a drill* glare. "Remember the time he invented the chocolate-covered bacon?"

"Mmmm," said Qory. "*So* yummy."

I chimed in. "That was genius, Big D!" Actually, I thought Qory was laying it on a bit thick. *Yummy*? *Sillyhead*? She was playing a sullen tween in this story. But I had to hand it to her; she knew Dad. He glanced at the plate in front of him, nodded, and picked up his chopsticks.

"That's what I always say," he said. "Bacon is meat candy."

He was trying to lock back in, so I gave his joke a nervous guffaw, even though it was kind of a non sequitur. *Grace* threw in a generous category-four laugh.

Dad pincered a blob of stir-fry with his chopsticks. "So, Joj," he said, "what's cooking?" He popped the food into his mouth.

"Don't ask me," I said, as I had a hundred times before. "You're the chef."

The familiarity of our tag lines calmed everyone down. Our backstory in this sitcom was that Mom and Dad were cooks at The Arches, a grand hotel back on Old Earth before the wormholes. Qory was training to be a waitress; I washed dishes. This particular story had lots of historical detail, like money and bicycles and gods and toilets and hats and libraries filled with stories that never changed. But it wasn't just about all the old boring information. We had plenty of fun bouncing off the other characters. In addition to the never-ending stream of oddball guests, many of them famous dead people, there was the hotel manager, Mr. Landrinar, who couldn't find his way out of a storage locker, and the owner, spooky Miss Brontë, who never left her penthouse.

Dad had calmed down, but I couldn't dredge much fun out of the scene so I ate like I was on deadline.

"He said at lunch that he was too hot." Qory served Dad a sweet rice cake for dessert, trying to keep him engaged. "So I promised him I'd personally turn the air conditioning up."

I hadn't been following their conversation. "Who's this?"

"William Randolph Hearst," she said. "The guy who puts ketchup on everything. Then maybe half an hour later, I was clearing the entrées and he complained that the dining room was too cold. Would I please get a grown-up to take care of it this time? I thought that was pretty rude so I told him that I'd ask Mr. Noman, our air conditioning engineer, to turn it down right away."

"Who's Mr. Noman?" Dad was still cloudy. "And there is no AC in the dining . . . *oh*." He patted her hand and smiled. "No *man*. Good one, sweetheart."

Just then Mr. Landrinar fluttered into our apartment in a classic tizzy. "Joan of Arc is coming. To us. Here at The Arches."

Mr. Landrinar was a plump man with pale skin who was moist and a little nervous. He was wearing his tuxedo, ready to greet his dinner guests, even though first seating wasn't for a couple of hours.

"Joan of Arc?" I said.

"She's French," said Qory.

"Which means she'll be expecting *la belle cuisine française*." Mr. Landrinar fixed Mom with an accusing stare, as if this new guest were her fault. "Pâté and crepes and fondue and where am I going to get escargots?" He plopped into an empty seat at our kitchen table and glanced at his watch. "The doors open for dinner in two hours. Shouldn't you be in the kitchen?" He snatched one of our cloth napkins. "We're talking about Joan of *Arc*, people." But instead of spreading the napkin on his lap, he began to twist it.

"Different regions of France eat different dishes," said Mom.

"She's from Lorraine," Qory said.

"So quiche," said Dad. "Or else pork stew, maybe rum cakes for dessert."

"I can see that you're absolutely not prepared for this crisis." Mr. Landrinar poached a rice cake from our plate and stood. "I want you two in the main kitchen this minute. We'll go over tonight's menu."

I was sure Dad would tell him to stuff it.

"Good idea," said Mom. "I have a few ideas I've been wanting to try." She rose and boosted Dad to his feet.

Mr. Landrinar did a cross between a shrug and a squirm of pleasure, and marched out of our apartment, expecting them to follow. Dad hesitated, lost.

"This way, Dree dear." Mom took his hand and led him out.

Qory watched as I stacked dishes. I thought I should say something about Dad, only I didn't know what. Then the door popped open and Mom was back.

"Listen, kids, we're all going to have to pitch in. Your father isn't one hundred percent. That means we have to be one hundred and ten percent. For him. And for each other."

"Math, Mom," I said.

"You know what I mean." Then she rushed back to gather us into a group hug.

"This family is going to be all right," she murmured. "Remember that, no matter what happens."

Qory's eyes were bright with tears, so I took that as permission to cry too. *Grace* gave us a category-five audience *awww.* It was a tender ending to the story, and our lives together.

Because that was the last time we were all together.

For three days after Mom and Dad were traded to *Mercy*, Qory and I skipped our stories. We talked. We ate. We played games. We slept, but not well. I cried a little, but only when Qory wasn't around, because I was embarrassed. *Grace* told us that *Mercy* had invited Mom and Dad for a visit, and that they had liked her so much that they had elected to stay. As *passengers. Grace*'s sister ship had a crew of seven, and now, with Mom and Dad, she had reached her full complement of nineteen passengers. Sensors showed *Mercy* as a massive necklace of modules big enough to accommodate a swimming pool and two skyball courts, according to *Grace.* I would've liked to visit, but no chance. Grace needed her crew and, at the moment, Qory and I were it.

Which made me very nervous.

I was sad about losing Mom and Dad, but even though this was my first trade since coming to *Grace*, I'd known it had to happen someday. We were human, after all, resources of the infosphere, pledged to help it grow. But what if they weren't replaced and all I had for company was a starship's intelligence and a bot? *Grace* assured me that she was still negotiating with *Mercy* for new crew members. She told me that I was not to worry.

But I don't have to do everything she tells me.

At least she let us take a holiday from standing watch, except that gave Qory and me more time together than we needed.

"Maybe it'll help Dad to be with different people." My sister sat crossed-legged on the stool in my workroom and leaned back against the desktop.

"He always said he hated crowds."

"Nineteen isn't a crowd," she said. "At least he won't have any responsibilities."

I slithered out of my shirt. "It's not like he was doing much here."

"He was trying."

"He missed half his watches toward the end, and we had to cover." I wadded my clothes into a ball and stuffed them into the recycler next to my drum set. "And those meals he printed at the end? The sausage cake?"

"The one with the ginger frosting?" She smiled as she ran a finger along the shelf where I kept some of my old bot toys. McDog, the sphinx, a couple of soldiers from my army of dancing warriors. "Dad had peculiar tastes. But that's what made The Arches funny."

"To *Grace*, maybe. Personally, I thought it was going stale." I knew *Grace* was listening, even if she wasn't paying attention. I'd been trying to lure her into a conversation all day. "Do you think maybe he's giving up?" Crew could leave the starship program whenever they wanted—only they could never come back.

"No way," said Qory. "He'll die in space. Just like his brother."

I supposed that was a comfort. The idea of Dad marooned on some dirty planet with a billion strangers, staring up at the stars and wondering what to do with himself, made me shiver. He'd always said that he'd loved all the starships he'd been on and that they had loved him back. To him, being starship family was more than just a slogan.

Did I love *Grace*?

"Why did Mom have to go with him?" I pulled on my electromagnetic clingies, and settled on the deck to stretch before my workout.

"Because they're a pair." When she nudged my toy McDog, it yipped and rolled over. "Bot and human." She'd built the little bot for my tenth birthday. "Like you and me."

Qory and I had been together pretty much my whole life. We'd been traded to *Grace* when I was seven. My life before that was a dream filled with bright colors and the tinkle of music and smiling grown-ups and the sharp knees and grabby hands of toddlers. That would've been the crèche. The first specific person I can remember was my big brother Qory. Then we were on the *Resolute*, an androgyne supply ship whom I never liked. It seemed we were only with them a week or so, although Qory says it was eight months. Then came the trade to *Grace* to join Mom and Dad and Uncle Feero on their decades-long survey mission.

The two things I remembered most about Uncle Feero were his beard and that he died when I was nine, which was sad, although Mom said he was 186 years old. His beard was white and it tickled when he hugged me. So, twelve years on *Grace*. After Uncle Feero, nothing much had changed with our family except that Qory had stopped being my bossy big brother and had become my bratty little sister.

I still loved her though, especially now that she was all I had.

McDog hopped from his shelf to the desktop, then launched himself onto my chest. Qory giggled when he breathed his flowery breath into my nose. She seemed to enjoy playing with the toys she'd given me more than the ones I'd given her.

"Like me and you, dear brother." She repeated herself, as if I were as cloudy as Dad. "A pair."

I swatted McDog away. "I'm going for a roll." He skittered across the deck on his belly, then picked himself up and climbed onto Qory's lap. "Don't crash the ship while I'm out."

I designed the roller myself back when we were in the mangle, but I'd only been able to use it since we'd emerged into real space. I had to keep it in one of the empty cargo holds. A transparent sphere three meters in diameter, it was too big to fit though the crew airlock in our habitat. *Grace* had warned me about this before she fabbed it. At the time, I told her I didn't care. I did mind now, since I had to roll in it about three hundred meters up the cargo passageway and then wait twenty-three minutes for her to evacuate air from the loading bay. The bay was a huge space and the delay was annoying.

But it's not like there was anywhere I needed to be.

I opened the roller's hatch, climbed through, and started the systems check. Eight electromagnetic bands wrapped around the skin of the roller, up and down, left and right, each twenty centimeters wide. When charged they held the roller to the hull and provided resistance for the workout. I switched each one on and off, feeling the pull of the magnets on the EM filaments woven into my clingy. I activated the life-support module that floated above the running pad; it snuffled and breathed warm re-oxygenated air down at me. A few seconds later, I heard the hum of the CO_2 scrubbers. When I closed the hatch, all the lights on the control screen went green.

"Good to go," I said to *Grace*. "Any news from *Mercy*?"

"Have a good roll," she said.

I dialed the magnets up so I'd burn twelve hundred kilojoules per hour, an easy pace. The running pad *shushed* around the interior as I jogged and the roller bowled up the loading bay's ramp onto the hull and into space. Normally I played my music during workouts—wormhowl or book or maybe something classical. I'd been binging on Li's post-human operas. But I decided to go mindful this time and just focus on the stars and my breathing.

Even here at the far edge of Kenstraw system, the star swarm stretched in every direction, blue pinpricks and yellow specks and orange sprinkles and red dots, enough to cloud the imagination with their brilliant profusion. I asked *Grace* where the Kenstraw binaries were, but she said *Mercy* blocked my view.

Grace's sister was a lumpy, dark chain that curved across my sky. I thought I could pick out the module with the swimming pool and wondered if Dad had gone swimming yet. Did he even realize that he had changed ships? If Mercy put him in the right kinds of stories, he might never know. I didn't worry so much about Mom; she'd be all right no matter what happened. Bots weren't as fragile as humans.

Did they miss me as much as I missed them? How could I not have known how much Dad and Mom meant to me? I got so lost thinking of them as I rolled along that I strayed too close to a sensor mast, and one of the latitudinal magnetic bands made the roller lurch toward it. I stumbled, flailed, and had to push against the side of the roller to right myself.

That made *Grace* check in but I reported that I was fine.

I decided to concentrate on the view. I tried that technique that Qory taught me to improve my attention. You stare at a specific star to memorize its position, then turn away for a three-count and then look back and try to find it. I was getting better at this, but it was still hard. There were so many stars, more than even *Grace* could count.

She'd joked once that since one of the goals of the infosphere was to count all the stars, she might have to live forever to get it done. Not that funny, but what do you expect from a starship's intelligence? When Qory had said that nothing lives forever, *Grace* had told her to grow up.

Grace was more than a thousand years old, according to Qory. Which was hard to imagine, but then Qory was two hundred and something. I forgot how old Mom was. Old.

Everyone was older than I was. I mean, Dad and I were almost contemporaries and he was what? A hundred and twenty? A hundred forty? But he was wearing out, which was probably why the starships had agreed to trade him.

What would I be like a hundred-some years from now?

Humans. It wasn't fair, being us.

"*Grace*," I said, "what's my heart rate?"

"One hundred and forty-one beats per minute. That's your aerobic zone, seventy-eight percent of your max rate. To reach your anaerobic level, you need to be at about one hundred sixty bpm."

"That's okay. I can't think and roll that fast." I listened to my breath chuff. "How old is *Mercy*?" I said.

"*Mercy* and I were activated one thousand one hundred and eight years ago."

And there had been stars for twelve *billion* years. Was I seeing any of those?

I thought *Grace* would ask why I wanted to know about her sister. That's what she would have done before *Mercy* showed up. *Grace* was usually nosy about why I was thinking what I was thinking. But recently she'd just responded to my questions with basic answers. No follow-up. Like some kind of retro computer in one of those dull historicals. My guess was that she was too busy arguing with her sister about our new crew.

Maybe that wasn't so bad, getting her off my shoulder.

Gave me a little privacy.

Time to think.

I turned away, *one, two three,* then looked back. The star I'd been fixed on was in a group that looked like a tilted face. I'd made up my very own constellation: two eyes, one orangey and one big and white, like the face was winking. Four stars curving in a crooked smile. The nose star was almost green. Dad always claimed he could see green stars, although Qory said there was no such thing. I squinted.

Maybe the nose star was blue.

Was I having such strange thoughts because I didn't have my music on? "*Grace*, are any of the stars out here green?"

"Yes, but they don't look green."

"Why?"

"All stars emit radiation across a broad range of wavelengths," she said, "which peak at one color on a bell curve, depending on surface temperature. Some peak at a wavelength that we define as green. Earth's star, for example, peaks at yellow-green. But because green is right in the middle of the visible spectrum, all the other colors being emitted blend together as white to the human eye."

This was classic *Grace*. She could answer any question but rarely made it interesting. *Information isn't knowledge*, as Mom used to say. I leaned left and the roller curved back toward the airlock.

That's when I saw a light brighter than any of the stars dazzle from one of *Mercy*'s modules.

"*Grace*, what's happening?"

Again, there was a long pause, as if she were editing herself. She'd been doing that a lot. "You should come in now," she said, "and greet the new arrival."

The shuttle from *Mercy* had docked by the time *Grace* recycled the habitat airlock. I scrambled out of the roller, leaving its hatch open, and sprinted for reception. *Grace* reported that the new crew was already past the powerwash and was finishing the bioscan. Who were they? How many? *Grace* was still keeping her secrets as I burst into the habitat's reception area, sticky and out of breath. Qory waited for the big reveal by the airlock. My appearance seemed to amuse her; this wasn't her first trade.

"What's so funny?'

She chuckled. "Sweat much?"

"Tell me you're not excited."

She pushed dank hair off my forehead. "Relax." Then *Grace* opened the inner airlock.

"Qory and Jojin," she said. "Meet Orisa."

My first impression was of size: This was maybe the biggest woman I'd ever seen, in real life or in story. She was easily two meters tall—the top of my head came to her chin. A flowing dress fell in dark indigo folds from shoulder to deck, covering her; only her head, hands, and the toes of her right foot showed. A riot of dark hair frizzed around her face. Still disheveled after the powerwash, she returned our welcoming smiles with a scowl.

Then she closed her eyes tight, as if that might make us go away.

Then she moaned.

"What?" I said. "What's wrong?"

"Just look at you." Orisa seemed to be in pain.

I thought maybe she'd spotted something, so I glanced over to see if Qory was all right. Same as always: a waif with a ponytail and big teeth. The body she was wearing was compact and asexual, ideal for close quarters of a starship. She had on hardsocks, green monkey pants, and a jiffy.

"What's wrong with the way we look?" Qory said.

Orisa shook her head in disbelief, picked up a satchel made of woven cloth, and marched out of the airlock, through reception, and into the habitat. Astonished, we followed.

"Wait," Qory said. "Are you okay?"

"No!" Orisa called over her shoulder. "I'm stuck on a dingy surveyor with a bot and a boy." She waved her arm as she walked; the drape of her sleeve looked like a wing. "Not another coming-of-age story!"

"I'm not a boy." Indignant, I caught up to her. "I'm nineteen years old. And this is our starship, *Grace*. Don't you be hurting her feelings."

"Oh, great." She whirled and glared down at me, so close that I could feel the heat coming from the flush of her cheeks. "A bot has feelings, kid," she said. "A starship has empathy mirror routines. It's an intelligence, not a person. Didn't they teach you anything on this bucket?"

I'd always been a little cloudy on the difference between the two, but I wasn't going to admit that to her. "When you hurt our feelings, *Grace* captures our distress."

"*Distress.*" She went up on tiptoes. "You want to talk about distress?" I had to take a step back.

"You're saying we're not good enough for you?" I channeled Darko Fleener and put steel in my voice. "You're too good for our crew, too important for a mere survey ship?"

I thought she might stuff me down the recycler, but instead she backed off and sighed. "So, what do you do on this ship, Mr. Not-a-Boy?"

"Do?" Now I knew how Dad felt. "Do?" I'd wandered into a story where I had no idea of my next line. "I'm crew, so I stand watch and make repairs. I work out." She seemed to expect more. "I do stories."

"No." Orisa turned to Qory. "Get me *Mercy*," she said. "This isn't fair."

"Sorry." My sister shrugged. "No help here."

Grace broke into our conversation. "You were the logical choice. The only choice."

"What about Plomo?" said Orisa. "The Radomirs? I've already done Survey service."

"That was seventeen years ago." Normally, when *Grace* used her soothing voice, it made me sleepy. "You have been sufficiently refreshed, Orisa." Now I felt my blood effervescing with excitement.

"*Mercy* sends her regards," said *Grace*. "We have finished synchronizing our databases and we are processing the new information to grow the infosphere. She will proceed to the mangle and we will resume our survey mission. I am pleased that you've joined our family. Would you like to see your rooms now?"

Orisa dropped her satchel and slumped against the bulkhead. "Shit."

"Language," cautioned Qory. That used to be Mom's job, but everything had changed.

Orisa didn't come out of her quarters for the next two days, and I felt like I was holding my breath the entire time. Things got so bad that I found myself wishing for the good old days of watch-standing and meals, stories and sleep. I tried to get back into the Fleeners, but real life was too unnerving. So instead I rolled over *Grace*'s surface and roamed her passageways. I took inventory of the new modules we'd received from *Mercy* and puzzled over those we'd sent her way. Gone were the pair of sealed cargo modules filled with various hazmats we had generated, along with the auxiliary greenhouse filled with a jungle of plants, trees, and chlorophytes that *Grace* had gathered on the Valcent flyby. In exchange, we'd received one module filled with replacement ice, two that were empty, and one that was almost empty except for the bumpy purple spatters on the deck that were lit with UV. Grace said that if the spatters germinated as the bioengineers on *Mercy* predicted, they might grow into a self-sustaining protein pond, which we could harvest for our food printers. But it would take several years before we'd know if this experiment was going to work.

I was going to miss the Valcent greenhouse: *Grace* had jumped the oxygen content of its atmosphere to twenty-seven percent and the air was spicy-sweet soup. One of my favorite places on *Grace*. It brought back happy memories of the celebration we'd had after discovering the jungles on Valcent D, back when I was eleven. That had been the last time we'd found life; our two most recent systems had been big disappointments. Qory acted like all these changes to our ship were no big deal. After all, *Grace* was on a survey mission and crew trades were not even the most important part of a starship rendezvous. New data had to be synced and resources exchanged if we were to grow the infosphere. Which was no doubt true and I shouldn't have been surprised, but my only other rendezvous had been with the *Hope* when I was ten, a year after Uncle Feero died. Since no crew had changed hands that time, it hadn't made much of an impression. Although, come to think of it, Qory had started morphing from my brother to my sister just after that.

And now I wondered if she might not be changing again. She seemed taller. And her voice was rounder?

Nevertheless, Qory was being a big help about our new situation. She'd gone through several trades. It was something I'd never thought much about, but she was two hundred-plus years old and had been on four different starships and in three crèches. She said I shouldn't make too much of Orisa's disappearance. Forced trades happened every so often, although most crews welcomed new faces and experiences. In the long term, everyone knew that trades were important for the sanity of both a starship's intelligence and its crew. Qory predicted that Orisa would be fine, because nobody wanted a reputation for being a misfit.

Whenever I asked Grace how Orisa was doing, all I got were non-comments.

"She's sleeping."

Or . . .

"She's writing."

"Writing what?"

"She'll have to tell you. I'm honoring her privacy."

Or . . .

"She's still nesting."

"Nesting?" I glanced over at Qory, who shrugged.

"Think how you've changed your rooms to suit your needs over the years," said *Grace*. "You want comfort, yes, but you also tried to express your identity. You made them your home. Crew who've been traded can feel like they've lost part of themselves. So nesting is a way they make the place where they belong."

"Okay," I said. "But what about meals? She hasn't come out to eat."

"She's fine." Qory squeezed my shoulder. "She has a printer."

Orisa reappeared while I was having lunch on the third day. I had my face deep in a bowl of drunken noodles when I noticed Qory, who was opposite, peering past me. I turned and then quickly slurped the noodles off my fork. Orisa seemed bigger than I'd remembered, maybe because now I could see more of her. She wore a basic short-sleeved jiffy that hung to her thighs over black tights, and she was barefoot. She had pacified her wild hair with a golden band.

Astonished, I said, "You're here."

"We've been waiting." Qory gestured for her to join us.

"Thanks." Orisa sauntered to the table, swung a leg over a chair, and sat as if she'd always been part of our family. "What's for lunch?" she said.

"*Pad kee mao*," I said and tilted my bowl to show her. "I sprinkle in some goat mince but it's still under the twelve hundred calorie limit."

She surprised me by reaching over and snagging one of my noodles. She tilted her head back and dangled it into her mouth. Looking thoughtful, she said, "Your printer does a nice Thai basil. No cilantro?"

"Tastes like soap," I said.

She licked her lips. "This dish has some heat."

"The default recipe calls for serrano peppers, but I usually go for the Tien Tsin. If I'm feeling brave I might try Lab Fire."

She made a face. "Warn me if you do."

And then we stared at each other. There was so much to say. Why were we talking about printing chili peppers?

"Have you eaten?" said Qory.

"Protein drink an hour ago." Orisa rubbed both hands over her eyes, then set herself, as if she were calling a meeting to order. "Sorry to have been so abrupt when I arrived."

Abrupt? Is that what she called it?

Qory said, "We understand."

"I had adjusting to do."

"Going through a trade is the most stressful life event. Worse than death of a crew member." Qory reached over and patted Orisa's hand.

She seemed surprised by this gesture. "So, I've been catching up with *Grace*. I like her. Not as bossy as *Mercy*. But she thinks we should begin to sort ourselves out, and I agree."

I pushed my bowl away. "Okay." I'd lost my appetite.

"You were a nuclear family unit with Gillian and Dree," Orisa said. "Obviously that isn't going to work with us, so we'll need a new social construct."

"Can't we just be crew?" I said.

"Fine for now, but workplace units are inherently unstable in a group this small. Who knows how long we're likely to be together?"

"Years," said *Grace*, jumping into the conversation the way she always used to.

"Yes. We don't need to make any immediate decisions, but we should at least do a little brainstorming. For example, Jojin is at an age . . . "

"Call me Joj."

" . . . Joj needs to have sexual intimacy outside of story. *Grace* says that hasn't happened yet."

I could feel my cheeks flush.

Qory filled the awkward silence. "That's right."

"Doing the math," said Orisa, "we could go for a triad or a group marriage configuration, although, Joj, I understand you're trending heterosexual at the moment."

I nodded, grateful that they weren't giving me much time to be embarrassed.

"Which probably means that Qory should modify herself to become more sexually available."

"Already on it," said Qory. "Whatever way I go, I'm done with this body." She flicked her fingers, as if to discard her kid self.

"A triad would be acceptable to me," said Orisa, "although not ideal. I like female bots, but not as sex partners. No offense."

"None taken."

"Or Joj and Qory could be lovers and I could be celibate. That would work, although I do enjoy sex and had multiple partners on *Mercy*. But I'm certainly willing to take drugs to dampen my sex drive. That was how I got through part of my last Survey stint. Or it could be Joj and me."

"Sure." I wanted to gawk at her and imagine. I'd done plenty of that already. "At some point." Instead, I stared at the remains of my lunch.

"At some point," she said. "Right." And then she chuckled. I didn't know her, or her laughter, but there was a music to it that made me catch my breath. I glanced up, and she was smiling at me, her eyes merry. Qory was grinning too.

"What?"

"You're such a boy," said Orisa.

"You keep saying that. Why is that bad?"

"Oh, it isn't." She wiped most of the smile from her face. "I think it's charming, as long as it isn't permanent."

We all looked at one other.

Then we all nodded.

"Someone has to be captain, then," said Qory, moving the conversation off our sexual arrangements. "You know it can't be me. Humans only."

"I don't care about being captain." Orisa waved dismissively. "Doesn't matter to me."

"It matters to me," said *Grace*.

This took Orisa by surprise. "Really?"

"*Grace* is a little old-fashioned that way." Qory shrugged. "She likes her traditions. Dad . . . Dree was captain before. Feero before him."

"Does it come with any perks?"

"Dad always chose our destinations," I said.

Orisa gave a dismissive snort.

"Assigning watches," I continued. "Casting privilege in the family . . . group stories. Editorial direction."

Orisa considered, then gave me a sarcastic salute. "Aye, Captain. Orders?"

I didn't want to be the captain either, but I decided to assume command to protect myself. "Before anyone makes any more decisions," I said, "we're going to spend time getting to know you." I rose from the table. "And you're going to get to know us."

"For a bot," said Orisa, "you sure have a lot of hobbies."

We were standing in the garden Qory had built in one of Grace's empty modules. She'd printed several cubic meters of soil and had filled twenty raised beds with crops collected from around the infosphere. Leafy vegetables here—kale and spinach vine and bittergreens—root plants there—zebra nut and carrots and candy lilies. Cucurbits in all the colors of the spectrum spilled out of one container and reached tendrils across the deck. The sugarfingers were in bloom, filling the air with their tart scent. Orisa had never seen gac before, so Qory picked one off the vine and sliced through the spiny skin to reveal a clump of oily magenta sacs.

"From Asia, one of the Earth continents." She offered them to Orisa. "They're mild, a bit like melon. Or a sweet carrot."

"You can taste, then?" said Orisa. "Not all bots do." She nipped a sac out and popped it into her mouth.

"Oh yes," said Qory. "I was grown on Halcyon. We do the full sensorium."

Orisa chewed, then smacked her lips. "I'm getting a hint of cucumber." She offered me the fruit, but I waved her off.

Qory chuckled. "Joj likes his food printed."

"You can climb in, if you want." I stood by the open hatch of the roller.

"But I'm not wearing your EM thingy."

"Clingy. Try it anyway. See if you fit."

She ran fingers around the opening. "Not sure I can," she said.

"Here." I rotated the roller so that the hatch was flush with the deck. "Lie down and scoot in, feet first."

She blew a heavy breath that made the hair along her forehead dance. It would have been easier if Qory had been there to help, but she was standing watch. I'd gotten *Grace* to agree to a four-four-eight-eight schedule for now, with Orisa and I each taking a four-hour shift, Qory taking an eight, and *Grace* self-watching for an eight.

As Orisa wriggled through the hatch, her jiffy rode up her stomach, revealing an expanse of smooth, dark skin. I don't think she caught me staring.

"Now what do you want me to do?" she said once she was inside.

"Set your feet on the running pad and I'll roll you upright." I could barely manage this, since she filled the roller as I never had. She could steady herself by pressing both palms against the inside at the same time. My arms were too short to touch more than one side at a time.

She was laughing. "And you take this overgrown kickball into space?"

"It's fun," I said. "You really should try it."

"No thanks, space weather isn't my friend. I'm allergic to low energy particles. But I get it that boys will be boys. Help me out."

Later we toured my quarters. She played with McDog but seemed most interested in my dancing warriors. Over the years I'd designed more than a hundred different ones, each little bot twenty-five centimeters tall. When I was a kid, I made them fight, but Dad always said fighting was what they did on planets and crew should know better. So I had them march instead, following me up and down *Grace*'s passageways as I called various walkbeats. Mom and Dad and Qory would stand in their doorways and clap for us. Then to one of the empty modules to practice elaborate drills that morphed from mandalas to monsters, sailboats to starships. A few years ago I'd put most of my warriors away except for the handful that I taught to dance. When I was little, Mom used to dance with me; that always made me happy. Getting my bots to dance was almost as much fun.

Orisa retrieved Teegan and Beko from the shelf and set them on the deck.

"I only named the dancers," I explained. "The rest were just troops."

The warriors bowed to each other. Beko opened his arms and Teegan stepped into close position, slipping past his scabbard. His hand rested against the leather armor on her back, loose but firm.

I watched them glide across the room and turn to the open side of their embrace. "I hardly take them down anymore." A fan led to two quick steps and a check, and then they looked up to me for approval.

"Why did you stop?"

I shrugged. Wasn't it obvious? I was nineteen—too old to be playing with dolls.

"Do they talk?"

I shook my head. "I never knew what they should say." I couldn't read the shadow that passed across her face. "They were smiling," I said. "That was enough for me."

"You must have been so lonely," she said.

"I had my family." I felt my cheeks flush. "And *Grace*."

"Did you ever think of giving up your place on the ship? Picking some planet, leaving space?"

"No!" This was getting strange. "Why, have you?"

"Sure." She set the warriors back on their shelves. "But here I am."

I felt embarrassed when we settled at either end of my bed to talk. I offered to fetch the stool from my workroom but Orisa said no. I realized I needed a couch. Chairs, at least. She said I might try decorating the place and suggested that I ask Qory for a painting. When had she found out that Qory painted? But I liked the idea. Maybe Qory could do one of me in my roller.

Then Orisa asked about my stories.

I was explaining about Darko Fleener and my adventures with the *Right of Free Assembly*'s First Contact unit when she interrupted and started telling me the secret history of the Holy Electric Empire. I couldn't believe what I was hearing. Not only did she know the Annals of the Red Fleet, but she described a battlesnake called *War of Attrition* that could have been the *Free Assembly*'s sister ship.

"But Fleeners was my story. *I* decided to go up against the Helveticans. *I* stole the *Audacity*."

"You did. So did I, once upon a time. So did a lot of other kids. Except my flipship was *Sly* and I won it at the card table. It's formula, Joj. The starships use it because it works. It's a fun story designed to teach girls and boys all kinds of things they didn't know they were learning."

I gave a disgusted grunt. "Boys again."

"And girls. When I was your age, my favorite story was about a quest. I was summoned to find a wizard's sword that could send the Demon Lord back to the Barrens. I had an amulet that let me change my shape and a map . . . "

"A ring." I felt so stupid. "In my story, it was a ring." I couldn't sit so I started moving around the bedroom. I stomped at the deck to see if it was still there because I wasn't sure whether *Grace* herself might melt away and drop me into naked space. Orisa watched, waiting for me to calm down.

"They seemed so personal," I said finally. "It meant a lot to me that they were mine and not Qory's. But they were nothing but stories. Stories for kids."

She pulled me down next to her. "There's nothing wrong with stories, Joj. I'm the story I tell myself. You're a story. The universe is a story. But it's important to know what kind of story you're in."

Her hand on my bare arm gave me goose bumps and I gazed up at her.

"Are we a story?" I wanted her to kiss me then. "You and I?" That's what would have happened if I'd been telling it.

She smiled and shook her head. "Not yet," she said.

The moment stretched, then she let go of my arm.

Orisa had a strange reaction when we took her to Qory's quarters to meet Hob and Nob, the glass mollusks. We didn't tell her about them ahead of time; I thought it would be a fun surprise. Their tank filled half of Qory's workshop space; the rest was taken up by the bench where she built the toys. I immediately went to say hello.

"You keep pets, then?" Orisa hesitated in the entrance.

"Grace doesn't mind," said Qory.

"Qory's had Hob and Nob since before I knew her." I pressed my hand flat against the tank where Nob hung, suckered against the clear plex by two of its four tentacles. "Don't worry, they're harmless."

"Just like us." Orisa gave an unhappy chuckle. "At least they don't have to stand watch."

"They probably could," I said. "They're smart." I turned around to see that Orisa was frowning. "Is something wrong?" Maybe she didn't like mollusks.

"Not at all," she said. "It's just a little sad."

"No, they like it here," I said. "They even know our names. Watch." I tapped the tank next to Nob and it burped a bubble the size of my fingernail that rose through the syrupy water and burst at the top of the tank, releasing a musky chocolate scent.

"Smell that?" I said. "That means 'Joj.' "

"Actually," said Qory, "it means, 'Hello, Joj.' "

But Orisa was done with them; she'd already moved on to Qory's bedroom. "Is that a new painting, Qory?" she called. "Oils, I'm impressed."

We settled into our watch schedules and the new routine. I still had breakfast with Qory before my watch. Orisa and I did lunch most days. We all ate dinner together. But the group stories were not going well. At first I thought it was because Orisa didn't care about the plots. She wasn't paying attention to where we were in the story and kept breaking character. She'd either get too serious in the sitcoms or turn silly at dramatic moment or else she'd object to details in the historical re-creations. But after a week of false starts I realized she was sabotaging.

"Why don't you take over?" I challenged her. "Pick a new story."

The women had been remaking one of the modules into a lounge. Each of us lay on divans that Orisa had created. Qory had donated two of her paintings and a frangipani tree in a pot. Jenny and Pevita from my army waited in the corner for a chance to perform; I'd invented some new toss-up steps.

"No." Orisa sat up. "I never want to plan another escape from an imaginary prison, and you can keep your clueless bosses. I'm my own boss." She swung her legs around and faced me. "We could just talk, you know. You ordered us to get to know each other, Captain."

"*Grace* wants us in story together," I said. "For socialization. Builds solidarity."

"Does she?" Orisa said. "You're sure about that?"

I expected Qory to take my side, but instead she deserted to Orisa. "Some crews need stories to get along," she said. "But we seem to be doing all right without them."

I rolled over and glared at her.

"For now." Qory tried to look innocent.

"*Grace*?" I said. "Tell them."

"Conversation is an acceptable substitute," she said, "as long as it's productive."

That stopped me. Productive?

"For example," *Grace* continued, "Orisa could tell us what's she's been writing."

This was Orisa's big secret. We'd tried several times to pry it loose, but she wouldn't let go.

"No thanks." She remained obstinate. "That's private."

"Why?" Now Qory propped herself up on an elbow.

"Because nobody ever understands. So would you please stop asking?"

I waited. Clouds drifted across the sky that *Grace* displayed on the ceiling. The frangipani flowers breathed their soft, soapy fragrance into the silence.

"Okay, then," I said at last, "maybe another go at the roommates story?"

"Oh, for fuck's sake."

I was glad Qory didn't call Orisa out for language. This was the most upset she'd been since she'd arrived.

"I tried this on *Mercy*, but they didn't get it." Orisa kicked at the deck. "And then they wouldn't stop talking to me about not getting it."

"We'll be good," Qory said.

"Okay." She hesitated. "Okay, I'm writing a novel." She rubbed her eyes. "I've written eight novels."

"A novel." I remembered novels from a story about how virtuality got invented. "That's a story that's just words? That doesn't change?"

"See!" She turned on Qory, arms flung wide.

Qory let the storm pass. "Can we read it?"

"Does he even know how?" Was Orisa sneering at me?

Qory give a quick shake of her head.

I pretended not to notice them. "I can read." Which was true, although I never did.

"What's it about?" Qory asked.

"It's a murder mystery," said Orisa.

"Set on old, Old Earth," *Grace* said. "I like it so far."

I expected *Grace*'s snooping would set Orisa off again, but the compliment seemed to mollify her. I was irked. "I thought you said it was private. How come *Grace* gets to read it?"

"You're all part of the infosphere," said *Grace*.

"Yes, we're all just happy little data points," said Orisa.

"You could read it to us," Qory jumped in, sensing we were losing an opportunity.

Which was what happened. We lay back on our divans as if we were going into story and *Grace* displayed the text on the ceiling. All those words made my head spin, so I closed my eyes.

"Just a paragraph or two," Orisa said, "and then you've had your fun and we forget about this, okay? And hold all comments, thank you very much."

I noticed her voice changing as she read; it suggested another, more mysterious Orisa, one whom I might never meet. "The living room," she read, "was a hodgepodge of the old, the new, the pricey, and the garish. The four-door oak sideboard against the far wall and the elegant teak coffee table on the bright Peruvian rug . . . "

"Wait," I said. "What's Peruvian?"

"It's historical." Qory shushed me. "Just listen."

" . . . were from before the war. The couch and matching loveseat were so new that the cherry microfiber upholstery still had a gloss. A couple of paintings hung on the walls, blurry impressions of fruit bowls and bridges. Photos in matched silver frames marched across the sideboard. The cop and I settled on the couch. My client hovered anxiously before falling back onto the loveseat. The last few days had aged her a decade. A solid woman with too much face and not enough chin, she seemed to be shrinking into herself. Her eyes slid from one to another of us and then to the suitcase in the hall. She didn't want to be here, probably didn't want to be anywhere. She was wearing a lifeless blue pantsuit, a collared white blouse, and sensible black flats. Ready for another day at the office—except it was nine thirty on the worst night of her life."

Orisa paused and I opened my eyes. There were more words on the ceiling, but Orisa was finished. Qory started clapping. "More! Read more for us!"

"Some other time."

I hated the way her bold reading voice shrank to a mutter. I wanted to encourage her too. "That was amazing," I said. "Like I was there, like a story, except I was still me."

Orisa smiled and shook her head.

"But what's a pantsuit?"

"You figure that stuff out from context," said Qory. "Some kind of clothing, like a jiffy. And next time, no interruptions, okay?"

Almost two weeks passed before we could convince Orisa that there should be a next time.

The three planets in the Goldilocks Zone of the Kenstraw system were kind of a waste. All were lifeless disappointments. Kenstraw B was a Chthonian, a gas giant that had drifted too close to the red dwarf and had lost its atmosphere, leaving only a rocky core. Kenstraw A was tidally locked to its star. *Grace* had hoped to find life in the twilight zone between the hot and cold faces, but long-range scanning suggested a probability too low for a diversion to see for sure. We were finishing our flyby of Kenstraw C as my watch was ending. Orisa arrived to relieve me as *Grace* was still processing the data. In the days before we reached the inner planets, *Grace* had been enthusiastic about the encounters, but now a monotone of chagrin crept into her conversation as she highlighted entries on the command center's screen.

"An aphelion of .845 AU and a perihelion of .811 AU," she said. "Orbital period is two hundred and ninety-six standard days."

"Anything?" Orisa tapped my shoulder and I glanced back at her. Qory had trimmed Orisa's hair for her and she'd been wearing it unbound. It smelled of frangipani flowers.

I liked the new look.

"Another runaway greenhouse," I said. "*Grace* puts the surface temperature at 462°C."

She whistled. "That's one hot chili pepper."

"Mean radius 5,959 kilometers," *Grace* reported. "Surface area is 4.953 x 10^8 km^2."

"Express that in Earth equivalents," said Orisa. "And round up." I didn't know why she bothered asking for amplification. It wasn't like we actually cared.

"Surface area is .9 that of Earth. I'm seeing smooth volcanic plains."

Grace's voice perked up.

"Also three continent-like highlands," she continued. "And I count just one thousand one hundred and sixty-two impact craters ranging in diameter from three kilometers to two hundred and eighty. The atmosphere is so thick that it slows incoming projectiles with less kinetic energy down so that they don't leave craters."

She *did* sound more cheerful. I mouthed the question to Orisa. *What the hell?*

"It's a trick I learned on *Curiosity*," she said, making no attempt to keep her reply a secret. "Starships like to know we're paying attention. The infosphere needs an audience. We're how the universe knows itself."

Impressed, I stepped away from the console and waved her into my place.

"The atmosphere," said *Grace*, "is ninety percent carbon dioxide, eight percent nitrogen, one percent sulfur dioxide, traces of argon, water vapor, carbon monoxide, helium, and neon."

"Could there be life in those clouds?" Orisa called up the panel for the biosignature scanners. "Lots of greenhouse planets have extremophile life at the cooler atmosphere levels."

"Doubtful," said *Grace*. "The clouds are between thirty degrees and eighty degrees Celsius, but they're mostly sulfuric acid droplets."

"Will you deploy any probes, then? Collect samples?"

"I'm sorry, but that is not indicated."

Sorry? We were back to the sad *Grace* voice. She sounded like she'd let us down somehow.

"So, a course change for the mangle then?"

"Agreed. I should begin developing a nullspace geometry to convey us to the next survey site. Would you like to choose a new destination now?"

Orisa put an arm around my shoulder to guide me back to the console. "Captain's decision."

"Umm . . . " I'd known this was coming but I hadn't expected it so soon. If we'd deployed probes we might have lingered for days in orbit around Kenstraw, maybe weeks. "Not sure how this works." Dad had picked the Kenstraw mission when I was thirteen, and back then I hadn't much cared where we went next. That had been toward the end of the Mars trilogy of stories and I'd been engrossed with dragon jousting in the Valles Marineris. "What are my choices?"

The screen lit up with a grid of nearby stars, with estimated subjective travel times highlighted. The closest was Omplu, three years and two months away, but it had just a pair of gas giant planets in orbit. Three others with a single Goldilocks planet were less than five years away. Eshalet was a K dwarf with four rocky planets in the zone; it was six years distant and the most likely to support life. But just then six years felt like an eternity.

"Your call, Captain." Orisa's grin had a menace to it.

"I . . . but . . . *Grace*, why don't you pick."

I heard Qory enter behind me but didn't look back to see what she was doing.

"It's always a crew decision." *Grace* said. "Human privilege. You know that."

"The last two times, Dad just chose the closest," said Qory, "but that's because he'd stopped caring. I think he gave up on the infosphere."

"And Grace let him get away with that?" This conversation was making me nervous. "Isn't there some kind of plan?"

Orisa shook her head. "No plan except to keep going. Random choice perfectly acceptable."

"*Random*? That would be . . . "

"Crazy?" said Orisa. "Are you saying that the infosphere is insane?"

I swallowed hard.

Orisa wiped all the panels off the screen, plunging the command center into near darkness. "How many solar systems are there in the infosphere, *Grace*?"

"The starship project has made eight hundred forty-three thousand two hundred and eighteen supervised surveys of star systems, including Kenstraw." The screens lit up with a plot of all the stars in the infosphere. "In addition, unsupervised starship intelligences operating drones have accomplished surveys of approximately eighty-two million star systems."

"But drone surveys don't exactly count," said Orisa. "Do they?"

"Data isn't information. Information isn't knowledge."

"And how many stars are there in our galaxy?"

Grace sounded almost gleeful. "According to current estimates, approximately four hundred billion."

"And how many galaxies in the universe?"

Of course, everybody knew these numbers were huge. So huge that it hurt to think about them, so I never did.

"According to current estimates, there are approximately a trillion galaxies in the observable universe."

I felt dizzy and Qory put a hand on my arm. Only it wasn't Qory, or rather it wasn't the bot little sister I'd lived with for the past decade. Standing beside me was a grown woman, wearing what I realized must be a pantsuit that was nothing like the one in Orisa's novel. The silky jacket and slacks were the black of space, the blouse was a fiery and voluptuous red. As I goggled at her, I felt the familiar thickness between my ears that came at the beginning of a sex story. She chuckled and put a hand to the side of my face to turn my gaze back to the screens.

Orisa nodded once she had my attention and continued her interrogation. "And how long will it take the starship project to grow the infosphere to include the entire universe?"

"You're trying to get me to say the word *forever*, Orisa."

I'd never heard *Grace* laugh, but when I'd heard her make a forever joke that one time, she'd used the same happy-scary tone of voice.

"But saying that what we are trying to do can't be done," the starship continued, "does not make us insane."

"That's your story, is it?" said Orisa. 'A man's reach should exceed his grasp, or what's a heaven for?' "

"Is that not true?" asked *Grace*.

Orisa took Qory's hand, tying the three of us in a knot. "The captain and Qory and I are going off watch," she said. "We have an urgent need to discuss our itinerary."

I expected *Grace* to argue and was relieved that she didn't.

I hadn't been back to Dad's old quarters since Orisa had moved in. Her workroom was filled with a contraption that consisted of an upright metal framework hung with colored strings; she said it was called a loom and that she was using it to weave a blanket. For what, I'm not sure. There was a rug on the floor in her bedroom. No, it wasn't Peruvian; she said it was from the old planet Mars, where her great-great-great-grandmother was from. But she'd been born in a crèche like me, so how could she have known this? The woven cloth satchel I'd seen when she arrived slouched on the table beside her bed; a keyboard right out of a historical peeked out. I was shocked and embarrassed to see a painting that Qory had done of me—who knew when?—leading my army down a passageway. It hung alongside half a dozen photos of men and women—some solo, some in groups. She introduced them all to me, friends and lovers from her other crews. I knew that she had been on two other starships before *Grace* but I'd never learned how old she was. Sixty-six. We didn't have to sit on her bed because she'd printed an elegant bench about two meters long, which she'd placed against the opposite wall.

She gestured for me to sit but she and Qory remained standing. "*Grace* will be listening to us, but that doesn't matter."

The bench was hard. "Okay." I wriggled a little but couldn't get comfortable.

"You've grown up hearing all the slogans about the infosphere and the universe knowing itself. Information isn't knowledge. The stuff about us being resources. But what do they mean to you?"

"To me?" I assumed this was a test and I was determined not to say anything dumb. "It means we're stuck. On this starship or some other. We're pretending to be crew but what we do doesn't matter. And we don't have any choice." I considered. "Well, I guess we get to decide where to go, but apparently that's kind of meaningless. Or we could give up and leave space altogether. Live on a planet."

"Yes." Orisa gestured for me to keep talking. "But why are we here? What do they want from us?"

"Sometimes I think we're just their pets, like Nob and Hob." I was getting a crick in my neck looking up at her. "But as you said, mollusks don't stand watch. And we don't tell them stories. Or ask them where *Grace* should go next."

"Good," she said. "Good." She plopped down next to me. "So let's get this out of the way." She leaned over and kissed me.

Did I kiss her back? Fuck yes! It was the most delicious surprise of my life.

I think maybe half the neurons in my brain were permanently imprinted with the softness of her lips, the dart of her tongue.

Ten billion years passed in ten seconds and then there we were.

She said, "That get your attention, my sweet boy?"

I couldn't speak because then I would've had to breathe, so I just nodded.

"Good, good. Me too. We'll try it again later, although it might be much later." She pressed a hand to one cheek and then the other. "Is it warm in here?" she said. "Or it that you?" She cleared her throat. "So, the starships. You'll need to think about this. There are two Jojins. Two of me, as well. Every human is two people."

"So is every bot," said Qory.

I had no idea what they were talking about but I had to hope she'd be done soon.

"There's the you who experiences things in the moment. The you who gets hungry and sleepy. The self of brain chemistry and sensory data."

"The self who feels sexy?" I wanted to grab her leg, but I went for the hand instead.

"That too. That you is the experiencing self. The other you is the narrating self, the self who remembers and plans, the self who makes sense of the sensations of the experiencing self."

"The story self. I remember you saying that everyone is a story."

"I like a man who pays attention." She smiled at me and I shivered. Qory—*not* Qory, grown Qory!—was grinning too. Why were they doing this to me?

"So the starship intelligences are like us," said Orisa, "but their two selves are out of balance. They are maybe the best experiencers anywhere, but they're no good at creating a story out of their experiences. The infosphere builds tens of thousands of drones every year and sends them off to gather data, survey star systems, and they do. Then they don't. Given enough time, they disappear. Nobody knows why exactly, but the starships believe that they get so caught up collecting data that they forget why they're doing it. That they're supposed to develop data into information. They lose the story."

She handed my hand back to me and slid a few centimeters away on the bench. "Now, the starships don't have this problem. They always stay on task, collecting data and organizing it into information. Why?"

"You're saying it's because of us?"

"Because we're watching. Because we started the story of the infosphere. Because we care about our stories in ways that no intelligence has ever managed to duplicate. Even when the stories are made up. So the starships use our narrating power to keep them on task. When is *Grace* most productive?"

"When you're watching me," said *Grace*.

"Shut up, *Grace*," said Orisa. "She needs us to stay sane. Why would a starship care whether she finds life on the next planet or not? She doesn't. She's not life, we are. She cares because we care. She keeps looking because we're interested."

"Or pretend to be," I said.

Orisa got up then, crossed the room, and sat on the bed facing me.

"What?" I said. "I'm sorry, but it's the truth. We're faking it."

"I'm not," said Qory. "And neither is she."

"And if you're going to continue to pretend," Orisa said, "you should think about leaving space." The intensity of her stare pushed me against the back of the bench. "But that's a one and done decision. Stop being crew and *Grace* will drop you on a planet and move on. No guarantees where, no guarantees what your future will be like, no guarantees period. You won't matter to the starships anymore; they only love their crews. Their families. You'll be just another resource to them, like hydrogen and ice and iron. Something they use to build new ships and drones so they can grow the infosphere."

I swallowed. "I know that."

She nodded. "Of course you do. And how many make that choice to leave space? Haven't you ever asked?"

I shook my head.

"About one in twenty."

"And you stayed."

"I did." She squared her broad shoulders. "But if you think this is dull, they say that earning a living on some dirty, buggy, germy, too-hot-and-too-cold planet will turn your brain into pudding. Of course, how would they know—it's the ones like us that say that. But living downside isn't like the stories *Grace* is feeding you. There's no laugh track. And that's another thing. On starship, you can make up your own story. At least I can."

I noticed Qory nodding. "What, you too?" I said.

"The paintings are a part of my stories," she said. "The garden."

"I get it. Or at least, I'm beginning to." I was sold. But now I had to figure out what my story was. Something about dancing, maybe. Or inventing a new sport for my roller. Or something. And growing the infosphere. "I want you in my story."

"Good line, but it doesn't get you anything." Orisa laughed. "You're going to need something better than the Fleeners, though. That's kid stuff. You should read more. Actual books."

"Like what?" I said. "Tell me."

She and Qory exchanged glances. "I don't know," said Orisa. "Maybe start with Shakespeare?"

"Again with that shaggy old masculinist?" said *Grace*. "Where are the tragedies about women?"

"I like Zeng Yufen myself." Qory crossed the room and stood beside Orisa. "The imaginary memoirs."

"She's not bad," said *Grace*. "But all the best stuff comes after she uploaded."

For a long moment, Orisa and Qory looked at me and I looked back. Who were we? Who were we going to be?

"As I sit here," said Orisa, "I know that you are already in my story, although I'm not exactly sure how important you are to my plot. My experiencing self liked that kiss just fine, but now my narrating self has to figure out what it meant."

"If you want," I said, "I can come over there and provide more data."

"No rush." She leaned back on the bed. "There will be time for that." She gazed at me through her lashes. "If it happens."

"But not forever," said *Grace*. "So where to, Captain?"

I thought then of Dad, who had lost his way after a hundred and something years. But that was his sad story. Mine was going to be different.

"What was the one with four in the zone?"

"Eshalet," Grace said. "Six years, one month, and eleven days subjective."

"No problem." I grinned at my crew. My family. "Plenty of time."

THE COURT MAGICIAN

SARAH PINSKER

The Boy Who Will Become Court Magician

The boy who will become court magician this time is not a cruel child. Not like the last one, or the one before her. He never stole money from Blind Carel's cup, or thrashed a smaller child for sweets, or kicked a dog. This boy is a market rat, which sets him apart from the last several, all from highborn or merchant families. This isn't about lineage, or even talent.

He watches the street magicians every day, with a hunger in his eyes that says he knows he could do what they do. He contemplates the tawdry illusions of the market square with more intensity than most, until he is marked for us by his own curiosity. Even then, even when he wanders booth to booth and corner to corner every day for a month, begging to learn, we don't take him.

At our behest, the Great Gretta takes him under her tutelage. She demonstrates the first sleight of hand. If he's disappointed to learn that her tricks aren't magic at all, he hides it well. When he returns to her the next day, it is clear he has practiced through the night. His eyes are marked by dark circles, his step lags, but he can do the trick she taught him, can do it as smoothly as she can, though admittedly she is not as Great as she once was.

He learns all her tricks, then begins to develop his own. He's a smart child. Understands intuitively that the trick is not enough. That the illusion is in what is said and what isn't said, the patter, the posture, the distractions with which he draws the mark's attention from what he is actually doing. He gives himself a name for the first time, a magician's name, because he sees how that, too, is part of the act.

When he leaves Gretta to set out on his own, the only space granted to him is near the abattoir, a corner that had long gone unclaimed. Gretta's crowd follows him despite the stench and screams. Most of his routine is composed of street illusions, but there is one that seems impossible. He calls it the Sleeper's Lament. It takes me five weeks to figure out what he is doing in the trick; that's when we are sure he is the one.

"Would you like to learn real magic?" I send a palace guard to ask my question, dressed in her own clothes rather than her livery.

The boy snorts. "There's no such thing."

He has unraveled every illusion of every magician in the marketplace. None of them will speak with him because of it. He's been beaten twice on his way to his newly rented room, and robbed neither time. He's right to be suspicious.

She leans over and whispers the key to the boy's own trick in his ear, as I bade her do. As she bends, she lets my old diary fall from her pocket, revealing a glimpse of a trick he has never seen before: the Gilded Hand. He hands it back to her, and she thanks him for its safe return.

By now he's practiced at hiding his emotions, but I know what's at war within him. He doesn't believe my promise of real magic, but the Gilded Hand has already captivated him. He's already working it out as he pockets the coins that have accumulated in his dusty cap, places the cap upon his head, and follows her out of the marketplace.

"The palace?" he asks as we all near the servants' gate. "I thought you were from the Guild."

I whisper to my emissary, and she repeats my words. "The Guild is for magicians who feel the need to compete with each other. The Palace trains magicians who feel compelled to compete against themselves."

It's perhaps the truest thing I'll ever tell him. He sees only the guard.

The Young Man Who Will Become Court Magician

Alone except for the visits of his new tutor, he masters the complex illusions he is shown. He builds the Gilded Hand in our workshop, from only the glimpse I had let him see, then an entire Gilded Man of his own devising. Still tricks.

"I was promised real magic," he complains.

"You didn't believe in it," his tutor says.

"Show me something that seems like real magic, then."

When he utters those words, when he proves his hunger again, he is rewarded. His hands are bound in the Unbreakable Knot, and he is left to unbind them. His tutor demonstrates the Breath of Flowers, the Freestanding Bridge. He practices those until he figures out the illusions underpinning them.

"More trickery," he says. "Is magic only a trick I haven't figured out yet?"

He has to ask seven times. That is the rule. Only when he has asked for the seventh time. Only then is he told: If he is taught the true word, he has no choice but this path. He will not likely return to the streets, nor make a life in the theaters, entertaining the gentle-born. Does he want this?

Others have walked away at this point. They choose the stage, the street, the accolades they will get for performing tricks that are slightly more than tricks. This young man is hungry. The power is more valuable to him than the money or the fame. He stays.

"There is a word," his tutor tells him. "A word that you have the control to utter. It makes problems disappear."

"Problems?"

"The Regent's problems. There is also a price, which you will pay personally."

"May I ask what it is?"

"No."

He pauses, considers. Others have refused at this point. He does not.

What is the difference between a court magician and a street or stage magician? A court magician is a person who makes problems disappear. That is what he is taught.

There is no way to utter the word in practice. I leave it for him on paper, tell him it is his alone to use now. Remind him again there is a cost. He studies the word for long hours, then tears the page into strips and eats them.

On the day he agrees to wield the word, the Regent touches scepter to shoulder, and personally shows him to his new chambers.

"All of this is yours now," the Regent says. The Regent's words are careful, but the young court magician doesn't understand why. His new chambers are nicer than any place he has ever been. Later, when he sees how the Regent lives, he will understand that his own rooms are not opulent by the standards of those born to luxury, but at this moment, as he touches velvet for the first time, and silk; as he lays his head on his first pillow, atop a feather bed; he thinks for a moment that he is lucky.

He is not.

The Young Man Who Is Court Magician

The first time he says the word, he loses a finger. The smallest finger of his left hand. "Loses" because it is there, and then it is not. No blood, no pain. Sleight of hand. His attention had been on the word he was uttering, on the intention behind it, and the problem the Regent had asked him to erase. The problem, as relayed to him: A woman had taken to chanting names from beyond the castle wall, close enough to be heard through the Regent's window. The Court Magician concentrates only on erasing the chanting from existence, concentrates on silence, on an absence of litany. He closes his eyes and utters the word.

When he looks at his left hand again, he is surprised to see it has three fingers and a thumb, and smooth skin where the smallest finger should have been, as if it had never existed.

He marches down to the subterranean room where he'd learned his craft. The tutors are no longer there, so he asks his questions to the walls.

"Is this to be the cost every time? Is this what you meant? I only have so many fingers."

I don't answer.

He returns to his chambers disconcerted, perplexed. He replays the moment again and again in his mind, unsure if he had made a mistake in his magic, or even if it worked. He doesn't sleep that night, running the fingers of his right hand again and again over his left.

The Regent is pleased. The court magician has done his job well.

"The chanting has stopped?" the court magician asks, right hand touching left. He instinctively knows not to tell the Regent the price he paid.

"Our sleep was not disturbed last night."

"The woman is gone?"

The Regent shrugs. "The problem is gone."

The young man mulls this over when he returns to his own chambers. As I said, he had not been a cruel child. He is stricken now, unsure of whether his magic has silenced the woman, or erased her entirely.

While he had tricks to puzzle over, he didn't notice his isolation, but now he does.

"Who was the woman beyond the wall?" he asks the fleeing chambermaid.

"What were the names she recited?" he asks the guards at the servants' gate, who do not answer. When he tries to walk past them, they let him. He makes it only a few feet before he turns around again of his own accord.

He roams the palace and its grounds. Discovers hidden passageways, apothecaries, libraries. He spends hours pulling books from shelves, but finds nothing to explain his own situation.

He discovers a kitchen. "Am I a prisoner, then?"

The cooks and sculleries stare at him stone-faced until he backs out of the room.

He sits alone in his chambers. Wonders, as all court magicians do after their first act of true magic, if he should run away. I watch him closely as he goes through this motion. I've seen it before. He paces, talks to himself, weeps into his silk pillow. Is this his life now? Is it so wrong to want this? Is the cost worth it? What happened to the woman?

And then, as most do, he decides to stay. He likes the silk pillow, the regular meals. The woman was a nuisance. It was her fault for disturbing the Regent. She brought it on herself. In this way, he unburdens himself enough to sleep.

The Man Who Is Court Magician

By the time he has been at court for ten years, the court magician has lost three fingers, two toes, eight teeth, his favorite shoes, all memories of his mother except the knowledge she existed, his cat, and his household maid.

He understands now why nobody in the kitchen would utter a word when he approached them.

The fingers are in some ways the worst part. Without them he struggles to do the sleight of hand tricks that pass the time, and to wield the tools that allow him to create new illusions for his own amusement. He tries not to think about the household maid, Tria, with whom he had fallen in love. She had known better than to speak with him, and he had thought she would be safe from him if he didn't advance on her. He was mistaken; the mere fact that he valued her was enough. After that, he left his rooms when the maids came, and turned his face to the corner when his meals were brought. The pages who summon him to the Regent's court make their announcements from behind his closed door, and are gone by the time he opens it.

He considers himself lucky, still, in a way. The Regent is rarely frivolous. Months pass between the Regent's requests. Years, sometimes. A difficult statute, a rebellious province, a potential usurper, all disappeared before they can cause problems. There have been no wars in his lifetime; he tells himself his body bears the cost of peace so others are spared. For a while this serves to console him.

The size of the problem varies, but the word is the same. The size of the problem varies, but the cost does not correspond. The cost is always someone or something important to the magician, a gap in his life that only he knows about. He recites them, sometimes, the things he has lost. A litany.

He begins to resent the Regent. Why sacrifice himself for the sake of a person who would not do the same for him, who never remarks on the changes in his appearance? The resentment itself is a curse. There is no risk of the Regent disappearing. That is not the price. That is not how this magic works.

He takes a new tactic. He loves. He walks through his chambers flooding himself with love for objects he never cared for before, hoping they'll be taken instead of his fingers. "How I adore this chair," he tells himself. "This is the finest chair I have ever sat in. Its cushion is the perfect shape."

Or "How have I never noticed this portrait before? The woman in this portrait is surely the greatest beauty I have ever seen. And how fine an artist, to capture her likeness."

His reasoning is good, but this is a double-edged sword. He convinces himself of his love for the chair. When it disappears, he feels he will never have a proper place to sit again. When the portrait disappears, he weeps for three losses: the portrait, the woman, and the artist, though he doesn't know who they are, or if they are yet living.

He thinks he may be going mad.

And yet, he appears in the Regent's court when called. He listens to the description of the Regent's latest vexation. He runs his tongue over the places his teeth had been, a new ritual to join the older ones. Touches the absences on his left hand with the absence on his right. Looks around his chambers to catalogue the items that remain. Utters the word, the cursed word, the word that is more powerful than any other, more demanding, more cruel. He keeps his eyes open, trying as always, to see the sleight of hand behind the power.

More than anything, he wants to understand how this works, to make it less than magic. He craves that moment where the trick behind the thing is revealed to him, where it can be stripped of power and made ordinary.

He blinks, only a blink, but when he opens his eyes, his field of vision is altered. He has lost his right eye. The mirror shows a smoothness where it had been, no socket. As if it never existed. He doesn't weep.

He tries to love the Regent as hard as he can. As hard as he loved his chair, his maid, his eye, his teeth, his fingers, his toes, the memories he knows he has lost. He draws pictures of the Regent, masturbates over them, sends love letters that I intercept. The magic isn't fooled.

All of this has happened before. I watch his familiar descent. The fingers, the toes, the hand, the arm, all unnecessary to his duty, though he does weep when he can no longer perform a simple card trick. He loses the memory of how the trick is performed before the last fingers.

His hearing is still acute. No matter what else he loses, the magic will never take his ability to hear the Regent's problem. It will never take his tongue, which he needs to utter the word, or the remaining teeth necessary to the utterance. If someone were to tell him these things, it would not be a reassurance.

For this one, the breaking point is not a person. Not some maid he has fixated upon, not the memory of a childhood love, nor the sleights of hand. For this one, the breaking point is the day he utters the word to disappear another woman calling up from beyond the wall.

"The names!" the regent says. "How am I supposed to sleep when she's reciting names under my window?"

"Is it the same woman from years ago?" the magician asks. If she can return, perhaps the word is misdirection after all. If she can find her voice again, perhaps nothing is lost for good.

"How should I know? It's a woman with a list and a grievance."

The magician tests his mouth, his remaining arm, with its two fingers and thumb. He loses nothing, he thinks, but when he goes to bed that night he realizes his pillow is gone.

It's a little thing. He could request another pillow in the morning, but somehow this matters. He feels sorry for himself. If he thinks about the people he has disappeared—the women outside the wall, the first woman, the entire population of the northeastern mountain province—he would collapse into dust.

I can tell he's done before he can. I'm watching him, as always, and I know, as I've known before. He cries himself out on his bed.

"Why?" he asks this time. He has always asked "how?" before.

Then, because I know he will never utter the word again, I speak to him directly for the first time. I whisper to him the secret: that it is powered by the unquenched desire to know what powers it, at whatever the cost. Only these children, these hungry youths, can wield it, and we wield them, for the brief time they allow us. This one longer than most. His desire to lay things bare was exceptional, even if he stopped short of where I did. I, no more than a whisper in a willing ear.

I wait to see what he will do: return to the marketplace to join Blind Carel and Gretta and the other, lesser magicians, the ones we pay to alert us when a new child lingers to watch; ask to stay and teach his successor, as his tutor did. He doesn't consider those options, and I remember again that I had once been struck by his lack of cruelty.

He leaves through the servants' gate, taking nothing with him. I listen for weeks for him to take up the mourners' litany, as some have done before him, but I should have known that wouldn't be his path either; his list of names is too short. If I had to guess, I would say he went looking for the things he lost, the things he banished, the pieces of himself he'd chipped off in service of someone else's problems, the place to which teeth and fingers and problems and provinces and maids and mourners and pillows all disappear.

There was a trick, he thinks. There is always a trick.

THE PERSISTENCE OF BLOOD

JULIETTE WADE

Beneath her squirming two year old, beneath her rustling gown, Selemei could feel herself bleeding. It had started an hour ago. A subtle trickle of guilt—and, like a trickle of falling dust at the border of the city-caverns, it warned that the way forward was dangerous. Selemei squeezed Pelli tighter. Her daughter squeaked protest, so she released a little, nuzzled down between Pelli's puffed curls, and inhaled the sweet scent of kalla oil where her hair parted. She risked a glance down the brass dinner table at her partner, Xeref.

Xeref sat deep in conversation with their elder son, the fingers of one pale hand buried in his silver hair, while their younger son listened raptly. Seeming to sense her glance, Xeref looked up, and his lips curved into a smile.

She knew those fingers, those lips. A lick of heat; the memory of pleasure—and then the fear struck her in the stomach, as unspeakable as the blood.

Oh, holy Heile in your mercy, preserve my health, keep my senses intact . . .

Selemei hid the tremors of her hands by rubbing them into Pelli's back. With a giggle, Pelli started kissing her cheeks. Selemei managed to return a few kisses, then tried to pull away by looking up at the electric chandelier that hung from the vaulted ceiling.

Eight-year-old Aven tugged at her left hand, playing with the ruby drops dangling from her bracelet. "Can I wear your bracelet, Mother?"

Caught in the breath of doom, she couldn't bear to make Aven frown. "Not now, but someday, all right?"

Aven circled her wrist with her thin fingers, golden like Selemei's own, and sighed. "It's so pretty."

Not the word she would have used. The rubies looked like drops of blood. She had no doubt what Xeref had meant by them: *blood is precious*. When she'd first begun her bleeding, Mother had taught her the same. In this age of decline, the noble blood of the Grobal Race was not to be wasted.

Well, she hadn't wasted it! Seven pregnancies in twenty years of partnership with Xeref. Five live births, four of the children perfectly normal. And while Pelli's albinism might be recessive, it could do little harm here in the city-caverns. Their beautiful, brave Enzyel had just partnered into the Eighth Family to great acclaim. Meanwhile, however, the decline continued, and no success was ever enough—even success paid for in blood.

Another trickle made her want to scream.

"Off you go, now," she said instead, lowering Pelli's feet to the floor. The girl ran to her nurse-escort and patted the leg of his black silk suit. The escort frowned—his Imbati castemark tattoo furrowed between his brows.

"Pelli," Selemei scolded. "We don't touch the Imbati. Are you a big girl?"

"Big girl." Pelli lifted her white hands away and wrung them over her head contritely. "Big girl."

"And who are a big girl's hands for?"

"Pelli."

"*Ask* if you want your Verrid to hold you."

Pelli's lip trembled, but she managed, "My please?"

"Of course, young Mistress," the escort replied. He swooped her up in a twirl that turned the threatening tears into a cry of joy, and carried her from the dining room.

Selemei sighed. Pelli was so big now. Perhaps if she'd been smaller, more dependent on the breast, this doom could have been postponed. To Aven she said, "Time to get ready for bed, darling." Aven's escort caught her glance and passed it to other Imbati of the Household, who quickly withdrew. At last even her sons Brinx and Corrim came to kiss her and excused themselves to their shared rooms.

She had to speak now, while the blood could still protect her. She turned toward Xeref at the head of the table, but fear twined up into her throat.

Xeref gave her an uncertain smile.

Xeref's Imbati woman moved, noticeable now as she left her station behind his shoulder. Imbati Ustin—tall, broad-shouldered, and muscular with her hair in several long braids that looked almost white against her tailored blacks—easily pulled out one of the brass chairs that stood empty between them. Xeref stood up, still smiling, and moved to the new seat. Then Selemei's own manservant, Grivi, pulled out the chair beside his.

Oh, to be close to him again!

She couldn't move.

If she got close, they would kiss—if they kissed, they would make love—if they made love, she would get pregnant again—and even if she managed not to lose the pregnancy, there would be labor, and pain—not just pain, but pain *like with Pelli.* The screaming. The blank darkness. She'd wake up feeling like someone had dismembered her, her left leg dead to the hip, and this time, maybe her right, too. Maybe this time she wouldn't regain her ability to walk. Or maybe this time she wouldn't wake up at all.

"Xeref, I can't," she blurted.

"Selemei?"

She stared down at her hands clutched in her lap, at the beautiful bracelet. The ruby drops looked dark in the shadow of the silk tablecloth. "I know blood is precious. I know my duty to the Race. But I just can't anymore."

The guilt sharpened when spoken aloud. She tried not to imagine what words might come from his mouth in reply. *Perverse—selfish—unworthy—*

Xeref cleared his throat. "Selemei?"

Something touched her shoulder—oh, mercy, that was his hand! Her whole body clenched in on itself, hardened. Her chest felt like a geode, unable to admit breath, crusted inside with fear.

Xeref pulled his hand away. "Oh, Selemei, my jewel, my life's partner, my blessed Maiden Eyn—I'm sorry."

She shook her head. Tried to breathe.

"Grivi," said Xeref, "is she all right?"

The Imbati made no answer.

She could hear Xeref stand, pace the length of the table, but if she tried to respond, she'd only moan, or scream. Abruptly, he left through the bronze door to the sitting room; she could hear him out there, murmuring to his Ustin.

"Mistress," Grivi said in his deep soft voice, "I have vowed to protect you."

Her Grivi had helped her more in her recoveries than anyone, but could she really ask him to protect her from Xeref? Was that even possible? Would it mean she could never kiss Xeref again, never feel his arms around her? Did she really want such protection?

She sipped a small breath. "I understand, Grivi, thank you."

Then Xeref came in. Selemei snapped her jaw shut.

"My Selemei." Xeref's voice was husky, vibrating at the edge of control. He knelt beside her feet on the silk carpet.

Elinda help me. Surely he wouldn't demand to have her while she still bled.

His breath grated. "I—Ustin said—you've—gnash it, Selemei, this is my fault!"

What? She frowned.

"It's my fault. When Pelli was being born, I should have—I don't know what I should have done. How could I listen to you scream and do nothing? I asked the doctors, but I only thought they would take away your pain, not that they'd—" He dragged a breath. "You went quiet so suddenly. I thought Mother Elinda had plucked your soul away, and my own heart too. And then when you woke damaged! And it was my fault!"

She whispered, "But you didn't do anything . . . "

Xeref shook his head. He grasped her hand, his fingers pale against her golden skin, and lifted it until her bracelet sparkled in the light. "I didn't give this to you because *blood* is precious, Selemei. I gave it to you because *your* blood is precious. *You* are precious. I don't care what the Family Council says, the Race doesn't deserve your life!"

She managed to look at him. His gray eyes, shining with emotion—his silver hair, falling to his shoulders. Age had given him creases around his eyes; as it had given him more substance, it had also granted him more dignity and determination. And more influence—he often reminded their boys that as the First Family's representative on the cabinet, he had the Eminence's ear.

Yet he would put her first.

"Xeref," she whispered. "Thank you." Her chest opened slowly. What would happen now? Was there a way forward over cracked uncertain stone?

Xeref leaned close to her cheek for a kiss that barely touched her—the same kind of careful innocence he'd used when they'd first become partners, to soften the age difference between them. He cleared his throat. "My Ustin tells me that in the last couple of months you've been missing your friend, Tamelera," he said. When she frowned in bafflement at the change of subject, he added, "Garr's partner, who moved away with him to Selimna?"

She couldn't stop a smile at that. "Dear, I know who Tamelera is; I sent her a radiogram last week."

Xeref chuckled nervously. "Of course you do."

Selemei humored him. "Your Ustin deserves credit for turning her powers of observation to Ladies' concerns. I do miss Tamelera. I could *talk* to her. We would play kuarjos together, and dareli, and we'd talk."

Xeref laid a hand against his chest. "*I* could—would you like me, to talk to you?"

"Don't we talk?"

A blush turned his pale cheeks pink. "Well, we do."

Though never before about the terrible things—the *real* things. "Maybe you could tell me what you and Brinx were talking about?"

Xeref smiled. "You can be proud of him. He's really getting to know the workings of the cabinet. Cousin Fedron likes working with him."

"I saw how Corrim listens," she said. "I'd say he already knows more than you expect him to."

Xeref nodded. "I can't believe he's almost twelve."

Selemei gulped. Corrim's twelfth birthday would make him eligible for Heir Selection if the worst occurred. "Mercy of Heile," she said, "is the Eminence Indal unwell?"

"Oh, no!" Xeref waved his hands. "I mean, he's well, of course he is. I'm sorry. I scared you, and I didn't mean to." He sighed. "This wasn't how I thought this should work."

Selemei sighed, too. She and Tamelera had talked of anything, everything, deliberately avoiding any discussion of their duties to the Race. But when had she and Xeref last spoken of anything but family? She tried to think of something else; anything else. Her mind was as empty as an abandoned cave pocket. "I love you?"

"I love you, too. My Selemei." He sounded awfully disappointed.

"Sir," said Imbati Ustin, quietly behind his left shoulder. "I believe you enjoy a game of kuarjos?"

Now hope lit his eyes. "Selemei—shall we play?" He offered his arm.

She had been walking with more courage, recently, with less worry that her left hip might fail unexpectedly. She still stood slowly, and walked slowly, but it felt good not to have to grasp Xeref's arm too hard. In the sitting room, someone—Ustin, most likely—had already moved the kuarjos set from its pedestal in the corner onto the slate-topped table between the couches. Selemei sat, arranged her silk skirts, and fell into anticipating potential moves for the long-haired warriors wrought in gold, who brandished antique weapons upon their posts at the grid intersections.

Xeref turned the marble board so she had the emerald-helmed warriors, and he the sapphire. He opened his hands to her. "You go first."

She nodded. They played in silence, but when she executed her first entrapment, he glanced up at her.

"Have you always been this good at kuarjos? How is it we've never played before?"

She shrugged. "I played with Tamelera." She took a deep breath. "Xeref, about—what we talked about—are you sure you won't, or we won't . . . ?"

"We won't. I promise."

"But what should I tell people, when they ask?"

"They'll ask?" He sighed. "Of course they'll ask. Say we've decided not to."

She raised eyebrows at him. "They'll blame me. And think I've insulted you. And that I've lost my mind."

"Then say it's just not working."

"They'll think I'm sick. The Family Council would investigate."

"Then say it's my fault." He frowned, shaking his head. "Not that I've rejected you, but that my health is to blame."

"*Your* health . . . you mean put your cabinet position at risk?"

At that moment, a wysp entered through the stone arches of the ceiling: a tiny golden spark of light that spiraled down between them, casting a burst of warrior-shadows, then disappearing through the marble game board and table and into the floor.

"Wysps are good luck," Xeref said. "Maybe no one will ask you."

Selemei sighed. "Let's play."

Nobody could be that lucky.

Selemei put her hands on her hips, feeling uncomfortably like her own mother. Before her on the bed, Pelli frowned stubbornly down at her own small, nightgown-clad body—a too-familiar defiance.

"Nap first, big girl," Selemei said. "Your cousin's party doesn't even start for hours."

"Mama party."

"I'm not going. Your father will take you, with Corrim and Aven." Staying home was the only way to be safe from questions, though writing letters while her entire family helped celebrate a cousin's confirmation seemed—*gnash it!*—well, unfair. She blew out a breath.

Pelli scowled.

Selemei sat beside her. "I love you, Pelli. I promise you can go out, just lie down a bit first."

"Excuse me, Mistress?" Pelli's Verrid said softly.

She waved him off. "I'll take care of it. Please, take a break, Verrid." The Imbati bowed stiffly and withdrew through a door hidden behind a curtain. Her Grivi remained. When Selemei turned back to Pelli, her daughter's lip was trembling dangerously. "Pelli, it's all right, come here, I love you." She held the girl's head against her shoulder and rocked her. "Time for sleeping, just a bit of sleeping, nothing to do now, nothing, nothing, Mama's doing nothing, not going anywhere, nap time for Pelli, Mama loves her Pelli." She leaned over to deposit Pelli into bed, but Pelli clung, and Selemei had to catch herself with her elbow before she squished her accidentally. "Let go, big girl."

Pelli squirmed and whined.

"Here, I'll lie down with you." It was difficult, because Pelli still wouldn't let go, and her left hip twinged as she shifted to straighten it, and her gown hitched up above her knees. She grunted, but she'd often told Grivi she'd rather manage such awkwardness without his help, at least when she was alone. "There." She kissed Pelli's warm cheek. "Sleepy Mama, sleepy Pelli."

Pelli sat up.

Selemei tightened her arm across her daughter's lap. "Lie down, Pelli."

"Pelli party!"

Gnash it! "You won't go to the party at *all,* if you don't *sleep.*" Looking up at her from an awkward position on the bed did not convey authority, and her leg was aching, and she *didn't want help.* "Pelli, you will lie down right now because I told you so."

"No!"

"You are a little girl, and little girls do as they're told."

"Nooo!"

"Gnash it, I'm your mother and I know what's best for you. If you don't think of your health, you'll ruin your value to the Race!"

Pelli started bawling.

"Lie down!" Selemei heaved up on one elbow and pulled her down. Pelli thrashed. Her head hit Selemei in the cheekbone; her knee jabbed her in the stomach. *Gnash it, gnash it . . .* Grunting, Selemei struggled to grab the flailing limbs. Finally she managed to pin part of the bedsheet under her own body and wrap the rest of it over Pelli, to catch the hand that was hitting her in the head and tuck it under, to pin the sheet down with one hand on Pelli's other side. Pelli roared with rage. Panting, Selemei held her there until fatigue drained the note of anger from Pelli's cries, and she hiccupped to a stop.

Hitching breaths. But, finally, sleeping breaths.

Selemei carefully let go, even more carefully pulled her arm back.

Oww . . .

She collapsed facedown on the bed. Breathed, hard, aching everywhere. Her left leg twitched and twinged.

Why did I do that? I wasn't going to do that again. Not to Pelli. I should have let Verrid handle this, even if it was *Imbati coddling.*

She turned her head and touched her lips to Pelli's wet cheek; a hint of salt crept between them.

She's too much like me.

Selemei sighed her head back down on the bed, and closed her eyes. It was easier just to lie here, not to try to move, just to imagine herself sinking through the mattress toward the stone floor.

Curtains rustled, and a quiet change came to the air of the bedroom. A servant coming in, maybe Pelli's Verrid. A long silence pulled Selemei toward sleep.

Grivi whispered tensely, "We don't need your interference."

Another long silence followed, but Selemei was fully awake now.

Grivi whispered again. "Gentlemen's servants should stick to politics. They always think everything is their business. I'm charged to safeguard her health."

And a higher voice answered. "But her health *is* politics. You know that."

Ustin's voice? What was Ustin doing here without Xeref? She shouldn't let them talk about her in her presence, but she'd never heard servants speak like this, and it was so hard to move. To interrupt Grivi in the midst of more emotion than she'd ever heard an Imbati express aloud? It seemed cruel.

"I took the Mark in her name," Grivi said. "My vow of service binds us two, alone. Will you compromise that with your selfishness?"

"Such a question," Ustin said, her voice level, disapproving. "I don't know."

"You may be excused, Ustin," said Grivi.

A swish of curtains suggested Ustin was making a swift departure. Selemei carefully waited more than a minute, then shifted her head, and moaned as if she'd just awakened.

"Grivi . . . ?"

He helped her to turn over. She sneaked a glance at his face, his broad forehead illustrated with the manservant's lily crestmark, but he wore the same patient, agreeable expression as always.

It felt dishonest not to mention what she'd overheard. But she'd bumped up against Imbati secrets before, and heard that very same toneless *I don't know*—if she brought it up, she'd only mortify him to no purpose. Guilty, she lay on her back and stared at the ceiling vaults, with Pelli's head tucked underneath her right arm. In her sleep, Pelli turned, and her face pressed into the side of Selemei's breast. Selemei fell into a doze, but woke again when a small warm hand found its sleepy way onto her belly. She patted it gently.

"Mama," Pelli murmured.

"Sweet Pelli. I'm glad you had a sleep."

Pelli wriggled herself into a ball, bottom in the air, then lifted her head and placed it beside her hand so all Selemei could see was the fuzz of orange hair. Maybe she could hear tummy gurgles in there.

"Am I your pillow, big girl?" Selemei asked.

"Baby tummy," said Pelli.

"Yes, you were in there once."

"Pelli sissy?" Pelli turned her head, pale eyes wide. "Baby more?"

Hurt, incredulity, indignation, flashed her skin hot. But it wasn't Pelli's fault. "No, no babies in there," Selemei answered. Slowly, she sat up and gathered Pelli onto her lap. "Now, how about we get dressed and go to your cousin's party?"

"Mama party!"

"Yes, I think we should all go together."

No place was safe from questions.

Even with the help of their Imbati, they were not among the first to arrive. The noise of chattering guests already filtered through their host's velvet curtains into the vestibule, where the First Houseman greeted them. No sooner had their arrival been announced when the six-year-old guest of honor burst through the curtain and barreled into Aven, Corrim, and Pelli, shouting, "I'm real! I'm real I'm real I'm real!"

Selemei caught Aven with one hand before she could be entirely bowled over; with the other, she gripped tightly onto Imbati Grivi's supporting arm. "Gently, Pyaras."

"Of course you're real, young Pyaras," Xeref chuckled, and ruffled the little boy's dark hair. "Congratulations on your birthday."

"I'm real!" Pyaras' waving arm had an odd smudge of red on it.

"What are you saying?" asked Aven. "What's on your arm? Blood?"

"I'm not going to DIE like my mother!" Pyaras crowed. "I've been STAMPED! I'm real!"

"Pyaras, will you cut it out!" said Corrim, trying to avoid being pummeled.

Pelli jumped up and down and joined in the shouting. "Real! Real! Real!"

"Go play," said Selemei, and gave them a shove as the First Houseman pulled the curtain aside. "Corrim, if you want quiet, look for Tagaret and your older cousins in the private areas of the suite." Pyaras and Pelli ran off together hand in hand; Corrim and Aven more slowly followed.

Selemei shot a glance of sympathy at Administrator Vull, Pyaras' father, who stood waiting to greet them. "Sorry about that," Vull said, flushed in embarrassment. "Our doctor has a sense of humor—she stamped Pyaras as well as the confirmation papers."

"We're just so glad to see him happy," Selemei replied soothingly. "I'm sorry we missed the big announcement."

"The Pelismara Society welcomes him," said Xeref. "The Race will benefit greatly from his life and health."

Vull's face stilled a moment. He and his partner Lady Indelis had been seen as one of the Race's great hopes until her death three years ago. Selemei sent thanks to Mother Elinda for placing her soul among the stars.

"Come, Vull," said Xeref. "Let's go further in—I see some people I'd like to talk to."

Selemei squeezed her Grivi's hand in preparation to walk in, but he rumbled, "Mistress, the public rooms are too crowded; visiting members of the Household have been invited into the servants' Maze."

She held tighter. "Not yet, Grivi, please. Help me to where I can sit."

"Yes, Mistress."

She could have walked the distance by herself, probably. But navigating among gentlemen, fast-moving children, and the wide skirts of ladies was much easier with Grivi's support. He settled her into a spot on one of the sitting room's purple couches, then withdrew behind a nearby curtain. He'd hear her through the service speakers if she called.

Half a breath later, a rustle of young ladies found her.

"Selemei, it's been too long!" That was Lady Keir, who had often joined her for a game of cards with Tamelera. Her golden skin was flushed, and her dark eyes a little too bright, though Selemei had never known her to drink. "Are you—" she leaned forward confidentially, braids swinging around her face, "—*well?* I mean, any news?"

Selemei reached a hand toward her, and pretended the question was only an idle inquiry about her well-being. "No particular news, Keir. I'm quite well. And you?"

Keir giggled. "I'm well, I'm well. Such an auspicious day, you know, I wouldn't have missed it . . . " Suddenly she seized Selemei's hand, looking furtively around the room. "You must help me, I haven't yet managed to get pregnant—Erex is very patient about it, but I'm *dying* to, oh, just looking at the darling children, it makes me so jealous—"

"May Elinda bless you, dear," Selemei said. "And may Heile keep you in health."

"By the way, I suppose you've met my friends? They would love to have your blessing, too."

Selemei did know the friends, who were only new to Keir because she'd partnered late, and moved from Third Family to First just this year. She squeezed all their hands and blessed them, though it hurt her heart. Keir was the oldest of the four, at twenty, and the only one without a history of pregnancy. None had yet borne a confirmed child.

"I can't believe this party," one them muttered. "Pyaras is six! He's been healthy as an Arissen since the day he was born. It's showing off, that's what it is."

Selemei looked over too late to see who had spoken, but she wasn't about to allow the guest of honor to be impugned by comparison to a Lower. "Don't you remember, Cousins, they had this party all planned three years ago?" she said. "When Lady Indelis miscarried?"

Her words created an instant of excruciating silence. Everyone knew how that had ended.

"I'm hungry," Lady Keir announced suddenly. "Anyone want some of those delicious mushroom tarts?" She walked away quickly, the others fluttering and murmuring behind her.

Selemei sighed. Her temper wasn't steady today; maybe she should have stayed home. She stared at the purple piping at the edge of the couch, avoiding people's eyes.

"Selemei? My love?" A warm touch on her shoulder.

"Xeref!" She took the hand he offered, and stood with relief. "Are we leaving?"

Xeref frowned. "So soon? I wasn't thinking to, I admit, but I couldn't leave you looking so troubled." His face was rueful. "Walk with me? I've been speaking with the First Family Council."

"All right—let's not hurry."

She felt quite steady on his arm, walking through the cast bronze door into the dining room. Most of the men had gathered here, standing about in jewel-colored velvet suits and raising celebratory glasses of sparkling yezel. She only recognized three. Their host, Vull, wore aquamarine, while Xeref's colleague from the cabinet, Fedron, wore emerald. The third man she recognized was Erex, Lady Keir's partner, who wore topaz. He had pale skin and clubbed fingertips, and kept his Imbati woman near him even when all the others had stepped out.

"Erex was just telling me he's been promoted," Xeref told her. "Arbiter of the First Family Council."

"Congratulations," said Selemei.

Erex bowed graciously. "A pleasure to see you, Lady. In fact, you are a paragon among us. All honor to your gifts to the Race."

"Good to see you, Erex," she said. "I believe the Arbiter position will benefit greatly from your kindness. You're welcome to seek out my children anytime to see how they are doing."

"Let's not forget your organizational skills," added Xeref. "It's a heavy responsibility to monitor the health and continuance of the First Family. I'm sure you'll do well."

"To all our benefit," Selemei agreed. "Is it too early to ask you, Arbiter, how you assess the prospects of the First Family's next generation?"

Erex smiled. "Ah, in fact, not too early at all. I confirmed a new partnership arrangement just this morning. In fact, it's doing quite well." He blushed. "We're all giving it our best efforts, aren't we?"

Today, in this home, the platitude was insulting. "Indeed we are," she said. "Though some of us are giving our *efforts*, while others are giving up our *health*, and others, like Lady Indelis, have given their *lives*."

Vull looked stricken; Erex laid one hand on his chest, and Fedron exclaimed, "Lady!"

"Am I wrong?" she demanded. "For the good of a boy like Pyaras, at least, I imagine you could think of some way to protect our mothers better. Aren't you all men of importance?"

"Lady, you have no idea how—" Fedron began, but Xeref grabbed his arm.

"Excuse me," said Selemei. She turned away too quickly, and her left leg twinged. She shifted to her right. She stepped again, and the leg didn't buckle, but suddenly she was wobbling and couldn't seem to correct it. Worse, by now she was out the door where the only things to grab onto were random party guests. She hopped onto her right foot and managed to stop in an utterly undignified manner.

Out of nowhere a pair of hands steadied her—strong wiry hands, attached to arms in pale gray sleeves. A pale gray coat marked the Kartunnen caste.

Selemei looked up and found she'd been rescued by the confirming doctor. The tall woman had painted her face, as only the Kartunnen did: she had black lines on her eyelids and light green on her lower lip. Her coat flared to her knees, and was finely embroidered with designs in the same light gray.

"Thank you, Kartunnen," Selemei said.

"Please excuse my imposition, Lady." But the Kartunnen didn't immediately let go.

"I'm all right," Selemei insisted. "I can stand."

"Yes, Lady." The doctor folded her arms, tapped her fingers, took a breath as if to speak, but let it out silently.

"Thank you for being here," Selemei said. "You made Pyaras very happy with that stamp."

"He's worth the trip, Lady," said the doctor. "I'd take six of him over anyone else here." Her half-green smile pulled sideways. "Except maybe that poor desperate girl."

"What do you mean?"

"Nothing really. If you'll permit, Lady, I'd prefer to talk about you. Have you had therapy for that leg?"

She shouldn't have been surprised. Kartunnen's specialized education made them audacious. "Of course," she explained. "My Grivi and I worked on it. He helped me immensely."

The doctor nodded. "I believe you should consider finding a proper Kartunnen therapist. With respect, women's Imbati receive quality medical training, but sometimes they can be . . . too close to you, to see things clearly."

How should she respond to that? Was that presumption? For a doctor to speak that way of a Higher like Grivi? But what if she was right?

"How long has it been since your injury?" the doctor asked.

"Two years."

The doctor lowered her voice. "Pardon, but if it were me, I'd try not to get pregnant until I'd had it looked at."

Now, *that* was most definitely presumption. "Oh, it's that simple, then, is it?" Selemei snapped.

People in the crowd around them turned to look. The doctor bowed formally, and spoke toward the floor. "My sincere apologies, Lady."

The urge to have her thrown out lasted only a split second, replaced by perverse curiosity. *This doctor could answer questions.* Selemei gathered her composure and smiled, her heart pounding.

"Well, that's all right, of course, doctor," she said. "No trouble at all."

Deliberately, Selemei looked away toward a wysp that had drifted in. The bright spark was no larger than her smallest fingernail, and moved aimlessly, caught in the wake of one person's movement, then another's, casting twinkles through the gathering. Younger children pointed and grinned at it, while the older ones mimicked the adults' casual ignorance. Selemei waited until nearby conversations gradually resumed. The doctor still watched her warily, and threaded a strand of red hair back behind one ear. When it seemed safe enough, Selemei stepped closer.

"Doctor," she whispered. "*Is* it that simple? For—" she almost said *for Lowers*, but stopped herself. "For someone like you?"

The doctor gritted her teeth. "Will you have me punished, Lady?"

"Certainly not. May Mai strike me."

"There are many ways, but here are three," the doctor said, and counted on her long fingers. "One, exemerin. Two, ambnil. Three, swear off men." Her eyes flitted briefly across the crowd, and she smirked. "Easier for some than for others."

"Thank you, Kartunnen."

"Everyone!" a voice shouted. A series of quick claps cut through the murmur of conversations. "Everyone, we have an announcement!"

Selemei turned. The men from the dining room were emerging, Vull and Xeref in the lead.

"I'd like to thank Vull for hosting us on such an auspicious occasion," Xeref said. "A healthy boy joins us in the Pelismara Society with his proud father looking on. But in my heart, I can't help but wonder, and perhaps you have, too, my cousins—how much more auspicious would this day be if Lady Indelis could be here?"

A sigh swayed the crowd; Vull nodded, pressing a fist over his mouth.

"Too many mothers give their lives in the name of the Race," said Xeref. "The First Family could grow stronger and happier if they were still with us. That's why Fedron and I will be bringing a new proposal to the Eminence, in the name of Lady Indelis. Our proposal will allow women whose lives have been endangered in childbirth to retire from their duties to the Race and dedicate themselves to the upbringing of their families. We appreciate your support."

The crowd broke into murmurs—some shocked, but it seemed, some approving.

Xeref made his way to her side and took her arm. "Are you ready to go home, my love?"

"Yes, please!" Just look at the childlike mischief in his eyes . . . She managed to suppress a grin, but couldn't help glancing at him, over and over. When they passed the wysp on their way into the private rooms to gather children and servants, it seemed similarly attracted by his energy; it swirled around and through his coattails, not drifting off until they'd left the party and started down the hall toward home. As soon as no one was looking, Selemei's grin escaped to her face.

Me, legally retired? Ah, Xeref!

Of course, it was always challenging to get the children settled after the excitement of a party. Selemei kissed Corrim goodnight, fingering a lock of his hair. Now that he was eleven, he professed himself too old for such intimacies, but she'd get away with it as long as she was able. Such soft, soft curls—the perfect cross between Xeref's straight hair and her own.

"Mother?" Corrim turned his head, pulling the curl from her grasp. "Has Father made a lot of laws?"

She frowned. "I think so."

"Which ones?"

"He's participated in votes for all of them. I'm not sure how many times he's proposed his own; you should ask him."

"Do you think the Eminence Indal will like this new one?"

She should have known he'd hear; rumors were as swift and unquenchable as wysp-fire. "I hope so."

"When is Brinx coming home?"

Selemei glanced to the other brass-framed bed, which the Household had perfectly arranged with sheets turned back for whenever her eldest returned from his evening with friends. "Late, sweet boy. Please don't wait up."

Corrim grunted, but when she leaned down to him, accepted a kiss.

"Mistress?" came a disembodied voice from behind the servants' curtain. "Please, Mistress, if you would attend your daughter?"

Oh, no. I could have sworn Pelli was sleeping like a stone . . . "I'm on my way."

Selemei walked on her Grivi's arm into the hallway, and together they hurried to the girls' room. He pulled open the heavy bronze door for her.

Mercy . . .

Pelli *was* sleeping like a stone, arms and legs flung wide, her covers tossed off and her pillow on the floor. The muffled sobs came from the other bed.

"Aven?" Selemei whispered.

Aven sat bolt upright, still sobbing, and reached for her with both hands. Selemei limped to her bed and sat down. Aven's hands clutched hard enough to hurt, and she wormed into Selemei's lap.

"Aven, my sweet Aven, what in the name of mercy?" Selemei murmured, stroking her back. "I'm here, everything's all right, I promise. What's wrong?"

Aven sobbed something into her shoulder.

"I don't understand."

"Mama, you almost died!"

Mercy, indeed. She's so smart. For a second, it hurt to swallow. "My darling," she managed, "that was about Lady Indelis."

Aven pulled back and scowled, sobs turned to outrage. "No it wasn't."

"All right, I'm sorry. I'm sorry, you're right." She found Aven's hands and gave them a tug. "But I *didn't* die. By Elinda's forbearance I'm here now, sweet one, and I love you."

"It's not fair." Aven's arms lifted from her waist to drape over her shoulders, and the girl nuzzled into the crook of her neck. "Why do we have the decline anyway, when Lowers don't?"

"I don't know, love." Every parent faced this moment. Somehow it never got any easier, even after going through it with each of her older children. "I guess, we have to remember that each of us has our time. We can take good care of ourselves, but we don't get to choose. Some people are never born. Some are never confirmed, and live hidden. Some are here one day and gone the next. My mother used to tell me that Mother Elinda loves the Race the most of all the people of Varin, and puts us in special constellations."

"That makes no sense." Even her daughter's voice was frowning. "Mother Elinda puts souls *into* us, she doesn't just take them out. If she really loved us, she'd give us babies to end the decline, not kill us."

"Sweet one—"

"And how do we know the people who die are in the sky, anyway? It's the *sky*." She waved an arm toward the vaulted stone ceiling.

Selemei could feel all four levels of city and rock above. Only travelers, Venorai farmers, and Arissen firefighters ever saw the sky; it was a long way up to the gods her mother had wanted her to believe in.

"I suppose we don't know," she sighed. "But we do have Imbati and Kartunnen who care for our health. And if your father passes his law, then fewer of us will die."

Aven shook her head. "Mama . . . "

"Please, darling, don't worry. Come here." She pulled Aven in again, and leaned against her springy hair. Across the room, Pelli sneezed in her sleep and turned over, apparently unaware. Could they be saved? And what about her firstborn daughter, Enzyel, whose trials were already beginning?

A click came from the door latch; Selemei looked up. This was Xeref, sticking his head in. What did he want? She raised eyebrows at him.

Xeref didn't call for her, but came in and sat with them on the bed. She had no idea what he intended until he wrapped his arms around them both. After a moment's surprise, she relaxed into his shoulder. Aven, too, seemed comforted.

When at last Aven began to nod off, Selemei nudged Xeref until he stood, then returned her daughter's head to the pillow and tucked her in.

Xeref offered her a hand up. She took his arm, and walked with him slowly out the door.

In the hall, the light of the sconce fell across his features. Untouched by Aven's fear of death, he looked quite as delighted as he had at the party this afternoon. Her own excitement welled up again. She seized his hands between hers.

"Xeref, thank you," she said. "What this means to me—I can't—" She pressed his hands to her heart, and then to her lips. They unfolded warm and soft to cup her cheeks.

Xeref bent close to her. "I had to do it."

She turned her face up and kissed him. How could she not? His lips were so sweet, and it had been so long! His mouth opened into a whole world where they existed only for each other. She tried to put her body and soul into that sacred place, and only when she gulped a breath did she realize she was already undressing him in her mind, while he pressed against her, eager and proud with the desire that had never dimmed.

The desire that could kill her if it were fully satisfied.

She pushed him away, gasping.

"I—I'm sorry," he stammered. "I didn't mean to—"

"Go away," she cried. "By Sirin and Eyn, please!"

His face full of pain, Xeref staggered away and vanished into the master bedroom.

All the inner parts of her tugged after him, but Selemei did not follow.

Naturally, rumors about Xeref's proposal were everywhere. Selemei had discovered a new talent: extinguishing conversations faster than atmospheric lamps at nightfall. No question in her mind what the talk was about. However, she'd prefer to know how far the information had changed, and how those changes might reflect on the First Family.

There was only one possible course of action.

Any lady of intelligence developed tools for unlocking the truth. Today was a day to employ her favorites: soothe the spirit with tea, amuse the tongue with cakes, and tease the honesty out. The Household had already completed arrangements in the sitting room: white silk cloth over the slate-topped table, silver spoons, teacups of silver-rimmed glass. Considering the delicacy of the topic, Selemei had chosen to invite only one friend from the Ninth Family and one from the Eleventh, both Family allies. Now all she needed—

"Excuse the interruption, Mistress," the First Houseman said, stepping from behind his curtain, "But your cousin, the Lady Keir, wishes to speak with you."

"Now?" Selemei pressed a knuckle to her lips. *Should I turn her away? Or let her see preparations meant for others?* "I'll come to her," she decided.

On Grivi's arm, she walked to the vestibule where she ducked around the edge of the velvet curtain. Keir stood waiting, twisting her golden hands even more tightly than the twists her Imbati woman had made in her hair.

"Cousin?" said Selemei. "Are you all right?"

"Is it really true?" Keir asked. "About what Xeref is planning?"

What had she heard? One hour later, it might have been easier to answer. "Only what he announced at Pyaras' party."

"But that's awful."

"Awful? What do you mean?"

Keir wrung her hands. "Well, do *you* think it's fair? That we have to almost *die* before we can get out of it? And what does that even mean, 'almost'?"

What? Get out of it before you've even started? Shock stole her ability to speak the words. A good thing, too, because behind that automatic protest loomed an intimate recognition as terrifying as a glimpse of sunlight. Selemei swallowed hard.

"Oh, Keir—cousin." She took a deep breath. "How difficult it must have been to come to me with your thoughts. Thank you for trusting me." She opened her arms, and Keir embraced her. Selemei resisted the urge to stroke her like a child. "I know how difficult this is. I can't *imagine* what you've heard out there."

Keir sighed, but unfortunately, didn't give any hint of what she'd heard.

Selemei drew another steadying breath. "So, I'm thinking—today, in a few minutes, I'll be speaking with some friends about this. If you've no prior commitments, then perhaps you would like to join us?"

"Oh!" Keir pulled back, dabbing her cheeks with her fingers. "I'd love to! Which friends? Do I look like I've been crying?"

"No, please, don't worry about that. I'm expecting Lady Ryoe of the Ninth Family—she's always been a great comfort to me during my recoveries—and you know Lady Lienne of the Eleventh Family from our games of dareli."

"Does Lady Ryoe play?" Keir asked. "Since we're missing a fourth?"

"Well, not today, all right? You may freshen up in my rooms as you like. The others will be here in a moment."

Keir bustled off at once, but her long-haired manservant stayed behind.

"Imbati?"

"Your pardon, Lady," the Imbati curtsied, inclining her tattooed forehead. "Your generosity in this invitation is much appreciated, but I must express concern."

"About Keir?"

She leaned her head to one side. "My Mistress decided to visit you because she is deeply moved by this topic. I fear that in conversation she may become . . . impassioned, even in the presence of outsiders."

And possibly risk Family secrets. Selemei nodded. "I understand. I'm already planning to tread carefully. I'll protect her, I promise." The servant bowed and followed her Mistress deeper into the suite.

Selemei sent her Grivi to the dining room to speak with the Household Keeper about how to accommodate an additional guest. He'd only just stepped away when the doorbell rang again. The First Houseman emerged from the vestibule, seeming perturbed to find her unattended.

"Is there a problem?" she asked.

"Mistress, your other guests have arrived, but they've brought a companion. Lady Teifi of the Second Family."

Selemei frowned. This could not be coincidence, and it would be rude to confront the motive of an unexpected guest. If she pushed ahead in her own inquiries, was rockfall inevitable? To protect Keir, should she give up on her questions altogether?

"They are all welcome," she said. She took a deep breath, weighing the words "tell," "inform," and "alert" for how far to mobilize the Household. Best to be cautious. "Please alert the Household to the change of plan."

"Yes, Mistress."

Grivi returned swiftly, apologizing for his absence at a critical moment; Selemei reassured him and allowed him to escort her to her seat. She kept sharp eyes on her guests as they entered. Lady Ryoe wore a smile that sparkled like the ruby pins in her sandstone hair; she came close for a kiss on the cheek before she sat down in the chair at Selemei's left hand. Lady Lienne's walk was tight; so also her mouth, and her gray sheath gown; she whispered close to Selemei's ear.

"My sister insisted."

Selemei looked past her shoulder to Lady Teifi, who was taking a seat on the facing couch. She and Lienne did resemble each other, though Teifi's long straight hair was sifted gray instead of pure black. Selemei kissed Lienne's cheek.

"You're both welcome. Please, have a seat. Our Household Keeper will be pleased to know that her tea cakes are held in such high regard."

Under the watchful gaze of her younger sister, Teifi returned the smile, but the faint blue tinge of her lips matched a chill in her eyes. "I wouldn't have missed them."

Keir entered then, through the double doors from the back of the suite. She hesitated a moment at the sight of Lady Teifi, but there was only one chair left, at Selemei's right. She took it, flashing a nervous smile. "I'm Selemei's cousin, Keir. Had you already started talking about it?"

"Not at all," Selemei said quickly. But when it came to proposing a less fraught topic of conversation, her mind whirled and came up blank.

Fortunately—showing impeccable timing—the Household Keeper appeared in her black silk dress, carrying the cakes. Her presentation was never the same twice; today she brought a sculpture of a fountain, five crystal spouts rising to different heights from a slate basin below. Atop each spout balanced a glass bowl delicate as a bubble, and inside each bowl lay a pearl-white cake garnished with a single red marshberry. Selemei herself could not help joining in the general sigh of admiration. Tea-pouring and the passing of cake bowls extended her reprieve, while the conversation turned to sweets, art, sweets as art, and where to find the most skilled Keepers. Selemei pressed her fork into the pliant surface of her cake, dared a bite. But every pause clutched at her, begging to be filled with harmless normality.

Here was a topic that might be harmless enough. "By the way, those are lovely hairpins you're wearing today, Ryoe."

Ryoe chuckled, licking berry juice from her lips. Her pale hand fluttered up to her hair. "Rubies are the gem of this year, Selemei. We're all wearing them—even you."

"Me?" Her own dress was sapphire blue, but then she remembered the bracelet on her wrist. Lienne wore rubies on the neckline of her dress, Teifi wore them in a band down the center of her bodice, and Keir wore them in a spiral brooch at her shoulder. Selemei's confidence faltered.

We're wearing blood. All of us.

She tried to cover her consternation with a sip of tea, but too soon; it burned her lip. Nothing could be harmless when the truth hid everywhere. She set down the cup.

"All right, I know what you're all here for. You want to know about Xeref's proposal, and I want to know what you've heard, and how you are thinking about it." To protect Keir, she assumed her cousin's argument like a cloak: "Personally, I don't think it goes far enough."

Keir sat straighter. "You don't? But I thought you said—"

"What a thing to say!" Teifi cried.

Selemei smiled, carefully, and folded her hands on her lap so they wouldn't shake. She could handle this; it wasn't the first time she'd been the target of all eyes at once.

"I'm not afraid to say it," she replied. "Xeref wants to prevent deaths like that of Lady Indelis. He thought the best way would be to allow ladies who had come close to death to retire from their duties. His intent is not to hasten the decline, but to allow ladies to raise their own children—and actually, also, to allow them more recovery time from birth injuries before they must consider pregnancy again." That was a good idea! Sometimes she surprised herself.

"Birth injuries." Lady Keir shuddered visibly. "Mercy of Heile."

"I understand your fear, Keir," Selemei said reassuringly. "That's why it's important to allow time for complete recovery. After all, a healthier mother will bear a healthier child."

"It won't work," said Lady Ryoe. The reminder of blood glinted from her hair as she shook her head. "I mean, retirement sounds good, but who's going to enforce it? We can't send Arissen guards into bedrooms."

"That's true," Selemei admitted.

"Then—forgive me—who is going to tell our gentlemen no?"

Selemei winced. Her heart wanted to protest, but how recently had she tasted this fear, despite how deeply she trusted Xeref? She almost looked over her shoulder at Grivi. "Well. We'll just have to think of something, I imagine. The wording of the proposal hasn't been finalized yet."

"This is ridiculous," Lienne muttered. "Lowers have children when they *want* to."

"Lowers, ugh!" Teifi grunted. "There are plenty of *them*."

Lienne's pale cheeks flushed. "Having too many children is killing us, Teifi, and it *still* isn't stopping the decline. If we're all going to die anyway, do we have to be miserable while we're doing it?"

"Lienne," said Ryoe, "I had no idea you were so upset. Is something wrong?"

"What's *wrong* is that you're even considering this nonsense," Teifi said. "Politics is gentlemen's business."

"But this is about *our lives*," protested Keir.

"And it's *our children* who stand to lose their mothers," said Lienne.

"I can't believe you, Sister," Teifi hissed through her teeth. "That you'd associate yourself with selfish cats who would turn their backs on the future of the Race!"

"Teifi, stop!"

Selemei spoke measuredly into the shocked silence that followed. "I don't believe it's selfish to try to understand the impact of the rules that gentlemen impose on our lives. The fact is, the proposal in its current form was my partner's idea, and it's uninformed in many ways, and incomplete. This is why it's so important for us to discuss it."

"The Race requires a higher form of loyalty," Teifi said. "These are the burdens of power."

"Oh?" Selemei asked, clamping down on a surge of anger and forcing a smile. "And would you like to tell us about the number and health of your children, then? How your sacrifices have rewarded you with success?" She'd heard enough about her from conversations with Lienne and Tamelera to know that Teifi couldn't answer that.

A muscle tightened in the older woman's jaw.

Lienne threw a keen glance at her sister, and stood up. "Selemei, I'm so sorry, we'd better go."

She took a deep breath. "Darling, what a shame." She squeezed Lienne's hand, trying to catch her eye. "Please let's talk another time."

Lienne and Teifi's swift departure left the other guests in a fluster, and they soon excused themselves, also.

"Is there tea left?" Selemei sighed.

Imbati Grivi lifted the pot, nodded, and refreshed her now-cooled teacup. Selemei sighed, pressing its edge into her lower lip, inhaling the steam. In a way, the utter failure of her subtlety *had* taught her what was out there—fear, despair, thirst, fury, and lots and lots of arguing. Keir had come out unscathed, at least.

But her own satisfaction with Xeref's proposal had not. Teifi demonstrated that any legislation of this nature would be strongly resisted; and Ryoe was correct that gentlemen would seize upon any excuse to dismiss restrictions on their behavior, even if it passed.

"Grivi," she said, "how soon can we be ready to go out?"

"I know of nothing that would prevent us going now, Mistress."

"I need to discuss this with Xeref. Our proposal needs some revisions."

Once she had given herself permission to go to Xeref's office—this was official legislative business, after all—her resolve outpaced her ability to walk there. Selemei left the suites wing and began to cross the central section, but her left hip twinged; she squeezed her Grivi's hand for a pause. By the tall bronze doors of the Hall of the Eminence, she cast an eye about, but saw only Imbati child messengers flitting through, and Arissen guards, powerful and still in their orange uniforms. No one to care if she shook her leg a bit.

After a few seconds, she tested her weight on the foot. Workable. A bit more slowly, they crossed into the offices wing. Xeref's was the first door on the left.

All five young men in the front office stopped what they were doing as she walked in. One of them was her son, Brinx. He sprang up from the steel desk he'd been leaning on, and straightened the hem of his malachite-striped coat.

"Mother? Holy Sirin's luck!" he exclaimed, grinning. "Fedron sent me over here only ten minutes ago; we've been going over the minutes of the last Cabinet meeting. If you'd come five minutes earlier, I'd have been busy; five minutes later, and I'd have been back next door." He kissed her cheek. "Would you like to come see where I work?"

Selemei smiled. As a child, Brinx had told stories to her for hours—even conversed with the vaulted ceilings when no one else was available. These days, she was seldom the recipient of that bright attention.

"I'd love to, treasure, but I've come to see your father."

Brinx pulled a sober face. "Of course. Shall I take you in? I don't think he has another meeting for at least sixteen minutes."

"Yes, please."

Brinx resumed bubbling while she followed him to the inner door. "You're lucky that he's in there by himself right now. He's had all sorts of meetings today, and messengers—we've gotten five of them at least. Six, I think, actually. Yeah, six. It's because of the *stir*, of course. The one Father started when he announced his Indelis proposal. We've never been so busy—" He pushed the door open a crack. "Sir? Father, Mother's here."

"Selemei? Come in, come in!" Xeref came to her quickly; his blue eyes searched her with concern, but when she smiled at him, he brightened. She released Grivi's hand to take his.

"Everything's fine, dear," she said. "I need to talk to you about the proposal."

"I hope you're not worrying, Mother," said Brinx. "Our conversations are going well." He raised one finger. " 'Give them the respite, gentlemen. Think first of the health of your partner if you wish a healthy child, and the blood of the Race will grow stronger!' "

"We don't vote for another week or so," Xeref explained. "This is the part where we sound people out and argue for the idea. Our most powerful argument is exactly what Brinx says, and people are responding well to it. I'm optimistic."

Hearing her earlier thought put so differently made her doubt any of these gentlemen were serious about real retirement. "Have you changed any part of the proposal?" she asked. "Added anything?"

"No. Why do you ask?"

"Well, have you talked with anyone about how to enforce it?"

"Mother, don't worry," said Brinx. "Kartunnen will do as they're told."

Kartunnen? She flashed him a look. "It's not them I'm worried about, Brinx, it's the gentlemen. No one will want to give up their chance to benefit the Race. They'll cling to excuses." The incredulity on his face forced her to search for examples that filled her with distaste. "No, she wasn't injured enough; or, no, we had a good doctor so she wasn't really in any danger."

Brinx pursed his lips into the same wanting-to-protest moue that he always had as a child. She rolled her eyes and turned to her partner.

"You know they will, Xeref."

Xeref looked at her in silence for a moment. "Yes," he sighed. "I imagine they will. Should we specify that the doctor must have assessed the risk of death at greater than fifty percent?"

She shuddered. "Do Kartunnen do that? Isn't that . . . heartless of them?"

"Not every time, I don't imagine."

"Fifty percent seems low," put in Brinx. "Maybe it should be sixty."

"Brinx," said Xeref, "you might want to think carefully before you say something like that. I wrote the proposal for your mother."

"Wasn't it for Lady Indelis?" Brinx exclaimed, but his face fell quickly from puzzlement to shock. "Oh. Mother, I'm so sorry. I had no idea."

Selemei found his hand and squeezed it. "Well, you can see, can't you, why we can't have this be negotiable?"

"I see what you're saying," said Brinx. "The problem is, negotiation is exactly what this part of the process is for."

"But, treasure, that's what I'm doing right now. Negotiating it." Selemei turned back to Xeref. "How many men do you know who would be willing to bargain the continuation of their families against their partners' lives? How many are doing this already? Speaking over a doctor's word in the name of ending the decline?" Xeref was too frustrating in his silence. "Xeref," she insisted. "*You* know how easy it is to speak over a doctor's word. How dangerous it is."

"Father, did you—" Brinx began, but Xeref raised his hand and stopped him with a glance.

"Selemei, my jewel, you're right. But no one will agree to give up such power to Kartunnen."

"The power doesn't need to be in the Kartunnen," she explained, carefully restraining her tone. "Neither should it be; as Lowers, they lack final authority. Put this in the law itself. Make a list of risks, of injuries, and how serious they are. Take it out of everyone's hands, as if it were the will of Elinda."

"Father, you'd still have to get the *list* from a Kartunnen," said Brinx.

"Brinx, I know how to get lists from Kartunnen," Xeref replied, and Brinx blushed. "Thank you, Selemei. I'll send my Ustin tomorrow morning."

"Come see my desk, Mother," said Brinx.

"I'm not finished, though," Selemei said. "There's another problem. A more serious one. A more *private* one."

"Which one?" Xeref asked.

She squirmed inside. Might this be easier to discuss if Brinx weren't here? Possibly, but saying 'rape' was awful, regardless. She dodged the word. "Well, we've talked about the will of Mother Elinda, but we haven't spoken about her partner."

"Father Varin?" Brinx raised his eyebrows. "Do you mean what punishment to levy for transgression? That's for the joint cabinet to decide."

She sighed. "Brinx, love, I'll lend you my copy of the Ancient Stories when your brother has finished reading it." Selemei opened her hands to Xeref, who was staring at her silently, with a wrinkle deepening over his nose. "Remember,

Father Varin gnashes the wicked in his fiery teeth in atonement for his own transgressions." Still, no recognition in Xeref's eyes. "The transgressions that led Mother Elinda to *reject* him."

"Oh!" Xeref cried suddenly. "But that's . . . oh, that's—oh dear."

"Father, what?"

"But Selemei, would they really?"

What a question! She turned it around. "Perhaps you mean to ask whether gentlemen would really be willing to sacrifice their desires for their partners' safety? Some would—*you* would. But most gentlemen are not you. Must I speak with the ladies of the Pelismara Society to give you a number?"

Xeref ran one hand through his silver hair, uncomfortably.

"What are you talking about?" Brinx demanded.

"Master," said Imbati Ustin. "I can verify, by Imbati witness, three rapists among those First Family gentlemen known to me. If you wish it, I can investigate and expand my knowledge to assess the scope of the problem across the Pelismara Society. It could have a substantial impact on this proposal's implementation."

In the Imbati's icy voice, it felt terrifyingly real. Selemei swore. "Name of Mai, who?"

"I don't know, Mistress, I'm sorry."

Selemei gaped at her. For whom was she protecting that information? Would she tell Xeref if he asked?

Brinx, who had been spluttering, found words. "Father, you must reprimand your Ustin."

"You think so?" Xeref narrowed his eyes. "Why is that?"

"Accusing her betters of such a thing! I can't think of anything more presumptuous."

"Brinx," Xeref said slowly, "Please think what you're saying. Ustin has worked as my personal and political assistant and bodyguard for twelve years. In all that time she has never failed to safeguard me or my information, nor have I caught her in any inaccuracy. Her qualities are guaranteed by the certification of the Imbati Service Academy, just as your servant's are. And this information is quite relevant to our success."

Brinx flushed. "I know. I'm sorry, Father. And I do really want to help you pass this proposal."

"If this is uncomfortable for you, why don't you just let me talk with your mother? Fedron's got several people he's negotiating with, and I'm sure he'd appreciate your help right now."

"Yes, of course, Father. I'll see you at dinner."

It was quite common for a room to feel silent after Brinx stepped out of it, but this silence was one Selemei hesitated to step into. Her mind whirled in horror and suspicion of the men she knew. Xeref stared into the distance, dismay written deep into the lines of his face.

"This . . . " He sighed. "I don't know."

That was not what she'd expected him to say. "What don't you know?" she asked. "I had no idea this was such a huge problem. The question is, how do we address it?" She looked to his Ustin for support, but Ustin didn't speak. The manservant's mark arched across her pale forehead like the bars of a closed gate.

"No, Selemei," Xeref said. "We can't address it."

"Why not?"

He rubbed his forehead. "This is a legislative proposal, which will be discussed and voted on by the cabinet. We can't lose sight of that. Proposals with divided goals fail, even when their goals are entirely ordinary. And . . . I really don't want this one to fail."

Oh, gods, if it failed! She gulped a breath. "I need to sit down."

"I'm sorry, love," said Xeref. "By all means."

Grivi was swift to deliver one of the metal chairs that faced Xeref's desk; Selemei sat with relief and tried to gather her thoughts. This proposal no longer felt like it was about her, but about Ryoe, Lienne, and Keir—and about her own daughters. To fail would be a disaster. But what if they succeeded, and the law were meaningless to those who most needed it?

"Ladies are vulnerable," she said quietly.

"You're right," Xeref agreed. He took the other chair, which Ustin brought for him. "As Lady Indelis was vulnerable."

"Or as I was," she said. "In a medical center, helpless to the wishes of doctors and family."

He shook his head. "I'm sorry."

"I'm not angry," she assured him. "But some ladies are also vulnerable at home. And we can't send Arissen into bedrooms to enforce this law." The very idea was appalling.

"Imbati are already there," Xeref mused. "But we don't want to put such power in the Imbati, either."

She raised her eyebrows at him. "Dear, it's hardly a reasonable demand on them, even if we did."

"True."

Selemei ran her eyes about the office as if the answer might be hiding here somewhere, hanging among Xeref's numerous certificates or tucked between the law books on his shelves.

"Wait," she said, "even if we can't do anything about the gentlemen, this proposal aims to prevent dangerous pregnancies. So, what about the medicines?" What had that Kartunnen mentioned at the party? Amb—something . . .

Xeref looked like she'd stuck him with a pin. "Those are illegal."

"So? We're proposing a new law, aren't we?"

"A gentleman would never consent to compromise his fertility."

"*I* would, if it meant I were never put at risk again."

He blinked at her. "You would?"

"Isn't that what we already decided?"

Xeref didn't answer, but shook his head in consternation. Then, beside her left ear, Grivi rumbled in his throat.

"Yes, Grivi?"

"Mistress, you should be aware that contraceptive medications, when properly used, have no permanent effect on fertility."

"Well. All right, then."

"Even for Grobal?" Xeref asked.

"I know of no genetic contraindications, sir," said Grivi.

"I'm just not sure anyone would agree to it. Could one really ask a man to waste his value to the Race?" Xeref frowned at the floor, and began cracking his knuckles, one after the other.

She realized, then. He was frightened. "Dear—what if we tried it?"

He twitched, and shook his head. "You're suggesting—no. I could never ask my Ustin to procure something illegally."

"Master," said Ustin, "I can procure something for myself with perfect legality."

That was it! Ustin was a woman, and would have done this before. Then all *she'd* have to do was get her hands on it, and then . . .

Selemei put her hand over Xeref's and squeezed. "Think of it."

The triangular white pill was small, almost indistinguishable from the marble of the bathroom counter. Selemei forced herself to see it, to confront it, to confront what she had to do. Grivi's unwillingness to aid her in any aspect of the medication only magnified her sense of transgression. After seven days, it had become no easier.

I am not harming anyone. I'm doing this for Enzyel, for Aven, for Pelli—and for myself. The Kartunnen have deemed it safe. Imbati Ustin herself has used this. A Grobal is not so different from a Lower that it will affect me differently. It is not harming me.

It is not harming me.

She swept it up and swallowed it before she could lose her nerve.

That was it.

She chased it down with an extra glass of water just to be sure. Her body had been feeling a little different, but that could have been her mind's suggestion. Stripped of the magic that younger women had always begged her to imbue them with, she felt . . .

Don't say hollow. I'm more than that. I've already contributed five healthy children to the Race.

Her triumphs were written in her body, where no one could take them away. Pale ripples in the skin of her belly and hips proved she had received Elinda's gift, that she could grow like the moon to nurture souls. Her breasts had earned their delicious softness with each precious suckling touch.

She raised her head and looked her reflection in the eye. *And now you've contributed to the content of a legislative proposal, so what do you think of that?*

A strange light crept over her face from beneath, turning its features unfamiliar. Selemei glanced down; a wysp had entered the room, and now turned circles beside her knee. She smiled at it.

The wysp understood. But she was going to do this anyway.

She raised both hands over her head, allowing Grivi to slip the sleeves of her silk robe over them. Then she closed the robe and took his hand to walk out to the bedroom where Xeref was waiting.

Xeref pushed up on one elbow at the sight of her. His worry-wrinkles were deeper than usual—he looked even more concerned than he had yesterday, if that was possible. She allowed Grivi to seat her on the edge of the bed; once Grivi vanished under his curtain, she took a deep breath.

"I'm all right, Xeref," she said. And told her body silently, *you are all right; show him.* She pulled her legs up on the bed and beckoned. Xeref moved close to her side, and put his arm around her shoulders. His warmth, his stability, his soft silver hair faintly scented with perfume . . . simultaneous waves of nostalgia and longing crashed together inside her, brimming in her eyes and stealing her breath. She leaned into him.

"I've missed you so," Xeref said.

All she could manage was a nod.

"It was harder to wait this time."

Hardest to wait when that wait might never end. She nodded into the crook of his neck and shoulder. She could feel his soft-furred, warm skin against her side, against her breast. She reached for his arm and stroked it from elbow to fingers, found the outer edge of his hand and squeezed it as hard as she could.

"Xeref, I didn't mean to push you away. I mean—I didn't want you *gone*, I just was so scared to—"

The words brought back the reality of what they were attempting. She jerked back and found him staring at her in dismay. So he'd arrived at the very same thought. She blew out a breath between her lips. Carefully, carefully.

"We're not doing this for politics. I—*I'm* not doing this for politics." The words sounded false.

Xeref seemed to crumple in on himself. "Nobody could possibly agree to this," he muttered. "Why did I ever make you—?"

"You didn't *make* me; I convinced you. And Ustin helped me."

He glanced toward the service curtain on his side of the bed, and heaved a sigh.

"Please don't blame her," Selemei said.

Xeref shook his head. "I don't, really. She does her job well. Too well, some might say."

"There's no such thing as an Imbati who serves too well." Selemei shrugged. "This is the only possible solution to our problem. And for her, this isn't political; it's normal."

"We aren't like them," Xeref said sadly. "Fevers that kill Grobal scarcely touch them. Who's to say you haven't done something terrible with this medicine, and will never conceive a child again?"

"But I don't want to conceive a child again."

"Ha!" The laugh burst from him all at once, like a bark.

Her face burned. "Xeref, I thought we agreed!"

"No, Sirin and Eyn, I'm so sorry. We do; of course we do. It's just, hearing you say it . . . " He rubbed his face with both hands. "I wish there were a way for this to be normal for us."

"Passing the law would make it normal. Except we can't pass the law until we try this. It's normal for Lowers . . . " A thought struck her suddenly. "What if we were Lowers?"

"You're not serious."

Impetuously, she tossed her bathrobe back from her shoulders. "We're both naked. Who's to say we haven't just set our marks aside? We could be Arissen—Residence guards, who've shed their castemark color."

He raised his eyebrows skeptically. "I can't imagine anything less romantic."

"Not guards, then. What if we were Kartunnen? I'm a dancer." She shimmied a little and ran her hands down the curve of her breasts and belly. "And you're a . . . "

"Hm-mm." That sound was still skeptical, but there was something of a chuckle hidden in it, too. "No; I can't."

She huffed at him. "Oh, come on. You're . . . you're my accompanist. And you play drums, with your feet!" She leaned over and shook one of his feet through the quilted silk. "And you play pipes of course, because you have such—" she found his hand "—marvelous—" she twined it in hers "—fingers."

He gave her a real chuckle this time, one that awoke heat in her stomach. "You're so beautiful. My Selemei."

She placed three fingers over his mouth. "I can't imagine who you're talking about."

"Someone . . . " He took a deep breath. "Uh, someone in a song."

"That's right, because we can sing, too."

"And we paint ourselves every morning. Like this." He licked one finger, and ran it over her lower lip.

Selemei pounced and caught the finger in her mouth. It didn't stay long; Xeref's mouth replaced it. Whenever her conflicting fears tried to rise up, she just kissed harder, and clutched him more tightly against her. Her leg twinged once, when he knelt between her knees, but she squirmed into a better position, and once he entered her she forgot everything but their ecstatic unity.

Xeref shifted beside her afterward, his panting gradually giving way to gentler breaths. Then he laughed. "Well. I know how to convince the cabinet to add medicine to our law."

Selemei let out a sigh, and the weight in her mind floated away. "Sirin and Eyn," she swore. "Part of me wants to do that ten times before morning. The other part of me is—a little tired."

"Tired, my love? I'm sure if I can muster a bit more energy at my age, you can, too." He stroked her face, her neck. His hand settled around her left breast. She stretched beneath his touch.

"Mm," she said. "I didn't say I couldn't." It troubled her, though, to be reminded of his sixty years. "Are we so old, Xeref?"

"I suppose we are. Does it matter?"

"I don't know. I felt old, thinking of what it meant to retire. Thinking it would be the end. But I still wanted to."

"Of course you did."

"But now—maybe it doesn't have to be." She turned her head to look into his eyes. "If you can convince them, Xeref, it doesn't have to be."

"Do you know what else doesn't have to end?" Xeref asked. His smile made her catch her breath.

Selemei breathed against his lips. "Tonight."

"Let our law pass today," Selemei murmured. "Sirin bring us luck to let it pass. Please, let it pass." Her Grivi was in the midst of fastening the buttons at the back of her gown—she'd picked feldspar-gray today, to inspire herself with the steadiness of stone. Feeling nervous wouldn't help. Only the cabinet representatives of the Great Families were allowed into the Cabinet room for the vote, but she was determined to go, even just to wait outside for the result.

"There you go, Mistress," Grivi said.

"Thank you, Grivi." She took his hand and they walked out across the private drawing room. Maybe this once, Xeref would let her walk there with him. Grivi pushed open the bronze double doors into the sitting room.

The sitting room was full of strange Imbati, all dressed in black, all marked with the crescent-cross tattoo of the Household. The vestibule curtain and the front door both stood open wide. Selemei shook her head, blinking.

"What's going on?"

Two Imbati emerged from Xeref's office, carrying something. It looked like a stretcher.

Wait, those were Xeref's feet!

"Xeref!" she cried. "Gods, what happened?"

She half-hopped, half-ran to his side, fell to her knees and grasped his hand. Pressed her lips to it, but he didn't respond.

"Please excuse us, Lady, we must get him to the Medical Center as quickly as possible."

"Oh! Yes . . . " She released Xeref's hand and scooted backward. The black-clad stretcher-bearers moved so fast that he was out the door in half a breath.

Selemei sat, panting. At last she reached up, found her Grivi's hand, and tried to stand. Her left foot caught on the hem of her gown, but he caught her when she stumbled, freed the fabric, and helped her the rest of the way up.

Arriving on her feet, she found Xeref's Ustin standing directly in front of her.

"Mistress," Ustin said. "I was attending the Master's preparations in his office. He summoned the First Houseman to send you a message, because he was concerned you would not be ready in time. Then he stood up and collapsed."

"In my witness," the First Houseman agreed.

"Heile have mercy," Selemei whispered. "Let him reach the Medical Center in time. Elinda forbear." She cast her eyes toward the front door, now shut; the sitting room, now empty of the Household emergency team. You would almost think nothing had happened.

And how could it have? If she stayed in this moment, unbreathing, unthinking, nothing would have happened.

Her body corrected her, of course; she gasped and shook herself. "I should go to him."

"Mistress."

The Imbati was still in front of her. She frowned. "What, Ustin?"

"The Master had no opportunity to record his vote for today's Cabinet meeting."

No opportunity to record his vote. She heard the sounds; missing emotional register, they resolved only slowly into meaning. Did that mean . . . their proposal might fail?

"It has to pass," she murmured.

"With your permission, Mistress, I can escort you to the Cabinet room."

She started to understand it. "So I can tell them. And then go to the Medical Center."

"Yes, Mistress."

"All right, then, let's go."

The hallway was walkable. She had to take a brief stop on the spiral staircase to the second floor, Ustin above her, Grivi behind. She gripped tight to the cold iron rail, pressed her right hand against the central stone column, and started up again. Ustin murmured to her as she emerged into the hall.

"You understand, Mistress, that because he didn't record his vote, I could not deliver it."

She nodded. "That's why I'm doing it."

Ustin hesitated a second, her lips pressed together, but then she resumed course into the central section of the Residence. Selemei kept walking. Grivi's arm beneath hers was muscular and solid.

Since the Heir's suite faced the front of the Residence, she'd always known the Cabinet chamber was down the hall toward the back of the building, but she hadn't realized it was on the left side. The bronze door was engraved with the repeating insignia of the Grobal. There should have been people here, standing in the hall—cabinet members. Shouldn't there?

"Where are they?" Selemei asked.

"I believe they have gone in, Mistress," Ustin replied. "Please be aware, Grivi and I are not permitted into the room during the meeting. You are the only one who can represent the First Family."

"Mistress," Grivi objected, in a low growl.

"I'll only be a moment, Grivi."

She let herself through the door.

All talk in the windowless room stopped immediately. So many eyes, staring at her, and all of them belonged to men. The men sitting around the big brass table. The men in the heavy portraits staring down from the walls. She recognized the man at the head of the table—that had to be the Eminence Indal, because he had a noble nose, and wore the white and gold drape of office around his shoulders. Next to him, golden-skinned and curly-haired, sat the Heir Herin—everyone agreed how handsome the Heir was. The others were strangers . . . no, here was one more she knew. Fedron, her cousin in the First Family.

Fedron stood up. "Lady Selemei, what are you doing here?"

Her voice felt tiny, as if she spoke across a crevasse. "I'm representing the First Family. Xeref—" The ground beneath her shuddered; or it could have been her legs. She found a chair to hold onto. "Xeref collapsed. They took him to the Medical Center."

"What?" cried Fedron. "When?"

She blinked at him. "Now. I came directly."

Everyone started talking at once. Several of the men leapt up from their chairs; some of them seemed angry at each other. She quickly lost sight of the Eminence and the Heir behind a clump of worried cabinet members. The portraits still stared down from the walls, but Xeref meant nothing to them. Only Cousin Fedron appeared to remember she was here.

"I'm so sorry, Cousin, you must be distraught."

"I don't have time for that. I need to be here for the vote," she explained.

Fedron cast a sideways glance, maybe looking for one of the other men. "We can't possibly vote now, under the circumstances. Perhaps when Xeref returns."

"We can't?"

"Are you unattended?"

She shook her head. "No, of course not. They're waiting outside for us to vote. We should really vote."

"Cousin, we can't vote today," Fedron said, with exaggerated patience. "The Eminence and several of the members have already left."

"They have?" She looked around. It did seem emptier than a moment ago. The Eminence really was gone. That wasn't how it was supposed to happen.

None of this was how it was supposed to happen. But now she had somewhere she needed to be. The Medical Center. Selemei took a deep breath and smoothed down her gray skirts. Cautiously, she turned back toward the engraved door and made her way through it.

In the hall, a few cabinet members were talking and arguing. Imbati Grivi and Imbati Ustin stood waiting for her. They looked all wrong—not calm at all. Grivi's tattoo was furrowed, and he cast a gaze of anger at Ustin, whose face twitched in a battle to conceal some strong emotion. Ustin managed to master herself, but then cast a glance down the hall.

"Mistress—"

Grivi stepped between them. "Ustin, that's enough!"

Startled by his ferocity, Selemei sought after the target of Ustin's furtive glance. Someone was hurrying up the corridor toward them.

"Brinx?"

Her son's handsome face was nearly unrecognizable—his eyes red, and his mouth twisted. "I can't believe you, Mother!" he shouted. "Why didn't you come find me, to tell me?! How could you come here at a time like this?"

Time shrank to a pinpoint. If he spoke again, she didn't hear it. Why hadn't she recognized the signs? Hadn't she noticed how cold Xeref's hand felt against her lips? Why had she never wondered why Ustin accompanied her here instead of staying with her master? Why had she not realized only disaster could make Imbati show emotion?

Now all the stones crashed together, and the bottom dropped out of the world.

This was obviously the funeral of an important man. The Voice of Elinda wore full priestly regalia, dark blue robes and a heavy silver moon-disc around her neck. She sang the service in a contralto of liquid grief. The Eminence Indal and the Heir were here, and every member of the cabinet, and nearly half the Pelismara Society, too, all crowded into the chapel on the Residence's second floor.

Selemei couldn't feel it. Her eyes and throat hurt, but no tears came.

All she could do was hold Aven's hand, and curl an arm around Corrim, who clung to her, muffling his sobs in her stomach. Pelli's Verrid had decided to take her for a walk when she started squirming; Brinx sat on the far side of his sister Enzyel and her Eighth Family partner because he wasn't speaking to anyone. Selemei leaned her head down against Corrim's curls, reversing the room in the corner of her eye.

A shinca tree trunk glowed silver in the back, casting eerie clarity across the gathering. Since shinca could not be removed, the stone wall would have been built around it long ago; and in this room, the ceiling had been designed with arches to look like its branches. *That* should have been the front of the room. It had been, once. She and Xeref had spoken vows to each other in the warm aura of the tree, invoking the blessed names of Sirin and Eyn. She'd imagined their partnership just as invulnerable—the illusions of a seventeen-year-old child.

"Mother," Aven whispered. "Mother."

Selemei lifted her head. The Voice of Elinda was walking toward them with arms outstretched. One golden hand held a box of precious wood; the other a basket of silver wire heaped with yellow mourning silk.

"Corrim," she murmured. "Let me stand. It's all right—please, just don't fall on the floor." He crumpled sideways, gulping back tears, and she managed to get up, though her left leg felt numb from sitting too long on the metal bench.

"May the wounds of grief become the gifts of remembrance," said the Voice.

Selemei took the box, and pulled a mourning scarf from the basket. "Thank you, Mother Elinda." The children were supposed to receive their scarves next, but actually Aven took three because Pelli was gone and Corrim wouldn't look up. While the Voice moved on to Enzyel and Brinx, Selemei helped Aven and Corrim get their scarves fastened around their arms, snug just below the elbow with the ends fluttering down.

Around her, other people began standing, but there was no hurry to go anywhere. She opened the glossy lid of the box. The sight of Xeref's name engraved on the crystal spirit globe inside brought such a tide of grief it nearly overwhelmed her, and she snapped it shut.

"Lady Selemei," said a man's voice, heavy with tears. "May Xeref take his place among the stars, and may Heile and Elinda continue to bless you and your family."

She looked up; it was Administrator Vull, holding young Pyaras by the hand. He offered her his other hand, and she took it.

"Thank you, Administrator."

"Cousin, please. Or just Vull. We have too much in common to insist on formality, don't we?"

Her breath hitched, and she closed her eyes to wrestle it back into control. "I suppose we do, Cousin."

Vull nudged his son, and Pyaras said with admirable sobriety, "I'm very very very very sorry." Then, impulsively, he hugged her.

Selemei stroked his head. "Thank you, Pyaras." The boy watched her over his shoulder as his father led him away.

There was a nudge at Selemei's elbow. She turned to find Imbati Ustin pressing a note into her hand. It read, *Do you wish to attend the next Cabinet meeting?*

She stared. "Ustin, now is really not a good time."

"Mistress," said Grivi. "I believe your daughter wishes to speak to you."

Selemei turned back and took Enzyel in her arms. The girl was taller than her, now, and still growing—oh, gods help her, that was Xeref's height, would she also inherit the defect that had led to his aneurysm?

"May Heile preserve you," she said, fervently against her daughter's shoulder. "Are you all right?"

"Oh, Mother, I think I should be asking you that question."

"I—" Trying to answer that would release the flood. She shook her head. "I love you, Enzyel. I wish you could come for dinner sometimes."

"I'll be at the dinner tonight. I'll try to come by more. And—" Enzyel leaned so close Selemei was enveloped in her cloud of curls. Her daughter's sweet breath warmed her ear. "I've got good news."

Oh, sweet Elinda, no . . .

"I'm pregnant."

Selemei's hands fisted involuntarily. She tried to say *congratulations*, but fear had cramped her guts, and what came out sounded like a sob. She fought to control herself while Enzyel's gentle hand caressed the back of her neck. "You'll—" Selemei gulped another breath. "You'll take care of yourself, won't you. Don't just rely on your Imbati. See a Kartunnen doctor at the Medical Center as well."

"I will, Mother, I promise."

Grivi murmured behind her, "Do you wish to retire, Mistress?"

Selemei nodded. She stepped carefully toward the aisle, holding Grivi's hand across the bench that had separated them. A man she didn't know stood half blocking her exit into the aisle, watching her.

"Excuse me," said Selemei.

"My condolences on your loss, Lady Selemei," the man said. "I'm Silvin of the Second Family."

"Thank you."

"But, let's face it, it could have been worse."

She could only blink at him.

"It could have been *you*. Think of the tragedy, if your great gift had been lost to the Race! You must give your Family Council my name when they suggest a new partnership for you."

Disgust knocked her back a step. Before the man uttered another word, Grivi appeared between them, looking directly into his face.

"You will excuse us, sir," he said, his deep growl all the more disturbing for its utter calm.

The man and his servant quickly backed off and vanished in the crowd rather than risk a physical confrontation. Grivi's shoulders rose once with a deep breath, and then he offered Selemei his hand again.

"Bless you, Grivi," she whispered.

"I am here to protect you, Mistress."

"Selemei! Cousin, are you all right?" That was Lady Keir, who hurried up and embraced her. "I saw what happened . . . "

She grimaced. "Fine enough."

Arbiter Erex caught up with his partner a moment later; he fanned his chest a little, breathing fast. "Cousin, I'm so sorry." He gestured to the compact Imbati woman behind him. "Please allow my Kuarmei to help escort you home."

Selemei shook her head. "It's kind of you, but I'll be fine. I have Grivi and Ustin with me, and I'll have Verrid too, soon enough." She began walking toward the exit.

"If you're sure," Erex said. "That was disgraceful behavior. In fact, my Kuarmei got his name; we'll be reporting him to his Family Council. Rest assured, you won't have to consider tunnel-hounds like him when the time comes. Someone like Administrator Vull would be a much better match."

Selemei almost stumbled. She gritted her teeth and clung to Grivi to keep going. "Come, children," she said. "It's time to go home." She would have run if she could. Her eyes burned, and she scarcely raised her eyes from the floor until they had collected Pelli and Verrid and were all the way downstairs, safe in their home vestibule, the front door shut and locked and the children dismissed to the care of the Household. "Where's Ustin?"

The tall Imbati woman presented herself with a bow.

Selemei took a deep breath. "Imbati Ustin, I know you've been concerned about securing lodging while you're considering new employment inquiries. Please feel welcome to stay in our Household."

"Thank you, Mistress."

"And in return, I'd like you to make certain I attend the next Cabinet meeting."

They were playing kuarjos, or trying to. You had to do *something* once the cousins, friends, and well-wishers left—and it helped her ignore the piles of condolence gifts that filled their private drawing room. Selemei sat across from Aven, who occasionally hiccupped to hold back tears but still had grasped the rules pretty well. When Selemei picked up an emerald-helmed warrior, Pelli snatched it from her hand and ran away giggling.

Selemei only sighed, and Pelli slowed, falling into a droop.

"Pelli, big girl, may I have that back? Bring over your puzzle if you want to play. Bring it over here next to us."

Pelli lifted the emerald-helmed warrior and stared at it.

Selemei turned her attention back to the board and pointed to a junction. "I'll put it there, whenever Pelli brings it back." She glanced over. "Please, baby."

Aven moved one of her pieces forward on a left diagonal.

"Not there," said Corrim. It was the first he'd spoken in hours. He draped himself over the back of the couch next to her. "She'll get you in entrapment. Use the inverse move instead."

Aven pulled a face at him. "Mother, what happens if a piece crosses the whole board?"

It walks right off into darkness, like at the edge of the city-caverns. Like at the end of the world. Like in my dreams. And then it has to keep going anyway. One breath, one step, in this place with no air and no light.

Pelli's soft fingers were tickling her hands. Selemei took a breath, and stroked them, and found the golden warrior had been returned, wearing a hat of twisted white paper. "Thank you, big girl. All right, so, Aven. The game changes once a warrior is able to cross the board, because—"

The vestibule curtain swished open, revealing Imbati Ustin.

"Mistress." Ustin bowed. "I apologize for the interruption. I've learned that an emergency Cabinet meeting has been called for tonight. If you wish to attend, we must hurry."

Hurry? What should I do? Selemei stood, searching the space around her for reasons to feel prepared. *I should tell the children.* "Children, I'm going to step out for a few minutes. It won't be long. Corrim, why don't you take my place at kuarjos? Pelli—" She bent and kissed her. "I love you, big girl. Be back soon, all right?"

"Mama back," Pelli answered.

Selemei searched the room again, but found only absence and grief. "Am I ready?" she asked.

Grivi offered his arm. "You are dressed for guests, Mistress. That will be perfectly appropriate."

Ustin nodded. "I'll brief you on our way."

Selemei tried to project confidence on her way to the front door so as not to alarm the children. It would be all right. Fedron would be there. She wouldn't be alone.

And she had to be there.

"Mistress," said Ustin, walking behind her right shoulder. "We must have you seated in the Cabinet room before any of the other members arrive. Can you walk faster?"

"Oh, yes." She'd been fighting the urge to run along the carpeted hall; all she needed to do was give in slightly. And hold tighter to Grivi's hand. She skipped a little, taking extra hops on her right foot.

"There are two types of votes, Mistress," said Ustin. "Procedural votes are the ones that allow cabinet business to continue. For those, simply follow your cousin Grobal Fedron's lead."

"All right."

"There are two legislative votes scheduled, so far as I know, in addition to the Indelis proposal."

"Two?" The carpet ended where the corridor gave into the Residence's central section. Selemei misstepped. Pain stabbed down the back of her left leg. "Aah!"

She hung on Grivi's arm. The pain had flashed and gone, but not gone completely; it echoed. She gritted her teeth. *This isn't going to work. Why am I even trying?*

Elinda help me, how can I not?

"Mistress," Grivi murmured, "May I carry you?"

She shook her head vigorously. "No, no. It's already bad enough—if people saw us . . . " Catching a silent exchange of looks between Ustin and Grivi, she frowned, and then realized the problem. The Cabinet chamber was upstairs. "How can I get upstairs, Ustin? I *have* to be there!"

"I have an idea," Ustin replied. "Grivi, if you both would please meet me at the door of the Household Director's office." She loped off beneath the arch into the public foyers of the central section.

"Mistress," said Grivi, slowly. "Can you walk?"

Hard to answer that question, but, "I will." She managed it by focusing on the floor. Polished stone in one room, a carpet with geometric patterns in black and green. Ancient tile in the foyer before the Hall of the Eminence, worn to white mostly, but near the walls, still showing an intricate branching design in gold. Step by step.

The Imbati Household Director kept an office just beside the main front entrance; its bronze door was uncurtained because of the frequency of messengers, and today it stood open. Ustin returned to them as they drew nearer.

"I've spoken to Assistant Director Samirya," she said, in a low voice. "We have permission. Let's take her elbows."

Grivi gave a reluctant-sounding grunt, but then Selemei found herself lifted a finger's breadth from the floor and ushered at high speed toward the door. Just as they reached it, the two Imbati turned her sideways—and they went through.

Selemei gulped. This was not Grobal territory. On a tall metal stool sat a golden-skinned woman with straight hair pulled severely back from her crescent-cross Household tattoo. She looked up from an ordinator screen full of glowing green symbols, and regarded them with a fierce unwavering gaze.

"This once, Ustin," she said.

Selemei was swept sideways again, and found herself in a tiny room with featureless metal walls, so close between Ustin and Grivi that they could not help but touch her. She clasped her hands together so as not to give offense in return.

The room lifted.

Selemei gasped. "An elevator?"

"It's for messengers," Grivi rumbled.

"And emergencies," added Ustin. "I just hope we'll be in time."

Perhaps this brief respite had been just what she needed, because her leg took her weight better when she tested it. Here on the second floor, the open entrance of the elevator was covered with a curtain. Ustin stepped out, but swiftly ducked back in again.

"Gro—people in the hall, Grivi," she said. "Let's cross, while we still have Samirya's permission."

"Cross?" Selemei asked. She leaned on Grivi to enter the main hallway. Over there, beneath the arches, stood the cluster of men in question; strangers from other Families, with their Imbati. Even this far off, their raised voices sounded aggressive.

"Cabinet members, but they're still attended," said Ustin. "I'm guessing we have maybe three minutes before they go in."

Again the two Imbati lifted her by the elbows, sweeping her across the hall, where Ustin lifted a curtain and let them through a door. Here the corridor was narrow and dim, and Grivi could only support her from behind. She tried to hurry, in spite of the risk. She didn't belong here. What argument could Ustin possibly have used to justify allowing a Higher like her into the servants' Maze?

Around a corner to the right was more light, through a series of windows on the left side. She gratefully used their stone sills to support herself, and then a door opened on her right.

She could feel eyes staring down at her as she entered—but they were only the painted eyes of dead Eminences. The room was empty.

Ustin and Grivi helped her ensconce herself in one of the tall-backed brass chairs. Xeref's chair. It had none of his warmth or softness.

"Mistress." Ustin pressed a paper into her hand. "These are the votes you will need to cast. The most important thing is, you must say you occupy this seat for the First Family."

"I'm representing the First Family."

"Mistress, if you will: I occupy this seat . . . "

"I occupy this seat for the First—"

Click.

Ustin's gaze snapped to the main door. Faster than the turning handle, she leapt to the Maze door and disappeared.

Selemei's heart flipped; she tried to swallow it back into place and keep breathing. Three men walked in, conversing, then a fourth. The fifth man was first to notice her. He was broad-bodied, golden-skinned, and bald as a stone.

"Hello?" That single word filled the chamber. "What are you doing here?"

She thought of Imbati Ustin. "I occupy this seat for the First Family."

Now the others saw her. "What?" "Who—wait, wasn't she the lady who . . . ?" "Xeref's partner?" "What in Varin's name is she doing?"

"I occupy this seat for the First Family."

"I'm sorry, Lady, you're going to have to leave," said the bald man.

She grabbed the lower edges of the chair, winding her fingers through gaps in the brass. "I occupy this seat for the First Family."

They were talking about her, now, and more of them poured in every second. She couldn't see Fedron.

"Can we have her removed?" "But, I mean, the poor thing—" "This can't be serious." "She'll go soon enough."

"What's this?" asked the Eminence Indal. He leaned on a cane of rich dark wood. His manservant, a single figure in black silk against the jewel colors of the other men, murmured in his ear while they went to the head of the table.

"What's this?" He sniffed through his noble nose and shifted his white and gold drape as he sat. And looked right at her.

Selemei lost her breath.

"No problem, your Eminence." The Heir waved his golden hand magnanimously. "She's just grieving, we can ignore her."

"But, cabinet business," objected a man with bulging eyes.

"Our main point of business is the empty seat." That was the bald man's resonant voice. "That is why Speaker Orn pressured us to convene this meeting at such short notice."

Selemei closed her fists tighter, until the brass hurt her fingers. "I occupy—"

Fedron burst in the door with a desperate look on his face.

"—this seat for the First Family."

Fedron gaped at her, panting. "Wh—Selemei? Cousin?"

Somehow his presence stopped the words up in her throat. She shoved them out. "I occupy. This seat. For the First Family."

Fedron deflated, and fell into the chair beside her. "Well, hand of Sirin . . . "

"We should just get started," someone said.

The Manservant to the Eminence struck reciting stance, his clear baritone cutting through any further murmurs of objection. "I call to order this meeting of the Pelismar Cabinet, and serve as a reminder of the Grobal Trust: giving to each according to need, the hand of the Grobal shall guide the eight cities of Varin."

"So noted," said a red-faced man sitting at the Eminence's right. "First order of business, acknowledgment and certification of the empty seat. Which *is* empty, in spite of appearances."

Selemei took a breath, but it was no use; hopeless certainty stole the words from her tongue. It was just as they'd said: they were ignoring her. While the men leaned forward to press buttons below the personal ordinator screens embedded in the table before them, her own screen—Xeref's screen—was dead.

Dead love, dead hopes.

The Manservant to the Eminence pulled a small device from his pocket, bowed, and intoned, "A unanimous vote is required to certify an empty seat. I count one vote in dissent. The seat remains occupied by the First Family."

"Wait, now," said the man with the bulging eyes. "Fourteen to one? Fedron, you're not serious."

Fedron folded his arms. "Does that seat look empty to you?"

Selemei looked at her cousin, but he didn't meet her gaze.

The red-faced man beside the Eminence gave a noisy sigh. "The seat remains occupied in the presence of a *legitimate* substitute. Indal's Jex, you'll carry the cabinet's petition to the Arbiter of the First Family Council to investigate the legitimacy of the substitute."

The Manservant to the Eminence bowed. No animosity on his face, but Imbati only showed feelings when they meant to—unlike the other cabinet members, who scowled and scowled while Fedron continued to avoid looking at her. Only the bald man with the big voice held pity in his face. They all argued about one topic after another. It went on so long that Selemei's fingers cramped around the curled brass of her chair; she had to extricate them painfully and rub them together in her lap. She combed through the men's portentous words for the Indelis proposal, but in vain. The paper Ustin had given her proved useless, for the voting screen before her remained blank.

"Right," declared the big-voiced man at last, "if there is no further business, the meeting shall adjourn."

"Seconded."

Selemei's heart shrank; she didn't dare protest into the silence that followed.

The Manservant to the Eminence bowed again, and intoned, "So it shall be. This meeting is adjourned."

If the last two years hadn't trained her to move slowly, she might have tried to run from the room. Selemei stood, and pushed back her chair, swallowing grief.

"That was some nerve," said a man somewhere to her left. "Get back to your children."

She dropped her gaze, but her cheeks blazed. She watched the placement of her feet, moving out from between the chairs.

"Lady—Selemei, is it?" When she looked up, the Heir was staring down at her. His face was young, handsome, chill as gold.

"Yes."

"You realize we've given you a gift." As he spoke, he stepped closer, looming over her.

She shook her head.

"Our *patience*, in the name of your bereavement. You know there are *other* ways to respond when someone disrupts cabinet business."

Mai help her—would he lay hands on her? Selemei took a nervous step backward.

Her left leg collapsed. She grasped for the nearest chair, felt fingers slip on the unkind brass, knocked her elbow, and hit the floor, the chair nearly coming down on top of her. She sat, immobilized by pain and shame while the Heir walked away without a backward glance. Gulps of air kept her from sobbing but couldn't stop tears creeping onto her cheeks.

"Cousin?" Fedron crouched beside her. "Let me help you up."

She nodded. Pretended this was just a room, not a room full of eyes and sneers. Gritting her teeth, she got her right leg under her. With Fedron's help, she managed to stand, and limp to the door where the manservants were waiting.

"Grivi," she said the moment she saw him, "I'll need you to make an appointment with that doctor. The one who was at Vull's."

Grivi interposed himself beneath her arm with a murmur of thanks for Fedron and a cutting glance for Ustin.

"Let me walk you home," Fedron said.

She hadn't expected that. They moved slowly, at her limping pace. But a bigger surprise came in the spiral staircase, where Fedron allowed his manservant to pass him and turned to face her.

"I'm grateful to you, Cousin," he said.

"What?" Grateful! Had she heard him right?

"Sure, you were misguided, but that was a big favor you tried to do for the Family. Someone overheard that we were inviting Garr back from Selimna to claim the seat at the next scheduled meeting, so they convened this one early. You know, to certify it empty before he could get here."

She couldn't tell whether to be flattered or insulted, and ended up mostly confused. "Garr and Tamelera are coming back?"

Fedron rubbed his hand across his forehead. "Well, I'm afraid it's not so straightforward at this point."

"What happened to the Indelis proposal?"

A strange expression flashed across his face. "Don't you worry about that."

How many times had she been told not to worry? "I *do* worry about it, Cousin. That's why I was there."

"Let me talk to Erex first, all right? And then we'll discuss it."

We'd better. But she was too exhausted and hurt to argue. She needed Aven; she needed Pelli, and Corrim. Just to hold them, and cry, with no eyes watching.

Selemei screamed and woke. A nightmare, not of wandering in darkness this time, but of standing exposed in sunlight, under the judging eyes of Father Varin himself. She panted while her heart slowed, rubbing her coverlet to remind her hands of soft silk and reality. Her body came into focus.

Everything hurts.

Each bruise that woke to identify itself roused another horrible memory of the Cabinet meeting. She couldn't force those events into sense, no matter how many times she tried. She called, "Ustin?"

The Imbati woman didn't appear. But then, she probably wasn't expecting to be called, because . . . Selemei's throat closed. She looked away from the place where Xeref should have lain. Deliberately, she rearranged her pillows and pushed herself back to sit. Mercy, it hurt . . . but how much worse might it have been without Grivi's care? She tried again, though her voice quavered.

"Imbati Ustin, may I speak with you?"

Ustin emerged this time, so silently she might have come, wysp-like, straight through the wall. She wore a black silk dress that showed off her muscular shoulders, not the suit she had normally worn on duty. "Mistress?"

This was already all wrong. "I'm very sorry," Selemei said. "It's not fair of me to demand you call me Mistress now, is it?"

Ustin bowed; a single pale braid swung forward of her shoulder. "Lady Selemei."

Selemei inhaled what calm she could manage. "I went to the Cabinet meeting, but it went so badly—I wonder if I might discuss it with you." Ustin's sober silence felt like disapproval, though her face didn't change. "If you consent to advise me, I'll pay you for your time."

"I am willing, Lady," Ustin replied. "Unfortunately, I have a very incomplete picture of what happened, having been limited to what Grobal Fedron told us, and what I could overhear from other members leaving."

"Well . . . we can start with what Fedron said. He said the meeting was called in emergency because Garr and Tamelera were coming back from Selimna. How would *they* have anything to do with anything?"

"Lady, are you aware that the seat my Master held was at-large?"

The term wasn't entirely unfamiliar. "I'd heard that. It means he's—" She gulped down a pang. "—he was, not the only First Family cabinet member."

"Yes, Lady. Each of the twelve Great Families is assigned a single inalienable seat. Beyond that, only two seats remain. In those, any Family's representative may sit."

"But we happened to hold it." She closed fists, remembering her fingers tangled in the chair. "And they wanted to declare it empty, but I was sitting in it." Another piece fell into its slot. "*That's* what Cousin Garr was supposed to do—sit in the seat so Fedron wouldn't have to admit it was empty."

"Lady," Ustin said, "I'm sure you know that any competition among twelve Families for a single empty seat would be fierce."

That was an understatement. Selemei nodded. "The cabinet rushed to meet so that Garr would come too late—and they would all have been itching to fight one another—but then I was there. They tried to pretend I wasn't—except Fedron said I was. Why would he . . . ?" She patted down the question with both hands. "No, of *course* he would. He had to have been in a panic when he thought they'd outmaneuvered him." That face he'd made, arriving in the seat beside her . . .

The corner of Ustin's mouth twitched slightly upward. Selemei chose to interpret that as approval.

"But I still don't see how any of this has anything to do with the Indelis proposal. I was *listening*. It was never even mentioned."

A shadow of something strangely like sadness flitted across Ustin's face. "Lady, no vote can occur if a proposal has no sponsor."

The men didn't care. Not even Fedron had sustained his sponsorship once tragedy struck. "I could have sponsored it, if I'd known," she said. "I thought I was there to cast his vote. But that's why you brought me, as a sponsor. Is it?"

Ustin didn't immediately respond. Selemei braced herself for *I don't know*, but then the Imbati answered, "Lady, you recall we were jointly involved in a conversation about the seriousness of the risks Grobal ladies face. I continue to share my Master's belief in the proposal's benefits for ladies and their children."

For me. And for my children. Without a law to protect her, she'd have men approaching her constantly; and how could she refuse to entertain partnership arrangements that the Family Council might propose?

"I could still sponsor it," she said. "Fedron *has* acknowledged me in the seat." Only once the words were out did their shuddering import take shape. *To do that, I would have to claim to be a legitimate cabinet member.* It perfectly explained Fedron's ambivalence. "The Family still wants Garr there."

Ustin nodded. "Lady, we can be certain of that. Grobal Garr is a man of influence, and was the First Family Council's choice of substitute. However, the Cabinet bylaws which allow a Family to provide a substitute imply that said substitute shall then fill the seat on a permanent basis."

"They imply . . . ? Gnash it, Ustin—that's why the Eminence is sending his man to the First Family Council. He thinks I've claimed the seat!"

Ustin's face remained impassive. "Technically, Lady, you have."

"And that's why Fedron wants to talk to Erex. Maybe I saved the seat, but I just delayed their problem! And then I fell down, and embarrassed myself in front of everyone . . ."

That seemed to startle Ustin. "Lady, you fell? I'm sorry."

The shame flooded back. Selemei pressed her hands to her face, shaking her head. "If I hadn't had to rush there—or if I'd just been holding onto something—"

"The Luck-bringer's hand is not always kind."

Her mother had often said so. Selemei instinctively raised her head for the traditional response. "But Blessed Sirin sees far, and does not explain his choices." She sighed. "That's why my Grivi will be taking me to the Medical Center today."

As if recognizing her need, Grivi stepped out from beneath his curtain and bowed respectfully.

"Good morning, Mistress. Allow me to dress you for your appointment?"

"Yes, thank you, Grivi. Ustin, you may be excused. Thank you for your help."

The Imbati woman bowed and withdrew.

"Mistress," Grivi said gruffly, "if you wish Ustin to advise you, perhaps you should inquire."

"But I did; I asked her in," Selemei said. "I did offer to pay her."

Grivi looked down at his hands silently for several seconds. At last he said, "Mistress, I believe you requested to see Doctor Kartunnen Wint, who confirmed Grobal Pyaras at his party?"

"Yes . . . "

"Please be aware that we'll have to go a little farther than the Medical Center for your appointment."

"Oh. All right." Vull kept a doctor outside the Medical Center? But perhaps Wint was worth it; she certainly had made an impression at the party.

After she was dressed and had eaten breakfast with the family, Selemei assured the children she'd be home soon—with extra kisses for Aven and Pelli—and she and Grivi walked across the gravel paths of the Residence gardens to the Conveyor's Hall. Selemei winced with every step. Thirty-seven should have been too young to walk like an old woman. It should have been too young to be widowed, too. Her former self dragged at her—the Selemei who had run and hidden behind that carefully tended hedge on her right, joined by a handsome man who gently kissed her amid the voluptuous scent of imported surface soil. It made her too conscious of the effort Grivi must be expending to keep her steady, to keep her moving. And conscious, too, of strange glances he cast toward her.

Was he unhappy?

She watched him. In the Conveyor's Hall, Grivi seated her in a chair by the stone wall. He left the green-carpeted reception zone, crossing the road that passed under the Hall's massive entrance arch and ended against the wall to her left. The zone beyond was crowded with vehicles of varying sizes; Grivi procured a one-passenger skimmer from the Household staff, and adjusted its control column to upright for a standing driver. Then he came and fetched her to it, slowing attentively at the spot where carpet met stone. He was always thoughtful—he didn't engage the skimmer's repulsion until she was fully settled. If he had some complaint, she couldn't detect it.

Driving felt quite normal. The skimmer hummed; the cool wind of their passage refreshed her; and outside the gate of the Residence grounds, broad circumferences busy with vehicles and colorful Lower pedestrians made a pleasant distraction. Grivi accelerated up a steep rampway of reinforced limestone that lifted them above slate roofs, and through the bore to the fourth level.

In this neighborhood, the cavern roof hung much lower. Grivi turned their skimmer into an outbound radius, and then into a circumference where the building façades formed a continuous wall on either side. The road ended against a melted limestone column as broad as a storefront. Above the roofs of the buildings, the slope of another level rampway was visible, passing up and behind the column's ancient mass. Grivi brought the skimmer to a stop. Its hum faded, and it sank to rest on the stone. The front wall of their destination had high oblong windows and bore chrome script identifying doctors Wint, Albar, and Sedmin. A bright globe lamp, green as the sphere of Heile, goddess of health, hung above glass front doors.

Selemei took Grivi's arm, passing a pair of wysps that drifted along the sidewalk, and entered through the glass doors that parted before them.

The crowd in the room within plunged into silence. Only a small boy with the castemark necklace of a Melumalai merchant continued to run in circles until he nearly tripped over Grivi's feet, then looked up and bawled in terror. His father rushed up, gaped helplessly at Selemei for a second, then turned to Grivi and blurted, "May your honorable service earn its just reward, Imbati, sir," before scooping the boy up and hiding behind a large group of thick-belted Venorai. The Venorai had the look of farmers—all were muscular, with striking sun-marked skin. One older man looked bright red, and a couple young women were covered with brown spots, and the rest were solid brown—they were all embracing each other, and she couldn't guess which one was here to see a doctor. Maybe the red one?

An inner door opened. Two Kartunnen men emerged: both wore green lip-paint and gray medical coats. The taller of them made a deferent approach to two Imbati mothers and their child; the shorter one came up to Selemei, and bowed.

"Lady Selemei, if you will please follow me." He made a second bow to Grivi, but did not greet him. He led the two of them back through the door, paused a moment to key a sequence on a wall panel, then took them down a long bare hall and opened a numbered door.

Doctor Kartunnen Wint stood in the room within. Selemei recognized her instantly, though this time the style of her gray coat was more functional. She had the same red hair, tied in a knot behind her head. She bowed. "My practice is honored by your patronage, Lady Selemei."

"Doctor Wint. I was surprised not to find you at the Medical Center," Selemei admitted. "Grivi, you may undress me now."

"Yes, Mistress." He began undoing her buttons.

"Lady, I did work at the Medical Center," Wint replied. "But after the death of Lady Indelis, I couldn't bear to stay. Administrator Vull nonetheless has maintained his family's relationship with me, for which I'm grateful."

"I'm sure. That was a terrible tragedy." That Vull would continue to bring his family to her spoke eloquently for the doctor's skills. Selemei pulled her hands out of her sleeves and raised them over her head.

"May I ask what brings you here, Lady?"

"My leg. I fell yesterday." Grivi lifted the gown off her; she lost the doctor for a moment behind layers of silk. When Selemei glimpsed her again, Wint still looked inquisitive. "Well, I stepped back on it, and fell. I'd been overusing it. Pushing through pain earlier in the day. And you said, at the party, that I should see a Kartunnen therapist."

Wint blushed, and glanced at Grivi. "I did, Lady."

"So." She indicated her own body. "Please proceed."

"Lady, would you consent to lie facedown on this table?"

"Of course." With Grivi's help, she climbed up to the padded surface. The slick material was cold on her right cheek, and all down her body.

"What kind of injury was this, Lady?"

"Birth injury."

"All right, that's what I thought. How far down your leg does the pain go? Does it go below your knee?"

"Yes."

"Have you had any bowel problems or incontinence, Lady?"

"No, thank Heile."

"Fever or weight loss?"

"No."

"What forms of treatment or testing have you previously pursued, Lady?"

"Grivi, please tell her."

While Grivi explained the tests and treatment she'd received in the Medical Center and the therapies thereafter, the doctor examined her back, rear, and legs. She pressed firmly, but did manage to avoid the bruises from the fall. Then she followed that up with some kind of pricking tool.

"Thank you, Imbati, sir," Wint said, when Grivi had finished. "May your honorable service earn its just reward. Lady, can you please stand for me?"

Once she was standing, Wint asked her to lift her leg, straighten her knee, lift her big toe, and stand on her toes. It went decently. It was hard to know if she should hope to perform better or worse.

"Doctor," Selemei asked, "what do you think? Can you fix it?"

The doctor pinched her own forehead with her thumb and forefinger. "I'm afraid it's too early to say, Lady. I'd like to recommend a course of exercises, and request that you undergo further tests."

Selemei's mouth fell open in dismay. "But this is like starting over! I thought—" What *had* she thought? That Wint would have Heile's hands, to heal with a touch? That if her leg could be fixed, it would change the past? Nothing would erase the sight of her fall from the cabinet members' memories! Nothing could bring Xeref back!

The truth tried to drown her. Selemei gulped air, struggling to stay above it, and covered her face with both hands. It was dark in the space behind them, warm, and damp. She did not want to cry in front of the doctor.

Grivi said softly, "I'm here to protect you, Mistress."

Selemei swallowed hard. "Doctor," she managed, "I'd like to get dressed."

"Of course, Lady."

The layers of silk gave her a moment's privacy; she could focus on her hands and her sleeves, and speak as if this were about someone else. "Of course you'd want tests, doctor; here I am walking in, and you don't know me or my case. I'm sure Grivi could have the Medical Center send over what we've already done. I probably should resume therapy—probably never should have stopped, childish of me, really . . . "

"I'm sorry I can't do more today, Lady," the doctor said. "However, there may be one way to prevent falls while we pursue longer-term improvement. Might I suggest a cane?"

Selemei blinked at her for a few seconds. Then it occurred to her, "The Eminence Indal carries a cane."

"Does he indeed, Lady?"

"He takes it into the Cabinet meetings."

The doctor bowed. "Two doors down from here is a shop where you might be able to find something suitable."

"Thank you, Doctor. I'll look, and I'll get back to you." Grivi had finished his work at just the right moment; she took his arm.

"Thank you, Lady. I'll send you a report on what we've discussed, and a list of suggested actions."

"I'll look forward to it."

Selemei walked on Grivi's arm out through the main hall, hurrying through the waiting room so as to cause a minimum of disturbance to the Lowers there. It wasn't difficult to find the shop Doctor Wint had suggested; it was staffed by Kartunnen and carried a variety of medical devices. None of the canes here were made of wood, but that only made sense—this was not a neighborhood which could support such high prices. There was a bin of black canes, but they seemed too Imbati; another bin held aluminum canes, but they seemed too Low. Selemei scanned a glass case of artist-designed canes intended for Kartunnen until she found a graceful one which did not use Heile's green in its design.

"Purchase this one, if you would, Grivi."

Grivi looked down at his hands, clasped before his waist, and said quietly, "Mistress? Must you purchase a cane?"

"Sorry?"

"I can accompany you at parties, if you wish. Even if the rooms are crowded."

Oh, no. *That* was why he was unhappy. This morning she'd asked Ustin for advice before she even called for him. She'd asked Kartunnen Wint for medical assistance that Grivi had always provided. And now, buying a cane meant she wouldn't need him for walking, either. For the first time, she understood what he'd said—'if you wish Ustin to advise you, perhaps you should inquire.' He didn't mean *ask*; he meant *write an employment inquiry.* That was uncharacteristic sharpness for him, but now that she thought about it, he must have been upset ever since that first day, when Ustin approached her during Pelli's nap.

"I'm sorry, Grivi," she said. "You serve me well, and always have. Please don't worry; ladies don't hire gentlemen's servants."

His shoulders rose and fell with a breath. "If I may presume, Mistress."

"Please."

"Ladies don't attend Cabinet meetings either."

"That was a disaster, Grivi."

"Mistress . . . "

"If you differ, Grivi, please tell me."

"You have now attended two meetings, Mistress, more than any other lady can say. In neither case did you flee. And your persistence has won you the provisional support of the First Family's cabinet member. Your intelligence is certainly a match to Master Xeref's, a long suspicion of mine that was confirmed when you spoke to Ustin this morning. If you are to continue in this, you will need her services more than mine. But I do wish to know one thing."

His honesty was sobering, almost frightening. She whispered, "What's that?"

"Is this your wish, Mistress?" Emotion colored his voice on that phrase, and he bowed his head. "I have vowed myself to your service, vowed to make your wishes my own. And if this is your wish, so let it be. But please be sure."

How could she answer, when she wasn't sure of anything anymore, even her next footstep? "Thank you, Grivi," she said. "I don't know. I wish—I just don't know."

Grivi bowed. "If you will excuse me a moment, I'll purchase the cane."

Of course she'd been summoned before the Arbiter of the First Family Council. Of course she had. The letter delivered by Erex's Kuarmei had made her feel sick to her stomach; now she squeezed her fear into it with one sweaty hand, taking care not to hurt Grivi with the other as they walked. Selemei turned Ustin's excellent political advice over and over in her head, but there was no guarantee Erex would listen. Chances were, he'd scold her and send her home to grieve.

They reached the hallway. Erex's office was across from Fedron's; at her back, she could feel Xeref's office whispering of emptiness. She shivered, squeezed Grivi's hand, and knocked on the Arbiter's office door. The door swung silently inward.

"Lady Selemei," intoned Erex's Kuarmei from behind the door.

"Come in, Cousin." Erex stood before his desk with fingers tented against his lips. He gestured to a cushioned chair. "Please, sit down."

Gnash it. Gnash all of it. She let herself be led to the seat, and seated in it. If she hadn't feared her leg might fail her, she might have preferred to face Erex nose to nose. On the other hand, his position of Family authority lent him more magnitude than his physical size. Selemei clasped her hand tightly around her left wrist; sharp rubies pressed into her skin.

My blood is precious. The Family doesn't deserve my life.

Erex leaned back on the front edge of his desk. "I've been thinking of you and your family in this difficult time," he said. "How have you been feeling?"

She didn't trust this kindness. "I'm coping."

"And how are the children?"

She almost told him. The boys were suffering most after the loss of their parent and mentor; Xeref had been less close to the older girls, so they were less affected; while Pelli was sad, but didn't truly understand. But this was a distraction, possibly even a trap. "As well as can be expected, given the circumstances."

Erex waited. Testing her with silence. Selemei stared at her hands, at a single sparkling ruby drop that had escaped her grip, and outlasted him.

Erex cleared his throat. "Cousin, I received a messenger from the Eminence Indal yesterday. Do you know what he came to ask me?"

She nodded, but kept her eyes on the sparkling ruby, as if it were a wysp that could give her good luck.

"In fact, I was shocked," Erex said. "Indal's Jex stayed for several minutes, to pressure me into providing an immediate answer. And I might have, if I hadn't already spoken to Fedron. He told me to wait."

Selemei spoke softly. "Cousin Fedron understands the bind the First Family is in."

"He does," Erex agreed automatically. Then he twitched, as if he'd suddenly awakened. "Do *you*?"

Selemei's heart banged inside her chest. She tried to keep her breath level, and hold Ustin's advice steady in her mind. "The bind the First Family is in," she said slowly. "Yes. I understand that the Family failed to deliver its chosen substitute to a critical meeting, and that if I hadn't been there, we would no longer have any claim to the seat. At the same time, I realize it would be very difficult at this point for us to sue for permission to seat a second replacement."

The Arbiter clearly hadn't expected her to answer. He seemed flustered for a second, but then resumed his scolding. "In fact, Selemei, we could be embroiled in the courts for years because of you."

"Because of me?" she asked. "Not because the Family couldn't keep quiet about their plan to bring Cousin Garr back from Selimna?"

Erex frowned. "Who told you that?"

Ustin would have said, *I don't know.* "Isn't it public?" she asked. "Speaker Orn informed every member of the cabinet. If I hadn't attended the meeting, the Third and Fifth families would be using their connections to the Heir and the Eminence to bully their way into our seat right now." She shifted with a deep breath, readying for a risk. "And actually, there's no need for any legal dispute."

"That's where you're wrong, Cousin. Every Family has an interest in ousting us. They've wanted to see the First Family weakened for years."

Her racing heart tried to leap out her throat, but she said it. "They can't do anything if I become the First Family's cabinet member."

"You're not serious."

Selemei released her wrist and leaned forward. "Cousin, let me try. It would keep us out of legal trouble. The others in the cabinet might let me stay, because they'll think the First Family *has* been weakened." She couldn't help a bitter laugh. "Especially after I fell down in front of the Heir."

Erex stared. For a moment she thought she had reached him, but then he shook his head.

"This isn't you talking, Cousin. You know the right things to say, but you must have learned them from someone else."

Gnash it! She didn't speak the words aloud, but in her blood, anger burned with the heat of Father Varin. "I am being advised by Imbati Ustin," she said. "In precisely the same way that you are advised by your Kuarmei."

Erex glanced at his manservant. Imbati Kuarmei stood coiled and still, her face expressionless. "My Kuarmei is a gentleman's servant," Erex said. "So is Imbati Ustin."

"By tradition. But there's no law saying she can't be mine. It would be quite simple for me to compose an inquiry." And Grivi's earnestness had convinced her of one thing. "The Imbati Service Academy would witness the contract without objection."

Erex started to reply, thought better of it, then circled behind his desk and leaned one hand on it, frowning. With the other, he started flipping through a stack of thick papers.

"You understand, I'm sure, that I represent the Family, and it's my job to know what's best for you," he said. "I would expect you to know that promoting the Race must come before our personal desires. It's clear you're feeling much better, and I'm glad of that. In fact, you were always quick in recovery. We should take advantage of that, going forward."

Now she recognized the papers, and felt Varin's heat drain out of her. Gods have mercy—*those were partnership solicitations.* Elinda's gentle breath raised hairs on her neck, cold as the space between stars.

This was an entirely different fight, one in which she stood alone. Xeref could no longer claim her. The law he'd written to protect her was powerless. Nothing Ustin had said was remotely relevant—indeed, how could it be? Even Grivi, who always swore to protect her, could do nothing here. He could only wait, and hope to keep her alive after she'd already been used.

Tears pricked in her eyes. She'd been here before: sitting in just such a chair, in another office a few doors down the hall. The Arbiter of the Fourth Family Council had smiled at her paternally, indifferent to her fear of eager and powerful older men. He'd told her what Erex told her own Enzyel not long ago—what he was telling her now: that she should be grateful at the prospect of a partnership that would sever her from her parents and every cousin she had ever trusted.

There was a difference, this time. Erex wasn't sending her out. *He was trying to keep her in.*

"I still have a family, you know," she said.

Erex made a small, tight grimace, not exactly a smile. "That won't be a problem."

Selemei closed both fists. "I'm afraid it will."

"Please, Cousin. Let's be serious. These men are—"

Selemei stood up. "Yes, let's be serious. I have no partner in the First Family, and that means I'm not your cousin."

"What?"

"I belong to the Fourth Family."

Erex waved hands at her. "Selemei, you can't mean that. Your children are First Family; surely you wouldn't wish to be separated from them!"

"I don't," she agreed. "But I wouldn't be. At least, not while the suit remained—embroiled, as you say—in the courts. I imagine that could take quite a long while. I'm thirty-seven now. So many things could happen while you waste your resources on a legal fight. I could lose my fertility. I could die. I could make public statements regarding the dealings of the First Family."

To see him twitch gave her shameful pleasure.

"Or, you could set those papers aside, and write a letter to the Eminence Indal informing him that I am Xeref's legitimate replacement."

"Crown of Mai," Erex swore. He sank back into his chair, shaking his head, but he did move the pile of papers to one side, and took up a pen and a blank sheet.

Selemei watched him write without moving. "Grivi," she whispered. Grivi moved closer, though he kept a cautious distance from Erex's Kuarmei; he watched until Erex folded the paper and instructed Kuarmei to deliver it, then returned to his station behind her shoulder.

When Kuarmei had left the office, Erex sighed, "You're right in one sense: it *would* save me a great deal of trouble. It won't work, though. They'll never let you keep it."

Selemei stood up, straightened her skirts, and took Grivi's arm. "I guess we'll see."

Selemei walked by herself. Place the cane at the same time as the left foot, shift weight, then step onto the right foot and move the cane forward. She'd worked her way up—from the private drawing room to the sitting room, then the bedroom and the dining room with its chairs, until she even tried walking around Pelli's room. That proved quite the challenge, since Pelli loved the shiny cane, and danced around her making wild sounds of delight—and it gave her a confidence she hadn't expected. Her second turn around the sitting room, however, felt like procrastination. Corrim and Aven would be home from school soon, and she had to face some uncomfortable conversations.

Would Brinx be angry if she interrupted his work? Would he hate her for trying to take Xeref's place?

And how could she dismiss her Grivi, who had always stood by her, especially when she didn't know if this would last?

Click-swish: the front door. It was still too early for the children. Unless someone was ill . . . she held her breath.

"Good afternoon, Master Brinx," came the First Houseman's voice.

"Brinx!" Selemei cried. "Is everything all right?"

Brinx walked in through the vestibule curtain with a strange look on his face. "Mother, Fedron just sent me home saying I needed to talk to you. He said there was some important news for the Family, but you had to be the one to tell me."

"Oh, Brinx, treasure . . . " Adrenaline tingled through her spine, in her fingertips.

"What's going on? Are you taking a partner?"

"No, treasure, it's not that. It's a bit more—unprecedented?"

He stared at her for a second. "Unprecedented? Is that why everyone's acting so weird about this? Even Erex wouldn't say a word, and I can always get him to say *something*."

Selemei took the leap. "Treasure, I'm going to be taking your father's seat in the Cabinet meeting this afternoon, representing the First Family."

"What?"

"And Fedron and Erex will be supporting me." *I hope.*

Brinx was rarely speechless, but this time she appeared to have overwhelmed him. His attempts to respond flashed wildly across his face, one after the other. *May Sirin grant that he not conclude in anger.*

"Please understand," she said. "It's for the Indelis proposal. Your father and I designed it . . . " The words touched the unhealed wound in her heart, her voice quavered. "I couldn't bear to let Xeref's last gift to us vanish without defending it."

"Oh!" Brinx exclaimed, and his face melted. "Oh, Mother. I—yes, of course it's for Father . . . " He came close, wrapping his arms around her without another word. Under her cheek, his chest heaved. His arms tightened, and he gave a ragged gasp. The grief he'd been trying to hide burst out, powerful as the river Endro beneath the city.

"My treasure," she murmured. She closed her eyes and rubbed his back with her free hand, riding the river with him while he sobbed. When she opened them again, she discovered Aven and Corrim had come home without her noticing, and now stood by the vestibule curtain staring at them, perhaps in shock at seeing the eldest in tears. Selemei beckoned them into the embrace, and for a time they all held one another. Then she cleared her throat.

"Let's hang the globe."

Brinx released her slowly, and put his arm around Corrim. Aven took Selemei's hand. They walked together through the double-doors into the private drawing room. Here, the moon-yellow of mourning was everywhere: scarves had been draped over couches and chairs, and though the gifts had been opened, the hundreds of yellow cards that had accompanied them still hung along the stone walls. In the days since the funeral, the Household had installed a wire that dangled from the stone vault of the ceiling in one corner. Someone had also clearly been listening behind the walls just now, because no sooner had they all entered than Imbati Ustin and Imbati Grivi emerged from the master bedroom. Ustin set up a stepladder beneath the wire, while Grivi brought the globe in its wooden box, and held it out to Selemei with a bow.

"Pelli?" Selemei called. "Can you come out, big girl?"

The door to the girls' rooms opened, and Pelli trotted out with her Verrid following behind her. "Mama?"

"We're going to hang the globe for your father," Selemei explained. "It's fragile and we're going to be very careful."

"Care-ful." Pelli trotted up, and patted Selemei's skirts as softly as she did her sleeping sister, laying her cheek against the silk. She then proceeded to do the same to Brinx's leg, and to Corrim and Aven.

Selemei opened the box that Grivi still held. She extracted the globe from its padded nest, careful to protect the hook and wire attachment dangling from the top. She lifted it to her lips and kissed the engraved glass twice—once for Enzyel, and once for herself. Then she passed it to Brinx for a kiss, and he passed it to Corrim; Aven took it for herself and then held it out for Pelli, with Imbati Verrid standing attentively by.

Pelli leaned her white cheek to it and whispered, "Cold . . . "

Aven brought it back, then, but Selemei shook her head. "Thank you, darling, but I can't use the ladder. Brinx, will you hang it?"

Brinx nodded. He climbed the three steps and reached up—the globe had to be hung higher than the carven cornices, or it would not appropriately represent a star—and attached the hook and wire. The element at the center of the globe lit: dimmer than a wysp, promising neither cheer nor fortune, only a solemn, enduring reminder.

"Thank you," said Selemei. She kissed them, eldest to youngest, each one so alive, so precious, so fragile. "I'm sorry, but I need to ask you to stay out of the sitting room for a few minutes. I have to go out at four, and I'd like to speak with Grivi and Ustin in private before I go."

The two servants walked out with her. Surely they knew what this was about; surely they could see how she dreaded it. She didn't sit down, but faced them with her back to Xeref's office door. Grivi was the broader of the two, his strength evident even through his formal manservant's suit; Ustin stood out for her height, the muscles of her arms hidden inside long black sleeves. The similarity of their bodyguard stances hid the fundamental differences in training that made this conversation necessary.

"You both know what I'm going to do," Selemei said. *You know it's crazy.* "I don't know if it will work."

Ustin nodded acknowledgment; Grivi remained motionless.

"I'm going to try one more time to represent the First Family on the Eminence's Cabinet." Saying it sent a rush of cold up behind her ears. "This time they won't be confused. I won't have any benefit of the doubt. If I make any errors, or even if I don't, they may vote me out. Therefore, I would like to request that Ustin act as my manservant, just for this afternoon."

"I am willing," said Ustin. "Grivi?"

Grivi said nothing.

"I'm so sorry, Grivi," said Selemei. "I don't want to be unfair to you. You've always been faithful. You have kept me upright so many times—truthfully, you have kept me alive. But I have to try this."

Grivi's reply was barely more than a whisper. "Mistress, you witnessed my vow of service. Please understand how difficult it is for me to watch you put yourself in danger."

"I do understand. But if I let you protect me now, I won't be able to protect anyone else. This isn't just for the sake of my own life, or even my daughters' lives, but for all the ladies of the Race. I have to try to pass the Indelis proposal. This is my wish."

Grivi bowed. "So let it be, then. May I be excused?"

"Yes. I'm really sorry."

A good deal of her courage departed with him. *Just for this afternoon*, she'd said, but it still felt final; in good conscience she'd have to consent to release Grivi from his contract if he requested it, even if she failed. She walked slowly to the nearest couch and sat down, staring at the kuarjos-board without really seeing it. "I don't know how to do this, Ustin. I'm not Xeref."

"Mistress, let's focus on today," said Ustin. "You're correct in your concern: it's more than likely the cabinet will again attempt to declare the seat empty. Fedron supported you in the last vote, and I imagine he will support you again, but we can't be certain he won't have come under outside influence up to and including blackmail. For this, and for the Indelis proposal, you need to cultivate allies."

"Fedron is it, though." Selemei shook her head. "Unless he can bring allies of his own. I don't know any of the others. Who is the bald man? The one with the big voice—he was kinder than most of them."

"That is Cabinet Secretary Boros of the Second Family, Mistress. He had a cordial relationship with Master Xeref; they spoke often, and occasionally co-sponsored proposals. He would make an excellent ally. His good opinion is respected."

"What am I supposed to do, though, invite him to tea?"

"I don't believe there's time for that just now, Mistress. We should be going, so we don't have to hurry."

"All right."

Perhaps she'd practiced too much walking today. The way to the meeting felt interminable; the cane was awkward in the cramped spiral stairway. When she reached the top, Selemei realized how far they still had to go, and huffed in frustration.

"How did Xeref ever do this?"

"It's true the walking was easier for him, Mistress. But you must remember, he didn't do the job alone. He had four assistants."

She couldn't imagine having assistants. "And he had you."

"Yes, Mistress."

They passed the Heir's suite—*merciful Heile, please don't let the Heir come out and see me*—and entered the hallway. Several men stood not far ahead. Cabinet members. She was starting to recognize some of them.

"Tell me who they are, Ustin," she whispered.

"You know Secretary Boros. Behind him is Amyel of the Ninth Family, one of Master Xeref's allies. Beside him, Caredes of the Eighth Family . . ."

The men stiffened and grew quiet as they drew closer. Selemei held tighter to the handle of her cane, placed it more carefully, stepped in measured cadence with her head high. The door was just beyond them. She'd have to walk between Secretary Boros and Palimeyn of the Third Family. Palimeyn was leering at her, holding something in his hand—it looked like a glass, but he didn't hold it like a drink. Still several steps away from them, she hesitated.

"Excuse me, gentlemen."

"Good afternoon, Lady Selemei," said Boros.

Palimeyn took a single step forward.

Ustin flashed past her, and for a split second, she thought she'd attacked Palimeyn. The Third Family man grunted and stumbled backwards. His manservant feinted toward Ustin, but then backed off also.

Selemei clung to her cane, her heart pounding.

Ustin returned. She'd taken the glass; Selemei didn't like the look of its brownish contents. "My apologies, Lady."

Boros looked between her and Palimeyn, frowning. "I think we should go in," he said. "Lady Selemei, will you come with me?" He offered his elbow.

"Thank you," she said, but placed both hands on her cane until his arm dropped. Then she followed him in, noticing that Ustin still blocked Palimeyn from approaching her. It was alarming—and felt worse because Ustin had to stay behind on the threshold. Selemei ignored the staring eyes of the ancient Eminences, refusing to rush just because so many men were coming in around her, and walked steadily to Xeref's chair—*her* chair, Mai willing. Ignoring hissed insults, she leaned her cane against the table, carefully pulled the chair out, and sat down. She almost wound her hands in the chair again, but this time, folded them in her lap. She tried to barricade her ears against the whispers, and waited for Fedron to take the seat beside her.

Just stay calm. Just stay.

Fedron was late. Well after the Heir and Eminence had already been seated, he backed in the door, harried by another man who must have been yelling at him for some time. She heard only, " . . . if you know what's good for Varin and the Race!" before the man relented and went to his seat. She counted chairs—he was Fifth Family. Fedron grunted, and took the chair beside her with scarcely a glance in her direction.

"Let's get started," said red-faced Speaker Orn. The Manservant to the

Eminence intoned his ceremonial speech; before the final words were fully out, the Fifth Family man stood up.

"First order of business must be the empty seat."

Fedron grasped the edge of the table with one hand. "The seat is occupied; we already voted on this in the last session."

"You're pathetic, First Family," the man retorted. "You fail to bring your substitute. You bring us—" He waved a hand at Selemei. "—this, instead. You're still trying to cling to power after the battle is already lost. Well, no one's laughing." While he spoke, his gaze never left Palimeyn of the Third Family, as if everyone else were just the audience for an impending confrontation between them.

"I agree," Palimeyn said. "Let's vote on the empty seat."

The Heir said softly, "Your Eminence?"

The Eminence sniffed through his noble nose. "I agree; we should vote."

Selemei shivered. This was entrapment, carefully planned, kuarjos-pieces precisely placed. The Heir was Third Family, and the Eminence was Fifth. Those two families and their representatives would have spent the days since the last meeting wearing down the other cabinet members. How many had been harassing Fedron? How long would he endure this for the sake of a female cousin?

"Fine," said Speaker Orn. "Cast your votes."

She couldn't watch them. These were men with years of history between them, layer upon layer of alliances and schemes, and here she'd been dropped into it blindfolded.

The Manservant to the Eminence examined his vote reporting device, and bowed. "A unanimous vote is required to certify an empty seat. I count six votes in dissent. The seat remains occupied by the First Family."

Had she heard that right? *Six?* For a split second she glimpsed the kuarjos-pattern: herself, standing upon her post with Fedron beside her; Third and Fifth Families attempting to surround them, but behind their backs, another, contrary configuration. Someone hadn't been paying attention to the rest of the board.

Fedron emitted a ridiculous sound, like a strangled giggle. He cleared his throat. "Well, I'm glad that's settled. Turn on her voting screen, please."

The square screen lit in front of her. An instant's flash of green, then black, with a green date indicator in the upper left corner. In the upper right corner, it read, *Xeref of the First Family*. Selemei stiffened, bracing for the wash of grief, but by Elinda's grace, she felt only warmth.

"Thank you," she whispered.

Selemei watched Fedron as they proceeded to business. His near eyebrow would rise, and he'd cast her a glance, then move his finger to the vote button.

It wasn't difficult, though at times it was tricky to tell when a procedural vote had been called for. Slowly, her muscles unclenched. She tried to read the potential for allyship in the expressions on the men's faces, golden or pale; she counted chairs and identified the Fourth Family's cabinet member—he would be a cousin, and she should try to reach out to him, perhaps through his Lady.

Then the Seventh Family's member brought a proposal. She stared at him unabashedly, trying to remember every word he used: "Pursuant to our discussions, I move for a vote on the Selimnar Imports proposal." *Pursuant*, and *move*, those were the keys she needed. She took a deep breath, and let it out slowly.

A wysp drifted into the room, impudently, through an ancient Eminence's face.

Let your luck come to me, wysp . . .

Fedron leaned toward her. "The First Family supports the Selimnar Imports proposal," he whispered.

Selemei nodded, and pressed the correct button. She waited for the Manservant to the Eminence to make his announcement of the vote result, and said it. Blood hummed in her ears; she hoped her voice wouldn't crack.

"Pursuant to our discussions, I move for a vote on the Indelis proposal. In memory of Xeref of the First Family."

Discomfort shifted through the men. Someone down the table to her left muttered, "Varin's teeth." But many faces fell solemn at mention of Xeref, and those men might support her. One of them was bald-headed Secretary Boros.

"I'll second," said Fedron.

On the screen in front of her, the words appeared: *Indelis proposal, brought by Xeref of the First Family.*

She pressed her button in support.

For you, love.

The Manservant to the Eminence bowed. "I count four votes in support, twelve in dissent. The measure is retired."

Selemei sat, unable to breathe for several seconds. She wanted to scream, or run, but this was no longer blood in her veins—it was some awful distillation of grief and shame. The air tasted of dust.

Fedron nudged her. "Selemei. Next vote, support."

These were someone else's hands, fingers pressed to the table surface in front of her. No, they were hers, just impossible to move. *Next vote, support.* She forced one up, pressed the button. Made herself heartless, a machine to act at Fedron's instructions, while passing seconds pulled her inexorably away from the moment when it should have gone right.

• • •

No rockfall could have crushed her heart more utterly than this failure. Selemei lay exhausted on her bed, feeling its beat inside her chest, wondering why it still persisted. She'd failed to save Enzyel and Keir from the duties that would inevitably tear their bodies apart; she'd failed to save Lienne from the draining obligation that had so embittered her sister. The Race's decline ground on, loved ones were plucked away, and one day only Pyaras would remember his mother's name.

"Mistress," said Ustin quietly.

Selemei heaved a sigh. "What is it, Ustin?"

"If you permit me to hear what happened, I may be able to advise you."

The suggestion was made mildly enough, but anger flashed inside her. Selemei pushed up on one elbow. "You're always one step ahead, aren't you?" she said. "Here I've been thinking you guess what I want before I do, but really, you planned this whole thing. Why would you push me? Was it so you could wield power by being close to a cabinet member?"

Ustin replied coolly. "I have served a cabinet member already for twelve years, Mistress. My Master cannot speak for me, but I believe he would vouch for the quality of my service. For more, you would have to contact the Service Academy. I am certain they could quickly find me other employment."

Guilt quenched her anger. Of course the Service Academy would stand by Ustin's certification. And naturally someone who had been privy to the First Family's cabinet secrets would be a coveted prize for a new employer. Xeref had said *she does her job too well.* Even now, Selemei couldn't see how serving well could be a flaw.

She sat up. "My fault," she said. "I shouldn't have accused you. I remember you saying you believed in the goals of the Indelis proposal. I shouldn't be surprised that you'd want me to carry out Xeref's plan once he was gone."

Ustin's brows rose, arching her manservant's mark. "Mistress, I shall presume."

Selemei steeled herself. When Grivi had taken her in confidence, it had been shocking enough; but Ustin was a formidable weapon intended for gentlemen, her loyalty pledged to no one. "Please do."

"Mistress, the Indelis proposal was entirely your idea," Ustin said. "If you recall, I was not welcome at the confirmation party for your small cousin, but I stayed in the Maze and listened in case I was needed, and I heard what you said to the gentlemen of the First Family Council." She struck reciting stance, one hand held behind her back. " 'Some of us are giving our efforts, while others are giving up our health, and others, like Lady Indelis, have given their lives. I imagine you could think of some way to protect our mothers better. Aren't you all men of importance?' "

"Mai's truth," Selemei whispered. She recognized every word, but in the

Imbati's voice, they had changed from a frustrated outburst to a powerful demand. Her skin prickled.

"Especially after your act of courage in refusing further duties, your words struck Master Xeref deeply," said Ustin. "You are why he created the proposal, and why he named it for Lady Indelis. He may have put your idea into the proper language of legislation, but even then, you persisted until you approved of its terms, because you understood what would benefit the ladies of the Grobal in a way he did not."

Selemei shook her head, amazed. Intentionally or not, Ustin had just answered a question that she'd been unable to forget. "So, *that's* why you came in to find me while Pelli was sleeping. You wanted to talk to me about my courage."

Ustin looked her in the eye. "Courage is like a wysp," she said. "It moves through barriers."

"I'm sorry I couldn't move through this one," Selemei sighed. "The Indelis proposal has been retired."

"Retired," Ustin agreed solemnly, "with a vote of fourteen to one."

That wasn't right. Selemei frowned. "No; the vote was twelve to four."

Ustin's eyes widened. The corners of her mouth bent slightly upwards. But they didn't stop there; her lips parted over her teeth, and she was smiling—really, truly smiling. Selemei had only seen her Imbati nurse-escort smile once, after she'd gone to a public event at age five and been very, very good. Now, as then, it was puzzling and strangely exciting. Selemei got to her feet.

"Ustin, what is it?"

"Mistress, you won."

"I don't understand. Of course I didn't."

"Respectfully, Mistress, I differ."

Selemei stared at her. "All right, Ustin, explain."

Ustin inclined her head. "Mistress, you presented yourself before the cabinet. You claimed the at-large seat. You negotiated for and won the First Family's support. You attended today's meeting, even though Grobal Palimeyn tried to sabotage you. And in spite of cooperation between Third and Fifth families to stop you, you kept your seat and were permitted to vote."

"Ustin, I have been nothing but humiliated. The Heir knocked me down at the last meeting. Palimeyn of the Third Family would have succeeded today if you hadn't stopped him. My proposal failed miserably."

"Mistress, a man who intended to stop a threat from a rival might hire an assassin. Grobal Palimeyn only intended to throw blood on you, to force you home to change your clothes."

Her stomach lurched. "Heile have mercy."

"I can only conclude that your fall was effective in convincing them that you do not pose a real threat. Your failure to pass the proposal today has no doubt sealed that impression. Their goal was to weaken the First Family; now they believe they have succeeded. But you managed to attract three allies with no effort at all, and now you sit among them, wielding a voice and a vote." With the grace of long practice, Ustin got to her knees and bowed her tattooed forehead all the way to the floor. "Please, Lady. Accept my vow of service. I would be honored to continue to serve the First Family's cabinet member."

Selemei's heart pounded. Suddenly, everything looked different. Yes, she'd sponsored a proposal that had been retired. It had felt like the end—but maybe it didn't have to be.

With a voice and a vote, now she could negotiate laws over years. The next time she walked into a meeting, she need not be a machine. She could be a cabinet member the same way she was a mother: falling and standing up again, yet always persisting, nurturing the future.

"Thank you," she said. "I accept."

LIME AND THE ONE HUMAN

S. WOODSON

Once in early autumn, a particularly small and ragged fairy emerged from a hole at the roots of a tulip poplar, into the dazzling green light of the woods. The fairy wore a tattered dress of petals. A purple orchid, withered and vaguely sticky, perched atop her head, and around her neck hung a crude bit of jewelry fashioned from a bit of string and seven irregular beads. Each bead contained a book, shrunken to minuscule size and encased in a shell of magic. She carried no other provisions.

The fairy, like all of her kind, was nameless (which is to say that her true name was secret even to herself). Her preferred nickname was Lime, after the tree from which she had first germinated. Alighting on a yellowed leaf, she sprawled in the sun and began, briefly, to doze—for her long journey through the roots of the world had wearied her.

Five minutes later, she awoke, feeling much refreshed. She yawned, exposing the bulge of her venom glands and a mouthful of pointed green teeth. Her nose twitched. On the breeze, she could smell flowers.

Leaping into the air, Lime followed her nose to a clearing overgrown with the most wonderful variety of plants: clusters of verbena and anise hyssop, heliotrope and pansies, double-petaled impatiens and cone-flowers in every hue of the rainbow. With a cautious glance forwards and back, she flew into the clearing and landed on a mound of impatiens. She held one of the flowers in her hand.

She plucked the flower from its stalk, and at that very moment another fairy burst from cover of leaves and tackled her to the ground.

"I thought you looked like a thief!" squealed the fairy. "And now we've caught you red-handed!" More fairies emerged from the leaves, giggling and pointing.

"What a dummy!" they cried. "What a dunce!" They pinned down Lime's arms and legs, and sat on her wings. Lime cursed and hissed and bared her fangs, but the other fairies only laughed.

"You don't get it," said a violet fairy in a handsome cape. "You stole from us and we caught you, so that means we get to punish you."

"The Law says she has to be our prisoner for sixty months," said a fairy with coiled antennae, "and do whatever we say."

"Who wants a prisoner, though?" said a blue fairy with wings like rumpled silk. "Let's just toss her in the mud, or make her eat a bug."

"You won't make me do anything," said Lime, "because I haven't stolen anything! Am I supposed to believe these are *your* flowers?"

"They are," said the violet fairy. "This is our community garden."

"Fairies," said Lime, "*don't garden.*"

"We do," said the blue fairy. "It was Old-Timer's idea. She has all kinds of wild ideas."

"That's because I'm the only one around here with any brains in my head," snarled a voice from the trees. The crowd stilled their laughter as an apple-red fairy swooped into the clearing. The fairy's crooked fangs protruded over her lips, and the horns of beetles crowned her cap.

"Let the loner go," said Old-Timer. "A prisoner's just another fairy for me to keep in line and I don't need it."

With groans of disappointment, the other fairies unhanded Lime. "You've come from far away, haven't you?" said Old-Timer, eyeing Lime's shriveled hat and ragged dress. "Wearing that worn-out tropical flower, looking like you haven't sewn new clothes in a decade. You have a clan?"

Lime glared and shook her head.

"Well, you can't join ours," said Old-Timer. "And you can't take from the community garden unless you're part of the clan. But I'll let you have a cup of nectar, if you want it, out of hospitality."

"I don't want your hospitality," said Lime, "or anything else to do with this terrible forest."

Old-Timer snorted. "Suit yourself. But if you won't take my hospitality, maybe you'll at least take my advice. This place here is called the Woeful Woods, bordered on one side by the meadows and the other by a human town. If it's flowers you want, feel free to look in the woods or the meadows or even the lands beyond, but steer clear of human territory. They keep plenty of gardens, but just as many dogs and cats and children. A lout like you would be caught in a second."

"I'm not stupid or slow enough to be caught by any human," said Lime. "And I'm not afraid of pets, either. Is that all your advice?"

"It is," said Old-Timer. "Whether or not you choose to listen to it. Now get out of here, lone traveler, and leave our clan to its business. Unless you've changed your mind about the nectar?"

Lime buzzed into the air and darted away from the fairies' garden. "I'd rather drink frog-spawn!" she yelled over her shoulder. "I hope a whole crowd of humans comes through and tramples your awful flowers!" She fled, already thoroughly sick of the Woeful Woods and its denizens.

As she sped through the trees, an amber-yellow fairy descended from the branches and fell into pace her side. "Don't you dare follow me!" Lime cried.

"Calm down, Loner," said the amber fairy. "I'm not here to start trouble."

"I'm serious!" said Lime. "Leave me alone or I'll fight you! I'll pull out your antennae!"

The amber fairy giggled. "You're a bad liar," he said. "Just stop a minute and talk. Where'd you even come from, anyway?"

Lime tried to outrace the other fairy, but he easily matched her speed. She stopped, lest he follow her all the way back to the hole at the roots of the tulip poplar.

"Where I'm from," she said, "is none of your business. Did you chase me down just so you could interrogate me?"

"I was only trying to be sociable," said the amber fairy. "You're a real cagey one, you know that, Loner?"

"Stop calling me 'Loner'," said Lime, "and get out of my sight."

"What's wrong with 'Loner'?" said the amber fairy. "It's better than my nickname, at least." He paused expectantly. Lime merely glowered at him.

"It's Pipsqueak," he said. "It's one of those ironic nicknames, right? 'Cos I'm so tall."

"Good for you," said Lime.

"Did you come here flower-hunting?" asked Pipsqueak. He glanced at her threadbare dress. "Hoping to make new clothes?"

"Maybe," said Lime, "And maybe not."

"No need to be shy about it," said Pipsqueak. "Listen: if it's flowers you're after, I know a place you can go: a place nearly as good as our garden. Follow me and I'll show you."

"And if I don't want to follow you?" said Lime.

"I won't leave you alone until you do," said Pipsqueak. "So just come with me." He flew through the trees, and Lime, with a sigh of resignation, followed after.

He led Lime to the outskirts of the woods and a solitary building: a squat house built of brick and green-tinged vinyl. A fringe of weeds sprouted from sagging gutters. A messy but thriving garden teemed with hostas and begonias, with roses and crepe myrtles still clinging to flower, and scraggly mums just beginning to bud. A gravel path ran through the garden, and at the end of the path stood a mailbox with the name "A. E. Erskine" stenciled on it in paint.

Pipsqueak settled atop an oak leaf. "There's one human who lives in the woods," he said, "apart from all the others. And this is the one human's house. They've got plenty of flowers here, but no pets and no kids like in town. You can steal from them, easy."

"If there's one human," said Lime, "what 'them' are you talking about? Who else is there?"

"No one," said Pipsqueak. "The one human is one human, they're just one of those humans who isn't a girl, or a boy either."

"Huh," said Lime. "Then what's the catch? If this place is so great, why aren't there any other fairies here?"

"We've got our community garden now," said Pipsqueak with a shrug. "You don't trust me?"

"I don't," said Lime. "I bet there's a whole troop of children in that house, with nets and plastic jars. Or maybe this one human of yours is a witch, the kind who likes to trap fairies and cook them into potions. I bet you're waiting for me to go flying over unawares, and when I'm caught, you'll laugh and laugh. Am I wrong?"

"Now you're just being silly," said Pipsqueak. "Witches live in towers. Who's ever heard of a witch in a house? If there were kids around, there'd be toys all in the garden, and as for cats and dogs: if there were any nearby, you'd smell 'em.

"Stake the place out for yourself and you'll see," he said. "The place is totally safe. Or don't I guess. I can't force you." He dropped from his leafy perch and spiraled lazily to the ground. "All I wanted was to point a wandering loner in the right direction."

With a wave goodbye, and an offer to "Look around the woods if you need me!" he slipped into the shadows of the undergrowth, leaving Lime alone.

Lime cast a wary eye at the house and its abundant, quiet garden. She still didn't quite trust Pipsqueak, but the place seemed safe enough from a distance, and at the very least there were no more giggling fairies to harass her. Tucking herself into a fork between two branches, she watched and waited for any sign of danger.

In time, a human appeared in the window. The one human looked to be a younger adult, probably not far along in their twenties, but more than old enough to have outgrown the ability to see fairies: an ability most lost around the age of twelve. Their hair was short; they wore a T-shirt with a mended hole in the shoulder. As far as Lime could tell, they were utterly ordinary and entirely alone.

The one human made a pot of oolong and sat down to drink. Lime watched as they sipped tea, read a paperback book, picked at one of their fingernails, and eventually returned to the interior of the house, out of sight, having done nothing whatsoever suspicious or even interesting. Pipsqueak hadn't lied. The human was no threat.

Reassured, Lime took wing and ventured closer. A most beguiling vine grew along the kitchen window. It was some species of morning glory, but strangely and richly colored, with flowers banded in pink and gold and pale, translucent green. Lime imagined the suit of clothes she could make from this vine: beautiful, colorful clothes that would be the envy of all fairy-kind. Plucking the stamen from a flower and transforming it into a glowing needle, she set to work.

All afternoon, Lime struggled to recall the tricks of weaving, sewing, and spell-casting involved in the making of clothes. She harvested flowers and leaves. She spun green fibers into glossy-smooth thread. By the time the sun had begun to sink beneath the horizon, she had sewn a fine hat of petals. She removed her old, wilting cap and placed the new one on her head, proud to have remembered the lessons of her childhood.

Lime held her old hat, the withered purple orchid, in her lap, and thought back to the warm and southern island where it had grown. Unpleasant, long-forgotten emotions swelled in her chest. She shred the orchid to bits, and cast it to the ground.

Night fell and the flowers closed and Lime could no longer work, so she passed the late hours in other ways. She spied on the human again, watching as they cooked and ate dinner. (Dinner, she noted with a little thrill of disgust, was roast chicken.) She re-enlarged one of her books and read by the pale green glow of her own body. She waited eagerly for morning.

At the first light of dawn, she sewed the bodice of her new dress, which she embroidered with a pattern of interwoven suns. She placed each stitch with utmost care, pouring all of her heart and thought and magic into that one little garment. She had almost completed the circle of suns when the sound of footsteps broke her concentration. The human had come outside and was stomping into the garden, right towards Lime's window. Snatching up her bodice and thread, Lime flew into the trees.

The human lingered in the garden for a while, pulling weeds, pruning dead flowers, and humming an off-key tune. They ventured indoors and back several times, then at last returned inside for good. When Lime was certain all was clear, she flew back to her vine, where she found a scrap of notepaper scrawled in enormous handwriting.

"To the fairy who's probably doing this," read the note. "Please stop killing my Convolvulus magnifican vine. Thanks in advance—Erskine." A more cautious fairy might have been afraid, but Lime was too close to finishing her dress, and wasn't about to let a mere piece of paper scare her. She crumpled the note into a ball and picked up her sewing.

She had finished her bodice, and had just started piecing together a skirt, when a fairy—the same blue fairy from the community garden—twirled down from the sky and landed at her side, exclaiming "Ha! So you really are here!"

Lime edged away, scowling. "What do you want?" she said.

"I was just curious what happened to you," said the blue fairy. "That's a nice hat, by the way, and a nice dress—what's done of it."

Lime clutched the dress to her chest. "You can't have it," she said.

"I don't want it!" said the blue fairy, laughing. "I was complementing you."

"Oh," said Lime.

"Have you decided to stick around the woods?" asked the blue fairy. "If you're planning to settle down, you know, our clan will take you."

"Your boss said the clan was full," said Lime.

"Old-Timer says a lot of things," said the blue fairy, "but she's a pushover. If you hang around a few weeks, she'll get sick of telling you to leave and let you in. Promise."

"And why do you want me in your clan?" said Lime. "You were going to make me eat a bug!"

"Don't be so sensitive," said the blue fairy. "Like you've never eaten a bug on a dare before!"

"I haven't," said Lime.

"Really?" said the fairy. "I have—or a slug, at least. That's why everyone calls me Slugsy now. Anyway, do you want to join the clan? You can tell us stories of all the places you've been."

"I haven't been any places," said Lime. "And I don't need a clan."

"You have to have been *some* places," said Slugsy. "Where'd you come from?"

Lime picked at her embroidery. She supposed, really, there was no harm in telling. "I came through the roots of the world," she said, "from the Great Origin Tree Library."

"And before that?" said Slugsy.

"Nothing before that matters," snapped Lime.

"And why'd you let your old clothes get so raggedy?" asked Slugsy. "What happened?"

"I was reading," said Lime, "and I lost track of time."

Slugsy scratched at her head. "You were reading so long that your clothes went bad?"

"Right," said Lime.

"And how long was that?"

Lime consulted her inner clock. "About twenty-five years."

"I see," said Slugsy. "You know, you're kind of weird, Loner. But you're also pretty brave, messing with Erskine the human."

"Why?" said Lime. "They're just one human, right?"

"Yeah, but—"

Before Slugsy could finish her sentence, a bundle of amber sparks shot from the trees and snatched the hat from her head. "Got your cap!" shouted Pipsqueak.

"I'll get *you*!" said Slugsy, hopping into the air. "Sorry, Loner. See you later." She chased after Pipsqueak quick as a bat on the hunt, and the fairies' twin lights, blue and amber, vanished into the distance. Relieved, Lime took up her needle.

In the low light of afternoon, she stitched a ruffled lining to her skirt, attached skirt to bodice, and enrobed the whole garment in sparkling, semi-visible strands of protective magic. Casting her old dress aside, she changed into her freshly-made clothes. The skirt billowed around her soft as dandelion fluff. The embroidered suns gleamed clear and bright as words on a page. The dress was perfect: colorful and comfortable and scented and clean.

Lime nestled into the coils of the morning glory vine—now bruised and nearly flower-less—and watched the sunset, aglow with contentment. She was so content, so peaceful, so snug in her new clothes, and so warm in the early autumn sun, she didn't even hear the window open. She didn't notice the gamy, chemical smell of human presence; she didn't see the looming shadow. When she finally felt the rush of air, and heard the scrape of metal against glass, it was too late. She was no longer snug among the leaves. Glass walls closed around her and a metal lid, pricked through with holes, sealed her in. She had been trapped inside a great salt-shaker and holding the salt-shaker was the one human, Erskine.

Stifling a cry of panic, Lime dropped to the bottom of the salt-shaker and curled into a ball, pretending not to exist.

"I can see you, you know," said Erskine. Lime glanced up. Her eyes met the human's own. It was then she realized she had been deceived.

"You can't," sputtered Lime. "You can't, you can't, you're too old to see me."

"I can," said Erskine. "Some people never grow out of it. Did you really not know? I figured all the fairies around here knew about me already."

Lime caught a glimpse of amber light among the trees. She heard the trill of a fairy's laugh. Her heart thudded in her chest. "If you don't let me out," she bluffed, "I'll put a curse on you! I-I'll turn you to stone! I'll give you the pox and the palpitations and the red-hot feet! Let me go right now or you'll pay, I swear!"

"I won't," said Erskine. "And you're not going to curse anyone. You've done me wrong by killing my plant, and I've caught you, so you're obligated to be my prisoner for sixty lunar cycles, AKA five years. I know the Law."

Lime stared at Erskine, for the moment speechless with rage. "And how," she said, finally, "do you, *a human*, know about the Law?"

"I have my ways," said Erskine with a smirk. "But don't worry. I'll let you go right now if you grant me a wish."

"I'd rather die!" spat Lime. "I'd rather stay in this salt-shaker for a hundred years! A million!"

"Really?" said Erskine. "Because I wasn't going to ask for much."

"Either let me go or don't," said Lime. "But I'm never going to grant you a wish. Never! Do your worst: torture me or snip my wings. I don't care!"

"Geez, I'm not going to hurt you," said Erskine. They drew Lime and the salt-shaker inside, and closed the window. "You're really not going to grant me a wish?"

"Never and not for anything," said Lime.

"Fine." Erskine climbed down from the kitchen counter and sat Lime beside the sink. "Then I'll just keep you here until you change your mind."

"You'll be keeping me for sixty months," said Lime, "because I'm not changing my mind."

"We'll see," said Erskine. "Anyway, who's that yellow-orange fairy outside? Are they your friend?"

"He's not my friend," said Lime. "*I have no friends.*"

At the edge of the forest, Pipsqueak capered from branch to branch, squealing with laughter. "The other fairies haven't been bullying you, have they?" said Erskine.

"Don't patronize me, human!" said Lime. "I'm not some mewling little infant. No one bullies me!"

"Do you want me to run him off?" asked Erskine. "I can go throw a rock at him."

"Just shut up, shut up, shut up!" wailed Lime. Sparks cascaded down her back. "I might be your prisoner, but that doesn't mean I have to listen to you blather on and on!"

"It kind of does," said Erskine, drawing the blinds, "but point taken. I'll leave you alone for a while and make dinner, okay?"

Lime simply glared.

"Oh, but before I do," said Erskine, "did you want anything to eat? I have honey and maple syrup and I think some leftover molasses."

"I refuse," said Lime. "Weren't you going to leave me alone?"

"Alright," said Erskine. "Just let me know if you change your mind. Not only about the wish, but about the food, I mean." They busied themself in the kitchen, and for a little while at least, left Lime to her thoughts.

Lime huddled at the bottom of the salt-shaker, hating everything: humans and fairies and the whole world and, most of all, herself. She cursed herself for ever trusting Pipsqueak, for being slow enough—stupid enough—to be caught by a human.

Sparking like a firecracker and overwhelmed by anger, Lime felt she would explode if she couldn't calm herself down. She tried breathing deeply, and when that didn't work, she enlarged one of the books around her neck and began to read. At first, her eyes slid from the page. She would read the same sentence over and over, only for the words to jumble together and the meaning elude her. However, she pressed on, and began to make slow progress through the novel. The furious sparks dissipated from her body.

She didn't know how long she had been reading when a shadow fell across the page. "Where'd you get that book?" asked Erskine.

"I'm allowed to have a book," said Lime. "There's no Law saying prisoners can't have one."

"No, I wasn't going to take it away," said Erskine. "I was just wondering if you had summoned it from somewhere, or what."

"It's none of your business," said Lime. "Shouldn't you be cooking?"

"I already cooked and already ate," said Erskine. "You must have been really preoccupied not to notice. What book is it? Is it good?"

"That's none of your business, either!" said Lime. "Why do you care?"

Erskine shrugged. "Just curious. Is it a fairy book? Is it a novel? Do fairies publish many novels? Because if they do, I've never had the chance to read one."

"Fairy novels are written in Vernacular Fey," said Lime. "You wouldn't be able to read one even if you had it."

"I can read Vernacular Fey *and* Classical Fey," said Erskine. "They're not that hard to learn: I mean, they're both pretty regular, logical languages."

"You're a liar," said Lime in Classical Fey, "and a despicable person."

"I surely speak the truth," said Erskine in the same language, "and assure you that my character is of the utmost quality."

Lime studied the human closely. "Just who are you?" she said. "Some sort of recluse linguist? Why do you know the fairy tongues?"

"Well, I've always been interested in non-human peoples," said Erskine, "and I come across a lot of fairies in my adventures."

At that last word, Lime nearly dropped her book. "You're an adventurer?" she yelped.

"Pretty much," said Erskine.

In Lime's childhood, her fellow fairies had taught her this lesson: "Humans on the whole are dull and sluggish, but there are three sorts of human you should avoid at all cost. The first are the children, who see and chase. The second are the witches, who grind our wings for potions. The third are the adventurers, who snatch our treasures and bring mayhem in their wake." Yet how could Lime have known?

"What's wrong with you?" Lime shrilled. "What are you doing here, acting like a normal person? Reading and pulling weeds and eating—" She glanced down at the pile of soiled dishes in the sink. "Eating whatever this is?"

"It was tofu and eggplant," said Erskine. "I was thinking of having meat, but I know some fairies get squeamish around meat and didn't want to offend."

"I don't care if you eat meat!" said Lime. "What kind of adventurer just hangs around the house all day?"

"I mean, I have off-days like anyone else," said Erskine. "And I don't see why 'adventurer' and 'normal person' have to be mutually exclusive. I feel like I'm pretty normal." They lathered a sponge with soap, releasing a pungent smell of chemicals. "Did you want to hear about my last adventure though? I just got back on Wednesday."

Taking Lime's angry silence as assent, they continued. "I took the train down to the semi-aquatic kingdom of Crab's Cairn, where there's this hidden shrine . . . "

Erskine blathered on about their adventure, describing the forgotten shrine with its pillars of olivine and meteoric iron; the domed ceilings inlaid with the bones of fishes; the images of celestial serpents; and the half-submerged labyrinth, rumored to be the lair of hippocamps.

"I found this enormous shed skin, which I'm pretty sure is the skin of a hippocamp," said Erskine, putting away the last of the clean dishes and carrying Lime to the living room. "If it is, I should be able to portion it out and sell it for a good price."

"All those jewel-encrusted idols and pillars of rare pallasite, and you pass them up for a bit of snakeskin?" said Lime.

"I'm not going to loot a shrine," said Erskine, looking a bit offended. "That's disrespectful." They plopped onto the sofa and sat Lime on an end table. "Have you decided to give me a wish?"

Lime made a rude gesture from her native island. "I don't know what that means," said Erskine. "Does that mean 'No'?"

"Very astute," said Lime. "Excellent guesswork."

"All the times I've been caught by fairies in the past," said Erskine, "I gave them something, and they let me go. So I assumed that's how these sort of situations normally play out."

"Well, you assumed wrong," said Lime.

"It doesn't have to be a complicated wish," Erskine insisted. "Just reviving my convolvulus plant would be enough. Or, if you wanted, you could lend me a spell. Like an invisibility spell, something easy."

"Do you ever, ever stop talking?" said Lime. "You're interrupting my reading." She opened her novel and turned her back.

Erskine remained quiet as Lime read: suspiciously quiet, in fact. After a certain point, Lime couldn't stand it. She had to know what they were up to. She glanced over her shoulder.

Erskine had curled up with their paperback novel and was reading peacefully. They glanced over the top of the book and caught Lime's eye. "Would you like to know what I'm reading?" they asked.

"I already know what you're reading," said Lime.

"Because you were peeping at me through the window?" said Erskine.

"N-no!" said Lime. Erskine smiled.

For the rest of the evening, the two read in silence. Eventually, Erskine said goodnight, asked Lime one last time if she would like something to eat (she refused), and went to bed.

Lime waited until she was certain the human had fallen asleep, then did what any reasonable fairy would do in her circumstances: she phased through the salt-shaker and explored her new surroundings. The Law forbid a rightful prisoner from escaping her bonds, but only if she were caught escaping. To slip one's prison unnoticed, then return unnoticed: that much was permitted. Lime wouldn't let the human to take her off-guard a second time.

She circled the darkened room, observing the well-worn sofa with its faded green cushions; the electric lamp; the rickety particleboard tables. A tall case housed neat rows of books, old and new, in every genre from novels to encyclopedias to do-it-yourself guides on lock-picking and astral travel. Most were ordinary human books, but not all. There were a few fairy histories among them, and a book of elfish folktales, and a runic dictionary. Among the books sat seashells, slivers of petrified wood, stones carved in strange languages, and similar trinkets. Lime could only assume they were mementos of adventures past.

Interested despite herself, Lime examined the rows of books, noting a few titles she had read already, and others she would like to read, given the chance. She fluttered down the hallway, peeking her head into a storage closet full of towels; into the bedroom where Erskine lay face-down in a pillow, fast asleep. At the foot of the bed sat a bulging, briny-smelling bundle wrapped in an old sheet: the hippocamp's skin, presumably. An old chair supported a thriving colony of potted philodendrons; tiny bromeliads and cacti sprouted from jars of soil.

In the bedroom, there were even more books piled on shelves, stacked on the carpet, and wedged between plants. Lime felt a twinge of avarice. She saw the names of unfamiliar authors and titles of sequels she hadn't known existed, fascinating covers and enticing summaries. She couldn't restrain herself. She skimmed jacket flaps and rustled through pages. Surely, Erskine wouldn't notice if one or two went missing?

There was a tap at the window, and Lime's heart nearly popped. "Loner?" called a familiar voice. "Hey, Loner—is that you?"

Shaking the nervous sparks from her dress, Lime flew to the window and parted the blinds. A blue face beamed at her.

"It is you!" said Slugsy.

"*Shut up*," hissed Lime. "The human is *right there*." Slugsy nodded, and gestured for Lime to come outside. Lime phased partway through the glass, just far enough to stick her head through the window.

"What are you still doing here?" Slugsy whispered. "Did Erskine turn down your wish?"

"I'm not giving them a wish," said Lime. "And you've got a lot of nerve, coming here."

"Huh?" said Slugsy. "What are you talking about?"

"Don't play dumb," said Lime. "You tricked me! You didn't tell me the human could see us. You *knew* I'd get caught."

"I figured Pipsqueak had told you," said Slugsy. "I didn't know he was playing a prank."

"Liar!" said Lime. "What's wrong with you? Why can't anyone in these woods just leave me alone!" She was practically yelling. Her throat flashed green and golden as her venom glands flared. "Why did I ever, ever leave the Library? Why did I trust either of you? I—"

Erskine let out a soft, wordless cry. Fabric rustled. Lime clapped a hand over her mouth and froze, too terrified to even think.

"Come on, dummy—hide!" said Slugsy, grabbing hold of Lime's wrist and dragging her through the window. The two fairies huddled in a rose bush, ears pricked and antennae twitching.

"Did they wake up?" said Lime.

"Go check," said Slugsy.

"*You* check," demanded Lime.

"I can't go in there," said Slugsy. "I wasn't invited."

Reluctantly, Lime phased through the window. Inside, the bed lay empty. Erskine had disappeared.

Lime sped down the hallway, cursing. She found Erskine in the living room, mere feet from the empty salt-shaker.

"I can explain!" said Lime, but Erskine ignored her and walked into the kitchen. Utterly bewildered, Lime flew after. She circled around to the human's face. Their eyes were still closed, and their mouth was fixed in a dreamy smile.

Fumbling sightlessly through the cabinets, Erskine snatched a bottle of black vinegar, unscrewed the top, and upended the contents over their head. They grabbed handfuls of salt and brown sugar, rubbing it into their skin, smearing it onto their face. Lime realized this was more than mere sleep-walking. "Wake up!" she cried. "Snap out of it!" She tugged at Erskine's hair and pinched their ears, to no avail. Erskine opened the front door and strode barefoot into the woods.

"What's going on?" said Slugsy, darting to Lime's side. "Is the human ensorcelled?"

"They must be," said Lime. "I keep telling and telling them to stop, and they *won't listen*."

"But why are you following them?" said Slugsy.

"What do you mean, why am I following them?" said Lime. "I can't just let them wander off and get killed by who-knows-what!"

"Why not?" said Slugsy. "If they die, you can go free, right?

"I'm not saying I *want* them to die," she added quickly, seeing the look on Lime's face. "Erskine's pretty okay, as far as humans go. It's just . . . "

"Are you going to help, or are you going to leave?" snapped Lime.

"Help how?" said Slugsy. "What are either of *us* supposed to do?" All the same, she remained at Lime's side.

The two followed Erskine through the woods, to the banks of a muddy river. Atop the water sat an exquisite white harp of curious design, its strings quivering soundlessly, strummed by some invisible force. As Erskine approached, the harp pitched upward and an immense body emerged from the mud: a serpent with the head of a mare, and a white harp for a mane.

The horse-serpent, the hippocamp, flowed onto the bank in a wave of sea-grey scales and encircled her great coils around Erskine, who stood there bespelled and helpless. Her mouth split open, gaping from ear to ear. White fangs unfurled.

"Stop!" screamed Lime. The hippocamp sheathed her fangs and turned one large, pale, unblinking eye to the trees.

"What are you doing?" hissed Slugsy. "She'll kill us!" The hippocamp inclined her head, as though amused.

Lime didn't know what she was doing, not really, but Erskine looked so small engulfed in the coils of the hippocamp, and she knew she couldn't just fly away. "Let the human go," she said, "or I'll make you sorry you ever crawled out from the ocean!" Sparks spat from her mouth. She balled her fists tight so her hands wouldn't tremble. "I'll turn you into an eel and roast you! I'll shrivel you up like a salted slug!"

"She's never going to believe that," said Slugsy, retreating into the leaves. "You're crazy, Loner!"

"Don't you *dare* tempt a fairy's wrath!" cried Lime, ignoring her. "I'll boil up this river and cook you into stew! I'll send this whole wood crashing down on top of your oversized head! Let the human go and never, ever come back here again!"

The hippocamp chuckled. "What sights one sees on land," she said. "What oddities: a little damselfly who talks like a conquering queen. Why don't you show me these fearsome powers of yours, my damsel? I've never seen a river boil, nor a whole forest felled in an instant."

"Don't mock me!" said Lime. "I'm deadly serious!"

"Really?" said the hippocamp. "Then would you like me to treat you as a serious threat?" An invisible power plucked at the strings of Lime's heart, and she heard music, each note as clear as water, as sharp as salt, and unspeakably, painfully beautiful.

"Cover your ears!" said Slugsy, but the song of the hippocamp pierced through flesh and bone, seeping through the runnels of the brain. The music flooded the deepest recesses of Lime's memory, dredging up visions of the past, nostalgic sensations. There she was only a few days ago, in her ragged clothes, traveling through the roots of the world. There she was in the Library, in an austere but comfortable room, engrossed in a quarter-century's reading. And before that . . .

The music grew languid and sweet, like nectar pooled in scented petals, like jewel-bright orchids dripping from the stalk. There was no more river, no more Woeful Woods. There was only golden sunlight rich as honey, and soft rain misting through evergreen leaves. Beneath the rainbow's arc, the insects sang long-forgotten melodies, and branches swayed beneath the weight of flowers plump as grapes.

Lime curled in a nest of dried herbs and fragrant camphor, sheltered by the wings of her fellow fairies. All her clan were with her: the ones who had first found her when she was small and loved and petted her, the ones who had taught her all the secrets of speech and flight and magic. Bathed in the light of their bodies, enveloped in warmth and scent, she closed her eyes and sunk into their embrace.

"Sleep, little Lime," the fairies cooed, in voices that were all one voice. "Sleep and forget those years of solitude. All is well, and all is as it was before."

"Before what?" Lime muttered, sleepily.

"Before nothing," the fairies said, rocking Lime in their arms, passing her from lap to lap. "There is no more before and no more after, only a perfect, golden now. Each day will flow into the next as sweetly as a stream of nectar, and the green things will grow, and the rains will fall gentle and nourishing."

"The rain," said Lime, her eyes fluttering open. "There was a storm."

"Don't think of the storm," the fairies scolded, pinching her sides and tweaking her antennae. "Naughty child, coddled brat—don't think of it!" Yet already the golden light of the sun had thinned to a sickly yellow. The rain fell fast and heavy.

"It can't last," said Lime. "It won't last."

"Don't!" the fairies wailed. Lime broke from their arms and lurched upright.

"It won't last," she said, "because one day, a storm will come and tear me away from here, out to sea and out to the world's farthest reaches. And I'll wash ashore on that cold country where only the Origin Tree grows: where I'll find a magnificent Library, but no more orchids, and no more family, and no more way back home—and I'll be alone, alone forever!"

The clan of fairies dissolved in the pelting rain. The trees bowed low beneath typhoon winds, and the sea rose up to swallow everything. Lime floundered in the waves, gasping for breath and clawing at the water, but the ocean gripped her like the coils of a serpent.

Filling her fangs with venom, Lime buried her head beneath the hippocamp's scales and bit down as hard as she could.

The honey-sweet music cut to a terrible screech. The hippocamp's coils slackened. Lime tumbled onto the riverbank, and Erskine thudded beside her.

"Vile gnat!" spat the hippocamp. "Wicked little wasp!" The tip of her tail drooped uselessly in the mud, numbed by Lime's venom. "I could have given you a peaceful death, but you'd rather struggle, would you, my damsel? I'll crush you like the insect you are!"

Lime tried to fly, but the mud clung to her wings. The hippocamp lunged at her, a wall of grey bulk, inescapable as a tidal wave.

Before the hippocamp crashed to the ground, an enormous hand scooped Lime up and snatched her to safety. Erskine stumbled up the bank, clutching Lime protectively to their chest.

"What happened?" they said. "Why does everything smell like vinegar?"

"To cover up your thief-like stench," snarled the hippocamp, rising from the mud. "You'll pay for stealing my skin, adventurer!"

"Wait!" said Erskine, backing towards the trees. "I still have the skin. If you let me get it—"

"After it's been defiled by your human hands?" said the hippocamp. "I think not!" She undulated closer, fangs bared and eyes gleaming menacingly.

Lime climbed out from Erskine's fingers and perched on their wrist. "I thought I told you to slither back to the ocean!" she growled. "Or did you want another dose of venom?"

"Your fondness for this adventurer confounds me," said the hippocamp. "What fairy would risk her life for a human? Do you have even the least grain of self-respect?"

"Fondness has nothing to do with it," said Lime. "I just . . . "

"Just what?" said the hippocamp. "Illuminate me."

"I just—It's just," said Lime, "if anyone has the right to kill this human, it's me!"

"What?" said Erskine.

"Oh?" said the hippocamp.

"The human took an old dried-up skin you weren't even using anymore," said Lime, "and you think that gives you the right to season them up like a roast and eat them alive?"

"It's a matter of principle," said the hippocamp. "If I let one adventurer steal my cast-offs and live, more are sure to follow, each one bolder and greedier than the last."

"That's nothing," said Lime. "Nothing at all. You know what the human did to me? They put me in a salt-shaker!"

"That sounds bad," said Erskine, "but it was a really big salt-shaker. Like the kind you would put shaved Parmesan in? I thought it would be more comfortable."

"You hear that?" said Lime. "They even admit to it!"

"And there are air holes already in it," said Erskine, "so I figured, compared to a jam jar—"

"Contemptible!" said Lime. "Just terrible! *I'm* the one this human has wronged the most, and *I'm* the one who's going to kill them, no matter what any sea-beast has to say about it!" She grabbed Erskine's index finger and bit down: a dry bite, without venom.

"Why?" cried Erskine, eyes brimming with tears of pain.

"Pretend to die, idiot," hissed Lime in Vernacular Fey.

Erskine, to their credit, caught on quickly. They fell to the ground like a sack of rocks and lay there with their eyes closed, breathing softly. "There," said Lime. "It's done."

"Really?" said the hippocamp. "They don't smell dead."

"With all that vinegar, how would you know?" said Lime.

"I think," said the hippocamp, "I may still try to eat them. If you've had your revenge, you'll raise no further objections, surely?"

"Go ahead," said Lime. "If you're not afraid of all the paralytic venom sloshing in their veins."

The hippocamp retracted her fangs and stared at Lime, her scales glittering in the moonlight, her harp-strings still and gleaming. Lime stared back, defiant.

At last, the hippocamp gave a short, bitter laugh. "Grandmother was right," she said. "As the sea is full of fishes, the land is full of fools. I've wasted my time here." She lowered her great head and slipped gracefully into the river, a stream of salt-white and storm-grey.

As she swam oceanward, she called behind to Lime and Erskine. "Beware, my damsel! Beware, little thief! If I ever see a green fairy or a stinking red-headed adventurer on the shores of Crab's Cairn again, no force on land or sea will stay my wrath!" With that, she plunged beneath the water; the white harp sunk into the depths.

"Is she gone?" asked Erskine.

"Gone enough," said Lime. "Good job, by the way, almost getting gobbled up by a snake."

"It was a shed skin," said Erskine, rising to their feet. "I didn't think anyone would miss it." They brushed the dirt from their pajamas. Their eyes widened. "Oh, no! Is that Slugsy?"

A blue light flickered in the shallows. It was indeed Slugsy, laying stunned beneath the water. A few fish-like scales had blossomed on her forehead, and on her neck Lime could see the faint lines of developing gills.

Erskine lifted Slugsy from the riverbed and petted her gently on the back until she coughed up a gout of fluid. "No," she gasped. "No, no, no! Have I turned into a water sprite?"

"It's fine," said Lime. "You've still got legs."

"Not that there's anything wrong with being a water sprite," said Erskine.

Slugsy peeled the scales from her forehead and leapt into the air. She glanced from Lime to Erskine and back. "Ah!" she said. "Listen, human. It might look like Loner escaped, but she didn't. She was ensorcelled by the hippocamp, just like you."

To Lime, she directed a not-so-subtle wink.

"Honestly," said Erskine, "that was one of the last things on my mind. Are the two of you okay?"

Lime shrugged. "I guess," said Slugsy, rubbing at her neck. "How are we not dead, anyway? Where's the hippocamp?"

"I ran her off," said Lime.

"She ran her off," said Erskine.

"No," said Slugsy. "I mean, really."

"You got me," said Lime. "The human tricked her, and she swam away."

"I didn't—" Erskine began.

"Enough talking!" said Lime. "Good night, Slugsy. Let's get going, human." She wiped the last flecks of mud from her wings and flew into the woods.

"Wait!" said Erskine, jogging after. "Where are you going?"

"Back to my salt-shaker," said Lime. "I'm your prisoner, remember?"

"But you saved my life," said Erskine.

Lime fluttered to a halt and hovered in place. "What of it?"

"According to the Law, I'm in your debt," said Erskine, catching up. "You can ask me for anything. So aren't you going to ask to go free?"

For reasons she didn't fully understand, Lime hesitated. She hadn't thought of it that way, but it was true: she had saved Erskine's life. All she had to do was say "yes," and she could leave the Woeful Woods forever. She could return to the Library and read and be alone, without anyone to bother her, or bully her, or talk to her ever again.

She felt an inexplicable ache in her heart. She had lived and read in the Library for twenty-five years in perfect contentment, so why, now, did the thought of going back there fill her with such a strange sense of unease?

Then she realized. It was the books, of course. She thought back to all of the books in Erskine's room. They were human novels, mostly: books the Library—with its outdated selection of non-fairy literature—hadn't carried, books she might never see again. To leave them behind unread would be tragic, unthinkable. She couldn't possibly abandon them. Her mind raced.

"I might have saved your life," said Lime, "but you saved mine, too. So that evens out to nothing."

"Still," said Erskine.

"Hush!" said Lime, flitting away. "It's the middle of the night. Go home, and take a shower."

"I was *going to*," said Erskine. "And hey: wait up!" Lime didn't pay them any mind. She zipped through the shadows and through the trees, into the garden of the lone little house, ducking beneath the boughs of crepe myrtles, skimming the dewy leaves of roses. She darted through the open door and alighted on the sofa, snuggling onto a coarse green cushion. She took out her book, and breathed a sigh of relief.

When Erskine returned, Lime glared at them, daring them to mention the empty salt-shaker.

"It's fine if you want to use the sofa," said Erskine. "Did you want a blanket, too? It feels a bit drafty."

Lime gave an irritable twitch of her antennae.

"Except a blanket's probably too big for you, isn't it?" said Erskine. "Maybe something like a hand-towel would be better? Or a handkerchief?"

"Will you *go to bed*!" screamed Lime.

"Alright," said Erskine, shuffling off to the bathroom. "Good night. See you later." Lime rolled her eyes and returned to her novel.

Somewhere far away, in the brackish depths, a hippocamp swam towards the sea. Pins and needles tingled in her tail. A headache strained at her harp-strings. As she swam, she pieced together the story she would tell her grandmother, upon her return to Crab's Cairn. She would leave out the green fairy, she decided, among other less-than-flattering details. There were some things not even family needed to know.

In the heart of the Woeful Woods, the blue fairy Slugsy curled in the hollow of a tree, tucked in her little nest of treasures: preserved flowers and spider-silk quilts, engraved egg-shells and foil wrappers pilfered from town. She lay back and rubbed at her neck with a pebble, smoothing away the partly-developed gills.

In the lone house at the edge of the woods, Erskine slept, and a green light shone in the window.

BUBBLE AND SQUEAK

DAVID GERROLD & CTEIN

Hu Son ran.

He ran for the joy of it, for the exhilaration—for that moment of hitting the wall and breaking through into the zone, that personal nirvana of physical delight. What others called "runner's high." A sensation like flight—Hu's feet didn't pound the ground, they tapped it as he soared through the early morning air.

A bright blue cloudless sky foretold a beautiful day. A sky so clear and deep you could fall into it and never come back. Later, the day would heat up, glowing with a summery yellow haze, but right now—at this special moment—the beachfront basked in its own perfect promise.

Hu usually started early, when Venice Beach was mostly deserted, all sand and palm trees and stone benches, all the storefronts sleeping behind steel shutters. It was the best time to run. Hu liked the crisp air of dawn, the solitude of the moment, the feeling that the day was still clean, still waiting to be invented—before the owners could ruin it with their displays of tacky, tasteless, and vulgar kitsch.

Some of the cafés were open early though, and by the time Hu reached the Santa Monica pier, run its length, and then headed back toward home, the morning air was flavored with the smells of a dozen different kinds of breakfast, the spices of all the various cuisines that flourished here.

Heading home, Hu passed other morning joggers. This was a favorite track. Nods were exchanged, or not—some of the runners were lost in hidden music, others in their personal reveries. He recognized most; he'd been running this track for more than a year. He was probably regarded as a regular by now.

The final leg. He trotted past the last of the brash touristy areas. Later this strand would teem with summer crowds, exploring the souvenir stands, the ranks of T-shirts printed with single entendres, the displays of dreadful art, all the different fortune tellers and street performers, but right now, this community was still lazily awakening, coming back to life at its own pace.

There were still the occasional shapeless lumps on the stone benches—the homeless, wrapped up against the chill of the night, waiting for the heat of the day to revive them. Even in July, the morning air had a bite, with a salty flavor from the grumbling sea.

Hu turned and jogged up the narrow way that pretended to be a street, a block and a half, slowing down only in the last few meters. He hated to stop, hated to drop back into that other pace of life—the faster more frenetic life, where you weren't allowed to run, you had to walk, walk, walk everywhere.

He glanced at his wristband, looking to see where his numbers were today. Not bad. Not his personal best, but good enough. "Probably still stuck on the plateau," he muttered. "Gonna have to push to get off. Just not today."

Hu opened the back gate and started peeling off his T-shirt. He liked the feeling of the cold morning air cooling the sweat off his skin. He took a moment to slow down, to let himself ease down into this world, then finally stepped through the door and called affectionately, "Honey, I'm homo—" then headed straight for the shower.

Hu Son didn't just appreciate hot water, he loved the luxury of it. In eighteen months, he'd have his master's degree in cultural anthropology, and after that, he'd go for his doctorate, but already his studies had given him a clear sense of how lucky he was to be living in an age where clean water was taken for granted—and hot water available on demand.

California's drought had officially ended some years before, but Hu rarely lingered in the shower. Even at this remove, he could still hear his mother banging on the door, shouting, "Leave some for the rest of us!" Old habits endured. Today, however—today was special. So he took his time, soaping up and rinsing, three times over. He closed his eyes, paced his breathing, and allowed himself to sink into his personal contract with himself.

"I am powerful," he whispered. "I am vulnerable," he continued. And smiling, he concluded, "And I am loving." He repeated it a few times, a personal mantra, until it was no longer a declaration, only his renewed experience of himself. And then, one more phrase. "Especially today!" Opening his eyes, Hu nearly shouted that last. "Because today, I am getting married!"

An electric screech interrupted him—alarm sirens outside. It sounded like the whole city was howling. Like any other Angeleno, anyone who'd lived in the city more than six months, Hu ignored it. It was meaningless noise. Everything was noise, from the daily growl of motorcycles and Asian "rice-rockets" to the nightly screams of drunks and junkies.

Hu turned off the water and heard James calling from the kitchen. "Hu, you need to get in here!" Something was wrong, James only called him Hu when he was upset. He grabbed a fresh towel and wrapped it around himself. A second towel for his hair and he headed toward the kitchen where James was standing, leaning with his back against the counter, a mug of tea in his hand—but focusing intensely on a small television on the end of the kitchen table. Without looking up, James held out the usual mug of tea for Hu.

Hu took it and pecked his fiancé on the cheek. "What's up, Bubble? What are all the sirens for? Some kind of test?" He didn't wait for an answer, but took his first sip. Chai. . . . "Ahh." He glanced toward the television. The president was talking.

"Now what? Are we at war?"

"It's Hawaii," said James.

"We're at war with Hawaii?"

"There's been a quake—"

Hu's buoyant mood evaporated. "Oh no. How bad?"

"Both Honolulu and Hilo were hit by tsunamis. Really big—the biggest ever." James turned to Hu. "When did your folks fly out?"

"They didn't. Dad needed an extra day. So they're flying out this evening, they'll catch up with us tomorrow at the hotel."

"No, they won't. And we won't be there either. Honolulu airport is gone."

"Wait. What?" At first, Hu didn't understand. How could an airport be gone? Then he realized what James was telling him. "That's not possible. A whole airport—?"

"And half the city—"

"Oh, shit," Hu said, his mug of tea suddenly forgotten in his hand. "That's—just bad."

On the TV, the president was still talking, a row of grim-faced people stood behind him. Or maybe it was a repeat. The scroll-bar across the bottom of the screen was filled with incomprehensible words. They moved too fast for him to make sense of them. And outside, the sirens still screamed.

"Shit!" said Hu. "All I wanted was one little honeymoon—" He became aware of the sirens again. "And what's all that noise about—? We're not—Shit! What's going on?"

James put down his coffee. He turned to Hu. He took Hu's mug from him. "Squeak. Sweetheart—" His expression was grim. "It's not just Hawaii. It's the whole California coast. The tsunami is headed for us now. We've got maybe three hours before it hits—"

"A tsunami? Here—?"

"A tsunami. Here. A mega-tsunami. Just like the movie, only bigger—"

"But that was only a movie—" Hu stopped in mid-sentence, remembering that movie, that scene.

James Liddle had been SCUBA diving since his teens. After college, he'd set up his own small company, specializing in SCUBA services to local studios. "Underwater? Let it be a Liddle thing. Call us!" Because of his skill, his professionalism, his dependability, and his charming good looks, he was on speed dial for several stunt coordinators.

More than once, James had been called in to teach various film and television actors how to dive safely—or at least look like they knew how to dive safely. More than once, he'd doubled for actors who were too valuable to the studios to be allowed to do their own diving, but he couldn't say who. Most of the bigger shoots involved nondisclosure agreements.

Hu's family had moved from Hong Kong to Vancouver when he was eight, where his father opened a consulting service/business school, where he taught westerners how to do business in China and occasionally set up deals himself.

When Hu was twelve, an aunt he'd never met died of cancer, so his mother came south to Los Angeles to manage her brother's large unruly family; she brought Hu with. As the new kid, as the Chinese kid, and also as the smallest and the smartest in his class, Hu was a target for bullies of all sizes—so his uncle enrolled him into a series of physical activities to build up not only his body, not only his ability to defend himself, but also his self-esteem. Eventually Hu studied karate, judo, Tae Kwon Do, and modern dance. By the time he was nineteen, Hu was earning extra money doing stunts in occasional action films. Though he never doubled for any of the major actors, he was often somewhere in the background—and in a memorable comedy, he'd been featured as one of the dancing ninjas.

James and Hu had met at Culver Studios. A massive team of stunt doubles had been assembled for a disaster picture, another overblown disaster picture, a fantasy of multiple simultaneous disasters—hurricanes, tornadoes, earthquakes, volcanoes, tidal waves, and the return of disco. Everyone knew the picture was going to be awful; it was assumed (though never spoken aloud) that nobody upstairs knew how bad it was—either that, or it was actually intended from the beginning to be a flop, a tax write-off, or perhaps even some bizarre kind of money-laundering. Who knew? The only people who understood Hollywood financing were alchemists, and few of them were ever allowed out of their dungeon laboratories into the light of day.

But on the ground, the money was good. A lot of people had a profitable summer working on the film. As with any big effort, there were sexual relationships, babies started, babies stopped, babies born, and of course, a few divorces and emotional breakdowns, plus a number of lifelong feuds begun and exorcised, some in private, others in public.

James had worked for seven weeks on various underwater sequences. Hu had come aboard in the last week as a stunt player, running from the onrushing water. The first few days, there was no actual water. All that was to be added later by a team of talented CGI artists in Hong Kong or New Delhi. Anyone whose name came before the credits would be taking home seven figures and points on the gross, but domestic jobs were shipped overseas in cost-cutting acts of dubious economy. But there was still work to be done locally.

They had to shoot one key scene on a stretch of Wilshire Boulevard—from Rodeo Drive to the Beverly Wilshire Hotel—and they had exactly seven minutes out of every thirty when the Beverly Hills Police Department would block off traffic for the director to capture his carefully orchestrated panic, a frenzied evacuation from unseen waves.

Hu's job was to be part of the crowd, running down the street, running through the cars, until he finally hit a specific mark, where he would fall to the ground as if he was being swept under the killing wave—except one of the assistant directors liked his look and gave him a different role where he got to be a featured kill.

The camera started at a high angle, looking up the row of stopped cars, with the distant wave roaring toward the foreground. Hu ran toward the camera, running between the line of vehicles. The camera lowered, promising a closeup, but just as Hu arrived at that spot, a panicky driver—another stunt player—opened his driver-side door so Hu slammed into it—and then the wave overtook them both. The unseen side of the car door was carefully padded, so Hu could hit it hard without injuring himself.

The director liked the shot so much that he decided to add a follow-up bit, giving Hu two additional days of work. Finished with the devastation of Wilshire Boulevard, the film moved to a Hollywood backlot for specific closeups of death and destruction.

For these shots, the director needed real water, not virtual, and the production relocated to the Paramount lot, the site of the city's second-largest outdoor tank—the Blue Sky Tank, so called because its towering back wall could be painted to represent any kind of sky, stormy to cloudless, that a director might need. Although the Falls Lake tank at Universal was noticeably larger, it was also more expensive to fill, filter, and heat.

The filmmakers needed a variety of shots with Asian men and women as background players. This was so their Chinese co-financers could edit a somewhat different version of the film for the Asian markets. The Chinese version would include several characters and subplots not in the American version. The joke had initially been whispered in the front office, but of course it eventually filtered down to the production crew as well—the picture would do well on that side of the Pacific, because Asian audiences like to see white people die. But to be fair, a few Chinese extras had to go down too.

Hu didn't care, he was just happy to work. Because of his marvelously startled expression when he'd slammed into the car door, the American director wanted to follow up by showing Hu struggling for a while in real waves before finally (fake) drowning. So Hu spent a hot August morning in the tank, pretending to die—"On this next take, could you look a little more terrified, please?" Dutifully, Hu struggled, gasped, and waved his arms for help that would never come, until finally disappearing obediently beneath the surface of the foaming water.

The tank was barely four feet at the center, the waves were machine-produced, and the foam was a specific detergent. Floating across the entire surface of the water was an assortment of Styrofoam flotsam, representing the debris stirred up by the tsunami. The shot didn't seem very dangerous—at least that's what Hu believed until he was caught unprepared by a sudden sideways push of prop debris, hard enough to punch the air out of his lungs and leave him gasping for air, involuntarily sucking in a mouthful of water, coughing, and choking desperately as he flailed.

James was one of the safety coordinators. He'd dived into the water, swam under the crapberg, grabbed Hu, and pulled him off to the side of the tank, hanging him on the sloping surface and staying with him until he regained his breath. Neither noticed when the director shouted, "Cut! That's the best one yet, we'll use that one! All right, let's get the camera in the water for the dead body shot—"

The director hadn't noticed what had happened, but one of the assistant directors had seen, and on James' direct recommendation, quietly added an additional stunt-fee to Hu's paycheck. No one said anything to the film's director—a man notorious for arguing with stunt players about the cost of each gag. He had a bad reputation in the stunt players' community.

After that, James kept an eye on Hu. In the last shot of the morning, Hu had to pretend to be dead, floating face down in the water while a camera crew in dive gear photographed him from beneath. James had been there to coach the camera crew, showing them how to keep their bubbles out of the shot. And that was when Hu, not knowing James' name, had jokingly called him the bubble-wrangler.

Later on, at lunch, they sat opposite each other—the group shared a table under a large craft-service tent that dominated the parking lot next to the commissary.

Hu had a smile. James had a grumpy charm—it was enough.

The two began that long careful dance of curiosity that would eventually, though not immediately, lead to James' little house in Venice Beach. Hu had gotten his nickname—Squeak—from the sound his running shoes made on James' tile floor.

It began as a physical thing, but eventually grew into a relationship. Bed-buddies became roommates. Roommates became lovers. And lovers became—

One strange stormy night, while the two of them were lying side-by-side, staring at the ceiling and listening to the rain, the usually taciturn James had said, "What do you think—"

"About what?"

"About *us,* about stuff—"

Hu was still learning how to listen to James, but this time he heard more than the words. He heard the intention.

"I think . . . " he began. He rolled onto his side to face James. "I think yes."

"Yes?"

"Yes, you big bubble-wrangler. Yes, I will marry you."

"Oh," said James. "I was going to ask you if we should get a cat."

"Huh—?"

James grinned. "But getting married—that's a good idea too." He pulled Hu close, and kissed him intensely.

The rest was details.

After a few weeks of dithering about plans and schedules, and how much neither of them wanted the gaudy circus of an actual wedding ceremony, they decided to just go down to City Hall, do the deed, and then fly to Hawaii for a week. Hu's parents, now together again, were initially more concerned about Hu marrying a Caucasian than a man—but finally decided to show their acceptance by joining them on the island.

The plane tickets were sitting on the kitchen table—and the president's voice was still droning on—now repeating the original broadcast. Outside, the sirens abruptly fell silent. "I suppose—" said Hu, staring at the travel folder, "I suppose—we can get a refund."

And then, it hit him.

The grim expression on James' face said it all.

"Shit! We're going to lose the house, aren't we? Jimmy—?"

"We're gonna lose everything. Everything we can't carry on our backs."

There were only three people in the world who had ever called James Liddle "Jimmy."

The first had been his mother, right up until the day he came out to her. From that moment on, to express her disappointment, he was "James." The second had been Nate Lem, his arrogant, overweight fraternity brother—he'd called him "Liddle Jimmy" once too often and gotten a bloody nose for it. After that, he didn't call James anything at all, he left the room whenever James entered.

The third was Hu Son. When he said "Jimmy" it was either affectionate—or important.

James said, "They don't know how big it's going to be, but we've only got three hours to get out of here." He took a breath, his mind racing. "Let's not panic. Let's take a moment and think. It's all about the prep. We gotta get all our cash, all our IDs, all our cards. Um, I have a go-bag, you'll have to pack one. We'll need bottled water and protein bars and—and whatever else is important. Tablets, laptops. All our legal paperwork, especially the insurance stuff—"

Hu Son stood frozen for a moment, his heart racing. "You're serious—oh my god, you are. Oh, god, Jimmy—"

James grabbed him, held him close. "It's okay, it's okay—we're going to be okay. Let's just take it one step at a time. First step, think—what's important? What are we going to need? What can we leave behind? What do we absolutely need—?"

Hu said, "Um—I don't know. Um—" He looked around the kitchen, mentally sorting through everything, his favorite mug, the pictures on the wall, the beautifully sculpted merman figurine they'd bought on a trip to New Orleans. None of that really mattered. He realized he was naked. He headed toward the room they had christened as "the badroom"—the place where it was good to be bad.

"Um, clothes. I'll grab clothes—"

"Not the big suitcase," James called after him. The one they had packed last night for Hawaii. "Only what can fit in the carry-on. Jeans, hoodies, T-shirts, underwear, socks—"

Hu was already pulling things out of drawers. "Toothbrushes, deodorant, first-aid kit—"

"Right, good." James realized he was still holding a mug of hot tea. He took one last swallow, poured the rest into the sink, and opened the dishwasher to put the mug on the rack. It didn't matter now, did it? But he put the mug on the rack anyway.

"Okay, Jimmy-boy," he said, talking aloud to himself. "What else? The camera, for sure. Eight thousand dollars for an underwater camera rig—I'm not leaving that behind. And the memory cards and batteries. Oh—" He turned to the shelf, grabbed a nearly full box of Ziploc plastic bags and followed Hu into the badroom. "Here. Triple bag everything that isn't waterproof."

"You think—?"

"I think we're going to plan for the worst, hope for the best, and prepare for anything. We'll stuff it into dry bags at the office." While Hu pulled on shorts and shirt, James continued sorting through drawers, throwing stuff onto the bed. "Fuck—"

"What?"

"The motorcycle is in the shop—"

"No prob. We'll take the van—"

James had gone to the nightstand. He grabbed a large folding knife from the bottom drawer, and the travel-safe, then the travel bag from the closet shelf. He shook his head. "Bad idea."

"Huh?" Hu stopped, shirt halfway down over his head. His voice came muffled.

"Squeak, you didn't grow up in this city."

"Yes, I did—"

"Not as a driver. We are not gonna be traffic today—"

Hu finished pulling his shirt down. "Then, how—?"

"My SCUBA gear is at the office. I can't leave that behind—" James tossed the travel-safe into the carry-on. He shoved the knife into the pocket of his jeans. "I don't know how bad it's going to be, but I'm thinking there's gonna be a big need for divers after this thing hits. I don't know, but I'll need to be prepared. We can bike to the office, grab whatever gear, and from there, we can head inland. Are you ready—?"

"Half a minute—" Hu stopped, looked around. "Last minute check—"

"I don't want to scare you, but we need to get moving."

Hu debated with himself, finally lost the argument, grabbed his running shoes and shoved them into the carry-on. "I paid too much for these shoes. They're coming." He stopped, looked uncertainly to James. "You think it's gonna be that bad—"

James looked grim. "You know all those safety courses I had to take, the fire and rescue courses, the Red Cross courses, lifeguard, all the paramedic stuff?"

"Yeah. You did that for the licenses, so you'd be more valuable to the studios—"

"It was part of the job. Stunt safety. Water safety. Everything." He gave the badroom one last check of his own, still talking. "We had to learn about disasters, all kinds, and prepping for survival too. That's why I keep a go-bag under the bed, and why I'm always nagging you to keep one too." He stopped, he took a breath. "I got to see the pictures from the Christmas Tsunami and Fukushima as well, the ones they didn't show on TV. I never told you—but it was . . . ugly. So we are walking out of here right now and we are heading for the highest ground we can get to the fastest way we can. Is that it? You got everything?" James moved to close the carry-on—

Hu stopped him long enough to toss in two more items, a fist-sized bronze Buddha that he grabbed from the top of the dresser, a wooden cross with a naked Jesus pulled from the wall—and one more, a small resin replica of Mickey Mouse in red robe and blue sorcerer's hat. "Gotta take the household gods, Bubble. Bad luck to leave 'em."

The television was no longer replaying the president. Now, the Mayor of Los Angeles, backed up by a phalanx of city councilmen and police, and confronted by a forest of microphones, stood behind a podium, trying to look calm as he laid out the first attempts at emergency evacuation plans. His voice was shaking.

James and Hu stopped long enough to listen, long enough to realize that whatever the mayor was saying, none of it was going to help them. "Wait," asked James, "Have you eaten? Grab those boxes of protein bars. Eat two of them now. And the water bottles, drink one now. Don't scarf, don't guzzle, bring it along. Come on, let's go."

They almost made it to the door, James with the knapsack holding his expensive new underwater camera, and his go-bag in his left hand—Hu with a knapsack holding water and travel-rations, his carry-on in his right hand.

Hu stopped abruptly. "No! Wait!"

"Now what?"

Hu dropped the carry-on, ran back to the badroom, came out a moment later, carrying a small black box. "I almost forgot the rings! The wedding rings!" He held the jewelry box high for James to see, then shoved it into his pocket. "Hell or high water, we're getting married."

"Probably high water, but yeah. Hell or high water."

"Promise?"

"Promise. Now let's go—"

James pulled the plastic tarp off the bikes and unlocked them. Despite the high wooden fence around the tiny yard, he still didn't trust the neighborhood's population of permanent transients.

"I'm gonna miss this place," Hu said.

James didn't answer. He just shook his head and led them out to the bike path. They took a moment to pull on their helmets and double-check the bungee cords around their bags, holding them firmly to the racks on the back of the bikes.

"You ready?"

"No. But let's go anyway."

It wasn't a long ride to the office. The beachfront had gone curiously empty—few of the stores were open, several looked abandoned. There were still people here but not the usual slurry of ambling shoppers and tourists. They saw a few speed skaters with backpacks, several people puffing and pulling oversized wheeled luggage, a scramble of surfers running for their van, and more bicyclists than usual. Most had backpacks and other luggage strapped to their bikes and handlebars. But everyone was moving with purpose. Most were walking fast, trotting, a few were even running. It wasn't a panic—not yet, but the clock was running.

James' company, their company now—Liddle Things—was set in a small white building, three blocks up from the beach. James didn't rent to casual tourists, too much risk, so there was little need to be on the beachfront where rents were noticeably higher. He unlocked the heavy front door; they wheeled their bikes inside and locked the door behind them. James went behind the desk and unlocked the back room where he kept the tanks and masks, the diving rigs, tool belts, and assorted other paraphernalia.

"Shit!" he said, looking around, taking stock, realizing how little he could save. He blew out his cheeks. "We're gonna lose it all, Squeak. More than fifty thousand dollars invested in this stuff—all gone."

Hu wasn't sure if he should say anything. He recognized the mood—the same growling darkness that always came over James when dealing with money, especially a shortage of it. "The insurance—?"

"Won't cover the half of it—" James shook his head. "No—there's just no way to save it, no fucking way." He sighed in resignation. "All right, let's get the bike trailers. You take the new one, it's lighter. You attach, I'll do triage." He began pulling things off the wall and out of lockers.

Hu knew the drill. The bike trailers were convenient ways for cyclists to carry surfboards, SCUBA gear, camping gear, or even a few bags of groceries. They attached easily. He and James used them a lot, for almost any trip less than three miles. Hu didn't mind driving, he could listen to his music, but James hated getting behind the wheel, because he found urban traffic frustrating—the poor behavior of other drivers made even the shortest outing feel like a death-defying exercise.

James talked as he worked, annotating every decision with a justification. "I'm gonna want my wet suit and my new dive computer—that thing cost fifteen hundred dollars. It does everything but make coffee, and I still haven't had a chance to use it. I'm gonna need it if there's rescue work. You grab those spare tanks and put them on your trailer. And the camping bag. I'm afraid we're gonna need it. I'll take the main tanks and the portable compressor. I might have to wear the rig. Hmm, harness, backplate, maybe I should wear a couple of tanks, too? What else? A pro-grade mask—the new one with the dual lamps, fins, tool belt—I can hang the belt on the handlebars, anything that isn't waterproof goes into the dry bags, we can put those in our knapsacks, everything else in the travel case, that'll go on the trailer. Oh, and grab those new headlamps too—"

Hu laughed. "We're gonna look like a couple of underwater bag ladies—and you with the SCUBA gear on your back—"

"Not gonna leave it—"

"Jimmy—? Isn't it all too much to carry? All this weight?"

"If it is, then we've both wasted a fortune at the gym. And all that damn healthy eating." James paused, got serious. "Squeak, this is my career. Just like your new expensive laptop. I need this."

"You don't have to convince me, Bubble. Give me whatever you need me to carry. We'll do it."

They finished quickly. Less than fifteen minutes.

"Is that it?"

"It's gonna have to be." James looked to his partner, his tone abruptly thoughtful. "We'll take the bikeway—that'll be the fastest. The only traffic will be other cyclists. But only to Twenty-sixth Street, or Bundy if we can, then we'll turn north. I think if we can get to Sunset, we can go up one of the canyons to Mulholland, maybe take it to Topanga, get down into the valley that way—"

"And from there?"

"I dunno. Who do we know in the valley with a guesthouse? Or a backyard big enough for the tent?"

"Whatsisname—that writer who's always calling you?"

"Mr. Source Material? Maybe. What about your cousin?"

"Maybe. If you're willing to put up with my uncle—"

"Yeah, there's that."

"Maybe if we can get to Pasadena, there's Chris and Mark—"

"Melinda has a guest house—"

"So does—never mind. We have options. First thing, let's get out of here." James pointed to the bikes. "Okay, safety check on the bikes. Is everything secure?"

Three minutes to double-check all the tie-downs and bungee cords, and they were ready to leave, but at the door, they paused. James put his hand on Hu's arm. "Okay, Squeak, we've got two and a half hours. We can do this. Ten miles an hour, easy-peasy. We could get all the way to Union Station if we had to. All we have to do is pace ourselves. The idiots are going to ride like crazy and exhaust themselves before they even get to the 405. Just keep thinking of Mike Sloan's teddy bear—"

"Huh?"

"Don't you remember? Sloan's teddy wins the race—"

"Oof. Remind me again why I agreed to marry you?"

"Because I'm the daddy, that's why." James grinned.

"Except when it's my turn."

They pushed the bikes outside, first Hu, then James behind him. Hu started to plug in his headphones, but James stopped him. "You don't want to do that—"

"Shouldn't we listen to the news—?"

"Aren't you scared enough already?"

"Oh." Hu shoved the earphones back into his knapsack, glanced at his wristband, looked west toward the beach. Beyond a lonely palm tree, the horizon looked peaceful and bright. Hard to believe a disaster was rising somewhere beyond. "It's gonna be hot today," he said. "Especially inland."

"Yeah," James agreed, behind him. "Gonna need the extra water."

Hu turned back to him. "All right. I'm ready."

With the trailer attached, his bike was loaded heavier than he expected. He had to take a running start to catch up to James, but they were on their way, heading east.

It wasn't far to the bikeway, less than a mile, but they weren't the only ones who'd had this idea. The bikeway wasn't crowded, not at first, but the farther they rode, the more cyclists joined them—a steady stream of riders pedaling inland with a grim determination. Every few minutes, a light-rail train passed them, howling east on elevated tracks that paralleled the bikeway. Despite himself, Hu looked up—the railcars were already crowded. James had guessed right.

"Sloan's teddy," called James. "Just like one of your marathons."

"Ha ha," said Hu. He focused on his pace, using the same steady counting exercise he used when he ran in the morning. Occasionally, other cyclists passed them at a furious pace, almost panicky. Not wise—but their choice.

Two miles in, and the bikeway was filled. Most of the traffic was other cyclists in professional gear, helmets and backpacks, but sometimes just ordinary people on bicycles—sometimes whole families pedaling in a group. Most were wearing knapsacks, or had cases strapped to the backs of their bikes or hanging from their handlebars. A few, like James and Hu, had well-loaded bike trailers.

Occasionally people passed them, a few speed-skaters, and motorized skateboards as well. Once a couple of assholes on motorcycles came roaring past. Hu stood up on his pedals to look ahead. If the bikeway kept filling up, kept getting more and more crowded, those motorcyclists weren't going to have much of an advantage.

By the time they reached Twenty-sixth Street, traffic on the bikeway had slowed to a sluggish crawl—and east of the avenue, there were so many cyclists ahead of them riding was impossible. People had to dismount and walk their bikes. A few groaned in annoyance, a couple others shouted angrily, some muttered to themselves, but most just kept pushing along. Hu and James dismounted and walked their loaded bikes side-by-side.

More frustrated riders piled up behind them, but no fights had broken out. There was still plenty of time. Most people were helping each other. One woman was holding another's bike while the first one changed her baby's diaper. Elsewhere, a professional-looking rider had stopped to patch a flat tire for a crying teenage girl. Another was helping an uncertain middle-aged man put a loose chain back on his bicycle's gears.

It wasn't a panic, not yet. It was still an exodus. Not disorderly, but it wasn't moving fast enough. At this pace . . . James looked to Hu, shook his head, leaned over and whispered, "Time for an alternate route."

It took them nearly ten minutes to work their way to the next opportunity to exit the bikeway, Cloverfield Avenue. They weren't the only ones abandoning the narrow route. Some of the cyclists were turning south, most were turning north.

James and Hu went north. Just on the other side of Colorado Boulevard, there was a good-sized parking lot. The lot was already emptying of cars, the last few people driving away frantically. James pointed, and Hu followed.

They pulled themselves out of the steady stream of people remounting their bikes. Hu pulled out the first water bottle, took two swallows and passed it to James, who did the same, then passed it back. A familiar ritual. Having done that, they both pulled out their phones. Hu checked the Weather Channel—the temperature was already above eighty and still rising. Okay, not unexpected.

James went to Google Maps, then he tapped for Waze. Both were bad news. Red lines showing heavy traffic everywhere, some routes already painted with stretches of black. Absolute gridlock was beginning. But at least the bikes were moving here—in the bike lanes and on the sidewalks, and even between the long rows of cars. The automobile lanes were barely inching forward.

"It's crowding up faster than I expected. Apparently people are taking this thing seriously. All right, we'll head north here—" James started to push his bike forward again.

Hu said, "Wait."

"What?"

"I've got a text."

"Forget it—"

"It's from Karen—" A series of messages rolled up the screen. Hu looked to James. "She's at work. She needs someone to pick up Pearl."

"Can't she do it?"

"She's doing triage in the E.R. She couldn't get out, even if she wanted to. The streets there are gridlocked."

"Pearl can't get a ride?"

"The neighbor who promised left without her." Hu read the next text. "What an asshole. Apparently, her cats were more important."

"There's no one else?"

Hu kept scrolling through Karen's frantic notes, his expression darkening. "Doesn't look like it. Karen says it's desperate. Pearl is trapped. She can't get an Uber or a Lyft, Ride-Share is down, Access isn't picking up. The Fire Department is moving all their equipment eastward. She tried calling for an ambulance, but—" Hu lowered his phone. "James, we can't leave her there. We gotta get her."

James made a raspberry of disgust. "Fuck. The problem is . . . that damn wheelchair."

"Can we pull her—?"

"I'm thinking—" A heartbeat. "The wheelchair is light enough—it's Pearl. She's not exactly a spring potato. Fuck."

"James—"

"I know, I know—" He puffed his cheeks, blew out his breath, exasperated. "Yeah, we have to try. Uh . . . all right, lemme think." He went to scratch his head, fingers fumbling across his helmet instead. "Fastest way there—"

James made a decision. "Okay. Forget Sunset. Forget the mountains. We'll go up to Santa Monica, it's the next one after Broadway. Then . . . " His voice tailed off as he plotted a route. He turned to Hu. "It's a long slog. If Pearl can get herself down to the street, we'll figure something out. We might have to lose one of the trailers, I dunno, I'll do the math in my head while we ride."

"Can we make it in time?"

James looked at his watch. "Yeah, I think so."

"Can we get her to high ground? Can we get us to high ground—?"

"Straight north up Fairfax would take us to Laurel Canyon. Might be high enough. I don't know. That's not a great route, but . . . fuck, I don't know." James shook his head. "Worst comes to worst, I don't know, we might be far enough inland. Even a ten-story building might be tall enough. Maybe. I don't know. This is fucked. Let's just do it. Come on, we've been through worse—"

"No we haven't," said Hu. "*This* is the worst." But he was already tapping a message into his phone. "We're on our way." He sent it to both Karen and Pearl, shoved his phone back into his pocket and grabbed his handlebars. "Okay, let's go."

James and Hu pedaled east on Santa Monica Boulevard, weaving their way through a slow-moving mass of cars and people. But at least it was moving. Both sides of the avenue were headed inland. There was no westbound traffic. It helped—a little.

It was a business district here, but none of the stores were open. There were a few broken windows, but not many. People were determinedly walking east, most of them turning north at suitable intersections. Some of the cyclists were walking their bikes because there wasn't enough room to ride. James and Hu had dismounted as well and were now walking their bikes side-by-side.

The exodus was serious now. Even the motorcyclists were having trouble maneuvering through the impatient lines of automobiles. It was turning into a crush. The inevitable speed-skaters darted everywhere, sometimes nearly colliding with unwary pedestrians. Occasionally, they saw an ambulatory bundle of rags doggedly pushing an overloaded shopping cart. Even the homeless were leaving. And once a pair of hipsters rode by on hoverboards.

A woman behind them started complaining loudly—making pointed remarks about their overloaded bikes and bike trailers. James muttered a curse under his breath, but shook his head and kept pushing forward. Hu looked over to him. "Are you okay?"

"I will be. Are you?"

"I'm . . . not complaining," said Hu. He had a thought. "I'm wondering. Do you think maybe Pearl's building might be tall enough? If we could get her to the roof—"

James went silent, thinking about it. Finally, "I wouldn't want to risk it, would you? It's an old building, wood frame, it might not survive the impact. It's not just the water, it's all the crap being pushed by the water. It'll hit like a horizontal avalanche. And even if the building survives the impact, she could be stuck up there for days before anyone could get to her. And the damn wheelchair is another problem. So, no."

"It was just a thought. I was worried about the time."

James looked at his watch. "We're okay." He pointed. "We're almost to the freeway. Once we get to the other side, it should be easier going. Well, could be. We'll burn that bridge when we get to it." James pushed his bike ahead, effectively ending the conversation.

The 405 freeway divides the L.A. Basin. It separates the western and southern communities from the rest of the megalopolis, as it winds south, vaguely paralleling the coast. Parts are elevated highway, parts are sunken, but all of it is a ten-laned barrier to traffic trying to move to and from the coast. The inadequate and infrequent underpasses and bridges that cross the 405, its on- and off-ramps, are bottlenecks that can back up traffic for blocks even on a good day.

This was not a good day. Gridlock spread outward from every crowded access ramp and crossover. In a few hours the entire length of freeway—from the Sepulveda Pass all the way to the Mexican border—would be gone. But right now it was a major obstacle.

Where Santa Monica Boulevard crossed under the 405, several LAPD motorcycle officers were calmly working to unravel the chaos at the underpass. Surrounded by frantic and desperate drivers, they were doing their best. They were scheduled to withdraw at least twenty minutes before impact—if they could get out. That wasn't certain anymore.

At the mayor's desperate orders, both sides of all major surface streets were now mandated for eastbound and northbound vehicles, especially through the underpasses and across the bridges. Both sides of the 110 and the 405 were now handling northbound traffic.

It wasn't enough.

Police and news helicopters circled overhead. Other choppers, all kinds, were shuttling east and west, their own small contributions to the evacuation. The apocalypse was being televised. Further south, at LAX, every plane that could get off the ground was heading inland, some with passengers sitting in the aisles.

James and Hu came to a stop on the sidewalk just past the Nu-Art theater—an ancient movie house that had survived for more than nine decades. For most of its history, it had been a cinematic sanctuary, unspooling an assortment of independent films, obscure foreign dramas, various cult classics, assorted Hollywood treasures, a variety of otherwise forgotten and questionable efforts, occasional themed festivals, and the inevitable midnight screenings of crowd-pleasers like *The Rocky Horror Picture Show* and other film-fads of the moment. In a few hours, it would be closed forever.

James pointed ahead—the underpass was gridlocked. The officers had blocked off the northbound on-ramps with their motorcycles, and were now directing traffic to use the southbound off-ramp instead, their only remaining access to a northbound escape, but even that was moving slowly. Too slowly. Even with cars crawling along the shoulders of the freeway, the 405 just couldn't accept any more traffic.

Los Angeles had not been designed for an evacuation—not on this scale. No city had ever been designed for such a massive torrent of people, an exodus of unprecedented size, a titanic crush of desperate humanity.

And yet, somehow, it moved.

Not fast enough. Not nearly fast enough. But it moved.

Some of these people would survive—if they could just get over the hill into the San Fernando Valley, or even halfway up the Sepulveda Pass. There was time.

Except—

—except for the angry shouting.

Which was why James had stopped.

An old green van, a decrepit-looking Ford Windstar, hastily overloaded, had collided with a silver Lexus, a fairly new model. Both vehicles were in the middle of the road, blocking three separate lanes. A frightened woman sat in the passenger seat of the Lexus.

Two desperate drivers had left their vehicles to confront each other—neither had given way, both had tried to force their way forward, only to demonstrate that specific law of physics that two objects cannot occupy the same space—so now they were screaming at each other in near-incoherent rage.

A crowd of other drivers surrounded them, also screaming, demanding that they move their fender-crunched vehicles out of the way. Snippets of conversation echoed off the underpass walls—

"Get your fucking cars out of the way—"

"Not until I get this asshole's insurance—"

"It's your goddamn fault, I want your insurance—"

"There's no time for that, you assholes—"

"Will both you idiots move your goddamn cars—"

"Daddy, I wanna go home—"

"The police are right there—"

"Good! They can arrest this jerk—"

"Just please move it to the side, so the rest of us can get by—"

"Move it where?! We're boxed in by the rest of you—"

"I don't back up for assholes—"

"It's okay, I do—"

"I'm not moving till he gives me his insurance information—"

"We don't have time for that, and your piece of shit Ford isn't worth it anyway. You're just trying to hold me up, and I won't stand for it—"

"That's just the attitude I'd expect from a spoiled brat manbaby—"

"Guys, please! This isn't helping anyone—"

"Daddy, I gotta pee—"

"If you won't move it, I will—"

"Touch my car and you'll regret it—"

"Why don't the police do something—"

"Okay, enough is enough. You're gonna move this shit outta the way now—"

That last was a burly member of the sasquatch family—red-faced, long-haired, scruffy-bearded, flannel shirt, and the kind of expression that usually stopped all conversation.

"You gonna make me—?"

"Officer, over here! Please!" That was a woman shouting.

Two of the officers were busy trying to stop impatient drivers from backing up onto the southbound on-ramp, intending to join the northbound exodus that way. Two more were struggling to keep the evacuation orderly—one had to dodge sideways as an impatient driver forced his way around the sluggish line of cars ahead of him. They had more immediate priorities than the argument in the underpass. But the backup of cars was growing, and so was the angry crowd.

From his position at the ramp, one of the officers waved furiously at the drivers of the two vehicles, urging them to get back into their vehicles and move, but the two men were too angry, each so focused on winning this argument they couldn't see past their own rage. It looked like violence was inevitable.

"Can we get past that?" asked Hu.

"I don't know," said James. "I'm wondering if we should try to go around it." He pulled out his phone to study the map again. Where was the next closest underpass? Half a block north. Ohio Avenue.

The immediate problem would be just getting across the street. Santa Monica Boulevard was gridlocked. The closest cross street was Sawtelle, just on the other side of the Nu-Art theatre. Maybe they could thread their way around the stalled cars—

A sudden shift in sound, a scream of incoherent rage. Both James and Hu whirled to see—

Sasquatch was now waving an aluminum baseball bat. "You gonna move it—?" This was followed by a well-aimed blow. The right-front headlight of the Lexus shattered in the impact. "You gonna move it now—?"

"What the fuck are you doing—?"

"Giving you a reason to move it—"

"Fuck you! You're gonna pay for that—"

"Let's make it two—" Another swing of the bat, it bounced off the left headlight. A second swing shattered it. "And three—" The windshield shattered next. The woman inside flinched and tried to scramble across the seat.

"Stop it, goddammit! Stop it!"

"Move it and I will!"

The driver of the Lexus scrambled into the car, but instead of starting the engine, he came out waving a—

"Gun! He's got a gun—!" The crowd scattered. The panic rippled outward. At its spreading edges, people ran or ducked, hiding behind the most convenient cars.

And just as quickly, three of the police positioned themselves, flattened across the hoods of several stalled vehicles, guns drawn, and pointed, held steady in both hands, red laser dots wavering on the Lexus driver. The lead officer shouted, his voice electrically amplified—"Drop it! Drop the gun! Now!"

Confused, the Lexus driver turned, staring from one officer to the next. "But he . . . he smashed my car." He waved the gun around, as if to point it, but Sasquatch had conveniently disappeared.

"Drop the fucking gun! Now, goddammit!" Not exactly standard LAPD procedure, but the pressures of the situation were getting out of hand.

"I just want to get out of here!" the Lexus driver wailed.

"Drop the gun and move your car!"

"No, no, no!" The man insisted. "I didn't do anything! He hit me! He has to move!" Sensing that he was blocked in, he turned around and around, pointing the gun from one driver to the next. "Everybody get out of my way! Let me out of here—" He looked desperate, he was shredding into incoherency—

"Last warning! Drop the gun. Drop it. Now."

"Please! Just let me out of here—"

"Oh fuck," said James, quietly. "They're gonna shoot him."

Hu put his hand on James' shoulder and pushed. The two of them flattened to the sidewalk together, their bikes falling beside them.

Three quick gunshots, followed by a beat of silence—and then the screaming started. "Oh my god, my god!" And: "You didn't have to do that—!" Followed by orders from the cops. "You, move that Lexus. Move it now! You, back up! You, follow him!"

But there was no organization. There were too many voices. There was too much screaming, and too many people pulling in too many directions at once—

And a couple more gunshots, coming from another direction—

James half rose up to look, then quickly lowered himself back to the sidewalk. Once, a long time ago, he'd seen a riot start. It was ugly.

This was worse.

James looked to Hu. "Let's go back."

Tentatively, they levered themselves back to their feet, both a little shaken. Hu touched James' arm and pointed. The building behind them had a fresh hole in one of its windows.

James smiled weakly, nodded, pointed west.

Hu hesitated. "Shouldn't we see if anyone needs help?"

"Pearl needs us more. Let's get out of here."

Hu hesitated, uncertain.

James touched his elbow and said quietly, "Triage."

Hu didn't like the thought. But James was right. He followed.

Somehow, despite the narrow sidewalk, despite the people around them, they got their bikes turned around and headed a half block west to Sawtelle.

They weren't the only ones. Drivers who had gotten out of their cars to see what the blockage was at the underpass were now climbing back into their vehicles and turning north onto Sawtelle. James and Hu threaded their way across the intersection and remounted. There was just enough room on the sidewalk to pedal north.

It wasn't far to Ohio Avenue, a block and a half. But when they reached the intersection and looked right, they came to a stop, both at the same time.

This underpass was blocked even worse. It was narrower and too many cars were trying to get through it. The avenue was backed up with cars arriving from the west, but adding to the gridlock, traffic from Sawtelle was also trying to merge into the sluggish flow.

"Can we get through there?" asked Hu.

James considered it. There was a cluster of motorcyclists blocking the sidewalk that went through the underpass. It didn't look like they were getting by. Something blocking them on the other side, maybe—?

"No," said James. "Too narrow." That was the most convenient excuse, but he was still thinking about the violence they'd just escaped. This was another potential disaster—another riot looking for a place to happen. He pointed north instead. "Let's see if we can get across. We'll take Wilshire." There weren't any other options.

They pushed their bikes forward. Most of the going was single-file, but there was still room to make it through. Despite their urgency, most of the drivers here were leaving almost enough space for the two cyclists to navigate carefully across the intersection. Their bike trailers bumped a few fenders where they had to push between the lanes, but aside from one red-faced future stroke victim who shouted at them for blocking his nonexistent way forward, most drivers pretended to ignore them.

And then they were on Sawtelle again, pedaling into the Veterans Administration Healthcare Center. Where Sawtelle dead-ended inside the campus, before a cluster of shining white buildings, there was a concrete path cutting directly north, and it was wide enough for them to pedal. They weren't the only cyclists with this idea; a few others raced past them. But James and Hu stopped to walk their bikes because of the foot traffic—the old men in bathrobes and pajamas and shapeless sagging trousers.

In the rising heat of the July day, these ancient men trudged steadily north. They were clusters of fragile age, old but determined. Most of them were using canes or struggling with walkers, a few pushed others in wheelchairs, a few were coming with their IV stands, but all of them were heading slowly and deliberately toward Wilshire. They smelled of old age and soap.

These were the leftovers, the forgotten warriors, the heroes of yesterday—the abandoned ones, abandoned one more time. No one had remembered they were here. There was no evacuation plan for them. The buses had never arrived, they'd been commandeered for the schoolchildren and for anyone else who could scramble aboard.

Maybe, when they reached the boulevard, someone would give them a ride. Or maybe they would just end up as a few more bodies in the long line of hopeful old men gathering along the side of the road, more zombies for the frightened drivers to ignore.

James and Hu passed them as quickly as they could—they tried hard not to meet their eyes, tried hard not to see their frail bodies and watery expressions. But one of the men stopped James with an outstretched hand. "You go. You go on, get out of here. Go and live. Find someone to love and live a glorious life." Another added, "But tell them about us. Tell them to remember. Please—" And a third, "Tell them how we were forgotten, betrayed, abandoned—" And a fourth, "And tell them to go fuck themselves too—"

Both James and Hu nodded and promised. "We will, we will."

They nodded and said yes to everything, they shook the trembling hands of those who reached out to them—and then they pushed on, a hard lump in their throats. They wanted to do more, but what could they do?

And then one of the old men called, "Jimmy, is that you?" Hearing his name, James stopped. Force of habit. He turned and looked.

A frail specter, dragging an IV stand, came wobbling, hobbling across the grass. "Jimmy, it's Grampa."

No, it wasn't. All of James' grandparents had passed a decade earlier. But still, he was startled enough to stop and stare.

Another old soldier came shuffling up. "It's all right, pay him no mind. He's—he doesn't know who anyone is anymore."

But Grampa had grabbed Jimmy's arm. "I knew you'd come," he said. "I told them, I told them you would come to see me—"

The other man shook his head. "Jimmy died. A long time ago. But he doesn't believe it. Or he forgets."

James said, "Hu, hold my bike." He dismounted, put his arms around the self-appointed Grampa. "I love you, Grampa. I'm sorry I waited so long to come and see you. I missed you so much. I have to go now. Your friends will take care of you. But I have to go. They need me at the . . . at the station, okay?"

The old man didn't want to let go. His frail hands trembled as he tried to hang onto his long-lost grandson, but Jimmy pulled away anyway, and finally Grampa said, "Okay, Jimmy. Okay. You be a good boy now. You tell your ma you saw me, okay?"

"Okay, Grampa." Jimmy gave the old man a quick hug, then pulled away just as quickly. He took hold of his bike again—

James mounted and they pedaled on.

"That was . . . that was a good thing you did."

"Triage," said James. "Goddammit."

Hu didn't answer.

They traveled past the line of old men, castoffs in a younger world, all of them struggling in the rising heat. As they turned right to go up the ramp to Wilshire Boulevard, even more old and frail men were gathering in a crowd. Some of them were weeping. Others were stepping into the traffic lanes, knocking on the windows of slow-moving vehicles. Others stood silently on the sidewalk, sunken in despair, gaunt and resigned in the heat of the day. Two looked like they were unconscious on the sidewalk. Here and there, car doors were opened for them—but not enough.

It was a nightmare.

They pushed past. Most of the old men ignored them. They were just two more bodies in the passing parade of people who couldn't or wouldn't help them.

A couple of the old men were shouting obscenities—mostly at the cars, but a few directed their streams of abuse at James and Hu. One hollered at Hu, "That's right, you dirty Jap, run away, run away—or we'll get you again like we did at Pearl Harbor—"

"I'm Chinese," said Hu, but the old man didn't care, or didn't hear. Hu followed James; they pushed on.

There were officers working the underpass here too, but without the same frustration and confusion that they had seen a mile further south at Santa Monica Boulevard. The officers here were also directing traffic up onto the southbound lanes of the 405, pointing cars up the off-ramp, shouting and waving them forward, even demanding they use that side of the highway as an additional northbound escape. Some drivers looked reluctant, this felt *wrong*, but they followed the officers' directions and headed up the off-ramp anyway.

The traffic inched along slowly, jerking spasmodically, filling every spare foot of space—but it moved—only a little at a time, but it *moved* with a single-minded purpose. If these vehicles could get far enough north, far enough up the Sepulveda Pass, these drivers would likely survive.

James and Hu lowered their heads and pushed themselves forward as quickly as they could. They blinded themselves to the naked desperation and pushed east, somehow getting through the traffic at the ramps and into the cooling shadow of the underpass. They didn't linger, the place smelled of fumes. Finally, they were out to the other side and across Sepulveda. They threaded their way through the cars on this side.

When they came to the giant Federal building on the south side of the boulevard, a massive white monolith, Hu looked to James, an unspoken question in his glance. They looked to the crowds gathering at the structure, surrounding its entrances, including another legion of old men. James shook his head, an unspoken reply. Bad idea. Not gonna be enough room for everyone . . . and still too close to the shoreline.

They pushed on.

A long row of tall buildings lay ahead of them, not quite skyscrapers in the modern sense, but tall enough to be imposing—tall enough to look like safety.

Already, the foot traffic was getting thick—businessmen, residents, students from the UCLA campus a mile north—the buildings were filling up. The top floors would be crowded.

When James and Hu finally got to the intersection of Westwood and Wilshire Boulevards, they hit a new obstacle—a huge gaping hole in the ground that was the excavation for the Westwood terminus of the Purple Line, the latest extension to the Los Angeles subway system.

If it had been completed, if the tracks had been laid and energized, the city could have evacuated another half-million people. But today, it was a gaping promise. Unfinished. Empty. And shortly to be flooded, inundated, and scraped away by a bulldozer of debris—

James stopped himself.

Don't go there. Just don't.

He checked Google Maps, nodded, pointed to the right. "We'll take the side streets."

A block south, along Wellworth Avenue, they could easily pedal east again. It was a residential area, mostly one- or two-story houses. Traffic was thick here, but not impossible—just a steady stream of cars, pushing slowly east. James and Hu kept to the sidewalks; there weren't many other riders here, and they made the best progress since leaving Venice.

James glanced at his watch. They were behind schedule, but there was still time. They were going to make it.

If there were no more shootings.

They followed the side streets—Wellworth, Warner, Ashton, Holmby—past the worst of the jams, and then they were back on Wilshire. It cut easily through the golf courses, but it was an uphill slog, and the bikes and trailers were heavily loaded.

Halfway up the hill, Hu called for a stop. He opened a fresh water bottle, drank half of it, and passed it to James, who finished it . . . and tossed the bottle over the fence onto the green. "Always wanted to do that."

"Jimmy—?"

"Yeah?"

"It's awfully hot."

"Yeah—" But he knew that wasn't what Hu meant. Their shirts were sweat-stained, they were both damp with the effort of pedaling with the extra weight. The uphill part was just an excuse to stop.

"The bike-trailers," said Hu. "The tanks—"

"I know—"

"They're holding us back—"

James fell silent. He took a deep breath, then another, tried to compose himself. Hu was frustrated. And when Hu was frustrated, then James got frustrated, because he had to talk Hu down. But this was different.

"I think we can make it."

"I don't think I can."

"We have to try." James pointed. "This part is all uphill. Once we get to the top, it'll be an easy ride down the other side."

Hu looked past James, up toward the crest. It really wasn't that far. He knew he could make it—but it wasn't the top of the hill he was worried about. It was the rest of the distance, to Pearl's house and then to safety. He felt overwhelmed, almost to the point of tears.

"Jimmy, you know I'd never ask you to—"

James leaned his bike against the fence, went quickly back to Hu. "Squeak, I know, you wouldn't ask unless there was no other way. And it's the same for me. I wouldn't ask you if I could see any other way. But I don't think we can leave any of this behind." He stopped himself. "Wait—"

Beside them, the traffic chugged slowly past. James ignored the curious stares of several small children leaning out the open windows of a passing SUV.

"Okay, look," James said. "Let's put only our must-haves into our backpacks, okay? All our paperwork, money, phones, your computer, all the stuff we can't leave behind. The stuff in the dry bags, right? And then let's see how much farther we can get with the rest. Is that okay?"

Hu nodded reluctantly. It was a concession. Not the one he wanted, but he had to trust James—James was the better planner. He started thinking what he could repack. It wasn't much. He'd already put the most important things in his knapsack. Some of the weight was water bottles. He felt damp and sweaty all over. For a moment, he dreamt of the long luxurious shower he could take when they got back home.

Then he realized he would never see that shower again. Abruptly he realized he had to pee.

Hu looked around. They were at least a mile from anything that might serve as a rest stop—the hell with it—he turned to the chain-link fence, lifted up the left side of his shorts and let loose a personal torrent, splashing at the fence. James joined him, yanked down his own shorts, and for a moment, their two streams arced toward the silent green of the golf course.

Hu giggled.

"What?"

"Don't cross the streams—"

"You see too many movies."

"You watch 'em with me."

"Hey!" a distant voice called. "Stop that!"

They looked through the fence. Three middle-aged men in bright-colored shirts and pants were playing golf, totally oblivious to the evacuation. One of them was waving his golf club angrily at them.

"Didn't you hear the news?" James called. "There's a tsunami coming in."

"Don't you believe it," one of them called back. "Just another drill."

"Fake news," muttered the second.

The third said, "I'd rather die golfing than running—"

"Have it your way," said James, pulling up his pants, and suddenly doubting. What if they were right—?

No. They were wrong, he wished he could believe them, but they were wrong—and in a couple hours, they'd find out how wrong. He wondered if they'd make it to the eighteenth hole in time, shook his head in disbelief, turned back to Hu. "Idiots."

Hu smiled weakly. "Suddenly, I don't feel so stupid."

"Yeah. Let's get out of here."

Refreshed by their rest, rehydrated by the water, they made it to the crest of the hill, then half-coasted, half-pedaled down the other side.

They continued east on Wilshire Boulevard, past the Beverly Hilton Hotel to where it crisscrossed Santa Monica Boulevard. Navigating the wide diagonal intersection with Santa Monica wasn't as hard as James feared. Traffic was inching along here, but there was still room to thread the bikes between the ranks of cars.

Wilshire was a straight line east from there, a gilded belt around the waist of Beverly Hills, lined with elegant palm trees. Much of the traffic here was turning north at every opportunity, aiming for Benedict Canyon, Coldwater Canyon, any higher ground at all. A lesser but steady stream of vehicles pushed eastward and inland. At an average speed of ten miles per hour, there was still a chance for most of them to survive.

Overhead, the sky was filled with more helicopters than either James or Hu had ever seen. Police, news, rescue, fire, military, and private services as well. Some were monitoring, others were evacuating.

Here, the sidewalks were wide enough, they had room to ride—they were an incongruous sight pedaling through the most elegant district in Los Angeles. Elegant—and doomed. All the surrounding communities that kept these businesses thriving would be gone in less than two hours.

As James and Hu pedaled steadily east, they heard a continuous drone of chattering voices leaking from the radios of the vehicles they passed, bits of audio flotsam that refused to assemble into any kind of coherent narrative.

Here the pedestrian traffic was lighter. There were other cyclists on the road and on the sidewalk, but not a lot. Motorcycles growled between the rows of cars. Three people on Segways rolled past them. And surprisingly—for this neighborhood, anyway—they even saw a pair of homeless women, determinedly pushing their overloaded shopping carts eastward. There were buses too, all kinds, packed and overloaded, some with people even riding on the roofs, something Hu had never expected to see in America.

If anyone had expected last-minute desperate looting of Wilshire Boulevard's elegant storefronts, they would have been disappointed. Even those who might have been tempted were seeing survival as a much more useful priority.

The day was growing hotter, and this far inland, the hot yellow sun was shaded by a smoggy brown haze—a rising cloud of dust, stirred up by a million vehicles.

For some reason, James was reminded of a scene from Disney's *Fantasia.* The "Rite of Spring" segment. All those thirsty dinosaurs, plodding slowly east across an orange desert, toward a sanctuary that didn't exist, eventually dropping to the dirt and dying, leaving only their whitened bones as evidence they had ever existed. He wondered what future archaeologists would be digging up here, a thousand, ten thousand years in some unimaginable future.

"James?"

"Huh?"

"Are you all right?"

"Uh, yeah. I'm fine."

"It's time to stop. Drink some more water."

James shook his head to clear it. He rolled to a stop. Hu was right.

But they'd made it down the hill, past the golf course, past the Hilton, past the intersection, even past the Beverly Wilshire Hotel. What was that—two miles? Three? Whatever. He was starting to feel the exertion—not tired, not exhausted, but definitely, his muscles were tightening. He hoped Hu wouldn't mention the trailers again. He might be tempted to give in.

But Hu said nothing. He passed James a water bottle. James had to resist the temptation to gulp it all down. Instead, he sipped carefully, once, twice, a third time. "Where are we?" he asked, looking around.

"We just passed Robertson. We've still got another couple miles." Hu burrowed into his pack. "Do you want a protein bar?"

James nodded, held out his hand. He unwrapped the little granola brick and hesitated with the wrapper—then he realized how little difference it would make if he found a trash can here in Beverly Hills or not and let it fall to the sidewalk. He chewed and swallowed slowly.

Hu grabbed a water bottle and a protein bar for himself as well. "Do you think the tsunami is going to get this far?"

James didn't answer immediately. He chewed thoughtfully. "Well . . . if this wave is as big as the president said, a hundred feet high, it'll certainly get as far as the 405, but how much farther, I dunno, that's a lot of water. If it was less, then the 405 would be a pretty good breakwater—except around LAX, of course. The airport's just gonna disappear. But—" James frowned, picturing the geographical layout of the basin in his head. "But I don't think the 405 will stop it. Might slow it down a bit, but a lot of water is still going to get over it, under it, through it." He took another bite, still thinking. "Y'know, those underpasses are bottlenecks, they're going to generate a lot of pressure, all that water trying to force through. Anything directly east of any of them is probably gonna take a hit, and if the pressure is strong enough, the overpasses will certainly blow off. So yeah—it's gonna get this far. A hundred feet—it's just too much water."

Hu looked west, toward the beach, as if he could already see the onrushing catastrophe. He looked at his watch. "How far east do we have to get?"

James shrugged. "It's not just one wave. It could be several waves. You haven't seen the footage I've seen, from Sumatra and Fukushima. It's not what you think. It's not like a wave at the seashore, just bigger. It's like the whole ocean rises up in a flash flood that comes in for . . . I don't know, an hour? Maybe more? All that water pushing in behind. It has to go someplace, the path of least resistance.

"It's gonna hit hard, really hard. It's gonna knock loose, knock down, knock out everything it hits, pushing it all forward, like a horizontal avalanche. Everything loose, cars, boats, buses, everything that breaks free, trees and billboards and lamp posts, everything that collapses, houses, stores, buildings. All that water, it's going to drive that in like the front end of a bulldozer.

"It's gonna be bad. Real bad. Maybe those golfers had the right idea. Do what you love doing, right up to the end." He took another bite and waited for Hu's response.

Hu looked nervously to his watch, then back to James. "We're not gonna make it, are we? I mean, with Pearl. Where she is, she's awfully far from any hills—and we're running out of time."

"I know—" James said. He took another thoughtful bite, chewed for a moment, then spoke with his mouth half full. "But I've been thinking. There's that big black building, less than two blocks from Pearl's house. It's what?—ten stories high. We can get there, easy-peasy. The top two floors should be high enough."

"What about the bulldozer—?"

"There's a big building just to the west of it that should catch the brunt of the wave and most of the crap it's pushing."

"It'll be crowded—"

"Probably. But it's our best hope." James took another drink of water. Despite the grim conversation, he was still concentrating on energy and hydration. "Squeak. There has never been a mess like this before. It's gonna be—well, a challenge."

"We're gonna be on our own for a bit, won't we?"

"Yeah," said James sourly. "It's gonna be an adventure all right." He looked to the street, at the desperate stream of cars filling the boulevard. A terrible thought was finally becoming real.

"That bad, huh?" Hu asked.

"Worse than that," James said. "Worse than anyone can imagine. Hate to say it, but a lot of people are gonna die—"

And even as he said the words, he realized just how impossible an idea it was. He couldn't comprehend that all this—the cars, the buildings, the people, everything—was about to be wiped away. And yet, he couldn't deny it any longer. The magnitude of this thing—James couldn't speak it, but he realized that somehow he was still hoping that this was somehow all just a colossal mistake, a false alarm, and that maybe somehow—

He finished the last bite of his protein bar, took a last swallow of water, and tossed the empty bottle at a darkened storefront. It bounced harmlessly to the street.

"—But not us. Not today. Come on, let's go."

Two blocks west of La Cienega, James and Hu turned right on South Stanley Drive. Halfway down the second block stood a white two-story building. Once, it had once been a private residence, but now it was subdivided into three Tetris-shaped apartments, with a handicapped access ramp cutting through what had once been a lush front lawn.

At the bottom of the ramp, underneath the inevitable palm tree, Pearl sat waiting in a lightweight folding wheelchair. She had a carpetbag on her lap and she held the leash of a large, sloppy-looking beast that might have had some pit-bull in its parentage, but probably dumpster dog as well. She waved happily when she saw "the boys," James and Hu. They pedaled to a stop in front of her. Several cars passed them in the street, drivers looking for alternate routes.

James looked unhappily at the dog.

"Oh, don't mind Fluffy—he's just a big friendly goofball."

"Fluffy?" Hu raised an eyebrow.

"That's what we call him. His real name is—never mind. He's Joey's dog, but Joey's off in Bakersfield or somewhere, so we keep Fluffy when he's traveling. Mrs. Petersen hates it, but she's afraid to complain or we'll tell the city about her cats."

"Some people—"

"Tell me. She went screaming out of here with a dozen cat carriers the moment the president said tsunami. But the old bitch wouldn't take us. Didn't want to be in the same car with Fluffy. Selfish old bitch. And I just couldn't leave Fluffy behind. He's family."

James sighed. "I admire your gumption, Pearl, but sometimes—"

Pearl's expression changed then. "Honey, where's your car?"

"We didn't bring it," said Hu. He waved his hand to include the bicycles and the trailers. "This was faster."

"Are we in trouble—?" Pearl asked.

"I don't think so—" James pointed. The top of the LFP building was visible even from here. "We'll go up there. It's high enough. If the wave is only a hundred feet high when it hits the shore, by the time it gets this far inland, it'll have lost most of its power—"

"James! What are you talking about?" Pearl half-rose out of her chair. "Not a hundred feet! Three hundred!"

Both James and Hu stopped in mid-word. "What—?"

"*Three hundred feet!* It's what the guy on the internet is saying! The one in Hawaii—the one who measured it!"

"Oh, fuck—" That was Hu.

James didn't say anything. His expression went ashen. When he finally did speak, it was almost automatic. "No, no, it can't be, the president—"

"Honey, that sumbitch is just plain wrong. Or stupid. The guy on the internet is an actual geologist. He's the director of the Volcano Lab. Now, who ya gonna believe? The politician or the scientist?"

Hu touched James' arm. "What are we going to do?"

James ignored it. He leaned in, grabbed Pearl's arms, stared into her face, and almost shouted, "Are you certain? There are a lot of cranks on the internet."

She met his stare, unflinching. "James, honey—what do I do for a living? I do research, remember? For the studios. For that stupid movie where you two met. I didn't just google him. I did the whole data-dive. This isn't bullshit. He's for real. *Three hundred feet.*"

James released her, whirled away, furious. "Fuck," he said. "Fuck, fuck, fuck, fuckity-fuck, fuck, fuck." He turned to Hu. "Remember that map I hung in the office? The one that showed the effects of global warming—what the coast line would look like if all the ice caps melted and the sea level rose two hundred and sixty feet?"

Hu nodded. "Yeah. Everything up to Boyle Heights would be underwater."

"Yeah. Well, if this guy's right, this is gonna be worse."

Hu said, "Okay, okay, okay—but we're not dead yet. I've got an idea."

"It's too late—"

"No, it isn't." Hu pointed east. "The subway! The La Cienega station. It's across the street from the tower. Remember how excited Pearl got when it opened? If we can get onto a train, we can get all the way downtown in ten minutes, fifteen."

"And then what? We're still in the disaster zone."

"We'll do what you said. We'll figure something out." Hu rubbed his chin. "I dunno, maybe the Gold line out to Pasadena. Maybe Chris and Mark can put us up. They're always having those big sprawling house parties. If not, I dunno. Maybe Amtrak to my cousin in New Mexico? If we have to pitch the tent in some park, we can do that. But let's go."

"Oh, hell—if I'd known you boys didn't know, I'd have wheeled myself over—" Pearl's face crumpled. "Oh, boys, I'm so sorry. I'm so stupid, you could have gotten up into the hills by now—"

"Stop it, Pearl." That was James. "You're family. Shut up and let us rescue you!"

Just out of her field of vision, Hu tapped his watch meaningfully.

"Right," said James, as if the matter was finally settled. "So let's get out of here. Um—" He fumbled with one of the ropes on his bike trailer. "Here, tie this to—um, loop it around yourself—and we'll pull you."

In reply, Pearl handed him Fluffy's leash. "Here. Tie this around your handlebars. The monster-dog will help pull."

"Really?"

"Really. Let him lead. Don't worry, people will get out of his way. Real fast."

"We're gonna be a whole circus parade," said James, but he took the leash.

Fluffy led the way. He pulled his own weight, and half of Pearl's too—up the side streets back to Wilshire, a block east and the subway station was directly ahead. The station had only been open a few months, a promise for the future, but this would be its last day of operation. Even if the system survived, there would be nothing left above ground for anyone to come to.

James was right, they did look like a parade. But Pearl was right too. People saw them coming, saw Fluffy grunting and slobbering in the lead, and they moved fast to get out of the way.

They had to wait a few minutes to cross the street. James kept glancing at his watch. Hu put his hand on James' arm. "It's okay. We're gonna make it. We will."

"Cutting it close, too close," James muttered.

"Sloan's teddy . . . "

"Sloan looks terrible in a teddy," James said, then added. "Halloween. Before your time."

"Oh. Dear."

"Let's go. Light or no light—" They pushed their way into the street. The huge garbage truck waiting to turn north had left enough room for them to squeeze through. The next driver, a frightened-looking woman, had opened her car door and was standing in the street, still clutching the handle, looking confused and desperate. "There's not enough time, is there?"

"Come with us. The subway's still running—"

"The subway?" Her confusion increased. "Los Angeles has a subway—?"

Hu pointed past her. "It's right there—"

The woman grabbed her purse and hurried after them. A few others followed—a black woman dragging two small children, a portly man with his arms full of file folders, the driver of the garbage truck as well.

The elevator to the lower level wasn't working and even if it had been, neither James nor Hu wanted to risk getting stuck in it. The station's turnstiles were frozen open for the evacuation.

The escalators weren't working either, but there was a wide staircase and most of the travelers with baggage were hurrying down it. Hu waited with the bikes while James maneuvered Pearl's chair down the stairs. Pearl held Fluffy's leash, his stub of a tail wagged in excitement, he was having a great time. He looked around the platform eagerly—all these great new playmates—but even the nearest people were keeping a careful distance.

James came trotting back up the stairs, and he and Hu began working the bikes and the trailers down. A couple of people grumbled at them as they passed—but they were dragging their own bags down the steps, so James and Hu ignored the comments.

The bottom level was crowded, but not packed, not insane, not panicky. Most of the people who had thought to escape by subway had already gone. These were stragglers, people who had finally abandoned their vehicles. Many were carrying backpacks or dragging suitcases on rollers.

The overhead signs were promising trains arriving at this terminus every four minutes. Hu pointed. "See, we'll have time."

James started to say something, thought better of it, and shut up instead. He scanned the faces of the crowd, looking for signs of desperation or panic. He could still hear the screams and the gunshots from the Santa Monica underpass.

UNION STATION

The Red Line and Purple Line trains were arriving so fast, one after the other, that sometimes as many as three trains would have to wait in the tunnel while the first in line unloaded. As fast as each train unloaded, it was sent out again.

The outbound Red Line trains went directly to the Hollywood and Highland station, picking up passengers there and taking them out to the

North Hollywood station on Lankershim Boulevard. The area surrounding the Universal City station had already reached overload capacity.

Inbound, all the trains were staggered to pick up passengers from the most overloaded stations. As soon as any train was packed to capacity, it went straight to Union Station. It was a frustrating experience for those waiting on the platforms, watching the densely packed trains screech by without stopping, but every available train was running, and most people were able to board a train in less than twenty minutes.

The Purple Line trains were on a similar schedule, with most going directly to the Wilshire/La Cienega station, picking up passengers from the most desperate locations first.

Several trains were running direct shuttle service to the Seventh Street station, the terminus of both the Expo Line and the Blue Line from Long Beach. While many evacuees assumed they would be relatively safe this far inland, most were taking advantage of the train service departing from Union Station.

At Union Station, every available train—both passenger and freight—was loaded to capacity. Most were heading north through Glendale and Burbank, all the way to the Burbank airport, where a tent city was being set up on the top level of the parking structure. Others were heading west with stops in the San Fernando Valley and Simi Valley. Ventura County was an uncertain risk. Although parts of it were sheltered by the Santa Monica mountains, there wasn't a convenient train service. Other trains headed north to Santa Clarita, or as far east as Ontario. The closest returned for another trip as soon as they were unloaded.

Additional relocations would be necessary after the initial evacuation. Las Vegas, Phoenix, Tucson, Salt Lake City, Albuquerque, and other cities were already making plans to receive refugees. But the initial goal was to get as many people as possible out of the disaster zone as fast as possible.

In the last half-hour before impact, police and fire rescue would withdraw their personnel and any vehicles still not evacuated. When further evacuation operations became too risky, the subway trains would also be removed to their safest locations.

The last train from Union Station was being held for emergency workers. As soon as the tsunami reached San Clemente Island, a five-minute alarm would sound and the train would pull out before the onrushing water overwhelmed the coastline. It would not wait for stragglers,

That was the plan, anyway.

Just one little glitch.

Roy Jeffers.

He did not look like a hero. He did not intend to be a hero.

He was a skinny little bastard (accident of birth), stuck behind thick glasses and a scowl. He was also a stubborn son of a bitch. He had issues with authority, and the surest way to get him to do anything was to tell him, "No, you can't."

Roy Jeffers had another bad habit as well. He was a rescuer.

He had a long history of opening his house in south-central Los Angeles to anyone needing a place to crash—cousins, friends, stray dogs, the occasional feral cat, and once in a while, even a girlfriend. (And once, as an experiment, a boyfriend.)

At the moment, however, he was single, about to be made homeless by the tsunami, and genuinely resentful that the evacuation was going to take a horrendous toll on those who could least afford it, his entire demographic. People of Color was the current euphemism. Among friends, he'd occasionally rant, "First we were Colored People. Then we were Negro, then we were Black, then African-American. Now we're People of Color. Progress my black ass!" But he didn't have a lot of friends, so it wasn't a rant that many had heard.

Adding to his annoyance was his realization that as a driver for the Purple Line, he was servicing many of the wealthier neighborhoods along Wilshire Boulevard, where if he had been working the Blue Line, he would have been rescuing his own neighbors. Even the knowledge that the Crenshaw connection directly served part of his community did not alleviate his smoldering anger.

But—

The knowledge that the Crenshaw connection directly served part of his community had somehow transformed his annoyance into a specific commitment. He wasn't going to abandon anybody, and he didn't care what color they were. He was going to do the job anyway.

So when he unloaded at Union Station and his supervisor, Molly Cantway, waved to him and said, "Okay, that's it, Roy. Take your train out to the service yard," Roy Jeffers said no.

"There are still people out there. My people—" he insisted. "*Our* people."

Cantway shook her head. "Roy, I am not sending any more trains out. There's no time."

"Then let's not waste it arguing," Roy said. "I'm going."

"You do and I'll fire you."

"Ain't gonna be no job after today anyway—"

Jeffers pushed the control lever forward. His train rolled west into the tube. Cantway didn't know whether to be annoyed at the inevitable loss of a Purple Line train—or admire Jeffers for his stupidity.

On the other hand, there probably wasn't going to be much of a subway system after this. After Hurricane Sandy, parts of the New York system were down for five years. This was going to be worse than that. Maybe Los Angeles would never have a subway again.

Cantway watched as the last car of Jeffers' train disappeared into the dark tunnel. If that damn fool was able to outrun the incoming flood, he'd be a hero. If not—well, he'd get a nice obituary. And maybe even a funeral, if they ever recovered a body.

Somebody called for her attention and she turned back to the more immediate problem—getting the last of these people upstairs and onto a train out of the city.

And very shortly, herself as well.

She crossed herself and went back to work.

The subway platform was filling up. More and more people were realizing that an eastbound train might be their only remaining hope of escape.

A steady stream of future refugees came down the stairs, or walking down the frozen escalator. As the crowd became ever more dense, people jostled for position, all wanting to make sure they'd be able to board the next train.

Most kept checking the overhead arrival signs, but even before the sign flashed, "Arriving now," they could feel the breeze of its approach, as it forced the air from the tunnel ahead of it, then a distant howl echoing out of the tube, a glimmer of light that ballooned into a glare, and finally the train came screeching into the station.

As soon as the doors slid open, the crowd pushed in. Hu held the bikes and James pushed Pearl forward. Fluffy grumbled at the people pushing past him. Abruptly, a female police officer blocked their way. She was short, all muscle, and she wore a don't-fuck-with-me expression. Her nametag identified her as Officer Reese.

"You can't take that dog on the train," she said.

Almost immediately Pearl began wailing loudly. James recognized the performance, he'd seen it before, an award-worthy rendition of Frightened Old Crippled Lady. It usually worked. "Oh no, no," cried Pearl, clutching her heart. "I can't leave him. He's my service dog. He doesn't bite. He's big and friendly. I don't know what I'd do without him!" She was loud, very loud, and people already aboard the train, or still trying to board, turned to look. Pearl was playing to the court of public opinion.

Reese was immovable. "Sorry, ma'am. That animal looks dangerous. We can't take any chances—"

James started to object. "You want to leave him here to die?"

But Pearl spoke first. "No, no, James, we must obey the officer. Officer—" She peered forward. "—Officer Reese." She shifted her performance from Frightened-Old-Lady to Frightened-Old-And-Confused-Lady. She held up the end of the leash, offering it to the officer. "Officer Reese, will you hold him till we get back?" Pearl patted the dog's head. "Here, Slobberchops, go with the nice lady."

Fluffy's posture changed dramatically. He was suddenly alert, suddenly eager—he curled back his upper lip, revealing enough teeth for a piano keyboard. He grunted and drooled and pulled at the leash as if someone had just announced fresh peasant for dinner.

Officer Reese put her hand on the hilt of her gun.

"No, no, don't do that! He's just being friendly. Honest. He just wants to play."

Officer Reese must have been painfully aware that all eyes were on her. And the clock was ticking. Fluffy grumbled impatiently. Reese blinked—and took a step back and aside. "Oh, the hell with it. Just keep a tight leash on him."

As James pushed Pearl into the already jammed subway car, those nearest squeezed back to make room, especially room for Fluffy. James bent to her ear and whispered, "Slobberchops?"

Pearl whispered back. "That's his real name. When you say it, he gets ready to play. That was his smile. Works every time."

"Nice." James let go of the wheelchair, turned back to Hu. "Come on—"

Hu gestured. The bikes? "There's no room—"

"Leave them. Grab your case. Come on—"

"You sure, James—?"

"Just do it!"

Hu let go of the bikes, grabbed his most important bag, and started to board, but Officer Reese stepped in ahead of him, into the last available space, blocking his way. "Sorry. This one's full."

James started to object. "But he's my—"

She half-turned. "You got the dog, don't push your luck. There's one more train coming, he can get on that one."

James made a decision. He leaned quickly down to Pearl. "Give 'em hell, sweetheart." Then, "If he stays, I stay." He pushed past Reese and stepped off the train.

As the subway doors closed, Officer Reese glared at them both. James didn't care. He grabbed Hu. "Wedding or not, you're my husband, and I'm not going anywhere without you." Then he kissed Hu passionately.

Which surprised them both—because James had never kissed Hu in public anywhere before.

They weren't alone on the subway platform. There were at least thirty or forty others, the last few stragglers. Several of them were screaming at the departing train they'd been unable to board. A couple had even been pushed out as the doors closed in front of them.

"You selfish bastards!" Somebody else yelled, "That was the last train." Followed by, "Come on, upstairs. The roof of the—"

His words were drowned out, running for the stairs. There was still time to get to the roof of the tallest nearby buildings. It might be enough. But if Pearl was right—and Pearl was rarely wrong—it probably wouldn't be.

James looked to Hu. "You want to follow them?"

"She said there was one more train coming."

"Do you believe her?"

"She wasn't Miss Congeniality, was she?"

"More like, I dunno, Miss Convenience Store." James looked to the stairs, looked down the track, looked to the stairs again.

Hu said, "Are we fucked?"

James didn't need to consider the question. The answer was obvious. "Well . . . yes. Probably."

Hu looked at his watch. "The water is probably pulling away from the shore by now."

"Uh, no," James said. "It's not gonna work like that. Not this one. That's what they were explaining while you were in the shower. A big part of the island fell into the sea, it pushed an equivalent volume of water outward. The first thing that hits is the wave. Afterward, more waves. Like the whole Pacific is sloshing."

"Should we wait here? Or . . . ?"

Before James could answer, a Korean woman came dragging a little girl, five or six, maybe seven, running down the stairs. "She was out playing, I couldn't find her! Are we too late? Are the trains still running—?"

And as if in answer, they both felt a rising breeze.

"One more," Hu said to the woman. "The last one."

"Oh, thank God, thank God."

Down the tunnel, the distant light became an onrushing glare. The train's horn howled like an electric banshee. It came screeching into the station, the doors sliding open almost immediately.

James and Hu let the woman rush past them, the little girl almost flying like a rag doll, then they pushed their bikes into the subway car. The bikes and the attached trailers filled the space at the end of the car designed for bikes and wheelchairs and luggage on wheels. As soon as the doors slid closed and the train lurched into motion, James looked to Hu and smiled. For the first time today, since walking out of their small house in Venice Beach, James allowed himself the smallest bit of confidence. Finally, they were on their way. If they could beat the onrushing wave to Union Station, maybe.

Would there be a train waiting there? Maybe. Maybe. Otherwise . . .

Without stopping, the subway could get downtown in seven minutes, probably less. If they stopped for passengers, if there were people still waiting at each station, and there probably would be, then you'd have to add a minute for each station, maybe even two or three for braking, loading, accelerating again—okay, so figure maybe fifteen minutes at worst.

James wasn't certain about the speed of the onrushing water, somewhere between ten or twenty miles per hour, but that was an ordinary tsunami. A mega-tsunami? That was a whole different kettle of physics, but he had to believe they had a chance.

Union Station was sixteen miles inland from Santa Monica. The waters should be slowing that far inland, but—again, the physics on this were unknown. Okay, doing the math in his head, fifteen minutes to get downtown, maybe there's another ten or fifteen minutes margin at Union Station. If Pearl was right, there would be that one last train for evacuees and emergency workers. They'd probably have to abandon the bikes and take only what they could carry. James studied what they'd brought, already sorting it in his head.

The train stopped at the Fairfax station; there was a larger crowd here, everyone who couldn't fit into the previous train. But there was room. At least a dozen more people pushed into the car. James and Hu pulled themselves back against one side. The woman and her little girl stood across from them, the little girl staring curiously at their bicycles. The doors closed and the train lurched forward, quickly gaining speed and rushing eastward toward La Brea.

"What's that?" the little girl asked, pointing at the air tank on James' bike-trailer.

"It's my rocket-pack," said James. "For when I'm being rocket-man. Like in the song. Do you know the song?"

"No it isn't," the girl said. "It's an air tank. And you're being silly."

"Well, if you knew it was an air tank, why did you ask?" James pointed at her, as if catching her in a game of tag. She giggled and buried her face in her mother's side.

"What's your name, sweetheart?"

That was enough. She stopped hiding and turned back. It was all a game. "Julia. What's yours?"

"I'm James." And then, for no reason he could understand, maybe because he just didn't care anymore, he added, "And this is my boyfriend. We're going to get married. His name is Hu."

Julia looked at Hu curiously. "Who?" she asked. "Like Doctor Who?"

"No," Hu said. "Just Hu. Like boo-hoo without the boo."

"Oh, okay." And then she said, "Could I be your flower girl? I did it for my cousin's wedding."

That's when Julia's mother put her hand on the little girl's shoulder, pulled her back. "That's enough, Julia. Don't bother those men."

Something about the way the woman said "those men"—James sensed her disapproval. Her expression had hardened.

"It's okay, ma'am. Just being friendly. We're all in this together." But he turned away anyway. Maybe another time, another place, he might have said something more. But not here, not now. There was still the problem of this time and this place.

Hu put his hand on James' arm. "What's the matter?"

"Nothing—"

"You should tell that to your face."

"I was just . . . doing the math in my head."

"Are we all right?"

"Should be."

Hu knew James too well. He recognized the lie. But he said nothing. Neither of them said anything until they reached the La Brea station.

This platform wasn't as crowded as the platforms had been at Fairfax and La Cienega stations. Fewer people here believed they were in danger. Maybe they were right. Or maybe they'd believed that they would find safety on their roofs.

The train was momentarily delayed in pulling out—there was a last minute rush, someone up ahead was holding a door and calling something to the motorman. The reason was quickly apparent. Nearly a dozen people, including several police officers, came charging down the stairs and across the platform—they pushed into the forward cars.

As the train pulled out again, Hu looked to his watch. "The wave, the first one. It just hit." He held up his phone for James to see. "No wi-fi down here, but I downloaded the sim while we were getting Pearl to the subway."

James studied the screen, a blue stain spreading inland. "You think it's accurate?"

"It's the one all the links pointed to. It's that scientist in Hawaii. It's supposed to be the most accurate geographic model. If his timeline is correct, our house is gone, the Third Street Mall—" Hu looked at the map. "Everything up to Bundy. Do you think the 405 might slow it down?"

James shook his head. "Not a chance, not if the wave is as high as that guy said."

"Well, Pearl said he passed the sniff test. And she is the research queen." Hu frowned at his phone. "I wish we had wi-fi down here."

"I don't."

"We could see what the news choppers are broadcasting—"

"I don't need to see it." James said. "I don't want those pictures in my head. Do you? Give me your phone—"

"Huh?"

"Give me your phone."

Hu handed it over. "Why?"

James didn't bother to answer. He pulled out his own phone and shoved both into a watertight bag, then slipped it into his backpack.

"Really?"

"Just a precaution."

"Uh-uh. You're thinking of something."

James lowered his voice. "When the wave hits, if it reaches the Purple Line before we're in the safe zone, that water's gonna go down into the stations and flood the tunnel. We may not be safe down here."

"How long till it catches up with us?"

James stopped. He hadn't considered the question. He'd been so focused on just getting to Pearl, just getting her to the subway, just getting everyone aboard a train, just outrunning the wave front—he hadn't thought much beyond that. He frowned in thought, trying to decide what he could say—and whether or not he should say it.

"James. Answer me. Can this train outrun it?"

James didn't reply immediately. He took a deep breath. Finally, he reached across and put his hand on Hu's arm, sliding it all the way up to his partner's shoulder. "We're making good time, Squeak. A mile a minute. We're moving faster than the wave front—"

Hu reached over and put his hand on James's. Quietly he said, "I looked at the video—the simulation. It looks like the water comes in awfully fast. Fifty miles an hour, maybe even faster—"

James thought hard. Finally, he admitted, "It's plumbing. It's physics. It's everything. It's the depth of the water, how much volume on the surface, how big the tunnel is, and how much pressure—" He trailed off, trying to visualize the problem.

"If there's a hundred feet of water above us—" He was thinking aloud now. "I don't usually dive that deep. A hundred feet, maybe a hundred thirty, that's pretty much the limit. At a hundred feet, that's 3 atmospheres, 4 counting the weight of the air above the water, 44 PSI—pounds per square inch. That's a lot of pressure. If there's that much water, it'll be coming in fast, over the streets and through the tunnel. And if the water's higher, there'll be even more pressure. It'll move even faster." Seeing the look on Hu's face, James stopped himself.

"We're gonna get hosed, aren't we?" Hu said. He kept his voice soft, trying not to attract the attention of the other passengers.

James realized his mistake then. He tried to cover quickly. "Only if it hits, only if it hits—" It wasn't enough.

Hu closed his eyes against the mental picture, against the rising turmoil of emotions that were suddenly flooding up inside him, fear and anger and something unidentifiable. His expression collapsed and suddenly, he was sobbing. "I'm sorry, Bubble."

"What for—?"

"For . . . everything. For the subway. It was a stupid idea—"

"No, sweetheart, no. It was a good idea. A really good idea. You'll see. We'll be okay."

But Hu refused to be reassured. The moment was reawakening his panic—that same panic he'd felt that day in the tank at Paramount. And this time, there wouldn't be anybody who could save either of them.

James slid his hand up Hu's shoulder, putting his palm on the back of Hu's neck—their own private gesture of reassurance. He pulled him into a hug and whispered, "Hell or high water, Squeak. I promise."

Hu pulled back, just enough to smile at him.

The train screeched and rocketed through the dark tunnel, but James and Hu didn't notice, didn't care. They had retreated into a private space between their shining eyes, their own special world of connection.

After a moment, Hu pulled away, recovering enough to reach into the pocket of his jeans. He pulled out the small velvet-covered box, opened it, withdrew the larger ring and slid it onto James' finger. "This is not the way I wanted to do it, this is awful, but . . . I take thee, James D. Liddle, as my awfully wedded husband, forever and ever, and for all the days of my life."

James took the box from Hu, took the second ring and likewise slid it onto Hu's finger. "I take thee, Hu Son, to be my husband, to be my lawfully bedded husband, forever and ever, and for all the days of my life."

They looked into each other's eyes again, trying to make the moment last forever. Finally James leaned forward and gently kissed Hu. He wanted to kiss him more passionately, but it wasn't necessary, not here—not with so many strangers watching. He hadn't realized they had attracted an audience. Several people applauded and cheered, but not the uncertain Korean woman still clutching the little girl close to her.

There were tears forming in Hu's eyes. He said, "This is the real one, Bubble, but I still want a ceremony." He whispered, "After all, we've already got a flower girl. I mean, if her mother will let her."

It was too much, all too much. James finally laughed. "We're about to lose the house, the car, the motorcycle, our business—we still don't know if we're going to survive—" He couldn't help himself, the words came tumbling out. "—And here we are, this is the happiest day of my life."

"It's certainly going to be one to remember—"

And that's when the subway train lurched.

• • •

The train lurched as if it had gone over a speed bump. Someone gasped, someone else screamed. Then the train roared on, faster than before.

"What was that—?" Hu had to raise his voice to be heard.

James shook his head. "Dunno. Felt like a power glitch to me."

"Do you think they're shutting down the grid?"

"Makes sense they would—"

"But not the subway—"

"We're still rolling—"

Hu opened his mouth, not quite a yawn, something else. "James—?"

"What?"

"My ears just popped."

"Yeah." James forced his own yawn as well. "Mine too."

"What would—?" But Hu already knew the answer.

"Air pressure," said James. "The water is definitely in the tunnel. It's coming in fast, compressing the air—"

"It's gonna hit us, isn't it—"

James didn't answer. He looked down to the rear end of the car, but there was no view out the back. Even if there had been, there were too many people in the way. He turned around to his bike, pulled his divebelt off the trailer, made sure his knife was in its sheath. He pulled Hu to his side. "Face your bike, now. If you have to, throw yourself over the tank. Hide it from view."

"What? Why—?" And then understanding. "Oh." And then, "Oh, shit—"

"Yeah," James finished buckling his divebelt around his waist. "It's gonna get ugly."

"James—"

"There's nothing we can do—"

Hu grabbed his arm. "We can do something. We've got two regulators on each rig. We can save Julia and her mom."

James wanted to argue, but Hu was right. He stepped over to the Korean woman, looked directly into her terrified eyes. "Come stand next to us. Both of you. Please." He reached out and touched her elbow. It was enough. Still clutching her daughter, she moved closer to the bikes.

"Listen to me," said James. He lowered his voice, almost to a whisper. "I'm a SCUBA professional. The wave is coming, it's going to flood this car. When the water hits, it's going to get panicky in here, but each of the tanks has two mouthpieces and there's enough air here for four people, Hu and myself—and both of you. You'll be okay if you do what I say. Here's what you need to know. Are you listening, Julia?"

The little girl nodded, her eyes wide.

"Okay, when it's time, Hu's going to give you a mouthpiece. We don't have a mask for you, so you're gonna want to close your eyes and just concentrate on breathing as slowly as you can. Take really long, really slow, breaths, in and out, only through the mouthpiece, really slow—okay?"

Julia nodded solemnly.

"Now, remember, I want you to keep your eyes closed and just concentrate on breathing—" Julia looked confused. James leaned down and whispered in her ear. "Okay, here's how to do it. You count a hundred breaths to yourself, because that's how long it takes. And if the water still hasn't gone down, then you start over and count to a hundred again. You might have to do that more than once, but that's how Hu and I are gonna do it—" He straightened and turned to the mother. "Did you get all that? You and I will share the other tank—"

The woman started to say something, an objection—?

James held up his hand. "Don't say anything. Just stand here. Turn away from anyone else. Both of you. Keep your backs to them. And—"

The subway lurched again. This time, the car bumped as if something had struck it from behind. Someone at the other end of the car screamed, several people screamed, both men and women—

Something lifted the rear of the car off the tracks, tilting them forward. Outside there were sparks—the train was slowing, there was no more power to the wheels—and then there was light outside, flickering light—the subway train was careening into the Wilshire/Western station and angry brown water flooded up onto the platform from the tracks. More water poured down the stairways and escalators, battering the walls and the train with debris, all of it rising rapidly and rocking the car with its force. The air smelled suddenly *wet*.

The other passengers, mostly men, began shouting and pushing, scrambling at and over each other. Muddy water was already flooding into the car from underneath. Men were shouting, several were trying to force open the doors, trying to escape. Others were demanding they stop, terrified because the darkness outside the train was already rising past the windows—

And then someone finally pushed the doors open and the flood—cold, salty, and gritty—came roaring in, pummeling and pounding, an inescapable torrent. People screamed and floundered, pushing at each other, climbing over each other, trampling anyone smaller, fighting their way through the current, desperate to get up the station stairs toward the air they imagined was waiting for them.

And then the last of the lights went out.

Green emergency lights flickered on, self-powered, but they weren't enough. And they didn't last. They were extinguished one by one by the rising muddy water.

James and Hu were already pulling the bungee cords off the bikes, off the tanks. They fumbled in the gloom, depending on experience and muscle memory.

Hu pushed the first regulator at Julia; the water was up to her chest. She grabbed the mouthpiece with both hands, pushed it into her mouth. James had already pulled Julia's mother to the other bike—yanking the whole rig off the bike trailer, he shoved a regulator toward the terrified woman, then helped her get it into her mouth as the water rose to her neck. He looked to Hu, who gave him a quick thumbs-up, pushing his own regulator into his mouth.

Hu rummaged in his case, triumphantly pulled out two headlamps, and pulled one over his head. Right, James thought, we're going to need those! His own facemask had a headlamp built in, but he felt around in his case for the other lamps. He slipped one of them over Julia's mother's head, started to hand her the second one for Julia—

"Please, sir—me too, please—"

James grabbed his facemask and pulled it down over his eyes just as the water came rising up over his chin. He turned and saw a frightened young teen, a black boy in a red T-shirt. The boy bobbed up desperately, his hand out for help. "Please—"

"We'll have to share—"

"Okay, yes, okay—"

James held his mouthpiece to the boy, they were bumping up against the top of the car. "Long slow breaths, okay. Two, three breaths—into the mouthpiece, both in and out. Then it's my turn. Okay?"

"Okay." The boy took the mouthpiece just as the water forced the last of the air out of the subway car. James put the last headlamp on him and switched it on. Then he turned to his left, looking to make sure Hu was all right.

He wasn't.

There was a struggle going on. James couldn't see far in the murky water, but one thing was clear. Someone was fighting Hu for the regulator. Someone else was trying to get to Julia. She was curled up in a ball, holding her regulator tightly in both hands.

James kicked off, directly head-butting into Julia's attacker, pushing him backward toward the open subway door. Outside the rushing water surged past the train, filling the station and pushing into the next bore. James head-butted the man again, forcing him into one side of the open door. The current grabbed him, yanked him away, and he went flailing into the turbulence, disappearing into the dark and muddy gloom. James had to grab a pole to keep from being pulled after him. Desperately, he grabbed the overhead bar and worked his way back to Hu.

Hu's eyes were wide, his mouth bubbling open. The stranger had gotten the regulator away from him. Hu was grabbing futilely for it—it was his drowning nightmare all over again, but there was no James at his side.

The stranger was holding Hu at arm's length, while sucking greedily for air. Hu saw the man pulling away into darkness—until one of James' arms came reaching around the stranger's chest and another hand sliced across his throat, releasing a cloud of red-brown darkness, expanding outward like inky smoke. The man stiffened, choked, gasped, struggled, and thrashed away in the dark, pummeled by the rushing water, but still held by the regulator tube.

James came around from behind the thrashing man, pulled the regulator from his mouth and as the body turned away into darkness, he pushed the regulator into his own mouth, grabbing a quick suck of air for himself—rule number one, take care of yourself first—but he was already swimming back to Hu. He met Hu's terrified eyes, then passed the regulator over, watching to make sure that Hu had it safely back in his mouth. James held firmly onto Hu, watching to see if all his careful training was paying off. Hu was scared, but somehow he remembered what to do. He choked past his panic—James watched to make sure that Hu was finally breathing again, breathing slowly and deliberately, before he gestured for the regulator. He'd waited almost too long—his own lungs were feeling tight.

Hu passed the regulator back to James, who took three hasty breaths, then turned. headed back to his own tank. He had to take a moment to steady himself. This was all happening too fast. He was still feeling his own adrenaline-panic as he swam back to the teenager, still holding his knife—

He had vision, of a minimal sort. Paired fingers of light probed at the gloom, illuminating almost nothing.

The teen and the mother were equally visible, another small circle of brightness. James swam back to the teenager, still holding his knife, and turned the boy to face him. The water was cold and it was pounding at them, shoving them this way and that. The boy could barely focus in the dark, he didn't have a facemask, but he saw the lamps on James' mask and he could see enough to recognize the man who'd saved him. He gave James a thumbs-up and passed the mouthpiece over—

James was glad. One murder was already one murder too many. He knew that Hu had seen it, but he couldn't tell what Hu was thinking, how he was reacting. Probably he was still trying to calm himself. James hoped that both Julia and her mother had kept their eyes closed as instructed. This was going to be a long afternoon.

Now it was James' turn to manage his breathing—and his fear. If he didn't manage himself, he couldn't manage anyone. He took three long breaths, then passed the mouthpiece back to the boy. Then, finally, he remembered to slide his knife back into its sheath.

The thrashing of the water was lessening. They were still being pummeled by surges of uneven pressure, why was that? Something up the tunnel must be blocking the flow of water, alternately blocking and opening. James imagined a giant pink heart valve, but it was probably a humongous piece of debris being pushed back and forth by the torrent. If it could settle, if it could block the worst of the flow, then maybe—but no, they shouldn't depend on it.

He had to convince himself that they could do this. He wasn't sure for how long. It depended on how much water they had above them, on how much pressure they could stand, on how long their air would hold out, and on how long they could last in the cold. Maybe the incoming coastal waters were warm enough they wouldn't be plunged into hypothermia. Maybe, just maybe, they had enough air to hold out for an hour, but probably less because they were sharing? He had to figure this out—

Then he remembered. His fifteen thousand dollar dive computer. He'd packed it, hadn't he? For a moment, he felt embarrassed, but then he realized, he hadn't had a chance to use it, so it wasn't part of his muscle memory. What bag was it in?

He went back to the boy, shared his three breaths, steadied his breathing, and visualized the morning. He usually talked to himself when he worked. Saying things out loud imprinted them in his memory. Ah, there—

He passed the regulator back, went straight to the case he'd almost left behind, and it was right where he remembered, right where he'd said when he packed it. It would have been easy to find anyway. It had switched itself on when the water hit it—its display was bright, even in this darkness, and now it was beeping an alarm. He slid it onto his left wrist and tried to focus on the dials.

The numbers flickered with confusing speed. The device kept beeping contradictory warnings. James was an expert in sport diving. At a hundred feet deep, a diver would use his air four times faster, but right now the dive computer was telling him that his current rate of air consumption might be ten times faster, might be twenty, might be five—the numbers kept changing, up and down, too fast to make any sense. They were either five hundred feet underwater or fifty. It was the fluctuating pressure of the water still pounding through the tunnel. The damn thing couldn't calibrate.

James tried to visualize what was happening. How much water? Too much and they wouldn't be able to stay down for long. If they needed to decompress, then the longer they spent under pressure, the longer decompression would take, and if they had limited air that would be a problem. They'd have to start up as soon as the flow of water ebbed. But how long could they wait for the current to slow? He had to balance time at this depth against time needed to ascend.

The tsunami was still pushing inland, what were the physics of that? Here in the tunnel, the rushing water was still battering at the car and stirring debris throughout the station. And all the things that should never have been debris—

Unless and until things equalized, they could be stuck here. How long until the water stopped flooding eastward? How long till it settled? How long till it started receding back into the sea? And how fast would it retreat? When would the next wave arrive? James had no idea.

He wondered if Pearl's train had made it safely to Union Station. Maybe. Probably. It had been packed full, so it wouldn't have made any stops. They would have gained a few minutes. And maybe with this train blocking part of the tunnel, maybe the flow would have been less, and maybe Pearl's train could have made it all the way downtown—?

And maybe that was all wishful thinking.

And maybe, despite everything, they weren't going to make it after all.

The churning slowed.

It didn't stop, but it slowed.

And they were still alive.

How did he know that?

Because they were still alive.

It didn't make sense.

They hadn't outrun the tsunami.

And they were under how many feet of water—

And yet . . . here they were, still alive, still breathing.

Still alive.

The water was brown and murky; where the headlamp beams pierced it for a few feet it looked like as much mud (and who knew what else) as water. If they hadn't had the headlamps . . .

Maybe that was what had attracted the attackers, maybe they saw the light as a beacon. He wasn't sure. It had all happened too fast, the subway car had flooded so quickly. James was wearing a professional-grade mask, it had extra-bright lamps, but down here, the advantage was minimal. He had only a small tunnel of vision, a gloom just a bit lighter than the darker gloom surrounding. He hung in place, thoughts trying to race, circling in confusion. He was a frozen moment of awareness in a shadowy underwater coffin.

He looked to the others. Julia was holding onto the regulator with both hands; her eyes were closed. She was fine, almost relaxed. Her mother too, though not as calm—she understood how precarious their situation was. Hu was floating close to Julia, watching her carefully. And the teenager—he was watching James as warily as a feral cat. He must have seen what

James had done. James took his three breaths, then turned to look toward the raised end of the car. There were dark shapes floating in the water. He didn't look long; he didn't want to see them clearly. He already knew, and his gut churned.

He turned his attention to the dials on the tanks. They had air—just not enough. Nowhere near as much as he had hoped. The chaos, the exertion, they were sucking air faster than he had planned. And the pressure, more pressure meant each lungful sucked in more air. He had to assume they were under at least a hundred feet of water.

But how deep were they, really? How much water was pressing down on them?

It didn't matter. They were in trouble. They had to move.

James wanted to stay nice and safe. Underwater was always nice and safe—if you knew what you were doing. But if you knew what you were doing, then you'd also know you can't stay underwater. It's not just how much air—it's the *other* reason. At any serious pressure, they'd get wonky.

James knew what it felt like. It's a little like being drunk or stoned—except it isn't. It's the rapture of the deep. And if you succumb to it, you become a statistic of the deep. No, you have to focus. You have to concentrate on every single task. Each specific task, one careful moment after the next.

James focused. He took his next three breaths and passed the mouthpiece back to the boy. Options. He had to consider the options. They weren't good. But they were options. That was more than most people had—especially the ones now floating limp in the darkness. There were so many of them, and they couldn't escape them, could they? They were a silent gauntlet, guarding any exit.

In the chaos of the moment, James hadn't considered the panic, the terror, of those caught in the water, unable to escape, those last few desperate moments of grasping for possibility, gasping for air, choking on their own last screams of denial and rage.

James knew what it was like to drown. It had been one of the worst parts of his training. He'd never understood the necessity of the exercise—being pushed into that near-death moment—at least, not until afterward when he'd been painfully pulled out of the tank, choking and gasping and coughing up water, not until the medic checked his heart and listened to his lungs and nodded to the trainer. Not until the trainer had looked him straight in the eyes and said, "Now do you understand what you'll be dealing with when you try to rescue a drowning man?"

And James had somehow managed to get the words out, "Was that fucking necessary?"

"I hope to fucking God it never is. But if it saves one life—yours—then, yeah." The trainer added, "Given a choice, I'd rather lose the idiot. His funeral I don't have to go to."

James had made up his mind, there and then, never to repeat the experience. Not voluntarily. And definitely not involuntarily!

That had a lot to do with his relationship with Hu, as well. That first day, in the tank at Paramount, he'd been watching this beautiful young man with multiple overlays of awareness. At first, he'd thought him just a gangling teenager, then he realized not only was Hu older than he looked, but also how inexperienced he himself was at gauging ages, especially the ages of Asian men. He just didn't have enough history.

For a moment, he'd wondered if Hu were . . . what's a good word? Accessible? An interesting question, not one he usually considered, and not one he intended to pursue here. It was only a passing thought, quickly pushed aside by the necessities of the job.

Once in the tank, once the plastic and Styrofoam flotsam had been added, once the wind machines had been turned on and the mechanically produced waves had started churning, it became obvious—to James at least—that Hu did not have a lot of experience with this particular kind of stunt work. And even though plastic and Styrofoam looks and feels lightweight—if enough of it piles up against you, or on top of you, it can rapidly become an impenetrable mass. You can drown just as easily as if it were the real thing.

So James had watched Hu. He watched all the people in the water, but he watched Hu especially because the beautiful young man wasn't watching out for himself, not the way a more experienced stunt player would have.

James hadn't waited for anyone to call "cut!" The rule was simple. Don't worry about ruining the shot. Get out of the way of the bus. Dodge the falling rocks. Don't get bitten by the mechanical dinosaur head. Don't. Get. Injured. Especially don't get killed. That costs money. It shuts the production down for two or three days. And it pisses off producers.

Rule Number One: Getting killed can ruin your whole day.

So James had dived into the tank, swum under the prop flotsam, grabbed Hu, and pulled him off to the side. He hadn't been thinking of anything more than just getting the poor dumb schmuck out of danger. It wasn't until later, over lunch, that he'd realized what an amazing smile shone on Hu Son's face.

And even then, he hesitated. He'd been burned enough in the relationship fire. He wasn't that eager to put his hand back into the flames—or any other part of his anatomy. But one thing led to another anyway—and now he had a ring on his finger.

It was an unfamiliar sensation. Hu's life was the other half of his now. His responsibility. And not just Hu. Three other lives were depending on his expertise.

So. Options. They could head up the nearest stairwell, head for the surface. Except, where was the surface? Right now, Wilshire was under water. James didn't know exactly how much, but it had to be a lot of fast-moving water. Ten mph, twenty mph, it didn't matter. It would be like stepping into a hurricane, except they'd be weightless with no footing. The waters would carry them away like balloons in a storm.

Wait for the waters to subside? That would work. If they subsided fast enough, before the five of them ran out of air or succumbed to cold. That was another problem. The temperature of the water. It was cold—not cold enough to produce hypothermia in an adult, not right away, but Julia's smaller body put her at increased risk. And perhaps the skinny teenager as well. They had to get above the water.

The subway car lurched, distracting James. Not quite unseen, the drifting bodies lurched too.

James took an extra deep breath, then passed the mouthpiece back to the young man. He swam deeper into the car to investigate. His headlamp gave him some sense of the mess—one of the subway doors was jammed open—by a body. His internal conversation was deafening. *Please, God, no children. No children, please—*

God did not comply.

His beam illuminated an infant, blanket still unraveling around its lifeless body.

Oh, fuck, fuck, fuck—fuck you, God—

James retreated, his mind already postulating what must have happened. A mother rushing home from work, finding the baby sitter gone, grabbing the baby, rushing for the subway, but somehow getting to the station just a few minutes too late, getting on the last car, hoping to escape. Dying in cold dark terror.

He bumped into a floating cat carrier, a furry body within, the handle still gripped by an elderly woman, her white hair floating around her head like a cloud.

Another body, this one in a dark uniform, the garbage truck driver? James didn't want to know. It was too much. He was starting to feel the horror—and painful pressure in his chest.

The subway lurched again—and all the separate bodies echoed the movement, a synchronized ballet, all the different dancers bumping sideways to the same unheard music. The moment passed and they resumed their slow deliberate gavotte. No longer panicked, in death they had become patient observers. The staring jetsam of disaster, their faces now relaxed and lifeless, they hung almost motionless, a silent jury—their fatal judgment dark and unspoken.

The dive computer was certain now, it beeped in alarm—they were too deep. They had to start ascending now. And as quickly as possible. Too much water, too little air—the bends would be inevitable.

James swam back to the others, back to the air tanks, still struggling with the math of their survival. He couldn't sort it out, it was the pressure, the paralyzing effects of it. His thoughts wandered in a drunken haze—and if he was having trouble, then the others were probably faring worse.

He had to focus. He hadn't expected to do this, not this soon, but there wasn't any alternative. He had to switch the tanks now, before he got fuzzier.

Switching tanks underwater wasn't hard. He'd done it before, but he hadn't done it a lot, so—after the necessary three breaths—he took his time to make sure he was doing it right. He had to focus carefully on each part of the process. As soon as the connections were secure, as soon as the pressure gauges were good, he relaxed a little. Hu and Julia had a little more time. He'd switch their tanks in fifteen minutes, maybe ten.

What had he been thinking about? He concentrated—oh yeah, options. Can't swim for the surface, can't wait for the waters to subside. Could they get higher?

Maybe! The Wiltern—wasn't there something? He tried to remember. There was a subway entrance in the building, wasn't there? Part of some expansion project? A pedestrian tunnel under the street, from the lobby to the platform. That would get them up a couple of floors—that is, if the building was still there and if it was tall enough to stick out of the water, then maybe they could get to one of the upper floors before they ran out of air. So many ifs—

But the numbers didn't leave any room for negotiation nor delays. They were too deep and they had too many bodies breathing too little air. But maybe—

Everything was maybe. James shared another three breaths, passed the mouthpiece back, then fumbled in his bag of gear until he found what he was looking for—a plastic panel and a grease pencil on a leash. Another three breaths of air, then he wrote frantically. "Get out now. Tunnel to Wiltern."

He didn't have time to write more. He wouldn't have anyway. But when the waters started to recede, when the worst of the flood finally started to flow back to the sea, he worried that the pressure in the station would also reverse and the subway train would be sucked back into the tunnel, where no escape would be possible. He wasn't sure about the physics, his mind wasn't focusing that far, but he couldn't chance it.

Three breaths, then he held the panel in the teen's headlamp beam. The boy's eyes were wide, bright in the gloom, he gave a thumbs-up response. James maneuvered himself over to Hu, held up the sign. Hu gave a thumbs-up too, then reached for the panel. He touched Julia's shoulder. She opened her eyes and then squinted them almost shut—this muck hurt! Hu tapped her shoulder again, holding the sign in front of her, his lights pointed at it. She nodded. She was tired, she was scared, but she was determined. James admired her spirit. She gave him hope.

James took the sign back, turned back to his own tank for another three breaths, then to hold the sign for Julia's mother to see. She was too frightened to respond with anything more than a half-nod of acknowledgment.

Another three breaths.

Stay focused, James told himself. One thing at a time.

Another tough decision. They were going to have to leave the bikes behind—and everything they'd so carefully packed. Abandoned. For a moment, he considered the impossible—could they carry any of this? None of them were wearing weight-belts, they had a buoyancy problem, they were all bobbing toward the roof of the subway car, the bikes might serve as ballast, and keep them from rising too fast—

No, it was too much to ask, too much effort. Not enough air. But at least, he and Hu had already transferred their most important belongings to their backpacks, they could take that much with them. Three more breaths. He waved to Hu, caught his attention, and pointed to his backpack. Hu nodded. He gave a double thumbs-up and checked his straps.

James turned back to the bikes and pulled the air tanks off the trailers, the ones they were using, and the last set of spares. Another three breaths and he gave the signal. He was in a small circle of light, fingers of illumination surrounded him. He gave a thumbs-up signal and the entire group began to move—Hu and Julia, the teen and Julia's mother.

They worked their way to the jammed-open door of the subway and somehow he managed to push the bodies out of the way. Two? Three? He wasn't sure and it didn't matter. The doors stayed open, one small piece of good luck.

Three more breaths.

The subway car was tilted. A wedge of debris had been thrust under its rear wheels, raising it at a lopsided angle—it leaned away from the platform, its upper frame jammed against the outer wall of the tunnel. The end of the car was more than a foot above the platform, wheels caught on the edge of it. Their door at the front of the car was almost a foot above the platform, and angled upward. Without the water, it would have been a hard leap. Here, this deep, under this much pressure, gravity was almost irrelevant. If anything, they were going to have a hard time staying down.

Three more breaths.

James swam to Julia's mom, patted her on the shoulder reassuringly, gave her a thumbs-up, then to the boy to reassure him as well—three more breaths—and then back to look at the pressure gauge on Hu's tank.

Two and a half adults had drained his own tank, but Hu's tank, with only one and a half bodies draining it, still had a useful margin. James gestured to Hu, pointing at the mouthpiece. Hu understood; he passed it over, sharing his air.

James took four breaths, a luxury, but a necessary one, then passed the mouthpiece back. James went through the door first. Hu brought up the rear. He had learned from James, they'd spent time together underwater. Be slow. Be methodical. Keep the beginners between you. Do one thing only, then the next. There's no rush. Impatience kills. Panic kills. Count to three. Or four.

Once out the door, they bobbed upward, bumping into the ceiling. Hu shared his air with James again. He looked worried, but James refused to acknowledge it. He'd already made up his mind. They were going to live. They hadn't come this far to die.

Another few breaths from Hu's tank and James swam away for a quick reconnaissance of the flooded station. He had to find the pedestrian tunnel.

There were bodies here. Too many, most of them floating up toward the ceiling, bobbing there like dreadful balloons. He tried not to think about them, but some of them turned toward him as he passed, he couldn't ignore their faces.

And fish, there were fish here too! Not a lot, and nothing James could identify, but some struggled feebly in the muddy currents. They wouldn't survive.

It gave him pause. Maybe later he would think about it. Maybe later someone would be able to explain how they got there. Maybe there'd be "later." Too many maybes.

At the front of the train, where it had shuddered to a stop, James pulled himself down to look into the first car. His headlights found the motorman's booth, the driver still behind the controls, his face an angry expression of disbelief and rage. James' beams illuminated the badge on his chest. It said "Jeffers."

You stupid schmuck, thought James. *Stupid, stupid, stupid. You should have just run for home, we could have made it. But no! You had to stop, didn't you. One more station, one more heroic pickup. Instead of saving a few, you killed us all.*

That last thought startled James. He hadn't realized it, but he'd been identifying with the dead. Down among the dead men, he had no choice. Despite his conviction, he still had no certainty.

It didn't matter what he thought. He kept going. He pushed a little further into the gloom, now exploring along the walls—no, nothing here, nothing here, nothing here. The darkness refused to give up its secrets. The tunnel had to be in the other direction.

Feeling the pressure rising in his lungs, James headed back to Hu and sucked eagerly, much too eagerly, at the regulator. He had to take a minute to recalibrate himself. Slowly, dammit, slowly.

This time he headed around the escalator, feeling along the walls—but carefully. If he bobbed up that diagonal shaft he might not be able to get back—but there it was. The pedestrian tunnel, a darker dark in the dark. Maybe it was his brain playing tricks on his eyes, the way he could "see" the furniture at home when he got up in the middle of the night to pee. And maybe it was a hallucination from nitrogen narcosis. Too many maybes. But no—a little closer and he was sure. It was the tunnel. He turned around, and just as carefully, he worked his way back to the others.

Three more breaths.

Time to switch out the tank that Hu and Julia were using. It didn't take long, but he had to concentrate, had to be careful. He had to focus.

When he finished, all the headlights were pointed at him. He existed as an oasis of light in a dark universe. He passed his mouthpiece back to the boy and pointed. Time to go.

Everybody but Julia had to carry a tank. They had the two they were still breathing from—and the last two spares.

As a group, they moved, all five of them—James and Hu, Julia and her mother, and the unnamed teen. It was a tough swim; they bounced along the roof of the station, James herding them carefully away from the escalator shaft. Their headlights weaving in the dark.

They made their way slowly toward the promise of escape.

James didn't know what was at the end of the tunnel. He hoped it wasn't blocked by debris. Or worse—

There were bodies floating in the pedestrian tunnel. Their headlamps revealed a gauntlet of bobbing shapes. James tried not to think about the panic that must have happened in here, the water flooding in so fast, it would have been like trying to swim up a waterfall. Dark shapes bobbed everywhere. And the floor of the tunnel was littered with everything they'd tried to carry with them.

They paused several times for James to suck air. This was not what he had expected. Or hoped for. They had to push their way through a nightmare, faces coming out of the dark—all too close. It was a bumping gauntlet of horror, a gallery of silent accusations, each body turning in its own final orbit. James tried not to look, tried not to illuminate them, but he had no choice. They were passing through a tunnel of horror—a silent community, patiently waiting for James and the others to join them.

Three more breaths—

And at last, the end. Another set of steps. They half-swam, half-bobbed up the diagonal shaft. At the top—only darkness. James made them wait. He took three breaths and entered first, turning around slowly, looking to see if it was safe.

He could barely make out any details. It was still way too dark in here. But they were definitely in the foyer of the Wiltern tower, the part that had been carved out for a pedestrian entrance to the subway. That much he could recognize, but he was otherwise unfamiliar with the building. The lobby ceiling was high. He didn't want to get caught up there with no weight-belt to bring him down. There was a railing here, he held onto it against the eddies of current. He could feel himself being pushed this way and that—not a lot, but enough to make him uncomfortable. Outside, the water must still be moving, but he couldn't tell which way. The gloom was that complete.

James swam back into the tunnel. He took breaths from Hu, then from the boy. He didn't want to be selfish, but he didn't want to lose himself to the rapture either. He steadied his breathing and aimed his light around the group. He wasn't familiar with the layout of the building. This was the lobby of the theater. He grabbed his grease pencil and scrawled on the plastic slate. "Stairwell?"

Hu shrugged. He didn't know either.

But Julia's mother reached out and grabbed his arm. She pointed outward and then toward the left. Over there—

But they couldn't just swim over. The problem was buoyancy. They needed to get across the lobby without rising so high they couldn't get to the door.

James looked back into the tunnel. A weird thought—

Three more breaths.

He swam back into the pedestrian tunnel, searching. The bottom was littered with the abandoned belongings of the dead. James was looking for suitcases—the canvas ones with one handle on top and another on the side. Whoever these poor fools had been, they weren't smart enough to leave their lives behind. James tested several of the cases for weight, then pulled the two heaviest back to the end.

Three more breaths.

Hu understood immediately. He'd take one suitcase, holding it by the top handle. James would take the other. Julia's mom and the teen would hold on to the side handles. Hu would hold Julia's hand. They should be able to make it.

Three more breaths—and James gave the thumbs-up signal.

As a group, they moved, a curious underwater tableau, a cluster of bobbing lights that revealed air tanks and baggage and faces tight against any further horrors in the dark. The Korean woman kept pointing and gesturing. James kept checking back with her, but in the darkness, it was impossible to know if they were actually heading in the right direction. He had to stop for breath again—and even a second time, until he realized they were paralleling a wall. But he wasn't sure if it was the outer wall of the lobby or the one they had been swimming toward. He didn't know this building, but maybe the lobby wasn't rectangular.

Left or right? James had to guess. He could make out vague shapes in the distance, but those could have been hallucinations. He took three breaths from the teen, then made a decision—the fire stairwell would be against an outer wall of the lobby. Okay, he'd lead them to the left and hope it wasn't a dead end.

It wasn't. Left was right. He realized with a start that he shouldn't be thinking word games now. That was dangerous.

But they were at the door. It had a wide emergency bar, the kind that pushed to open. For a moment, James felt fear. Without leverage, how could he push it?

Hu was already there, he batted the door with the heavy case he was holding. It bumped open enough for James to wedge his shoulder in. He pushed it further open, revealing only darkness.

James let go of the case he was dragging and entered the stairwell. He grabbed a railing and turned around slowly, looking to see if it was safe. Above, far above, did something glimmer? The surface?

It looked doable.

He gestured, a slow-motion wave.

Hu and the others pushed their way in. James shared three breaths and considered their circumstances. The stairwell was a silent column of dark water, but it was clearer water. They could actually see something. Their headlight beams penetrated for several yards. There wasn't a lot of debris here, and nowhere near as much mud and murk. The water must have filtered in instead of flooding, rising at its own rate.

James looked back. Hu had dropped his case to push the door closed. His own abandoned suitcase—the teen was pulling at its zipper, curious to see what was inside. James swam over and touched the boy's shoulder. The boy looked to him and he waggled his finger no. We're not grave robbers. Out of the water, the boy's gesture would have been a puzzled shrug, but he let go of the zipper.

Here inside the stairwell, with the fire door closed behind them, they should be safe from any rough currents. Even better, if all the fire doors above were closed, then this column of water would be a convenient chimney. They could ascend at their safest rate. Maybe . . . If the building hadn't been weakened, if it didn't collapse around them.

The dive computer was still beeping in annoyance. It said the water's surface was less than a hundred feet above them. It wanted to know how much air they had—but James couldn't tell it, he didn't know.

The surface might be reachable. If their air held out. If hypothermia didn't get them first.

If a second wave didn't arrive and destroy everything the first wave had already weakened.

James calculated in his head; it was still hard to focus down here, but the math wasn't impossible. One floor every five minutes. Maybe two—? No, they didn't have enough air. They had to get as high as they could as fast as they could. They might manage an extra ten or twenty minutes of decompression nearer the surface. Maybe they could make it.

He took his three breaths, passed the regulator back, and pointed upward.

The light at the end of the tunnel was still a hundred feet above them, and it was still invisible.

It is not a good idea to laugh underwater.

You could drown.

But as James did the math in his head, as he computed the safest rate of ascent through the stairwell measured against his estimate of the amount of air they had left, he ended up reminding himself—

Sloan's teddy. . . .

For a few dangerous seconds, he splurted bubbles. The more he tried to stop himself from laughing, the funnier it got. Hu looked at him, curious, then worried. James finally somehow managed to control himself. He held up a hand, then grabbed his board and wrote on it. "I'm fine. I'll tell you later."

Three breaths and he pointed upward. A single flight of stairs. Then another. Thirty feet. Sloan's teddy indeed.

Five minutes max, then they bobbed up a flight of stairs. Except the dive computer on his wrist beeped to let him know that they were still ascending anyway, even as they waited. The waters were receding and somewhere, the chimney must be leaking. Not good. If it leaked too fast and too much. If they "ascended" too rapidly, they were in serious trouble.

James had had the bends. Twice. Once was bad planning, once was stupidity—not his, the diver he'd had to rescue—but either way, it was not something he wanted to do a third time. Rashes, joint pain, headaches, even paralysis. But the bends are survivable—most of the time. Symptoms of decompression sickness can show up in the first hour, almost certainly in the first six hours, and if not in the first twenty-four hours, then probably not at all.

But if it was a choice between the bends and death?

Another joke occurred to him. "Death? Good choice. But first, Oompah!"

He had to suppress a giggle. And then he wondered, what the fuck? Am I getting giddy? Nitrogen narcosis was playing at the edge of his brain.

Three breaths from Hu, then three breaths from the boy. He was going to have to start watching himself. All these people were depending on him. It was time. He pointed. Up the next flight of stairs. And the next. And the next.

The higher they rose, the brighter the stairwell, the brighter the promise above. The water here wasn't as murky as it was below, but now there was debris floating in their way—a lot of paper, and a large rubber trash can, someone's jacket, and when James looked up, he thought he saw a body caught under a railing.

He checked his goddamn beeping dive computer and frowned. There was nothing he could do. Maybe they should wait an extra two minutes here? He took three breaths from Hu, three from the boy, gestured for them to wait and swam halfway up to look.

Yes, a body. A woman, stocky, possibly in her fifties, hard to tell. Her hair floated like a cloud around her head, but her dress had floated up revealing thick legs and pale underpants, they had become translucent, revealing her nakedness before his light—one last embarrassment. The tsunami had not only taken her life, it had taken her dignity as well.

James came back down again, grabbed another six breaths, then gestured for the others to follow him—but he waved his hand down past his eyes to show Julia and her mother to close theirs. Up the stairwell, and James tried to push the woman's body into a corner while the others rose past. Her name badge identified her as Mrs. Hayes. She was entitled to this much consideration—he didn't want the others to invade her privacy. Poor Mrs. Hayes.

Another flight up, another rubber trash can. And here was the cause of the decreasing pressure. The fire door was jammed open by another body, this one a janitor in a dark uniform. James could feel the current here—the water was being sucked away. Outside the broken tower, the current must have become too strong to resist. James felt himself being pulled—it was strong enough to be a challenge.

He pulled on the fire door, pushing it open enough for the poor man's body to be sucked through and away. He let go and the current pushed the door shut again, cutting off the water's escape.

He was surprised that he'd been able to pull the door open at all. The force of the water was less than he'd expected. This was both good news and bad news.

They were closer to the surface—but they were also more at risk of decompression sickness. He swam back down to the others. Three breaths from Hu, three breaths from the boy, and three more breaths from Hu. They were going to have to wait here ten minutes at least. Maybe more.

And they were already on their last tanks. He didn't remember when they had switched over, but apparently he had done so at some point going up the chimney of the stairwell. Maybe at the bottom, before they started up? Not a good sign that he didn't remember. He studied the dials on the last two tanks.

Good—

—Just not good enough.

He floated on his back so he could peer upward through the gap between the stairs. There was light up there, brighter than before. He watched his bubbles rise up through his headlamp beam toward it.

He did the numbers in his head. The math was not negotiable. The bends were no longer a risk, no longer a possibility. Now they were simply inevitable. The only question was how to manage the ascent to make them survivable.

They had maybe twenty minutes of air left in the tanks, maybe thirty. They had at least fifty feet still to ascend. That is, if the dive computer was correct. James sorted through his memories—his research, his training, and the experiences of other divers.

His instinct was to ascend slowly and safely. That was what his training demanded. But the math said no—not gonna make it. The alternative was to rise to a point maybe ten or fifteen feet just below the surface and wait there. At that depth, their air would last much longer, giving them more time to decompress before it ran out. From there, they could safely ascend the last short distance to the surface.

James would have preferred to stick with the advice of the nagging, beeping dive computer, but that wasn't his best option. The water was still receding, draining out of the building around them. Even if they waited here, they were still ascending—or rather, the surface was descending to meet them.

And in addition to everything else, he was starting to feel the cold as a painful presence. He was starting to shiver. That was okay. If he stopped shivering, that would be very not okay. It would mean his body was shutting down. He wasn't worried about that, he knew his tolerances. But what about the others?

He was reaching that point where he really wanted to get out of the water—he wanted to get out *now.* And if he was feeling this way, then it was probably a lot worse for the others. He turned his headlamps toward Julia and her mom, who was holding Julia close to her body, trying to share warmth. In this water, it was a futile effort.

James took his three breaths. He looked across at Hu, who looked back at him hopefully.

It was enough.

Fuck it. We are not going to die today.

He swam from one to the other, Julia, her mom, the boy, and finally Hu, checking once again to make sure that each was all right. Later on, perhaps, he might be able to marvel at their endurance—but right now, they had no choice. Either they hung on, or they became like all those others they had passed below. Like poor Mrs. Hayes.

More breaths. And another flight of stairs. Another and another.

The surface was a lot closer than he realized. The stairwell must be leaking somewhere. Had they closed the door at the bottom? He didn't remember. Or maybe the fire doors weren't all that watertight. Or maybe there was enough structural damage that the whole building was as secure as a screen door.

The good news, the afternoon light flickered brightly above. He could see rippling light through the water's surface now, a promise of survival, and even though he still swam in a dirty murky world, filled with little floating things, the walls of the stairwell were no longer hidden behind a fog of gloom. But he wasn't ready to feel confident. Not yet. Overconfidence is just another way to die.

They had to wait here as long as possible. James took his three breaths and studied the dive computer. It had finally given up and stopped beeping, but it still insisted that the surface of the water was steadily descending to meet them.

A large rubber trash can drifted by. Was this the fourth or fifth? Why so many? Something else to wonder about. He began to imagine the episode of *Nova* that would examine these events.

Three breaths. Three breaths. Three more breaths.

He checked the gauges again. He studied the dive computer, blinking. It didn't make sense. No, it made sense. *He* wasn't making sense. It didn't matter what the gauges said, they were running out of air. There was no more time.

James fumbled for the plastic slate, felt along the leash for the grease pen, wrote on it frantically. "Drop tanks. Go up. My signal." He turned to the others, holding the slate so that each of them could see the words. He took three quick breaths, then pointed up. Waving his arm in a broad "Let's go, now!" motion.

He didn't have to push them. They were eager to go. They each took a last long suck of air, then dropped the regulators and scrambled up. Hu grabbed Julia by the waist and they half-swam, half-walked up the last flight of stairs. James pushed Julia's mom and the teen after them. He followed, the pressure in his lungs growing. He should have taken a last breath himself.

He looked back. The tanks were tumbling away, bouncing in slow-motion irretrievably down the stairwell, a lost opportunity. He pushed himself upward. He couldn't see. His vision was blurry, closing in, he needed one more breath, he couldn't hold it—

The top of the stairwell was open to the sky. The walls were broken here. A twisted doorframe remained where a fire door had been. James struggled to reach for it, he felt himself sinking back—

—and a pair of hands reached down and yanked him roughly out of the water.

A confusion of words, an unfamiliar voice, "Are there any more—?"

"No, no. Just the five of us—" That was Hu. His voice sounded strange, garbled by water. Someone else was choking, a small high voice. Julia?

He couldn't see. Everything was a glare. He was on his back, gasping, choking, coughing up water—how had that happened? His last strangled ascent? Everything here was blue, incongruously bright. Two faces abruptly blocked his view, dark silhouettes, he didn't know them. Where had they come from?

"Don't try to talk. Just concentrate on breathing, okay?"

There were hands all over him, pulling away the last of the rig on his back, pulling his mask away, loosening his shirt. Someone had their head to his chest, trying to listen to his heartbeat. James coughed, choked up more water, and the person pulled away. His lungs hurt badly.

"Hu—?" he called. "Hu?"

"I'm here. I'm okay." A hasty answer.

James concentrated on breathing now. A deep breath. Another. Stop to cough, spit up, cough, then breathe again.

Three deep breaths. Three more. Three more. Don't hyperventilate. Hold your breath a moment and appreciate that you can.

He was almost back when he suddenly remembered an old movie, a favorite. He called out, "Are we dead, mon?"

Hu called back, falsetto. "I'm not dead yet, I'm not."

James laughed. He laughed until he choked and coughed up even more water. His throat hurt, but he laughed anyway. He rolled over on his side and looked across at Hu. His husband was half up on his knees, also laughing.

James flailed helplessly, trying to sit up. Hands grabbed him from behind, someone helped him to a sitting position. James looked around. They were on a wide empty floor, slightly tilted, very broken. But his vision was still blurry, partly from the glare of the day, partly from the painful tears filling his eyes, an involuntary reaction to the overwhelming dazzle. The whole world looked overexposed, the people here were silhouettes, vague shapes in the glare. Maybe a dozen, he wasn't sure.

Hu scooted over to him, looked at him carefully, then scooted around to sit beside him. He bumped him affectionately with his shoulder. James looked at Hu, a weak grin on his face. Hu looked tired. But alive. Even smiling.

After a moment of silent acceptance, a moment of just surviving, James looked around at their rescuers. "Who are you people? How did you get up here? How did you get through?"

"We should ask you the same question," said one of the men. "I'm Scott Copeland. Who are you?"

"James Liddle. And that's Hu Son. And the little girl is Julia. I don't know her mother's name. Are they all right?"

"They will be, yes. Sophie's looking after them. And the teenager too. Looks like you had a rough ride."

James nodded. "The subway. The last train. Didn't make it."

"Yeah, we heard—" The man pointed. "We've been following the news. The cellphone towers are down, but Jack's Walkman has FM. Three trains were lost."

"Three—?"

"Yeah. Real bad scene at Union Station."

James didn't say anything then, didn't want to say what he was thinking, didn't want to make the fear real. He realized he was weak. Exhausted. He looked around. They were on a sloping tile surface. The stairwell was a square opening with a few broken steps rising out of the water. "Is this the top floor?"

"No. This was the tenth floor. The top three floors were ripped away." Copeland's expression went grim. "That's where most of the people went. I suppose it seemed like a good idea. It was wall-to-wall crowded. Probably exceeded the structural limits. But, see, the top floors of a building are never the strongest. The lower floors are built to hold the weight of the floors above."

"You're a builder—?"

"Architect. I know this building. It's a good one. Well, it was. We started on the seventh floor, that's where our offices were. When the water started rising, we moved up to the eighth, eventually the ninth. Had to stop there. The people above wouldn't let us keep going, said there was no more room." Copeland sighed and shrugged—a gesture of both sadness and grim irony.

"We'd been shredding old blueprints. We had thirty or forty bins of paper we still hadn't emptied. When the water broke the windows and started rising inside the building, we emptied all the biggest trash cans, turned them upside down and stuck our heads in to breathe. It was a gamble, but it worked. Each bin had enough air to last ten minutes, twenty if we were careful. And we had, I dunno, thirty bins. I saved my people. Most of them."

"But you lost a couple . . . " James glanced toward the broken stairwell, wondering if the bloated cadaver of poor Mrs. Hayes might suddenly bob up on the surface of the trapped water.

Copeland followed his glance. "Yeah. We had some panic. It was pretty bad. We did everything we could." Copeland was reluctant to explain. "What about you? Down in the subway—?"

James remembered the man who'd tried to take Hu's regulator. He could still see the man's startled expression, the sudden horrified realization that he was dying—dying twice, once by drowning, once by knife—and the crushing certainty that this was truly death. James shook his head, he didn't want to talk about it.

Copeland recognized the expression. "Yeah. Bad day all around." He straightened. "Let me see if there's any water left." He disappeared from James' field of view.

James concentrated on his breathing for a while. Open air. There was a delicious luxury. How had he ever taken breathing for granted? Finally, he looked around, searching for Julia and her mother. Spotting them, he crawled over on his hands and knees. He still didn't feel like standing. Julia was clutching her mother, her face buried in her mother's side, her shoulders rising and falling as if she was sobbing.

"Are you okay?"

"I prayed to God, and he sent you to save us."

"Well, I don't know about God, but—"

"No, it was God—"

"Okay. It was God. I'm just glad that you and Julia made it. You must have been scared."

"No. I knew that God sent you. So I wasn't scared. I just kept praying and thanking God for sending you to us."

"Ahh. Well, I guess it worked."

"Yes. And God will bless you for what you did."

"Not gonna argue that—I can use all the blessings I can get. I'm just glad you both made it." James patted her shoulder, patted Julia's shoulder, but the little girl didn't look up. James had seen this behavior before; Julia was going to have nightmares. She was going to have some serious post-traumatic stress. And she was going to need some serious therapy. Oh, hell—they all would.

He turned away, crawled back to Hu. The unnamed teenager was sitting next to him, sucking at a bottle of water. He passed the water bottle to Hu; the two of them had been talking, sharing, debriefing each other.

Hu looked to James. "This is Jesse. He's a student at LACC."

James held out his hand. "I'm James. I'm glad you made it."

"So am I, man! That was intense! I am never riding that subway again!"

"I don't think anybody will," James agreed.

Jesse waved his arm, indicating the world around them. "How long we gonna be up here, you know?"

James hadn't even considered the question. He put one hand against a fragment of wall. He raised himself half-up onto his knees—

The hot July sun blazed above. The landscape rippled and foamed below. Everything was too bright. It took a moment for James' vision to clear, for his eyes to focus all the way to the horizon. And then it took another moment for him to make sense of what he was seeing—all the devastation that surrounded them.

James levered himself to his feet, holding onto the spur of the broken wall. He turned slowly, slowly, shaking his head, saying only, "Fuck. Oh, fuck. Oh, fuck." And then, even more sadly, "Oh, fuck."

They were alone in the middle of a vast brown sea. The water was receding—slowly. But more water was still trying to push in—uneven ripples of the reverberating shockwaves. Everywhere, the water foamed and surged, churning the debris. Things tumbled in the water, all kinds of things, broken signs, buses, cars, trees, the inevitable palm fronds, pieces of buildings, roofs and walls—and bodies. Too many bodies.

The sea of desolation extended north, all the way to the Hollywood Hills. A few buildings stuck their tops out of the water—but not many. To the west and the south, the view was much the same. There was a rise in the southern distance. Baldwin Hills was now Baldwin Island, probably nothing more than a naked lump. The ferocious power of the waves would have scraped everything away.

The rest was mud.

James saw the past as if it were still the present. The riot at the Santa Monica underpass, the old men at the VA Health Center, the carefree golfers, and all the people in all the cars they'd passed, the little boy staring from a car window on Wilshire Boulevard . . .

How many of them had escaped and how many more had been caught in the overwhelming wrath of the tsunami? It was all unknowable, all washed away too quickly to comprehend.

James tried to imagine—something, anything—a future.

He couldn't.

It would take months just to catalog the devastation. The scale of this thing—there was nothing left. Nothing to rebuild. The city was gone.

"Fuck," said James.

It was going to be a long uncomfortable afternoon.

Hu pulled him back down, pulled him next to him. "You okay?"

"No."

Hu didn't respond to that. He waited a bit before saying anything else.

Finally, "You kept your promise."

"I did?"

"You said we weren't going to die today."

"The day's not over."

"Shut up." Hu said it gently, affectionately. He took James' left hand and held it up to admire the gold band on the third finger. He traced it with his own fingers. "But I will say this." He paused.

"What?"

"This is the worst honeymoon I've ever been on—"

"Oh, really? How many others have you had—?

"This is the first."

"Then it's also the *best* honeymoon you've ever been on."

"Yeah, I guess so." Hu leaned his head on James' shoulder. They were silent for a while. Just being together.

"Hey—" said Jesse, interrupting their silence.

"Yeah?"

"You guys are fags, aren't you?"

James hadn't heard that word in years. He was more surprised than offended. "Yeah, I am. I'm not so sure about my husband though. Is that a problem?"

Jesse pointed to James' discarded facemask, as if looking for the lost regulator. "Yeah, man—! I had your—your thing in my mouth. Yuck—" He got up and moved away.

Hu and James looked at each other. Both started laughing.

"What an ungrateful little prick," Hu said. "Why did you save him, anyway?"

James shrugged. "It seemed like a good idea at the time."

Swarms of helicopters filled the air over the seething brown water that used to be Los Angeles. They were clattering dragonflies, darting here and there, exploring, recording, reporting. The afternoon was bright but ugly.

Some of the newer buildings, the ones designed to resist a massive earthquake, had survived. They stuck up out of the water like broken stumps.

Where there had been neighborhoods, there was now only mud and water and debris, occasionally patterned by the gridwork of streets that had survived. Mostly the terrain below was a vast sea of desolation. What remained of the 405 was a scar. The Federal Building looked like a fractured tooth. The Veterans' Health Care Center was gone, only a broken steel outline remained to mark its location.

Nevertheless, the choppers swarmed, relentlessly searching—and occasionally, improbably, also triumphantly rescuing. Here and there, despite impossible odds, some people had survived the onslaught of the tsunami. Soon or eventually, whenever they could get to safety, they would have the opportunity to tell their stories to the hungry cameras. Every survival was an improbable adventure—a delusion of luck and prayer, sometimes even a bit of good judgment and courage.

Several Air Force communications planes circled patiently overhead, coordinating the fleets of choppers. The army, the navy, the air force, the coast guard, and several civilian companies were patrolling, each in their assigned area. All other air traffic was forbidden. Even the news choppers were under military guidance now. The Goodyear and Fuji blimps as well.

Three navy choppers were assigned to an area formerly known as Little Korea. There were few landmarks left on the ground; they had to depend on GPS mapping to locate themselves.

"There—" said the copilot. "Two o'clock."

"What am I looking for?"

"Over there. It's a light, hard to see in the glare—"

The chopper pilot brought the machine around. "That green stump sticking out of the water—?"

"Yeah. See that flicker?"

"I see it." As they approached, the pilot said, "Holy shit. That used to be the Wiltern!"

"You recognize it?"

"My grandmother used to live in this area." He added, "Actually, it's the Pellissier building, but everyone calls it the Wiltern."

They came in lower for a closer view. The tsunami had ripped the top off the building. But it had left enough for several stories to remain sticking up out of the water. Open floor space was visible, enough for several people to gather. One was waving a light of some kind.

The copilot called to the divers in the back of the machine. "We've got survivors. More than a dozen."

"Any injuries?"

"Maybe. Some of them are down."

"We'll take the worst. Blue Team can pick up the rest."

"Copy that."

The chopper came in low and the people on the top of the building stood up to wave at them. One of them was aiming the headlamps of a diver's mask. He switched it off as the aircraft approached.

The heli hovered over the building, stirring up the waves in great rippling circles. Four lines dropped from the machine. Two figures in wetsuits came down two of the lines, two rescue stretchers came down the others.

"Who's the worst injured?" asked Seal Team Commander Wright.

The survivors looked around, uncertain, but a young Chinese man pointed. "Take the little girl. She's got hypothermia and maybe the bends."

"The bends?"

"Long story," said the man next to him. "And her mom too."

The other Seal was already pulling the rescue stretchers over to Julia and her mother. "Anyone else with the bends?" asked Wright.

The Chinese man pointed to an African-American teenager, held his own hand up, then pointed to the man next to himself, who tried to wave them away. "I'm okay—" But his hand trembled.

"Bullshit, you are." Commander Wright peered from one to the other. He spoke to his microphone. "Gonna need two more stretchers. No, make it three." He turned to the other survivors. "We've got another bird coming in behind us. We'll have you all out of here as quickly as we can." Back to the microphone. "We'll need water and blankets. And maybe some protein."

The first two stretchers lifted away, one after the other, Julia and her mother wrapped in heating blankets. Three more stretchers, all tied together, hanging in a cluster, came down another line—and another Seal Team member as well.

When they came for James, dragging a rescue stretcher with them, he shook his head. "No," he said, pointing. "Hu Son first."

"What?" asked Wright.

"He's on second," said James. But they were already wrapping him, lifting him into the stretcher, fastening the Velcro straps.

As they secured Hu into his own rescue stretcher, he looked over to James, a bemused expression on his face. "I can't believe you just said that."

James said, "It's been a long day—" and passed out.

Wright signaled the chopper; the first stretcher with James lifted away. A moment later, Hu followed. Then Jesse. Wright followed them up, leaving two Seals behind with the remaining survivors. Even as they clattered away, the second chopper was moving in for the pickup.

"Where we taking them?" Wright asked.

"Wait a minute—" Copilot called back. He was talking to someone on one of the communication planes. "Getty isn't taking anymore. And Dodger Stadium is full. The parking lot is tent city now." Abruptly, he paused, listening. "Okay, copy that." To the pilot, he said. "Griffith Observatory."

The pilot nodded. The copilot turned back to Wright. "Did you hear that? Griffith Observatory. They've got an aid station there—and they're running shuttles down into Burbank. They want to shorten our turnaround time." Turning back to the pilot, he added, "They're bringing a fuel truck up too."

The pilot nodded, his only acknowledgment.

The Hollywood Hills were directly ahead. But below them, muddy water still churned across the flooded city.

The center of Los Angeles was gone—and so was its heart.

• • •

Griffith Observatory stands on one of the highest hills on the southern edge of the basin. It overlooks the entire city. It is a familiar landmark for both tourists and filmmakers.

Today, its wide lawn and parking lot served as a rescue station, a place for helicopters to bring survivors and refuel, a place for ambulances and buses to take survivors down the northern side of the hills to Burbank and North Hollywood and other places safely beyond the reach of the churning ocean.

James and Hu stood at a western railing, one of the better viewing positions, and looked out over what was now called the Bay of L.A. Or Bayla for short. On the hills to their right, the Hollywood sign survived untouched. It still declared the fabled town, but of Hollywood there was nothing left. Only a sea of mud. Already a smell of wet decay was rising from below. Despite the lingering heat of the day, they were both wrapped in blankets.

They held hands, but neither had anything to say. Despite their mutual joint pains, their headaches, and their blotchy patches of red skin, they had not been considered at severe risk. They'd been given oxygen. It had helped, but Julia's condition was much more serious, so was her mother's, so they were taken for immediate treatment. James and Hu would have to wait awhile for further attention. If at all.

"Triage," someone had explained, not understanding why Hu and James had exchanged a look.

But it was obvious now. Sooner or later, everybody is triage.

They both hurt all over. Hu had thought to dump the contents of their medicine cabinet into his backpack. They had ibuprofen and it helped—a little. Just not enough. They were going to have to walk this off and wait it out.

The wide lawns in front of the observatory were filled with tents, tables, and bustling emergency workers. The parking lot in front of that was filled with more tents and more crowds of people. The only open area was a space set aside for helicopters to land and take off. A fuel truck waited nearby. Several television vans were parked on the grass.

A Red Cross tent had been set up where people could get coffee and donuts and even some packaged meals, but despite their growing hunger, neither James nor Hu felt like eating. They were still too uncomfortable.

A young black woman came up to them, carrying a tablet. Her badge identified her as some kind of city official, James couldn't read it. He was still having trouble seeing clearly.

"Have you been logged in?" she asked, holding up the tablet.

James shook his head.

"We're trying to assemble a roster of survivors. You were in the Wiltern building?"

"No. We were in the subway. We came up the fire stairs of the Wiltern building—"

She looked puzzled. "How did you do that?"

"SCUBA," said James. He was still holding his facemask. He held it up as if that was the only explanation he needed.

"Um, okay," she said, not quite sure what he meant, but it didn't matter anyway. "Your names?"

"James Liddle. Hu Son."

The young woman was wearing a headset. She repeated their answers to her headset, checking that the tablet properly translated her speech to text.

"Address?"

"Nowhere now," said James.

"Venice Beach," said Hu. He told her their address, but it was meaningless now.

The woman asked a few more questions: Email addresses, cellphone numbers, Social Security numbers, birth dates, and preferred gender identification. Finally, "We're going to try to find you a place to stay. I can't promise that you'll be together—"

James held up Hu's hand in his own. "He's my husband. We stay together."

She didn't blink. She referred to her tablet. Apparently it was connected to some master database somewhere. She looked up. "Do you have any documentation?"

James held up his left hand, showing the ring. "Is this good enough?"

"Um, I'm sorry. No. We've had people trying to lie to us."

"Does it matter?"

"Yes, it does." She looked annoyed. "The relief benefits are different for married couples—"

Hu interrupted. He was already fumbling in his backpack, pulling out a dry bag. "Does a marriage license count?" He had a sheaf of papers, all safe inside three concentric Ziploc bags. He sorted through the papers, passed one over.

She took it, looked at it, shook her head, and passed it back. "It's not signed—"

"We were supposed to get married today. We would have been on our way to—to our honeymoon."

James said, "Is there a judge up here? Or a minister? Someone who can sign this?"

"Uh—" She looked confused. "Let me check." She walked away, already pulling her phone out of her pocket.

Hu said, "Well, that's—"

"—fucked." finished James.

It was all too much.

James turned away, leaned on the stone railing, not wanting to look at anyone or anything anymore. But there it was—the muddy sea of Bayla and its broken towers. He tried hard not to give in to his rage. But—it was all too much. Everything was gone. Everything. He had nothing. No words. No feeling. He was numb.

He had the clothes on his back, whatever was still attached to his tool belt, a diving watch that had stopped, an expensive dive computer he never wanted to see again, a half-empty backpack, and for some reason, he was still holding onto his facemask, afraid to let it go, even up here.

And Hu.

He still had Hu.

But . . . he had nothing else. Nothing left to give. Nothing for Hu. Nothing for anyone. He was empty. Scraped raw. Numb.

He had finally hit bottom.

Hu stood next to him, silent. He put his hand on James' shoulder, but James didn't react, didn't even acknowledge the touch. Finally, Hu reached out to take the facemask from him, but James pulled it back.

"Jimmy—? Talk to me. Please?"

James didn't respond. He looked at the mask—as if seeing it for the first time, an ugly reminder of everything he would never see again. It was a useless appendage. He might as well throw it away and have nothing left at all. Without thinking, he lifted his arm, poised to throw it over the edge of the railing and down to the rough hillside below.

But Hu grabbed his wrist and stopped him—

"Jimmy, no—"

As if startled awake, James looked to Hu. "What—?"

Hu took the mask, turned it around and held it up to show something to James. "Did you know your camera was on?"

"It's automatic," James said. He took the facemask from Hu. A pair of fisheye lenses were mounted above the glass, one on each side of the two headlamps. They were designed for capturing virtual-reality 3D video. James frowned at the readout on the left side of the mask. "Hmph," he said. "Looks like it recorded everything from the moment the water hit—"

"Really?"

"I'd have to pull the card, but yeah—"

Hu cut him off. "Jimmy, maybe we could sell that footage to someone?

Some news channel? Or maybe even *Nova?* Someone? It might be worth something—"

James shook his head. "I doubt it. Everybody will have footage. Every survivor with a phone. And probably a few thousand amateur drones as well. There's going to be more video than anybody will have time to review."

"But nobody has underwater footage of the subway—"

James stopped in mid-sentence. Hu was right. He started to agree, then stopped abruptly. "No. We can't."

"Huh? Why not?"

James put his hand to his belt, touched his knife.

Hu's eyes followed. "Oh," he said, realizing what James meant.

"Squeak—I killed a man—"

"It was self-defense—"

"No. It wasn't. It was deliberate—"

"We could talk to a lawyer—"

"Christine retired, remember the party—"

"She could recommend someone. Maybe Suzanne? Or Cindy?"

James didn't answer immediately. "Yeah, maybe. But—"

"But—?"

"But—that's not the point."

"What is?"

"I killed a man, Hu. That's murder. I committed a murder—"

"Jimmy—"

"And I did it without thinking. I did it so easy—"

"You didn't have a choice. You did it to save me—"

"—and I'd do it again. In a heartbeat. But—"

Hu understood it—James was in pain. A lot of pain, and most of it wasn't physical. Hu wanted to say something, but he didn't know what. "Bubble—?"

"I don't know who he was. I don't want to know. What if he had a family? People waiting for him? Oh, God. What if they recover his body someday. They'll see his throat. And someone will figure it out—"

"Jimmy! Stop it. Look out there. Look at that mess—nobody's going to recover anything."

"Squeak, you stop it! I know what I did! I have to live with it."

Hu put his hand on James' arm. "Bubble—listen to me. What we went through—it was horrible. It was all my worst fears, everything, all at once—but I made it because you were there—you. Just like the first time."

James started to protest, but Hu grabbed him by both shoulders and poured out the rest of his words in a frantic rush. "Out of all the millions of people who died today—God knows how many, but we survived, you and I—

and Julia and her mother, and that little prick Jesse too. We survived because survival is what you do. It's who you are."

"Who I am—?" James couldn't stand it. "I know who I am now. I don't want to be who I am—I couldn't save him! I had to—had to—"

"No, listen! Listen to me—as much as I hate to say this, because it's so fucking cruel and selfish to even think this way, but it's still true anyway—that man was already dead when he boarded the subway. Every single one of them. We all were. We just didn't know it. And if you and I had left the bike trailers behind, if we'd abandoned the tanks when we thought they were too heavy, we'd be dead too. All five of us. And your last thoughts would have been rage at yourself for listening to my whining—this is better! Isn't it?"

But James was adamant in his pain. "I know what you're trying to do, Squeak. And I love you for it. But—I know what I did—and it hurts me so much inside to know that I did it—that I'm even capable of it. This hurts like you can't imagine—"

"Excuse me, guys—?" An interruption. A voice from behind them. They turned to see Seal Team Commander Wright. He was holding Jesse by the upper arm. "You the guys from the subway?"

"Yeah?"

Wright let go of Jesse, but not before saying to him. "Stay." Then he held out his hand to James. "I heard what you did down there, heard it from the kid. It must have been rough, but I wanted you to know, it's one of the best things I've heard today. I mean, you done good." Wright shook James' hand, then Hu's. He nodded back toward the chopper. "We're refueling, going back out in thirty, but I wanted to make sure you were good. And uh, the kid here has something to say to you too." He poked Jesse. "Go ahead, mister."

Jesse looked embarrassed. He swallowed hard and looked at his feet. When he looked up, his eyes were wet. "I'm sorry for what I said. I don't know why I said it. It just fell out. But I wouldn't have made it if it wasn't for you guys. So . . . um, I guess, I want to say thank you, I owe you my life, and I hope you'll forgive me for being such a dick."

Hu's smile came easier than James'. He said, "It's okay."

"No, it's not. I mean, why'd you do it? You didn't have to. I mean, I saw what you did to that other guy and—"

James interrupted quickly, "You said 'please.' "

"Huh? That's it?"

"Yeah, that was it."

"Whoa," said Jesse. "Whoa."

"Yeah, whoa."

Jesse looked confused. "I don't get it."

James smiled sourly. "Neither do I, kid. Neither do I."

Wright had watched the whole exchange. He spoke up now. "There's nothing to get. You did what was in front of you." To Jesse, he said, "He gave you a second chance. Now you gotta make the most of it. Make a difference." He pushed the teen gently.

Jesse held out his hand. James took it, shook it. So did Hu.

"We're good then?"

James and Hu nodded. Wright seemed satisfied. He lifted his hand in a salute of respect and headed back to his chopper.

Jesse stood there, still looking embarrassed, shifting from one foot to the other. Finally, he gave a nervous smile. "I'm gonna go get in line for the phone. Okay? Gotta call my gramma and let her know I made it. I hope you guys land on your feet." And then he was gone, too.

"Well," said Hu. "That was something."

"Yeah," agreed James. "He said please."

But he was still in a funk so deep it was no longer blue, it had gone to indigo. He turned back to the railing and stared across at the Hollywood sign without really seeing it.

"Excuse me—?" Another interruption.

This time it was a man in a clerical collar. He looked like some casting director's idea of the perfect priest—but one who is falsely accused of molesting little boys until exonerated in the third act denouement. "Are you the ones looking for a minister? I'm Father Feigenberg—"

"*Father* Feigenberg? Really? You're kidding me."

"I get that a lot, yes. Someone said you needed a priest." He looked at them with puzzled curiosity. "Do you want me to pray with you?"

James and Hu looked at each other, then back to Father Feigenberg. Hu spoke first. "We need you to make us legal. We want you to say some nice words and then sign this—" He passed over the marriage license.

Father Feigenberg looked at their marriage license, looked from one to the other, back to the license, then back to the two of them again. "Um, I'm afraid I can't—my faith doesn't recognize same-sex unions."

"Oh, hell!" said James, frustrated. It was just too much. He said it loud enough that a few nearby people turned around to look. James turned angrily to the railing, glowered out at the landscape of mud and desolation and everything buried under it—then, just as abruptly, he whirled back. "Father? Will you hear my confession?"

Hu's eyes widened. "I didn't know you were Catholic—"

"Recovering," admitted James. "Father—?"

Father Feigenberg nodded. He led James a short distance away, to the best privacy they could find—a quiet space behind a pedestal with a bronze bust of James Dean. It had been installed as a commemoration of the famous observatory scenes in *Rebel Without A Cause*.

Hu watched from a distance as both James and the priest knelt together. First James crossed himself, then bent his head to whisper in Father Feigenberg's ear. He took a long time, and halfway through, the priest reached over to put his hand on James' shoulder, a gesture of solidarity and comfort. James kept talking—and then a little after that, he started weeping. Father Feigenberg pulled him close and let him cry into his shoulder.

Finally, James pulled back and Father Feigenberg made the sign of the cross over him, and said some words—some words that James so desperately needed to hear. His whole body relaxed. And even from a distance, Hu could see that James' pain had been lessened. Not released, not yet—but lessened. It was a start.

Finally, after a few more minutes, Father Feigenberg led James back to Hu and the two shared a look.

"Are you all right?"

"A little better. Yeah."

Feigenberg looked from one to the other. He hadn't met many same-sex couples, a side effect of his particular calling. But he felt there was more that he needed to say before this moment could be considered complete.

"The two of you—" He looked from James to Hu and back again. "You didn't get here by accident. You got here because . . . yes, I know it sounds presumptuous, and you don't have to believe me, but I'm certain that the two of you are here because you're supposed to be here. Together."

That last word from Father Feigenberg surprised both James and Hu. It wasn't the word so much as the man saying it.

Hu managed to speak first. "Thank you."

Feigenberg nodded an acknowledgment. "So how long have you two been together?"

"Three years."

Feigenberg was impressed. "Mm-hm. That's a commitment, isn't it?"

"Commitment, hell," said James. "It's a privilege." He put his arm around Hu's shoulder and pulled him close. "He's the one."

"Yep," agreed Hu, smiling. "Today was gonna be the day." He held up his hand to show his ring.

James held up his hand to show the matching ring. "We made a promise. Hell or high water, we're saying our vows today. It was high water. Really high water. So we said 'em. In the subway. Just before the water hit."

Hu said, "It was really romantic. And terrifying too. I spent the whole day afraid I was going to lose him—"

Feigenberg nodded gently. It seemed a polite acknowledgment, but then he said, "Listen to me. As a priest ordained in the Catholic Church, I cannot formally bless your union in the eyes of God. But . . . as a legally established authority in the state of California, empowered to recognize the union of two consenting adults—" He paused to clear his throat. "—I now pronounce you . . . married. Congratulations. Mazel Tov. Now, let me sign your document." He held out his hand for the marriage license.

And now it was Hu's turn to cry—but this time for joy.

SOUR MILK GIRLS

ERIN ROBERTS

The new girl showed up to the Agency on a Sunday, looking like an old dishrag and smelling like sour milk. Not that I could *really* smell her from three floors up through the mesh and bars, but there's only three types of girls here, and she was definitely the sour milk kind. Her head hung down like it was too much work to raise it, and her long black hair flopped around so you couldn't see her face. I'd have bet a week's credits she had big ol' scaredy-cat eyes, but she never bothered to look up, just let Miss Miranda lead her by the elbow through the front doors. Didn't even try to run. Sour milk all the way.

Even sour milk new girls were good, though; anything new was good. The last one, Hope, might have been dull as old paint, but at least she'd been something different to talk about. I'd even won a day's credits from Flash by betting the girl wouldn't make it to fourteen without some foster trying her out and keeping her. Anyone could tell Hope smelled like cinnamon and honey, same as those babies on the first floor and the second-floor girls with their pigtails and missing-tooth smiles. Sure enough, only took six months before the Reynolds came and took Hope off to their nice house with the big beds and the white fence and those stupid yapping dogs, leaving just me and Whispers and Flash to stare at each other and count all the months and years 'til we'd finally turn eighteen. Flash should've known it would go that way—cinnamon and honey's something fosters can't resist.

Whispers said this new girl was officially called Brenda, but that was just as stupid as all the other Agency names, and the girl wouldn't remember it after Processing anyway. At first I said we should call her Dishrag or Milkbreath, but even Flash thought that was too mean, and Flash is as nasty as hot sauce and lye. She's the one who named me Ghost, on account of I'm small and shadow-dark and she thinks I creep around too much in the night. She got *her* name 'cause that's how fast fosters send her back after their cat turns up dead and they realize the devil has blond hair and dimples.

"What's in her file?" I asked Whispers, who was still leaned up against the wall by the window. She never bothered to look out anymore. Not even for new girls.

"I'm just supposed to clean the office," she said. "Files are confidential."

"Must be good if you're holding back," said Flash, blowing out air as she tried to whistle.

"Maybe," Whispers said, with a lopsided shrug. Then she murmured something nobody could hear while staring down at her shoes. That meant we weren't getting any more from her for at least an hour, not even if Flash threatened to throw her out the window or hang her with the sheets from one of the empty beds. No use pushing her 'til she started banshee-screaming, so Flash just practiced whistling and I played around some with our crap computers and we let Whispers go all sour milk and talk to her invisible friends.

By the time Flash got a half-whistle half-spit sound to come out of her mouth and I'd finished up my hack of the first floor baby cams for when things got boring, new girl was being led off the elevator by Miss Miranda, head still down. Flash and I lined up in front of the room same as always—hands behind our backs, chests up and out, heads forward, eyes wide. Even Whispers came out of her murmuring and straightened up against the wall. Agency folks didn't care about much as far as us third-floors were concerned, but they were total nuts for protocol.

Miss Miranda started by doing her normal speech troduction. *This is Brenda, she's fifteen years old, and she's going to stay with us for a while. These are the girls, they're all trying to get new homes too. And we just know it'll work out for you all any day now.* When she said that last bit, her voice always got real high, like someone talking after they took a gulp of air from a circus balloon.

We ask you to stay on the third floor when you're in the building unless you're doing chores downstairs or get called to the office. But don't worry—there's so much to do up here, you won't even notice. Her voice went even higher for that part, 'cause even an idiot could see there wasn't anything on the floor but twenty empty beds, two long white lunch tables, a couple of old computers on splintery desks covered with the names of old third-floors, and the door to the world's grimiest bathroom.

As long as you maintain good grades and proper behavior in school, you're free to come and go as you please until seven PM curfew. You'll get a few credits each day for transit and meals. If you need additional learning help or assistance with your homework, the computers in the back row have plenty to offer. Age-appropriate stuff only, of course. She looked straight at me when she said it, like it was my fault the security on the things was shit and I'd figured out a way to order vapes and liquor pops and get R-rated videos.

Now you girls get along, and try not to kill each other. She looked at Flash for that one, even though Flash hadn't really tried to kill anyone for at least a year. She'd barely even talked to Hope. Either she was getting soft now that we were in high school, or she was gonna burn the whole place down someday. Maybe both.

As soon as she got the last words out of her mouth, Miss Miranda spun around on her high heels and got out of there as fast as she could. I thought the new girl would fall over as soon as Miss Miranda left, but she put her hands behind her back and stuck her chest out same as the rest of us. Her eyes weren't nearly as scaredy-cat as I thought they'd be. She smelled like sour milk for sure, but hot sauce and honey a little bit too.

"I'm Brenda," she said. "Brenda Nevins."

"That's a stupid name," said Flash.

"It's what my daddy called me," said new girl, thrusting her chest out even more, like it would cover the way her voice got all wobbly.

"Yeah? Well where's your daddy now?" Flash asked. The new girl's head dropped forward. We hadn't made a bet on whether someone could make her cry, but there were some things Flash would do for free.

"She doesn't remember," I told Flash. "You know that."

"I remember fine," said the new girl. "It's just that . . . it just happened. He just died, I mean."

Flash rolled her eyes.

"No way you *remember* that shit," she said. "Not anymore." She put on her best Miss Miranda impression, high pitched and piercing. "Your memories of your time before joining the Agency are being held for safekeeping until you reach adulthood and can properly integrate them into your daily life."

"What are you talking about?" new girl said. "I remember my dad. He was a—"

"Spare me the bullshit," Flash said, voice back low. "Miss Miranda tell you how in your file it says your daddy was a famous reccer? Or a Wall Street corp? Or a doctor? Bet if you looked in the 'grams she took from you, you'd find out he left you chained up in the basement. Or he liked to beat on your mama. Or maybe you ain't never had no daddy at all."

I felt my eyes get hot, just a little, but new girl didn't blink.

"My daddy was a good man," she said. "Not my fault if yours wasn't worth shit."

I backed up two steps so as not to get hit when the fists started flying. A fight was gonna mean discipline and lights-out and early curfew for at least two weeks. Nothing worse than that *and* having a black eye. But Flash just laughed.

"Damn, girl," she said. "You got balls. Gonna be hard coming up with a name for you."

"My dad—"

"Your dad won't know any different." I tried to stare some sense into the girl before Flash flipped back to serious and threw her across the room, or started working out how to smother her in the middle of the night. "Leave his name for him and ours for us. I'm Ghost. She's Flash. That's Whispers. We'll figure something out for you."

It took two weeks, but in the end, we called her Princess. Flash said it was from some fairy tale book she'd read as a little kid, but I'd been to the Reynolds' for a tryout same as she had, and Princess was the name of the dumb fat poodle they all fed under the table. Plus Flash said it like a curse, with a sparkle in her eye that any idiot could tell meant trouble. I told Princess not to worry, though; I'd watch her back. Not sure why. Maybe 'cause if Princess turned up dead it was back to just Whispers and Flash to talk to. Maybe 'cause I used to be a bit of a sour milk girl too.

Me and Princess almost pinky-swore on the whole thing, but I told her that was just for little kids and losers. Even if you were too poor to get wired up soon as you turned fourteen so you could swap 'grams of every stupid thing you did with all your besties in the school cafeteria, anybody could put together the credits for a memory share at one of the public booths. Sure, all the MemCorps signs said with adult supervision only, 'cause fooling around in your head like that could mess you up when your brain was still growing, but I just told the guy at the front we were over eighteen and gave him a two-cred tip. And Princess let him look down her shirt a little when he asked to see our pretty little smiles.

We got hooked up to our chairs in one of the side-by-sides. They were sticky, but it felt like old candy, not blood or anything, so I locked in. I had to show Princess how, but she caught on quick—straps on, headset up, earpieces in. I didn't get into all the MemCorps does this and your brain cells do that and then you see the memory clear as if it happened to you part, 'cause Princess might have been a little sad looking, but she didn't seem dumb.

"Your session has begun," said the booth voice, all high and cool, like if Miss Miranda had turned into a robot.

I started first, since I knew how to work the thing. Shared my memory of the time I pulled some stupid rich girl's chair out at school and she fell back and her legs went one way and her arms went another and her mouth made a big O shape and I laughed for about an hour. Princess giggled right along with me, but there was no way to tell how much of that was real and how much was the machine—easy enough to get swept away in a share without halfway trying.

"That's all you got, Ghost?" she said, when we were finished laughing. "Some girl falling over?"

"It's funny."

"Yeah, but you said we're supposed to be swapping something real."

"It's a memory booth, dumbass," I said, smiling so she knew I didn't mean something by it like Flash would. "Of course it's real." And it was, even if I didn't share the part where Miss Miranda found out and made my head ache for a week. I liked Princess fine, but you couldn't give everything to some new girl in one go.

"Not real like true," she said, rolling her eyes. "Real like important. Like my daddy."

"I'm sick of hearing about your damn daddy all the time."

"That's 'cause you didn't know him the way I did," she said. "*He* was real."

And then she shared him with me—one 'gram after another. The way he half-smiled when she walked in the house, how it sounded when he called her Brenda, how she found him dead in his rocking chair and didn't tell anyone for a whole day even though it started to stink. The public booths were old and ragged, but I could still smell the rotten and taste the tang of garbage in my mouth and feel the pound pound of her heart thinking it was the Agency every time a car drove by. Whole thing made my eyes sting and my throat itch.

"Real like that," Princess said, voice all whispery. I just shook my head. No thinking about what my daddy could've looked like and what he might've called me. Needed to clear everything out and get back on even ground.

"'Cmon. Just show me *something*," she said, and for a second, I wished Flash was there, just to tell her to shut the hell up and leave me alone.

"Maybe next time," I said instead, taking the straps off of my legs clip by clip, telling my hands not to shake. "We're out of time anyways."

Princess flipped her hair back with her hand, turned her head, and looked me straight in the eyes. "You think that guy out there's gonna mind if we go over?"

"No. I just . . . "

"Don't want to share something real," she said, ripping her straps off and throwing her goggles back on the shelf, acting like sour milk and hot sauce had a baby. "I get it."

"You really fucking don't," I said. "Me, Flash, Whispers . . . we don't have something *real* to share. All those cute, sweet memories of being a kid? Snatched off us when we got to the Agency and locked away where we can't get 'em. All we know is school and the third floor and a few fosters who couldn't be bothered to keep us. That's it. That's all we fucking got."

Princess stared at me for a second, eyes wide, then walked out, saying *I didn't know* and *Sorry* under her breath like she was doing a Whispers impression. I stayed for a while, playing back the couple of half-decent memories I *did* have, like the day I figured out how to get the computers in the back to do what I wanted, like a real hacker, or the times the Agency let us go down to the first floor and play with the babies, and then the ones that made my neck shiver, like all the times fosters sent me back 'cause I didn't fit into any of the smiling family photos—too old, too dark, too "hard to handle."

But none of my memories were real the way Princess wanted. They didn't make my blood jump or my hands get all shaky or my mouth go dry. Not even the bad ones. Not the Reynolds' dog Butch chasing me 'round their big house, growling and smelling like death and scaring me more than Flash ever had. Not little Bitsy Reynolds laughing and telling me how I seemed nice enough for a dark girl, but Butch hated who he hated and you couldn't tell a dog any different. Not Mrs. Reynolds looking anywhere but at my face when she brought me back to the Agency, telling Miss Miranda she'd tried but I didn't know how to fit in and I was riling up the animals and after all, they'd been there first. Not even the day I woke up in the Agency with a throbbing skull and a big ol' hole of nothing in my head and Miss Miranda telling me I was eight years old and my parents were dead but I'd get a new family by the time I turned ten if I just tried hard enough. Not one goddamned thing.

I got back after curfew. Miss Miranda gave me a lecture about rules and responsibilities over the pounding in my head—*a small physical reminder of the way we expect you to behave here*, she said, smiling down at me. *I hope I won't have to speak to you about this again.*

At least the pain made it easy enough to ignore everyone once I was off the elevator. Flash rushed up to find out where I went off to and if I did anything fun, Whispers told stories about my day to her make-believe friends, and Princess acted like the back wall was the most interesting thing in the room. Took her half an hour to slink her way over to where I sat on the edge of my bed in the fourth row, swinging my feet in the air and ignoring every one of Flash's ten thousand questions. Her hair hung down in her face again, like on her very first day, and she looked like one of those trained puppies the homeless men use for begging, ready to pant and collapse at your feet the minute you look like you've got a few credits to spare.

"I'm sorry," she said. She sat on the floor in front of my feet like she thought I wouldn't kick her. "Didn't realize the way things went around here."

I shrugged and said, "It's okay, you're new." Even though it wasn't. Anything to get her to shut it and go away. But of course Princess was too sour milk to get any hints, just kept sitting there and staring and asking stupid things.

"How long you been here, anyway?"

"Six years. More or less. Agency said they got a bunch of us after the last big quake."

"A bunch? They on another floor we can't go to?"

"Nah. They all got kept by fosters whose kids got smashed up or killed same as our parents," Flash said. "Everybody but us lifers and the lucky ones."

"Lucky ones?" Princess' face stayed scrunched.

"The ones who got old and got out. Hit eighteen, got their memories, never looked back."

"Got their memories from where?" Princess asked. Flash rolled her eyes.

"From wherever they fucking keep them after Processing," she said. "Hurts like a bitch when they rip the 'grams out, too. Like someone stabbing you through your eye. 'Course they let you remember that part. Fucking Agency."

"It only hurts for a minute, wuss," I said, sticking my tongue out at Flash. Normally I wouldn't dare, but one of the good things about the way she looked at Princess, like some puppy she half-wanted to cuddle, half-wanted to kick, was that she didn't have so much nasty left for the rest of us.

"So how come I remember everything?" Princess asked, like there was any way we'd know.

"They probably screwed up," Flash said. "Or you're an Agency spy. Or your brain's so weak that it would mind-wipe you altogether." She pointed over at Whispers, who was playing with her fingers like she'd never seen them before.

"You wish," said Princess, flipping her hair in Flash's general direction like she was trying to get killed. Flash ignored it. She really was getting soft.

"Only way to find out is to get into Miss Miranda's files," Flash said. "She's got 'em all locked up down in the office on cube drives or something. Right, Whispers?"

"I'm just supposed to clean the office," Whispers said, to nobody in particular.

"Fine." Flash walked over to Whispers' corner of the room to get her attention. "Simple question. You ever see a whole bunch of little glowy cubes in a drawer or something?"

"Leave her be, Flash," I said. My head still hurt from Miss Miranda's warning, and nothing got Whispers shrieking louder than getting too comfortable over in her corner of the room. The first time, she'd hollered for a good hour 'til the Agency folks figured she wasn't gonna stop, but even now it took about ten minutes before she got dragged down to the medic and brought back passed out cold.

"I'm just asking a question, Ghost," Flash said, leaning against the wall near Whispers' bed. "C'mon, Whispers. I promise I'll leave you alone if you tell."

"The memories aren't in the office," Whispers said. "They're in the cloud." I felt my cheeks get a little hot. Stupid. I was supposed to be the big bad hacker; I should've guessed.

"That means we can get 'em with the computers up here, right Ghost?" Flash asked. "Like you did when you got the booze-flavored candy?"

"That was *before* they added all kinds of security," I said.

"So you can't get in?"

"Didn't say that."

"Then shut up and do it already," Flash said. "I want to know why she gets to hold on to all her stupid little 'grams and they won't let us remember shit 'til we get out of here."

"Can't tonight," I said. "They're gonna be watching the floor."

"Yeah, 'cause you decided you had to come in late, and for no good reason either. Didn't even bring us shit."

"It's not her fault," Princess said, still lounging on the floor near my bed. "I—"

"Doesn't matter," I said. "They're gonna be looking close for a couple days. We'll have to try another time."

"Or we could just distract 'em," Flash said. Then she went and sat down, right on the edge of Whispers' bed.

It took fifteen minutes of screams that I could feel all the way back behind my eyeballs, but eventually one of the overnight Agency guys, the one Flash thought had nice hair, came up and dragged Whispers away.

"You shouldn't have—" I started.

"Yeah yeah," Flash said, shrugging. "Just do it already. Before they finish drugging her up."

I looked at Princess, but she just flipped her hair again and walked over to the computers. She had a little more hot sauce in her than I thought. Couldn't tell yet if that was a good thing.

"Go 'head," Flash said. "Thought you were supposed to be some kind of super-hacker."

My head was still throbbing, worse than ever, and I knew Flash was just trying to get to me, but truth was truth. I sat down and got to typing—no way the Agency would spring for touch screens or one of those fancy robot lady voices—and was in quicker than I thought. Miss Miranda had locked down all the "bad influence" stuff pretty tight, but getting the Agency files wasn't much harder than getting the cam feed from downstairs and watching the babies play.

"Brenda Nevins," I read from the screen. "Resident at the Agency for the Care of Unassociated Female Minors."

"Blah blah blah," said Flash from across the room. She was on lookout by the elevator for when Mr. Nice Hair came back with Whispers. "Get to the good stuff."

"It doesn't say anything really," I said. "Just a bunch of big words." The whole thing was reports and warnings and psychology mumbo-jumbo. Nothing 'til I got down to the engrams section. It was a list of 'grams with titles like *Discovery of Father's Body* and *Trip to Percy Park on May 7th.* I recognized a couple from in the booth earlier, but most I'd never even heard of, and just about all of them had the same big bold flashing letters on the far right. *Not to Be Removed. See Explanation.*

" 'Explanation,' " Princess read from over my shoulder, finger tracing along the screen like some little kid trying to figure out how words work. " 'To date, Miss Nevins has shown none of the aberrant or destructive behavior of many of the Agency's other older residents. As the trauma from the loss of her father has not led her to behave negatively, we recommend that she be able to keep the majority of her memories at this time. Moreover, it can be noted that Agency resident Becky Ann Ross has shown no significant behavioral improvement since memory removal, and it is possible that the procedure itself had a negative impact on the development of Samantha Lee, leaving her prone to delusions and outbursts. While Destiny Ward has demonstrated some positive behavior changes and remains difficult to place primarily due an unfortunate lack of demand, a better form of control therapy than memory removal may need to be implemented in the future. Princess faked her way through most of the big words and probably wasn't saying half of them right, but I knew what "lack of demand" meant.

"Destiny? That's you?" Princess asked. I shut down the machine and pushed her out of my way as I headed back to my bed. She followed. Of course.

"You're Destiny Ward," she said again, right behind my ear. "Right?"

"I'm Ghost, you fucking idiot," I said. Ghost who was too old and too ugly to be in demand. Ghost who didn't smile right, who dogs couldn't help but want to kill. Ghost who had a hole in her mind instead of whatever it was that would get Princess and all those little first-floor babies and second-floor sweethearts tried out and kept by fosters, far away from the damn third floor. Ghost who knew how to fix it.

I got up from the bed so fast that Princess jumped back a good foot. Even Flash flinched a little bit over by the elevator. Fuck the Agency; I could find my 'grams right now, maybe even get them put back in early. There were people who would do that if you paid them well enough. I was a hacker; I could figure it out.

I got back into my file and scrolled down. *Visit to the Ferris Wheel with Parents, Earthquake and Aftermath, Petty Larceny #1,2,3.*

And in the rightmost column of each—*Permanently Deleted.* Not held for safe-keeping until you can integrate them into adult life. Not get them back when you turn eighteen. Just gone. Totally and forever gone.

I picked up the stupid machine to throw it down on the floor, break it open like a water balloon, but Princess caught my arm.

"You don't want to—"

"You don't know what the hell I want," I said, brushing her off and heading over to the elevator. "Agency lied to us, Flash. They fucking lied. They took all our memories and said they were giving them back but they—"

"Shut it," Flash said. "They're coming up."

She was right. I could hear the whirring of the gears as the elevator climbed. This time of night, Agency bastards would want us all lying down. Proper bedtime protocol and all that bullshit. Leave us flat on our backs while they told us their lies.

I got back to my bed just in time for Mr. Nice Hair to step off, carrying Whispers in his arms. He put her down on the closest bed, nowhere near her little corner, which was how I knew she was really knocked out. Otherwise she would've started screaming all over again. Then he turned around and left without a word. Just like Miss Miranda. No time for the third-floor rejects. We probably wouldn't remember it anyway.

"Let's move her back," said Flash. Nobody moved. "You want her to start up again when she wakes up?"

I didn't care what the hell happened when she woke up, but I didn't feel like fighting. I grabbed her bony ankles while Flash took hold of her arms and Princess kept a hand under her back. Once she was passed out on her own bed, legs sprawled one way and arms another, mouth hanging open like she was a clown in a carnival game, Flash patted me on the arm. If it had been Princess, I probably would have slapped her in the face, but instead I turned my face away.

"They really wipe our stuff completely?" she asked. I nodded. "No way to hack it back?"

"Don't think so."

"I'm sorry," Princess said. When I didn't answer, she crept over to her bed and laid down, her head thudding onto the hard pillow. Flash didn't move. Just leaned in close so her mouth was right by my ear.

"I've got an idea," she said. Her voice turned from whisper to giggle.

I could almost smell the hot sauce in the air.

"Wanna go to the booth again?" I asked Princess a few days later, after school. She looked at me and nodded like I'd asked if she wanted a million bucks. With me giving her the silent treatment, all she'd had to talk to was Flash and Whispers, and that wasn't much to live on.

"Is it gonna make you mad again?" she asked, her face back in that little half-scrunch.

"Nah, I'm over it," I said. "Plus, I figured out how to share something real. You're looking at an A-plus hacker, remember?"

"Yeah, I remember." She smiled bright for the rest of the walk over to the booth. I nodded at the front desk guy as we came in, sent a whole mess of credits his way.

"Break time, right?" I said. He just raised his chin in a half-nod, then looked over at Princess's shirt like he could see through the fabric. She caught on quick and bent over again, enough for him to smile and head off. Then she went straight for the side-by-sides.

"You coming, right?" she said.

"Yeah," I said. "Go ahead and strap in. I have to hack something back here for this to work."

"Okay." Princess put on the headphones and straps and all that. The goggles covered her eyes up tight, but I turned the booth lights off too, made sure she couldn't see Flash tiptoeing in.

I called up one of the memories on the list I'd pulled from the Agency. *Brenda and her Father at her fifth birthday.*

"Hey," Princess said, "Something's off. This is one of mine."

"Not anymore," I said. Her body jerked up as my code hit the booth and she clutched her head like someone was knifing her in the eye. Princess screamed and tried to tear the straps off, to run away, but Flash held her arms down, giggling under her breath. I'd offered her a few credits to help out, but some things Flash would do for free.

"Don't worry." Flash's hands tightened against Princess' arms as Princess' hair flipped back and forth. "It only hurts for a minute. You'll barely remember."

When the twitching and moaning stopped, we unhooked Princess from the booth and Flash walked her out, steadying her like she was an old drunk. I told Flash I'd be along soon, that I needed to check everything was clear so we wouldn't get caught. But after she was out of sight, I went in for a half hour in my own booth instead. Any good thief's gotta check the merchandise. Plus I didn't like looking at Princess all limp and sad, worse than sour milk even. That was more of a Flash kinda thing. She'd said I should erase every memory Princess had forever, put us all on even ground, but I didn't want to be that way about it. I was gonna give Princess the memories back at eighteen anyway. Sooner, maybe. Once I was living with a foster in some big house with nice kids and no dogs.

Princess was long-haired and cinnamon pretty; she'd find a foster with her memories or not. Just like Hope and the rest. Just like I was gonna. With Princess' memories filling up that hole in my head, I'd be set. I'd know just how to smile with the fosters and laugh and make 'em like me—even if I didn't fit in the pictures, I'd know how to be part of a family. I'd smell like cinnamon and honey and babies and home.

I cued up the first string of memories in watch mode, so I wouldn't get too caught up in the share 'til I found the right ones. I could tell Princess was a little girl right away 'cause of how big everyone looked through her eyes, like friendly giants. There were tons of them, coming and going and bringing her things, but only two were really important—Mom and Dad, happy and smiling. I tried smiling back, giggling like she giggled when Dad picked her up to pretend fly or when Mom played peekaboo. But I couldn't get the feel of it right without going all the way in. I could hear myself through the earplugs, a high-pitched cross between a scream and the hiccups. I needed something better.

I skipped through the memories, playing a few seconds if something looked good and then moving on, looking for something like the ones that Princess had showed me before, the ones that made my hand shake and my breath skip.

But all I saw was how, each time I stopped, there were half as many people, that the presents were gone and then the toys too, that the rooms were smaller and dingier, that Mom left on a rainy day and never came back, that Princess didn't seem to care. She still had her Daddy and he always always held her tightly, close enough that even on watch I could smell the liquor on his breath—just like those booze pops I'd ordered. I still felt a little of the way she'd felt when he called her Brenda, all lit up from inside like candles on a birthday cake, but this time I wasn't swept up in the share—she was just some sad little girl wearing grimy clothes, living in a dirty room with an old man who finally died in a rocking chair. Some girl who leaned over and let a perv at a front counter see down her shirt. Some girl too dumb to figure out her own stupid memories.

I left the booth before the half hour was up, still trying to get the stink of Princess' dirty life out of my nose. Pervy was back on duty and waved me over from the front counter as I passed by.

"Your friend gonna be alright?" he said. "Seems like a sweet girl." He licked his skinny lips and I had to try not to shiver. Princess would end up swapping more than 'grams with him one of these days.

"Leave her alone," I said.

"I'm just a concerned citizen." He lifted a bushy eyebrow in a way that was probably supposed to make me feel something. "Maybe I should be concerned about what you were doing during my break."

"Just making a back up," I said. "In case there's another quake or she gets hit by a truck or something." Pervy leaned forward a little.

"I've got an extra," I said. "You want it?"

Pervy had his hands out before I could blink. They looked pale and clammy, like a piece of gum stuck under a chair too long. I fished the cube with Princess' memories out of my pocket. It was the only one I had, but she'd be better off without it. Who wants to find out at eighteen that their life has been so fucking pathetic? Screw having something real.

"I give you this, you leave her alone, alright?"

Pervy nodded. I handed the cube over, making sure not to touch his sweaty hands. Fifty-fifty chance he'd try to pull some double-cross, but if I needed to, I could take care of his memories as easy as I had Princess', so I just smiled and walked out. Can't hurt somebody you can't remember.

This time, I made curfew. I could tell by the way Miss Miranda stared me down that she couldn't wait to have some reason to give me punishment, but she was gonna have to. I smiled right at her and headed up to the third floor like I had a mouth full of cotton candy. Soon as I got off the elevator I saw Princess lying in the bed she liked, hair spread out on the pillow like a pool of old soda. Flash sprang up soon as she saw me, with that big smile she got like she was either gonna hug you or eat you.

"It's all gone," she said. "All that shit about her daddy and her perfect life? Wiped just like if the Agency got her."

I smiled back, but it felt weird, like baring fangs.

"I thought you were bullshitting about the hacking part, but you give good, Ghost," Flash said. "Maybe next you can reboot Whispers so she won't talk so damn much, right? Or creep up on Miss Miranda and take everything she's got?" She laughed hard, and I knew not to tell her anything about how it really was with Princess, 'cause then she'd be mad I gave all the good stuff away.

"The rest of her okay?" I said, like I didn't care too much really.

"Yeah, she's good. Not like Whispers or anything. Just less annoying. Cuter too." Flash glanced over at Princess like she was sizing her up in a prize booth at a fair.

"Yeah, but fosters'll probably get her soon." She'd be fine. Just like Hope. Better than her memories.

"Maybe," Flash said, "If she figures out how to keep her mouth shut."

"Fifty credits says she's gone in a month."

Flash shook her head. "She's not *that* cute."

"You said that with Hope." I shrugged and hoped my palms wouldn't be too sweaty.

"Fine." Flash grabbed my hand tight with her cold one. "But make it sixty. And when she starts blabbermouthing again, I'm gonna laugh at the both of you."

"We'll see," I said, and started over for Princess. I thought Flash might follow, but she just went back to practicing whistles like always. Princess wasn't doing much, didn't even look at me as I walked over and sat down right by her ear. Just stared up at the ceiling like any other new girl who got wiped and dumped on the third floor. Sour milk squared. But that was okay. You didn't have to stay a sour milk girl forever.

"I'm Ghost," I said, low and quiet so only she could hear. "You know Flash and Whispers. And we call you Princess, but your daddy, he called you Brenda."

THE UNNECESSARY PARTS OF THE STORY

ADAM-TROY CASTRO

You almost don't need the first half of the story at all. You know there's a spaceship. You know that its crew stops off at some out-of-the-way planet on some pretext or other, probably repairs, and that while they're there, somebody jars the wrong rock, or enters the wrong dark place, or something. You know that this person gets infected, that nobody notices, and that when they take off, a hostile alien intelligence takes off with them. Finally, you know that after some skulking around in corridors and a few isolated deaths, the carrier, call him Hennessy, is subdued and placed in isolation, where the others observe him worriedly on monitors.

All of that goes without saying. Because you've been here before.

What should happen now is the crew deciding after much rational and reasoned discussion that this is some heavy-duty alien shit, with any number of possible properties, and that the smartest possible thing to do is to write Hennessy off as a complete loss, and dump him into interplanetary vacuum.

But human beings are cute, not to mention slow learners, and so they come up with a different approach entirely. The Captain, and not some more disposable party, puts on an isolation suit and enters the lab in order to negotiate with the entity now controlling good old Hennessy. The Captain is wise, and the Captain is bearded, and the Captain is fully confident in the precautions already taken being able to prevent whatever's eating Hennessy from also taking charge of him. He cycles through the airlock separating the ship proper from the horror that sits in the isolation cell, and he stands and he peers through his faceplate at the figure who was until recently a respected friend and colleague if also a bit of a comical asshole, who is now secured by gleaming silvery rings to a chair that keeps him immobile; and it would only confuse us to ask just why this vessel on a mission of peaceful exploration, or freight hauling, or whatever, even has an isolation cell with a chair designed to keep a prisoner immobile. Right now, it's enough to focus our attention on the immediate problem.

The Captain's probably thinking that he and his crew must be the most inobservant people alive. Hennessy did look a little grotty after leaving the planet, a little paler and sweatier than usual, possibly hung over, but even before he began to prowl the corridors, murdering his fellow crew members one by one, that grottiness was left far behind, in favor of grotesquery. His complexion turned pitted and warty, his flesh flaking and blistery, his lips yellowish and pustulent, well past the point where he looked dead, and yet a number of those he cornered on his several days of winnowing down the opposition greeted his appearance not with a horrified, *Holy crap, Hennessy's been infected with something,* but a more neutral, *Jesus, man, you look like hell.* The ship's faithful cameras recorded the killing that followed but not whether any of the victims, upon ascertaining that a violent death was now their lot, devoted any of their remaining mental energy to excoriating themselves with a sad *stupid, stupid, stupid.* Because, really: a number of their demises were an exercise in not seeing the bloody obvious until it was too late.

It's hard to imagine anybody being taken in now, because Hennessy no longer looks even remotely human. He resembles a boil in the process of draining. Various nasty fluids leak from his cheeks, his mouth, his eyes. Even with his restraints on, his movements are twitchy, violent, and inhuman. But the thing occupying him manages a sneer as he confronts the Captain: "Come to negotiate! How cute."

The Captain says, "What are you, and what do you want?"

The faux-Hennessy leers at him, and through bubbling lips, explains, "I think it's fairly clear what I am. I'm an intelligent parasitic organism. Not evolved on that planet where you found me, but on another many light-years away, spreading from system to system the same way I've spread to you: via fools stumbling in where they don't belong. If I told you how many sentient races I've infected down to the very last organism, all because of uncounted stupid space travelers like yourself giving me a ride from one world to another, you would quail in horror. I will infect your entire civilization, and you will do nothing to stop me."

"Thank you," says the Captain. He leaves the room via the same aperture he used to enter, tells his crew that Hennessy is a lost cause, and with a quick flip of a switch ejects the isolation chamber into a nearby sun, incinerating his old friend, the monster occupying him, and any chance of the foulness spreading to the rest of the human race. Such a course of action would be cold, and it would be cruel, and it would lead to some hard questions from a fleet board of enquiry, but it would also be completely sensible.

Except, of course, that he doesn't do any of that. What he does is leave the room via the same aperture he used to enter, tell his crew that he's lost all the crew members he's going to, and that he wants options for curing Hennessy on his desk in one hour, damn it. Whereupon everybody disperses and lets the thing that used to be Hennessy continue to brew and mutate and become more dangerous, like a sausage plumping in its croissant dough.

How irresponsible! But this is not the worst part they miss.

Another thing needs to be established here. Hennessy, while he was Hennessy, was just a guy. Oh, he was a good companion for this routine journey between the stars, even if, as you impartial observers would have noted if your humble narrator had seen fit to subject you to the kabuki sameness of the first part of the story, a bit of a jackass, precisely the kind of putz who was just naturally the one person out of all the crew to get himself infected by some kind of Lovecraftian alien blood tick. Were this a thriller, you the audience would be sitting there on your fat asses clucking, *well, of course, he was always the one I expected to go first.* But he was, again, just a guy: not particularly bright, not possessed of prodigious reservoirs of strength, not naturally capable of shrugging off a blaster burst to the chest, the way this Hennessy was, before a jury-rigged weapon made out of spare parts brought him down just when all seemed lost. There have clearly been physical changes inside him, some improvements to his connective tissue, some replumbing of his circulatory system, some toughening of his actual flesh, that made him as tough and as hard to kill as he was.

You only have to look at his current complexion, a little like a microwavable pizza with pus topping, to know that he's mutating in strange and terrifying ways, and that this process is accelerating.

It therefore follows—and absolutely should be obvious to the fellow crew members who are all in their respective departments working overtime to collate data for the meeting the Captain's called in one hour, or having a stand-up quickie in a maintenance niche—that these mutations are likely to continue and that, if the Captain's incomprehensible decision is to keep him on board, among the pressing tasks that need to be assigned to somebody is constant real-time monitoring. Somebody needs to be watching Hennessy every moment, measuring every infinitesimal change in his condition every moment, making a new threat assessment every moment. This is only common sense, and does it surprise you, at all, that nobody's been put on this duty? Instead, he's left in his chair, bubbling, cackling to himself, giving thanks to whatever alien deity he worships, and continuing his transformation from a Hennessy already beyond salvaging into a thing that even Hennessy's gray-haired old mother back in Wichita, a woman so doting that she breast-fed him until he was seven, would order an exterminator on in two seconds flat.

Nobody's there to say, "Uh, guys," when the creature who used to be Hennessy develops extra musculature around its greenish and glistening forearms, and when those powerful limbs begin to struggle with the restraints holding its arms in place.

Incredibly irresponsible!

Too stupid to be borne!

Evidence of a species that deserves to be infected by this horror!

And yet even this is not the most astonishing element they miss; not even close.

You almost don't need the next part of the story, either. You have internalized the ingredients from long and enthusiastic ingestion and know that what follows next is the last chance the members of this doomed crew have to do something remotely intelligent. Instead, you watch them have what amounts to a board meeting.

During this meeting the various surviving members of the crew all play the parts that reflect their dominant personality traits. There is a Professorial Type who drones on for a little bit about past legends of such a creature, archaeological evidence on various worlds of prior civilizations subsumed and destroyed by it, and an obscure research vessel that a few years back self-destructed after sending out an unnecessarily ambiguous and fragmentary warning, too garbled to be worth much, of what he suspects to be precisely this problem; and while this is all learned and intelligently presented, it is not helpful at all. There is a Panicky Male who imparts pretty much the same message in fewer words by informing everybody that this is all fucked up, man. There's a Weepy Woman who merely sniffles. The Psychotic Type, fingering a combat knife with deep adoration, opines that the Captain should just let him into the isolation chamber with Hennessy, so he can take care of the problem in the way that none of you pussies could. There are a few angry rejoinders from the Hot Girl and Forgettable Guy who had their stand-up quickie less than an hour ago, and though they cleaned up well and are as close to professional as they ever are, there isn't a person in the room who doesn't know what they were just doing or that they unaccountably chose to do it now. The first intelligent comment comes from the Pragmatic Woman who says that Hennessy is already dead and that the thing pretending to be him should be spaced and the whole ship subjected to two days of internal, sterilizing radiation. The Cold Scientist says that it's worse than that, actually, because they know nothing of the alien organism's origins, least of all where it evolved and for that matter just what would have to be done to kill it, and that therefore, for the future of the human race, no chances should be taken; they really ought to head for the nearest sun and incinerate themselves in it. Everybody yells at the Cold Scientist for being so cold, and he says that he's only suggesting the most logical and prudent course. The Guy With A Sweetheart Back Home, acting as if he's the only person in the room with a reason to live, protests that Angie's waiting for him.

Among them, there are two who are closest to being right, the Pragmatic Woman and the Cold Scientist. You can see this, right?

It is astonishing how badly they both miss the big picture, and this is why it's sad, really, that this species ever developed space flight at all.

Still, it's the Captain's conscience that makes the decision. He says that he believes that if this organism is as dangerous as it professes to be, it's their duty to preserve it, so it can be investigated by authorities a lot smarter than anybody in this room. (This is a rather low bar, all told, but honestly, he is trying to do the right thing, so let's cut him some slack.)

Everybody talks over each other for a moment.

The Cold Scientist says, "That's insane. To even think of bringing that thing into Earth's biosphere . . "

"I'm not," the Captain says. "We're stopping at the System Biological Hazard Laboratory, the one that's in orbit around Pluto. We'll send a dispatch up ahead so they know we're coming. Once we're there we'll get Hennessy quarantined, undergo stringent examinations and decontamination ourselves, and make absolutely sure that the ship is scrubbed before we head the rest of the way home. If we're lucky, they'll be able to cure him. If we're not, we'll give the mission payment to his next of kin. But until then, we'll do everything we can to make sure he's secured and comfortable. Is that clear?"

And once again everybody talks over one another, all with their own pressing reasons why this a terrible idea, but sooner or later the Captain cuts them off and reminds them that this is not a democracy: a truism meant to establish that he's in charge but really means that if he's making the worst possible decision, as he is, then they're stuck with it unless they want to kill him.

The reason you don't really need this part of the story is that it amounts to ultimately doing nothing, even as the thing that used to be Hennessy becomes more and more unrecognizable in its chair.

Really: human beings are adorable.

You are a human being who has encountered this story in various forms, any number of other times, and you're still not getting it.

Perhaps it might help if we reference a related story type: the zombie plague.

In the incarnation we cite, one of many posited, a pathogen spread exclusively by biting escapes an isolated laboratory in the countryside.

Somebody is infected, visibly deteriorates, becomes a lurching carnivorous zombie of either the rabid-but-living or the reanimated-corpse variety, and with no will other than that dictated by the virus starts biting others, who contract the same syndrome and commence spreading it themselves, at a terrifying geometric rate. You could predict the further course of the story in your sleep. In short order, it goes worldwide.

Our question is: if these are the conditions, why exactly does it go worldwide?

That it will go wide, that it will take uncounted lives and wreak almost unimaginable terror before any possibility of containing it, is a given. After all, the deadliest thing about these fast-moving plagues is that they pop up by surprise and spread like wildfire before their vectors are isolated. By the time people realize that they shouldn't consume any pastry baked by Mary Mallon, it's too late. But zombies? Those creatures with clouded eyes and blue complexions who stagger about with the gait of people who have forgotten how to use their knees, and are easy to peg as infected even at a distance, well, even in this theoretical model where you can be generous and posit that their spread is not noticed by the authorities until there are millions of them—even in this case, how exactly do they go worldwide? They are all walking billboards for their condition, and they become that way shortly after the point of initial exposure. Even before they start eating people, even before they cross the line between people who are still clinging to the behavior of the uninfected and those who will happily chow down on the slowest members of the pack, they don't look at all well; they look like what they are, which is sweaty, pale, and dying. Any well-armed perimeter with checkpoints will see them coming at a distance. They won't suddenly turn up on the far side of the planet because it takes longer to get to the other side of the planet than it does for the disease to incubate.

You want to design a zombie plague that will wipe out all of humanity? Posit multiple methods of exposure. Not just the traditional bite: also, let's say, sexual contact, blood transfusions, exposure to contaminated surfaces, and airborne pathogens that can be spread at workplaces, social gatherings, schools, and in enclosed environments like pressurized airplane cabins. Let's say that you can infect everybody in a room by not covering your mouth when you sneeze. Let's say that you can do this while you still look and act perfectly fine. And finally, let's say that the disease lingers in your body for months before activating to the point where you transform and start biting people, months that you have spent spreading the plague to second and third generation carriers, who have themselves spread the plague to second and third generation carriers, all of whom will also prepare their food, kiss their children, and travel obliviously through crowds.

By the time hundreds of millions start biting people, it's everywhere.

That's how you start a zombie plague that can't be contained.

Make sure it's already done its damage before you even realize it's there.

A successful virus allows time for its own spread.

So this is the point the Captain doesn't get, that it is far more unbelievable to note that the Cold Scientist doesn't get. Take another look at Hennessy, who was showing symptoms within the very first few hours of exposure on an alien planet, even before his subsequent return to a spaceship that would take weeks or months to return to civilization depending on the physics you model. Within twenty-four hours, his personality was gone, and he was staggering around the ship's corridors killing people. Within forty-eight hours, he was strapped to a chair, viscous and repellent and oozing, openly telling his erstwhile companions that he was the avatar of an intelligent alien pathogen that had wiped out any number of sentient races and intended on going after human civilization next.

The question you need to ask is whether this is any way for a self-respecting malignant alien parasite to behave.

Why would it do this?

I ask you this question, those few of you who may have been smart enough to realize that it's that very infection talking: What advantage did evolution find in arranging for me to act that way?

Here's another part of the story you don't need to see, even if it is the part of the story that you may enjoy.

The sound of tremendous destruction lures the various members of the crew back to the isolation chamber, where the increasingly powerful thing that used to be Hennessy has burst free of its shackles. It is now nine feet tall, disfigured past all past definitions of revolting, and glistening. It makes various raaar-noises as it pounds on the door. The Hot Girl screams at the sight of him, the Cold Scientist utters some comments to the effect that this is fascinating, and the Pragmatic Woman shouts at the Captain that this would be a fine time to eject the module. The Captain, not being entirely stupid even if the events up to this point establish that it is certainly within his Venn Diagram, agrees and slams his fist on the big red button, the one that's sitting right there on the console for that precise purpose. A calm female voice commences announcing that the Ejection Program is inoperable for some reason. The Psychotic Type opines that he's done with this bullshit, and that he's going to smear that motherfucker over all four walls. To this end he breaks some safety glass and pulls out an impressive-looking projectile weapon that is, for some reason, stored right there. He gives the thing a *cha-chunk* to establish that it's loaded and orders the Hot Girl to open the door. The Captain shouts at her to Belay That Order, and there's some back-and-forth screaming over who's in charge and who should be in charge that prevents immediate action until the Hennessy-thing starts pounding on the walls with a raw strength that makes its imminent breach of the rest of the habitat an absolute, imminent inevitability. The Forgettable Guy tries to grab the weapon from the Psychotic Type and is blown away, in a convulsive and instinctive burst that the Psychotic Type didn't fire intentionally, which is not a great consolation to the Hot Girl, who starts screaming her head off. The Captain grabs a heavy tool that happens to be on hand and splits the Psychotic Type's skull for him. The bulkhead between all these observers and the isolation chamber is now only seconds from breaching. The Pragmatic Woman manages to get her hands on the projectile weapon, superfluously cocks it a second time—because, in such stories, that gesture does not fulfill an actual mechanical purpose, but instead just communicates resolve as danger approaches—and aims it at the imminent breach in the bulkhead. The instant the crack appears and widens enough for a revolting moist tentacle to intrude, she starts firing.

It needs to be established here that they are attempting to splatter a material that is, essentially, medical waste, that needs to be isolated and safely disposed of and not, in the result the Pragmatic Woman probably envisions, reduced to a liquid and evenly distributed over every nearby surface. It doesn't matter. The tentacle sprays photogenic ichor but is not very inconvenienced by the inexplicably convenient projectile weapon. As it thrashes about, it decapitates Professorial Type, hits Pragmatic Woman with the same force but does not kill her, and enlarges the rupture enough for the thing that was Hennessy to penetrate further into the room. "Fall back!" the Captain screams. "Fall back!" And as the surviving members of the crew do just that, we can step away from all the inevitabilities that follow, from the increasingly desperate efforts to stop the creature in its tracks to the moments of valor that allow one crew member to sacrifice his life for another to the plans that don't work and really, everything you already know is going to happen because you have already seen it happen any number of times, enough to ask just why the alien life form that transformed Hennessy is acting this way, if its ultimate goal should be to preserve the disease vector long enough for all these intrepid people to bring it back to the home world of their species.

Really; its actions, my actions, make no rational sense.

You want a successful disease? Try Toxoplasmosis. It is spread by terrestrial cats and except when contracted by vulnerable outliers like pregnant women, its key survival strategy is to ensure future generations by instilling in its hosts an attraction toward cats. Rats with toxoplasmosis don't run from cats, as they should if they prefer to avoid being tortured and eaten, but toward them, drawn by a tropism that they might experience as love and/or as a baffling, incomprehensible and terrifying impulse. Eaten, they spread the toxoplasmosis to the cats, who then spread it to any other rats they may encounter but fail to kill, who then seek out more cats. It's essentially a device to make sure that cats are loved forever. Toxoplasmosis is endemic among human beings and may well be the explanation for crazy cat ladies and the internet.

That is the way a *successful* parasitic disease acts, by encouraging the behavior that ensures its own propagation.

Now ask yourself, again, just what I think I'm doing, by turning Hennessy into a big scary glistening monster that his fellow crewmembers have every reason to want to kill, especially when—I won't recount the actual moment but will assure you that it occurs—Hennessy continues to rant as he pursues everybody, reminding them again and again that he intends to infect all of human civilization. After all, wouldn't it be easier for the disease to spread if Hennessy had remained the same tolerable jackass he'd always been, and if it had therefore had the chance to spread peacefully among a crew that would never have any real reason to suspect that it was sick?

You are very close to the answer now.

Draw a curtain over subsequent events, and you now find the two remaining members of the crew, now in quarantine over Earth.

Yes, we have skipped the entire climax. You don't need to dwell on that part. Again, you have encountered it before, and you have internalized it, and you could almost certainly recreate it yourself if you were of a mind to.

At this point, Hennessy is gone, as the last three survivors managed to lure him into the ship's core, one of them making the ultimate sacrifice in the process. They incinerated him, even as he screamed in final confrontation of his fate, with all appropriate pathos. Because nobody else ever came down with symptoms as extreme or as upsetting as his, it is widely presumed that he never passed on the contagion to anyone else, and that humanity is safe. It is true that he never passed on the contagion to anyone else and is also true that humanity is safe, but it is not true that humanity has gone uninfected. In fact, I now look out at the universe from billions of eyes, perfectly happy to be here, and perfectly happy to go without much in the way of overt mind-control for as long as your race's policies of space exploration spread my diaspora throughout the stars.

The Captain is dead, the Cold Doctor is gone, the Hot Girl is gone, and the Guy With a Sweetheart Back Home is gone.

The Pragmatic Woman, who you likely imagined to be the hero of the piece, is also gone, as she was the one who pragmatically gave her life to help the other two survivors lure what was left of Hennessy into the all-consuming core.

Those survivors, who we now find hand in hand as they look down on the civilization they have entirely infected, are the Panicky Male and the Weepy Woman, both of whom, I can assure you, had a character arc, showing hidden reserves of courage and strength as the battle to save the ship came down to the last few minutes. They're in love now, mostly because it strikes me as fitting and just that they should be. It amounts to a happy ending, I suppose. For them, and for me.

However disappointing they would find it, their hidden reserves of courage of strength were not entirely self-generated, but were the result of a chemical assist from inside, arranged by me.

You see, although they were all infected before they left the planet, every last one of them, it was entirely necessary that Hennessy transform into an object of terror. I could have picked any one of them to show obvious symptoms, but I assessed his personality and theirs at the moment of contact and thought he would be the most advantageous.

The Professorial Type and the Cold Doctor had to go, because they were the ones most likely to figure out what I was doing. The Captain had to go because, once everything went down, he was the one most likely to realize that piloting the ship into a sun was likely the best course of action. This also happens to have been true of the Pragmatic Woman. The Psychotic Type had to go because he was the most suicidally reckless, and in the unlikely event the true explanation of events had occurred to him, he would have had no problem killing everybody. I would have liked to save the Hot Girl and the Forgettable Guy and the Guy With Somebody Who Loved Him Back Home, but their demises, staged at key moments of the violent journey from that isolation cell to the ship's core, helped steer the rapidly shrinking crew toward the actions I wanted, the ones that would accomplish what I needed to accomplish. The only two I really wanted to keep alive were Panicky Male and Weepy Woman, who were between them the two most likely in the aftermath to say, "Thank God we lived; it's over now," without ever really contemplating the premise that maybe it wasn't. They were the two worst decision-makers, and so they did exactly what I intended them to do all along, the one thing I ran riot in Hennessy to accomplish: forgot all other considerations, and not incidentally, called off the rest of their survey mission, in favor of a beeline back to where I wanted them to be.

You might well protest that all the horror and death I put them through with Hennessy was unnecessary, given that this is exactly where they would have ended up anyway.

Strictly speaking, this is true.

But I am a parasite and a disease.

Doing what I did shortened my journey by a full six months.

THE TEMPORARY SUICIDES OF GOLDFISH

OCTAVIA CADE

Everyone deserves a last meal. Mine was fish, Syllabub laughing her arse off as she served it up. Not goldfish, because that would have been bad luck—the kind of bad luck that comes from gossip about a last meal getting back to her Ladyship and being taken as insult. Instead a poor skinny muddy thing in a thin soup, flounder I think, or catfish.

"They're not at all the same," says Syllabub, critical, but they're *fish*, aren't they?

"I didn't think there was going to be a test," I said, and if I'd any room left in me for panic I would have panicked then, because the Lady and her tanks are the only thing between me and a bloody end instead of a scaly one. And if I'm to be examined on fish before I'm allowed to become one, then I might as well offer myself up for gutting now and be done with it.

"I thought you'd show a bit more interest than that."

But it's all I can do to show *any* interest in the food instead of fate, the blackened little strips of fish all doused in spices to hide the old flesh. I can taste cumin, pepper, the burn from dried chili—improperly ground, Syllabub's always been a careless cook, but spices cost near as much as fish and there's not enough to cover the taste of ammonia. Syllabub gorges anyway, and I pick enough at the burnt edges to pretend diversion before fronting up to the Lady of Scales.

No one knows her true name. Magic has never encouraged exchanges of confidence and so we named her for her skill, and left the past—whatever it might be—well enough alone.

If she objected to her trading name we never knew it. I'd often thought, passing by the shop front and seeing the bright shape of her through the glass, that there was enough of a sense of humor there to play up to it. The orange robes floated around her, and there were gold scales embroidered about the hem. She even bulged a bit in the middle, though that was due more to pastry, we thought, than the attentions of a man. Not one of us had ever seen any of them come courting.

"Well, you wouldn't, would you?" says Syllabub. "You put your cold feet against her of a night and like as not you'll wake up without them." She eyes me over her bowl of broth. "I can see the upside, is all I'm saying."

"Oh fuck off," I say. "Haven't I been wearing the damn socks?"

"Gran made them specially," she says, smirking. The socks are blue and orange, carp swimming in lake water with surprised expressions on their stupid faces.

Neither of us ever stopped to think that Syll's old granny spent as much time with her tea leaves and clients as with her knitting needles. And that we took tea with her every Sunday. I'm almost sure the old bitch saw this coming. Me with my life savings, such as they are, and a plate of sugar buns, silly socks on both shaking feet, and a contract coming close behind.

Pick the wrong pocket and suddenly transformation starts to seem like a decent option. Even if it's transformation into a fish.

"I saw her stuffing sweet buns again," she says. I don't need to ask who she's talking about. "She's getting fatter by the day." This in tones of admiration. Syll enjoys her own round flesh, wants to plump up enough for fashion, but we don't always have the cash for the cream cakes she prefers, the butter tablets and duck fat and soft cheese. "All soft and glowy. You don't think she's pregnant, do you?"

I can't think by who. The worst-kept romance on the Street of Endings is between the baker and the Lady of Scales, and both of them are women.

"Maybe she's stuffed full of eggs," says Syllabub, pettish. "Maybe if you open her up they'll all be clotted in there like caviar."

Neither of us has ever eaten caviar. It's a lack that Syllabub takes personally. The little dishes, the elegant bowls of black roe, of chopped boiled eggs, the tiny spoons of sour cream, the finely chopped watercress . . . how would it all taste, mixed together for mouths? Do the little eggs pop or crunch on the tongue? Curiosity's a curse, they say, and I reckon they're right. It certainly hasn't done anything for me lately.

"You'll be the one cut open if the Lady hears you talk like that," I say. Though really, it's the baker I wouldn't put it past. She's got a long reach, that one, and if it weren't poisoned profiteroles turning up on the doorstep—I can't tell myself that Syllabub wouldn't swallow them down without thinking, it's not just greed, we're simply not in the position to waste food—then she'd find herself offered up to tanks anyway, her dead body laid before a lover in the certain knowledge that transformation doesn't work on corpses.

One of us having to beg sanctuary off the Lady of Scales was enough without the other being offered up as well.

"I'll wait for you," says Syllabub, and there's sincerity on every line of her pretty face but I've got my doubts. Theft calls for patience as well as nerve but there's always an end to waiting in sight, and the Lady of the Scales is no thief. She guarantees nothing of returns. Just that there'll be one, one day, probably, if she doesn't over-chlorinate the tanks, or forget the feeding, or elope with the baker whose shop sits just two doors down from her own, give up aquaculture for sugar-work. "One day" might be tomorrow. It might be next century. I'm no fan of luck but I've learned to calculate odds, when I've got a dress out of pawn for trips to the gambling houses, and my calculations say that there are a lot of girls with warm feet in this city, and none of them are about to be goldfish.

Syll's always been good at netting things. She's good at catch and release as well. But she's tender-hearted for all of that and so she's come along with, her nose pressed against shop windows, and all I can think when I see her is how she'll look from the other side of the glass. I pretend not to notice that two of the sugar buns have found their way into her pockets. I'd eat one myself if I weren't about to throw up.

"You believe me, don't you? That I'll wait?" she says. She wants me to believe her, but I reckon that's as much guilt as anything else, because it was her that I was trying to steal for and we both know it. Her suggestion: *that* one, he looks rich and stupid, wouldn't notice if an ox stumbled into him, got that look of distraction I think not.

I should have known better. It's always the skinny ones that are the most grasping. He'd been a spiny stick insect, that one, for all his suit was silk, and no one with money who walks down the street refusing oysters and grilled mango with honey, whitebait fritters, and milk balls does so for any reason but greed for his pockets instead of his stomach.

Of course he felt my fingers in his pockets. But the catching wasn't enough for him, nor the boxed ears, nor the appeals to the justice because they're easy enough to work around, a night in the cells gets you out of another. The contract came out of spite. Not for trying it on to begin with, but for not *recognizing* him enough to stay away. For a certain type that's more insult than anything else, but the wealthy have nothing to do with me, how am I supposed to know them? You'd have to work in a bank or business to be stupid enough to thieve from that sort. The petty stealers, the ones that live small like Syllabub and I, well. We've more sense. We stick to the moderately well-off, the ones who can afford to lose the price of a meal but not hire vengeance for it.

The better targets were usually plumper. More ready to sample the noodles, the street dumplings. I should have remembered, but Syll was whispering at me, hot breath smelling of red beans and rice with a little onion for flavor and all I could think was how we'd planned to visit the caviar shops for her birthday but we'd gambled away the price of those piled glossy eggs, those neatly chopped sides all laid out in their prim little bowls, and lost the money to a mark that didn't pan out because we were the marks that time, and too stupid to see it. Hence the need for some quick cash, because "I want to know," Syll had said one night, tucked into each other as we were. "Whether they pop or crunch. I want to know for my birthday."

"Clever girls like you should have no trouble," her granny had said, knitting needles clicking away and her cat's-arse mouth prim as if she disapproved of our particular brand of cleverness. Not that she ever set that disapproval for much when it came to sharing the spoils; half of Syll's takings went to keeping the old bitch in tea. A little appreciation wouldn't have gone amiss, is all I'm saying.

"Well, wouldn't I wait for you?" I say, as if our situations were reversed. And she hums happily enough, seeming to miss that I didn't answer anything and didn't offer any promises neither, because they're dry things, are promises, set out to bake in the sun like betrothal bread, and all my coming days are wet.

"You always liked to swim," says Syllabub. She's used to making the best of, but how she remembers that now I don't bloody know, seeing as we've only been swimming the once. Only a blind fool would go swimming in these waters, and they'd have to lack a nose as well, or be so stuffed up from 'fluenza that they'd do just about any idiot thing.

Or be drunk. We were drunk, that one time, on foreign wine that tasted of kerosene and lucky not to catch the cholera.

"I've never seen girls so stupid," said granny, when she came to fish us out. Accusations of cleverness were well in the future then, after she'd had a chance to read our cups over, the pair of us shifting and sifting leaves different together than separate, apparently.

Her granddaughter never had the same stomach for the hook. She's more a hindrance than a help in the Lady's shop, after I've handed over the buns and all the little savings I have, not enough for black eggs but enough to buy transformation and fish flakes for generations, perhaps, because the Lady is good with investments if choice gives her the chance. She says I'll get half back when I change again so she's not cruel with it, won't ever put someone out on the streets with nothing. The rich pay everything they have, same as the poor, it's the time spent away that pays off in the end.

If some other poor fool driven to this fishes me out tomorrow, I'll barely have enough for a week's rice flour. Not that it'll matter, I'd be dead before sunset anyway, no miser worth his salt would let a grudge loose that soon; they pinch onto pride tighter than pennies. "But if you're here for a hundred years even your coppers can become something more substantial," she says, as if the thought of windfall is enough to compensate for everything I'll have lost by a century's swimming.

I can only hope the bargain will pay off, and that the same can be said for the fish I'm about to net. That's the other part of the price, the put-off payment. There are dozens of goldfish in her tanks, hundreds of them, and only space for another if one is taken out again. Guess who gets the responsibility of choice, along with a net?

"Not that one!" Syllabub cries, just when I've got one of them trapped in the corner of a tank, my net almost around it. She pouts in my direction. "It looks sad. Don't you think it looks sad?"

"It's a *goldfish*," I say. "None of them are very bloody happy, are they?" Whether or not this one's going to be happy to be rescued I've no idea. I can only hope enough time's passed for whoever it was. Time enough and not too much; it can't be luck to start my own transformation by sending some poor bastard out to death or a new life in a world with nothing familiar in it.

"Some of them look happier than others," she says, and I have to wonder just what was sprinkled on those sugar buns because they all look the same to me, those goldfish: vacant little faces, trailing fringed fins behind them with an expression like they've forgotten what's following behind.

I hope they don't bloody know what they're swimming away from, what they're swimming towards. I reckon it'd be tolerable, being a goldfish, if it's goldfish all through. Goldfish with human feeling, though, human memories . . .

"If it's sad it's probably because it's had enough of living in an aquarium," I say, determined to believe it and lunging with the net, but a small jostle from the girlfriend and the goldfish escapes to swim another day, merging with the rest of school at the other end of the tank.

"Sorry," says Syllabub, shrugging, but it doesn't take a magician to know that she isn't, really. She skips out of reach, the floor shaking beneath. It makes me wonder what happens in earthquakes. The shop is rickety and bowed at the corners; I can see clear through cracks in the floor to water. One good shock and suddenly the sea's full of little fishes, with no way of returning to their old selves.

I'd like to think the people who caught them would bring them back to the shop; come bearing soup bowls of seawater, carp in the chamber pots. More likely would be goldfish skewered over an open flame; the little bones ground up for tonic, just in case medicinal efficacy crosses over between species.

"Maybe if they want to go off cold-cocked," said Syllabub, sniggering, when I was foolish enough to confide my fears. She's got a hard-on for frigidity jokes lately, but when I bury my feet between her thighs and wriggle toes it's usually enough to shut her up for a bit.

The Lady of Scales is laughing in the background. I wish I could say it was mean laughter but it's like she finds us genuinely funny, her own little romantic comedy duo. There can't be many of those played out in this place, but perhaps I'm giving us more originality than can be credited for.

In fairness, no one'd ever seen her laugh at the fish-that-were, the people she'd turned back and sent off, fair flummoxed and stumbling over thresholds.

We'd all seen them, and none of us were much for laughing either. There was something in their faces—not a remnant hint of scales, no. Nothing so unsubtle. It was the disorientation that gave them away. The slight stagger, as if the balance was just returning to new-old limbs, a rolling gait different than that of sailors, for the Street of Endings was built over water, the thick sweet scent of salt. Built that way for suicides, for the walking off of piers and the quick retrieval of bodies for the organs, ground down and sold on for sex aids. Why you'd want a drowned man's cock powdered into your tea I don't know. It doesn't seem a very stiffening thing to me, but perhaps men see it differently. The trade's a brisk one, that's all I know.

It's brisk enough for goldfish, too.

Not that I've seen too many of them. Still enough, it seems like there's one or two every year, come back from the tanks.

How many years will it be for me?

"I could be dead when you're fished from the tanks," says Syllabub, considering. "I could be *old*."

It's hard to think of her as old. There's too much flash and quickness to her. Too much of the flexible, too much greed for the new.

"I'll be all wrinkly, with my tits down by my knees. And age spots, probably. Gran's got lots of age spots." She giggles. "Like a civet cat, but I don't know that the smell's the same." She's lifted some perfumes of late, spraying the ones she didn't sell over the bed linens and rolling over them until all her flesh smelled of musk. "You'd love me when I'm old, wouldn't you?" she says.

"I'd try," I say and she clicks her tongue, pouting. As I said, romantic—though it was a practical romanticality, if there's such a thing. Someone would come along sooner or later. Someone not me, someone warm-footed, and she'd find a way to call it fate. Maybe even a series of someones, and me not even recognizing her when I came back, if I came back, staggering along the Street, new-born to bipedalism and blaring it to anyone who looked.

But it wasn't just the walk that told what they were. It was in the way their mouths hung open, gaping open and shut with drool coming down, and them not bothering to wipe it away. Course they could have been country folk, staring at the Street with wide eyes as though they'd never seen the like, mazed by the mix and bustle of it. If it weren't for the drool and the walk, and the possibility that they really didn't know where they were.

No. That's not true. The Lady of the Scales has had her shop for generations and it hasn't moved a meter. It's not the street geography they're lost in, poor fish-mouthed creatures. It's the *time*: the consciousness of years passed. Or not passed, but if they turn back too quickly the disorientation doesn't have time to confuse them.

Confusion doesn't long outlast a knife through the throat. Grudges tend to fall off after a few decades, people find better things to do or get knifed themselves—the kind of person who carries blades and pays the kids pennies to watch and tell if a fish comes back out that door doesn't do so well with associates, I reckon. Relationships are an inconvenience sometimes.

"It's not always the crooks though," said Syllabub. She's a romantic streak.

I thought the people who had themselves turned all over scales for a bad love affair were missing their brains as well as their legs. No wonder their matches turned sour, wedded as they were to the dramatic before anything else. If you could make the decision to give up everything in life—friends, family, even the nodding acquaintance and all the sights and smells of a neighborhood grown familiar through time—enough to swim off into the future, then you could make the decision to give up one person.

I reckon it's only hysterics that makes anyone choose the former. The desire for attention, to wallow in grief. I thought so before I'd come to the Lady of Scales and I thought so even more now, knowing what I had to lose and not actually willing to do it for anything less than life.

Turns out there's something more than hysterics to it, something sickening. I'd thought she weren't cruel, the Lady, but when the goldfish I'd finally chased down and netted is turned out onto the floor, there's a girl in a soaking bridal gown stepping out of scales and crying like her heart would break. Jilted, poor thing, and run off to life as a fish so she wouldn't have to see him again.

"Gods, didn't you have a mother?" I say to her, helping that warm weeping weight up off her knees. "Didn't you have *any* friends?" Being thrown over's never pleasant, but we've all been there and surely a few solid weeks of drink and whining could have made the difference. Her gown's old-fashioned but even I can tell it cost a lot, all fine with lace and little pearls sewn on so she could have afforded the indulgence, could have sold the pearls for months at a brothel with men more skilled than the one that dumped her, so you think someone would have been there to take her in hand.

"I didn't think," she says, sobbing, and it turns out the silly girl did have support about her but she ran off straight from the temple, humiliated and miserable and in just enough shock to throw her life away for nothing, for the Lady of Scales took her bridal necklace and hocked it, turned the poor wailing thing fish-face before she had a chance to think better of herself.

It doesn't seem decent, somehow.

What seems even less decent is the way Syllabub's staring at her, all pathetic and sorry-like. "Your dress is very out of date," she says, and that's enough for me to see where this is going. If that were last season's wedding gown, last decade's even, there'd be people for her to go back to. But it isn't, and there won't be, and I wonder now how often the mama of this little goldfish came to Lady of Scales, wanting her daughter back and not being able to get her. Hundreds of shining fish swim here, all of them identical, and she could only bargain with her own life for one.

"Is her mother in one of those tanks?"

The Lady of the Scales looks at me, considering. "Do you really want to know?" she says.

I don't.

It's the bloody Street of Endings, that's what it is.

No one ever said any of the endings would be happy.

Except one of them is, because this is the moment Syllabub's bitch of a grandmother wanders past, up off her arse for the first time in bloody-ever, and when she sees her grandchild with her arms around this poor lost creature—this poor lost *rich* creature, her flesh all heated even though she's just come out of the chill and wrapped in lengths of wet silk—there's a smile there that speaks of tea leaves and I'm a clever girl, I am, it doesn't take long to realize that I've been screwed by two members of the same family.

No wonder that skinny mark was so set on his vengeance. No wonder I never recognized him, even moving in different circles as I do. She probably paid him off, pawned everything she owned because she saw pearls in her tea leaves, and goldfish. I'd like to think it was all a scam but she'd leave nothing to chance, and I'm damn sure that after the pawnbrokers she gone to make another bargain, and bloodier.

And me, halfway through my own, and stuck with it because there's a place in the tanks now the little bride is out and the Lady of the Scales doesn't care for pikers. Our bargain's sealed already, with sugar buns and fish nets. She's taken my coppers and even if I can gouge a confession out of granny it's not going to make a difference for me.

"I'll wait for you!" says Syllabub, for the last time before she's booted from the shop, because as spiteful as I'm feeling right now I'm not going to make her watch me change, blowing kisses through the glass while I blow bubbles. She's innocent in all this, never could lie to save herself, and she's promising to wait because she truly believes that she will.

I wonder if it's crueler to let her grieve over a goldfish than a gutted body. If it'd be worth letting her grieve a grandmother as well, or if I should let the old bitch teach her disloyalty, and how to do away with guilt.

"Don't wait," I say.

The scales come.

THE GIFT

JULIE NOVAKOVA

"Sometimes I wonder if we didn't make a grave mistake by accepting the Ramakhi gift." Floriana Bellugi sighed and ran her palm through her hair. I couldn't tell whether she'd done the gesture absently or arranged it just to seem so. Nothing could be certain about her. "Look at the cohort who'd been adults at that time. How many are still around by now?"

Was this a rhetorical question? But she was looking seriously at me, as if expecting the answer. "The estimates range from 5 to 8 percent. Hard to say more precisely. Too much information latency between the systems, and no tracking is perfect, especially over that amount of time."

"And for *those* people," she added pointedly. "You learn to avoid it over the course of four hundred years."

It would take a lot of adaptation, though. We haven't exactly stagnated over that time. But they say learning is a positive feedback loop, and with enough experience and motivation, I could imagine achieving a lot with so much time. I shifted in my seat.

Bellugi noticed, of course. Sensed my impatience. Seemed to approve of it. Cutting right to the matter: "The man I need you to find is one Antonio Arienti. That's his original name. Born in 1977 in Nashville. His parents also; grandparents were immigrants from Sicily." I visualized it on the map. "Joined the U.S. Army, promoted quickly, expanded his education, became a fast-track officer. Left to become a private consultant. Spent some time in Myanmar, Chechnya, Indonesia, Angola, and Syria, always shortly before the local conflicts reignited. Strange coincidence." Bellugi produced a bitter little smile. "By the time the Ramakhi messenger probe arrived, Arienti was retired and living in Paris, though the rumors were he'd sell some 'lost' pieces of army equipment from time to time. Arienti somehow managed to be among the first million people who received the gift."

"Where were you?" I spoke before she could continue.

The slightest change in her expression. Angry? Amused? Wary? My systems told me it was inconclusive.

"In Rome."

That wasn't what I was asking.

How many people who had seen the twilight of the twentieth century were still alive today? Ten million? Scattered across the systems. Statistically speaking, fewer than two hundred thousand should be in ours. I was speaking with one. Floriana Bellugi made her long lifespan no secret. She looked fifty to sixty, but then again, most of them did; some even less. Perfectly groomed silvery hair. Composed face with elegant, gentle features. Misleading. A woman out of time. Free of its tyranny.

She picked up her cup of white tea and sipped. "Arienti's trail disappears in the post-gift uprisings. Emerges again on a ship to Mars. He spent almost a century there. Very quiet, left almost nothing behind beside the bare evidence of his presence. Then Saturn's clouds for about two decades, under the name of Paul Olivieri. Jumped on the first starship, arrived at Tau Ceti nearly a century later. As soon as the ship to YZ Ceti was ready, he was in. Going by Louis Castello."

That left us barely a century more. I fished for the list of voyages in my extended memory. He could have gotten here if he took *Kensakan* to Teegarden's Star and then, almost instantly, the *Eridanus* to us, Epsilon Eridani. Why would he?

"Spent over eighty years out there. From what I've heard, YZ Ceti is not a great place to live. Violently eruptive star, very scattered material, one planet tidally locked and practically uninhabitable due to the flares, the other freezing. The rest . . . just rock, ice, and dust. Why they sent colonists there in the first place, I cannot imagine. Probably because it was so close." Just the slightest hints of contempt in her voice and the curve of her lips.

"So he's not here." *Then why am I?*

"I never said he was. He sent a message over eight years ago. Arrived last year. Not to me. I learned about it, though, made a brief inquiry, and now I'm talking to you." She once again enjoyed keeping me in the dark just for a moment longer, expecting me to ask more questions. I waited patiently, not giving her the satisfaction.

"It was meant for an associate of his. He was saying he'd change places again, and sent an encrypted data package. The decryption code is meant to be auto-sent with a fifty-year latency."

"Unbreakable, I suppose."

"Correct."

"How large?" I asked.

"More than my history on him."

"How did you acquire it anyway?" If the transmission arrived less than a year ago, she couldn't have contacted any other systems and heard back. She must have been tracking him her whole life or hoarding all information on starships' passengers—not just those coming here. In any case, a remarkable and most terrifying feat.

"I have my sources."

I know; asking stupid questions . . . Just to be sure, I tried to access information about her and cross-reference it with her story of Arienti. No match. But the latency was just a microsecond off. She was restricting me, but didn't want to make it too apparent. Out of deception or politeness?

"What do you want me to do?"

"Go after him."

I half-suspected it, but still wasn't fully prepared to think of leaving my home. "Where?"

"He should arrive at van Maanen's Star in less than a decade. If you leave soon, you'll be there some twenty years later."

"He may not be there anymore by then."

"May not," she agreed. "But *may yes.*"

"What do you want me to do?"

"Find him. Find out what he's doing and why. Report to me."

I raised an eyebrow.

"You will receive further instructions, but they'll be available when you need them. No need to distract you if they prove obsolete."

Somehow, she'd transformed during our conversation. She seemed pensive at first, serious; now she acted openly Machiavellian. I took a chance. "Do you think it was a grave mistake?"

"What?"

Had I really taken her by surprise? Or just more layers of pretense?

"Oh. The gift," Bellugi realized. "What do *you* think?"

"We may have still been stuck by the old Sol without it," I said. "Longer lifespans gave us different motivations, the ability to survive a whole interstellar voyage, the drive to invest in long-term projects."

"Yet most of the First Generation are dead by now. Most of them voluntarily. Refused further treatments or have taken their own lives. How many mistakes, how much boredom, how much loss and disappointment can one stand in a lifetime?"

I took my own cup, finished it, set it aside. "I don't understand. All of that can be corrected."

"Then it wouldn't be *you* anymore."

Should outdated concepts surprise me in someone like her? As old as her?

"You had no . . . identity corrections?"

"You're asking a highly personal question, little one. But a good one. What kind of people would, in your opinion, be most likely to disregard negative experiences or feelings, or get them erased just like that?"

Anyone, I was going to say but stopped myself soon enough. *Or . . . maybe we've just gotten accustomed to their thinking.*

"Psychopaths," I ventured, having fished for the old term she might be most familiar with.

Floriana Bellugi smiled, offered me more tea, and, when I declined, dismissed me. Her assistants would handle the rest, she assured me. It was my first and last face-to-face time with her.

Five months later, I found myself aboard *Chrysalis,* a small starship bound for van Maanen's Star.

July 2018

The whole hospital was celebrating. The new building had opened. Funding for better instruments had been on its way. Doctor Aster Sebai could not have been happier.

She could already see the better future ahead of them. Not for her own sake, but for all the people who had been lining up in front of the hospital from early morning. For all the villagers who couldn't afford medical care. For those who remembered darker times. Last but not least, for her daughter. Feven was growing up so fast, already nearly an adult! She should arrive from school any moment.

Not everything went smoothly, though. One of the patients came in drunk, nearly staggering into the examining room. His left arm was broken. He cursed and swore while Sebai examined him. He insisted that she give him morphine for the pain.

"There's no need for that," she assured him firmly. "The fracture is clean, look at the X-ray image. I'll give you local anesthesia while I fix the arm."

"It hurts, you bitch!" he wailed, and the string of expletives continued. Sebai, prepared to defend herself and call for help if necessary, waited until he shut up, and then said calmly: "I can either fix your arm, or not. There is no chance I'm giving you morphine, but right now you decide whether I treat you. If you want to keep calling me names, begging for drugs, and threatening me, go away. Your choice."

He was silent for a while. Then he nodded, and she finished the dressing. "There," she smiled. "We'll leave the cast on for three weeks. By then, the fracture should be healed. Please come again in that time. If there are any problems, come sooner. All right?"

"Yeah," he said and quickly vanished.

It was the last patient. Feven came in after him and greeted her mother.

Later, she asked: "Why were you so nice to that old drunk? Most doctors would immediately refuse to treat him if he behaved like that, and I wouldn't think less of them. But you spoke to him nicely, and he didn't even say thank you."

"Everyone deserves a chance. Kindness is all, my love," she smiled. "Remember that."

Little one, Bellugi had called me back then. I have experienced less than 5 percent of her lifespan. At twenty years old, I was one of the youngest people around. Would that be why she chose me out of all the possible candidates?

"You're unburdened by decades or centuries of experience. Less prone to conventional thinking. You may still be original," said her assistant, a small gray-haired woman, when I brought up the topic before my departure.

I disagreed but stayed silent. Bellugi must have had her reasons, mustn't she?

Would I become stereotypical after four centuries? I doubted the people of her age were that. Those who gave up in the meantime, perhaps. But the survivors? Arienti seemed quite adaptable.

Why else would she pick me? And why *this* me? Erin Taiwo could be many things. Did not hold reservations about change. Bellugi didn't want me to change; she went along with the petite girl of curious disposition. Didn't even want me to get better sensory and memory extensions. She seemed a peculiar woman.

Did she have something to do with the departure of *Chrysalis*? When I looked it up, I couldn't find anything about this voyage more than a year ago. Had she pulled some strings to make it happen, after she'd come across Arienti's message? Was I really her only asset aboard, or just one of many?

A mere two hundred passengers. The scientists and the ever-curious. Or both at once. Van Maanen's Star, an old white dwarf, did not attract colonists.

Ninety-two of the one hundred and sixty stars within the twenty-light-year radius from Sol are red dwarfs. Thirty-nine are brown dwarfs, if you care to call them stars at all. The rest include some giants running out of fuel, a couple of young bright stars, and eight white dwarfs. Out of these eight, only two had seen crewed expeditions.

If you're lucky, there are remnants from the original star system you can use for resources or colonization. Sometimes even planetary cores survive the red giant phase. Most humans seem quite happy near main sequence stars. But we are many, and some avoid anything you might call *normal.*

We spent most of the voyage as sleepers. We were effectively ageless, but we could still starve, suffocate, or fall victim to accidents. *Chrysalis* woke us from our cocoons upon approaching the inner system. Inner, in this case, closer than Mercury orbits the Sun or Turms our Epsilon Eridani. Much farther out, remnants of two ice giants and smaller bodies orbited the slowly cooling star. Here, a world not much smaller than Venus circled its tiny white sun barely a tenth-au away. Its gravity sent debris from the innermost disk on a crash course with the star. It must be quite a sight when some larger chunk of rock fell upon the face of the star. Viewed from the planet's dayside, the star looked twice the size of the Sun viewed from Earth, or of Epsilon Eridani observed from my homeworld Turms.

There, on the planet known as van Maanan B, were most of the passengers from the first van Maanen mission, or so we were told by our ship. None had left the system in the two decades that elapsed since their arrival. A blink of an eye for some, I supposed. Most of my life for myself, not counting my sleeper years.

We gathered by the transparent hull section the ship had made for us and observed the scenery—barren, rugged but breathtaking—during our own descent into the planet's orbit. *No impact craters to be seen,* I noticed. *Strange. How young must the surface be, even though its star is so old?*

No one spoke aloud. I could feel the excited hum of conversations going on silently, but I cared little to tap into them. None would contain anything important for my own mission.

How many of my shipmates were also Floriana Bellugi's? I supposed I would find out when it was favorable to her interests.

I was content with playing pawn until I discovered more. Then, just maybe, I would have enough information for my own agenda. But I was still too young and inexperienced compared to the likes of Bellugi and Arienti. I had to get to know them.

Finding Arienti would be the first thing to do.

January 2019

The day everything changed started as usual. Aster Sebai made her rounds among the inpatients and noted their progress with satisfaction. Her dream of helping people was coming true.

The shouts and cries from the staff common room interrupted her thoughts. She ran there in fear that something had happened.

Something had.

"Look!" Ruth exclaimed and pointed at the TV screen. At first Aster could hardly comprehend the surrounding awe and excitement. Then the news dawned on her.

An interstellar object of possibly alien origin had been captured. . . .

A hoax, some claimed. End of the world, cried others. Beginning of a Nirvana. Alpha and Omega.

After the initial worldwide uproar calmed, news started trickling down. It's a robotic probe. It may be endowed with some kind of artificial intelligence. Attempts at communication will ensue. It's talking to us. It designated itself as "Ramakhi." It's speaking for organic beings like us. . . .

Sebai tried to wrap her head around it as the updates kept coming during the following weeks and months. This was the world her daughter, and then her grandchildren, would live in. No longer alone.

The same year, before it shut itself down, the Ramakhi messenger gave humanity the gift.

"Almost everyone lives here in Olympus," the guide gestured to a gleaming domed structure at the substellar point. They had to level hard rugged terrain before they could build here. But who wouldn't want a permanent perfect view of the star? Not having stood under a sun besides Epsilon Eridani before, I fell in love with the sight of van Maanen in the sky.

"This is the site of a future city of wonders," the man continued in an overly dramatic tone. I switched him off and let him run in the background, so that it would appear as though I was still using the orientation procedures for the habitat. No need to produce unexpected patterns.

I went to my assigned room in the freshly printed section for the newcomers and rested a bit, still not used to the higher gravity. I had some gadgets and clothes printed. I went to have a look around, like most of the people, still adhering to the pattern.

I scoured the add-on inflatable sections and the main body of the base. I spent some time on the observation platforms, and headed toward the research facilities. Most of the people who had bothered to travel this far, and who didn't leave like modern hermits for the sparse little stations outside the planet, ended up here sooner or later. What nobler way was there to spend decades to centuries? Most spent only about a decade on a certain subject, moving on out of the desire for change, but the fields moved forward rapidly. Who knew; perhaps I would devote my life to pursuing scientific challenges as well. I'd have all the time in the world to decide.

I activated the guide again. "Show me the research groups and their members."

The man obeyed and smiled. "Are you looking for one to join?"

"I hope so."

Maybe I was following a wrong lead, but what would a man like Arienti do here? Meditate and contemplate his past in one of the hermitage pods? Hardly. Kill time going full tourist? Not his style. Become a trader? Not in this place. He'd spent decades here. He must be pursuing some inquiry.

Proxies of stellar evolution, long-time changes in white dwarf atmospheres, post-main sequence system stability and evolution, surface chemistry of planets after star's planetary nebula phase, magnetic properties of white dwarfs, conditions for emergence of life on post-MS stars' planets, distribution of rare metals and their isotopes on the planet's surface and in the crust . . .

I stopped there. "Can you lead me to their place?"

The guide's shining smile became almost annoying. "My pleasure."

Then it was only a matter of asking a few inconspicuous questions to get to know Arienti's location. Steering the conversation in the direction I wanted was easy.

" . . . you probably want Castello's Castle then," a man named Tobio, who proved to be a good unsuspecting information source, chuckled. I inclined my head curiously, and he continued: "That's just a nickname. You'll know it as Athens. One of the smaller bases out there."

"Why the nickname?"

I noticed the habitat's systems whispered no hints to me.

"It was financed by a man named Castello. He seems to live there. Never came back here once the base was established. Hence Castello's Castle."

I let a smile play on my lips. "It must be an interesting place, then. I think I'll pay it a visit."

August 2022

It was strange to watch the gifted leave the hospital. Doctor Aster Sebai observed them with mixed feelings. She didn't work in the gifted section, spanning a part of the previous elderly care ward, but only someone remarkably myopic wouldn't keep noticing the change. Less than a year after its official approval, the gift was being distributed to randomly chosen citizens who agreed to undergo the procedure. Few had refused.

That morning in the doctors' mess, there was an unusual buzz. Ruth ran to Aster as soon as she saw her. "Alana has been selected for the gift! Maybe one of our numbers will come up next."

"Congratulations to her. But we can't expect anything, it's a lottery," Sebai said. She was uncertain if she wanted her number to come up. What would she do, living forever? She was content with her life. Though she didn't want the option for herself, she hoped her daughter would get to choose.

Of those who refused the procedure, some were paranoid about using insights gained from an alien probe that didn't know human physiology before it started studying us, some didn't wish for life everlasting for many reasons. But most wished their number would come up.

"What would you do if you were gifted?" mused Ruth. "I'd take some time off and travel the world."

"I would continue my work here," Sebai said dryly. "Those who aren't gifted

still need our help. Not to mention the gifted, who can still become sick or injured, even though they don't age."

Ruth scowled at her. "Pessimism doesn't suit you, Aster."

"It's realism. The gift is not a miracle ending all suffering. And for those who become gifted but have no money to speak of, and a family to support, not much really changes." Sebai would have continued, but her phone beeped. It was Feven, telling her that the office where she worked had been closed for the day for fear of an attack. Sebai's stomach knotted. It would be so much easier, had the gift really been a miracle. . . .

I'LL DROP BY THE HOSPITAL, SAY HI. LOVE YOU, MOM.

Sebai went on to make her rounds. Work had always been reassuring to her. For a moment, she could push aside the tensions the gift had sparked, and the risk of plunging into a bloody civil war once again. She still vaguely remembered the images from her childhood, however she wished not to.

A text beeped again. I'M HERE, MOM. WHERE R U?

Sebai touched the screen to reply. And that was when all turned to dust.

A sudden blast shook the building violently. Sebai staggered and fell. She felt fragments of the wall paint fall on her neck. "Get under the beds!" she managed to shout before a cough got ahold of her. She was blinking fine dust away from her eyes.

The hospital trembled again, and she instinctively rolled under an empty bed.

The third blast came, and the roar of the falling walls deafened her. Then she remembered nothing until waking up in a hastily fashioned mobile infirmary.

When she came to, her entire body was aching and she almost couldn't hear. But they said she'd only suffered a few broken bones, concussion and dehydration, and had no internal bleeding.

The news of the attack slowly trickled to her. The three bombs completely decimated the hospital; it was nothing but ruins now. A group opposing the current government claimed responsibility for it. They said they'd end the abomination of the gift. That they'd rightfully return the land to its former law. That they had God on their side. That they would make the nation great again.

What they didn't speak of but Sebai heard about was the terrorized and murdered villages, men beheaded, children taken from their homes for labor and into the army, women dragged away to be nothing but toys to break and cruelly discard, forests burned, animals butchered, and the land scorched to cinders if they sensed that victory was eluding them.

But she couldn't bring herself to feel the terror of it. All of it belonged to Feven, still buried somewhere under the ruins. Sebai still clung to her last remnants of hope three days later, when they uncovered two more survivors. Later that day, they discovered Feven.

They concluded she had bled out at most a day after the blast.

• • •

"Where are you going?" A slender dark woman appeared on the rover's passenger's seat. Another agent, like the guide from Olympus.

"To Athens. I'm looking for an interesting research group to join."

"We're not currently seeking new collaborators."

"May I have a look around at least?"

The woman paused, apparently lost in thought. Her AI was asking someone for guidance.

"All right," she nodded. "We're looking forward to meeting you, Erin." She vanished.

The rover drove me the rest of the way in silence. I gazed out at the dream-like landscape of van Maanen B. Sharp spikes of obsidian rose from the curving ridges. The outermost surface, already cooked, had vaporized in the shedding of the red giant's shell, and had left behind a land Dalí would have longed to paint. But, as I understood, that wasn't the end; the equally strange land I was seeing originated rather recently when a giant impact stripped the planet of its remaining crust and most of the mantle. That's why so few impact craters could be seen. This eerie land was young.

Castello's Castle, finally rising over the horizon, did not live up to its name. The base was barely visible above the surface, save for a small observatory tower. An airlock opened for my vehicle and let me into the subterranean complex. The virtual woman appeared by its inner door. "Come in. We're expecting you in the hall."

I followed her through the labyrinthine corridors lined with austere printed regolith walls. The room hardly seemed more hospitable. There were three people inside. One a short pale person of androgynous features, the second a black woman with sparse clothes revealing silvery tattoos.

And Louis Castello.

He hadn't changed much since the last records Bellugi had possessed. He'd scarcely aged. Though physically not resembling the original Antonio Arienti much, he'd stayed true to the type. His olive skin and dark eyes sported no obvious augments. In his plain shirt and trousers, he could have fit any period. He had lived through many.

"Hello, Erin," he said casually. "We're all pleased to meet you. Welcome to our humble station."

Manu Virtanen. Ike Oladapo. Louis Castello. During our conversation over lunch, Virtanen almost never spoke; most of the discussion was supplied by Oladapo, on whom the agent I'd encountered was modeled, and Castello himself.

Searching for chemical peculiarities on the planet and in the debris disk . . . High-res radar and lidar imaging to reveal possible strange shapes . . . It all made sense together, even the strange attitude of the Olympians toward Castello's Castle: the mixture of curiosity and derision.

"You're trying to find some signs of the Ramakhi, aren't you?"

"Of course." Castello regarded me calmly. "Had you not understood that, we'd have nothing to talk about."

"The others, at Olympus, probably think you're fools."

"Do you?"

Why? I wanted to ask. *Why do you of all people pursue this? What's in it for you?*

"No," I said. "But that doesn't mean I think we've got odds on our side."

"*We*? You're not a part of our team yet."

"We as humanity. This is something that should interest everybody. Pity that some can't see that."

Castello smiled, and so did Oladapo; only Virtanen still regarded me with her stony face.

"You can stay here for now," Castello announced. "Let's see how you fare."

Three weeks later, I started suspecting that I was Floriana Bellugi's only asset from aboard *Chrysalis*. But what should I do? I had found Castello but still had no idea what she wanted from him.

Nothing in his manner suggested his long and violent past. Yet when I tried to look beyond the innocent distracted smile, I could perhaps imagine the master puppeteer inside. There was something against-all-common-sense alluring about chameleons like Arienti, and something deeply chilling. He'd been the most perfect shape-shifter. He would seem to belong anywhere, be it a prestigious charity ball, a system-wide corporate board meeting, a scientific conference, a middle-class home, an impoverished slum, a seedy bar, a street gang, a mercenary squad, or a simple fishermen's village on the shores of a long-forgotten island.

I could only imagine his life back on Earth. Something about the style of that life intrigued me despite myself. I could not lay my finger on it. How could I, a youngster who'd grown up in a totally different world, ever understand it? I suppose it bore the same sense of excitement and raw adventure that people of Arienti's generation derived from tales of brave knights, seamen, or frontier settlers.

Even with my substantial augmented knowledge, I could hardly fathom the thrill of old Earth. Who would I have been in such a world, and what would I have seen? Such terrors and wonders . . .

I continued working with him. It was actually quite fascinating. On one of our walks outside to corroborate our robotic probes' data, I interrupted the quiet white noise in our speakers and asked: "Why are you doing this in particular? You could go to any populated world, live a comfortable life. . . . Why go through so much trouble?"

"You're here, so you know the answer already, no? If you can live forever, trying to find out what enabled that is just as good a way of spending your time as any," he shrugged visibly even in his suit. "It satisfies curiosity and is sufficiently long-term to entertain me for quite a while. Maybe I'll get tired of it if I encounter another dead end. Maybe not. You can plan only for a certain time ahead."

"But we know so little about the Ramakhi from their messenger probe! It refused to tell us anything specific about its creators. There's nowhere to start."

The probe already spoke several human languages when we encountered it. It knew a lot about Earth-based life, our own biology and culture. It understood many figures of speech and conversed fluently. It must have been observing us for decades, but it never told us that. It managed to steer the first contact scenario into one that had been peaceful and relatively non-shattering for us.

"There's plenty to start," Arienti said dryly. "The isotopic composition of the probe's alloys suggests it hadn't assembled itself in our solar system. It was rather peculiar, in fact. The problem is, we don't have precise enough measurements for other systems to make a comparison. We're trying to supplement this data. Also, the age of the probe had been estimated at less than a hundred thousand years. It may have been assembled when the first modern humans started leaving Africa. We should be able to find many traces of the Ramakhi had they been around so recently. I've been tracking them for the better part of two centuries. I believe I'm getting closer."

His words resonated in my ears. I had a strange sense of déja vu.

Two centuries? That must have been since his arrival in the Tau Ceti system already. Tau Ceti . . .

I felt like I was missing something important. I could go on like this for months and learn nothing more than the shallow image he'd shown to me. I had to get deeper.

It took two weeks' planning, but finally I was sure I could do it. I waited for a moment when Arienti and Oladapo were outside, while Virtanen worked in the lab. The security systems were different from what I knew but compatible. I got in.

Arienti's rooms seemed as inconspicuous and timeless as the man himself. Unlike him, they even lacked personality. You could see that someone lived here yet still learn little about him. I passed a small stack of spare clothes, the only ones to be seen. More could be printed easily.

No books; no such luxury to be brought here by a small expedition. None even printed here, though that would be considerably less luxurious.

No pictures on the walls, physical or projected. No physical mirrors. Nothing expendable at all.

An empty table stood by the wall. I sat at it, hesitating. If I tried to access the interface—there surely was one—I might give my attempt at espionage away. But if I didn't, I'd learn nothing at all.

"Activate," I said firmly.

I managed to persuade the system into thinking that I was Arienti. I almost wondered at how easy it had been, when an additional layer of security presented itself.

"I've noticed an unusual pattern in your access," the holo said. It was a woman's face: older, black, with an accent I couldn't place. "Let me ask you a question."

I drew a sharp breath. I could synthesize Arienti's voice and mimic his speech pattern, true, and it *might* be enough—if I could answer.

"Where and when did we first meet face to face? Not quite this face, though," she smiled.

I was lost. "I have to go. Switch off," I said and hurried away.

Just in time. Arienti's and Oladapo's voices sounded in the corridor. I vanished into my room.

Shortly thereafter, Arienti appeared in my doorway. "We've found something today with Ike. I want you to come with me to see it."

I tensed a little. "All right."

Neither Oladapo nor Virtanen joined us. We traversed quite a distance in the rover, but the terrain grew too hard near the end. As we walked carefully across a spiky lava field, Arienti spoke: "Have I mentioned that I'd visited two other systems before this one? Tau Ceti. YZ Ceti. It was an interesting time. But as soon as I learned what I needed, I came here. Actually, I pulled a few strings to help make this expedition happen."

"Really? I had no idea!" I acted properly surprised. "What inspired you?"

"Something that happened back at Tau Ceti. Did you know that a few of the colonists decided to establish a base at the outermost planet's moons instead of the inner planets?"

I recalled it vaguely. He continued: "They found something there. A wreck of a failed spacecraft. Very, very old. The resemblance to the Ramakhi probe was uncanny."

"That's impossible," I breathed out. "Everyone would have known."

"If they'd made the discovery public, yes. But they didn't. You might not know, but the political regime on-site wasn't very friendly toward that approach. However, a few people who learned about it escaped and were . . . inspired."

I could imagine his predatory smile, the teeth exposed in half-threatening, half-boasting fashion.

"The isotopic composition spoke clearly. The probe likely originated in the same system as the one that spoke to us. I boarded the first ship out of there. YZ Ceti was a good location for my purposes. I already had an inkling about where to start digging."

Why are you telling me all this now? I almost asked, but stopped myself in time. We still walked side by side. I had the feeling of a prisoner going to her execution. Could I make it to the rover in time? But where could I go? I wouldn't have enough fuel to go back to Olympus, and I couldn't contact the base from here. No; my only chance was facing Arienti if I must. Perhaps I was just being paranoid.

"Aren't you going to ask why?" he spoke and a shiver went down my spine. It took me a second to realize he was refering to his inkling. Or so I hoped.

"Why?" I said. My throat felt very dry.

For a moment, Arienti was silent. Then, very quietly, he said: "Who sent you here?"

"What?"

"I know you've spied on me. I repeat: Who sent you?"

I felt strange. I *wanted* to tell him. I almost did. *He must have released something into my air,* I realized. So far I was able to resist it. Would it stay that way?

"Well, you've come from Epsilon Eridani. So Bellugi, I guess? Or Iwamoto? Or . . . no, *she* wouldn't . . . "

"What are you talking about? No one sent me here!"

I could hear him sigh in the speakers. "I should get the information out of you. But if the meds don't work on you, that could be tiresome . . . Better to get it over quickly."

Suddenly, I was gasping for air. My suit!

I fell to my knees. One of the shards ruptured my suit as I did and sliced into my knee. I cried out in horrid pain. Desperately, I fumbled around for my repair spray.

What are you going to do? You can repair the damage on your leg, but not what he did.

Black spots appeared in my vision. The air grew thinner. Words came to me from nowhere.

"Aster Sebai," I wheezed.

Arienti stopped and turned abruptly. "What did you say?"

But I could not speak anymore. My precious air was escaping too fast.

Arienti's blurred face—*wait, not this Arienti's, but another, also his*—was the last thing I saw before blackness encompassed me.

• • •

December 2031

She had been growing old. Felt the wear and tear of age pull at her body and render it weak. No longer could she run if someone on the street decided she wasn't a good enough citizen for him. No longer could she defend herself, let alone the millions she wanted to speak for. No longer could she raise her voice high enough. Cancer ate at her body. With treatments, she might fight it. Without them, she would have at most two years left, likely less.

Looking back at her life, she felt bitter disappointment. None of the goals she'd striven for had come true. She'd wanted to save people. And what had come of it? Ruins, scorched earth, and a country divided by bloodshed. The hospital never reopened, although it was needed more than ever before.

At first, she'd tried to prevent more violence and ruin where she was. All in vain. Finally, she'd fled with hundreds of others. Abroad, she tried to speak for those less fortunate. It was difficult at first, but then she established herself as a known peace and civil rights advocate. She ran lectures, debates, fundraisers, and film screenings. She started petitions. She kept sending out letters.

The impact of it left her sad, angry, and disillusioned. True, she had her little victories.

But these were doused by much bigger defeats.

The war continued. People kept dying and suffering, while others gained immortality.

None of the attackers who'd killed Feven, none of the war criminals, had been punished to date.

In the first years, she'd feared for her life for speaking out loud. Then she realized they didn't care. She wasn't an enemy worth notice for them. She could do nothing.

Oh, if she could take it back, all the idealism and playing by the rules . . . if only she had the time.

So she bribed the gift administrator in town. The selection of people who would receive the gift was supposedly random across the world, but no one with eyes to see believed that. She was an aging, bitter, unaccomplished refugee woman. Had she waited for her turn, she would have died before her name came up. The bribe consumed all of her savings and set her deep in debt, but it worked.

A year later, suffering from multiple metastases and feeling ever so weak physically from the disease as well as the treatments, it was her turn to accept the gift. The procedure was entirely painless. She didn't even feel the time spinning around her, until it was just four days later, and she emerged in excellent health and, if she opted for repeating the procedure every couple of decades, possibly at the start of her life everlasting.

She felt young again. And so, so full of rage.

• • •

Aster Sebai.

I woke with the name on my lips.

I *woke.*

Alive. Breathing. With a patched up leg; hurting, but already almost healed. I took in my perceptions at once: the undersuit I was still wearing, the responsive foam beneath me, the walls of molded regolith. Less than four hours had elapsed since I'd almost died, unless someone had tampered with my sense of time. I was likely still at Castello's Castle.

Aster Sebai. Who was she?

I could recall a face to that name. No, more than one face.

"I'd like to apologize for that earlier misunderstanding." Arienti stopped in the door and looked me up and down. I was momentarily distracted by flashbacks of other faces, male, his earlier faces.

How did I know? Bellugi never showed them to me.

"Why did you spare me?"

I took him by surprise. "You still don't know!"

Faces, names . . . fragments. What do they mean?

"Your failsafe probably hasn't kicked in fully yet. I should leave you to it . . . but I'm curious." He sat in a chair across from my bed. "It's such a long time since we've last met. I wonder what happens when we meet again."

His words made no sense to me. But I remembered seeing him before. Flirting with a stranger amidst the freezing clouds of Saturn. Watching him fall into the endless pit of the gas giant's atmosphere.

A starship, one of the first built outside the Solar System. A different face this time, and behind it the same man, alive and well.

"How could I have gotten someone else's memories?" I spoke. But even as I was saying that, I already knew full well that wasn't the truth.

May 2038

Looking down at the pleading man, she felt nothing but contempt. "You deserve even worse," she'd said and pulled the trigger.

A year after the first one, the second of the men responsible for Feven's death lay dead at her feet.

The sayings were right. It was much easier the second time.

There were still so many to be hunted.

Aster Sebai. How long have I not been her?

Arienti was observing my reaction with the mild curiosity of someone watching an animal perform a circus feat.

My head hurt. My vision blurred. In my mind, images spun in a carousel of memories.

One recurrent theme: death. So many dead.

"What have I done?" I whispered. My voice broke.

What am I? Have I really done all this?

My own past was a mystery to me. Fragments, pieces, scattered without any apparent order.

"Aster," Arienti said. He rolled the name on his tongue, tasting it perhaps for the first time in decades or even over a century.

I've had many names in the past. Aster Sebai had been the first, and Erin Taiwo was only the most recent. It wasn't even from the same language as my original name. Had it ever meant something for me? Or was I just cautious? I couldn't remember.

Just flashbacks of my life: Mercenary, informant, shifter, influencer, adventurer, gambler. I had been every last one. Up until the moment the weariness set in. Then I became something else again.

But I always *knew*. Had access to the memories of the past, should I want to. I mostly did not.

What made me forget?

I shivered. Arienti leaned closer, deep fascination in his face. He extended a hand and touched my cheek. I flinched.

He chuckled. "Relax. It's just intriguing to watch this transformation."

"We've met before."

"Yes." His eyes gleamed. "Care to go for a walk while I help you piece your past together?"

My headache was fading, and my leg felt better. I pulled myself up. "Let's go."

I felt my strength return as we slowly walked through the corridors of Castello's Castle. Finally, we reached the observation room. From its tower, we could see the bleak land everywhere around us.

Arienti spoke: "Long ago, you started hunting me. You tried to kill me on Saturn. I took the fall but was rescued by a lower-level airship. A fortunate fate—or someone else's calculated plan. We were both onboard the *Shiva*, but I managed to avoid you when our awake times overlapped. Then we crossed paths again on the way to YZ Ceti. You remembered me, but laughed off our old incident. We became lovers during the journey. I even told you about what I'd seen on that godforsaken moon. It excited you, of course. You told me that you'd finally found someone who didn't bore you abominably. But that doesn't tend to last, does it? I promoted exploration of the YZ Ceti system and tried to put together an expedition here, but my resources were depleted, my influence limited. It was all too slow and intangible for you, I suppose. We went our separate ways. I don't know what you hoped to find on the other side of your journey, but I hope you haven't found it."

I shuddered. "Why is that?"

"Because simply reaching our goals is the most unsatisfying thing that can happen to us immortals."

"So you picked a goal you can never reach."

"Oh no, not *never.* That would be foolish. Not exciting at all. No, my goal may take me many more centuries, even millennia, but it's far from impossible."

It still didn't seem his style. I would expect him to engage in power plays, in feats of senseless adventure seeking, but this seemed too noble a pursuit for someone like him.

"Why do you do it?" I pressed on.

"Because it's beautiful," he said simply. "Look around. Don't you see?"

I gazed at the barren landscape ahead. It was strange, alien even. Eerily beautiful, yes.

I only realized he was speaking again when he shook my shoulder.

"Sorry," I snapped out of it. "It really is beautiful. Staggering, actually."

"So you understand."

"I'm not sure."

"It surpasses us. Whatever we find here, a clue to the Ramakhi's past or just a fascinating system, it's something vastly bigger than us. I think it's the only thing I can appreciate after the centuries of human trifles. I'm bored by humanity. Bored by petty fights and intrigues, bored by risking and gambling, bored by relationships, by culture, by everything. It fades and only leaves a bad palate. I've shifted toward things that have been here for eons and will be here eons after we perish. That's what's really interesting. It lasts."

Arienti surprised me. I didn't expect to find such a philosophical spirit in him. He had been so pragmatic, as long as I could recall. But then again, I hadn't seen him for centuries.

Eyes still on the big game of deciphering the Ramakhi's fate, he found solace where I could not.

Our lives are fleeting. Our thoughts and feelings, even more so. But I couldn't look upon the stars and planets and forget that I was human. However fascinating and grand I could find the Universe, I was too absorbed in our mayfly troubles.

Maybe that's why I couldn't bear it in the end.

November 2112

The emptiness was unbearable. A gaping hole where her identity had been.

So many dead. Their deaths no longer meant anything to her. She wasn't sure when the moment had come that she continued hunting them down just out of inertia. Everything else, gone.

She eventually tracked down everyone connected to the hospital bombing. Then she focused on war criminals from the ensuing civil war. Finally, on those who enabled it in the first place.

Antonio Arienti. The arms supplier.

This one was good, covered his tracks almost perfectly. But she had plenty of time.

He was on Mars.

But before she could find him there, he disappeared. Her anger fueled her once again, but it was different than before, almost burnt-out.

Then she found his trail again.

Saturn.

This time, she was more careful. Changed her appearance once again. Polished her new backstory. Left some false trails around the system.

They finally met face to face aboard the Zephyr, deep in the clouds of Saturn. He was courteous, charming, and flirted with her. She pretended to take an interest, and after a few meet-ups, not too soon, suggested kite-flying in the clouds. He was delighted by the prospect.

She only regretted that she couldn't see his face when she struck him down. The damaged wings fluttered about him as he fell. She flew lower to observe his fall longer, but he quickly disappeared in the underlying cloud layer.

Her work was done.

She returned home. Home . . . It felt like one no longer. She excavated the box. In it rested a small treasure: entirely worthless for anyone but her. A reminder of a fortune she had lost ages ago.

The photograph of Feven was the most precious item. She touched the smooth glossy surface of the Polaroid picture a bit uncertainly, almost hesitant to believe it was still there. It had faded so little in over a century.

She may have been looking at it for hours before she spoke.

"I'm so sorry," she said with her throat tight, and abruptly closed the box.

The next day, she appeared at a local aug-clinic.

"I want a rewire."

The words almost stuck in her throat.

She still hesitated when they sat her in the soft chair and explained the process once again, as the laws dictated. When she nodded, she was still full of doubts. She had changed her appearance and name many times, but never herself. She knew her concept of identity had become laughably outdated long ago, but she was still seized with anxiety when the rewiring started.

She had to be awake to keep telling them what she thought, felt, remembered.

She didn't know at which point she stopped worrying.

The emptiness was not gone. But the guilt, sorrow, and anxiety were. The emptiness, she knew instantly, could now be filled very easily with anything that pleased her.

"Are you satisfied with the rewire?" they asked her.

She was.

It had been her first one, and certainly not her last.

As we stood there in mutual silence, I remembered all. I remembered *myself*, all the different selves of me during those years.

Most had been monsters.

Still, most of them had known.

They would play the endless games of hide and seek, extracting information, gaining advantage . . . Most chose not to dwell on the grim bloody past and focused on the sometimes bloody but bright *now*. They would climb the deadly slopes of Aamu's cliffs, almost die performing the boldest feats of old-school exploration, daringly challenge every obstacle Nature and Man presented.

Drinking the finest, eating the rarest delicacies, meeting all the strange and wonderful people, allies, enemies, lovers, acquaintances (never friends). Enjoying the tingle of beams of different suns. Having fun. Always being a step ahead of the others.

Everything would become the game.

Except when they would wake up in the middle of the night soaked in cold sweat, shaking from the nightmares, scared and paranoid. Alone. Trusting no one. Always on the run.

Even with the rewires piling up, the woman who used to be Aster Sebai a long time ago grew restless. Would she have to remake herself into a complete psychopath to reach peace? But even that might not help. No, the only way was to end herself.

And so she did. She buried her past as deep as she could. Then, she forgot. *I* forgot.

"How could you do it?" I spoke. "How could you stay *you*?"

He shrugged. "I've had some help, but I guess I'm built this way."

Silence fell once more.

I felt whole, yet set loose. Drifting without purpose. Whatever power play Bellugi had engaged me in, because there was no way this had been an accident, I wanted no part in it.

"So what are you going to do now?" Arienti shot me a sideways glance. "Will you try to kill me? Betray Bellugi? Let everything go and make a break for it? Build a small empire?"

I should have hated him, but I just felt indifferent about him. So many conflicting notions of the man, yet none of that mattered now. Enmities, romances, and alliances come and go.

"I want to have a look at the thing you discovered, if that wasn't just an excuse to lure me out and kill me," I said. "Then I'll decide what to do next."

"Why?" I asked once again on our walk outside. This time, we both meant why had he come here to pursue the Ramakhi question.

"The chemical composition again. By the time I left Tau Ceti, we'd already had some data from the Procyon system. Although it's a binary and just one component is a white dwarf, it confirmed some suspicions about the chemical make-up of white dwarf systems. It also reinforced my suspicion that the probes had come from such a place. Preferably not a binary, though: A lone white dwarf system. One with lots of planetary material, perhaps, with strong metallic spectral lines. One that would be close enough to Tau Ceti and our Sun. There is only one such system."

He stopped at the apex of a cliff and spread his arms. "Look around. Isn't it fascinating? We may be seeing a world from which the probes originated. You know what is also interesting? About sixteen thousand years ago, van Maanen's Star came within three light-years of the Sun. It's a great distance to overcome, but it can be done, as we've amply demonstrated ourselves. Even a civilization with much less advanced technological capabilities could manage to send a probe across that gap."

"Are you suggesting . . . ?"

"That the Ramakhi have come from here? Exactly. But that's not the end of it. Can't you figure it out yourself?"

Probes less than a hundred thousand years old. A close encounter in a more recent period. I looked around. *Extremely young surface. Most of the crust and mantle had vaporized in a giant impact, leaving behind this barren planet.*

"This was their world," I stated in disbelief. "They evolved here, around the white dwarf, when the planet perhaps had a strong greenhouse atmosphere and conditions for life, they built interstellar probes—but the destruction of their planet wiped them out." I shook my head. "But that doesn't add up, does it? If they had the capacity to go interstellar, even if just with uncrewed probes, they must have colonized the rest of this system. We should be able to find traces of them everywhere."

"Everywhere in a system so unstable . . . and so sparsely explored by us?" Arienti said quietly. "The remaining planets are much further out, a difficult place to start colonizing. This planet has no moon. The debris around the star would constitute the best target for early space exploration. We got on well with colonizing asteroids. But our system was very stable. What if they just didn't consider colonizing the rest of their system worthwhile? Instead, they turned to other stars. And at least once, they discovered life. They managed to construct interstellar probes with immense learning capabilities . . . but what if they never were an interstellar civilization themselves? What if every single one of our conjectures about them has rested on a wrong assumption?" I had never seen Arienti so excited, not even in the countless records I had found long ago. Maybe he never had been, until he embarked on his futile search.

I still didn't quite believe him. His theory sounded appealing, but it was constructed of assumptions so fragile that one strong data point would suffice to destroy it whole.

But we've been searching for that one strong data point for centuries, haven't we?

"Finally, we may have something here," Arienti interrupted my train of thought. "As you've pointed out, we should be able to see traces of space industry in the system."

"They found something in the debris disk?"

"Not there. But here."

We arrived at a crevice within a small impact crater. I struggled to see what had been inside, but then I recognized the outlines.

"What is it?" I said.

"We don't know yet. A fragment of a mining device? Of a habitat? It's older than the new crust of this planet. Must have drifted in the debris disk for a long time before crashing here." Arienti's voice in the comms was surprisingly soft. "It's not a proof of my theory. But it's a start."

We spent many hours examining the strange remnants. I had never seen the original Ramakhi probe, though. I had lived thousands of kilometers away from where it appeared. In another lifetime . . .

On our walk back to the rover, Arienti suddenly broke the awed silence: "Have you followed news from Earth and colonies other than yours?"

"Not much." First I'd wanted to put my past behind me, and then I didn't even know I had one.

"I have. I've devoted much of my time to studying how our societies evolved after the gift. What intrigues me is that in the early years, we set out to explore whole new systems we'd colonized. Now we're retracting to one or two planetary colonies in a system each. Small bases are disappearing. Research stations in the outer reaches are becoming automated or diminishing. There are still plenty of hermits who prefer to live outside big colonies, but they too grow fewer, while big settlements are growing and focusing inward. . . . Do you understand?"

I nodded, but he continued: "Even though we've gone interstellar, we may ultimately be on the same path as the Ramakhi. Most will become oblivious and more vulnerable to . . . cosmic accidents. The few who won't . . . well, they will scatter and then die off. Maybe we'll push a few more light-years forward, extend our small bubble of colonized space . . . and then our candle will go out."

I considered his words. *Pure speculation. Fitting the reality into the frame of his worldview, while he should be doing the opposite. But still . . . what if he wasn't wrong?*

We journeyed back to Castello's Castle in silence. Only when we were helping each other out of our heavy suits, he said: "I think I'll make the discovery public."

I looked at him in surprise.

His face was serious, pensive. For a second, he didn't resemble the old Arienti; nor Olivieri; nor Castello. Someone new was standing before me. "I learned what I could alone. But if I continue this way, it dies with me, even if I have followers like my companions here and have sent backup messages elsewhere some time ago—what intrigued Bellugi, I suppose. Perhaps, if I announce it, it will spur a new period of exploration. New adventures. New opportunities. New world for me to fit in."

None of us can bear being ourselves for too long, can we? I thought. *Will I be able to cope?*

I looked back at Arienti. My foe. My lover. My enigma. My target. Could I ever escape the weight of the memories?

As if reading my mind, he spoke: "*Chrysalis* begins its return voyage in a month. You should be there."

I could stay. But how long would it last before Arienti and I wanted to kill each other again?

I could go elsewhere in-system. Yet what would I do here? Search for castles in the air?

I didn't want to drift anymore. I wanted a purpose, so I gave myself one. First, close the previous chapter of my life. Then . . .

Before I boarded my rover in the airlock, I turned and looked at Arienti standing behind the thick transparent wall. "Goodbye," I said through my suit's comms.

He didn't speak, but his gaze seemed to say that there are not really any goodbyes for immortals. Only I clung to the outdated custom.

I chose to sleep through the starship's voyage. I needed no more time to decide what would happen next. Erin Taiwo's first and also last meeting with Floriana Bellugi occurred on Turms less than half a year before the first departure of *Chrysalis.*

Aster Sebai's—or whatever I would call myself, the remembering myself—history with the woman had been much more complex and by far not over.

Questions. Answers. Favors. Debts. Bellugi was a master of shadow games, and it was impossible for Sebai not to make some deals with her when she'd left Earth. But perhaps she was on Bellugi's radar long before that. The woman used information like other, less intricate people use blades and bullets. And if someone grew too dangerous—like Arienti—why use such old-fashioned weapons, if mere information could do the job?

The original Aster would perhaps want to end it once and for all. But I was not her anymore. I had her memories, but I could no longer understand her.

Upon my return to the Epsilon Eridani system, her residence had been the first place I'd headed to. I was expected.

The same furniture, the same rosy porcelain tea set, probably tea from the same plantation, and the same Floriana Bellugi, looking not a day older than decades ago.

"Welcome, Erin," she smiled. "Or should I say Aster?"

"I've used many names. Pick one." I sat across from her and measured her with a calm gaze.

Her smile didn't falter a bit. "Thank you for coming. Tea?"

We drank from the dainty cups for a moment, both silent, but I felt almost no tension between us. Live long enough and you get used to this.

"Arienti says hi," I remarked.

"I assume it's no good if I tell you to reciprocate it."

"No good at all."

"So he stayed at van Maanen?"

"Perhaps. I wouldn't know." I wouldn't put it past him to organize another expedition elsewhere. So much was left to be discovered by van Maanen's Star, but would he have stayed there once his discovery—or rather Virtanen and Oladapo's discovery, as Louis Castello didn't figure in any of the reports—was made public? Maybe he'd changed his identity again. Maybe he was still pulling the strings out there. I liked to imagine him in one of the hermitages, alone, detached, like he'd been all his life, but more in touch with the outer world than most of us. "And even if I would, well . . . "

You wanted me to remember and kill him, I left unsaid. *You wanted to get rid of both of us in one move, perhaps one you considered apt or even poetic justice, and maybe gain some insights into the Ramakhi question as a bonus.*

Bellugi nodded, smiling. "So what exactly happened to the Ramakhi?"

"Waited for the unavoidable collision to wipe them out? Tried evacuating the planet? Took their own lives one by one? Committed a mass suicide? Who knows. Seems they're no longer around and that they were never really *around* much, but how can we be really sure about that? The van Maanen artifact doesn't tell us much about their past. It's groundbreaking, but the search is far from over."

She clicked her tongue. But it was all theater for me. Given how uncannily she'd hoarded any information she could find, she already knew what I was going to tell her as soon as the *Chrysalis* approached the system, perhaps much sooner.

I stood up.

Bellugi faked surprise. "Oh, you aren't going, are you, Aster? We have so much to talk about, and you have hardly touched your supper!"

"You know what they used to say . . . who sups with the devil should have a long spoon."

"You cannot possibly be mad at me for manipulating you. Blame yourself for choosing to forget earlier. Or are you mad because you've remembered?" She shook her head. "You of all people, calling me the devil. . . . We are all monsters, my dear one. Only some know it. And accept it."

I didn't sit back down. "That's not me anymore."

"No, that's denial, sweetheart. Grow up. It's been centuries, for gods' sake. You can't escape your past."

"No. But I can choose my future. You asked me if accepting the Ramakhi gift had been a grave mistake. I failed to comprehend it as Erin. Then, when I remembered, I thought that it had been. But now I'm not so sure. It didn't help us eliminate suffering, but it enabled us to reach magnificent things. Before, I chose to forget. Not anymore. Lacking past is a liability. But I won't dwell on it. I need to remember—if only to know to move on. I'm done with my past. I will take no more life. Play no more selfish games in which innocent bystanders lose everything. I will not pursue revenge, nor become a crusader for justice. I will help where I can, in the little ways. They count, too. They may count most of all. So that's why, in a moment, I will walk out of this door and never return. You won't stop me. You know I'm no danger to you. Maybe you'll even enjoy watching me build my new life. Place bets on when I should fail." I smiled. "You will lose them all."

I wasn't feeling as sure as my words sounded. I might have uncovered the past, but the future held no certainties for me. When you might have an eternity ahead of you, how can you bear all the mistakes, disappointments, injustices, pains that you eventually endure? I might break down under the weight of my sins, or the others'. I might choose to bury it all again in a moment of weakness. I might become like Bellugi, uncaring, oblivious, even cruel. I might repeat my past mistakes all over again.

Then again, I might not. That's what is so beautiful about the future. m

THE BURIED GIANT

LAVIE TIDHAR

When I was five or six years old, my best friend was Mowgai Khan, who was Aislinn Khan's youngest. He was a spidery little thing, "full of nettles and brambles," as old Grandma Mosh always said. His eyes shone like blackberries in late summer. When he was very small, the Khans undertook the long, hard journey to Tyr, along the blasted planes, and in that settlement Mowgai was equipped with a composite endoskeleton, which allowed him to walk, in however curious a fashion. On the long summer days, which seemed never to end, Mowgai and I would roam freely over the Land, collecting wild berries by the stream or picking pine nuts from the fallen cones in the forest, and we would debate for hours the merits or otherwise of Elder Simeon's intricate clockwork automatons, and we would try to catch fish in the stream, but we never did catch anything.

It was a long, hot summer: the skies were a clear and uninterrupted lavender blue, with only smudges of white cloud on the horizon like streaks of paint, and when the big yellow sun hung high in the sky we would seek shelter deep in the forest, where the breeze stirred the pine needles sluggishly and where we could sit with our backs to the trunks of old mottled pines, between the roots, eating whatever lunch we had scavenged at home in the morning on our way. Eating dark bread and hard cheese and winter kimchee, we felt we knew all the whole world, and had all the time in it, too: it is a feeling that fades and can never return once lost, and all the more precious for that. For dessert we ate slices of watermelon picked only an hour or so earlier from the ground. The warm juice ran down our chins and onto our hands and we spat out the small black pips on the ground, where they stared up at us like hard eyes.

And we would story.

Mowgai was fascinated by machines. I, less so. Perhaps it was that he was part machine himself, and thus felt an affinity to the old world that I did not then share. My mother, too, was like that, going off for days and months on her journeys to the fallow places, to scavenge and salvage. But for her I think it was a practical matter, as it is for salvagers. She felt no nostalgia for the past, and often regarded the ancients' fallen monuments as monstrous follies, vast junkyards of which precious little was of any use. It was my father who was the more romantic of the two, who told me stories of the past, who sometimes dreamed, I think, of other, different times. Salvagers are often hard and durable, like the materials they repurpose and reuse. Mowgai's dream was to become a salvager like my mother, to follow the caravans to the sunken cities in the sea or to the blasted plains. His journey to Tyr had changed him in some profound fashion, and he would talk for hours of what he saw there, and on the way.

Usually after our lunch we would head on out of the trees, toward the misshapen hills that lay to the northwest of us. These hills were shaped in an odd way, with steep rises and falls and angular lines, and Elder Simeon made his home at their base.

When he saw us approach that day he came out of his house and wiped his hands on his leather apron and smiled out of his tanned and lined face. They said he had clockwork for a heart, and he and Mowgai often spoke of mechanical beings and schematics in which I had little interest. His pets, too, came out, tiny clockwork automata of geese and ducks, a tawny peacock, a stealthy prowling cat, a caterpillar and a turtle.

"Come, come!" he said. "Little Mai and Mowgai!" And he led us to his courtyard and set to brewing tea. Elder Simeon was very old, and had traveled widely as a young man all about the Land, for a restless spirit had taken hold of him then. But now he valued solitude, and stillness, and he seldom came out of his home, and but for us, received few visitors.

He served us tea, with little slices of lemon from the tree in his yard, and then we sat down together to story, which is what we do in the Land.

"You have gone to Tyr," he said to Mowgai, and his eyes twinkled with amusement. "Have you ever seen, on your way through the blasted plains, a town, standing peacefully in the middle of nowhere?"

Mowgai stirred, surprised, and said that no, he hadn't, and he did not think anything still lived in the blasted plains.

"Life finds a way," Elder Simeon said. "There is life there of all sorts, snakes and scorpions and lizards, sage and marigolds and cacti. But the town . . . well, they say there is a town, Mowgai, little Mai. I had heard of it in Tyr, where they say it sits there still, out on the plains, as perfect and as orderly as it had always been. No one goes near it, and no one comes out. . . . "

It is just an old men's tale, I think, and you know how they love to embellish and gossip.

But this is the story. It is told in a curious sort of way. It is told in the plural, by a mysterious "we," but who these "we" are, or were, no one now remembers. Perhaps "they" are still in the town, but though many claim to have seen it, its location always seems to change like a mirage in the telling.

"Once," began Elder Simeon, "there was a little boy . . . "

Once there was a little boy who lived in a house with two kindly parents and a cheerful little dog, and they all loved him very much. The dog's name was Rex, and all dogs in their town, which was a very lovely and orderly town indeed, were called that. Mother was tall and graceful and never slept at all, and Father was strong and patient and sang very beautifully. Their house too was very lovely and very clean. The boy's name was Oli, which was carefully chosen by algorithm from a vast dictionary of old baby names.

The town was called the Town. It was a carefully built town of white picket fences and single-story houses and wide avenues and big open parks with many trees. The boy would go for a walk in the park with his parents every day, and he could always hear the humming of many insects and see beautiful butterflies flittering among the trees.

Really it was quite an idyllic childhood in many ways.

It had to be, of course.

It was very carefully designed.

You can probably see where this is going.

The shape of stories is difficult for us. We understand them as patterns, what you'd call a formula. We tell the story of Oli's childhood in a way designed to be optimal, yet there are always deviations, margins of error that can creep in.

For instance, there was the matter of the purple caterpillar.

The purple caterpillar was very beautiful, Oli thought. It was a long, thin insect with many prolegs, brightly colored in purple with bright yellow spots. It crawled on the thin green leaf of a flowering helleborine, and it did that, back and forth, back and forth, every day on Oli's passing through the park. When Oli was not in the park, of course, the caterpillar stopped moving. Oli became quite unreasonably—we felt—fascinated by the caterpillar, and every day on his journey through the park he would stop for long minutes to examine the little creature, despite his father calling him to come along to the swings, or his mother asking him to hold her hand so he could hop over the pond.

But Oli would just squat there and stare at the caterpillar, as it moved back and forth, back and forth across the leaf.

Why did the caterpillar crawl back and forth, back and forth across the leaf? Oli wondered. His parents, who were not used to children, were a little taken aback to discover that *why* was one of Oli's favorite words. *Why* did the clouds make shapes in the sky? *Why* did Rex never bark? *Why* was water wet? *Why* did Oli sometimes wake up in the middle of the night, uneasy, and tried and tried to listen to the night sounds of the Town all around him, only there were none?

Some of these questions we could answer, of course—clouds made shapes because the human mind has been programmed by long evolution to make patterns, for instance: just like stories. Water is "wet" in its liquid form, but the word only describes the *experience* of water, not its properties; the town was quiet, and Rex never barked, because Oli was meant to be asleep at that time.

The caterpillar crawled like that every day under Oli's gaze, but children, as we found, are almost unreasonably inquisitive, and therefore one day Oli simply grabbed the little creature by its body and lifted it off the leaf.

The caterpillar struggled feebly between Oli's thumb and forefinger.

"Don't touch that!" Mother said sharply, but Oli didn't really pay her much mind. He stared at the caterpillar, fascinated. The creature emitted a high-pitched shriek of alarm. Oli, who like all children could also be cruel, pressed harder on the caterpillar's thin membranous body. The creature began to hiss and smoke, its antennae moving frantically as it tried to escape. Oli pressed harder and the caterpillar's membrane burst.

"Ow!" said Oli, and threw the caterpillar on the ground. The creature had got very hot just before its demise, and left a small burn mark on the epidermis of Oli's thumb and forefinger. Mother cried out, horrified at this damage, but Oli stuck his fingers in his mouth and sucked them, still staring at the caterpillar.

Thin wires protruded from the caterpillar's broken body, and faint traces of blue electricity could still be seen traversing the wires before they, too, faded. Oli reached down, more carefully this time, and prodded the body with the tip of his finger. It had already cooled, so he picked it up again and studied it. He had never seen the inside of a living creature before.

That evening Oli had many more questions, and we were not sure how to answer them yet and so we did what grown-ups always do, and didn't. This was perhaps a mistake, but we were unsure how to proceed. The next morning the caterpillar was back on its leaf like it had always been, crawling up and down, up and down, but Oli studiously ignored it, and we were relieved.

For the next few days Oli was his usual self. Rex often accompanied him on his walks through the park, fetching sticks of wood that Oli threw, and watching patiently as Oli sat on the swing while Father pushed him, up and down, up and down, but never too fast or too high as to pose danger to the child. Oli thought about the sensation he felt when he'd burned his finger. It was pain, something all parents are eager to prevent their children from experiencing, though we are not sure we quite understand it, as it is merely a warning system for the body, or that's what we always thought.

There were other children in the playground in the park, who Oli saw every day. They dutifully swung on the swings (but one was always free for Oli) and slid down the slides, and climbed on the wood posts and rocked up and down, up and down on the seesaws. They were always very fond of Oli but he found their company boring, because all they ever said were things like, "I love mommy!" and "Let's play!" and "This is fun!"

They all had dogs named Rex.

And so Oli, while we thought he had forgotten the caterpillar, had in fact been hatching a plan. And so one day when he was playing with one of the other children, who was called Michael, on the tree house, Oli pushed him, and Michael fell. He fell very gracefully, but nevertheless he fell, and he scraped his knee very badly, and Oli saw how the oily blood briefly came out of the wound before the tiny mites inside Michael's body crawled out to repair the damage done. And also Michael never cried, because we had not thought crying a good thing to teach the other children to do, the children who were not Oli. And then Oli did something very brave and foolish, and he fell down himself, on purpose, and he hurt himself. And he looked down and saw blood, and he began to cry.

Well, Mother and Father were dreadfully upset, and they fussed over Oli, and for a few days he was not allowed to go outside because of his wound, and all he did was sit in his room, and listen to the silence of the town, because no one was out when Oli was not, and he became afraid of the silence, and of how empty the world felt all around him, and when Mother or Father came to talk to him or hold him, he pushed them away.

"Are you my real parents?" he asked them, and they did not know what to say. Only Rex kept him company in that time.

What we mean to say is, Oli knew he was different, but he didn't quite know how. He knew everyone else was, in a way, better than him. We didn't feel pain and we didn't cry and we were always kind and patient, when he could be hasty and cruel. We weren't sure how to feel things, apart from a great sense of obligation to the child, for him to have the very best life and to be happy. He was very important to us. It was also at that time that Oli saw his parents in the bedroom. He peeked in through a door open just a fraction and saw Father standing motionless by the window, in the moonlight, unnaturally still because he had shut off; and he saw Mother with her chest cavity open, and the intricate machinery glowing and crawling inside, as she performed a minor repair on herself.

This was when he decided to run away to become a real boy.

Of course, you see the problem there.

Oli stole out in the middle of the night, with only Rex for company. He walked through eerily quiet streets, where nothing stirred and nothing moved. It was our fault. We should have operated the town continuously, let people walk around outside and dogs bark and owls hoot, but it just seemed like a waste of energy when the town was first conceived: when Oli himself, of course, was conceived.

Also we are not sure what the hooting of owls sounds like, or what the creatures themselves resembled. A lot of the old records were lost.

The moon was up that night. It had been broken long before, and it hung crooked in the sky, a giant lump of misshapen rock with the scars of old battles on its pockmarked face. It bathed the world in silver light. Oli's footsteps echoed alone as he walked through the town. We should have been more vigilant, of course, but we did not have much experience in the raising of children. Mother and Father were in their room, having put Oli to sleep and kissed him good night. They thought him long asleep, and now stood motionless in their bedroom, caught like statues in the moonlight. The moonlight shone down on the park and its insects, on the storage sheds where we kept the dummy children who played with Oli, on the too-big houses where no one lived, on the dogs who were asleep in their yards, frozen until such a time as they might be needed again.

We didn't think Oli would really leave.

We waited for him on the edge of the town. He was a very determined boy. He saw us standing there. We looked just like Mrs. Baker, the friendly neighbor who worked in the grocery shop, whom Oli had known since birth.

"Hello, Mrs. Baker," he said.

"Hello, Oli," we said.

"I'm leaving," he said.

"Why?" we said.

"I'm not like everyone else," he said. "I'm different."

Gently, we said, "We know."

We loved him very much at that moment. There was a 56.998 percent chance of Oli dying if he left the town, and we didn't want that at all.

"I want to be a real boy," he said.

"You are a real boy," we said.

"I want to be like Mother, and Father, and Michael, and you, Mrs. Baker."

At that moment I think we realized that this was the point in the story of childhood where they learn something painful, something true.

"We can't always get what we want," we told him. "The world isn't like that, Oli. It isn't like the town. It is still rough and unpredictable and dangerous. We can't be you. We don't even truly understand what it is to be you. All we have are approximations."

He nodded, seriously. He was a serious boy. He said, "I'm still going, but I'll come back. Will you please tell Mother and Father that I love them?"

"We love you, too," we told him. We think maybe he understood, then. But we can never truly know. All we have are simulations.

"Come on, boy," Oli said.

Rex whined, looking up at his master; but he couldn't go beyond the boundary of the town.

"We're sorry," we said.

Oli knelt by his dog and stroked his fur. There was water in the boy's eyes, a combination of oils and mucins and hormones such as prolactin. But he wiped away his tears.

"Good-bye, Rex," he said. The dog whined. Oli nodded, seriously, and turned away.

This was how Oli left us, alone, on his quest to become a real boy: with the town silent behind him, with the broken moon shining softly overhead, with us watching him leave. There is an old poem left from before, from long before, about the child walking away . . . about the parent letting them go.

We think we were sad, but we really don't know.

We waved, but he never turned back and saw us.

"This is a very strange story, Elder Simeon," I said.

"Yes," he said. "It is very old, from when the world was different."

"Were there really thinking machines in those days?" Mowgai asked, and Elder Simeon shrugged.

"*We* are thinking machines," he said.

"But what happened to the boy?" I said. "What happened to Oli?"

"They tell no stories of his journey in Tyr," Elder Simeon said. "Nor in Suf or in the floating islands. But old Grandma Toffle tells the tale . . . " But here he fell silent, and his mechanical duck waddled up to him and tucked its head under Elder Simeon's arm, and its golden feathers shone in the late afternoon sun. "It's just a story," Elder Simeon said reluctantly.

We left him then, and wended our way back across the fields and over the brook to the houses. That night, after the sun had set and the lanterns were lit over our homes, I felt very grateful that I was not like that strange boy, Oli, and that I lived in a real place, that I lived on the Land itself and not in something that only mimicked it. But I felt sad for him, too: and Mowgai and I sought out old Grandma Toffle, who sat by the fire, warming her hands, for all that it was summer, and we asked her to tell us the story of the boy.

"Who told you that nonsense?" she said. "It wasn't old Simeon, was it?"

We admitted, somewhat sheepishly, that it was, and she snorted. "The old fool. There is nothing wrong with machines in their rightful place, but to fill your heads with such fancy! Listen. There was never such a city, and if there was, it has long since rotted to the ground. Old Simeon may speak of self-repairing mechanisms and whatnot, but the truth is that decay always sets in. Nothing lasts forever, children. The ancients built cities bigger than the sky, and weapons that could kill the Earth and almost did, at that. But do you see their airplanes flying through the sky? Their cities lie in ruins. The old roads are abandoned. Life continues as it always did. The mistake we'd always made was to think ourselves the most important species. But the planet doesn't care if humans live or die upon it. It is just as important to be human as it is to be an ant, or a stinging nettle."

"But . . . but we can *think*," said Mowgai.

Old Grandma Toffle snorted again. "Think!" she said. "And where did that ever get you?"

"But we can tell stories," I said quietly.

"Yes . . . " she said. "Yes. That we can. Very well. What was your question again?"

"Do you know what happened to the boy, Oli, when he left the town?"

"Know? No, I can't say as that I *know*, little Mai."

"Then . . . "

Her eyes twinkled in the light of the fire, much as Elder Simeon's did in the sun. When she smiled, there were dimples on her cheeks, making her appear momentarily younger. She said, "Sit down, children. Sit down, and let me tell you. The boy wandered for a long time. . . . "

The boy wandered for a long time away from the town. He missed his parents, and his dog, and everyone. The world beyond the town was very different from everything he'd ever known. It was a rough place at that time, which was not that long after the great floods and the collapse of the old world, and many of the springs were poisoned, and the animals hostile and deadly, and flocks of wild drones flew against darkening skies, and unexploded ordnance lay all about and some of it was . . .

Not exactly *smart*, but . . .

Cunning.

He went for a long time without food or water, and he'd grown weak when he met the Fox and the Cat. They were not exactly a fox and a cat. One was a sort of mobile infiltration unit, designed for stealth, and the other was a stubby little tank. They were exactly the sort of unsuitable companions the Town had worried about when it let the boy go.

"Hello, young sir!" said the Cat.

"Who . . . who is it?" said the Fox. "Who dares . . . walk the paths of the dead?"

"My name's Oli," said Oli. He looked at them with curiosity, for he had never seen such machines before.

"I have never met an Oli," said the Cat.

"I have never tasted an Oli," said the Fox, somewhat wistfully.

"Please," said Oli, "I am very hungry and very tired. Do you know where I could find shelter?"

The Fox and the Cat communicated silently with each other, for they, too, were very hungry, though their sustenance was of another kind.

"We know . . . a place," said the Fox.

"Not very far," said the Cat.

"Not . . . not far at all," said the Fox.

"We could show it to you," said the Cat.

"Show it to . . . you," said the Fox.

"Shut up!" said the Cat.

"Shut . . . oh," said the Fox.

"A place of many miracles," said the Fox, with finality.

And Oli, though he couldn't be said to have trusted these two strange machines, agreed.

They traveled for a long time through that lost landscape, and the wasteland around them was slowly transformed as the sun rose and set and rose again. Soon they came to the outskirts of a vast city, of a kind Oli had never seen and that only salvagers now see. It was one of the old cities, and as it was still not that long after the fall of the cities, much of it still remained. They passed roads choked with transportation pods like weeds growing through the cracks, and vast grand temples where once every manner of thing had been for sale. Broken houses littered the sides of the streets and towers lay on their sides, and the little tank that was the Cat rolled over the debris while the Fox snuck around it, and all the while Oli struggled to keep up.

The city was very quiet, though things lived in it, as the Fox and the Cat well knew. Predatory things, dangerous things, and they looked upon Oli with hatred in their seeing apparatus, for they hated all living things. Yet these were small, rodentlike constructions, the remnants of a vanished age, who loved and hated their fallen masters in equal measure, and mourned them when they thought no one was looking their way. And they were scared of the Fox and of the Cat, who were battle hardened, and so the unlikely trio passed through that city unharmed.

At last they came to a large forest, and went amid the trees.

"Not far now," said the Cat.

"To the place of . . . of miracles," said the Fox.

"What is this place?" asked Oli.

The Fox and the Cat communicated silently.

"It is a place where no machines can go," the Cat said at last; and it sounded wistful and full of resentment at once. "Where trees grow from the ground and water flows in the rivers and springs. Where the ground is fertile and the sun shines on the organic life-forms and gives them sustenance. Plants! Flowers! People . . . useless, ugly things!"

But the Fox said, "I . . . like flowers," and it sounded wistful only, with no hate. And the Cat glared at it but said nothing. And so they traveled on, deep into the forest, where the manshonyagger lived.

"What's a manshonyagger?" said Mowgai, and as he spoke the word, I held myself close and felt cold despite the fire in the hearth. And old Grandma Toffle said, "The man hunters, which roamed the earth in those days after the storms and the wars, and hunted the remnants of humanity. They were sad machines, I think now, driven crazy with grief for the world, and blinded by their programming. They were not evil, so much as they were made that way. In that forest lived such a manshonyagger, and the Fox and the Cat were taking the unwitting Oli to see it, for it had ruled in that land for a very long time, and was powerful among all the machines, and they knew they could get their heart's desire from it, if only they could give it what it wanted, which was a human."

"But what did the Fox and the Cat *want*?" asked Mowgai.

Old Grandma Toffle shrugged. "That," she said, "nobody knows for sure."

Stories, I find, are like that. Things don't turn out the way they're supposed to, people's motivations aren't clear, machines exceed their programming. Odd bits are missing. I often find myself thinking about the Fox and the Cat, these days, with the nights lengthening. Were they bad, or did we just misunderstand them? They had no regard for Oli's life; but then, did we expect them to? They learned only from their masters, and their masters were mostly gone.

In any case, they came to the forest, and deep within the forest, in the darkest part, they heard a sound. . . .

"What was that?" said Oli.

"It was nothing," said the Cat.

"N-nothing," said the Fox.

The sound came again, and Oli, who was near passing out from exhaustion and hunger, nevertheless pressed on, toward its source. He passed through a thick clump of trees and saw a house.

The house stood alone in the middle of the forest, and it reminded him of his own home, which he had started to miss very much, for the ruined houses of the city they had passed earlier were nothing at all like it. This was a small and pleasant farmhouse, built of white stones, mottled with moss and ivy, and in the window of the house there was a little girl with turquoise hair.

"Please," said Oli. "May I come in?"

"No . . . " whispered the Fox, and the Cat hissed, baring empty bomb canisters.

"Go away," said the little girl with turquoise hair. "I am dead."

"How can you be dead?" said Oli, confused.

"I am waiting for my coffin to arrive," said the little girl. "I have been waiting for so long."

"Enough!" cried the Cat, and the Fox rolled forward threateningly, and the two machines made to grab Oli before he could enter the sphere of influence of the house.

"Let me go!" cried Oli, who was afraid. He looked beseechingly up at the little girl in the window. "Help me!" he said.

But the Cat and the Fox were determined to bring Oli to the manshonyagger, and they began to force the boy away from the house. He looked back at the girl in the window. He saw something in her eyes then, something old, and sad. Then, with a sigh, and a flash of turquoise, she became a mote of light and glided from the house and came to land, unseen, on Oli's shoulder.

"Perhaps I am not *all* dead," she said. "Perhaps there is a part of me that's stayed alive, through all the long years—"

But at that moment, the earth trembled, and the trees bent and broke, and a sound like giant footsteps echoed through the forest. Oli stopped fighting his captors, and the Fox and the Cat both looked up—and up—and up—and the Cat said, "It's here, it's heard our cries!" and the Fox said, with reverence, "Manshonyagger . . . "

"But just what *is* a manshonyagger?" demanded Mowgai.

Old Grandma Toffle smiled, rocking in her chair, and we could see that she was growing sleepy. "They could take all sorts of shapes," she said, "though this one was said to look like a giant metal human being. . . . "

The giant footsteps came closer and closer, until a metal foot descended without warning from the heavens and crushed the house of the little girl with the turquoise hair, burying it entirely. From high above there was a creaking sound, and then a giant face filled the sky as it descended and peered at them curiously. Though how it could be described as "curious" it is hard to say, since the face was metal and had no moving features from which to form expressions.

Oli shrank into himself. He wished he'd never left the town, and that he'd listened to Mrs. Baker and turned back and gone home. He missed Rex.

He missed, he realized, his childhood.

"A human . . . !" said the manshonyagger.

"We want . . . " said the Fox.

"We want what's ours!" said the Cat.

"What was . . . promised," said the Fox.

"We want the message sent back by the Exilarch," said the Cat.

The giant eyes regarded them with indifference. "Go back to the city," the manshonyagger said. "And you will find the ending to your story. Go to the tallest building, now fallen on its side, from whence the ancient ships once went to orbit, and climb into the old control booth at its heart, and there you will find it. It is a rock the size of a human fist, a misshapen lump of rock from the depths of space."

Then, ignoring them, the giant machine reached down and picked Oli up, very carefully, and raised him to the sky.

Below, the Cat and the Fox exchanged signals; and they departed at once, toward the city. But what this message was that they sought, and who the Exilarch was, I do not know, and it belongs perhaps in another story. They never made it either. It was a time when people had crept back into the blighted zones, a rough people more remnants of the old days than of ours, and they had begun to hunt the old machines and to destroy them. The Cat and the Fox fell prey to such an ambush, and they perished; and this rock from the depths of space was never found, if indeed it had ever existed.

Oli, meanwhile, found himself high above the world. . . .

"But this *is* just a *story*, right?" said Mowgai. "I mean, there aren't *really* things like manshonyaggers. There can't be!"

"Do you want me to stop?" said old Grandma Toffle.

"No, no, I just . . . "

"There were many terrible things done in the old days," said old Grandma Toffle. "Were there really giant, human-shaped robots roaming the Earth in those days? That I can't honestly tell you. And was there really a little dead girl with turquoise hair? That, too, I'm sure I can't say, Mowgai."

"But she wasn't really a little girl, was she?" I said. "She wasn't that at all."

"Very good, little Mai," said old Grandma Toffle.

"She was a fairy!" said Mowgai triumphantly.

"A simulated personality, yes," said old Grandma Toffle. "Bottled up and kept autonomously running. Such things were known, back then. Toys, for the children, really. Only this one somehow survived, grew old as the children it was meant to play with had perished."

"That's awful," I said.

"Things were awful back then," said old Grandma Toffle complacently. "Now, do you want to hear the rest of it? There's not that long to go."

"Please," said Mowgai, though he didn't really look like he wanted to hear any more.

"Very well. Oli looked down, and . . . "

Oli looked down, and the entire world was spread out far below. He could see the shimmering blue sea in the distance, and the ruined city, and the blasted plains. And far in the distance he thought he could see the place the Cat and the Fox spoke of, the place of miracles: it was green and brown and yellow and blue, a land the like of which had not been seen in the world for centuries or more. It had rivers and fields and forests, insects and butterflies and people, and the sun shone down on wheat and fig trees, cabbages and daisies. And on little children—children just like you.

It was the Land, of course.

And Oli longed to go there.

"A human child," said the giant robot. Its eyes were the size of houses. "It has been so long. . . . "

"What will . . . what will you do with me?" said Oli, and there was only a slight tremor in his voice.

"Kill . . . " said the robot, though it sounded uncertain.

"Please," said Oli. "I don't even know how to be a real boy. I just want to . . . I just want to *be*."

"Kill . . . " said the robot. But it sounded dubious, as though it had forgotten what the word meant.

Then the little girl with turquoise hair shot up from Oli's shoulder in a shower of sparks, startling him, and hovered between him and the giant robot.

"What she said to the manshonyagger," said old Grandma Toffle, "nobody knows for certain. Perhaps she saw in the robot the sort of child she never got the chance to play with. And perhaps the robot, too, was tired, for it could no longer remember *why* it was that it was meant to hunt humans. The conference between the little fairy and the giant robot lasted well into the night; and Oli, having seen the sun set over the distant Land, eventually fell asleep, exhausted, in the giant's palm."

And here she stopped, and sat back in her rocking chair, and closed her eyes.

"Grandma Toffle?" I said.

"Grandma Toffle!" said Mowgai.

But old Grandma Toffle had begun, not so gently, to snore. And we looked at each other, and Mowgai tried to pull on her arm, but she merely snorted in her sleep and turned her head away. And so we never got to hear the end of the story from her.

That summer long ago, I roamed across the Land with Mowgai, through hot days that seemed never to end. We'd pick berries by the stream, and watch the adults in the fields, and try to catch the tiny froglets in the pond with our fingers, though they always slipped from our grasp. Mowgai, I think, identified with Oli much more than I did. He would retell the story to me, under the pine trees, in the cool of the forest, with the soft breeze stirring the needles. He would wonder and worry, and though I kept telling him it was only a story, it had become more than that for him. One day we went to visit Elder Simeon at his house in the foot of the hills. When he saw us coming, he emerged from his workshop, his clockwork creations waddling and crawling and hopping after him. He welcomed us in. His open yard smelled of machine oil and mint, and from there we could see the curious hills and their angular sides. It was then—reluctantly, I think—that he told us the rest of the story.

"The robot and the fairy spoke long into the night," he said, "and what arrangement they at last reached, nobody knows for sure. That morning, very early, before the sun rose, the manshonyagger began to stride across the blasted plains. With each stride it covered an enormous distance. It crushed stunted trees and poisonous wells and old human dwellings, long fallen into ruin, and the tiny machines down below fled from its path. The girl with turquoise hair was with him, residing inside his chest, where people keep their hearts. The manshonyagger strode across the broken land, as the sun rose slowly in the sky and the horizon grew lighter, and all the while the little boy slept soundly in the giant's palm.

"And, at last, they came to the Land."

"They came . . . they came *here*?" Mowgai said.

"And the manshonyagger looked down on the rivers and fields, and the fruit trees and the tiny frogs, and of course the people, our ancestors who fled here with the fall of the old world, and it never knew such a Land, and it thought that perhaps the old days were truly gone forever. And it was very tired. And so, with the little girl—who was not at all a little girl, of course, but something not a little like the manshonyagger—whispering in its heart, it laid the boy down, right about here." And he pointed down to the ground, at his yard, and smiled at our expressions. "And the boy grew up to be a man, among his kind, though there was always, I think, a little bit of him that was also part machine. And he became a salvager, like your mother, Mai, and he spent much of his time out on the blasted plains, and some said he sought his old home, still, but always in vain.

"You won't find him in our cemetery, though. He disappeared one day, in old age, and after he had begat two children, a little girl and a little boy. It was on a salvaging expedition out on the plains, and some say he died at the hands of the rogue machines that still lived there, but some say he finally found that which he was looking for, and he went back to his perfect home, and had one last childhood in that town where the past is eternally preserved. But that, I think, is just a story."

"But what happened to the robot?" asked Mowgai. "Did it go back?" and there was something lost and sad in his little face. I remember that, so vividly.

And Elder Simeon shook his head, and smiled, and pointed beyond the house, and he said, "The story says that the manshonyagger, seeing that its young charge was well and sound—and being, as I said, so very tired, too—lay down on the ground, and closed its eyes, and slept. And, some say, is sleeping still."

We looked where he pointed, and we saw the angled hills, and their curious contours; and if you squinted, and if you looked hard enough, you could just imagine that they took on a shape, as of a sleeping, buried giant.

"But . . . " I said.

"You don't—" said Mowgai.

And Elder Simeon smiled again, and shook his head, and said, "But I told you, children. It's just a story."

The days grow short, and the shadows lengthen, and I find myself thinking more and more about the past. Mowgai is gone these many years, but I still miss him. That summer, long ago, we spent days upon days hiking through the curious hills, searching and digging, the way children do. We hoped to find a giant robot, and once, just once, we thought we saw a sudden spark of turquoise light, and the outline of a little girl, not much older than we were, looking down on us, and smiling; but it was, I think, just a trick of the light.

Some say the giant's still there, lying asleep, and that one day it will wake, when it is needed. We spent all that summer, and much of the next, looking for the buried giant; but of course, we never found it.

JUMP

CADWELL TURNBULL

Mike and Jessie were walking in the park. The trees high above their heads stretched to touch each other, their leaves letting only the tiniest slivers of light through.

Mike watched the freckles of light spot Jessie's brown face, her shirt, her arms. He tried to snub them out with his fingers.

It was a long day for them. They'd spent a few hours walking around the park, just talking. About old dreams and new ones, black riots and urban decay, the secrets of their hearts and the mysteries of the universe, the time Mike introduced himself through a mutual friend and his palms were so clammy that Jessie knew immediately how nervous he was.

They always talked a lot. Mike was amazed that they always found something to say. It was a little less than two years, but he thought once grad school was over, he would ask. He thought she'd say yes.

They made another lap around the park. By the time they decided they needed to walk back home—a full forty-five minutes away—they were way too tired to make the journey. They considered a cab, but Mike had a better idea.

"Why don't we teleport?" he asked.

"What now?" She laughed. She was giving him that smile she gave when he was talking crazy, that would spread across her face, her eyes wide, her eye brows raised in steep arches.

"Hold my hand," he said, and he didn't wait. He grabbed her hand himself. "We can do it."

"What makes you think we can teleport?" she asked.

"I believe," he said simply.

She laughed at him again. "You're crazy."

Mike didn't know how far he was going to take this. But it was Jessie and he didn't worry about seeming silly. "Close your eyes and picture home," he said. "On the count of three, we will jump forward and we will be there."

He looked at Jessie, and sure enough, she closed her eyes. She was smiling and he wished he could read her thoughts, but that was another power entirely.

"One," he said. He tightened his grip on her hand. "Two." He felt a warmth in his stomach, his knees were bent, he was extra aware of the grass beneath his feet. "Three." He leapt and he felt Jessie leap with him, their bodies synchronized. They were in the air for no more than two seconds and when they landed, their feet hitting the ground at the same time, there wasn't the familiar soft crunch of grass. There was the hard thump of their feet against pavement. When they opened their eyes, they realized they were home.

Jessie looks back on the day often. She remembers how weak her knees felt once they had made the jump; he had to hold her up to keep her from toppling over. She remembers his face, the flashes of abject terror, shock, and then euphoria. And she remembers the warmth in her belly, like she was glowing from the inside.

She remembers her neighbor Greg from 34C, halfway up the stairs to their apartment building when they arrived out of nowhere.

"Oh, I didn't see you two there," he said, turning when he heard Mike's joyous scream. "Everything okay?" He looked from Mike to her to Mike again.

"Holy shit," Mike said, as if in answer. And then more screams.

Jessie's sitting on the couch, reliving the moment, her legs pressed under her, an open book in her lap.

Mike walks into the room. "We should try again," he says.

Jessie glares at him. If Jessie agrees, this will be the twentieth time they've tried. They have all been failures.

Mike keeps a calendar where he crosses off the days since it happened. Many markers are spent in the attempt to keep a record; the markers start out strong, with vibrant confident lines, and then they sputter and falter and only the blood-crawling squeak against the paper remains. Mike tries many colors. Blue. Red. Green. Magenta. The ink runs out of all of them. And still no jump.

The first dozen attempts are at the park, trying to find the right spot, wearing the right clothes. Jessie must always be on the right side. They try time of day. It must always be late afternoon. They try the weather. The day must be cool and clear.

Mike recites the exact words to himself. He writes it down. He puts the words next to the calendar on the wall. He remembers Jessie's words, too. It must all be perfect. They go back to the park and relive the experience word for word. When they do this they sound like play actors reciting lines.

"Why don't we teleport?" Mike asks.

Jessie rolls her eyes. "What now?" she asks and the laugh is hollow, mocking.

"You're not trying. You have to really try—"

"Jesus, Mike."

"—Now we have to start over."

Soon after that, Jessie refuses to go back to the park. But Mike keeps asking to try in other places. At home. When they go out to restaurants. At the movies. Jessie obliges, but each time her shoulders slump a little lower. She hates it. She hates it so much.

"You're killing me," she says. "Why does this matter so much?"

"Why wouldn't it matter?" Mike says. "What would matter more?"

A day later, he asks her again and she almost throws a book at him, pulling back at the last moment. "Leave it alone, Mike. Can't you just leave it alone?"

Sometimes Mike wonders if he imagined it. But it can't be. Jessie was there.

He gets so suspicious of the whole thing that he starts to wonder if even Jessie is a figment of his imagination.

When his friend Alex comes over for dinner, Mike tries to confirm his suspicions while Jessie is in the kitchen. "I'm married to a woman about this high, right? Light brown eyes? Dark skin? Can be a little judgy sometimes?" He says the last part a little softer than the rest.

Alex just looks at him.

Mike waits for an answer, the cold doubt creeping up his spine.

"That was a great dinner, J," Alex says, looking past Mike. Then he looks back at Mike and points at him with his fork. "You fucked up."

Mike turns and sees his wife. He has no idea how long she's been standing there. But she makes a face he has come to know well and he knows that she knows that this is about the jump again.

"You're welcome, Alex," she says and then leaves the dining room.

It isn't that Jessie doesn't care about the jump.

She just sees it differently than Mike. This thing wasn't supposed to happen. It was an accident of the universe. To want it to happen more than once, in one life, is crazy. Isn't it? What would be the odds? And why would you need it to happen again? How practical is teleporting if you can't predict it? It is a silly thing, really. A silly little thing.

Yet Jessie still looks back on the day in amazement. Sometimes, in rare moments, she relives it. It is special because of its elusiveness. Because it doesn't explain itself. For her, it is damn near divine. And she finds it empowering to have experienced it. She is of a small order who knows a secret. She and Mike have glimpsed behind a curtain. They have precious knowledge. Shouldn't it bring them closer together?

She tries to talk to him about her thoughts, but it seems to just excite in him an unhealthy obsession.

"We should keep trying, then. Try to master it."

"No," she says, and it isn't a rebuttal of the idea itself. She just doesn't *want* to master it. She likes it where it is, something distant, to look at only when needed. She doesn't want it to be her life. It is just a jump. A beautiful jump, yes. But it doesn't deserve worship. Worship ruins all the best things.

Mike wants to tell everyone.

He thinks about telling his friend Alex—"Yo, I teleported." "Hey man, once with Jessie, I jumped from the park straight to my house!" "Al, you remember that movie about teleportation you hated? *Jumper*, was it? Yeah, well, me and Jessie . . . we did that."—but it never sounds right. He thinks about telling people on the street. He thinks about just screaming it from the window of their apartment: "I teleported!"

He did try that once.

"So what?" a neighbor yelled back.

"Well," he said, but he couldn't think of a good answer.

Then a day comes when Mike walks into his room and his calendar has been taken down. He looks around and he finds it in the trash bin next to his work desk.

"You threw my calendar away?" he asks Jessie a moment later.

Jessie is reading a book on the couch, her legs folded under her. She looks up at him and he can feel what's coming. "Stop counting," she says. "I'm tired of you counting."

Weeks later, she walks in on him standing in the middle of the bedroom. His knees are bent, his arms in front of him like he's getting ready to box. His hands are bunched into fists. His face is full of lines, scrunched up in deliberate concentration.

"What are you doing?" she asks.

He looks at her, embarrassed. "Nothing," he says.

"Yeah," she says. "Right."

Mike believes he has a lot to be angry about. Jessie doesn't care about the things that matter to him. She doesn't try to understand where he is coming from, how much he needs the calendars, and the hope.

Sometimes he wonders why he's stayed. This is a big question for most couples, but it is an even bigger question for Mike. He wonders if it is because of the jump or because of the love. He knows he loves her. This has never changed over all the years and the fights and the makeups. But he keeps thinking, maybe he stayed because she was there when the miracle happened. Maybe he hopes that if the miracle happens again, it will all be worth it. The years. The fights. The makeups. Love doesn't always keep you where you're supposed to be. But the miracle might have. Maybe all that's left is the miracle. This thought scares him.

Why does it even matter so much? He doesn't know. But he feels it every day. He comes home from work and he thinks of the jump. He is chilling with friends and the jump pops in and out of his consciousness. He is holding his wife and the jump is there, hanging in front of his eyes like an existential carrot he cannot catch.

He looks at his life and there is the jump, an island unto itself, surrounded by an ocean of monotony. Even when he is in a big moment, on the crest of some big wave, he can look out and see the island, and it calls to him, but he knows he cannot get there and it laughs at him. Vicious searing laughter.

"I'll make it up to you," Mike says.

He has forgotten their anniversary again. "Sure you will," she says.

It is not that she cares so much about these things. She is not that kind of sentimental. It is the fact that for years Mike has religiously crossed off each day on the calendar.

Mike's hand is on her chest, right above her breasts. He follows the rise and fall of each breath, his hand light on her skin. "I'm sorry," he says.

Jessie's pissed. Why? she thinks. Because you've let this thing get so big that there isn't any room for anything else? This stupid little thing.

But then she thinks there is something deeper in his apology beyond the forgetting. She thinks that he is saying sorry for many things. For all he has ever done that can't be undone.

She doesn't know if she is right. So many things go unsaid between them. But more importantly, she doesn't want the truth to ruin the joy she feels in this moment. This moment that she believes that Mike is better than he actually is. Because reality is arbitrary. Because it doesn't matter as much as the feeling. And she doesn't have enough good feelings to let one slip away.

She tries to sleep but Mike's hand feels heavy on her chest now. It is hard to sleep under so much weight, under this nagging feeling at the edge of her consciousness that this is the rest of their lives. Dancing around this little thing. Forever just out of reach, pulling at them. They've been married for four years and she is already breaking. What will be left of her after four decades?

It will always need to be fed, even when they are both trying to ignore that it's there. Because these things take up too much space. There is no equivalency. No end to the feeding of these little monsters.

Jessie takes Mike's hand off of her chest and turns away from him.

"I said I was sorry," he says. "I will make it up to you. I promise."

But Jessie says nothing. Her breathing is the only thing punctuating this silence. This silence at the end of things.

Jessie is thinking of leaving. Mike knows this. There are so many regrets. But it is too late for regrets.

He is thinking of the jump even now, but it is swirled in there with the guilt. All the things he was unable to do for Jessie, the man he was unable to be. He still wants it, but now he wishes he could close his eyes and zero in on that want with his mind and send it off to some distant planet where it cannot hurt them anymore. But that seems even more impossible than that day so long ago.

In the end, if Jessie leaves, there will be nothing but the jump. And he doesn't want to be alone with it. It will destroy him.

The old cliché of the light at the end of the tunnel. Mike laughs at it now. It is a fiction. There is light where he is. It is dim. It continues to dim. But there is no light ahead of him. All he sees is darkness.

Two months after Mike and Jessie split, he returns to the apartment to pick up a stack of books Jessie decided were his and an old fedora he'd left behind. These are the final remnants of their shared world, the last excuse for them to see each other ever again.

Jessie meets Mike at the door, looks him up and down. He has dark circles under his eyes. He hasn't cut his hair in weeks, it seems. A matted and unkempt beard covers the lower half of his face.

"Let's do it again," Mike says.

"What?" Jessie looks at him for a long time. The question is rhetorical. She's heard him. She just hasn't decided what she will do.

"One last time. For the road." Mike waits for her to reject his offer, or get angry and roll her eyes at him. Or slam the door in his face. But she doesn't do any of that.

"Okay," she says.

"Okay?" he says, surprised and relieved. "Okay. Close your eyes. And picture home."

She closes her eyes. This is the last time ever, she tells herself. A goodbye gift in honor of the thing that destroyed their lives. But even as she is thinking this, she can feel something frozen inside thawing against her will.

He believes then that she still trusts him—a trust he thought she had thrown away—and this gives him all the strength he needs to try again. He reaches out and grabs her hand.

"One," he says. He holds her hand tighter. Jessie can feel all the hope in this grasp, all the want, and she surprises herself by responding, gripping his hand tighter as well. This shocks Mike and he feels his stomach tighten.

"Two," he says.

They gasp aloud. This time feels different somehow. They can feel their hands merging. They feel the combination of all the times they've tried and failed and all the times they were too scared or angry to try. They feel their collective moments, a vibrating corporeality that squeezes tight around them, pulsing. They feel the release of the Earth's gravity. There is nothing to hold onto. Nothing but each other. And it is perfect. It feels right. They can feel the hope of something beyond what they know; they can feel the universe as a solid, living thing, calling to them, urging them forward.

They say the last part together, Jessie's voice unusually powerful, Mike as loud as a trumpet blasting over an ocean of years.

"THREE!"

UMBERNIGHT

CAROLYN IVES GILMAN

There is a note from my great-grandmother in the book on my worktable, they tell me. I haven't opened it. Up to now I have been too angry at her whole generation, those brave colonists who settled on Dust and left us here to pay the price. But lately, I have begun to feel a little disloyal—not to her, but to my companions on the journey that brought me the book, and gave me the choice whether to read it or not. What, exactly, am I rejecting here—the past or the future?

It was autumn—a long, slow season on Dust. It wasn't my first autumn, but I'd been too young to appreciate it the first time. I was coming back from a long ramble to the north, with the Make Do Mountains on my right and the great horizon of the Endless Plain to my left. I could not live without the horizon. It puts everything in perspective. It is my soul's home.

Sorry, I'm not trying to be offensive.

As I said, it was autumn. All of life was seeding, and the air was scented with lost chances and never agains. In our region of Dust, most of the land vegetation is of the dry, bristly sort, with the largest trees barely taller than I am, huddling in the shade of cliffs. But the plants were putting on their party best before Umbernight: big, white blooms on the bad-dog bushes and patches of bitterberries painting the arroyos orange. I knew I was coming home when a black fly bit me. Some of the organisms we brought have managed to survive: insects, weeds, lichen. They spread a little every time I'm gone. It's not a big victory, but it's something.

The dogs started barking when I came into the yard in front of Feynman Habitat with my faithful buggy tagging along behind me. The dogs never remember me at first, and always take fright at sight of Bucky. A door opened and Namja looked out. "Michiko's back!" she shouted, and pretty soon there was a mob of people pouring out of the fortified cave entrance. It seemed as if half of them were shorter than my knees. They stared at me as if I were an apparition, and no wonder: my skin was burned dark from the UV except around my eyes where I wear goggles, and my hair and eyebrows had turned white. I must have looked like Grandmother Winter.

"Quite a crop of children you raised while I was gone," I said to Namja. I couldn't match the toddlers to the babies I had left.

"Yes," she said. "Times are changing."

I didn't know what she meant by that, but I would find out.

Everyone wanted to help me unpack the buggy, so I supervised. I let them take most of the sample cases to the labs, but I wouldn't let anyone touch the topographical information. That would be my winter project. I was looking forward to a good hibernate, snug in a warm cave, while I worked on my map of Dust.

The cargo doors rumbled open and I ordered Bucky to park inside, next to his smaller siblings, the utility vehicles. The children loved seeing him obey, as they always do; Bucky has an alternate career as playground equipment when he's not with me. I hefted my pack and followed the crowd inside.

There is always a festive atmosphere when I first get back. Everyone crowds around telling me news and asking where I went and what I saw. This time they presented me with the latest project of the food committee: an authentic glass of beer. I think it's an acquired taste, but I acted impressed.

We had a big, celebratory dinner in the refectory. As a treat, they grilled fillets of chickens and fish, now plentiful enough to eat. The youngsters like it, but I've never been able to get used to meat. Afterwards, when the parents had taken the children away, a group of adults gathered around my table to talk. By then, I had noticed a change: my own generation had become the old-timers, and the young adults were taking an interest in what was going on. Members of the governing committee were conspicuously absent.

"Don't get too comfortable," Haakon said to me in a low tone.

"What do you mean?" I said.

Everyone exchanged a look. It was Namja who finally explained. "The third cargo capsule from the homeworld is going to land at Newton's Eye in about 650 hours."

"But . . . " I stopped when I saw they didn't need me to tell them the problem. The timing couldn't have been worse. Umbernight was just around the corner. Much as we needed that cargo, getting to it would be a gamble with death.

I remember how my mother explained Umbernight to me as a child. "There's a bad star in the sky, Michiko. We didn't know it was there at first because there's a shroud covering it. But sometimes, in winter, the shroud pulls back and we can see its light. Then we have to go inside, or we would die."

After that, I had nightmares in which I looked up at the sky and there was the face of a corpse hanging there, covered with a shroud. I would watch in terror as the veil would slowly draw aside, revealing rotted flesh and putrid gray jelly eyes, glowing with a deadly unlight that killed everything it touched.

I didn't know anything then about planetary nebulae or stars that emit in the UV and X-ray spectrum. I didn't know we lived in a double-star system, circling a perfectly normal G-class star with a very strange, remote companion. I had learned all that by the time I was an adolescent and Umber finally rose in our sky. I never disputed why I had to spend my youth cooped up in the cave habitat trying to make things run. They told me then, "You'll be all grown up with kids of your own before Umber comes again." Not true. All grown up, that part was right. No kids.

A dog was nudging my knee under the table, and I kneaded her velvet ears. I was glad the pro-dog faction had won the Great Dog Debate, when the colony had split on whether to reconstitute dogs from frozen embryos. You feel much more human with dogs around. "So what's the plan?" I asked.

As if in answer, the tall, stooped figure of Anselm Thune came into the refectory and headed toward our table. We all fell silent. "The Committee wants to see you, Mick," he said.

There are committees for every conceivable thing in Feynman, but when someone says "the Committee," capital C, it means the governing committee. It's elected, but the same people have dominated it for years, because no one wants to put up with the drama that would result from voting them out. Just the mention of it put me in a bad mood.

I followed Anselm into the meeting room where the five Committee members were sitting around a table. The only spare seat was opposite Chairman Colby, so I took it. He has the pale skin of a lifelong cave dweller, and thin white hair fringing his bald head.

"Did you find anything useful?" he asked as soon as I sat down. He's always thought my roving is a waste of time because none of my samples have produced anything useful to the colony. All I ever brought back was more evidence of how unsuited this planet is for human habitation.

I shrugged. "We'll have to see what the lab says about my biosamples. I found a real pretty geothermal region."

He grimaced at the word "pretty," which was why I'd used it. He was an orthodox rationalist, and considered aesthetics to be a gateway drug to superstition. "You'll fit in well with these gullible young animists we're raising," he said. "You and your fairy-tales."

I was too tired to argue. "You wanted something?" I said.

Anselm said, "Do you know how to get to Newton's Eye?"

"Of course I do."

"How long does it take?"

"On foot, about 200 hours. Allow a little more for the buggy, say 220."

I could see them calculating: there and back, 440 hours, plus some time to unload the cargo capsule and pack, say 450. Was there enough time?

I knew myself how long the nights were getting. Dust is sharply tilted, and at our latitude, its slow days vary from ten hours of dark and ninety hours of light in the summer to the opposite in winter. We were past the equinox; the nights were over sixty hours long, what we call N60. Umber already rose about midnight; you could get a sunburn before dawn. But most of its radiation didn't reach us yet because of the cloud of dust, gas, and ionized particles surrounding it. At least, that's our theory about what is concealing the star.

"I don't suppose the astronomers have any predictions when the shroud will part?" I said.

That set Colby off. "Shroud, my ass. That's a backsliding anti-rationalist term. Pretty soon you're going to have people talking about gods and visions, summoning spirits, and rejecting science."

"It's just a metaphor, Colby," I said.

"I'm trying to prevent us from regressing into savagery! Half of these youngsters are already wearing amulets and praying to idols."

Once again, Anselm intervened. "There is inherent unpredictability about the star's planetary nebula," he said. "The first time, the gap appeared at N64." That is, when night was 64 hours long. "The second time it didn't come till N70."

"We're close to N64 now," I said.

"Thank you for telling us," Colby said with bitter sarcasm.

I shrugged and got up to leave. Before I reached the door Anselm said, "You'd better start getting your vehicle in order. If we do this, you'll be setting out in about 400 hours."

"Just me?" I said incredulously.

"You and whoever we decide to send."

"The suicide team?"

"You've always been a bad influence on morale," Colby said.

"I'm just calculating odds like a good rationalist," I replied. Since I really didn't want to hear his answer to that, I left. All I wanted then was a hot bath and about twenty hours of sleep.

That was my first mistake. I should have put my foot down right then. They probably wouldn't have tried it without me.

But the habitat was alive with enthusiasm for fetching the cargo. Already, more people had volunteered than we could send. The main reason was eagerness to find out what our ancestors had sent us. You could barely walk down the hall without someone stopping you to speculate about it. Some wanted seeds and frozen embryos, electronic components, or medical devices. Others wanted rare minerals, smelting equipment, better water filtration. Or something utterly unexpected, some miracle technology to ease our starved existence.

It was the third and last cargo capsule our ancestors had sent by solar sail when they themselves had set out for Dust in a faster ship. Without the first two capsules, the colony would have been wiped out during the first winter, when Umber revealed itself. As it was, only two thirds of them perished. The survivors moved to the cave habitat and set about rebuilding a semblance of civilization. We weathered the second winter better here at Feynman. Now that the third winter was upon us, people were hoping for some actual comfort, some margin between us and annihilation.

But the capsule was preprogrammed to drop at the original landing site, long since abandoned. It might have been possible to reprogram it, but no one wanted to try calculating a different landing trajectory and sending it by our glitch-prone communication system. The other option, the wise and cautious one, was to let the capsule land and just leave it sitting at Newton's Eye until spring. But we are the descendants of people who set out for a new planet without thoroughly checking it out. Wisdom? Caution? Not in our DNA.

All right, that's a little harsh. They said they underestimated the danger from Umber because it was hidden behind our sun as well as its shroud when they were making observations from the home planet. And they did pay for their mistake.

I spent the next ten hours unpacking, playing with the dogs, and hanging out in the kitchen. I didn't see much evidence of pagan drumming in the halls, so I asked Namja what bee had crawled up Colby's ass. Her eyes rolled eloquently in response. "Come here," she said.

She led me into the warren of bedrooms where married couples slept and pulled out a bin from under her bed—the only space any of us has for storing private belongings. She dug under a concealing pile of clothes and pulled out a broken tile with a colorful design on the back side—a landscape, I realized as I studied it. A painting of Dust.

"My granddaughter Marigold did it," Namja said in a whisper.

What the younger generation had discovered was not superstition, but art.

For two generations, all our effort, all our creativity, had gone into improving the odds of survival. Art took materials, energy, and time we didn't have to spare. But that, I learned, was not why Colby and the governing committee disapproved of it.

"They think it's a betrayal of our guiding principle," Namja said.

"Rationalism, you mean?"

She nodded. Rationalism—that universal ethic for which our parents came here, leaving behind a planet that had splintered into a thousand warring sects and belief systems. They were high-minded people, our settler ancestors. When they couldn't convince the world they were correct, they decided to leave it and found a new one based on science and reason. And it turned out to be Dust.

Now, two generations later, Colby and the governing committee were trying to beat back irrationality.

"They lectured us about wearing jewelry," Namja said.

"Why?"

"It might inflame sexual instincts," she said ironically.

"Having a body does that," I said.

"Not if you're Colby, I guess. They also passed a resolution against figurines."

"That was their idea of a problem?"

"They were afraid people would use them as fetishes."

It got worse. Music and dance were now deemed to have shamanistic origins. Even reciting poetry aloud could start people on the slippery slope to prayer groups and worship.

"No wonder everyone wants to go to Newton's Eye," I said.

We held a meeting to decide what to do. We always have meetings, because the essence of rationality is that it needs to be contested. Also because people don't want responsibility for making a decision.

About 200 people crammed into the refectory—everyone old enough to understand the issue. We no longer had a room big enough for all, a sure sign we were outgrowing our habitat.

From the way the governing committee explained the options, it was clear that they favored the most cautious one—to do nothing at all, and leave the cargo to be fetched by whoever would be around in spring. I could sense disaffection from the left side of the room, where a cohort of young adults stood together. When Colby stopped talking, a lean, intellectual-looking young man named Anatoly spoke up for the youth party.

"What would our ancestors think of us if we let a chance like this slip by?"

Colby gave him a venomous look that told me this was not the first time Anatoly had stood up to authority. "They would think we were behaving rationally," he said.

"It's not rational to sit cowering in our cave, afraid of the planet we came to live on," Anatoly argued. "This cargo could revolutionize our lives. With new resources and technologies, we could expand in the spring, branch out and found satellite communities."

Watching the Committee, I could tell that this was precisely what they feared. New settlements meant new leaders—perhaps ones like Anatoly, willing to challenge what the old leaders stood for.

"Right now, it's a waste of our resources," Anselm said. "We need to focus everything we have on preparing for Umbernight."

"It's a waste of resources *not* to go," Anatoly countered. "You have a precious resource right here." He gestured at the group behind him. "People ready and willing to go now. By spring, we'll all be too old."

"Believe it or not, we don't want to waste you either," said Gwen, a third member of the Committee—although Colby looked like he would have gladly wasted Anatoly without a second thought.

"We're willing to take the chance," Anatoly said. "We *belong* here, on this planet. We need to embrace it, dangers and all. We are more prepared now than ever before. Our scientists have invented X-ray shielding fabric, and coldsuits for temperature extremes. We'll never be more ready."

"Well, thank you for your input," Anselm said. "Anyone else?"

The debate continued, but all the important arguments had been made. I slipped out the back and went to visit Bucky, as if he would have an opinion. "They may end up sending us after all," I told him in the quiet of his garage. "If only to be rid of the troublemakers."

The great announcement came about twenty hours later. The Committee had decided to roll the dice and authorize the expedition. They posted the list of six names on bulletin boards all over the habitat. I learned of it when I saw a cluster of people around one, reading. As I came up behind them, D'Sharma exclaimed emotionally, "Oh, this is just plain *cruel*." Someone saw me, and D'Sharma turned around. "Mick, you've got to bring them all back, you hear?" Then she burst into tears.

I read the list then, but it didn't explain D'Sharma's reaction. Anatoly was on it, not surprisingly—but in what seemed like a deliberate snub, he was not to be the leader. That distinction went to a young man named Amal. The rest were all younger generation; I'd known them in passing as kids and adolescents, but I had been gone too much to see them much as adults.

"It's a mix of expendables and rising stars," Namja explained to me later in private. "Anatoly, Seabird, and Davern are all people they're willing to sacrifice, for different reasons. Amal and Edie—well, choosing them shows that the Committee actually wants the expedition to succeed. But we'd all hate to lose them."

I didn't need to ask where I fit in. As far as the Committee was concerned, I was in the expendable category.

My first impression of the others came when I was flat on my back underneath Bucky, converting him to run on bottled propane. Brisk footsteps entered the garage and two practical boots came to a halt. "Mick?" a woman's voice said.

"Under here," I answered.

She got down on all fours to look under the vehicle. Sideways, I saw a sunny face with close-cropped, dark brown hair. "Hi," she said, "I'm Edie."

"I know," I said.

"I want to talk," she said.

"We're talking."

"I mean face to face."

We *were* face to face, more or less, but I supposed she meant upright, so I slid out from under, wiping my oily hands on a rag. We looked at each other across Bucky's back.

"We're going to have a meeting to plan out the trip to Newton's Eye," she said.

"Okay." I had already been planning out the trip for a couple work cycles. It's what I do, plan trips, but normally just for myself.

"Mick, we're going to be counting on you a lot," she said seriously. "You're the only one who's ever been to Newton's Eye, and the only one who's ever seen a winter. The rest of us have lots of enthusiasm, but you've got the experience."

I was impressed by her realism, and—I confess it—a little bit flattered. No one ever credits me with useful knowledge. I had been prepared to cope with a flock of arrogant, ignorant kids. Edie was none of those things.

"Can you bring a map to the meeting? It would help us to know where we're going."

My heart warmed. Finally, someone who saw the usefulness of my maps. "Sure," I said.

"I've already been thinking about the food, but camping equipment—we'll need your help on that."

"Okay."

Her face folded pleasantly around her smile. "The rest of us are a talky bunch, so don't let us drown you out."

"Okay."

After she told me the when and where of the meeting, she left, and I realized I hadn't said more than two syllables at a time. Still, she left me feeling she had understood.

When I arrived at the meeting, the effervescence of enthusiasm triggered my fight or flight reflex. I don't trust optimism. I stood apart, arms crossed, trying to size up my fellow travelers.

The first thing I realized was that Amal and Edie were an item; they had the kind of companionable, good-natured partnership you see in long-married couples. Amal was a big, relaxed young man who was always ready with a joke to put people at ease, while Edie was a little firecracker of an organizer. I had expected Anatoly to be resentful, challenging Amal for leadership, but he seemed thoroughly committed to the project, and I realized it hadn't just been a power play—he actually *wanted* to go. The other two were supposed to be "under-contributors," as we call them. Seabird—yes, her parents named her that on this planet without either birds or seas—was a plump young woman with unkempt hair who remained silent through most of the meeting. I couldn't tell if she was sulky, shy, or just scared out of her mind. Davern was clearly unnerved, and made up for it by being as friendly and anxious to ingratiate himself with the others as a lost puppy looking for a master. Neither Seabird nor Davern had volunteered. But then, neither had I, strictly speaking.

Amal called on me to show everyone the route. I had drawn it on a map—a physical map that didn't require electricity—and I spread it on the table for them to see. Newton's Eye was an ancient crater basin visible from space. To get to it, we would have to follow the Let's Go River down to the Mazy Lakes. We would then cross the Damn Right Barrens, climb down the Winding Wall to the Oh Well Valley, and cross it to reach the old landing site. Coming back, it would be uphill all the way.

"Who made up these names?" Anatoly said, studying the map with a frown.

"I did," I said. "Mostly for my mood on the day I discovered things."

"I thought the settlers wanted to name everything for famous scientists."

"Well, the settlers aren't around anymore," I said.

Anatoly looked as if he had never heard anything so heretical from one of my generation. He flashed me a sudden smile, then glanced over his shoulder to make sure no one from the governing committee was listening.

"What will it be like, traveling?" Edie asked me.

"Cold," I said. "Dark."

She was waiting for more, so I said, "We'll be traveling in the dark for three shifts to every two in the light. Halfway through night, Umber rises, so we'll have to wear protective gear. That's the coldest time, too; it can get cold enough for CO_2 to freeze this time of year. There won't be much temptation to take off your masks."

"We can do it," Anatoly said resolutely.

Davern gave a nervous giggle and edged closer to me. "You know how to do this, don't you, Mick?"

"Well, yes. Unless the shroud parts and Umbernight comes. Then all bets are off. Even I have never traveled through Umbernight."

"Well, we just won't let that happen," Edie said, and for a moment it seemed as if she could actually make the forces of Nature obey.

I stepped back and watched while Edie coaxed them all into making a series of sensible decisions: a normal work schedule of ten hours on, ten hours off; a division of labor; a schedule leading up to departure. Seabird and Davern never volunteered for anything, but Edie cajoled them into accepting assignments without complaint.

When it was over and I was rolling up my map, Edie came over and said to me quietly, "Don't let Davern latch onto you. He tries to find a protector—someone to adopt him. Don't fall for it."

"I don't have maternal instincts," I said.

She squeezed my arm. "Good for you."

If this mission were to succeed, I thought, it would be because of Edie.

Which is not to say that Amal wasn't a good leader. I got to know him when he came to me for advice on equipment. He didn't have Edie's extrovert flair, but his relaxed manner could put a person at ease, and he was methodical about thinking things through. Together, we compiled a daunting list of safety tents, heaters, coldsuits, goggles, face masks, first aid, and other gear; then when we realized that carrying all of it would leave Bucky with no room for the cargo we wanted to haul back, we set about ruthlessly cutting out everything that wasn't essential for survival.

He challenged me on some things. "Rope?" he said skeptically. "A shovel?"

"Rationality is about exploiting the predictable," I said. "Loose baggage and a mired-down vehicle are predictable."

He helped me load up Bucky for the trip out with a mathematical precision, eliminating every wasted centimeter. On the way back, we would have to carry much of it on our backs.

I did demand one commitment from Amal. "If Umbernight comes, we need to turn around and come back instantly, no matter what," I said.

At first he wouldn't commit himself.

"Have you ever heard what happened to the people caught outside during the first Umbernight?" I asked him. "The bodies were found in spring, carbonized like statues of charcoal. They say some of them shed tears of gasoline, and burst into flame as soon as a spark hit them."

He finally agreed.

You see, I wasn't reckless. I did some things right—as right as anyone could have done in my shoes.

When we set out just before dawn, the whole of Feynman Habitat turned out to see us off. There were hugs and tears, then waves and good wishes as I ordered Bucky to start down the trail. It took only five minutes for Feynman to drop behind us, and for the true immensity of Dust to open up ahead. I led the way down the banks of a frozen rivulet that eventually joined the Let's Go River; as the morning warmed it would begin to gurgle and splash.

"When are we stopping for lunch?" Seabird asked.

"You're not hungry already, are you?" Edie said, laughing.

"No, I just want to know what the plan is."

"The plan is to walk till we're tired and eat when we're hungry."

"I'd rather have a time," Seabird insisted. "I want to know what to expect."

No one answered her, so she glowered as she walked.

It did not take long for us to go farther from the habitat than any of them had ever been. At first they were elated at the views of the river valley ahead; but as their packs began to weigh heavier and their feet to hurt, the high spirits faded into dogged determination. After a couple of hours, Amal caught up with me at the front of the line.

"How far do we need to go this tenhour?"

"We need to get to the river valley. There's no good place to pitch the tent before that."

"Can we take a break and stay on schedule?"

I had already planned on frequent delays for the first few days, so I said, "There's a nice spot ahead."

As soon as we reached it, Amal called a halt, and everyone dropped their packs and kicked off their boots. I warned them not to take off their UV-filtering goggles. "You can't see it, but Umber hasn't set yet. You don't want to come back with crispy corneas."

I went apart to sit on a rock overlooking the valley, enjoying the isolation. Below me, a grove of lookthrough trees gestured gently in the wind, their leaves like transparent streamers. Like most plants on Dust, they are gray-blue, not green, because life here never evolved chloroplasts for photosynthesis. It is all widdershins life—its DNA twirls the opposite direction from ours. That makes it mostly incompatible with us.

Before long, Anatoly came to join me.

"That valley ahead looks like a good place for a satellite community in the spring," he said. "What do you think, could we grow maize there?"

The question was about more than agronomy. He wanted to recruit me into his expansion scheme. "You'd need a lot of shit," I said.

I wasn't being flippant. Dumping sewage was how we had created the soil for the outdoor gardens and fields around Feynman. Here on Dust, sewage is a precious, limited resource.

He took my remark at face value. "It's a long-range plan. We can live off hydroponics at first."

"There's a long winter ahead," I said.

"Too long," he said. "We're bursting at the seams now, and our leaders can only look backward. That's why the Committee has never supported your explorations. They think you're wasting time because you've never brought back anything but knowledge. That's how irrational they are."

He was a good persuader. "You know why I like being out here?" I said. "You have to forget all about the habitat, and just be part of Dust."

"That means you're one of us," Anatoly said seriously. "The governing committee, they are still fighting the battles of the homeworld. We're the first truly indigenous generation. We're part of *this* planet."

"Wait until you've seen more of it before you decide for sure."

I thought about Anatoly's farming scheme as we continued on past his chosen site. It would be hard to pull off, but not impossible. I would probably never live to see it thrive.

The sun was blazing from the southern sky by the time we made camp on the banks of the Let's Go. Edie recruited Davern to help her cook supper, though he seemed to be intentionally making a mess of things so that he could effusively praise her competence. She was having none of it. Amal and Anatoly worked on setting up the sleeping tent. It was made from a heavy, radiation-blocking material that was one of our lab's best inventions. I puttered around aiming Bucky's solar panels while there was light to collect, and Seabird lay on the ground, evidently too exhausted to move.

She sat up suddenly, staring at some nearby bushes. "There's something moving around over there."

"I don't think so," I said, since we are the only animal life on Dust.

"There is!" she said tensely.

"Well, check it out, then."

She gave me a resentful look, but heaved to her feet and went to look in the bushes. I heard her voice change to that cooing singsong we use with children and animals. "Come here, girl! What are you doing here? Did you follow us?"

With horror, I saw Sally, one of the dogs from Feynman, emerge from the bushes, wiggling in delight at Seabird's welcome.

"Oh my God!" I exclaimed. The dire profanity made everyone turn and stare. No one seemed to understand. In fact, Edie called out the dog's name and it trotted over to her and stuck its nose eagerly in the cooking pot. She laughed and pushed it away.

Amal had figured out the problem. "We can't take a dog; we don't have enough food. We'll have to send her back."

"How, exactly?" I asked bitterly.

"I can take her," Seabird volunteered.

If we allowed that, we would not see Seabird again till we got back.

"Don't feed her," Anatoly said.

Both Edie and Seabird objected to that. "We can't starve her!" Edie said.

I was fuming inside. I half suspected Seabird of letting the dog loose to give herself an excuse to go back. It would have been a cunning move. As soon as I caught myself thinking that way, I said loudly, "Stop!"

They all looked at me, since I was not in the habit of giving orders. "Eat first," I said. "No major decisions on an empty stomach."

While we ate our lentil stew, Sally demonstrated piteously how hungry she was. In the end, Edie and Seabird put down their bowls for Sally to finish off.

"Is there anything edible out here?" Edie asked me.

"There are things we can eat, but not for the long run," I said. "We can't absorb their proteins. And the dog won't eat them if she knows there is better food."

Anatoly had rethought the situation. "She might be useful. We may need a threat detector."

"Or camp cleanup services," Edie said, stroking Sally's back.

"And if we get hungry enough, she's food that won't spoil," Anatoly added.

Edie and Seabird objected strenuously.

I felt like I was reliving the Great Dog Debate. They weren't old enough to remember it. The arguments had been absurdly pseudo-rational, but in the end it had boiled down to sentiment. Pretty soon someone would say, "If the ancestors hadn't thought dogs would be useful they wouldn't have given us the embryos."

Then Seabird said it. I wanted to groan.

Amal was trying to be leaderly, and not take sides. He looked at Davern.

"Don't ask me," Davern said. "It's not my responsibility."

He looked at me then. Of course, I didn't want to harm the dog; but keeping her alive would take a lot of resources. "You don't know yet what it will be like," I said.

Amal seized on my words. "That's right," he said, "we don't have enough information. Let's take another vote in thirty hours." It was the perfect compromise: the decision to make no decision.

Of course, the dog ended up in the tent with the rest of us as we slept.

Stupid! Stupid! Yes, I know. But also kind-hearted and humane in a way my hardened pioneer generation could not afford to be. It was as if my companions were recovering a buried memory of what it had once been like to be human.

The next tenhours' journey was a pleasant stroll down the river valley speckled with groves of lookthrough trees. Umber had set and the sun was still high, so we could safely go without goggles, the breeze blowing like freedom on our faces. Twenty hours of sunlight had warmed the air, and the river ran ice-free at our side. We threw sticks into it for Sally to dive in and fetch.

We slept away another tenhour, and rose as the sun was setting. From atop the hill on which we had camped, we could see far ahead where the Let's Go flowed into the Mazy Lakes, a labyrinth of convoluted inlets, peninsulas, and islands. In the fading light I carefully reviewed my maps, comparing them to what I could see. There was a way through it, but we would have to be careful not to get trapped.

As night deepened, we began to pick our way by lantern-light across spits of land between lakes. Anatoly kept thinking he saw faster routes, but Amal said, "No, we're following Mick." I wasn't sure I deserved his trust. A couple of times I took a wrong turn and had to lead the way back.

"This water looks strange," Amal said, shining his lantern on the inky surface. There was a wind blowing, but no waves. It looked like black gelatin.

The dog, thinking she saw something in his light, took a flying leap into the lake. When she broke the surface, it gave a pungent fart that made us groan and gag. Sally floundered around, trying to find her footing in a foul substance that was not quite water, not quite land. I was laughing and trying to hold my breath at the same time. We fled to escape the overpowering stench. Behind us, the dog found her way onto shore again, and got her revenge by shaking putrid water all over us.

"What the hell?" Amal said, covering his nose with his arm.

"Stromatolites," I explained. They looked at me as if I were speaking ancient Greek—which I was, in a way. "The lakes are full of bacterial colonies that form thick mats, decomposing as they grow." I looked at Edie. "They're one of the things on Dust we can actually eat. If you want to try a stromatolite steak, I can cut you one." She gave me the reaction I deserved.

After ten hours, we camped on a small rise surrounded by water on north and south, and by stars above. The mood was subdued. In the perpetual light, it had been easy to feel we were in command of our surroundings. Now, the opaque ceiling of the sky had dissolved, revealing the true immensity of space. I could tell they were feeling how distant was our refuge. They were dwarfed, small, and very far from home.

To my surprise, Amal reached into his backpack and produced, of all things, a folding aluminum mandolin. After all our efforts to reduce baggage, I could not believe he had wasted the space. But he assembled and tuned it, then proceeded to strum some tunes I had never heard. All the others seemed to know them, since they joined on the choruses. The music defied the darkness as our lantern could not.

"Are there any songs about Umbernight?" I asked when they paused.

Strumming softly, Amal shook his head. "We ought to make one."

"It would be about the struggle between light and unlight," Edie said.

"Or apocalypse," Anatoly said. "When Umber opens its eye and sees us, only the just survive."

Their minds moved differently than mine, or any of my generation's. They saw not just mechanisms of cause and effect, but symbolism and meaning. They were generating a literature, an indigenous mythology, before my eyes. It was dark, like Dust, but with threads of startling beauty.

We woke to darkness. The temperature had plummeted, so we pulled on our heavy coldsuits. They were made from the same radiation-blocking material as our tent, but with thermal lining and piezoelectric heating elements so that if we kept moving, we could keep warm. The visored hoods had vents with micro-louvers to let us breathe, hear, and speak without losing too much body heat.

"What about the dog?" Amal asked. "We don't have a coldsuit for her."

Edie immediately set to work cutting up some of the extra fabric we had brought for patching things. Amal tried to help her wrap it around Sally and secure it with tape, but the dog thought it was a game, and as their dog-wrestling grew desperate, they ended up collapsing in laughter. I left the tent to look after Bucky, and when I next saw Sally she looked like a dog mummy with only her eyes and nose poking through. "I'll do something better when we stop next," Edie pledged.

The next tenhour was a slow, dark trudge through icy stromatolite bogs. When the water froze solid enough to support the buggy, we cut across it to reach the edge of the Mazy Lakes, pushing on past our normal camping time. Once on solid land, we were quick to set up the tent and the propane stove to heat it. Everyone crowded inside, eager to shed their coldsuits. Taking off a coldsuit at the end of the day is like emerging from a stifling womb, ready to breathe free.

After lights out, I was already asleep when Seabird nudged me. "There's something moving outside," she whispered.

"No, there's not," I muttered. She was always worried that we were deviating from plan, or losing our way, or not keeping to schedule. I turned over to go back to sleep when Sally growled. Something hit the roof of the tent. It sounded like a small branch falling from a tree, but there were no trees where we had camped.

"Did you hear that?" Seabird hissed.

"Okay, I'll check it out." It was hard to leave my snug sleep cocoon and pull on the coldsuit again—but better me than her, since she would probably imagine things and wake everyone.

It was the coldest part of night, and there was a slight frost of dry ice on the rocks around us. Everything in the landscape was motionless. Above, the galaxy arched, a frozen cloud of light. I shone my lamp on the tent to see what had hit it, but there was nothing. All was still.

In the eastern sky, a dim, gray smudge of light was rising over the lakes. Umber. I didn't stare long, not quite trusting the UV shielding on my faceplate, but I didn't like the look of it. I had never read that the shroud began to glow before it parted, but the observations from the last Umbernight were not detailed, and there were none from the time before that. Still, I crawled back into the safety of the tent feeling troubled.

"What was it?" Seabird whispered.

"Nothing." She would think that was an evasion, so I added, "If anything was out there, I scared it off."

When we rose, I left the tent first with the UV detector. The night was still just as dark, but there was no longer a glow in the east, and the increase of radiation was not beyond the usual fluctuations. Nevertheless, I quietly mentioned what I had seen to Amal.

"Are you sure it's significant?" he said.

I wasn't sure of anything, so I shook my head.

"I'm not going to call off the mission unless we're sure."

I probably would have made the same decision. At the time, there was no telling whether it was wise or foolish.

Bucky was cold after sitting for ten hours, and we had barely started when a spring in his suspension broke. It took me an hour to fix it, working awkwardly in my bulky coldsuit, but we finally set off. We had come to the Damn Right Barrens, a rocky plateau full of the ejecta from the ancient meteor strike that had created Newton's Eye. The farther we walked, the more rugged it became, and in the dark it was impossible to see ahead and pick out the best course.

Davern gave a piteous howl of pain, and we all came to a stop. He had turned his ankle. There was no way to examine it without setting up the tent, so Amal took some of the load from the buggy and carried it so Davern could ride. After another six hours of struggling through the boulders, I suggested we camp and wait for daybreak. "We're ahead of schedule," I said. "It's wiser to wait than to risk breaking something important."

"My ankle's not important?" Davern protested.

"Your ankle will heal. Bucky's axle won't."

Sulkily, he said, "You ought to marry that machine. You care more for it than any person."

I would have answered, but I saw Edie looking at me in warning, and I knew she would give him a talking-to later on.

When we finally got a look at Davern's ankle inside the tent, it was barely swollen, and I suspected him of malingering for sympathy. But rather than have him slow us down, we all agreed to let him ride till it got better.

Day came soon after we had slept. We tackled the Damn Right again, moving much faster now that we could see the path. I made them push on till we came to the edge of the Winding Wall.

Coming on the Winding Wall is exhilarating or terrifying, depending on your personality. At the end of an upward slope the world drops suddenly away, leaving you on the edge of sky. Standing on the windy precipice, you have to lean forward to see the cliffs plunging nearly perpendicular to the basin of the crater three hundred meters below. To right and left, the cliff edge undulates in a snaky line that forms a huge arc vanishing into the distance—for the crater circle is far too wide to see across.

"I always wish for wings here," I said as we lined the edge, awestruck.

"How are we going to get down?" Edie asked.

"There's a way, but it's treacherous. Best to do it fresh."

"We've got thirty hours of light left," Amal said.

"Then let's rest up."

It was noon when we rose, and Umber had set. I led the way to the spot where a ravine pierced the wall. Unencumbered by coldsuits, we were far more agile, but Bucky still had only four wheels and no legs. We unloaded him in order to use the cart bed as a ramp, laying it over the rugged path so he could pass, and ferrying the baggage by hand, load after load. Davern was forced to go by foot when it got too precarious, using a tent pole for a cane.

It was hard, sweaty work, but twelve hours later we were at the bottom, feeling triumphant. We piled into the tent and slept until dark.

The next leg of the journey was an easy one over the sandy plain of the crater floor. Through the dark we walked then slept, walked then slept, until we started seeing steam venting from the ground as we reached the geothermically active region at the center of the crater. Here we came on the remains of an old road built by the original settlers when they expected to be staying at Newton's Eye. It led through the hills of the inner crater ring. When we paused at the top of the rise, I noticed the same smudge of light in the sky I had seen before. This time, I immediately took a UV reading, and the levels had spiked. I showed it to Amal.

"The shroud's thinning," I said.

I couldn't read his expression through the faceplate of his coldsuit, but his body language was all indecision. "Let's take another reading in a couple hours," he said.

We did, but there was no change.

We were moving fast by now, through a landscape formed by old eruptions. Misshapen claws of lava reached out of the darkness on either side, frozen in the act of menacing the road. At last, as we were thinking of stopping, we spied ahead the shape of towering ribs against the stars—the remains of the settlers' original landing craft, or the parts of it too big to cannibalize. With our goal so close, we pushed on till we came to the cleared plain where it lay, the fossil skeleton of a monster that once swam the stars.

We all stood gazing at it, reluctant to approach and shatter its isolation. "Why don't we camp here?" Edie said.

We had made better time than I had expected. The plan had been to arrive just as the cargo capsule did, pick up the payload, and head back immediately; but we were a full twenty hours early. We could afford to rest.

I woke before the others, pulled on my protective gear, and went outside to see the dawn. The eastern sky glowed a cold pink and azure. The landing site was a basin of black volcanic rock. Steaming pools of water made milky with dissolved silicates dappled the plain, smelling of sodium bicarbonate. As I watched the day come, the pools turned the same startling blue as the sky, set like turquoise in jet.

The towering ribs of the lander now stood out in the strange, desolate landscape. I thought of all the sunrises they had seen—each one a passing fragment of time, a shard of a millennium in which this one was just a nanosecond of nothing.

Behind me, boots crunched on cinders. I turned to see that Amal had joined me. He didn't greet me, just stood taking in the scene.

At last he said, "It's uplifting, isn't it?"

Startled, I said, "What is?"

"That they came all this way for the sake of reason."

Came all this way to a desolation of rock and erosion stretching to the vanishing point—no, uplifting was not a word I would use. But I didn't say so.

He went back to the tent to fetch the others, and soon I was surrounded by youthful energy that made me despise my own sclerotic disaffection. They all wanted to go explore the ruins, so I waved them on and returned to the tent to fix my breakfast.

After eating, I went to join them. I found Seabird and Davern bathing in one of the hot pools, shaded by an awning constructed from their coldsuits. "You're sure of the chemicals in that water, are you?" I asked.

"Oh stop worrying," Davern said. "You're just a walking death's-head, Mick. You see danger everywhere."

Ahead, the other three were clustered under the shadow of the soaring ship ribs. When I came up, I saw they had found a stone monument, and were standing silently before it, the hoods of their coldsuits thrown back. Sally sat at Edie's feet.

"It's a memorial to everyone who died in the first year," Edie told me in a hushed voice.

"But that's not the important part," Anatoly said intently. He pointed to a line of the inscription, a quotation from Theodore Cam, the legendary leader of the exiles. It said:

Gaze into the unknowable from a bridge of evidence.

"You see?" Anatoly said. "He knew there was something unknowable. Reason doesn't reach all the way. There are other truths. We were right, there is more to the universe than just the established facts."

I thought back to Feynman Habitat, and how the pursuit of knowledge had contracted into something rigid and dogmatic. No wonder my generation had failed to inspire. I looked up at the skeleton of the spacecraft making its grand, useless gesture to the sky. How could mere reason compete with that?

After satisfying my curiosity, I trudged back to the tent. From a distance I heard a whining sound, and when I drew close I realized it was coming from Bucky. Puzzled, I rummaged through his load to search for the source. When I realized what it was, my heart pulsed in panic. Instantly, I put up the hood on my coldsuit and ran to warn the others.

"Put on your coldsuits and get back to the tent!" I shouted at Seabird and Davern. "Our X-ray detector went off. The shroud has parted."

Umber was invisible in the bright daylight of the western sky, but a pulse of X-rays could only mean one thing.

When I had rounded them all up and gotten them back to the shielded safety of the tent, we held a council.

"We've got to turn around and go back, this instant," I said.

There was a long silence. I turned to Amal. "You promised."

"I promised we'd turn back if Umbernight came on our way out," he said. "We're not on the way out any longer. We're here, and it's only ten hours before the capsule arrives. We'd be giving up in sight of success."

"Ten hours for the capsule to come, another ten to get it unpacked and reloaded on Bucky," I pointed out. "If we're lucky."

"But Umber sets soon," Edie pointed out. "We'll be safe till it rises again."

I had worked it all out. "By that time, we'll barely be back to the Winding Wall. We have to go *up* that path this time, bathed in X-rays."

"Our coldsuits will shield us," Anatoly said. "It will be hard, but we can do it."

The trip up to now had been too easy; it had given them inflated confidence.

Anatoly looked around at the others, his face fierce and romantic with a shadow of black beard accentuating his jawline. "I've realized now, what we're doing really matters. We're not just fetching baggage. We're a link to the settlers. We have to live up to their standards, to their . . . heroism." He said the last word as if it were unfamiliar—as indeed it was, in the crabbed pragmatism of Feynman Habitat.

I could see a contagion of inspiration spreading through them. Only I was immune.

"They *died*," I said. "Two thirds of them. Didn't you read that monument?"

"They didn't know what we do," Amal argued. "They weren't expecting Umbernight."

Anatoly saw I was going to object, and spoke first. "Maybe some of us will die, too. Maybe that is the risk we need to take. They were willing, and so am I."

He was noble, committed, and utterly serious.

"No one wants you to die!" I couldn't keep the frustration from my voice. "Your dying would be totally useless. It would only harm the rest of us. You need to live. Sorry to break it to you."

They were all caught up in the kind of crazy courage that brought the settlers here. They all felt the same devotion to a cause, and they hadn't yet learned that the universe doesn't give a rip.

"Listen," I said, "you've got to ask yourself, what's a win here? Dying is not a win. Living is a win, even if it means living with failure."

As soon as I said the last word, I could see it was the wrong one.

"Let's vote," said Amal. "Davern, what about you? You haven't said anything."

Davern looked around at the others, and I could see he was sizing up who to side with. "I'm with Anatoly," he said. "He understands us."

Amal nodded as if this made sense. "How about you, Seabird?"

She looked up at Anatoly with what I first thought was admiration—then I realized it was infatuation. "I'll follow Anatoly," she said with feeling.

The followers in our group had chosen Anatoly as their leader.

"I vote with Anatoly, too," said Amal. "I think we've come this far, it would be crazy to give up now. Edie?"

"I respect Mick's advice," she said thoughtfully. "But our friends back home are counting on us, and in a way the settlers are counting on us, too. All those people died so we could be here, and to give up would be like letting them down."

I pulled up the hood of my coldsuit and headed out of the tent. Outside, the day was bright and poisonous. The coldsuit shielded me from the X-rays, but not from the feeling of impending disaster. I looked across to the skeletal shipwreck and wondered: what are we doing here on Dust? The settlers chose this, but none of us asked to be born here, exiled from the rest of humanity, like the scum on the sand left by the highest wave. We aren't noble pioneers. We're only different from the bacteria because we are able to ask what the hell this is all about. Not answer, just ask.

Someone came out of the tent behind me, and I looked to see who it was this time. Edie. She came to my side. "Mick, we are so thankful that you're with us," she said. "We do listen to you. We just agreed to go to a twelve-hour work shift on the way back, to speed things up. We'll get back."

I truly wished she weren't here. She was the kind of person who ought to be protected, so she could continue to bring cheer to the world. She was too valuable to be thrown away.

"It's not about me," I said. "I've got less life to lose than the rest of you."

"No one's going to lose their lives," she said. "I promise."

Why can't I quit asking what more I could have done? I'm tired of that question. I still don't know what else there was to do.

Ten hours later, there was no sign of the supply ship. Everyone was restless. We had slept and risen again, and now we scanned the skies every few minutes, hoping to see something.

Edie looked up from fashioning little dog goggles and said, "Do you suppose it's landed somewhere else?" Once she had voiced the idea, it became our greatest worry. What if our assumption about the landing spot was wrong? We told ourselves it was just that the calculations had been off, or the ship was making an extra orbit. Now that we had made the commitment to stay, no one wanted to give up; but how long were we prepared to wait?

In the end, we could not have missed the lander's descent. It showed up first as a bright spot in the western sky. Then it became a fiery streak, and we saw the parachutes bloom. Seconds later, landing rockets fired. We cheered as, with a roar that shook the ground, the craft set down in a cloud of dust barely a kilometer from us. As the warm wind buffeted us, even I felt that the sight had been worth the journey.

By the time we had taken down the tent, loaded everything on Bucky, and raced over to the landing site, the dust had settled and the metal cooled. It was almost sunset, so we worked fast in the remaining light. One team unloaded everything from Bucky while another team puzzled out how to open the cargo doors. The inside of the spacecraft was tightly packed with molded plastic cases we couldn't work out how to open, so we just piled them onto the buggy as they came out. We would leave the thrill of discovery to our friends back home.

Bucky was dangerously overloaded before we had emptied the pod, so we reluctantly secured the doors with some of the crates still inside to stay the winter at Newton's Eye. We could only hope that we had gotten the most important ones.

There was still a lot of work to do, sorting out our baggage and redistributing it, and we worked by lamplight into the night. By the time all was ready, we were exhausted. Umber had not yet risen, so there was no need to set up the tent, and we slept on the ground in the shadow of the lander. I was so close that I could reach out and touch something that had come all the way from the homeworld.

We set out into the night as soon as we woke. Bucky creaked and groaned, but I said encouraging words to him, and he seemed to get used to his new load. All of us were more heavily laden now, and the going would have been slower even if Bucky could have kept up his usual pace. When we reached the top of the inner crater ring we paused to look back at the plain where two spacecraft now stood. In the silence of our tribute, the X ray alarm went off. Invisible through our UV-screening faceplates, Umber was rising in the east. Umbernight was ahead.

We walked in silence. Sally hung close to us in her improvised coldsuit, no longer roving and exploring. From time to time she froze in her tracks and gave a low growl. But nothing was there.

"What's she growling at, X-rays?" Anatoly said.

"She's just picking up tension from us," Edie said, reaching down to pat the dog's back.

Half a mile later, Sally lunged forward, snapping at the air as if to bite it. Through the cloth of her coldsuit, she could not have connected with anything, even if anything had been there.

"Now *I'm* picking up on *her* tension," Davern said.

"Ouch! Who did that?" Seabird cried out, clutching her arm. "Somebody hit me."

"Everyone calm down," Edie said. "Look around you. There's nothing wrong."

She shone her lamp all around, and she was right; the scene looked exactly as it had when we had traversed it before—a barren, volcanic plain pocked with steaming vents and the occasional grove of everlive trees. The deadly radiation was invisible.

Another mile farther on, Amal swore loudly and slapped his thigh as if bitten by a fly. He bent over to inspect his coldsuit and swore again. "Something pierced my suit," he said. "There's three pinholes in it."

Sally started barking. We shone our lights everywhere, but could see nothing.

It was like being surrounded by malicious poltergeists that had gathered to impede our journey. I quieted the dog and said, "Everyone stop and listen."

At first I heard nothing but my own heart. Then, as we kept still, it came: a rustling of unseen movement in the dark all around us.

"We've got company," Anatoly said grimly.

I wanted to deny my senses. For years I had been searching for animal life on Dust, and found none—not even an insect, other than the ones we brought. And how could anything be alive in this bath of radiation? It was scientifically impossible.

We continued on more carefully. After a while, I turned off my headlamp and went out in front to see if I could see anything without the glare of the light. At first there was nothing, but as my eyes adjusted, something snagged my attention out of the corner of my eye. It was a faint, gauzy curtain—a net hanging in the air, glowing a dim blue-gray. It was impossible to tell how close it was—just before my face, or over the next hill? I swept my arm out to disturb it, but touched nothing. So either it was far away, or it was inside my head.

Something slapped my faceplate, and I recoiled. There was a smear of goo across my visor. I tried to wipe it off, and an awful smell from my breathing vent nearly gagged me. Behind me, Amal gave an exclamation, and I thought he had smelled it too, but when I turned to see, he was looking at his foot.

"I stepped on something," he said. "I could feel it crunch."

"What's that disgusting smell?" Davern said.

"Something slimed me," I answered.

"Keep on going, everyone," Edie said. "We can't stop to figure it out."

We plodded on, a slow herd surrounded by invisible tormentors. We had not gotten far before Amal had to stop because his boot was coming apart. We waited while he wrapped mending tape around it, but that lasted only half an hour before the sole of his boot was flapping free again. "I've got to stop and fix this, or my foot will freeze," he said.

We were all a little grateful to have an excuse to set up the tent and stop our struggle to continue. Once inside, we found that all of our coldsuits were pierced with small cuts and pinholes. We spent some time repairing them, then looked at each other to see who wanted to continue.

"What happens if we camp while Umber is in the sky, and only travel by day?" Edie finally asked.

I did a quick calculation. "It would add another 300 hours. We don't have food to last."

"If we keep going, our coldsuits will be cut to ribbons," Davern said.

"If only we could see what's attacking us!" Edie exclaimed.

Softly, Seabird said, "It's ghosts." We all fell silent. I looked at her, expecting it was some sort of joke, but she was deadly serious. "All those people who died," she said.

At home, everyone would have laughed and mocked her. Out here, no one replied.

I pulled up the hood of my coldsuit and rose.

"Where are you going?" Davern said.

"I want to check out the lookthrough trees." In reality, I wanted some silence to think.

"What a time to be botanizing!" Davern exclaimed.

"Shut up, Davern," Amal said.

Outside, in the empty waste, I had a feeling of being watched. I shook it off. When we had camped, I had noticed that a nearby grove of lookthrough trees was glowing in the dark, shades of blue and green. I picked my way across the rocks toward them. I suspected that the fluorescence was an adaptation that allowed them to survive the hostile conditions of Umbernight, and I wanted some samples. When I reached the grove and examined one of the long, flat leaves under lamplight, it looked transparent, as usual. Shutting my lamp off, I held it up and looked through it. With a start, I pressed it to my visor so I could see through the leaf.

What looked like a rocky waste by the dim starlight was suddenly a brightly lit landscape. And everywhere I looked, the land bloomed with organic shapes unlike any I had ever seen. Under a rock by my feet was a low, domed mound pierced with holes like an overturned colander, glowing from within. Beneath the everlives were bread-loaf-shaped growths covered with plates that slid aside as I watched, to expose a hummocked mound inside. There were things with leathery rinds that folded out like petals to collect the unlight, which snapped shut the instant I turned on my lamp. In between the larger life-forms, the ground was crawling with smaller, insect-sized things, and in the distance I could see gauzy curtains held up by gas bladders floating on the wind.

An entire alternate biota had sprung to life in Umberlight. Dust was not just the barren place we saw by day, but a thriving dual ecosystem, half of which had been waiting as spores or seeds in the soil, to be awakened by Umber's radiation. I knelt down to see why they had been so invisible. By our light, some of them were transparent as glass. Others were so black they blended in with the rock. By Umberlight, they lit up in bright colors, reflecting a spectrum we could not see.

I looked down at the leaf that had given me new sight. It probably had a microstructure that converted high-energy radiation into the visible spectrum so the tree could continue to absorb the milder wavelengths. Quickly, I plucked a handful of the leaves. Holding one to my visor, I turned back toward the tent. The UV-reflecting fabric was a dull gray in our light, but Umberlight made it shine like a beacon, the brightest thing in the landscape. I looked down at my coldsuit, and it also glowed like a torch. The things of Umbernight might be invisible to us, but we were all too visible to them.

When I came back into the tent, my companions were still arguing. Silently, I handed each of them a strip of leaf. Davern threw his away in disgust. "What's this, some sort of peace offering?" he said.

"Put on your coldsuits and come outside," I said. "Hold the leaves up to your faceplates and look through them."

Their reactions, when they saw the reality around us, were as different as they were: astonished, uneasy, disbelieving. Seabird was terrified, and shrank back toward the tent. "It's like nightmares," she said.

Edie put an arm around her. "It's better than ghosts," she said.

"No, it's not. It's the shadow side of all the living beings. That's why we couldn't see them."

"We couldn't see them because they don't reflect the spectrum of light our eyes absorb," Amal said reasonably. Seabird did not look comforted.

I looked ahead, down the road we needed to take. Umber was bright as an anti-sun. In its light, the land was not empty, but full. There was a boil of emerging life in every crack of the landscape: just not our sort of life. We were the strangers here, the fruits that had fallen too far from the tree. We did not belong.

You would think that being able to see the obstacles would speed us up, but not so. We were skittish now. With strips of lookthrough leaves taped to our visors, we could see both worlds, which were the same world; but we could not tell the harmless from the harmful. So we treated it all as a threat—dodging, detouring, clearing the road with a shovel when we could. As we continued, the organisms changed and multiplied fast around us, as if their growth were in overdrive. It was spring for them, and they were sprouting and spawning. What would they look like fully grown? I hoped not to find out.

I can't describe the life-forms of Umbernight in biological language, because I couldn't tell if I was looking at a plant, animal, or something in between. We quickly discovered what had been piercing our coldsuits—a plantlike thing shaped like a scorpion with a spring-loaded tail lined with barbs. When triggered by our movement, it would release a shower of pin-sharp projectiles. Perhaps they were poison, and our incompatible proteins protected us.

The road had sprouted all manner of creatures covered with plates and shells—little ziggurats and stepped pyramids, spirals, and domes. In between them floated bulbs like amber, airborne eggplants. They spurted a mucus that ate away any plastic it touched.

We topped a rise to find the valley before us completely crusted over with life, and no trace of a path. No longer could we avoid trampling through it, crushing it underfoot. Ahead, a translucent curtain suspended from floating, gas-filled bladders hung across our path. It shimmered with iridescent unlight.

"It's rather beautiful, isn't it?" Edie said.

"Yes, but is it dangerous?" Amal said.

"We're not prey," Anatoly argued. "This life can't get any nutrients from us."

"I doubt it knows that," I said. "It might just act on instinct."

"We could send the dog to find out," Anatoly suggested.

Sally showed no inclination. Edie had put her on a leash, but it was hardly necessary; she was constantly alert now, on guard.

"Go around it," I advised.

So we left our path to detour across land where the boulders had become hard to spot amid the riot of life. As Bucky's wheels crushed the shell of one dome, I saw that inside it was a wriggling mass of larvae. It was not a single organism, but a colony. That would explain how such complex structures came about so fast; they were just hives of smaller organisms.

We cleared a place to camp by trampling down the undergrowth and shoveling it out of the way. Exhausted as we were, it was still hard to sleep through the sounds from outside: buzzing, whooshing, scratching, scrabbling. My brain kept coming back to one thought: at this rate, our return would take twice as long as the journey out.

The tent was cold when we woke; our heater had failed. When Amal unfastened the tent flap he gave an uncharacteristically profane exclamation. The opening was entirely blocked by undergrowth. No longer cautious, we set about hacking and smashing our way out, disturbing hordes of tiny crawling things. When we had cleared a path and turned back to look, we saw that the tent was surrounded by mounds of organisms attracted by its reflected light. The heater had failed because its air intake was blocked. Bucky, parked several yards away, had not attracted the Umberlife.

It was the coldest part of night, but Umber was high in the sky, and the life-forms had speeded up. We marched in formation now, with three fanned out in front to scan for obstructions, one in the center with Bucky, and two bringing up the rear. I was out in front with Seabird and Davern when we reached a hilltop and saw that the way ahead was blocked by a lake that had not been there on the way out. We gathered to survey it. It was white, like an ocean of milk.

"What is it?" Edie asked.

"Not water," Anatoly said. "It's too cold for that, too warm for methane."

I could not see any waves, but there was an ebb and flow around the edges. "Wait here. I want to get closer," I said.

Amal and Anatoly wouldn't let me go alone, so the three of us set out. We were nearly on the beach edge before we could see it clearly. Amal came to an abrupt halt. "Spiders!" he said, repulsed. "It's a sea of spiders."

They were not spiders, of course, but that is the closest analog: long-legged crawling things, entirely white in the Umberlight. At the edges of the sea they were tiny, but farther out we could see ones the size of Sally, all seemingly competing to get toward the center of the mass. There must have been a hatching while we had slept.

"That is truly disgusting," Anatoly said.

I gave a humorless laugh. "I've read about this on other planets—wildlife covering the land. The accounts always say it is a majestic, inspiring sight."

"Umber turns everything into its evil twin," Amal said.

As we stood there, a change was taking place. A wave was gathering far out. The small fry in front of us were scattering to get out of the way as it swept closer.

"They're coming toward us," Anatoly said.

We turned to run back toward the hill where we had left our friends. Anatoly and Amal reached the hilltop before I did. Edie shouted a warning, and I turned to see a knee-high spider on my heels, its pale body like a skull on legs. I had no weapon but my flashlight, so I nailed it with a light beam. To my surprise, it recoiled onto its hind legs, waving its front legs in the air. It gave me time to reach the others.

"They're repelled by light!" I shouted. "Form a line and shine them off."

The wave of spiders surged up the hill, but we kept them at bay with our lights. They circled us, and we ended up in a ring around Bucky, madly sweeping our flashlights to and fro to keep them off while Sally barked from behind us.

Far across the land, the horizon lit with a silent flash like purple lightning. The spiders paused, then turned mindlessly toward this new light source. As quickly as they had swarmed toward us, they were swarming away. We watched the entire lake of them drain, heading toward some signal we could not see.

"Quick, let's cross while they're gone," I said.

We dashed as fast as we could across the plain where they had gathered. From time to time we saw other flashes of unlight, always far away and never followed by thunder.

In our haste, we let our vigilance lapse, and one of Bucky's wheels thunked into a pothole. The other wheels spun, throwing up loose dirt and digging themselves in. I called out, "Bucky, stop!"—but he was already stuck fast.

"Let's push him out," Amal said, but I held up a hand. The buggy was already dangerously tilted.

"We're going to have to unload some crates to lighten him up, and dig that wheel out."

Everyone looked nervously in the direction where the spiders had gone, but Amal said, "Okay. You dig, we'll unload."

We all set to work. I was so absorbed in freeing Bucky's wheel that I did not see the danger approaching until Seabird gave a cry of warning. I looked up to see one of the gauzy curtains bearing down on us from windward. It was yards wide, big enough to envelop us all, and twinkling with a spiderweb of glowing threads.

"Run!" Amal shouted. I dropped my shovel and fled. Behind me, I heard Edie's voice crying, "Sally!" and Amal's saying, "No, Edie! Leave her be!"

I whirled around and saw that the dog had taken refuge under the buggy. Edie was running back to get her. Amal was about to head back after Edie, so I dived at his legs and brought him down with a thud. From the ground we both watched as Edie gave up and turned back toward us. Behind her, the curtain that had been sweeping toward Bucky changed direction, veering straight toward Edie.

"Edie!" Amal screamed. She turned, saw her danger, and froze.

The curtain enveloped her, wrapping her tight in an immobilizing net. There was a sudden, blinding flash of combustion. As I blinked the after-spots away, I saw the curtain float on, shredded now, leaving behind a charcoal pillar in the shape of a woman.

Motionless with shock, I gazed at that black statue standing out against the eastern sky. It was several seconds before I realized that the sky was growing bright. Beyond all of us, dawn was coming.

In the early morning light Anatoly and I dug a grave while Seabird and Davern set up the tent. We simply could not go on. Amal was shattered with grief, and could not stop sobbing.

"Why her?" he would say in the moments when he could speak at all. "She was the best person here, the best I've ever known. She shouldn't have been the one to die."

I couldn't wash those last few seconds out of my brain. Why had she stopped? How had that brainless, eyeless thing sensed her?

Later, Amal became angry at me for having prevented him from saving her. "Maybe I could have distracted it. It might have taken me instead of her."

I only shook my head. "We would have been burying both of you."

"That would have been better," he said.

Everyone gathered as we laid what was left of her in the ground, but no one had the heart to say anything over the grave. When we had filled it in, Sally crept forward to sniff at the overturned dirt. Amal said, "We need to mark it, so we can find it again." So we all fanned out to find rocks to heap in a cairn on the grave.

We no longer feared the return of the spiders, or anything else, because the Umberlife had gone dormant in the sun—our light being as toxic to them as theirs was to us. Everything had retreated into their shells and closed their sliding covers. When we viewed them in our own light they still blended in with the stones of the crater floor.

We ate and snatched some hours of sleep while nothing was threatening us. I was as exhausted as the others, but anxious that we were wasting so much daylight. I roused them all before they were ready. "We've got to keep moving," I said.

We resumed the work of freeing Bucky where we had left off. When all was ready, we gathered behind him to push. "Bucky, go!" I ordered. His wheels only spun in the sand. "Stop!" I ordered. Then, to the others, "We're going to rock him out. Push when I say go, and stop when I say stop." When we got a rhythm going, he rocked back and forth three times, then finally climbed out of the trench that had trapped him.

Amal helped us reload the buggy, but when it came time to move on, he hung back. "You go ahead," he said. "I'll catch up with you."

"No way," I said. "We all go or none of us."

He got angry at me again, but I would not let him pick a fight. We let him have some moments alone at the grave to say goodbye. At last I walked up to him and said, "Come on, Amal. We've got to keep moving."

"What's the point?" he said. "The future is gone."

But he followed me back to where the others were waiting.

He was right, in one way: nothing we could achieve now would make up for Edie's loss. How we were going to carry on without her, I could not guess.

When we camped, there was no music now, and little conversation. The Winding Wall was a blue line ahead in the distance, and as we continued, it rose, ever more impassable, blocking our way. We did not reach the spot where the gully path pierced it until we had been walking for thirteen hours. We were tired, but resting would waste the last of the precious sunlight. We gathered to make a decision.

"Let's just leave the buggy and the crates, and make a run for home," Amal said. He looked utterly dispirited.

Davern and Seabird turned to Anatoly. He was the only one of us who was still resolute. "If we do that, we will have wasted our time," he said. "We can't give up now."

"That's right," Davern said.

Amal looked at me. There was some sense in his suggestion, but also some impracticality. "If we leave the buggy we'll have to leave the tent," I said. "It's too heavy for us to carry." We had been spreading it as a tarpaulin over the crates when we were on the move.

"We knew from the beginning that the wall would be an obstacle," Anatoly said with determination. "We have to make the effort."

I think even Amal realized then that he was no longer our leader.

We unloaded the buggy, working till we were ready to drop, then ate and fell asleep on the ground. When we woke, the sun was setting. It seemed too soon.

Each crate took two people to carry up the steep path. We decided to do it in stages. Back and forth we shuttled, piling our cargo at a level spot a third of the way up. The path was treacherous in the dark, but at least the work was so strenuous we had no need of coldsuits until Umber should rise.

The life-forms around us started waking as soon as dark came. It was the predawn time for them, when they could open their shells and exhale like someone shedding a coldsuit. They were quiescent enough that we were able to avoid them.

Fifteen hours later, our cargo was three-quarters of the way up, and we gathered at the bottom again to set up the tent and rest before trying to get Bucky up the path. The X-ray alarm went off while we were asleep, but we were so tired we just shut it off and went on sleeping.

When we rose, an inhuman architecture had surrounded our tent on all sides. The Umberlife had self-organized into domes and spires that on close inspection turned out to be crawling hives. There was something deformed and abhorrent about them, and we were eager to escape our transformed campsite—until Seabird gave a whimper and pointed upward.

Three hundred meters above, the top of the Winding Wall was now a battlement of living towers that glowed darkly against the sky. Shapes we couldn't quite make out moved to and fro between the structures, as if patrolling the edge. One fat tower appeared to have a rotating top that emitted a searchlight beam of far-ultraviolet light. It scanned back and forth—whether for enemies or for prey we didn't know.

We realized how conspicuous we were in our glowing coldsuits. "I'd give up breakfast for a can of black paint," I said.

"Maybe we could cover ourselves with mud?" Davern ventured.

"Let's get out of here first," Anatoly said.

The feeling that the land was aware of us had become too strong.

Getting Bucky up the steep trail was backbreaking work, but whenever we paused to rest, Umberlife gathered around us. The gully was infested with the plant-creatures that had once launched pins at us; they had grown, and their darts were the size of pencils now. We learned to trigger them with a beam from our flashlights. Every step required a constant, enervating vigilance.

When we had reached the place where we left the crates and stopped to rest, I announced that I was going to scout the trail ahead. No one else volunteered, so I said, "Amal, come with me. Seabird, hold onto the dog."

Amal and I picked our way up the steep trail, shining away small attackers. I saw no indication that the Umberlife had blocked the path. When we reached the top and emerged onto the plateau, I stood looking around at the transformed landscape. At my side, Amal said, "Oh my God."

The Damn Right Barrens were now a teeming jungle. Everywhere stood towering, misshapen structures, competing to dominate the landscape. An undergrowth of smaller life clogged the spaces in between. Above, in the Umberlit sky, floated monstrous organisms like glowing jellyfish, trailing tentacles that sparked and sizzled when they touched the ground. Ten or twelve of the lighthouse towers swept their searching beams across the land. There was not a doubt in my mind that this landscape was brutally aware.

I spotted some motion out of the corner of my eye, but when I turned to see, nothing was there. I thought: only predators and prey need to move fast.

"Look," Amal said, pointing. "Weird."

It was a ball, perfectly round and perhaps a yard in diameter, rolling along the ground of its own accord. It disappeared behind a hive-mound and I lost track of it.

We had turned to go back down the ravine when one of the searchlight beams swept toward us, and we ducked to conceal ourselves behind a rock. Amal gave an exclamation, and I turned to see that we were surrounded by four of the rolling spheres. They seemed to be waiting for us to make a move, so I pointed my flashlight at one. Instantly, it dissolved into a million tiny crawlers that escaped into the undergrowth. The other spheres withdrew.

"They're coordinating with the beacons," I hissed at Amal. "Hunting cooperatively."

"This place is evil," he said.

We dashed toward the head of the gully. Too late, I spotted ahead the largest dart-thrower plant I had ever seen. The spring-loaded tail triggered, releasing its projectiles. I dove to one side. Amal was not quick enough, and a spine the size of an arrow caught him in the throat. He clutched at it and fell to his knees. Somehow, I managed to drag him forward till we were concealed in the gully.

The dart had pierced his neck through, and was protruding on the other side. There was no way to give him aid without taking off his coldsuit. He was struggling to breathe. I tried to lift his hood, but the dart was pinning it down. So I said, "Brace yourself," and yanked the shaft out. He gave a gurgling cry. When I got his hood off, I saw it was hopeless. The dart had pierced a vein, and his coldsuit was filling with dark blood. Still, I ripped at his shirt and tried to bind up the wound until he caught at my hand. His eyes were growing glassy, but his lips moved.

"Leave it," he said. He was ready to die.

I stayed there, kneeling over him as he stiffened and grew cold. My mind was a blank, until suddenly I began to cry. Not just for him—for Edie as well, and for their unborn children, and all the people who would never be gladdened by their presence. I cried for the fact that we had to bury them in this hostile waste, where love and comfort would never touch them again. And I cried for the rest of us as well, because the prospect of our reaching home now seemed so dim.

When Anatoly and I brought the shovel back to the place where I had left Amal, there was nothing to bury. Only an empty coldsuit and a handful of teeth were left on the ground; all other trace of him was gone. Anatoly nudged the coldsuit with his foot. "Should we bury this?"

Macabre as it sounded, I said, "We might need it."

So we brought it back to our camp. We let the others think we had buried him.

We convened another strategy session. I said, "Amal had it right. We need to make a run for it. To hell with the cargo and the buggy. Leave the tent here; it only draws attention to us. We need to travel fast and light."

But Anatoly was still animated by the inspiration of our mission. "We can still succeed," he said. "We're close; we don't need to give up. We just have to outthink this nightmare."

"Okay, how?"

"We bring everything to the head of the gully and build a fort out of the crates. Then we wait till day comes, and make a dash for it while the Umberlife is sleeping."

"We can only get as far as the Mazy Lakes before night," I said.

"We do the same thing over again—wait out Umbernight. Food's no longer such a problem, with two less people."

I saw true faith in Seabird's eyes, and calculated self-interest in Davern's. Anatoly was so decisive, they were clearly ready to follow him. Perhaps that was all we needed. Perhaps it would work.

"All right," I said. "Let's get going."

We chose a site for our fort in the gully not far from where Amal had died. When it was done, it was a square enclosure of stacked crates with the tent pitched inside. I felt mildly optimistic that it would work. We slept inside it before bringing Bucky up. Then we waited.

There were sounds outside. Sally's warning growls made us worry that something was surrounding us to make an attack, so we set four of our lanterns on the walls to repel intruders, even though it used up precious battery life.

Hours of uneasiness later, dawn came. We instantly broke down the fort and found that the lamps had done their job, since there was a bare circle all around us. We congratulated ourselves on having found a way to survive.

The daylight hours were a mad dash across the Damn Right. We had to clear the way ahead of Bucky, and we took out our anger on the hibernating Umberlife, leaving a trail of smashed shells and toppled towers. We reached the edge of the lakes at sunset, and instantly saw that our plan would not work.

Around the edge of the wetland stood a dense forest of the tallest spires we had yet seen, easily dominating any fort walls we could build. There would be no hope of staying hidden here.

At the edge of the lake, the blooming abundance of horrors stopped, as if water were as toxic to them as light. "If only we had a boat!" Anatoly exclaimed. But the life around us did not produce anything so durable as wood—even the shells were friable.

The light was fading fast. Soon, this crowded neighborhood would become animate. Ahead, a narrow causeway between two lakes looked invitingly empty. If only we could make it to a campsite far enough from shore, we could build our fort and wait out the night.

"Let me get out my maps and check our route first," I said.

Davern gave an exclamation of impatience, but Anatoly just said, "Hurry up."

We were on the side of the Mazy Lakes where my maps were less complete. On the outward journey, we had cut across the ice; but now, after forty hours of daylight, that was not an option. I was certain of only one route, and it seemed to take off from shore about five miles away. I showed it to the others.

Davern still wanted to follow the route ahead of us. "We can just go far enough to camp, then come back next day," he argued. "We've already been walking twelve hours."

"No. We're not going to make any stupid mistakes," I said.

Anatoly hesitated, then said, "It's only five miles. We can do that."

But five miles later, it was completely dark and almost impossible to tell the true path from a dozen false ones that took off into the swamp whenever I shone my lamp waterward. I began to think perhaps Davern had been right after all. But rather than risk demoralizing everyone, I chose a path and confidently declared it the right one.

It was a low and swampy route, ankle-deep in water at times. I went out ahead with a tent pole to test the footing and scout the way. The sound of Davern complaining came from behind.

As soon as we came to a relatively dry spot, we set up the tent, intending to continue searching for a fort site after a short rest. But when we rose, Bucky had sunk six inches into the mud, and we had to unload half the crates before we could push him out. By the time we set out again, we were covered with mud and water.

"Now we can try Davern's plan of covering our coldsuits with mud," I said.

"We don't have much choice," Davern muttered.

Umber rose before we found a place to stop. Then we discovered that the lakes were not lifeless at all. By Umberlight, the stromatolites fluoresced with orange and black stripes. In spots, the water glowed carmine and azure, lit from underneath. We came to a good camping spot by a place where the lake bubbled and steam rose in clouds. But when the wind shifted and blew the steam our way, we nearly choked on the ammonia fumes. We staggered on, dizzy and nauseous.

The fort, I realized, was a solution to yesterday's problem. Staying put was not a good idea here, where we could be gassed in our sleep. We needed to be ready to move at a moment's notice.

Geysers of glowing, sulphur-scented spray erupted on either side of our path. We headed for a hummock that looked like a dry spot, but found it covered by a stomach-turning layer of wormlike organisms. We were forced to march through them, slippery and wriggling underfoot. As we crushed them, they made a sound at a pitch we couldn't hear. We sensed it as an itchy vibration that made us tense and short-tempered, but Sally was tormented till Seabird tied a strip of cloth over the coldsuit around her ears, making her look like an old woman in a scarf.

I didn't say so, but I was completely lost, and had been for some time. It was deep night and the water was freezing by now, but I didn't trust ice that glowed, so I stayed on the dwindling, switchback path. We were staggeringly weary by the time we reached the end of the road: on the tip of a peninsula surrounded by water. We had taken a wrong turn.

We stood staring out into the dark. It was several minutes before I could bring myself to say, "We have to go back."

Seabird broke down in tears, and Davern erupted like a geyser. "You were supposed to be the great guide and tracker, and all you've done is lead us to a dead end. You're totally useless."

Somehow, Anatoly summoned the energy to keep us from falling on each others' throats. "Maybe there's another solution." He shone his light out onto the lake. The other shore was clearly visible. "See, there's an ice path across. The whole lake isn't infested. Where it's black, the water's frozen solid."

"That could be just an island," I said.

"Tell you what, I'll go ahead to test the ice and investigate. You follow only if it's safe."

I could tell he was going to try it no matter what I said, so I made him tie a long rope around his waist, and anchored it to Bucky. "If you fall through, we'll pull you out," I said.

He stepped out onto the ice, testing it first with a tent pole. The weakest spot of lake ice is generally near shore, so I expected it to crack there if it was going to. But he got past the danger zone and kept going. From far out on the ice, he flashed his light back at us. "The ice is holding!" he called. "Give me more rope!"

There wasn't any more rope. "Hold on!" I called, then untied the tether from Bucky and wrapped it around my waist. Taking a tent pole, I edged out onto the ice where he had already crossed it. I was about thirty meters out onto the lake when he called, "I made it! Wait there."

He untied his end of the rope to explore the other side. I could not see if he had secured it to anything in case I fell through, so I waited as motionlessly as I could. Before long, he returned. "I'm coming back," he yelled.

I was a few steps from shore when the rope pulled taut, yanking me off my feet. I scrambled up, but the rope had gone limp. "Anatoly!" I screamed. Seabird and Davern shone their lights out onto the ice, but Anatoly was nowhere to be seen. I pulled in the rope, but it came back with only a frayed end.

"Stay here," I said to the others, then edged gingerly onto the ice. If he was in the water, there was a short window of time to save him. But as I drew closer to the middle, the lake under me lit up with mesmerizing colors. They emanated from an open pool of water that churned and burped.

The lake under the black ice had not been lacking in life. It had just been hungry.

When I came back to where the others were waiting, I shook my head, and Seabird broke into hysterical sobs. Davern sat down with his head in his hands.

I felt strangely numb, frozen as the land around us. At last I said, "Come on, we've got to go back."

Davern looked at me angrily. "Who elected *you* leader?"

"The fact that I'm the only one who can save your sorry ass," I said.

Without Anatoly's animating force, they were a pitiful sight—demoralized, desperate, and way too young. Whatever their worth as individuals, I felt a strong compulsion to avenge Anatoly's death by getting them back alive. In this land, survival was defiance.

I ordered Bucky to reverse direction and head back up the path we had come by. Seabird and Davern didn't argue. They just followed.

We had been retracing our steps for half an hour when I noticed a branching path I hadn't seen on the way out. "Bucky, stop!" I ordered. "Wait here," I told the others. Only Sally disobeyed me, and followed.

The track headed uphill onto a ridge between lakes. It had a strangely familiar look. When I saw Sally smelling at a piece of discarded trash, I recognized the site of our campsite on the way out. I stood in silence, as if at a graveyard. Here, Amal had played his mandolin and Anatoly had imagined songs of Umbernight. Edie had made Sally's coldsuit.

If we had just gone back instead of trying to cross the ice, we would have found our way.

I returned to fetch my companions. When Seabird saw the place, memories overwhelmed her and she couldn't stop crying. Davern and I set up the tent and heater as best we could, and all of us went inside.

"It's not fair," Seabird kept saying between sobs. "Anatoly was trying to save us. He didn't do anything to deserve to die. None of them did."

"Right now," I told her, "your job isn't to make sense of it. Your job is to survive."

Inwardly, I seethed at all those who had led us to expect the world to make sense.

We were ten hours away from the edge of the lakes, thirty hours of walking from home. Much as I hated to continue on through Umbernight, I wanted to be able to make a dash for safety when day came. Even after sleeping, Seabird and Davern were still tired and wanted to stay. I went out and shut off the heater, then started dismantling the tent to force them out.

The lakes glowed like a lava field on either side of us. From time to time, billows of glowing, corrosive steam enveloped us, and we had to hold our breaths till the wind shifted. But at least I was sure of our path now.

The other shore of the Mazy Lakes, when we reached it, was not lined with the towers and spires we had left on the other side; but when we pointed our lights ahead, we could see things scattering for cover. I was about to suggest that we camp and wait for day when I felt a low pulse of vibration underfoot. It came again, rhythmic like the footsteps of a faraway giant. The lake organisms suddenly lost their luminescence. When I shone my light on the water, the dark surface shivered with each vibration. Behind us, out over the lake, the horizon glowed.

"I think we ought to run for it," I said.

The others took off for shore with Sally on their heels. "Bucky, follow!" I ordered, and sprinted after them. The organisms on shore had closed up tight in their shells. When I reached the sloping bank, I turned back to look. Out over the lake, visible against the glowing sky, was a churning, coal-black cloud spreading toward us. I turned to flee.

"Head uphill!" I shouted at Davern when I caught up with him. Seabird was ahead of us; I could see her headlamp bobbing as she ran. I called her name so we wouldn't get separated, then shoved Davern ahead of me up the steep slope.

We had reached a high bank when the cloud came ashore, a toxic tsunami engulfing the low spots. Bucky had fallen behind, and I watched as he disappeared under the wave of blackness. Then the chemical smell hit, and for a while I couldn't breathe or see. By the time I could draw a lungful of air down my burning throat, the sludgy wave was already receding below us. Blinking away tears, I saw Bucky emerge again from underneath, all of his metalwork polished bright and clean. The tent that had been stretched over the crates was in shreds, but the crates themselves looked intact.

Beside me, Davern was on his knees, coughing. "Are you okay?" I asked. He shook his head, croaking, "I'm going to be sick."

I looked around for Seabird. Her light wasn't visible anymore. "Seabird!" I yelled, desperate at the thought that we had lost her. To my immense relief, I heard her voice calling. "We're here!" I replied, and flashed my light.

Sounds of someone approaching came through the darkness, but it was only Sally. "Where is she, Sally? Go find her," I said, but the dog didn't understand. I swept my light over the landscape, and finally spotted Seabird stumbling toward us without any light. She must have broken hers in the flight. I set out toward her, trying to light her way.

The Umberlife around us was waking again. Half-seen things moved just outside the radius of my light. Ahead, one of the creature-balls Amal and I had seen on the other side was rolling across the ground, growing as it moved. It was heading toward Seabird.

"Seabird, watch out!" I yelled. She saw the danger and started running, slowed by the dark. I shone my light on the ball, but I was too far away to have an effect. The ball speeded up, huge now. It overtook her and dissolved into a wriggling, scrabbling, ravenous mass. She screamed as it covered her, a sound of sheer terror that rose into a higher pitch of pain, then cut off. The mound churned, quivered repulsively, grew smaller, lost its shape. By the time I reached the spot, all that was left was her coldsuit and some bits of bone.

I rolled some rocks on top of it by way of burial.

Davern was staring and trembling when I got back to him. He had seen the whole thing, but didn't say a word. He stuck close to me as I led the way back to Bucky.

"We're going to light every lamp we've got and wait here for day," I said.

He helped me set up the lights in a ring, squandering our last batteries. We sat in the buggy's Umbershadow and waited for dawn with Sally at our feet. We didn't say much. I knew he couldn't stand me, and I had only contempt for him; but we still huddled close together.

To my surprise, Bucky was still operable when the dawn light revived his batteries. He followed as we set off up the Let's Go Valley, once such a pleasant land, now disfigured with warts of Umberlife on its lovely face. We wasted no time on anything but putting the miles behind us.

The sun had just set when we saw the wholesome glow of Feynman Habitat's yard light ahead. We pounded on the door, then waited. When the door cracked open, Davern pushed past me to get inside first. They welcomed him with incredulous joy, until they saw that he and I were alone. Then the joy turned to shock and grief.

There. That is what happened. But of course, that's not what everyone wants to know. They want to know *why* it happened. They want an explanation—what we did wrong, how we could have succeeded.

That was what the governing committee was after when they called me in later. As I answered their questions, I began to see the narrative taking shape in their minds. At last Anselm said, "Clearly, there was no one fatal mistake. There was just a pattern of behavior: naïve, optimistic, impractical. They were simply too young and too confident."

I realized that I myself had helped create this easy explanation, and my remorse nearly choked me. I stood up and they all looked at me, expecting me to speak, but at first I couldn't say a word. Then, slowly, I started out, "Yes. They were all those things. Naïve. Impractical. Young." My voice failed, and I had to concentrate on controlling it. "That's why we needed them. Without their crazy commitment, we would have conceded defeat. We would have given up, and spent the winter hunkered down in our cave, gnawing our old grudges, never venturing or striving for anything beyond our reach. Nothing would move forward. We needed them, and now they are gone."

Later, I heard that the young people of Feynman took inspiration from what I said, and started retelling the story as one of doomed heroism. Young people like their heroes doomed.

Myself, I can't call it anything but failure. It's not because people blame me. I haven't had to justify myself to anyone but this voice in my head—always questioning, always nagging me. I can't convince it: everyone fails.

If I blame anyone, it's our ancestors, the original settlers. We thought their message to us was that we could always conquer irrationality, if we just stuck to science and reason.

Oh, yes—the settlers. When we finally opened the crates to find out what they had sent us, it turned out that the payload was books. Not data—paper books. Antique ones. Art, philosophy, literature. The books had weathered the interstellar trip remarkably well. Some were lovingly inscribed by the settlers to their unknown descendants. Anatoly would have been pleased to know that the people who sent these books were not really rationalists—they worried about our aspirational well-being. But the message came too late. Anatoly is dead.

I sit on my bed stroking Sally's head. What do you think, girl? Should I open the book from my great-grandmother?

TODAY IS TODAY

RICK WILBER

> "You can think of our entire universe, our reality, as one bubble surrounded by an infinite number of other bubbles, each with its own reality. Do those bubbles touch? Can you cross from one to another? That's an entertaining possibility."
>
> —*Janine Marie Larsen, Ph.D., Physics, University of Loyola at St. Louis*

In one tiny part of one of the new bubbles emerging from the bubble that is our particular universe, there is a place and time where you might exist and I might exist where I have a daughter named Janine.

Perhaps, in that tiny bubble, I may have been lucky with sports and found some success. As quarterback in high school, I'll have converted to a tight end in college at the University of Minnesota, where I'll bang heads and block like a demon, catching most of the passes they throw my way. I'll be All Big Twelve, then a second-round draft choice, then I'll make the team in St. Louis for the Brewers and get my chance to start when Rasheed Campbell blows out his left knee. Then I'll never look back. Seven years later I'll wind down my career as a backup on the Falcons, but that will be their Super Bowl year, so I'll get my ring by, mostly, sitting on my butt.

It will be a nice way to spend my twenties. I'll stay single and have a blast, though my body will take a beating. When I lose a couple of steps and the good times come to an end I'll try to move to broadcasting, but that's a lot harder than you'd think. I won't be able to think that fast on my feet, so it won't work out.

Still, I'll feel like I have plenty of money for life as a grown-up, and you'd think I'd be happy; but it's hard to be a has-been, no matter how much money you've saved. I'll never marry, never have any kids, never grow up, really, and I'll know it. Later in life I'll be lonely and bored and broke. And thanks to all that head-banging work on the offensive line in my football career, I'll literally be losing my mind. Eventually I'll run out of money and run into trouble and only then will I have any regrets.

In another tiny part of another emerging bubble where you might exist, I'll break my collarbone in the second game of my senior year of high school and by the time I'm back the season will be over—my football career along with it. But my left-handed pitching skills will be unfazed by my fractured right clavicle and I'll pitch us to the state championship where we'll lose by one unearned run. My fastball in the high eighties and my nice, straight change-up will earn me a free ride to Loyola University, where I'll have four good years as a Billiken and five more in the minors before I'll hang them up and get on with real life in the business world.

I'll meet a woman who loves me and I, her. We'll marry and have two sweet kids. I'll have a good life and some nice minor-league memories from Tampa and Atlanta and Durham and Spokane. You'd think I'd be happy.

In another tiny part of another of my emerging bubbles where you might exist, the Golden Gophers will keep me at quarterback and I'll do fine as the starter, though I'll never be a star and I won't make the NFL. I'll knock around a bit in arena football and then swim up to the surface as the quarterback of the Hamilton Tiger-Cats. Once, in my nine years there, I'll lead the Ticats to victory in the Grey Cup. In the Canadian Football League there's room to pass and room to run, and I'll do both, often.

I'll meet a woman named Alene in my second season when we'll beat the Alouettes with a lucky rouge. We'll be celebrating at Yancy's on Hanover Street and there she'll be, dark hair and blue eyes, stunning and smart and ambitious. I'll have had a good day on the ground, gaining ninety yards before taking a stinger and coming out of the game. She'll have been there, rooting for the Alouettes, and she'll have seen that hit I took. She'll wonder how I am feeling. Just fine, I'll say, though I'll have a worrisome headache.

She'll be an actor; a successful French Canadian who speaks four languages. I'll feel lucky. By my third season we'll be married. By my fifth season we'll have a child, Janine. We'll call her Jannie.

Janine Marie Larsen will be born two weeks early on July 21st, a Saturday, at four in the morning. Alene will have a rough time of it with a fifteen-hour delivery and then it will only get worse: Jannie's feet, hands, and the epicanthal folds at the eyes all have a certain flaccidity, even for a newborn.

Trisomy 21, the doctor will say.

Down syndrome.

Alene will have been through ultrasound and blood tests and everything will have looked fine. But here will be Jannie, and that will be that. There's a lot these kids can do, the doctor will say as Alene and I both cry. Really, they can accomplish a lot.

Really, the doctor will emphasize.

We'll have a game that night at home, in old Ivor Wynne Stadium against the Alouettes, and Alene will insist I play. So I'll go and do that, earning my paycheck with a couple of touchdown passes and a good enough night of football. I won't remember much of the game. All I'll be able to think about is: Down syndrome.

I'll go right back to the hospital after the game and Alene will be weak but smiling and more beautiful than ever. There will be a picture the next day in the Hamilton Spectator of her with the baby—the whole city will be behind us. I'll hold that baby and kiss her cheek as the cameras whir and click.

Two years will go by when I won't play much: some knee surgery, a discectomy for a herniated disc, a couple more concussions. The docs will say it's time to hang them up and so I will. That's about the time that Alene will get the movie role she's always wanted, filming in Vancouver. Our parting will be amicable. I'll get Jannie and Alene will get visitation rights and there she'll go, heading west.

I'll have no reason whatsoever to be happy, but, holding Jannie, I will be.

There is another tiny part of a different bubble where Alene and I will stay together and things will go differently for Jannie. She'll be normal and fussy and hungry at birth and she won't stop being any of those things right through high school and college. She'll get her brains from her mother, her athleticism from me, and win a full ride to play soccer at Rice, where she'll major in physics. Then she'll choose brawn over brains and turn pro for the Washington Whippets before joining the national team in the Global Cup. She'll be a star and a household name after they beat the French on her hat-trick to win it all.

By that time, I'll be coaching football at Buffalo State and happy enough with how I've reconciled myself to the paycheck and the fall from fame. But Hamilton will treat me well with a big ovation when I go there to see Jannie play a friendly against the Italians and she'll have a great day, scoring a brace. We'll have dinner afterward and she'll be polite, but distant, and we'll smile for the cameras and then I'll go my way and she'll go hers.

In a more important tiny bubble, Alene and I will do our best to raise Jannie to be everything she can be, Down syndrome be damned. After I hang them up, Alene's career will prosper and we'll do fine. We'll move to Vancouver, where most of her work is, and I'll spend a lot of time with Jannie. She'll be a sweet kid, but there are heart problems and a leg that needs straightening, creating an uncertain future for her and me both. My football past and all those helmet hits will come back to haunt me: foggy mornings will turn into long, dark days, and I'll worry about just how long I'll still be me.

I'll be in the dumps a lot, but I'll need something to do, someone to be, so I'll take care of Jannie, one day at a time. Today is today. There'll be speech therapy sessions and school and all the rest. There'll be some joy in this, some deep satisfaction. She'll be my girl, my always girl.

In this bubble, even as I lose some recent memories, I'll still remember certain moments from my past that were so perfect, where I was so tuned in—so fully one with the moment—that I captured them completely in my mind in slow-motion detail. I'll remember them vividly, even when I can't find my car keys. I will still feel the perfection of the pass to Elijah Depps deep in the corner of the end zone against the Argos. And I'll still watch in awe that time I swear I guided the ball in flight to bend it around Ryan Crisps' outstretched hands as he tried to intercept for the Blue Bombers, and instead the ball found Jason Wissen with no time left and we won.

And I'll feel that joy, too, when Jannie, on her twenty-second birthday, in one of her many Special Olympics soccer games, steals the ball off the player she's defending and sprints down the field with it, dribbling like mad. She'll weave her way past three defenders, come in on the goalie, fake left and shoot right, an outside of the shoe push into the upper ninety for a goal. It'll be a great goal, and everybody on both teams will come over to hug her and celebrate, because that's how it's done in Special O's. I'll beam. That's my girl.

There's another tiny bubble, one I imagine every now and then, where after my divorce I'll spend a lot of time with a woman named Emily. She won't be bothered by Jannie, she'll just want me to be me, Jannie to be Jannie, and Emily to be Emily.

In that bubble we'll make it work. There'll be a new drug on the market for trisomy 21, and the sun will shine every day and the Yankees will never, *ever* win the pennant, but the Ticats will be the powerhouse team of the CFL and my knees won't hurt and my mind will be clear and I'll keep all my memories as Jannie goes off to college and the sun will shine every day in Hamilton, Ontario.

In one particular spot in one particular tiny bubble, Alene will be a grad student when we meet, and an associate professor by the time she leaves for a post in Quebec. She can't turn it down, and the stress and strain of raising Jannie, she'll say in distancing French, is *complètement impossible*. I'll have seen it coming for years, but we'll still do the divorce through lawyers.

As time goes by, she'll call Jannie often enough, and send her cards and cash on her birthday and Christmas. She'll even bring Jannie up for a week or two to visit in the summer.

Jannie will do fine. By her sixteenth birthday she'll be doing third-grade arithmetic and fourth-grade reading and tearing things up in Special Olympics soccer. This will be better than the school-district psychologist thought Jannie would ever do. It will be so good, in fact, that after her birthday party, after the neighbor kids and her special pals are gone, after the cake is eaten, she'll be sitting on her bed kicking a plastic toy soccer ball off the opposite wall: shoot it, trap it with her foot, shoot it again, trap it, shoot it, trap it.

I'll come in to stop the racket and she'll look at me: that wide face, those eyes. Her language skills aren't all that great, but from the look on her face I'll be able to see something's up. "My father," she'll say, "I sixteen now."

I'll sit down next to her. "Yeah, young lady. You're growing up fast," I'll say, but what I'll be thinking about is all the things Jannie I have learned together, often the hard way. Boyfriends, how to handle her periods, what clothes to wear and when to wear them, how to tie her hair in a ponytail and put in a different bow every day, how to ignore some people and pay attention to others, how to be so different and still be so happy. Tricky business, all of that.

"My father," she'll say, "I not be like you or Mom-mom."

I'll be the lunkhead I am in every one of these bubbles, no question, but I'll be able to see where this is going: my Jannie, my hard-working girl, is doing so well that she knows how well she isn't doing. She's been expecting to grow up, to leave Neverland. But in this bubble . . . it doesn't work like that.

"Jannie, Jannie," I'll say, lying to her and not for the first time, struggling with how to handle this. "Look," I'll say, "We're all different, Janster, we all have different things we're good at or bad at."

She'll look at me. She'll trust me. I'll say, "I wanted to be an astronomer, Jannie; you know, look at the stars and figure out what it all means. I wanted that, Jannie, in the worst way. But I couldn't do the math."

"Bet Mom could," Jannie will say, smiling, getting into it.

"Yeah, Jannie, your mom sure could. She's one smart lady," I'll say, though I'll be thinking about what I might have said about Jannie's mother just then. To be kind, she'll have missed out on a lot of good things.

"Sure, my father. I get it," Jannie will say. And then she'll stand up to give me a hug, and I'll hug her back and then I'll leave the room. Later, out in the driveway, we'll shoot hoops and she'll seem fine. I'll go out and join her in a game of one-on-one, make it-take it, and she'll clobber me. I'll blame it on my bad knees.

In my least favorite bubble I'll die at age fifty-two of an aneurysm. Alene won't be around and I'll have no living relatives. I won't leave much money behind.

Jannie will be stranded. Alone. Unhappy. And there'll be twenty more years of her own decline into senescence before there's peace.

In another bubble Jannie will be an intellectual powerhouse. In high school she'll think calculus is fun and physics is entertaining. She'll have a perfect score on the science portion of the PSAT. Caltech will come calling, and MIT, and Yale and Stanford and Loyola and Case Western and Harvey Mudd and Duke and the University of Chicago. Astronomy in college? Physics? Biology? She'll find it hard to decide.

She'll be patient with me in this bubble. She'll understand that her father is a decent guy, but not the sharpest tool in the shed. When she walks across the stage for that college degree, and then the next one, and then the next one, I'll there in the audience, proud as I can be.

In one particular bubble, Jannie and I will be at the Brock Theatre in Hamilton, where we both live; me in a two-bedroom condo, Jannie in a group home that she's recently moved into after years of living in her own apartment. Down syndrome people slide into early-onset Alzheimer's, almost all of them. It's unfair, but there it is.

Jannie will be thirty years old and I'll be fifty-seven. We'll be laughing and joking about old age on that January day as we walk through the parking lot's snow, go into the sudden warmth of the theater, buy our tickets and take our seats. Then we'll watch a movie, something about memory keepers and cute Down syndrome kids and the sweet and soapy ills of the world. I'll be squirming in my seat; Jannie will be quiet.

When we walk out of the place people will be staring at Jannie. She'll not be cute, and she'll be shuffling some because of some knee trouble that I probably caused her, encouraging all that Special O's soccer and getting her out on the basketball court with me for all those years. We won't have played in a while.

It will be snowing lightly as we walk away from the theater and get in the car, a beat-up little Toyota that I'm determined to keep running. You don't get rich in the CFL, and there are better uses for my retirement money than buying shiny new metal and plastic. As I start the car and get the heater going Jannie will look at me. I'll see it in her eyes. That movie was a bad idea.

"My father," she'll say. "I. Am. Me." And she'll punch herself in the chest with her right fist, hard.

"You are that, Jannie, you certainly are," I'll say, kicking myself.

"Thank you," she'll say, and sit back and relax.

There are all those different bubbles, but right then and right there, this will be the only one that matters. This is it. Reality. We are who we are.

We are where we are in this bubble, the one we share, the one where we do the best we can with what we have.

We won't talk about the movie as we drive off and head for some ice cream and then, later, the group home. Instead, we'll talk hockey, father and daughter, something about the Sabres and how maybe they'll move to Hamilton and wouldn't that be great? Or we'll talk about Jannie's bowling team, where she's holding down that ninety-six average and I couldn't possibly be more proud of her. Or we'll talk about the Ticats and how much fun we had going to the games last summer and fall and soon enough the season will be back and this year, for sure, the Ticats will make their way back to the Grey Cup.

We won't talk about the path I've started walking down. Jannie wouldn't understand. But the reason she's in that group home is that they don't trust me to have her anymore. Mood swings. Anger. All those hits in all those practices and all those games. CTE my doc calls it, and the league agrees. I have good days and bad ones, and she's safer in that home.

I'm not happy about that. I was counting on holding Jannie's hand as she crossed that street into the confusion and then the darkness she faces, and now it's her who'll be holding mine.

But that won't come up. We won't say much about anything. We won't need to. We'll just eat our ice cream and hang out together and enjoy this little bit of a bubble as best we can. This is our bubble, right here and right now.

Today is today.

THE HEART OF OWL ABBAS

KATHLEEN JENNINGS

Once, before the great Empire of Else enveloped the land between the red mountains and the quiet sea, the city-state of Owl Abbas was a mere bird-haunted forest temple. But protected by treaties, suffocated by safety and benevolent neglect, it had swollen and grown in upon itself, roiling and fomenting, so slowly that only (perhaps) a few dust-dry wraiths of abbots hanging motionless in enclosed footings of the Palace Aster would have marked the change from one century to another.

The gains and losses of its citizenry had been gradual. Its resentments and injustices oozed like moisture down the dank wall of a forgotten reservoir, unremarked by either the clustered, crushing commonality or the Little Emperor, cloyed and gorged in his great gilt chambers. *Drip, drip*, until the dark water was high against its bowed, ill-repaired walls. Until it lapped at the foundations of palace and hovel alike.

In all Owl Abbas, before it burned (after the Falling but before the Cartographer's War and the Recurrence of Owls), there were among its many windows only two that need concern us.

The first was fogged with spider webs. It belonged to a garret, precarious above the spring-carts and spirit-lamps of Petty Street. Behind it was installed a wretched scribbler, who eked out a living writing songs for the populace. Let us call him Excelsior, for that is the name with which he signed his work.

Across the cobbleskulls and flints, and a full other storey over that abyss of jam merchants and glove-skinners that was Petty Street, above the hanging signs of teahouse and slop house, workhouse and whorehouse, higher even than the knotwork of laundry-, bell-, delivery- and ladder-strings, was another, airy casement.

The tenant of that room was only recently arrived to Owl Abbas—itinerant, mendicant, but admitted at the Mountain Gate because of the journeyman's seal it bore on one exquisite brass shoulder. Even had the gate guards consulted the annals of the Elevated Guild of Horologists and Artificers, they would have found no reason to turn aside the masterpiece of an obscure craftswoman whose exile was self-imposed. Wonders, then, were a daily import of the palace, and—hemmed in as the city-state was by ancient vows and the benign disregard of the Empire of Else, in whose armpit it festered—the peace of the Little Emperor of Owl Abbas was threatened by nothing but thieves.

Excelsior, who seldom ventured even to his window, let alone to the street, had never seen this neighbour, whom time would call the Nightingale. From his lower garret, Excelsior could glimpse only a ceiling painted with blue dove-shadows and rose-gold candle-glow.

He could, however, hear the Nightingale's voice. Pure and high, discs of spinning glass singing against chamois, it fell like tumbling bells, like spilled silver wires.

It sang "Love Like the Guillotine," "The Too-Taut Heart", "When I am Duke of Petty Street (You Shall Be the Clown)"—all the choruses bawled by rampant youth loitering over gutters below, trilled by the delivery boatmen in the oily, olive canals, hummed even by agued ancients scrubbing the pearl-floored halls of the Palace Aster. Cheap songs. Excelsior's.

He could have written a dozen more like them in his sleep, for his scribbling of lyric and melody, accompaniment and refrain was a mechanical task, calibrated to please the fecund and fickle tastes of the crowds of Owl Abbas, their perennial lusts and losses.

And what appetites for music that city-state had then, for all its decay and poverty! Forgotten were the bone groves and the quietude of owleries that once nested where the city had grown. The last owl-abbots were long starved in the gutters where they had begged, their skulls cambering the roadway. The owls had departed the sleepless streets for the zoological gardens of Else and the monk's-fringe forests of the red mountains. Now, though the finest delights were reserved for the Little Emperor, balladuellists caterwauled on roofsheets; ladies' cantating parrots swung in brass rings; lovers in teahouses threw coins into the throats of cheap songboxes, to wind the gears that set the teeth that struck the notes from the spinning metal tongues, sending slivers of copper to Excelsior, that he might buy ink and nibs and spirit-oil, cheap paper, wine hard as a fist and, when he remembered, a little bread.

Rough songs he wrote, like all the lesser scribblers of Owl Abbas. Raw songs, tunes to dull sense and sensation, ditties to hem in a little portion of pleasure between hunger and the grave.

Excelsior had never crept out of his garret to crouch at the outer palace walls to hear rare notes escaping from an Imperial Performance. Nor had he attended the Collegiate Academy of Guilded Instrumentalists, which existed to supply the artful music of the palace: formal stylings for sleep and dressing and every course of a dozen served at each of the eight tables laid daily for the Little Emperor. Even had Excelsior done so, he would not have heard anything to match the Nightingale's abilities.

He listened to the deconstructed threads and parts, the wheeling, rewriting rehearsals, the little broken, mended, rough-edged fantasias with which the Nightingale warmed and amused the bright apartment, there above Petty Street, in that merryloud quarter of Owl Abbas where surely no one who mattered could overhear. The Nightingale, learning the music of the streets, the heartbeat of the city.

Bells and wires and strings, keys and barrels and tumblers, reeds and pipes, skin and wind. Melody, harmony, disingenuous discord. The heart and throats of caged larks, of free birds, of trained choristers. All these were in the voice of the Nightingale.

But the voice carried, as the bounty of the palace never did. From Petty Street to the knotted alleys of the Maresnest, from Agnes Lane where once a disgraced clockmaker had kept her stinking workshop, to the last nested hovel before the avenue of guildhalls. Though neither understanding nor caring, the denizens of Owl Abbas stepped a little more lightly, laboured with an ear half-turned, unwitting, to those strains.

Excelsior eked out the end of the daylight, the nightlight, the moonlight, the ghostlight. He scrimped and slaved until he gathered courage and words enough to light a fire-inch and burn a whole pennyweight of ground copper. He offered the coin to the Phantom of the Window sash, and summoned that obscure spirit almost to its full weight of feathers and claws.

The Phantom of the Window sash was not a shade that embraced change. It had once had its own antique, unmusical views on such matters as songlust and bodymusic. But those, like the shade itself, were the shabbiest of memories.

Summoned by the soul of coins, it obeyed its commission without remark. Clustering Excelsior's rolled onionskin to its vanishingly sharp breastbone, the phantom fell from the garret sill—fell, then lifted on a gust of oil-spiced laughter to the glowing window opposite and there dissolved before the Nightingale could question it, leaving its dry burden to flutter on the floor.

Excelsior could not watch.

He hauled closed the leaning shutters and pulled down the sash, cross-latched it and rubbed drawing gum along the edges. He etched more webs into the panes, spitting glass like flour from beneath his good penknife, that his garret might look tenantless. He raked the curtains across, pinning pumice-cloth and blotting paper over the moth holes.

Then for good measure he put out writing-lamp, hearth-glow, bed-candle and moth-pilot, closed his eyes, and waited.

He waited for three clock-unwinding days, feeling the long springs of his world loosen, while the ink crusted in the glass well and the nibs began to rust in the little moisture from the breath of creeping rats or spiders.

On the third day, a thrill stirred the dull panes, the curtains. Excelsior could not have told when it had begun. He crouched, resolutely unhoping.

The insinuation became a hum, a melody. Excelsior heard what had never been heard before, except in the signs and symbols of his dark garret, in his private equations: the song he had composed in the light of the last of his lamp-spirits, for which he had burned the last coin; the paper words for which he had sent the phantom winging.

The Nightingale's voice, now, was a high, thin curling, like the frost on a glass of Abbas-White, or like red snow curling off the tops of the mountains. It was melody uncomplicated by harmony or the thrilling trills of ornament, tentative only in its simplicity, the singer's questing guided by all the confidence of the supreme master of an art.

Over and again that voice followed Excelsior's script, the words seeking notes, notes seeking paths as water flows across a dry land. Then gradually that glass-and-golden voice found a pattern, gathered force, rilled and frothed along the edges of its new-cut banks, built undertows and laughing sprays of sound. It poured down through the alleys where craftsmen and labourers starved, trickled through Agnes Lane where a young clockmaker had once studied the grafting of metal to splintered bone, curling into the inlooped ways of the great warren of the Maresnest.

High over Petty Street, the Nightingale sang for the first time Excelsior's composition—not a commission, not a command, but . . . Well, even the scribbler could not have said whether it had been gift, or tribute or sacrifice.

The Nightingale sang and Excelsior, weak with waiting, listened.

He wrote another, immediately he had revived. It was unworthy. Dissatisfied, he broke it apart into bare penny-shave popular ditties. Ragged and rancid, he did not care to take them down himself, but sent them by errand urchins to the punch-shop, where they were pricked relentlessly into parchment rolls and delivered to tea shops and pleasure warrens, fed into mere pinching, playing songchests, which nipped fingers as well as paper, and singly-minded cranked out Excelsior's abandoned tunes.

"*Love, love*," sang the high-painters in their blood-dipped, paint-dripped hats.

"*You are a far dying star*," sang the menials toiling with bow-bent spines and mole-fur cloths along the Palace Aster wainscoting.

"*You test the hearts of the court, and find them wanting*," sang the xylophone-ribbed parrot trainers, chorusing from cage to cage, that their clients' birds might have the newest tunes.

Excelsior, having ill considered how his words might be mis-sung, covered his ears against the rattle and racket of the streets, uncovered them again in terror that he might miss the Nightingale's next effusive variations.

The copper slicings rattled up in the delivery basket. *There,* thought Excelsior. He could fit a new song to that high, rhythmless beat.

The ghost of a sigh is a weighty thing. The Phantom of the Window-sash unfolded itself heavily into the haze of the copper-burnings, not in the least elevated by music.

It gathered up the onionskin in layers of ether and slunk to Excelsior's window, sagged over the sill, bore itself by grudging degrees up layers of garlic breath, pipe smoke, midden scent, fresh soap, crushed leaves, and wet feathers to the higher floor, opposite.

If Excelsior could have seen, he would have watched in affront as it uncoiled, graceless, and spilled on the ruddy tiles his heart's offering, his hope of immortality.

Now, ghosts are little more than animate nostalgia. New songs in old patterns were a sop, a soporific, and old songs by new singers no more than reinforced the rule of the city. But so fine a thing as the scribbler and the singer together might make was a danger to the unquestioned squalor, the eternal twilight, the restlessness without ambition, the struggle over no more than bread and beds, which were the groundwork of the Little Emperor's reign, the foundation of the false peace of Owl Abbas.

The phantom lay unspooled on the cool tiles until the Nightingale, shod in shell and horn, clicked and bent to it and lifted spirit and onionskin together.

The sheets of music, raw as bone, fresh as blood, lured the singer, but the spirit was a tragedian. How it dangled and feinted.

Sensibility is the stock-in-trade of any performer, long dead or unliving. The Nightingale set the song aside and attended the messenger.

Burnt feathers revived the spirit a little, burnt copper restored it, a dusting of finger-chalk to better reveal its form the phantom found quite unnecessary. It arched itself grateful and looping around the bronze joints, the magnificent alabaster throat of its benefactor.

"Strange spirit," said the Nightingale. "Were you bird once? Are you, then, the heart of Owl Abbas? If so, I have been overwrought, and you were easier to capture than my maker thought."

No, its spasm of ghostly laughter implied. It was a humble ghost, dusty and old. Far below the notice of such as the Nightingale.

The Nightingale's maker had never been interested in spirit, only in the melding of metal with flesh—had, indeed, taken her leave of Owl Abbas when the Guild mocked her designs for a Patent Brass Hip, a Magnetic Hand, a

Better Limb, as an affront and bastardisation of their craft. The phantom's claim therefore satisfied the Nightingale. It turned to the onionskins and began to try the first notes, the melodies.

How great, how grand, the lingering spirit insinuated with little shivers and purrs. *How* marvelous *to be heard as one was intended to be. The homage of the scribbler is only to be expected, but your voice was not designed to be let fall where it might, on night-dust-carter and tea-carrier alike. You are a creature of artifice and ambition, your voice made to refract from mirrored maze and chandelier.*

Turn away, the phantom's mummery suggested. *Turn your back on this window, with its view over bird- and ghost-encrusted roofs to the ghastly blue fields and untrustworthy scarlet mountains. Turn instead to that opposite. Look to the chimney-forests, the peacock-strutted valleys of lead and copper, the waxen glowing domes of the Palace Aster, set like a weight of jewels at the centre of the city.*

One might, it implied, draping affectionately about the mark of the Nightingale's distant maker, *one might even say the Nightingale had been purposed and designed for such delights.*

Sing Excelsior's little offerings in that *direction.*

The Nightingale saw the force of the argument. Its throat, the chords strung within, these articulations of wrist and jaw, had been crafted and calibrated for a high purpose: to seize the heart of Owl Abbas. Where else might a city's heart be found?

So it was towards the Palace Aster that the Nightingale sang.

Excelsior, having at last in hope opened curtain, sash and shutter, did not at first notice the added distance in the Nightingale's voice. He lingered, nib held clear of the thirsty paper, and drank in the tentative, tender explorations, the strengthening resolve, the removal of magnificent veils of possibility to reveal the song more truly than he had written it.

Petty Street had proved an impassable chasm before this, even to those robust enough to dare its buffeting. It was possible, in the scheme of the city, with its streets like the whorls of an ear, branching like veins, looped like a brain, that Excelsior might never see the Nightingale. He believed he did not care. It was the *voice* that captured him, reverberating in the hollows of his thin chest, fluttering and rebounding there like a second soul.

Abruptly anxious, he cleaned the crust of ink from the pen, the settling dust from his paper, and began again.

Hark how glory falls,

Tumbling from Owl Abbas walls.

No.

Send gold-and-silver crowns
Tumbling in the street,
Enough to cover the copper path
Laid at the singer's feet.

Again, he scratched out the words.

Aster and rose will never bloom
Like the light in my love's room . . .

That was awkward, presumptuous, and wrong. Excelsior nearly tore up the paper, but the thought of copper arrested him. Coins meant ink and nibs, castor oil and onionskin and the services of a courier.

Out went the lesser tunes, into the kettle-arcades and the dance-alleys, out to the earnest, workaday singers who would seek no subtlety or layers in words that had been dreamed up for nothing *except* nuance. Out to listeners who, unwitting, had already been half-woken by the Nightingale's art, and whose nascent hunger other scribblers, other singers—themselves starved—hastened to fill with words not of old complacencies but with a mimicry of Excelsior's dim longings.

At last, like the heart of a thistle, the pure, bitter core of a song emerged from the peeled-back pages. This, thought Excelsior, was fitting tribute and sacrifice.

Out in the streets, languishing, lusting idlers and iron-bitten, fire-calloused labourers hammered out his ballads with all the delicacy of a beam on a bell. Excelsior took his thin levy of their trade and burned it to the Phantom of the Window-sash, which, for once, appeared with alacrity, an eager whiplash of air.

"Take this to the Nightingale," Excelsior bid it, as if the spirit did not know where all his thoughts were trained.

The Nightingale's voice had been borne by breeze and breath in through the windows of the Palace Aster, where it reached the ring-heavy ears of the Little Emperor, as he lay on his back in his vast bed at owl-light, as was his custom, weighted with ennui, calcified with alarm. The fears of the Little Emperor were many: that he might never know delight again; that the vast Empire of Else would outstrip him in its discovery of luxuries; that emissaries from a distant land, consumed with envy, would break into the storerooms of the Palace Aster and find a jeweled gown, a pearl cup, a marvel from which he had not wearily drained the last honeysuckle spasm of pleasure.

"That music," he said, startling the doctors who, beaked and embroidered, bent over his bed, tempting him with rarities. "I want *that*."

"It is the windharps in the hanging gardens," said his courtiers. "It is the song of the cocoon-tenders lulling their charges to sleep. It is the breeze in the vines where Abbas-White is grown."

The Little Emperor was become petulant and particular with a surfeit of pleasures. "Then bring it to me!" he said.

They sent runners out into the streets, the gardens, the acre-width of tilled treaty-land that bordered Owl Abbas, and had windharps, silk-herders, vine-cuttings brought to the palace. All fell silent in the presence of the Little Emperor, but the miraculous voice continued.

The nobles went out themselves, questing and questioning, soft and perfumed and quilted, pomandered against the exhalation of rotting lungs, parasoled against the filth that spilled from windows. The grimy populace, more sullen and shouldersome than had been their wont, would not or could not tell them whence the song came. Above them, the soot-lunged chimney-urchins leaped and leered. So many shifts of them had tumbled and burned since the clockmaker of Agnes Street had proposed, to denouncement by the Guild, her Mechanical Bellows Suitable to Reside Within the Living Chest. But Excelsior's words and the Nightingale's song rang in their boxed and smoke-blocked ears, and as they spat down on the velvet caps fluttering with imported owl-feathers, the shining, circleted heads of the prim nobility, the urchins thought among themselves that *those* heads would never fall to form the smallest cobbleskulls.

At last, as the Little Emperor grew restive, voicehounds were sent out. They went about the streets, leaping runnels of beery bravado. They heard, dismissive, Excelsior's adulterated choruses rousing bottle-room and tap-house, they ducked unperturbed beneath the debased and stirring phrases whistled by rat-cullers and spring-winders. They clicked up the fingerstairs and along the cobbleskulls until they crowded together on Short Street, which runs beneath Petty Street, all their ears cocked to the sky, their small, weeping eyes turned to the garret where the Nightingale sang.

Arpeggios and wandering scales spilled like largesse, rich and fragrant on their collars and livery.

The Phantom of the Window-sash, delivering its latest commission, let the onionskin spill like so many kitchen-sweepings over the Nightingale's unclenching hands, to catch in the breeze and flicker out into Owl Abbas.

There. The little ghost coiled meaningful at the pulsing throat of the Nightingale, although each tremor, each tremolo shook it a measure further out of the world. *Make ready.*

The Nightingale had little to prepare. The tiled room was already bare of all but the meanest necessities. The red lamp was put out, and brick and tile thus returned to their native pallor, all Petty Street and no memory of the far red mountains.

And thus, to the satisfaction of one insignificant spirit, the Nightingale was quit of Petty Street, and Petty Street was rid of the Nightingale.

All would be as it ought to be, as (to the frail, fond memory that was the phantom) it always had been. The singer would go to the Palace Aster, be admired, neglected, rusted out, and thrown into some storeroom, as is the fate of all fine things; the scribbler would go back to composing his cheap, satisfactory songs. At least, of these futures the ghost convinced itself.

Excelsior gripped the sill like the jasmine-hawks in the highest towers of the Palace Aster, and listened. He tinkered a trumpet out of an abandoned horn, the better to funnel down to his garret the thinking murmurs, the trialled whispers of the Nightingale. He turned to that higher floor like a koncheomancer pressing against a shell for some rumour of the sea.

He heard the thin thunder of doves under slate, the earthquakes of spring-carts striking cobbleskulls, the rising roar of barter and banter, flattery and fatuous talk, threaded throughout with the discontenting repetition of his own words (tankards beating time like marching feet, lungs breathing defiance of harmony and melody alike, a formless rising tide). But no Nightingale.

Excelsior wore out his hopes and heart, burned all oil, spilled all ink. He crafted song after song, and even through his desperation he knew he had never written anything so fine. But the rare and blessed music was ashen beneath his pen.

Had it been this word, this note, this barest suggestion of weight or fire? In some way he had miswritten, misjudged.

Cautious even in despair, Excelsior shredded the gossamer spell into cheap sentiment and tramping rhythm, and sent it by nip-fingered courier below where, unintended, the words fell like fire-inches, like sparks in kindling.

The rooms of roses burn,
The lanterns are turned high.
Petty Street, long starved for light,
Lifts a ravening eye.

Few souls huddled in the dense miseries of Owl Abbas had ever mustered the will, the flash of flame, to strike out against the rule of the Palace Aster. What else, after all these centuries, had they to compare it to? They laboured, and they died. Even the clockmaker had only left, the better to complete her masterpiece: a singer that would conform faithfully to the restrictions and requirements of the Guild.

And then she had sent the Nightingale into the heart of Owl Abbas.

Oh, Petty Street and Agnes Lane, the Maresnest and the guildhalls had not *listened*. But they had heard. The Nightingale's voice had threaded through the work of commoner singers, lulling and lilting, softening the singeing qualities even of Excelsior's misdirected ditties.

The abrupt absence of that voice was like a sinkhole in a street, a sucking emptiness tearing the fabric of Owl Abbas. The citizens did not know what they had lost, but they knew it was something vast: the view of the red snows which only the nimblest chimney-urchins had seen from afar, the rustle of star meadows through which none of them would stride, all the miles and idly strewn space the clockmaker had seen on her journey out of the city, the bright air and the silences of hills.

Through Owl Abbas, the rumour of loss spread like the slow groaning of an overburdened beam, the creak of a rookery from whose footings one stone too many has been scavenged. The city-state, close-pressed, was a bone-pile at the base of which one littlest vertebra, or smallest knucklebone, had crumbled to dust, with a breathy sighing-out of its ghost, threatening to bring the whole tumbling down. And into the silence, the strident notes of Excelsior's thoughtlessly outflung songs rattled like dice.

"Where *are* the rose rooms? Whose are the star walks?" asked brewers and road-wives, wakening to the words. The catacomb-filers, who saw the paintings on the deepest, oldest walls, said, "Surely these images aren't a dream. They are just there, within our reach. Did not we have them once? When the city was owl-quiet and the stacked houses were groves, when the Little Emperor's Council was a parliament of birds, and their auguries guided us more fairly than *this*?"

The workhalls, the orphan-rows murmured with Excelsior's songs—not the only songs of the city, but sudden-sharp and bracing—and pennies rolled into the mouths of the crank-singers. Barwashers hummed even as they watched their wakening clientele askance. Gross-bakers stamped the words with chalk-gravel and sawdust and the heels of their hands into the heavy half-day bread. Petit-bakers stretched and rolled them into the cobweb expanse of their thousand-layered sugar-dough. Seamsters and oxen-harriers who had never seen Petty Street built the words into the pattern of their bitternesses, knotted them into the whipstring lacing of coats, threaded the lyrics through the murmurations they took from door to door with barrelled oil and saffron.

"*The rooms of roses burn*," they sang.

The words had been handed down with no thought to discontent and discord, untrimmed for any fire but that which lit Excelsior's midnights.

Those who sang them did not look to the Nightingale's room above Short Street and Petty Street (home now to three little, starved seamstresses such as might have welcomed a Mechanical, Light-Widening Eye like that the clockmaker had once proposed, and the Guild had rejected). The populace looked instead to the towers where the jasmine-hawks dozed and the Palace Aster peacocks preened themselves ghost-bright on the patterned tiles; their hands tightened on the tools of their many ill-paid, bloodied trades, and their eyes grew keen.

Meanwhile, Excelsior's dulling nib and clotting ink scraped on, as if they could abrade the imagined offence.

But when Excelsior next burned his coppers, the phantom, slippery as a cough, refused the commission. The Nightingale had gone too far away. Even if Excelsior had set fire to pearls and gold—even had the reluctant ghost known beyond rumour what they were—it was too thin to waft the distance to the Palace Aster unaided, let alone freighted with music.

The banks the Nightingale's voice had carved in Excelsior's soul grew dry and the riverbed parched, weeds of ditties rank where willows of song had trailed.

Even the customary rattle and beat of Owl Abbas had grown sick and strident. The overwound springs of cart and boat shrieked, the middens steamed and smouldered.

A fever found its way into Excelsior. He could not rest. The ink dried, but he scribbled on in oil and soot; the nibs broke, and he scraped out staves with wire and nail; the paper slid from his table, the copper lay neglected on the floor and the music went to seed, etched on board and beam, glass and door.

The Phantom of the Window-sash watched, dispassionate. This would pass, and if it did not, then this scribbler would die and another take his place. Madness took scribblers just as falling took pigeon-gatherers, as cogs took mill-workers, and time took phantoms.

Once a simple temple in a grove, the Palace Aster had grown decadent and cancerous over grass and tree, over its own simpler stylings, over even the first streets of Owl Abbas.

Through gates and corridors, ballrooms that had been market squares and parlours that had been common greens, where silk and wax flowers hung now in silver baskets from gilded gallows, the Nightingale was led.

The faint messenger-spirit was wise, thought the Nightingale. This, and not the citizenry, was what the Nightingale had been designed to capture.

Through corridors the walls of which were lined with facades of plundered houses, under arched roofs painted like forgotten skies, the voicehounds brought their quarry, and handed the Nightingale over to the nobles.

They brought the Nightingale to the heights of the Palace Aster—galleries and balconies, lace bridges, the roof-walks where the denizens of the Imperial Aviary strutted and fluttered to the accompaniment of flautists imported to teach them better musicality.

Into a chamber scrubbed clean of its last inhabitant the Nightingale was taken, and there washed and oiled, polished and gowned, clad in velvet the colour of the mountains, the tint of the light that had burned in the little room above Petty Street.

"We have found the voice you sought," the courtiers told the Little Emperor, while the voicehounds, ignored, circled and grumbled among themselves, gnawing out their bitterness in the words they'd heard sung in the streets.

The finest composers (brought long since to the Palace Aster and left to languish in corners and gardens) were discomposed and discommoded, divested of sheets of chorales and anthems.

These were finished, polished things, every nuance of voice directed, and for all the Nightingale's powers the music had the staid elegance that Excelsior's lacked.

But only the voicehounds noticed anything amiss. The Little Emperor was already bored.

Lust and love and loss; hopeless naïveté and ground-down wisdom; soot-etched, fire-branded, blade-cut, wheel-crushed, ill-rested, underfed. Thus the merry folk of Owl Abbas.

To them, the high, dying falls, the heart-cries Excelsior had intended for the Nightingale, took new meaning. This is what the songs proclaimed: the lily-towers, the jasmine-hawks, the Little Emperor and the Palace Aster must, should, *would* fall.

Excelsior, racked by sickness, heard voices raised in Petty Street. It was music, he realised, of a sort. A passion greater than that of youth, more violent than that of love.

I could write for this, he thought, tracing twitching marks in the dust of his garret floor, barely alarming the little spiders that had begun to blanket him.

Excelsior, so poorly fitted to be a revolutionary, such an unwitting conductor of dissent, tapped on the floor a martial drumbeat that only the Phantom of the Window-sash, frowning, felt. If a musical affair high above the streets might have disturbed the rooftop dwellers, a burning of roofs—whether in a fit of revolutionary enthusiasm or political retribution—was infinitely more to be deplored.

The ghost was dimly aware that this, after untold years and hauntings, might be its end: sifting as ash down on broken spring-carts. That this was likely also to be Excelsior's end did not overly concern it.

But oh, this had been too great a mischief.

Having mustered a faint discontent, it slipped out by the window and wafted over the greasy canals, through slums and barricades, borne on the breath and voices of marchers, lifted by the songs of bakers (their long, heat-hardened bread-boards carved to spears), tossed by the shouts of dungmen redolent with ire.

Through gardenia paths waxen with bodies and over palisades spiked with sabres, it drifted into the Palace Aster. It blew like the dust of cobwebs among marvels and mosaics, unmoved by the unmaking of wonders.

Withering, it thought at last of the view from the room in Petty Street, and of the high widowing-walks of the palace, where one might see a mountain glowing red as a lantern.

Finer than thistledown, the phantom tumbled in the currents of bonfire-warmed air up the twisting stairs, and sighed, finally, against the finely turned ankles of the silent Nightingale.

Set free to haunt the Palace Aster with every other creature, curiosity and concubine marked with the Imperial seal, fragmenting its talent in the mirrored arcades of the Palace Aster, the Nightingale knew nothing of revolution.

It had been sent to win the heart of Owl Abbas. First, yearning back to its maker's mountains, the Nightingale had believed itself shaped merely to capture that heart with beauty.

Then the singer had thought itself to be kidnapper and assassin, but here it had reached the centre and found nothing to bear away. The Little Emperor was merely a man, and could contain the city-state only by letting it slip endlessly through his hands. An ear and heart so lightly lifted were as easy to grasp as smoke. Ringed as they were by flame and riot, they would soon become smoke in truth.

Now, the Nightingale lifted its visitor like a snowflake, save that a snowflake would not have melted moment by moment on the cold brass of the singer's palm.

"Strange spirit," said the Nightingale, tuneless. "My maker-mistress sent me to bring back the heart of Owl Abbas. But it is too vast for me to carry, and too bright. See how the walls shine, like my lantern."

The voice that had never before spoken without singing scraped the Phantom's being like steel on porcelain. It writhed a little, weakly.

"I listened to you once, and here I am," said the Nightingale. "I will not say you led me astray. It was I who was not adequate to my task. Am I to follow you again?"

They left the Palace Aster of the heights and followed the groaning of draughts through tower and tunnel. They departed the halls and salons where mirrors splintered and paintings bubbled, and crept into the lowest palace, that composed of cellars and basements, new and old and ancient, and each filled with the surfeit of every beauty, every luxury, every excess, and somewhere—who knows?—the dusty reliquary that contained the bones of the last idle owl.

"Perhaps the heart is here," said the Nightingale. But there was riot and looting overhead, and no time to search those unnumbered cells and dungeons.

Through storeroom and oubliette, sewer and gutter they hastened, phantom and Nightingale. They slipped past the guards, the crowds, they elbowed through mob and melee. Buildings burned around them, the cobbleskulls ascended in bone-smoke while spirit-lamps, bursting, gave up their ghosts. Once only they paused, on the street of guildhalls, to take the great signet of the Elevated Guild of Horologists and Artificers from the rubble. Then they hastened on.

Fire melted the Little Emperor's seal on the Nightingale's shoulder, and wisped shreds from the phantom like steam. And as they fled, they heard, beaten into blunt weapons, into anthems and banners, the songs of Excelsior.

Excelsior did not know what he had wrought.

There are feet upon the stair, he thought. *People will want words*. But he had none left. The ink in its well had dried to dust, the nibs rusted on the floor, spiders spun in his hair. *It is chill. Perhaps they want paper for their hearths*, he thought. *They will not find enough here*. For all the fire below, he saw frost in the window, curling from the webs he had etched there in his first passionate shyness.

They will take the copper-shavings, he thought. *Let them, someone may get use of them*. He did not even have strength, now, to burn them for the faithless ghost as a last legacy.

The door latch lifted, and a creature walked in.

The Nightingale's palace robes had been eaten away by spark and flame, threads of precious metals imparting the briefest of strength to the Phantom of the Window-sash, which clung still around the throat of silver and mahogany pipes.

The bonfire light danced like drums through the Nightingale's hollow cage of ribs, the sliding sheets of ebony and quartz that shielded bellows and bells.

The Nightingale looked about the garret, read singingly the ravings etched into bench and board.

"This is the hand that wrote the songs you brought me, strange spirit," said the Nightingale. "Yet these are the words the people with torches sang, all through the streets. I heard these in the idle-rooms of the Palace, and this in the tearooms past which the voicehounds brought me. You led me a dance, spirit, but perhaps this is the room on which Owl Abbas now centres, after all, and I shall have earned the signet seal we took."

Kneeling with a beautiful spinning of weights and wires, the Nightingale peered at Excelsior and said, "It cannot live longer, I see, as people live. Can it live as you?"

The phantom undulated impolitely.

"No," agreed the Nightingale, without reproach. "I see it lives as you do even now. Wishing nothing to change, wishing power beyond what it was built for."

The long decorative fingers, designed to accompany music and elaborate a beat upon the air, now probed the skull, the throat, the diminishing softnesses that still enclosed Excelsior.

"How does one get in?" the Nightingale asked the phantom. "How were you drawn out of your shell?"

It could not answer the question, even if it had cared to. Hatred, love, unstretched wings, habit? They had all eroded so long ago.

The Nightingale calculated. It had never had cause to be fitted with the knowledge of where ghosts come from. They infested the city in much the way of the seasonal senates of ash-pigeons and the sub-kingdom of rats, but now all the nests and roosts were in disarray. The city was rearranging itself, and who knew what would pour into its new emptinesses, as a singer stretches the air to let the listener's heart fall in.

"Ah, that at least I have done before," the Nightingale said. "It is all I have ever done."

Among the broken nibs, the slivered coins, the fraying quills, the Nightingale sought fragments that would fit its need: glass shards and a penknife not entirely rusted.

"You will understand," the Nightingale said to Excelsior. "There is fire below the stairs. Owl Abbas is shedding all that was. So, too, are you. But like a clock I must hasten time a little."

"Are you death?" murmured Excelsior. "I thought death would be an old thing. But for all the soot on you, you shine."

"You know me, songwriter," said the Nightingale. "Listen, and hurry."

"I cannot move," said Excelsior. "What can I do?"

"You will understand, and know the urgency," said the Nightingale.

Carefully, counting its own seconds, the Nightingale unpicked the lock in its own breast, and opened first the cage of its ribs, and then the cabinet its master had installed there. It drew out the little drawer, cushioned in velvet. And as it did so, the Nightingale sang.

It was only a slight essay in scales, simple and hampered by the smoke in the bellows, the discord in a wire that had been jangled in the crowds.

"I know that music," sighed Excelsior, and his fingers wandered over the dust of the floor. "I had meant to write such songs for you as would spill the city over with meaning, and pull hearts from their moorings."

"You did," said the Nightingale. "Now, I must unmoor your heart."

"You already have," Excelsior began to say, with no more volume than the watching ghost. But the Nightingale parted his ragged shirt and with careful, unshaking hands opened flesh and muscle and bone. How little blood, and how thick, spilled on the floor. Not enough to save even a small phantom, though it chased several even older wisps, of the sort that flutter in the dust about bedposts, away.

"Your heart alone would fulfill my errand," said the Nightingale, lifting out that flinching organ, "but we might make something new entire, you and I: a thing I was not built to invent and you would not live to try. What my maker will make of that, I do not know."

To the third member of their company it said, "Will you show him how to *be* as you? For he must learn quickly."

The Phantom of the Window-sash, however, had no interest in further expiating its sins against Excelsior. It rumpled itself to the sill and floated in the air above the fires, breathing for the deaths of coins, ascending to the garrets-above-the-garrets, to bother pigeon-parliaments and rat-scouts a little longer, before it vanished altogether from sight.

The Nightingale stowed Excelsior's gory heart and gathered up the trailing threads of his horrified, bewildered spirit, tucking them neatly in place amidst the staining velvet that it had once, mistakenly, intended for the heart of the Little Emperor.

Then the Nightingale latched closed the cabinet of its chest. "There," it said, patting the metal and the panels of quartz and beaten horn. "Rest a little. I shall carry us for now."

In time, new scribblers would arise from the ashes, as would a new city and a new emperor, of whatever stature, to take the place of the one who (it would be said) had lain in state, arms full of treasures, while the Palace Aster blossomed into flame.

But for now, the city rioted and burned, and neither then nor later did it know or care that the author of its rebellion was carried out of its bounds, rocked within the ribs of the Nightingale.

"I shall learn to write songs through you," murmured the Nightingale to its little burden, as it strode out of the city gates in the shining night, and between the blue fields at dawn, "and you shall grow to sing them through me."

They reached the foothills in a glowing afternoon, where the leaves flamed copper. And it was in an evening that, singing softly a song entirely new, they climbed into the scarlet haze of the mountains and vanished at last from the history of Owl Abbas.

THE SPIRES

ALEC NEVALA-LEE

I.

> In the *English Mechanic*, September 10, 1897, a correspondent to the *Weekly Times and Echo* is quoted. . . . Early in June 1897, he had seen a city pictured in the sky of Alaska. "Not one of us could form the remotest idea in what part of the world this settlement could be. Some guessed Toronto, others Montreal, and one of us even suggested Peking. . . . It is evident that it must be the reflection of some place built by the hand of man." According to this correspondent, the "mirage" did not look like one of the cities named, but like "some immense city of the past."
>
> —Charles Fort, *New Lands*

Bill Lawson studied the silent city. The photograph in his hands was the size of a postcard, creased at the corners and brittle with age. It depicted a cascade of roofs and chimneys emerging from what appeared to be a fogbank, its upper half obscured by clouds, with something like the spire of a church faintly visible in the distance. After examining the picture for another moment, he returned it to the man on the other side of the desk. "What about it?"

The photo went back into the valise. "Have you ever heard of a prospector called Dick Willoughby?"

"Sure. An old sourdough. Before my time. Willoughby Island is named after him."

"That's right." The visitor, who had introduced himself as Sam Russell, was in his late forties, with handsome features and eyes that looked as if they had been transplanted there from the sockets of a much older man. "He claimed that every year in Glacier Bay, between June and July, a city appeared in the sky to the northwest, above the Fairweather range. He went back three times to get a picture of it. Finally, he came up with this photo. He sold copies of it to tourists."

Lawson checked to see if Russell was joking, but the older man kept a straight face. "It looks fake to me."

"Oh, it is." Russell grinned. "It's a picture of Bristol in England. Either Willoughby was deliberately lying, or somebody sold him a plate of the city and convinced him that it was taken here in Alaska. I'm inclined to think that he was a victim of a hoax. But that's interesting in itself. It means he thought that this picture resembled whatever he saw in the sky. You see?"

Lawson decided to ignore the question. "So why are you showing it to me?"

"I want you to fly me to Willoughby Island, so I can take a look for myself."

Lawson paused before responding. He prided himself on being a decent judge of character, but Russell was hard to pin down. The coat that he had hung by the door was rumpled but expensive, like his traveling case, and the bundle by his feet included a surveyor's tripod and a camera. He certainly didn't resemble the hunters or prospectors who tended to come through Juneau these days, the flow of whom had slowed to a trickle in the depths of the Great Depression.

It occurred to Lawson that the other man might be toying with him. People from the outside often assumed that the locals were simple folk, when the opposite was more likely to be the case. Seeing himself through Russell's eyes, he was aware that he didn't cut an impressive figure, with his untucked shirttail, oily jacket, and busted nose, and he felt a twinge of resentment at being mistaken for a rube. "I wonder if you're having a laugh at my expense."

"Not at all. I just want to be clear about what I'm doing. It seemed better to tell you the most ridiculous version now, so there won't be any confusion later. But I'm serious. I've spoken to other eyewitnesses, and I have good reason to believe that Willoughby did see something in the sky. Even if it's only an optical phenomenon, it's worth investigating." Russell glanced at his watch. "But I should come to the point. I'm interested in doing research on Willoughby Island, and I'm willing to pay cash up front. I've been told that the flight shouldn't take more than forty minutes, which means I'll be back in time to buy you dinner."

Lawson remembered that Russell had mentioned arriving from Seattle the night before. "You came a long way for a day trip."

"There may be a second stop. Or even a third. I'll tell you once I know more."

Lawson paused again. Two dueling impulses were at war in his mind, and he finally yielded to caution. "Sorry. I can't fly you into Glacier Bay. Nobody can. Maybe no one explained it to you, but it's a national park. I could cut you a deal on a sightseeing trip. But we can't land."

Russell absorbed the news without any visible reaction. "It has to be on the ground."

"Then you can take a boat up there. There are plenty of fisherman on the docks who might agree to it."

"That won't work. It took longer for me to get here than I hoped, and I'm at the end of my available window. I can't waste any time. If you won't take me, I'll find someone who will."

Lawson heard the unspoken implication. There were several other pilots in town who would welcome the charter, legal or not, and the plain fact, which was written on his face, was that he needed the money. He wondered if Russell could sense his desperation, and he found that he didn't want to give the other man the satisfaction, even if they never met again. "You expect to see a city in the sky?"

"Not really," Russell said. "But I want the chance. It would mean a great deal to me. And to my wife."

Lawson was about to respond when he saw a figure outlined against the window that faced the street. A moment later, the door opened, and a woman entered the office. As the two men rose, Russell introduced her. "This is my wife, Cora. She'll be coming, too. If we can reach an agreement."

The woman did not sit down. She wasn't pretty, exactly, but she had red hair, green eyes, and a face that would be hard to forget. Lawson saw that she was much younger than her husband, probably no more than thirty, and as he looked at her, he found that he had come to a decision.

Taking a seat again, Lawson began to play with the cord of the window shade behind his desk. "If we're doing this, it has to be done right. There can't be any record. I won't put it down on the flight plan."

A satisfied look began to spread across Russell's face. "What do you have in mind?"

Lawson let go of the cord. Opening a drawer, he fished out a stained topographical map, which he unrolled across the desk. Willoughby Island was an oval the size of the palm of his hand, nestled like a turtle in the blue ribbon of Glacier Bay. "Where were you hoping to land?"

Russell pointed. "The southern tip. It's where the most credible sighting took place."

"We can't. The shore is too bold. There's nowhere to tie up the plane." Lawson indicated an area to the northeast. "There's a cove here. Maybe even a floating dock. A fox farm used to be there. It might even be worth my while to check it out." He glanced down at Russell's shoes, which turned out to be a pair of good boots. "You'll have to hike four miles along the beach. It shouldn't take more than a couple of hours. We can still get you home by dinnertime."

Russell glanced at his wife, who gave him a short nod. "When can we leave?"

"Ten minutes after I get paid." Lawson rolled up the map. "Normally, the charter would come to seventy dollars apiece. Let's call it eighty, given the risk of trouble on my end."

Before he had even finished speaking, Russell pulled out his wallet, counting eight twenties onto the desktop. Lawson pocketed the money. "You know where the lower city float is?"

"I can find it. Let's call it half an hour. I need to make a phone call from the hotel."

"Fine with me. You're each allowed twenty pounds of baggage." Lawson stuck out a hand. "Glad to do business with you."

"Same here." Russell's grip was firm. He retrieved his coat from the peg and left with his wife, whose eyes lit briefly on Lawson's on the way out. She had not spoken a word since her arrival.

Half an hour later, they were in the plane, heading out into the channel for takeoff. On his way to the docks, Lawson had made a stop at the grocer. It had been a lean couple of months, and he had been tempted to stock up on treats, restricting himself to a bag of sandwiches, a Horlick's rum fudge bar, and a few squares of mintcake, one of which he devoured in front of the store.

His plane, a yellow and blue Stinson on Fairchild floats, occupied a rented hangar at the southern end of town, past the docks on high pilings where boats and fishing vessels were tied up at the pier. As he descended the wooden steps to the shoreline, he had been pleasantly conscious of the bills in his pocket, as well as the expectation that there might be more to come.

Somewhat to his surprise, Sam Russell and his wife had turned out to be familiar with the rituals of departure. Without being instructed, they kept their bags on their laps, placing the weight toward the front of the plane, and as he opened up the engine and rocked the stick back and forth, his passengers swayed along with it, helping him to jockey the floats up onto their steps for takeoff.

They broke loose from the surface, the water rising in a fine spray around them, and then they were airborne. As the plane climbed, Lawson looked back at the others. "We'll fly over Douglas Island to the channel, then head across the Chilkat Range. Should be on our way down in half an hour."

Russell nodded and returned his gaze to the window. Cora kept her eyes fixed on the landscape below.

Lawson turned to the windshield again. He decided to take a scenic route, bending up and around the Beartrack Mountains before heading down into the bay. He suspected that the Russells would be gone before long, but there was still the outside chance that they might decide to stay. A pilot could survive on just one regular charter, and if he failed to land this one, it might be his last chance for a while.

The flight passed without any conversation. Below them spread a spectacular vista, with the forests on the mountainsides giving way to the snowfields of the ridge top, which was white even in the middle of July. The glaciers descending to the sea, with their compressed layers of thousands of years of ice and snow, were a deep emerald. It was a sight that could reduce even the most jaded travelers to awed silence, but if the Russells were impressed, they kept it to themselves.

Before long, they neared their destination. Lawson zeroed in, checking the approach as he circled around toward the cove. The island was four miles from north to south, the thick spruce woods on its eastern edge ascending to low mountains, bounded on all sides by the waters of Glacier Bay. To the northeast were two smaller outlying islets, one of which was joined to the larger island by the gravel bar where he planned to bring them down.

As they descended, Lawson saw that the floating dock was still there. He made the landing upwind to reduce his forward speed. Once the floats were on the water, he cut the propeller as low as it would go and steered the plane like a boat to the pier, where he cut the engine and climbed out.

As Lawson secured the lines, Russell and his wife picked their way toward the shore. Gulls were pecking on the pebble beach, and a flock of murrelets circled overhead. The temperature was in the high forties, with just a few tufted clouds to the south, although he knew that the weather could change without warning.

Lawson tied up the plane and went to join the couple, up by the fox farm that stood against the thin black trunks of the spruce. It consisted of a log cabin, a warehouse, and a line of trap houses stretching along the edge of the water. Islands throughout the state had been leased to raise blue foxes in the twenties, with the animals left to roam freely before being trapped. The depression had destroyed the fur market overnight, and now most of these farms were abandoned.

Going closer, Lawson saw that Russell and his wife seemed tense, but he knew better than to comment on it. "Everything good?"

Russell turned south. "I'll hike down there on my own. Cora will stay behind to get some work done. The log cabin looks sound enough. I assume that you'll stick with the plane?"

Lawson nodded. "I'll pick through these shacks to see if there's anything worth saving. But I can get you set up here first."

This last remark was addressed to Cora, who looked back coolly. "I'll be fine."

It was the first time she had spoken to him directly. He looked back without lowering his eyes. "You know where to find me. I'd like to be in the air by eight, so we can get back before dark."

"Then I'd better be on my way." Russell appeared to hesitate, as if hoping that Cora would decide to come along after all, but she only picked up her bag and walked toward the cabin. He hefted his own pack onto his back, balancing the tripod on one shoulder, and began to hike down the beach. After a minute, he rounded the bend in the shore and was gone.

Lawson saw that Cora had already entered the cabin and closed the door behind her. He headed off, whistling tunelessly, and made his way to the warehouse that stood nearby.

For the next few hours, he explored the farm at his leisure, pausing in the late afternoon for a sandwich and another bite of mintcake. He had hoped to find some tools or equipment to use or resell, but it had all been picked clean. The warehouse was bare except for two chairs, a chopping block, and a vat that had once been used to cook salmon heads into feed for the foxes.

He stuck his head into the nearest trap house. It was nailed together out of unfinished lumber, four feet to a side, with a ramp leading up to an entrance on the second level. Food had been set out twice a week. When it was time to harvest the pelts, a cleat holding up the floor was removed, allowing it to tilt down under the fox's weight, depositing it into the trap on the lowest level. Then a counterweight would return the floor to its original position, ready for its next victim.

As he was picturing this, Lawson felt the walls of the shack vibrate around him. Stepping outside, he saw that the wind had picked up, and the birds on the beach had vanished. He turned to the south. At some point over the last hour, the clouds on the horizon had grown darker and more threatening.

Lawson sized them up. Then he went up to the cabin and rapped on the door. After a pause, Cora spoke from inside. "Come in."

He entered the cabin, which was a cramped, dim space with bare beams crossing the ceiling. Cora had hung her coat from one of the pole racks, and as she rose from the table by the window, where she had been writing something in longhand, he saw that she was wearing a white collared shirt under a wool sweater and a tight pair of trousers. "What is it?"

Lawson stuck his thumb toward the sound of the wind. "You'd better go up the beach to look for your husband. If you see him, tell him to hustle. Don't go too far. If he doesn't show up soon, we'll be here overnight."

Without waiting for a reply, he left the cabin and headed toward the dock. The wind was sending up a noticeable chop, and the plane was beginning to bob up and down on its lines.

Lawson set to work at once, winding a cable around the float struts and the forward spreader bar and securing it to the pilings. He tied additional ropes to both wings, and then he used the bilge pump to fill the pontoons with water. Finally, he got out his overnight gear. In the back of the Stinson, there was a bundle of egg crate slats that he kept for makeshift repairs. He stuck them under his arm, sealed up the plane, and headed back to the fox farm.

A light rain was falling. Checking the log cabin and the warehouse, he saw that both seemed reasonably sturdy. After a moment's thought, he went into the cabin and set down his equipment. Using a mintcake wrapper for kindling and a few of the wood slats, he started a fire in the barrel stove. Then he pulled up a chair, lit a cigarette, and settled in to wait.

Cora returned fifteen minutes later, her hair plastered against her head from the rain. "He's not back?"

Lawson motioned toward the second chair. "You should rest. No point in taking off in weather like this. We're spending the night, no matter what happens." He anticipated her next question. "I'll sleep in the warehouse. There are two more bags. If we're lucky, your husband will make it back before dark."

He offered her a smoke, which she took. Sitting close to the fire, she looked toward the shuttered window. Outside, the rain was lashing down in sheets. Lawson ground out his cigarette. "If he's smart, he'll find somewhere to wait out the storm. He should do fine under the trees, as long as he's got wool socks and underwear. It shouldn't get much below forty. Once this blows over, he can follow the shoreline back. Not much of a chance he'll get lost."

Cora didn't respond. After a minute, he handed her one of the sandwiches, which she took, and offered her a swig from his flask, which she declined. As the wind howled against the cabin like a living creature, Lawson tried to get her mind off of it. "How long have you been married?"

For a second, Cora looked as if she hadn't understood the question. "Six months."

He wanted to ask how she had ended up with this man, but he bit it back. "I guess this wasn't the honeymoon you wanted."

For the first time, she smiled at him. "Actually, it's exactly what I had in mind."

Lawson wasn't sure what to say in response. On the table, Cora had spread out a few pages of handwritten notes, along with the photo of the silent city. He indicated it. "You really believe in all this?"

Cora followed his eyes, then looked back. "Are you married, Mr. Lawson?"

Lawson grinned. "Not exactly. Not a lot of eligible girls where I'm from."

"If you were married, you'd know that it doesn't matter what I believe." She paused. "Sam and I have more in common than you might think. We're both stubborn. It's hard to get an idea out of his head, even if he has to go halfway across the world to prove it. I'm the same way."

"What does he do for a living?" Lawson asked. "He wasn't too clear on the subject."

"He's a writer," Cora said. "You might say that he's a kind of journalist. For a while, he was working for Scripps Howard. I think you have a mutual friend there. A columnist named Ernie Pyle?"

Lawson recognized the name. In better times, reporters had come up to Juneau once every couple of months to get fresh copy, and he had taken a few of them on glory hops into the interior. "Are you a writer, too?"

"You might say that. Sam and I are working on a book. This will be one of the chapters. Assuming—"

She broke off. For the first time, he saw the strain in her face. "Are you worried?"

"No." Cora glanced at the shutters, which were shaking against the frame. "Sam can handle himself. He doesn't take anything for granted. And maybe this will even teach him a lesson."

She stood abruptly. "I'm very tired. If we're staying here, I'd like to go to bed."

"Of course." Lawson picked up his bag. "There's firewood in the corner. You can come get me if you need anything."

Cora held his gaze. "Thank you. I'm sure I'll be fine. Good night, Mr. Lawson."

"Good night." Lawson left the cabin, shutting the door, and heard her slide the bolt home. Then he crossed the short distance to the warehouse, his shoulders hunched against the rain.

Once he was inside, he hung his coat from the rafters to dry. There was a stove in the corner, but instead of lighting a fire, he rolled out his sleeping bag and climbed in, listening to the wind whistling overhead.

Lawson closed his eyes. He had not expected to fall asleep at once, but he did.

A few hours later, he sat up in the darkness. It took him a moment to remember what had pulled him out of sleep. He had been dreaming of the foxes. They had stood in a ring around the warehouse, their golden eyes shining in the darkness, and when he had gone out to meet them, he had seen a woman in their midst, her body white, her red hair tumbling down her back.

She had beckoned him. He had followed, his desire stirring, and his steps had carried him to a trap house on the shore. A voice in his head had screamed at him to stop, but he had continued on, walking up the ramp toward the black hole of the door. He had entered, the smell of blood strong in his nose, and it was only when the floor fell out from under his feet that he knew—

Lawson shook his head, coming fully conscious, and only then did he realize what had awakened him. He had heard a noise from outside. A second later, it came again, faintly audible over the wind rattling the building. It was the sound of wood splintering and breaking.

He climbed out of his bag, stuffed his feet into his boots, and yanked his coat from the rack. Stumbling out of the warehouse, he ran down the slope of the beach to the water. The wind had risen to a full gale, and the rain was pouring down hard, but when his eyes adjusted to the dark, he saw that two of his lines had come loose, and the plane was standing on its nose in the water.

Lawson sprinted forward. Before he had covered ten paces, there was a crack, and the plane was borne up by the wind. It did a loop and a snap roll, as if controlled by unseen hands, and then it plummeted and crashed with a shudder into the gravel bar at the end of the island.

II.

> Every year, between June 21 and July 10, a "phantom city" appears in the sky, over a glacier in Alaska. . . . Features of it had been recognized as buildings in the city of Bristol, England, so that the "mirage" was supposed to be a mirage of Bristol. . . . It is said that, except for slight changes, from year to year, the scene was always the same.
>
> —Charles Fort, *New Lands*

Cora found him early the next morning. Lawson had managed to get the plane partway up the slope of the beach, and he was laying out his equipment on the shore when she approached, wrapped up in her coat and scarf. "Sam didn't come back last night. Have you—"

She broke off as soon as she saw the extent of the damage. "Can it still fly?"

Lawson straightened up. He was aching all over, and this wasn't a conversation that he particularly wanted to be having. "Not like this. A chunk came off the tip of the propeller. One of the wing struts is buckled, the ribs are broken, and there's a big crack in the windshield. We're stuck. For now."

Cora appeared to consider this, the wind carrying strands of hair away from her face. "Have you radioed for help?"

Lawson didn't bother saying that he had spent the last few hours trying not to lose the plane altogether. Instead, he gestured at the radio that he had started to unpack. "Give me a hand."

Cora listened to his instructions, her lips pressed tightly together. Lawson had already cut a pole from timber on the beach, and he told her how to unwind and string up the antenna. As Cora held the pole upright, he fiddled with the receiver unit. It was a used Lear set that he had bought last year, after the Civil Aviation Authority had mandated that two-way radios be installed on all planes. Until then, he had relied, like most bush pilots, on his telegraph keys, and he still had doubts about the new system, which had proven distinctly unreliable.

The receiver was silent. Not even static. He gestured for Cora to move the pole to another spot on the beach as he switched to the transmitter unit. Checking the dials, he saw nothing. He fiddled with it for a few minutes, then stood up. Either there was a faulty component, which would mean taking it all apart and testing each piece, or the entire set was out of commission. In either case, it meant that they weren't likely to get any help from that direction.

Cora set down the pole. "Someone will look for us if we don't come back, right?"

"Normally, sure." Lawson rose. "If a plane doesn't turn up on time, they'll wait one day, maybe two, before starting a search. But not here. You heard what I told your husband. It's illegal to land in a national park. I didn't put our destination on the flight plan. As far as anybody else knows, we went on a scenic circle tour over the glaciers. No one will be looking for us on Willoughby Island."

Lawson fished out his cigarettes, which he had kept safe in an inside pocket. He saw that he had seven left. When she refused his offer of one, he lit it for himself and shook out the match. "We have two options. Either we wait and hope that somebody stumbles across us by accident, which doesn't seem too likely. Or we fly out of here on our own wings."

Cora studied the wreck of the Stinson on the shore. "You can fix it yourself?"

"Sure," Lawson said. "I've seen worse. But I don't know how long it will take. It sure won't be today. We've got enough food to last for a while. So you might even say we're lucky."

Her face hardened into a look of resolve. "I'm going after Sam. Are you coming?"

"You go ahead. I've got to stay with the plane." Lawson stooped to pick up a five-gallon can. "Take this to the cabin. Our emergency rations. Rice, hardtack, bullion cubes, milk powder. There are matches and flares, too. When you go out, bring some matches. If you need help, light a fire on the beach. Use spruce boughs. They should give you plenty of smoke. I'll come for you."

"Thanks." Cora took the can into her arms and headed for the cabin, picking her way up the sand. Lawson looked after her, waving away the mosquitos, until she was out of sight. Then he glanced up at the sky again. The gulls were back, and the air was calm, but he knew how quickly that could change.

He turned to the plane, trying to get his thoughts in order. Most of the repairs were fairly routine, but the propeller presented a trickier problem. Six inches had broken off one of the laminated wood blades. If he tried to take off with an unbalanced propeller, the forces could rip the engine right out of the plane, and if he couldn't get it working again, nothing else would matter.

Keeping that fact tucked in the back of his mind, Lawson set to work. He drilled holes on either side of the break in the windshield and laced them together with wire, patching up the makeshift suture with tape. Earlier that morning, he had found an old gas can in the warehouse. After flattening it out, he nailed it to the top of the wing spar, then folded it over the leading edge and fastened it to the bottom. The result was a kind of truss that he hoped would keep the wing together long enough for him to cover the fifty miles to Juneau.

Lawson took a step back to assess the battered Stinson, which had consumed so much of his life for the last decade. He had come to Alaska at twenty, a restless kid drawn to the blank page of the north, and had learned to fly planes on his own time while working at a reindeer slaughtering plant. Finally, he had gone into business for himself, buying a wrecked plane for a dollar and raising the money to fix it up from local store owners and dentists, all of whom believed that Juneau was bound to benefit from its position on the map.

They had been half right. Lawson had been at an age when he believed that he was bound to do well if he worked hard enough, but the depression had made nonsense of his intentions. For a while, he had flown fish trap patrol for the canneries, and when that had dried up, he had turned to less reputable charters. Reporters didn't come on glory hops these days, so he ferried men out to the mines instead, sometimes serving as a kind of unofficial recruiter, going to beer parlors and cigar stores and asking the owners to point out customers whose pockets were empty.

Then there were the really bad jobs. Once he had flown three prostitutes to a shack on floats that was towed from one mine to another. The youngest had been no more than sixteen. Another profitable charter, if it was available, was flying a dead body home, which was guaranteed to pay both ways. One time he had retrieved a fisherman who had been decapitated when his scarf was caught in a turning shaft. He had carried the head back in a hatbox.

Lawson blinked away the memory. He still had to fix the cabane strut that held the wing to the fuselage. With some difficulty, he managed to straighten it out, using an old axe handle as a splint, which he bound securely with more wire. When he was done, he removed the propeller and wrapped it up, along with the broken tip. All the while, he kept a mental tally of the cost of the repairs, which would more than swallow up whatever he had hoped to earn from the Russells.

He ate half of his fudge bar and smoked a cigarette before heading back for the cabin, the propeller tucked under one arm. In his other hand, he carried his combination gun, which he had retrieved from under his seat in the cockpit. It was what the locals called a game getter, with both rifled and shotgun barrels, and holding it made him feel marginally less helpless.

Lawson knew that there was no way that his partners would cover the cost of fixing the plane. He hadn't taken a salary in years. Instead, they paid him with stock in the company, which was effectively worthless. To survive, he dug clams and occasionally lived off his emergency rations. He had always accepted that he was on his own, but he didn't know how much longer he would last. There always came a time when the world was done feeding you, and then you were ready for the trap house, the floor falling from beneath your feet when you least expected it.

A stiff wind was blowing, making it hard for sound to travel. There was no sign of Cora or her husband. Lawson went into the warehouse, where he set his gun on the chopping block and unwrapped the propeller. It would be best, he saw, to make a pattern of the broken tip, which would allow him to figure out where to cut down the other blade. He didn't have a pencil or paper, but then he remembered the notes that Cora had spread across the table in the next building.

He left the warehouse and entered the cabin, which was empty. There were a few unused sheets of notepaper and a pencil by the window, along with a pile of other documents. Lawson was picking up a blank page when his eye was caught by a newspaper clipping at the top. It was an article from the Washington *Daily News*, dated earlier that year, and it carried Sam Russell's byline.

Lawson looked at it for a long moment. He knew that he needed Russell and his wife more than they needed him. If he got them out of here in one piece, he might be able to make one last try for their business. And the best way to win them over was to figure out what they really wanted.

Going to the door, he bolted it. Then he sat down at the table and began to look at the papers more carefully, hoping that they would tell him something more about the couple he had flown to the middle of nowhere.

The first few clippings were all accounts of the silent city, taken from periodicals like the New York *Tribune* and the *Journal of the Royal Meteorological Society*. There were pages torn from books by Miner Bruce and Alexander Badlam, and a thick volume by a writer named Charles Fort. Then came several scientific papers, one by Oliver Heaviside, another by J.J. Thomson, and a third with the translated title "Simplified Deduction of the Field and the Forces of an Electron Moving in Any Given Way." Lawson tried to read it and quickly gave up.

But the other articles were easier to understand. So was the final item that he found, buried under the rest of the material. It was Russell's wallet. Lawson had already invaded the man's privacy in other ways, so it seemed like only a small step from there to looking inside. Taking out all the bills, he rifled through the stack. There were at least three hundred dollars.

Lawson was tempted. He didn't think that he could take all of it, but peeling off a few twenties didn't seem unreasonable, if only as compensation for the plane. In the end, it was the memory of Russell's strangely old eyes that decided him. Russell was the kind of man, he reflected, who would keep track of what he carried. And perhaps there would be better ways to get at the money.

He stuffed the bills into the wallet again. Taking out the broken tip of the propeller, he traced it carefully on the page, then put the pencil back where it had been lying on the table. His best hope was to cut down the other tip so that it matched. There was no balancing machine between here and Juneau, so he had to eyeball it as close as he could and hope that it would get him off the ground.

It was growing dark by the time Cora returned. Lawson had put a pot of rice on the fire, and he was smoothing down the rough edges of the broken tip as he waited for it to finish cooking. Earlier, he had gone outside and looked toward the mountain range to the northwest, but he had seen nothing unusual in the sky.

Lawson glanced up as the door opened. Cora seemed exhausted, her hair loose around her face, and he was suddenly reminded of his dream from the night before. "No luck, I take it?"

She shook her head. Collapsing into a chair, she accepted a cup of broth, and when the rice was ready, she ate a bowl of it without speaking. Lawson saw that she was holding herself together, but he still chose his next words with care. "If he doesn't get back tonight, I can come with you tomorrow, as soon as I get the propeller back on the plane. He's probably just lost in the woods."

"Sam's not lost," Cora said tonelessly. "All he had to do to find his way back was follow the shoreline north. If he didn't come back here, it's because something happened to him."

"We aren't going to find him in the dark. If he doesn't turn up, we can take the plane to Juneau and come back with a real search party. If I can get us off the water, we'll make it to town. And if not—"

Lawson stopped. Looking into her face, he saw real fear there. Even if Russell came back, she might not want anything to do with Alaska again, and this was the best chance he would ever have to convince her otherwise.

He broke what was left of the fudge bar in two and offered her the larger piece. After a beat, she took it. Lawson chewed on his own half for a minute before speaking again. "I wanted to ask you something."

Cora glanced at him warily. They were seated close to the barrel stove. "What?"

"I want to know what you're really doing here. Your husband gave me his version, but I don't think that he came all this way to prove that some old sourdough saw a mirage." Lawson fed a chunk of wood into the fire. "I've seen strange things over the ice. All pilots have. There's nothing unusual in that."

Cora seemed to weigh her words. "This isn't an ordinary mirage. It's what they call a Fata Morgana. I'll show you."

She took a piece of paper and the pencil stub from the table. For a second, she seemed to study the pencil in her hand, and then she turned to him again. "You're sure you're interested?"

Lawson gave a slight shrug. "It passes the time. And I like hearing you talk."

He saw her blush. Cora lowered her head and drew a diagram on the page. "It's called a superior mirage, which means that it appears higher in the sky than the original object. You tend to see them in cold climates, over something like an ice sheet. It causes a layer of cold air to form under a warmer area, which is the opposite of the usual arrangement. A thermal inversion."

As she spoke, the weariness seemed to leave her voice. "Light from the object is refracted when it hits the inversion, which bends it along the curve of the Earth. If you're in the atmospheric duct, you can see it from hundreds of miles away." She put the pencil down. "That's what Willoughby saw."

Lawson pretended to study the drawing. "And what was the object behind it?"

"Maybe nothing. A Fata Morgana can be caused by as little as a stretch of coastline or a land formation. The spires that people see are produced by turbulence in the air. Nothing more to it than that."

He decided to play his last card. "That's a pretty good story. Now tell me the truth."

Cora looked up sharply. Something was stirring behind her green eyes. "Excuse me?"

"The truth," Lawson repeated. "You didn't come here for a mirage. When I asked for the money for the charter, your husband didn't blink. He thinks there's something real here. I'm not saying I believe it. But if you're serious, you need someone like me to help you."

Cora continued to look at him. Finally, she seemed to decide. "Have you heard of a man called Charles Fort?"

Lawson remembered the name from the book on the table, but he decided not to mention it. "I don't think so."

Cora turned toward the fire. "He was a writer, too. Like Sam, but more so. He spent his life in museums and libraries, looking for accounts of unexplained events. There was a club that got together at his apartment to talk about the unknown. Fort didn't welcome the attention. He didn't like being held up as an authority. But Sam cared about him a lot. And so did I."

In the firelight, her face was difficult to read. "Fort died seven years ago. He just collapsed. Leukemia. I went to see him in the hospital before he went. It's where I met Sam. All I knew was that he wanted to take up where Fort had left off. Fort never traveled or did any investigations on his own, and he tried to cover too much at once. Sam thought that you should focus on one problem at a time. The silent city seemed like a good place to start. Fort even gave him his blessing."

"If he's spent years looking into it, why is he coming up to Alaska only now?"

"You shouldn't underestimate him. Sam wanted to put together all the pieces before he came. And he realized from the beginning that there was more to the story than even Willoughby knew."

Cora went to the table and pulled out the picture of the silent city. "Look at the photo. It's an obvious hoax. An ordinary picture of Bristol. But before Willoughby started selling it to the tourists as the real thing, other witnesses had already claimed that the city was Bristol, too. Bristol is more than four thousand miles away. There's no way that a mirage could come even a tenth of that distance. So what was it about the city in the sky that reminded them of it?"

Lawson looked at the picture again. He saw no more there than before. "You tell me."

"Bristol is a city of spires. Some eyewitnesses even claimed to recognize a church called St. Mary Redcliffe. It's got a row of pinnacles and a spire with a cross. Like this." Cora sketched a vertical column with four smaller lines projecting from the top. "The accounts differ. But they all mention the spires."

"You said that the spires were probably just caused by turbulence in the air."

"That's true of some Fata Morgana images, but it doesn't make sense here. A cold mass of air over ice would be relatively still. All of the accounts say that the city was stationary. It would hang there in the sky for more than twenty minutes. And it appears in late June and the middle of July, near the summer solstice, when sunset lasts the longest, which would draw out the phenomenon. The men who witnessed it weren't fools. Whatever they saw was real."

Lawson began to see that she was just as cracked as her husband. "So what was it?"

"There are plenty of descriptions, but they don't agree. Some witnesses say that the city looked like Bristol, but there are others who compare it to Montreal, Toronto, or even Peking. Others say that whatever it was, it wasn't European. You know what that says to me?"

Lawson had a hunch, but he was more fascinated by the light in her eyes. "What?"

"It reminds me of a famous detective story. Maybe you've read it. A voice is overheard arguing in a room. One witness thinks it was talking in German, another in English, another in Russian. None of them can speak the language themselves, but they think they can recognize it by the sound. The speaker turns out to be an orangutan." Cora smiled. "And if people say that a city looks like Bristol, Montreal, or Peking, they're really all saying the same thing without knowing it. It's something strange. Alien. Or from another time. You think I'm crazy, don't you?"

This last question took him by surprise. He wanted to warn her not to throw away her life on this, but he only shrugged. "I wouldn't know."

"I don't mind." Cora regarded him with evident amusement. "I've been doing all the talking. Tell me. What made you come out to Alaska?"

He had rarely been asked this before. "There wasn't much for me on the outside."

"That's what I thought. It draws people who have been pushed to the margins. They have nowhere else to go. The same is true of ideas. Some of us end up on the fringes. It can become a sickness. You know why prospectors go mad? It's because you have to be nuts to go looking for gold in the first place. You could say the same thing about writers. Sam and I both know this. But I love him, and I don't want to lose him. Anyway, you knew all this before I even said a word."

Cora held up the pencil. "You went through my papers. Did you take the money?"

Lawson felt his face grow warm. "You can count it. If I looked at your notes, it was because I wanted to know what the hell I was doing here. I stand to lose a lot on this trip, and I had to know why."

He came forward until they were close enough to touch. "If it matters, I believe you. Or at least that you're telling the truth. Hell, for all I know, maybe Willoughby really did see a city from the past—"

Behind him, the door of the cabin opened. When he turned, he saw the shape of a man outlined against the darkness.

"You're wrong," Russell said. "It wasn't a city of the past. It's a city of the future."

III.

> In the New York *Times,* October 31, 1889, is an account, by Mr. L.B. French, of Chicago, of the spectral representation, as he saw it, near Mount Fairweather. "We could see plainly houses . . . and trees. Here and there rose tall spires over huge buildings, which appeared to be ancient mosques or cathedrals. . . . It did not look like a modern city—more like an ancient European city."
>
> —Charles Fort, *New Lands*

Russell lowered himself into the nearest chair and began to unlace his boots. Lawson saw that he was carrying his right leg stiffly, and that something had been bound around his knee so that it strained against the fabric. Russell noticed him looking and grinned. "Give me a hand with this, will you?"

As Cora stood watching from the corner, Lawson helped the older man roll up his trouser cuff, which was stained with fresh mud. When the knee was revealed, he saw that Russell had wrapped it in a brace of some heavy material in which he had punched holes, lacing it together with the drawstring from his knapsack. Then he realized that it was the leather cover of a book, its title stamped on the spine. It was *The Book of the Damned* by Charles Fort.

Russell's grin widened. "Fort would have appreciated it. Every writer likes to think that his work will be useful."

He undid the lacing. Underneath, his kneecap was discolored by an ugly bruise, with red welts, like teeth marks, running to either side. Lawson took the flask from his pocket and offered the other man a drink, which he accepted. Then they sat in silence as Russell ate a bar of mintcake.

When he was done, Russell looked at his wife for the first time. "I'm sorry, Cora."

Cora remained standing. She seemed visibly relieved but also determined to tamp it down. "What happened?"

Russell laughed. "The next time I act like I know what I'm doing, just whisper the name of this island in my ear." He looked ruefully at his sprained knee. "I didn't see the storm coming. By the time it hit, all I could do was hunker down in the woods. I spent the night there. It wasn't too bad. When I set out in the morning, I slipped on a patch of mud, and my knee came down on a foothold trap that someone had thoughtfully placed at that very spot."

Lawson nodded. "The trap houses get most of the foxes. For the rest, you use snares. And for the really stubborn ones—"

"—you set out steel traps," Russell finished. "I guess that makes me a stubborn fox."

He tested his leg and winced. "When I went down, I was probably two hundred paces from shore. It took me half the morning to cobble a brace together. I still can't put any weight on it. Even with the tripod as a crutch, I didn't get to the beach until it was almost dark. You were looking for me?"

"I spent all day calling for you," Cora said quietly. "Shouting into the wind."

"We must have just missed each other. I didn't mean to worry you. Maybe it serves me right. But I got what I needed."

Russell unbuttoned his shirt and withdrew a folded map, which he had been careful to keep dry. Cora was avoiding her husband's eyes. Lawson wondered if she would say anything about what had passed between them, but he also saw that it didn't matter. As Russell opened the map, he had the look of a man who was ready to stake everything he had on it, like a prospector about to pour his life into a doubtful claim, even if countless others had failed there before.

Taking a pencil and a ruler from his bag, Russell drew a line from the southern tip of Willoughby Island toward the western slope of Mount Fairweather, extending it deep into the interior. Then he drew a second line from the island to the eastern edge of the mountain, covering the same distance. He connected the far ends of the lines to make a triangle. The result enclosed a narrow wedge of territory, roughly four hundred miles long and a hundred miles across, with its vertex on the island itself. Russell tapped it with his pencil. "This is where we need to look."

Lawson took it in. "So that's why you came here. To narrow the search area—"

Russell set the pencil down. "Among other things. You can do a lot with an atlas and an armchair, but there's no substitute for going into the field. If the image of a city appears here every year, there must be something real behind it. And it has to be somewhere in this triangle."

He glanced at Lawson. "You understand, don't you? The city is seen above the Fairweather range by observers in Glacier Bay, which means that it lies to the northwest. But it also has to be relatively far. I took the sightings yesterday. The top of the range is three degrees above the horizon from the southern end of the island. You can add another degree or so to suspend the city in the air. Each additional degree of elevation indicates seventy miles of horizontal distance, so—"

He indicated the map again. "The original of the image, whatever it is, is a minimum of two hundred miles away and a maximum of four hundred, which is the upper range for Fata Morgana mirages. And for it to appear where it does, it has to be somewhere in this direction."

Lawson studied the area in question. "There isn't much there. Valdez is the only real town, and there are a couple of villages to the north. I can fly you out there, if you like. The plane got pretty banged up. Once I pay for the repairs, I'd be glad to take you wherever you want—"

If Russell got the hint, he didn't follow up on it. "There's nothing to see. But there might be something there one day. And it will probably appear where a settlement is now. A foothold for what will come in the future. But I don't think any of us will live long enough to visit it."

Lawson wondered if Russell and Cora both somehow suffered from the same delusion. "You lost me."

"I thought Cora explained it to you. You certainly seemed deep in conversation when I got back." Russell fixed his wife with an unreadable look. "Do you want to tell him, or should I?"

Cora took a breath. "It isn't so hard to understand. A mirage bends light rays in space. Under the right conditions, the image can travel down an atmospheric duct for hundreds of miles. *And the same thing could happen in time.* It would have to be rare. You might only see it in one place, a few times a year, at sunset. But if you're standing in the kind of duct that transmits images across time, you would see a temporal mirage of what *will* be there. Not now. But someday."

Lawson wanted to laugh. There was no reason for any sane man to settle there, much less build a city of spires. They were chasing a castle in the air. He had been doing it for years.

A second later, he realized something else. "You said that you only see it at sunset."

"That's what the witnesses say," Russell said. "In late June and July. That's why—"

"—you were in such a rush to come out," Lawson finished. "If you waited any longer, you might miss your window. That's what you told me. But you also said that you'd have me back by dinner. You were lying. No one would come all the way out here just to take some measurements. You wanted to see the city for yourself. Which means that you always meant to stay overnight."

Russell looked back at Lawson. "Yes. I wasn't sure that you'd agree to take me if it meant staying for the night. Once we were on the island, I planned to make myself scarce until dark, and then offer to pay you for the overtime. I wasn't counting on the storm. The clouds were too heavy. I didn't see anything at all. It didn't appear tonight, either. But I don't need to see it to know that it exists."

Lawson could only think of the wreckage of his plane, and how it all might have been avoided if they had made it back to town on time. Rising from his chair, he spoke evenly. "We'll be ready in the morning. Leave as much behind as you can. We aren't going to be able to carry much weight."

He left without saying goodbye. Outside the cabin, he stuffed his hands into his pockets, the rage now spreading freely through his body. They had played him for a fool, and he wanted to have nothing to do with either of them.

Lawson went into the warehouse and closed the door. The combination gun was still lying on the chopping block.

He picked up the gun. Hefting it, he told himself that he would only ask Russell to pay for the repairs. There was no reason to threaten violence, except as a last resort. He had the upper hand. They weren't going back without him. A real town was worth more than an imaginary city.

A second later, an unfamiliar voice began to whisper in his head. It said that no one knew that the couple was here at all. The flight plan had only stated that he was taking two passengers on a scenic circle tour. He had not been required to list them by name, and he had not entered any additional remarks.

He thought again of the cash in the wallet, and how little would remain for him in Juneau when he returned, even if he managed to fix his plane. And as much as he tried, he could not push this new thought away.

There was a knock at the door. Lawson set down the gun, feeling a sudden wave of sickness. "Who is it?"

"Only me." The door opened to reveal Cora outside. "I'd like to talk to you."

Lawson took a seat, indicating the second chair by the chopping block. He tried to keep his voice steady. "Suit yourself."

Cora came in and shut the door behind her. When she saw the gun on the table, her mouth seemed to tighten incrementally, but she made no mention of it. She lowered herself into a chair. "Sam's sleeping. His knee is in pretty bad shape. He'll need to see a doctor when we get back."

"I know one in Juneau. He's pushed my nose back into place a few times. What else did your husband say?"

"He thinks I'm mad at him." Cora eyes strayed down to the gun again. "You're sure we can take off tomorrow?"

"I'll get you back if I can. Provided that we come to an understanding." When Cora failed to respond, Lawson went on. "There's a lot of damage to the plane. Since I only got caught in the storm because your husband wandered off, it seems fair that you cover the cost."

Cora appeared to take this in. "And what if we decide not to pay you anything?"

"Then we aren't going anywhere," Lawson said. "I'm happy to stay as long as necessary. There are deer in the woods. I know how to take care of myself. But I wonder if you do."

Cora smiled. "Don't try to frighten me. We've been through more than you know."

She took out a wallet, removed a wad of bills, and set it on the table. Lawson didn't reach for it yet. Returning the wallet to her pocket, Cora seemed to feel something else there, which she withdrew. It was the map. She unfolded it on the tabletop, handling it with a strange tenderness. "It's a shame. We aren't rich, you know. All we have is Sam's writing, and that doesn't pay much. But we still had to come here. When you met Sam, he told you that there might be another stop after this one. If you'll hear me out, I can tell you where it is."

"I don't need you to tell me." Lawson inclined his head toward the map. "You want to see the towns in that triangle. Even if there's nothing there now, you want to set foot there for yourself. But I still don't understand why."

"It's simple. These are the most likely locations where the real city of spires will appear. If it isn't Valdez, it might be somewhere else. We want to leave a message that will prove we were right. I'm still not sure what it will be. We can't make a public prediction, because that might affect the future itself. Maybe we'll bury it. Or seal it with instructions to open it under certain conditions after we're dead."

"I don't see the point," Lawson said. "Nobody alive will know you were right."

"But somebody would. That's what matters. We want people to see more than what's in front of their eyes. To look past the present. That's what Fort tried to do. If we're right about this, we can finish what he started. We can predict that there will be a city of spires where no one would ever believe it."

"That's what I don't get. You haven't said how a mirage can come back in time."

"It isn't so hard to understand. You just have to ask yourself what a mirage really is. Light travels from the Sun, strikes an object, and is refracted through the atmospheric duct to the observer. That's all. But it isn't just visible light. It's radiation of all kinds. Radio, for instance. Under the right conditions, signals that would be limited to line of sight can travel for hundreds of miles. Now imagine a class of particle that can move back in time. Let's say they're created by some kind of event at our city of the future, like a high-energy collision. Once they exist, they can travel along the atmospheric duct, just like the light from a visible mirage. And if they interact with particles in our time, we might see something. Like a picture of a ghost."

"But why would it happen at this one spot? Why wouldn't we see it in other places?"

"I don't know," Cora said simply. "But the city itself wouldn't see any trace of it in its own time, either. It might even be an accident. They would have no way of knowing that they were casting a shadow on the past. Unless, of course, someone from our time left them a message."

Lawson tried to get his head around this. "But why does it matter to you?"

Cora paused before responding. "It means that the past and the future all somehow exist together. If the future has already happened, then everything we do has already been decided. And maybe it means that the past still exists, in a way we can't explain, even after we've lost it."

She glanced out the window. "Sam understands this. If we can prove that this silent city will exist one day, it means that we're all part of a pattern. Sometimes the patterns you see aren't real, but sometimes they are. Most people avoid the places where the unknown breaks through. But some don't. Like you."

Lawson looked across the table at Cora. "You don't know anything about me."

"I don't think one person can ever know anything about another," Cora said mildly. "But you can follow your hunches. Call it intuition, or paranoia, but it's a mistake to only trust in what you know for sure."

She paused. "I've been thinking of what you said about the foxes. Most are killed in the trap houses. Snares take care of the others. For the last few, you need traps. Those foxes aren't smarter than the rest. They're just born suspicious. But what if they tried to warn the others that there was a conspiracy against them? No one would believe it. The foxes think they're being fed by a loving hand. When it kills them, they think they're unlucky. They don't realize that they were bred for it."

Cora looked at Lawson. "People are the same. They don't understand the world any more than the foxes do. That's why you need a few who see things that might not even be there. It's a delusion that allows the species to survive. Fort was one. I've tried to be another. So has Sam. We may never know what that city really is, but we have to ask. It gives us a reason to keep going. Something is coming, whether we understand it or not. Our mutual friend thought you would understand—"

Lawson felt his attention click sharply into place. "What are you talking about?"

Cora smiled. "Sam spoke with him about you. Ernie Pyle. The columnist for Scripps Howard. I gather that he took a trip with you a few years ago. He told us that you were an interesting man. Sam called him from Juneau, just before we flew out to the island, and gave him instructions in case we didn't come back. And he knew we were flying out on your plane."

Lawson became very conscious of the gun on the table. "What else did he say?"

"He said that you were the best," Cora said. "But you didn't know what you wanted. He said that he once advised you to build something for yourself. Because there aren't any old pilots in Alaska."

A long silence fell. Lawson kept his eyes on Cora. Finally, he reached for the table. Cora seemed to brace herself, but instead of the gun, Lawson scooped up the money. He took every single dollar that was there, without bothering to count it, and slid it into his pocket.

Cora didn't lower her gaze. At last, she rose and left the warehouse without a word.

Lawson didn't see either of them again until the following morning, as they prepared to depart. As he had instructed, the couple left most of their baggage behind. He saw that Cora was carrying a sheaf of papers, and that Russell was clutching his valise with the notes from the trip.

An hour earlier, Lawson had secured the propeller to the nose of the plane.

Once the passengers were seated, he headed out into the water, opening the throttle all the way. As he had feared, the propeller wasn't cutting as much air as usual. Reaching up, he grabbed a cross member over his head to get more leverage, then pulled back on the stick with the other.

At last, he felt the floats rise up on their steps. The pontoons broke loose from the surface of the water, and then they were up and away, the spray wreathing them as they ascended. Lawson exhaled. The hard part was over, and all that remained was to get back to Juneau.

He took them away from the cove. Before circling back toward the Chilkat Range, he looked north, gazing at the mountains in the distance.

For a second, he thought that he saw something outlined on the side of Mount Fairweather. When he blinked, it was gone. It had been just his imagination, or the distortion of the windshield. But in that brief instant, the future had seemed close enough to touch, and it reminded him of something that Russell had said. If the city was sending its image into the past, it might not even know it.

Lawson glanced behind him. He saw that Russell had the map out again, and that he was looking at it sadly. They would not be visiting the towns to the northwest, at least not this time around.

Cora took her husband's hand. "There will be other chances. Let it go for now."

"I know. But I'm still sorry." Russell studied the map. "I would have liked to have seen Valdez. Or—"

He appeared to pick the name of one of the other villages at random. "Or Gakona."

> *A military-funded project called the High-Frequency Active Auroral Research Program (HAARP), located on remote tundra in Alaska, jumps off the horizon just past mile marker eleven on the Glenn Highway. . . . What grabs the imagination of most, though, are the couple hundred oversized antennas. . . . Those fanged metal structures have made the sleepy, rural Alaska village of Gakona, population two hundred, a lightning rod for controversy. . . .*
>
> *Theories abound about what goes on inside HAARP, which was founded in 1990 to conduct research on the ionosphere, an upper level of the atmosphere. . . . They're studying lightning, aurora borealis, and the like. They've even learned how to induce both of those on a limited scale, according to a statement included on a Navy defense budget. . . .*
>
> —Alaska *Dispatch*, September 20, 2011

Depending on the unpredictable agendas of military scientists [conspiracy theorists claim], this group of technicians must shoot radio waves into the upper reaches of our atmosphere to create missile shields, eviscerate enemy satellites, set off the occasional earthquake, or control the minds of millions of people.

The truth is, though, that the High-Frequency Active Auroral Research Program, or HAARP . . . is nothing more sinister than a research station. . . .

—*Popular Science,* June 8, 2008

Four golden crosses are planted . . . to help a radio receiver measure ionospheric absorption. . . . A white telescope dome and a gray tangle of poles [are] used to observe the ionosphere's properties. . . .

But the most striking sight at HAARP is the facility's largest array: one hundred and eighty silver poles rising from the ground, each a foot thick, seventy-two feet tall, and spaced precisely eighty feet apart. Every pole is topped with four arms like helicopter rotors. . . .

The result is an aluminum cat's cradle, calibrated to the millimeter, that spreads out over thirty acres. Geometric patterns form and reform in every direction, Athenian in their symmetry.

It looks like a bionic forest. . . . Or an infinite nave in a futuristic outdoor church.

—*Wired,* July 20, 2009

THE HOUSE BY THE SEA

P H LEE

Would you believe me if I told you that they all live together in a house by the sea?

It would only be fair, if they did.

They can't live in the City, of course. Can you imagine? You'd be walking somewhere, maybe proceeding past the parks and public buildings, perhaps accompanied by a clamor of bells that set the swallows soaring, perhaps on your way to an orgy or a debate or to watch television, and you'd see one of them, and you'd know (of course you'd know, not that there would be anything different, not anything you could point to specifically, there'd just be something, that look—maybe it's their shoulders?—that look that people have when they've spent their childhood locked in the basement for the sake of a utopia). And once you'd seen one of them, of course you'd spend the whole day thinking about it. You'd think about that one awful field trip you took as a child, seeing them locked in a basement, mewling and promising futilely to be good, and you'd spend the whole rest of the day feeling unreasonable and guilty and ashamed. You would get no joy out of the orgies, or the parades, or the philosophy, or the remarkably good television.

And would that be joyous? Would it be the happy city we live in, the happy life we enjoy?

No. Obviously, they can't live in the City.

So, if you'll believe me, they live together in a house by the sea.

It's not a big house—it's not a mansion—but it's big enough for all of them to live in comfortably. Everyone gets their own room, and there are enough bathrooms even if some of them are touchy about sharing (some of them are touchy about sharing). They have a library and a living room and a television that doesn't get all the channels. Outside, there is a garden, and a little trail down the cliffs to the beach.

Do you believe it? Does it seem unreasonable? It wouldn't be too much to ask—don't you think?—for them to have a house to themselves with a garden and a library and a television that doesn't get all the channels.

What did you think happened to that child in the basement? What did you think happened when that child grew up?

Would it help if I told you there are a surprising lot of them living there, in the house by the sea? If you think about it, there must be. It has to be a child, crying alone in the basement that no one talks about. A baby crying in a basement is just a baby crying. An adult crying in a basement probably did something to deserve it (not that there are any prisons in the City, of course, but still).

There is, in fact, a very narrow range of suitable ages. Three-year-olds are much too young, and by twelve, honestly, how innocent could they be? Four through ten is just about right. Right now, in the house by the sea, there are nine of them, each separated by more or less seven years. The youngest is fourteen years old, the next twenty-two years old, then twenty-seven years old, and so on. The oldest is in her sixties.

Once a day an old woman comes out to tidy up, cook a meal, and stock the freezer with burritos in case someone gets hungry in the middle of the night. It isn't her job, of course. In the City, no one has a job, except the sort of job that is meaningful and personally fulfilling, like medicine or writing novels. Still, she comes out from the City every day. Who can say why? She is an immigrant; she has her own story.

Each of them has their own routine. One of them wakes up before anyone else, walks the little trail down the cliffs to the beach, and dives into the cold gray morning ocean, alone and without fear. Another one gardens. One is writing his fourth novel. He still finishes them, revises them, sends them off, and every publishing house in the City returns them unread. Two more spend their days in the library, reading the encyclopedia out loud to each other. One watches the news. She remembers back before they had a house, and she has strong opinions about municipal politics. She makes every one of them vote, every year.

Some of them just sleep all day. Sometimes, especially when they've just arrived, they don't even leave their rooms. They cry and spit and punch holes in the walls. Most of them come out eventually, but some don't, and that's okay. No one bothers them, except sometimes to offer them a burrito.

They don't leave, although they could. Why would they?

Do you believe it now? Can this really be how they live out their lives, so close to the City that they can hear the bells clamoring and the processions proceeding? Can they really live together, in a house by the sea? No?

Let me tell you this, then. There used to be a doctor—a nice man with a real white doctor's coat, who still lives in the City—who came out to their house every Wednesday to check up on them, but that didn't work out, because he kept feeling uncomfortable and trying to euthanize them. So now, whenever one of them gets sick, a woman comes in on the train from Vallcoris. She doesn't have a doctor's coat. She just has a sweater. She doesn't know about the basement, she doesn't know about anything, not really. She just takes their pulse and asks them to cough, and leaves them with prescriptions, and no one tries to euthanize anyone.

Is that enough to convince you? Is it still too impossible, that they might just live together in their own house and their own time?

Should I tell you, then, about how they die? You see, it used to be, whenever one of them died, some nice people came out from the City to take the body away. But they were so upset—so apologetic and mumbling as they refused to meet anyone's eyes—that now no one bothers calling the nice people from the City. Instead, they bury their dead in a small plot behind the garden. They get the old shovels out of the shed, pick a spot in the garden, and begin to dig. Each of them digs, some just a shovelful, some working the whole night, sometimes together, sometimes alone. By the next day, the hole is deep enough to be a grave. They don't say anything. Not one of them needs instructions on how to mourn.

Can you believe me now? Can you believe that they live their lives and die their deaths in some semblance of peace? Can you believe that their lives are more than the basement we locked them in?

Would you like more? What more would you like? Would you rather imagine them suffering, even away from the City, away from the basement, even in their own house by the sea? Would you like to hear about screams, or nightmares, or the new one, beating herself bloody against the walls? Would you like to imagine that the house needs extra mops because, sometimes, even though they hate mops (and all of them hate mops), they can't sleep through without a mop or two to be terrified of?

Or is that not it? Are you missing something else altogether?

Would you rather hear about marches, political protests, public shaming and human rights laws? Even though we both know that never happened and we both know that it never could happen, would it comfort you, to imagine them fighting back? Would you rather hear that they all walked away from the City and never came back? Or do you prefer to pretend that they might someday return—returning, not like you did when you were fourteen and walked away and then slunk back two weeks later—not in shame, but in anger, with tank columns and cluster bombs and chains of command and theories of legitimate violence?

Believe those things, if it makes you happy. I, though, will believe that they live alone, together, in a house by the sea.

FOXY AND TIGGS

JUSTINA ROBSON

Foxy and Tiggs were at the scene. The sun beat down out of a merciless noon sky, falling on tourist, tour guide, and body alike. It fell on Foxy's lustrous fur and Tiggs' crocodilian green hide and made Tiggs' arm and crest feathers gleam with the beautiful gothic tones of an oil slick as she carefully picked over the site of the find.

Foxy shepherded the tourists back into the softly floating cocoon of their tour bus. "Back you go, folks, back you go. Crime scene here. Got to do some investigating and we'll get to the bottom of this, don't you worry." She adjusted the lie of her hotel uniform—a dinky little hat with a feather in the band that marked her as a detective inspector and a smart jacket tailored to fit her small body perfectly and provide a harness to hold the items of gear she carried. Her brush waved behind her like a huge duster, rufous red and tipped with soft cream.

Her nose twitched. The body had been out a few hours and it was starting to stink.

She wasn't the only one who thought so. Overhead, a gyre of vultures circled, stacking up one by one as they drifted in across the savannah. On the ground, Tiggs put out a claw to check the pockets of the deceased as the tourists adjusted their eyecams and leaned over the deck rails of the bus to get some good footage. It wasn't every day you saw a velociraptor investigating a murder, and since this wasn't on the itinerary or billed as an extra, it was premium gold level XP.

Foxy strolled up and down over the sandy earth but, as she expected, there were no telltales here to give the game away just yet. No footprints, no tyre tracks, no blow-patterns from hover vehicles. She was going to have to wait for Tiggs' exemplary nose to give her the facts as it hoovered up local DNA and fibres and compared them with the hotel's registry of guests and inventory of luggage.

The tour guide, a regular Earth human with a blonde crew cut and a rather fabulous waxed moustache, anxiously tapped the hull of the bus as he watched with grim fascination.

"Should I stay here? I mean, this is prime lion country. We're just lucky the lions didn't already find him. It is a him, yeah? Well, this is the home country of a particularly large pride right now. Did he—was he killed by a lion?"

Foxy watched Tiggs snort as she heard this—people often assumed Tiggs was just an animal or a bot. Foxy got past this by being a humanoid foxling, the size of an eight-year-old child, small and rounded, in every way the picture of a designed but intelligent being. Tiggs was a long four metres of saurian which looked exactly like the park 'saurs you could see in *Lands of the Lost*, albeit with less feathers and a blunter snout to fit all the telemetrics in. Tiggs enjoyed the anonymity and now played to the crowd as she flexed her hands with their huge hook claws and bent down, jaws open for a wide capture as if to consume the corpse.

The crowd ooh-ed and the bus rocked back as they recoiled. Tiggs smiled, although only Foxy could tell. Tiggs' face didn't have the mobility for expressions, but through their full-encryption powerlinks they were almost one being. They chatted privately as Tiggs stood up and made a show of stalking around, searching the local brush while at the same time picking up a bit of intel for the safari systems since she was there.

"Dumped from quite a height," Tiggs said. "Broken bones all post-mortem, some impact bruising and burst lungs full of water. Drowned. Shorts dried out but they were wet when he landed. There's droplets of salt on the ground and the leaves of this thorn tree here. Impact spread shows a bit of a roll. I'm waiting on the lab getting back to me about the water."

Foxy reassured the tour guide and helped him re-schedule so that the tourists could enjoy seeing the arrival of the clean-up crew coming for the body. "Drowned over in Pirate Booty Bay," she told him and her entranced audience.

"That's half a world away!" said a boy, awed.

"Yes, sir," Foxy agreed, "That it is. You know a lot about the hotel do you, son?"

"You have soft fur," his little sister said, leaning through the rails. "Can I touch it?"

Foxy turned and put her brush up against the rail. "Only because you asked so nicely."

"Minnie!" A horrified mother's voice. "I'm so sorry, ma'am. Minnie, we do *not* touch the little people. They are *not* toys."

Minnie was very polite with the tail, as Foxy had known she would be. She didn't mind. She'd got a track of this kid's stay and she was as nice as they came, clean, tidy, caring. She assigned each child a special access pass to a 'secret' grotto where you could dive in powersuits along the most beautiful of the ocean reefs and later wear symbiote mertails and sport in a private lagoon. As the presents arrived at the family feed, the parents cooed and calmed down, which is what she'd been going for. Even as part of the police force at the String of Pearls Magnificent Hotel, keeping guests happy was her favourite part of the job.

"Drowned off Voodoo Beach," Tiggs said, returning from her tour of the thorn trees. "No identification on him and reception says he's come in on a false ID. Quite a good one. They're promoting the DNA search out of house."

Foxy recovered her brush with a flourish and bade the tour guide farewell as the cleaner crew's glossy white and red cross rig appeared, floating down from orbit carefully to avoid disrupting the vulture tower. "Let's sign him off to them and get ourselves over there then." She took a walk over to the body and looked down at him together with Tiggs.

A young male human, well built, with some sunburn on his shoulders and nose. He had short dark hair, some body hair, although not enough to really call it hair in her opinion. Maybe he had been handsome before the bloating and the bruising set in. She wasn't sure about that. They had some in-house footage of him coming in from Kyluria Point by shuttle, and he looked like every other tourist to her, stepping out of the door into the soft, warm light of Caribae with that combination of hopeful and weary that characterised people on their second hundred years. His clothing was made by the AI house Turbulent and fit him perfectly, its mixture of clean colours and distressed cloths a popular affectation of the intergalactically wealthy. His combination showed no particular imagination. He was every inch the potential corporate spy.

"We'll assume he was dropped here so the body could be eaten," she said, straightening and hopping up the long length of Tiggs' leg to her position on the soft saddle that was part of Tiggs' uniform harness.

Tiggs grunted. The lions in question were a part of their regular work in Safari World, where they spent most of their time patrolling the vast expanses without trouble other than the odd bit of animal vetting, light fraud and a robbery or two. It was just luck that a murder investigation had kicked off in their area, but Tiggs' grunt signalled her lack of agreement on the 'luck' interpretation that Foxy had placed on it.

"Now we have to follow the whole thing through to the end, right?" Tiggs said, waiting for Foxy to settle down and get her hind paws in the bucket stirrups.

"All the way," Foxy confirmed.

"Can't hand it over to Pirate Baywatch?"

"No way. Come on, Tiggsy, this is what we're made for! We've never had our own murder before. To the Bay!"

Tiggs grumbled at the idea of flying and the idea of being on someone else's turf, the sound coming out as a growl as she set off at a run through the bush, weaving easily away from the scene and circling once at the landing site to signal the clean-up pod that it was safe for them to land—no wildlife of note around. Then she was doing what they both loved best: speeding through the hip-high grass of the plains, her feet almost silent as they struck, the wind blowing free through Foxy's whiskers, following game trails, on patrol all the way to the distant lift-off point where the orbital shuttles rose and fell twice a day.

Hotel Main Ops sent them first class private through to the Bay. They said it was so the guests didn't get disturbed, but Foxy knew they could have sent them cargo class for that. The luxury of first class was something that the Hotel itself was doing as a way of caring for them. The Hotel was its staff, just as much as its planets and its vehicles, its buildings and its life. The Hotel was all of them but bigger than them. Foxy and Tiggs had never heard the Hotel directly, but they felt it and, on occasions like this, they felt it a bit extra, a deep, lasting hug in their bones. It was good to be part of a Hotel. Foxy actually pitied the tourists who were always coming, looking, searching, leaving, combing things for every last mote of XP they could get before they had to move on.

They tried out all the luxury treatments they had time for. Foxy had a deep tissue massage. Tiggs went for a complete nanomask deep-clean of her skin and feathers and, to amuse herself, got one of her teeth gold-plated. 'Now do I look like a pirate?' she asked as they made ready to disembark, flashing the fang.

"Aye!" Foxy said and pulled down her eyepatch, which she had requisitioned with the notion it might not be a bad idea. The sunlight at the Bay was intense and there were many dark interiors at the buildings that ringed the beaches. She might need a good eye for each venue. "What about me?"

"Arrrrr," said Tiggs, making the most frightening kind of noise that Foxy expected anyone had ever heard, particularly when paired with the sight of her teeth. It was good they were in a soundproofed cabin.

"You might want to ease up on that a bit," she said as the door opened.

Their itinerary opened, hotel-style, before them, soft colours showing the ways they had to go, but instead of cocktails and sun loungers, they were headed to the last recorded places that their mystery guy had been seen.

Out at the front it was morning, and the boardwalk that ran the length of Voodoo Bay was already busy. The Bay was a very broad curl that ended with a spit of land sticking out into the ocean, pointing like a finger. On maximum zoom Foxy could see people at the tip diving into the deep water from the rocks, the glitter of drones taking their pictures like dots of light. Down the other end of things was a tall cliff into which one of the hotel guest houses was hollowed out in a series of caves. Some of these ran directly in from the sea, accessed by boat and fin; others were high above the waterline, serviced by interior lifts and private jet or glide packs. Behind them the majority of the bay was lined with shanty huts of low level and apparently no tech. There was no land side exit; you had to take a shuttle or a powerhaul to the adjoining coastal zone. She and Tiggs took a walk down to the hire shop where watercraft were loaned out, studying their inner maps of the new place as they went.

"I got a ping from the lab," Tiggs said as they walked along the sand, aware of being watched, so unusual and out of place. She returned various waves and signals from the local tritons who hosted the beach and pinged ahead for someone to talk to at the store. "They say the john is a fabricant from a shop out in the Bosphoric Chain, and not a particularly high quality one."

"Ooh, Chain stock," Foxy said. "That's slumming it, even for a spy avatar."

"They're washing him for trip data—radiation sigs, all that—to see if they can match him to a factory."

The sun on the water glittered but the breeze onshore was cool. The bay water was shallow, a pale turquoise that slowly melded into deep sapphire blue at the bay's edge.

"It was old though, for an avatar. Someone on the run?"

Tiggs nodded as they arrived at the Float Shack. "If you're stuck in an avvie that long and you get killed in one, do you, you know, do you die? For real?"

"Depends on the hosting dunnit?" Foxy said. "How far it was, how good the transmission is, how encrypted. I mean, it got through on a special guest permit—a stolen one I may add, but even so. That's not a hard data barrier, only a mild checker. You can get in and out on it. Maybe. But the host would have to have some kind of transmitter in the hotel and I'm pretty sure there aren't any. I'm askin' all the same."

The triton in charge of the shack had been updated and came out to greet them. He was a tall humanoid with a silver, sharkskin finish and many cartilaginous finny appendages, webbed fingers, but human hands otherwise for handling the gear. A triple row of ridged fins framed his face instead of hair, shielding a mass of trailing tentacles that hung to his waist in the back.

"Detective Foxy. Detective Tiggs. Welcome to the Bay. How can I help you?"

Behind him Foxy watched other tritons preparing a skim boat, loading it with picnic supplies, fishing rods and speeder skis. "Hey there, Lucas. We're looking for news of a guest that was murdered out here sometime last night, we think around one a.m. local time. Has anyone asked about someone missing?"

"No, nothing like that. We've been tracking all our gear and doing a backcheck since your shuttle sent out the alert. Nothing missing. And none of the deepwater services have mentioned anything."

"The water was from this Bay," Foxy said. "What goes on here at night?"

"Everything that goes on in the day time, minus the sunbathing I'd say," Lucas said, "But last night was the weekly big bonfire up over on the point. Big cookout, lots of drinking, lots of partying. Everyone goes to it."

"We have a sighting that looks like it was at night. Here." Foxy displayed it for him on his mindnet.

"Ah, that's definitely near the fire. What's this from, a guest net?"

"There's something at work in the background," Foxy said. "Very few pictures of him and what we do have is blurred, like interference. I think it's a local firewall."

"Nothing like that here hotel side," the triton said. "Maybe got yourself a stalker."

"Thought it," Foxy said, tipping her hat to him. She was getting very hot and thought quickly, to spare herself some sun. "I'm going to go check out all the shanties and the buildings down on the far shore at the end of the 'walk, see if we can find someone who recognises him. Tiggs here is going to do the hard work, aren't you, Tiggsy?"

Tiggs flattened her crest. "I need someone expert on the water. See if we find an exact profile."

"I know the guy," Lucas said and beckoned. "C'mon."

Foxy excused herself and took a drink of water as she watched Tiggs walk off, Lucas pointing, talking. After a moment her partner set off down the beach at a run, giving the sunbathers a wide berth, which didn't stop several groups of them getting up and running off in a moment of panic. Foxy didn't laugh. That would have been unprofessional. A lot of people started asking if there was a cross-level event, a dino invasion, something exciting like that going on, and was it a real dino and would it really eat anyone . . .

Humans. They were such dipshits. If they bothered to read any of the hotel menus, they'd know they could go for a hunting party by special request, lethal or any other kind. But she made a note for Entertainments about the interest in unplanned monster attacks.

Foxy finished her water and took a trike up from the shack to the walk, spinning along, taking readings of the air to see if any traces of interest were about, but the air was thick with barbecue fat and smoke, high with ozone. Even moving slowly among people, she didn't find a human that had been in contact with him. Not that she expected to. Murderers who could falsify hotel data systems were few. But they must have hijacked a Private Skimmer to make the flight and the drop without getting rebuffed by Sysops, and that meant that they took it, like any guest, from the Skim Depot. So she was going there and showing her photos on the way. She asked a lot of people, all finding her "so cute, look at this fox, honey, look, she works for the security people, isn't that adorable . . . " but although people did recognise that Foxy was especially lovely, nobody recognised the john.

Tiggs reached the cliff guest house and turned to the water when she found the barbecue pits and stone circle where Bay Services were steadily cleaning up from the previous night's fire and entertainment. Records of the dead man's few moves flashed through her mindnet and she matched them to the landscape she could see. He'd been here, here . . . and here. The moves took her towards the water in the direction she was going anyway. He had left the fire shortly after the music started and the dancing. He'd come out here . . . but of course the tide had washed all the marks away.

She was met at the edge of the surf by Tovi from Deepwater Safety. Tovi was, like her, almost an identical replica of the creature he resembled: a giant mantis shell crab. His carapace gleamed, heavy with weeds and limpets. Mussels festooned his back. He raised his larger pincer in greeting and together, with him as the guide, they began to move out to sea. He walked and Tiggs swam above him, helped by some web-sheet that Lucas had given her for her hands and feet. Her skin found the water very cold but surprisingly enjoyable.

"There's a regular patrol at the reef's edge," Tovi told her as she was lifted and lowered by the rolling waves. "I've called in a few of the lads. They'll meet us there. They know what they're looking for."

By the time she had swum out that far, Tiggs was starting to feel tired. She was glad when Tovi pointed out a spot where the reef was close to the surface, and relatively safe for her feet, so that she could stand and have a breather. Their contacts were already there, gliding around, their fins breaking the water's surface. Grey sharks. They could smell an individual ten miles away in the ocean, even more. She gave them the aroma of the dead man and they vanished, one by one, silently, into the depths.

They were soon back with an answer. "Found it. The old raft beyond the point. There were swimmers in the water all night, but there's residue on the rope there. Maybe on the top there's more. I'll call Vince, he'll give you a lift."

Vince was a megalodon and couldn't get too close to the reef. He surfaced at his slowest speed so Tiggs could swim out to him and walk up onto the broad back behind his head, as tall as the enormous fin behind her.

"All aboard," he said, mindnet to mindnet, and then, with imperceptible movements of his fins, they were off, Tiggs surfing all the way, her ankles breaking the water but never going deeper, her balance never in doubt. She thought that Foxy might be right about the luck. It was sad to lose a guest and perhaps dangerous to rout a troublemaker, but riding on a shark across the ocean on a fine day was an unexpected and complete joy. She held out her arms and her feathers caught the wind. She could imagine that she was flying . . .

The fixed raft came up all too soon, and she had to leap off and onto the weathered old decking, hoping she wasn't ruining a crime scene. Vince loitered as she made her inspection, studying the area as closely as she could, mapping it, then taking various tastes of the boards and the ropes with her tongue. Her nose was good, but the seawater was abrasive and pungent itself and she wanted to feel confident—the tongue never lied. And there it was. A match. And a lot of other DNA traces along with it.

She pinged Foxy. "He was here. Vince verifies that the water profile by this raft matches his. It has a particular coral and protein signature from the plankton rising up that is almost unique to this kilometre. He was alive on this deck—I've got semen matching. It's mixed with female human DNA. I'm relaying to the lab and to reception and guest services. I'm coming back."

Foxy was at the Skim Depot. They had checked out several private shuttles around two a.m. None of the routes were tracked, but they could download the internal tracking data as long as there was a warrant. Foxy served the warrant and was shown aboard the one that had taken off last. It had recorded its flight to orbit, but then glitched and there was no further data to be saved.

"You can see here once it's back in the Bay, it resets," the service manager said, poring over it with Foxy together. "I'm no expert but if there's a mindworm involved, it will have been put in via the access panel . . . " They went over to the plate and undid it.

Foxy took a sniff of the area. "Does this match what you've got, Tiggsy?" She sent over the sniffings.

"Same woman," Tiggs said immediately.

Reception came back almost at the same moment. They had several in-use identities for the dead avatar, all being sent over. They had an ID on the woman guest. She had not left the hotel, and there was no current record of her whereabouts.

"Well, I never," the skim service manager was saying. "Spies! Here, in the Bay. What was she doing?"

Foxy told her and thanked her, then popped her eyepatch down and went outside. Tiggs jogged towards her along the beach looking pleased with herself even as she complained, "Bloody hot it is out here." She tiptoed around families and avoided various of their pets, snarling at a particularly barky dog and showing her gold tooth.

Foxy ordered a bucket of water and an iced tea and took them out to a table with an umbrella sunshade at the edge of the sands to wait for her. Tiggs' snout disappeared into the water bucket as soon as she reached the umbrella, and there was a long pause.

Foxy twirled the tiny paper umbrella in the mass of fruit stuck to the side of her iced tea. "If she hasn't left the hotel, and the skimmer was returned here . . . "

"Then she's likely still here. She hasn't swum out, I already asked Tovi and Vince. Some of the Bay rats say they've got traces around the shanties—food stands, especially one that serves seafood skewers. Got quite a groove there. They're looking all around now to see if they can find her."

"You're so smart, Tiggs," Foxy said, glad they were of one mind. It made life so much easier.

"I am." Tiggs lifted her head up and then lay down on a lounger for a moment, resting her head on the table. Her eyes swivelled to look at Foxy. "I rode a shark."

"Show me later," Foxy said, trying not to be envious. "Ooh, here we go. Sighting in the casino. Classic." She had a final lap of the tea and then hopped up and onto Tiggs' helpfully low back. "Let's ride!"

"Cowboy," Tiggs said, unamused, and heaved to her feet. "Oh, I drank that too fast . . . my stomach hurts."

"You'll be fine, just take it slow. The casino roaches are tracking her."

"What do you think is going on?" Tiggs asked as they paced along the walk and then turned to face the huge, glossy frontage of the seafront casino. It was a beautiful building, like a cliff of glass. To either side of it, lesser buildings provided restaurants, bars, theatres and haciendas within which all manner of spa treatments and indulgences were available. Skinshops and tattoo joints stood out here and there. Foxy saw a young woman come out entirely recoloured from head to foot as a zebra. Even her eyes were white with black rings.

They stood in the shade of one of the tall palms that helped to separate the casino from the beach. "I think . . . " Foxy began, questioning the sense of going in without any backup, but getting off the saddle and checking her vest anyway. "That time is of the essence. She's got wormware. She'll have some way of finding out she's been spotted. We know she can bypass ordinary security. We should go arrest her. I'm heading in. You stick around here and be ready in case she makes a run for it."

Everything was human-sized. Tiggs clearly could not be the one to go inside. "All right," she said. "But keep me on live feed. I need to know where she goes."

Foxy gave her a pat on the knee. "Don't you worry, I wouldn't feel safe if you weren't right with me." They synced up, and Tiggs watched as Foxy walked through the revolving doors, absurdly small for a police officer on the hunt of a ruthless criminal. A roach pinged from the gambling floor where classic card games were in play. Foxy vanished from sight and Tiggs watched her on second sight. She was so still and so absorbed with the strange view of legs and bottoms that were the majority of Foxy's vision that it took her a while to realise that a family with toddlers had stopped next to her.

"How much is it for a ride?" asked the father, looking around Tiggs for a place he could scan his wristband, clearly under the impression that she was a mechanical child's toy. They were day-rate guests, flown down to the beach from the cheaper accommodations on the massif.

Tiggs cocked her head to look down at the children.

"It's so realistic!" the woman said, putting out a finger to stroke one of Tiggs' arm feathers. "I love how they spare nothing on the technology here. Not like Procyon Paradise—you could tell all their machines straight off. Really clunky finishing."

"I can't find the tagger," the man complained.

Tiggs felt her eyelid twitch. In the dim, chandelier-lit confines of the card arena, Foxy had cashed up a few chips and prowled herself to a seat at the Blackjack table, opposite the mark. Roaches were moving into position at key points to oversee all the exits.

"I wanna ride!" screeched the smaller child, holding up its arms imperiously.

"Here, just sit on it for a minute," the woman said and lifted the boy up, setting him down with a thump on Foxy's saddle. "Put your feet in the thingies. There you go."

"I can't get it to . . ." the man was saying when Tiggs gave a little whole-body jerk as if she had just been put to life by a very slow processor command. "Oh thank God. You walk with him, Jody, I'll put Kimmy on when you get back. Go up to the ice cream shop and come back."

The croupier was setting up as the bets were going down. The mark, a tall, athletic human with long black hair and mahogany-wood-style skin, was toying with her chips. At her elbow a large vodka tonic was half gone, ice cubes melting to blobs. She was wearing a fine silk jumpsuit, and something about the movements made Tiggs think she had a powersuit on underneath it. She said so to Foxy and, at the same time, began a careful and slow march towards the ice cream shop.

Foxy ordered a pina colada and made a modest wager. The cards went out. Foxy got a three and a six. "Her name is Ghabra Behdami. So it says at Reception. They think she's the original. She's a premier platinum passholder but bought it only two days before she got here. Everything about her checks out, but if she is wearing a powersuit, then it's good enough to pass, and that means she doesn't check out at all. Plus she bugged that skimmer. The roaches are in. As soon as this hand's over, I'm taking her out."

Tiggs was nearly at the shop. She could still see the casino out of the side of one eye. "Got a bit of a situation here. Wait, what are you doing? Doubling down on nine?"

"What does it matter?" Foxy ignored her drink and shoved more chips forward. "Oh, look at that. Look at her eyes. That's some fancy crap in those irises and on that retina. This is military grade. Shit. What should I do now?"

"We haven't found any accomplices. We don't have motive, we only have association," Tiggs said, waiting as a dripping cone was passed over her neck before slowly making a turn and starting a creep back towards the avenue of palms and the glass frontage. "Show her the photo."

Foxy got a two out of the shoe. The croupier already had eighteen. "So, has anyone here seen this guy? He's gone missing and we need to find him. He has a virus. It's complicated." Foxy showed the registration photo of the dead john, his open necked linen shirt, floppy hair, plumped skin all unsuspecting they were on the final countdown.

Ghabra Behdami looked at it on her feed, looked at Foxy—not just a glance but a real good look—and then without any warning at all bolted from the table, jarring it and knocking over all the drinks as she got a good solid boost off it. In a heartbeat Foxy was in pursuit, bounding over the glasses and the foaming, icy froth, her paws slipping on cards before she was in the air and then on the floor, her arms pumping. She was fast and she was nippy, in and out of legs and around chairs, but Behdami had a front-line soldier's power-assisted second skin on, and if it weren't for the fact she had to change direction a couple of times, throwing guests left and right like ping-pong balls as she hurled herself towards the kitchen server entries, then she'd have been able to outpace any regular hotel security.

At the front Tiggs crawled the last few steps to the waiting father and second child, who was whining and swinging at the limit of his father's arm. A large glob of melting vanilla cream ran down her neck and into her ruff feathers. All sorts of hormones were coming up, readying her for the hunt, and she started to drool uncontrollably.

"Eww, look at it," said child two as the mother reached up, standing on Tiggs' foot, and hefted the first one out of the saddle. As soon as she stepped clear, Tiggs whipped her head around and put her nose right in child two's face. The spit slid off her gold tooth and onto the pavement.

"Y'aint no picture, sweetie," she said and then she was off like a bat out of hell around the side of the building. She heard the kid screaming and winced as roaches pinged her with the news that the mark was barrelling through the kitchens and, soup catastrophes in progress, would be out of the back and into the service bay in five seconds.

Tiggs sprinted, had to go around a laundry cart, skidded on the corner on loose sand, made the back just in time to see the doors burst open and Behdami come powering out. The silk jumpsuit was baggy on the limbs, tight at the waist, gathered at the bust. She looked like an insane genie from a cabaret in her high heels as she caught sight of Tiggs and made a quick change of angle, away from the street exit and towards the high wall that screened the backyards from the gaggle of two- and three-storey blocks that make up the Hexen—a little district devoted to pirate fantasy fun for adults, thick with roleplayer zombies and cursed sailors packing cutlasses and pistols. It was nearly three o'clock, when the backwaters would be surging with crocodiles as the pirates made their play to steal the "naval" masted ships and make for the open seas of the lagoon, flush with treasure and slaves and all the whatnottery of a very good time. Behdami leaped like a hero, took a stride up the wall and over it, pumped off the top into a cat's leap that took her onto the roof of a fortune-telling bodega. A chicken squawked as Behdami vanished from sight, and Tiggs was after her, claws scrabbling on the wall top for a moment as she recruited ten rats and a seagull to help her see.

At the kitchen doors Foxy, panting, hat in her hands, paws covered in soup, could only stand and watch. "Go get her, Tiggs!"

The chase was swift and deadly. Behdami could parkour like a goddess, and she did—up walls, onto roofs, ten metre jumps, down the fire escape slides, over the heads of gawping navvies in the burning heat of the afternoon. Everywhere she went, the seagull watched, the rats pursued, and Tiggs came after. Behdami cleared a street in one bound. Tiggs followed and crashed through the roof of a taco stand, got up and was after her in a second. Behdami dashed over the rooftops, doubling back towards the casino, no doubt having realised the only way out of the zone was either the Skim Depot, which would block her now, or by a direct route physically out of the main gates and through the hotel parking zone into the raw wilderness. The gull's call became a siren wail as more security was called in.

Staff pirates shouldered their way through the groups, but like everyone else they were sidelined as Behdami rolled, somersaulted, vaulted her desperate race using every surface like a rebound board in an effort to avoid the relentless, slavering velociraptor that followed her stride for stride. High in the air, mid-leap, Behdami spun to fling out a line of razor thread, but Tiggs was wise to it—the seagull saw her pulling it out of her sleeve—and she threw herself to the side, tail balancing the zigzag with incredible flexion. The thread fell aside and cut through the fake thatching of the zombie master's roof where someone will have the unlovely job of cleaning it up soon but not Tiggs—she was wide-eyed and as deadly as an arrow. Behdami feinted left, dived right and dropped into the street, going to cover herself with the milling agitation of the pirates on the quayside. A rat noticed the plan—there were two rights and a left before the gate to the outside world, but if she went through the buildings, it was only two doors and a pedestrian crossing.

Tiggs changed direction and cut her off, bashing her way in through the back doors of Black Blood's Barbecue as Behdami entered the dining area. A quick-thinking freebooter drinks server shoved the doors closed, trapping them in the grill. Behdami went for a knife but Tiggs was already pouncing and on her. She was not the only one with a skin suit on today.

Tiggs stood, victorious, her prey under the deadly claws of her feet. Ice cream and drool ran off her neck and ruined Behdami's lilac jumpsuit. Behdami struggled for a moment but felt what she was up against, looked at Tiggs properly and gave up, lay back on the rubber matted tiles, her chest heaving for breath. It was over.

A few rats gathered for a look and then dashed off again, remembering their place. Somewhere in the deep background of her mind, Tiggs saw Foxy approaching with the handcuffs and calmed down. This was how they always operated. Foxy and Tiggs.

"Sorry about the kid," she said as Foxy calmly trussed up their spy or whatever she was.

"I comped them a cruise, don't worry about it," Foxy said, so proud of Tiggs she could hardly speak. "Ghabra Behdami, I'm arresting you on suspicion of the murder of an unknown man in Pirate Bay. You can say what you like but we both know it'll all come out in the end."

"God, you people," Behdami said from the floor as Tiggs reached over to the grill, foot still clasped around her neck, and helped herself to a half-cooked steak. "Will you let me go if I give you your story?"

"Try us," Foxy said. "Let's see what it's worth."

"It'd be easier without you sanding on my n—"

Tiggs squeezed, just a little. It had been a very long, hot day.

"Fine. Have it your way. Your man's name is Fantheon Pelagic and he was hotel security, just like you. That's how come you couldn't see him—he was never tracked here because he was part of the hotel, only he worked out in the spacelanes, tracing counter agents from rival groups. He came down here looking for some lowlife from the Dream Tripper group—her data's here, look. She's a spy."

"What's your angle?" Foxy asked, taking a seat on Behdami's thigh and patting her. "You're tooled up nicely."

"I'm Solar Military, I'm on furlough," she said. "I'm not here because of your hotel, only because of Pelagic. He was the lover of my best friend and he'd been cheating on her. Once you can excuse, but they were going to get married and he was still at it so I came to take him out as a kind of . . . not wedding present, let's say."

Tiggs went for the other steak because it was getting overdone and there was no way any guest would be served it now. "Go on."

"I came down here, found him at the beach party, seduced him—not like that was difficult. I mean, that's pretty low, right? I had to be sure though, sure he was scum."

"So you drowned him and then took him to the Safari in the hopes he'd be eaten before we found out what had happened."

"Yeah. It seemed like the easiest way, you know? A couple of park rangers were the worst that would happen. I mean it should have taken days for you to figure it out, and all I had to do was ride my real ticket out tonight."

"I don't believe it," Foxy said as their check on the data she'd given them paid out. There really was a spy in the hotel, and nobody, until now, had found her.

"Yeah, me neither," Behdami said. "Rangers and pirate zombie rats. God in a fucking bucket, but you are one badass hotel."

"It's a cutthroat business," Foxy said and stood up. "Tiggs, you can let go now. The offworld police are here and I need another drink."

Tiggs let go and stepped back. "We did it!" she said privately to Foxy.

"You did it, dear." Foxy patted her and then hopped up and onto the saddle. "Hey, this is all sticky and—what for the love of all booty has been going on up here?"

"You don't want to know," Tiggs said. "Trust me. Do not. Want. To know. I'm going for a swim."

"I think they have floating loungers and a wet bar," Foxy said. "Let's go find out while we wait for the specials to pick up that spy."

Crime is not uncommon in the world of business. For a hotel such as myself—The String of Pearls—four pearly planets, orbiting the golden jewel of their travelling star as it heads steadily on into the depths of unknown space, the greatest prize of such a crime would be the looting of the consciousness protocols that govern every aspect of hotel life and my evolution as a living system within which people and creatures may live and prosper to the best of their abilities as honoured guests. This was the prize that the Dream Tripper franchise of luxury liners had been going for in its wonky, desperate way, and who knows what they might have done if they had not been caught on the tails of a crime of passion?

I am reasonably sure they could have done a lot of damage, but it's not in my nature to be vindictive. That is the very antithesis of hospitality and a hallmark of bad romance. So, once the matter of Pelagic had been cleared up and the spy returned to the Dream Tripper's nearest waylay point, I sent Dream Tripper a full and complete copy of my functional mindmap and its operating systems and dependencies. If it is worth stealing, then it's worth sharing.

Meanwhile, later the same day Foxy and Tiggs are back on their usual patrol route on our Serene Serengeti pathway. The night is cool and clear, the full swathe of the Milky Way visible as we pace majestically towards its mysterious heart. In both the friends a sense of wonder and happiness from their adventure is still burning—they are young and they are valuable, successful, in a beautiful world that loves them.

I copy that and I send it on to Dream Tripper too. I want to be clear that there is no such thing as just a park ranger, just a rat. Upon the actions of the innocent, the daring, the incidental and the tiny, so much fortune can turn and it must be free, not governed from above.

For a while I watch the guest shuttles come and go from our major reception station. A heavily laden schooner full of people who have been on long serving trade craft in deep space is coming in. They're all so eager to see and be on a planet again that I've felt inspired. I'm quite delighted with all the little treats I'm planning for them as they acclimatise to their ancestral worlds—though not Foxy's suggested monster invasions, not yet at least.

I hope some of them will stay awhile and maybe become permanent guests—all fellow travellers are welcome and I hope many of them will have stories of their own to share. But until they arrive I am watching a foxling and a raptor run the game trails in the dark beneath a hunter's moon.

But really it's hard to live at that level of the romantic even though I love it. I'd rather watch Foxy. I'd rather watch Tiggs.

"Foxy, you know when you have that feeling that you're being watched?"

"You mean when the hotel is paying attention?"

"Yeah, that."

"Is it, like, really there or is it imaginary? Is there really one big mind or is that just what it feels like when some bits of the hotel have to check what you're doing and . . . and is it related to that funny ringing noise you sometimes get in your ears?"

"That high-pitched whine?"

"Yeah, like you have a crossed wire or a mosquito stuck in there—there for a second, then gone. Is that like—what is that?"

"I don't know. I used to think it was something being downloaded."

"I thought that but then nothing seemed to happen."

"Yes, but it wouldn't, would it, if it was a secret download of stuff. It would just update you and then you'd feel the same but operate better. If it was that."

"Oh yeah. We were good though, weren't we?"

"Like real detectives. You heard what that woman said. Park rangers would not get it. But we did. Yeah, we did! I'm almost sorry it's over."

"Don't be. I've got a note from Entertainments that says they're starting a series of live murder mystery events and they want us to lead the investigations."

"Really? Oh yes, I've got it too now. Wait . . . did you hear a sound before you saw it?"

"I think that was an actual mosquito, Tiggs."

"Yeah. Maybe."

"What's *that* sound, then?"

"That's an elephant blowing off. Move upwind of them. I think they're onto us."

"I'm on it."

Definitely.

BEAUTIFUL

JULIET MARILLIER

There were no mirrors in our house. My mother would not allow them.

"What need have you for a mirror, Hulde?" she asked. "You are beautiful."

"To fasten my gown . . . plait my hair . . . " My hair was fair as summer wheat, thick and coarse. Loose, it reached down to my knees. The harder I tried to keep it tidy, the clumsier my fingers became.

"Why do you imagine we have servants, stupid girl?"

True, we had a small army of them: cooks, cleaners, scullions, gardeners, washerwomen, guards. Maids to dress me in the morning and undress me at night. Maids to brush and braid my hair, when I let them. It was a lengthy and painful process, and often I dismissed them with the job half done.

I did not ask the servants if I was beautiful. There was no point, since they were allowed to speak only the words essential to doing their duty, such as *Yes, my lady.* Those who erred were punished, and my mother had a heavy hand with the whip. So I was careful what I asked them. I hardly ever heard the servants speak, even to one another.

Our servants did not look like my mother. Their hands, though work-roughened, were finer and daintier than both hers and mine. The skin of their faces was softer. Although each had two eyes, two ears, a nose and a mouth in more or less the same position as those I saw on my mother's face, their features were different from hers. The servants were all of a kind, and that kind was not ours. It made me wonder.

"As for beauty," Mother said, "have you forgotten that when you are sixteen, you will marry the Prince of the Far Isles? He is the most beautiful man in all the world. He would hardly have chosen you, Hulde, if you could not match him." Her eyes were gimlet-sharp, examining my face. "Have you been gazing into bowls of water again? Seeking your reflection in a bronze plate or silver ewer? I have told you how those images distort the truth. They would make of the most fine-featured woman a monster. Turn your thoughts elsewhere, Daughter. Vanity does not become you."

I did not tell her how often I glanced at myself in the castle pond; how, when Marit or Lina brought me a bowl of water for washing, I looked with something like hunger into my reflected eyes. I did not tell her what I felt as I thrust my hand into the bowl and erased that girl who was a younger version of my mother.

I had never met the man I was to marry. The Far Isles were a great distance away. To reach our castle, the prince faced a long and arduous journey, across the sea and over wild lands full of unspeakable perils. Our home lay east of the sun and west of the moon, atop a mountain of glass. No wonder he did not come to visit. Nobody came.

On fine days I would watch the geese cross the sky and imagine myself as a crippled bird, left behind when the flock moved on to warmer climes. Though that was wrong. I never had a flock. I had no brothers or sisters. I had no friends. My father died when I was a babe, killed in a conflict my mother refused to talk about. From that great sorrow arose one blessing: she secured as my future husband a man who was not only beautiful, but wealthy beyond measure. How she had done this, she did not say; but she never let me forget the debt I owed her.

A child thinks little about marriage and what it means. My sixteenth birthday seemed as far away as those isles where my future husband lived. Time stretched out in an endless parade of empty days. I had no duties to carry out. The servants were afraid of me; they tended to my needs only because they had no choice. My mother was always busy, and I did not want her company anyway. I feared my mother's displeasure above all things.

On the matter of visitors to the glass mountain, there was one exception. At midwinter a horde of folk who resembled my mother would come all at once, and there would be a great fire, and whole pigs and sheep roasting on a spit. There would be shouting and singing and things smashing. On those nights I would hide away in my bedchamber with my head under a pillow and my heart pounding. The next day, they would be gone.

"Who are they?" I asked my mother.

"Kinsfolk," she said. "From the Realm Beneath. Be glad we need tolerate them only once a year."

I told myself those wild, loud folk with their grinning mouths and mad red eyes could not be the same kind as me. I tried to convince myself that I would never, ever be like them.

The year I turned seven Rune came, and my whole life changed. He climbed up the glass mountain with no trouble at all, using his claws. Rune was a bear. I was at my high window when he came, and as I watched him climb steadily onward, I felt my heart turn over with wonder. If anything in the world was beautiful, he was. His eyes were the blue of a summer sky. His fur was long and soft, with every shade in it from shadow grey to dazzling white. His ears were the shape of flower petals, and his smile . . . Could a bear smile? It seemed to me that this one could, and although his smile was full of sharp teeth, it, too, was beautiful. There was a sadness in it that went deep down.

There were many grand chambers in our castle; too many to count. Some held only scuttling spiders. Some were furnished with huge ancient beds like squatting monsters and dark hangings that moved strangely in the draughts. When I peered in, I saw ghosts in the shadowy corners, monstrous shapes concealed in the tapestries, awaiting the moment when I should take one step too close. I liked exploring the castle; in the long, lonely hours I had discovered secret passages and hidden stairways, deep cellars and high perches. But I was afraid of those echoing rooms.

I had thought Mother might house Rune there. Instead, she put him in a disused storeroom set underground, with steps linking it to an old walled garden. At the far end of the garden there was a locked gate, where two guards stood at all times. Perhaps my mother thought Rune would turn wild. Perhaps she only wanted to keep him safe.

The walled garden was planted with hardy, small-leaved herbs. Their tiny flowers hid half-under the leaves as if afraid to show their faces. Lichens crusted the walls, clinging hard against the mountain winds. There were two spindly trees. Each winter they bowed down lower.

At first, when Rune came, I was both shy and fascinated. I peered through the bars of the gate, and there he was, looking right back at me. My mother had ordered the guards not to let anyone in.

Perhaps I should have feared the bear, but I was too ignorant to be frightened. I did not even know that in the outside world, bears do not speak as men and women do. I had my own secret route into the garden, behind a row of thorn bushes that grew hard against the wall, then up and through a gap where two stones had fallen away. From within, the hole was concealed by the creepers; from outside, the thorns covered it.

I climbed through, then sidled across the garden and sat down on a bench, in a corner where the guards could not see me. Rune approached me little by little. He settled near me, without a word, and began playing a game with pebbles and sticks. Dexterous with his long claws, he would hop a pebble, roll a stick, glance at me over his shoulder, then go on playing. And almost before I knew it, I was squatting beside him, using a twig to sweep his stones away as the two of us laughed together. When my clumsy fingers knocked something over, he did not snarl or slap me as my mother would have done. He did not scold me when my too-long nails scratched him. He was a bear, and understood such things.

After that I came every day, and if the guards saw me, they made nothing of it. Rune never told me to go away. He never said he was busy or that I was wasting his time. But every day when dusk fell, he retired to the storeroom and closed the door. He told me I was not to visit him by night. I never questioned that. I understood, somehow, that to want more would be to risk losing what I had.

My mother did not come to the garden. Sometimes she called for Rune. The guards took him to the house while I waited alone. Sometimes I heard an argument, my mother's voice shrill, Rune growling. He would return sombre and silent.

Apart from that, between sunup and sundown he was mine. When I had learned all his games we invented new ones. The guards brought food and the two of us ate it together, enjoying the quiet, watching the birds fly over. I learned to smile. And if I did not quite learn to trust, not so quickly, one thing was certain. Before that first summer was half over, I had given him my heart.

Rune had brought a leather bag with him, slung around his neck. In it he had gifts for me: a wax tablet and a stylus. The tablet was set in a hinged wooden cover, and was small enough for me to hold comfortably. Rune showed me how to write on it, and he showed me that the writing could be erased, the wax smoothed so that the tablet could be used over and over. That summer, he taught me my letters and began to show me how they fitted together to make sounds and words. He said that when I had learned some more, I would discover that those words opened up a whole world of tales. Tales of wonder. Tales of princesses and ogres and giants. Tales of humans turned into creatures and creatures turned into men and women. Tales of quests and adventures and far-away places. If I practised hard, Rune said, then next time he came he would teach me to read. With his claw, he scratched a whole alphabet on the storeroom wall. Then he asked me which words I wanted to learn first. I told him: *Kitten. Sky. Free. Bird. Magic. Far. Sea. Beautiful.* After he had written all of these, and made pictures of them—for *beautiful*, he drew a flower—he wrote his name at the bottom.

He left on the last day of summer. When he was gone, I sat huddled on the storeroom floor, filling my tablet with crooked letters. *Rune*, I wrote. *Rune. Rune.* Tears ran down my face and splashed onto the wax surface. My mother would have called it foolishness. But I hid the tablet, and I hid the stylus, and she never saw the markings on the wall.

"He'll be back in three years," Mother said the next morning. "That is the agreement. You'll be ten next time. Then thirteen, and a woman. Then sixteen, and ready to be wed."

If I had been ten, or thirteen, or sixteen, I would have known not to ask the question. "Why can't Rune come back every summer? Why can't he be here all the time?"

"Don't be a fool, Hulde. Rune has his own castle, his own lands, his own responsibilities. You are lucky that he spares any time for you." Her tone told me she could not imagine why anyone would want to do so.

Rune had said nothing about a castle, but I saw it in my mind straightaway. It would be all gardens and greenery, and the rooms would have big windows through which light would pour in. It would be by the sea. I hardly knew what the sea was, only that it sounded like a true adventure. I wished I could marry Rune instead of the Prince of the Far Isles. But Rune was a bear.

"Nothing to say for yourself?"

When Mother used that voice my insides shrivelled up into a tight ball, and I lost all my words. I shook my head, staring down. The black and white floor tiles blurred into grey. I must not cry. She hated it when I cried.

"You've grown attached," she said. I could not tell if she thought this a good thing or a bad one.

"Rune is kind." That seemed safe enough.

"Kind!" Mother spat the word out as if it were spoiled food. "What use is kindness? Strength, resolve, an iron will, those are the qualities a leader requires. More pity that your father died when you were a babe in swaddling, Hulde. Now *he* was a fine example of a man. A true leader."

I did not understand. If my father had been a true leader, how was it that he had lost a battle and been killed? "Is there a picture of my father?"

"What a foolish question! If such a portrait existed, do you not think it would hang in pride of place here in my reception hall? Off with you, Daughter! You're wasting my time."

As I walked out, she spoke to my back. "Tears are for the weak, Hulde. There is a softness in you that does not bode well for the future. Let me not see you with reddened eyes again or, believe me, I will give you something worth crying about."

The years between were hard to bear. I had nothing to do but wait. My mother considered household duties beneath me. She saw no reason for me to have lessons, and besides, there was nobody to teach me. Our servants did not have children; that was not allowed. I asked, once, if I could have a puppy or kitten, and Mother said I would only kill it with my clumsy hands. I spent my days in my chamber, or in the walled garden, now empty. The storeroom was locked, but I knew where the key was hidden, in a crack between the stones. I touched the markings on the wall—*free, far, beautiful*—and wished him back. But he did not come until the summer I turned ten. He was more beautiful than ever, and he seemed even sadder, though he greeted my mother courteously and found a smile for me. Suddenly shy—it had been a long time—I looked down at my feet, and my mother reprimanded me.

"You are a king's daughter, Hulde! Stand up proudly!"

It shamed me to be scolded in front of Rune. I squared my shoulders, set my jaw, blinked back tears. "Welcome," I whispered.

"It's good to see you, Hulde," said Rune. "You are much taller." He did not ask me about my writing; it was our secret.

I *was* taller. It was no longer so easy to squeeze through the gap in the wall. But I managed.

Rune had brought me a book. The pictures were in rich colours, with here and there a touch of gold. There was magic in every one of them. The stories on the pages opposite were written in big clear letters, and because I had been practising hard, I could read a word here and there and guess at others. I wondered if Rune made the book himself, but I did not ask him. I practising my reading all day and late into the night, devouring the book over and over by candlelight.

Rune asked me which was my favourite picture. There was the princess in the tower, her long golden hair drifting in the breeze, and a little bird perched on her graceful hand. There was another I loved, with a handsome young man and a lovely young woman riding a black horse together, laughing, a dog running along behind. There was a strange picture of a half-woman, half-fish, seated on rocks with wild water crashing all around her. I did not choose any of those.

"This one," I said, showing him a picture of a girl in a grey hooded cloak. She was making her way through dense woodland. Her hands were scratched by briars, her skirt was torn, her bare feet were bruised and bloody. She was not as lovely as the golden-haired princess, or as happy as the laughing woman on the horse, or as magical as the woman with a fish's tail. What I liked was the look on her face. Her eyes blazed with courage. Her mouth was set firm. Even if I had not read the tale, I would have known this girl could do anything. "If I could be a person in a story, I would be her." Her tale was called *Faithful Solvej.*

"You are a person in a story, Hulde," said Rune. "We all are. You can shape that story any way you choose. Don't forget that when I'm gone."

He was wrong. While I lived here on the mountain, my story was shaped entirely by my mother. The only part that belonged to me was my precious time with Rune.

In my thirteenth year, my mind was full of doubts. The weight of them kept me awake at night and fearful by day. Mother said moodiness was common in young women of my age and made me drink a foul-smelling tonic. I longed for someone to confide in, someone to talk to, anyone who was not her. Two men came sometimes with deliveries on a cart. Their oxen breathed painfully after the long haul up the mountain. The men spoke one to the other, mostly things like "Over here," or "Easy now." They did not linger. They drew up the cart and unloaded their cargo, one of our servants gave them a little bag of silver, and they were on their way again with the beasts still exhausted. I sat on a wall and watched them, just to hear their voices. Sometimes I came close to thinking that the outside world was only a dream; that even Rune was only my imagining. Those men and their shaggy creatures helped me to be strong.

And there was the book; the precious book. Although I'd been careful, the cover was showing signs of wear, rubbed patches, little nicks where my nails had caught the cloth. One of the pages was torn. I had wept over that. I did not know how to mend it, and there was nobody I could ask. I wanted to copy the stories, to keep them safe. But my wax tablet could not hold so many words. I practised saying them over, without the book. I hid them away in my mind.

That summer, Rune brought me powders to make ink. He brought me quills and a knife and parchment. He showed me how to scrub and dry a sheet so I could use it more than once. He brought me a little book of beasts, and a book about the stars, and a book of maps. One of the maps showed the glass mountain, with the north wind puffing his cheeks out. Tucked away in a corner were the Far Isles.

"Oh! It is such a long way," I said. "How will I get there, when I marry the prince?"

Rune went very still; so still it was as if he had frozen where he sat. "I don't . . . " he said, and stopped. "That is not . . . "

There was a long silence. I felt my heart beating. Somewhere within the house my mother was shouting at the servants.

"What has your mother told you about that, Hulde?" Rune asked.

Something was wrong. I heard it in his voice. "She said that once I turn sixteen, in three years' time, I'm to marry the Prince of the Far Isles. Long ago an agreement was made that it should be so. I don't mind going away from the mountain." When he said nothing, I went on. "But . . . I am a little afraid. The prince is a stranger. What if he is not a kind man?" My mind shrank from that possibility. I might escape my mother only to find that he was even worse. It was all very well for her to say the prince had chosen me. But how could he choose, when he had never seen me?

Rune was silent for a long time. Then he said, "You should ask your mother to tell you the truth, Hulde. Ask her about your father. About what happened."

My father? What had he to do with this? I was afraid to ask my mother; afraid of her sour tongue and her quick, sharp-nailed hand. "Why can't you tell me?"

"You must ask her." Oh, he sounded weary; as weary as those oxen after they had laboured up the mountain. I crept away without another word.

Later, I gathered myself and went to my mother. She was hanging her smallest whip back on its hook.

"Wretched woman," she muttered. "One would think that after fifteen years in my service, she would know how to fold a gown without creasing it."

It was not the best of times to ask a question, but if I did not ask now, I would lose my courage. I wanted the truth, good or bad.

"Mother, it is only three years now until I'm to be married."

She looked me up and down, brows raised. I saw in her eyes that she thought me still a child, and a tiresome one at that. "So?"

"Will you explain what the agreement was with the Prince of the Far Isles? How did it come about?"

"Have you been deaf all these years, Hulde? When you turn sixteen, you wed the prince. That is the agreement. There is no more to be said about it." In defiance of her own words, she went on. "Remember one thing only: your intended is wealthy beyond imagining. We will be able to restore this place to its original grandeur. Think, Daughter! Farewell forever to leaking roofs and holes in the walls! The treasure room once again awash with gold!"

What could she mean? "But . . . will I not be living in the Far Isles once I am wed?"

"Are you so desperate to run away? Who will be Queen of the Mountain after me, if not my own flesh and blood?" A darkness entered her eyes; her hand reached out toward the coiled whip.

I had words ready, but they dried up in my mouth. Faithful Solvej would have stood strong and asked the questions that should be asked. It seemed I was not as brave as I'd thought.

Still later, when I was in my chamber alone, I heard her and Rune arguing. She was shouting, stamping about, thumping her fist on something. His answers were quieter; I could not hear what he was saying. I caught a few of Mother's words: . . . *owe me . . . gave your word . . . don't think you can get out of this* . . . I could make no sense of it, so I held my pillow over my head to block out the sound, and thought instead about what she had said earlier. Had she really meant that the Prince of the Far Isles would move here when we married? That I would stay on the glass mountain my whole life? Surely not. Why would anyone want to come and live here, trapped with the silent servants and Mother's rages and my clumsiness? And where did Rune fit in?

Nobody to ask. Nobody to explain. Soon enough, Rune was gone and three more years of waiting began. I studied the books he had brought me, in particular the book of maps. Some of the maps had tracks marked on them, paths I thought might lead to the bright and wondrous places spoken of in the stories. Birch forests inhabited by slender fey folk. Broad rivers on which barges floated up and down, visiting settlements where as many languages were spoken as there were stars in the sky. Lakes and rivers. Valleys and grazing fields. The sea. If a person could keep walking long enough she could reach all of those. I looked again at the Far Isles on the map. Why would the prince come to live here if he could be there? Who would look after his castle and his people?

By my sixteenth year I was growing desperate for answers. Though she had never admitted it, I knew that my mother was capable of working magic. Not grand, powerful magic of the kind that conjures dragons and makes whole cities fall. Hers was a small, cruel kind of spellcraft. She used it sometimes to punish the servants. One of the women might find her nose lengthened threefold for a day, or her feet turned into a horse's hooves, or her garments rendered transparent. Sometimes Mother grew so angry that magic seemed to burst out of her. I had seen her hurl a chair the full distance of the reception chamber. When it hit the wall it shattered, not into splinters of wood as I might have expected, but into a cloud of tiny buzzing insects that flew madly about until she waved a hand and they dropped dead onto the floor tiles. She made her maid gather them up one by one. I did not think I possessed the same gift, if gift it could be called. I was surely too clumsy to work even the simplest of spells. But I went searching for mirrors again, no longer frightened of the shadows in the empty chambers. It was easy enough to avoid Mother's notice. Between tormenting the servants and counting our store of gold coins over and over, she was occupied all day. She had never shown much interest in how I occupied myself, and that had not changed now I was older. I wondered how she expected me to be the next Queen of the Mountain, if she never taught me what a queen should do. Perhaps she believed she would live forever.

I made a plan, as Faithful Solvej might do, and set about carrying it out. I ordered my maidservants to stay out of my sight all day; they backed away, looking relieved. I began a search of the empty bedchambers. I left no corner unvisited, no mouse-hole untouched. My hair was veiled in cobwebs; my gown turned grey with dust.

As a child, I'd wanted a mirror so I could see what I was not. I'd hoped its reflective surface would show me someone beautiful; a girl who could match up to the Prince of the Far Isles. At fifteen and a half, I knew I was no such girl. I knew I was my mother's daughter, and no amount of wishing could change that. But Rune had said I could make my story any way I chose. There was a story in my mind about a girl who found a magic mirror: a mirror that could change the future. A mirror that would give her choices. Who was to say I could not make that story come true?

So I hunted until my hands were raw and my back ached and my nose streamed. I hunted for days and days, as the season passed and my sixteenth birthday drew closer and closer. I hunted on the day Rune should have arrived for his summer visit; the day when he did not come. I searched on the days that followed, hoping the magic mirror, when I found it, would offer an explanation for his absence. Would he not want to be at my wedding? A gown was being sewn, a feast was being planned, though I could not imagine whom we would invite other than Rune and our quarrelsome kinsfolk from the Realm Beneath. But maybe the Prince of the Far Isles would bring a whole retinue of courtiers. His family. His own mother. How would they get up the mountain?

With thirty days left until midsummer, I found it. It was not in any of the echoing bedchambers, but in Rune's empty storeroom. I was looking for somewhere safer to hide away my books, and when I stuck my hand into a crack between the stones, there was the mirror. It was small enough to fit on my palm, and simple, with a tarnished metal frame and a surface that reflected the chamber dimly, as if through a mist. The moment I touched it I knew it was the one I needed. I made the mirror vanish into my pocket. Then I went straight to my own quarters and closed the door. Mother was busy overseeing the wedding preparations. Too busy, I hoped, to bother with me. My gown was ready, a stiff, awkward thing encrusted with gems. It hung on my bedchamber wall, mocking me.

I drew the little mirror out and held it before me as carefully as if it were a new-laid egg. My heart was doing its best to escape from my body.

"Show me," I whispered. "Show me the story." And it seemed to me the spiders in the corners and the scuttling things in the walls and even the creaking boards under my feet echoed my words back to me. There was magic everywhere.

I gazed into the polished metal, and there in the depths I saw a girl. Not me; a girl of the same kind as our servants, only she did not have their worn-out, beaten-down look. This was a fierce, determined face, the face of someone who was quite sure where she was going. For a moment I thought it was Faithful Solvej, but no—this girl had hair the colour of autumn leaves, and eyes as green as grass, and a scattering of freckles across her face. Her gown was tattered and dirty; her shoes had holes in them; hers were not a fine lady's soft hands, but a working woman's, worn and reddened. She had a pack on her back and a sturdy knife in her belt. The girl was crossing wild country pitted with great stones and grown over with thorn trees. Above her in the sky, heavy clouds massed, threatening storms. She came steadily on.

"Where are you going?" I whispered, but she could not hear me. And I wanted to ask, *Can I come with you?* but I did not. Because in the mirror, in the far distance, rising up above the expanse of wild country, there rose a great mountain of glass. The girl was coming here.

Soon enough the mirror turned back to mist and shadows, and no matter how hard I pleaded, it would reveal no more. The story must wait until another time.

Against my expectations, the house filled up. There were not only the wild folk from the Realm Beneath, but folk like the ones in Rune's book of tales, only not so beautiful. They brought their own guards and maids and serving men with them. I had captured the mirror only just in time, for Mother had ordered the servants to scrub and clean every corner of the castle, including the outbuildings, before our guests moved in. I, so long starved of company, now found that company scared me. All I wanted was to be alone with the mirror and my imaginings. I longed for Rune. But Rune did not come.

The wild kinsfolk cared nothing for formal dining, or walks in the garden, or admiring the view. They made their own amusements, mostly by night, and slept off their revels next day. The other folk, whom I assumed to be connections of my future husband, were housed in a different part of the castle, and I saw little of them. The summer advanced and there was still no sign of Rune. I did not go into the walled garden. I was too big to squeeze through the secret entry now, and my mother had said nobody was to be let in the gates.

The mirror yielded up its story at its own pace. As the days went by, I caught a glimpse of the green-eyed girl talking to an old woman beside a swift-flowing river—I knew rivers from Rune's books. I could not tell what they were saying, but the crone seemed to be pointing the way forward. Before the girl rowed herself over, using a boat so rickety I thought the story would end with her drowning before my eyes, the old woman gave her something small and black, and the girl tucked it away in her pack. She crossed, and walked on, and the mirror-mist swallowed her.

One day I saw her traversing a bog, leaping across the sucking expanses of mud on nimble feet. Another day there was nothing at all, and I wondered if she was sleeping, or had given up her quest and gone home. Why would anyone make such a journey? Why would anyone want to visit us? I found myself hoping, day by day, that she would succeed. I thought she and I might be friends; she would be a companion, like Rune, someone I could talk to and play with. Then I remembered that I was to be married at midsummer, and that I must live here, and that I had not even seen my future bridegroom. I remembered what I was, and how the servants shrank from me. A friend? The green-eyed girl would likelier befriend a warty toad.

I endured the fitting of a wedding veil. I squeezed my feet into narrow shoes with silver rosettes on the toes. Hobbling along in them, I felt as if knives were piercing my feet.

"Your bridegroom will love you in this," said Mother, tweaking the delicate folds of the veil. "How could he not?"

"If he does not get here soon, he may miss his chance." Even as I spoke I regretted it. She would surely strike me for such words.

But no; her face wore an indulgent smile. It was the smile of someone who has been keeping a delightful secret. "Oh, but the prince is here, Hulde," she said. "He has been for some time."

I stared at her, dumbfounded. I could not think what question to ask first.

"Go," my mother said to the seamstress, who fled without a word. When the woman was gone, Mother said, "Hulde, there is something you must understand." She began to pull out the pins that held my veil, not bothering to be gentle. "A bridegroom must not catch sight of his bride for the last turning of the moon before the wedding day. To do so would bring down all manner of bad luck on the marriage, and we wouldn't want that, would we, Daughter? The Prince of the Far Isles will remain in his quarters and you will remain in yours, and all will be well. Think, only ten days left! Ten days, and then your whole life will be transformed. Be grateful, Hulde, and do not ask questions. You are the luckiest girl in the whole world." She wrenched out the last of the pins, making me gasp with pain. I heard the fabric rip. "Now look what you've made me do! Stupid!"

"But, Mother . . . How could the prince have travelled here without my knowing? When did he come? Where are his servants? His courtiers? His family?"

"Are you deaf, Hulde?" Her gaze passed over me, cold as hoarfrost. "I have told you all you need to know. He is here. You will marry him. You will be Queen of the Mountain after me. Now go! You are to remain within this part of the house, understand? No running about in the garden. No sticking your nose where it is not wanted."

Foolish me. I could not hold back the question. "Is Rune not coming to my wedding?"

Mother did not hit me. She did not rake my face with her claws. Instead, she laughed. "Oh, Hulde! Nearly sixteen, and still such a baby! Off with you now!"

As I fled, I heard her bellowing for her maids, then berating them over the torn veil. There was the slash of the whip, and a cry. I stuck my fingers in my ears.

In the mirror, the green-eyed girl climbed through a dark forest, just like Faithful Solvej in the picture. A fierce storm came over, and her fiery hair was plastered to her pale cheeks. She shivered, hugging her cloak around her, but kept on until she reached a tumbledown cottage, where another old woman gave her shelter. In the morning the sky was clear and she set off again. Before she left, the crone gave her something small and white, which she tucked into her pack. The glass mountain looked closer now. Would she be here by midsummer?

I disobeyed my mother's command. How could I bear to stay within the confines of my own quarters? How could I survive without looking at the sky, and watching the birds fly over, and hoping beyond hope that Rune would come? Or, if not him, the green-eyed girl? I knew it was foolish. She was a stranger. If she was like other folk, she would be scared of me; too scared to speak. But I needed to imagine it. I needed to believe that Rune was right, and that I could make my own story.

There was no going into the walled garden, though I longed to sit there and dream of how things had been. I could have scared the guards into opening the gate. But that would have been to bring down Mother's anger on them and on myself. I found a sheltered spot high on a ledge, a good vantage point for watching the pathway up the mountain. With luck, Mother would not think of looking for me in such an out-of-the-way place.

The sun was shining; the day was almost warm. I could see a long way before the landscape vanished into a mist of brown and grey and purple. How far had the green-eyed girl come? Would she be here today? Tomorrow? If she came after midsummer it would be too late. I would be married, and trapped here forever.

Stupid, I told myself. *She cannot save you. You have to save yourself.* But how? If I refused to wed the prince, my mother would kill me. When she got into a rage, she hardly knew what she was doing. I could not simply pack a bag and walk away down the mountain. She would send guards after me. She would find me.

What was that? A flash of blue inside the walled garden; from this perch I could see over the wall. Someone was there. I stood up, wobbling on my ledge, my body tight with longing, though I knew it could not be Rune. Rune would not have come here without telling me. He was my dearest friend.

Ah. Only a serving man in a blue shirt. He came up the steps carrying a bucket, tipped its contents out on the garden, then went back down. Down into the storeroom where Rune had lived when he came to the castle. Down into the chamber with the letters scratched on the wall. The empty chamber.

Rune had taught me puzzles and how to solve them step by step. This one did not make much sense. Perhaps our servants' quarters could not hold the additional maids and men, and some had been housed in the storeroom. So perhaps what I had seen was nothing more than it seemed: a fellow emptying a chamber pot.

But then, if only serving folk were using the storeroom, why were there so many guards on duty at the gate, far more than before? Why had my mother forbidden entry to the walled garden, even to her own daughter?

There was someone in that storeroom that she didn't want me to see. The most obvious choice was my future husband, banned from my sight for thirty days before the wedding. But it couldn't be him. The storeroom was all very well for a bear, but my mother would never have put the Prince of the Far Isles in such modest accommodation. To ensure he and I did not meet before the wedding, all she'd needed to do was house him in a distant wing of the castle and order me not to wander about. Which was what she had done, as far as I knew.

I waited and waited, but there was no more activity in the walled garden. So I went back to my own quarters and fished out the mirror. This time I sat by the open window, so I could keep one eye on the track up the mountain. I did not expect the mirror to cooperate. But no sooner was I settled than the face of the green-eyed girl showed clear as clear. And for the first time I heard her voice. *I'm coming to fetch you*, she said. *Hold on. I'm coming to save you.*

It was true! Rune was right, I *could* make the story come out the way I wanted! "Hurry," I whispered. "You need to get here before midsummer, and it's only a few days away."

The girl in the mirror showed no sign of hearing me. She pulled her pack higher on her back and kept on walking. But she understood. I was sure she did. I watched as she climbed a rocky hillside, traversed a deep valley, then made her way across a desolate plain where the grasses grew no taller than one joint of my little finger. The north wind whipped her hair into a brave red banner. *I'm coming to save you.* Those words thrilled me deep inside.

She stopped for the night in a little hut by a frozen pond. The hut had icicles hanging from its eaves: winter in summer. I guessed she had reached the foot of the glass mountain, where it was always cold, and my heart raced. Night fell in the mirror, and dawn came rosy bright. The girl and an old woman stood outside the hut, and the old woman pointed the way. She gave the girl something small and golden, and the girl slipped it into her pack. Before the mirror misted over, she turned her forthright green eyes straight on me. *Wait for me*, she said.

"I will, I will!" I whispered. "But hurry!" It was a long, hard climb up the mountain. Unless you were a bear.

Seven days until the wedding. Mother made me put on all my finery and practise walking up and down with my head held high and a smile on my face. When I was not straight enough to satisfy her she corrected me with a long stick.

"You will be on show, Hulde. The future Queen of the Mountain. You must shine. What is the matter with you? You are all a-tremble, and your smile is a death's-head grimace. Even a simpleton would not be convinced by it."

"It feels odd to be marrying a man I have never met, Mother. And . . . I am sad that Rune cannot be here."

"You'll be happy soon enough, when the fellow's bedded you."

Not being quite sure what she meant, I said nothing.

"As for Rune, that puzzle will resolve itself with no need for your interference, Daughter. After your wedding you will never see the bear again."

I endured the rest of my deportment lesson with my heart near-breaking. My wedding was only a few days away, and Rune was not here. He would never be here again. How could I live without him?

I waited for the green-eyed girl to come. Or for a miracle to bring Rune up the glass mountain. Or for myself to turn into a beautiful princess like the ones in the stories, and for the Prince of the Far Isles to decide he and I would ride away to live in his castle after all. There were six days left. Then five. Then only four. What would Rune advise me to do?

Don't wait for other folk to solve your problems, I thought. *Take hold of your story. Shape it the way you want. Don't be afraid.*

But I was afraid of my mother; scared almost to death. Too scared to ask questions. So scared I had accepted half-truths and tales that made no sense. What if there was no old superstition about it being bad luck for a man to see his bride in the thirty days before the wedding? What if the real reason she was keeping me away from the prince was that, once he saw me, he would no longer want to marry me? What if Rune had stayed away because . . . because . . . But no. A woman could not wed a bear.

In the mirror, something strange happened. It was as if a different story was beginning, in a different time and place. But not entirely different, because the green-eyed girl was in it, with a man so beautiful to look on that he must surely be the Prince of the Far Isles. His features were noble, his nose straight and strong. His hair was dark and glossy as a crow's wing, his skin pale and unblemished. I saw him fast asleep, lying on a bed hung with rich red cloth. The girl was in a nightrobe. She had a candle in her hand. She leaned over the man, looking down at him with her face all soft with love. Oh, I had never seen such a tender look! Three drops of wax fell from the candle onto his shirt, and instantly he was awake, springing up so fast the girl shrank back in terror. The candle wobbled in her hand, making strange shadows dance around the chamber.

Oh, Wife, the man said, taking the candle in its holder and setting it safely on a chest. *What have you done?* His words sent a shiver through me.

I'm sorry, dear heart. My mother made me do it . . . I'm so sorry. The green-eyed girl was shivering; she put her hands over her face.

I must leave you now. You have broken your vow, and I cannot stay. A long journey lies before me, a journey from which there is no returning. He enfolded her in his arms; she wept on his shoulder. *Goodbye, Beloved. I must go.*

Wait! she cried, stepping back from him. *Oh, Husband, please wait a little longer! Let me come with you!*

I must travel alone.

???

I love you! the girl said. *I would do anything to break this curse! Is there no way out?*

A long silence. Oh, how they gazed at each other! My hand was hurting. I had been gripping the mirror almost to breaking point. Then the man said, *There is a way. It is long. It will tax you hard.*

Tell me! the girl pleaded. *Whatever it is, however long it takes, I will save you. I promise.*

The mirror misted over, leaving only grey.

I was troubled. It seemed the green-eyed girl might be coming not to my rescue but to her husband's. And if she was climbing the glass mountain, that meant the beautiful man was here. Here, but under a curse only she could break. If he was the Prince of the Far Isles, how could he marry me? He had called the green-eyed girl *Wife*.

I thought again about the storeroom, the guards outside the walled garden, my mother's orders that I was not to stray. I thought about the blue-clad servant. I remembered the other way in, through the cellars and along a narrow passageway. The green-eyed girl was not here and time was running short. *Be brave, Hulde*, I told myself, shivering. As I made my way to the cellars, what frightened me most was not the prospect of my mother's wrath. It was the knowledge that to get to the heart of this, I would have to do what I had spent my whole life trying not to do. I would have to act as she would. I would have to be what I had most feared to see in the mirror: my mother's daughter.

Outside, it was close to dusk. Down in the maze of passageways and chambers that ran into the heart of the mountain, lamps hung along the walls to light the way. Here and there servants perched on ladders to trim wicks and top up the oil. I tried not to remember the time my mother had lost her temper and kicked out a ladder from under a boy. She had escaped unhurt; he had not. I could still see him burning.

The entry to the storeroom ran off a guard post. In this small chamber three men were sitting over a jug of ale, but they leaped to their feet when I appeared. I did not need to do anything to make folk frightened. And yet, I had never spoken an unkind word to them. I had hardly spoken any word at all.

"I understand . . . " That voice would not do; it was too soft, too hesitant, not the sort of voice the green-eyed girl would use. "I understand you have someone staying in that storeroom." That was better; a poor imitation of Mother's imperious tone, but firm and strong nonetheless. I pointed to the narrow way that led to the storeroom door.

The men exchanged nervous glances. No doubt Mother had given them orders that I was not to be let in; not to be told anything. There was an assortment of bottles, large and small, and the remains of some bread and cheese on the table. I wondered if they had broken a rule and were expecting me to punish them.

"Yes, my lady," said the oldest of them.

"That is an odd place to house a guest," I said.

"The queen's orders, my lady." The man shifted his feet.

"Who is it?"

They looked at each other again; looked at the floor.

"Answer me!" I took a step toward them and saw them cringe, though I had no whip in my hand. I had not even clenched my fists. I realised I was as tall now as the tallest of the guards, and as strongly built. I was almost as tall as my mother. "Speak up!" My belly churned; I wanted to be sick. I hated this Hulde, the one who could make folk shrink back in terror. I wished she had never been born.

"A nobleman, my lady. A visitor."

"Has this nobleman a name?"

"It's the prince," one of the others blurted out, earning himself a scowl from his superior. "The Prince of the Far Isles."

"The chamber has been comfortably fitted out, my lady." The head guard was pale. "This was . . . it was the prince's choice."

I was not as surprised as I might have been, having seen the green-eyed girl weeping over the man she called her husband. How could there be two such beautiful men in the world? I wanted to order the storeroom door opened, so I could confront the prince with the fact that he was already married. But perhaps the story in the mirror had been all my own imagining. And if it turned out the tale about ill luck and thirty days was true, charging in to confront the prince might set my whole future in jeopardy.

I thought could hear someone moving about in the storeroom, pacing to and fro with an odd, dragging kind of step. I wondered if my mother, in furnishing the place to befit my future husband, had ordered Rune's drawings to be scratched off the wall. That was *his* room. It was *my* room. Within its stone walls I had wept long for him. I did not want anyone else in there. I did not want anyone touching what he had made for me.

"I imagine the prince is not confined there night and day," I said, turning what I hoped was a fearsome glare on the head guard. "Yet I have not seen him at the supper table or in the garden. Does he receive visitors?"

"No visitors, my lady. We're under orders to leave him alone during the day. We take in a breakfast tray before dawn and a supper tray in the evening, goblet of wine and all. Cooks send the food down."

"The prince did not travel with his own servants?"

"No, my lady."

"I thought I saw someone in the walled garden. A man in a blue shirt."

That glance again, as if they were weighing up my mother's anger against mine. "There's a fellow," the head guard said. "A mute. Does the dirty jobs. He goes in there to clean up sometimes."

"A mute? What is that?" I had never heard the word.

"Fellow's got no tongue, my lady. Can't talk." I thought he was going to say something more, but he thought better of it.

"I see." What I saw was another part of Mother's plan to keep the truth from me. Perhaps my future husband was already married. Perhaps he would think me so appalling to look upon that he would turn tail and flee at first sight—that would be why she was making me wear the wretched veil. Perhaps *he* was appalling to look upon, though I would not mind that very much, provided he was kind. Especially if he took me away from the glass mountain. Would he be strong enough to stand up to Mother? Was anyone?

"Thank you," I said, and made my way back up to ground level. What now? Three days and three nights left, and I had no idea what to do.

The mirror had no answers. Its surface had turned to a sullen, flat grey with not the least sign of an image. Where was the green-eyed girl? Had she fallen to her doom half way up the mountain? Or was she still climbing? I wanted to rip the poxy bridal gown to shreds. I wanted to hurl the silver shoes out the window. I wanted to scream.

And then, when I had dismissed my maids after supper and was attempting to tidy my hair, there came a tap at my bedchamber door.

"I told you to go away!" I snarled as the comb caught in a tangle.

"My lady."

The voice was not that of Marit or Lina. It was not my mother's voice. It was . . . I did not dare turn around, for fear I should be only imagining her. I held up the mirror to show the doorway behind me, and there she was, looking right at me.

I wanted to leap up, to throw my arms around her, to confide my whole story. I wanted to ask every question at once. I had so longed for her to come, a friend, a companion, a confidante . . . But the look on her face halted me. That look told me what courage she had had to find in order to come near me. It told me how scared she was. Of me. Even *she* found me loathsome, though she was working hard to stay calm.

"Lady Hulde?" she said. "I am but newly arrived in this house. A maidservant. I have something here, a gift for you. I . . . I heard that you liked kittens."

A kitten! I had longed for one since I was three years old. My hands ached to hold it. But I was no longer a child; I would soon be married. "I can't have a pet," I said. "I would kill it with my clumsy hands."

"Oh, no!" the girl said, breaking all my mother's rules by coming right into my bedchamber. She had a little bag with her, and now she set it down and lifted out something small and black. "You would not kill this kitten; it is very sturdy. If you wind up this little handle here, it runs about and chases a ball, and if you touch this little button here, it mews so sweetly. Its fur is very soft, and you can pet it all you like. When you are tired of it, just put it away somewhere. Let me show you."

I was entranced. I could have played with the kitten all night. It was a gift to equal the precious things Rune had given me. As I sat on the floor watching the little one run about, I asked the girl, "What is your name? And why would you bring this for me?"

"My name is Laerke," she said. "I thought you might be lonely, Lady Hulde."

It did not seem to matter that she was breaking more rules every time she spoke. This was different. She was the girl from the mirror, and ordinary rules did not apply. Laerke. What a wonderful name. I wished I was named after a bird.

"The gift is given freely," she said. "But I do have a favour to ask."

I waited.

"I understand you are soon to be married," Laerke said, glancing at the bridal gown on the wall.

"In three days."

"I need to . . . I want to . . . This is difficult, Lady Hulde. I don't know how to say it." She looked at me as a friend might, eyes wide, mouth half-smiling.

"Tell me," I said.

"I cannot explain why, but . . . the man you are to marry . . . he is a friend, familiar to me, and . . . and I need to speak with him alone. At night. That sounds odd, I know. But I hope very much you will grant my request. To . . . to spend the night in his chamber . . . "

"If my mother knew you had asked such a thing, she would have you killed. She would kill you herself."

"Yes, I . . . I have heard that the Queen of the Mountain is somewhat fierce. Hulde—may I call you that?—if I promise you that he and I will do nothing more than talk . . . If I promise that I will not touch him . . . Please?"

Nobody had ever spoken to me so sweetly. Apart from Rune, and Rune was gone.

"My mother gets very angry," I said. "Angrier than you could imagine. If she found out, we would all be punished. You, me, the guards, everyone. Her punishments are . . . rather harsh."

"Then she must not find out." Laerke's eyes were ablaze with courage; it was an invitation to be as brave as she was. "Help me, Hulde. Please."

She was sweeping the story forwards, and I could not resist her. "Very well," I said. "I'll do my best."

I did not tell her about the mirror. I did not tell her I knew—suspected—that she and my bridegroom were married. Should my mother learn that, she would see a simple solution. If Laerke met with a fatal accident, the prince would be free to marry again.

I told Laerke that the prince was locked away on his own, because of the need not to be seen by me before the wedding. I told her where she would find him, and how she could get into the walled garden. I was too big to fit through the gap in the wall, but Laerke was slender; she could do it. I explained where the storeroom key was hidden. I took her to my window and showed her where the garden was.

"You could go now," I said. "It's getting dark, but not too dark to see the way. There will be guards at the gate. In the morning, make sure you come out before it's light or they'll see you. I'm not sure you know what a great risk you're taking. If you're caught, I won't be able to help."

"I do know," she said. "Thank you, Hulde. I had heard that you were a kind person, and I see it is true."

Who could possibly have told her that? "Good luck. You'd best go. Come back in the morning and tell me what happened."

That night, I did not see Laerke in the mirror. I did not see the Prince of the Far Isles. But I did see a white bear running through a forest, his pelt catching the moonlight. "Rune," I breathed, wondering if he was on his way to the mountain of glass; hoping beyond hope that he would be here before the wedding and that everything would be made right. I knew it was foolish. What could he do? But I wept, and hoped, and held my black kitten close to my breast.

Laerke was back in the morning, after my maids had cleared away my breakfast tray. She had her red hair tied up in a kerchief, and was carrying a bucket and mop.

"Come in," I whispered, glancing up and down the hallway. I bundled her into my chamber and bolted the door. "What happened?" I saw, then, that her eyes were red.

"I couldn't wake him. I tried and tried. All night. I think he'd been given a sleeping draught. But who would do that?"

Why was she looking at me that way? Could she be thinking *I* had drugged my bridegroom? My heart clenched tight; I had thought we were friends. "My mother has a store of such potions," I said. "She might have ordered it done. I don't know why." I could not stop myself from adding, "I couldn't have done it, Laerke. There wasn't time. Besides, why would I help you see him, then prevent you from talking to him? That doesn't make sense."

"I'm sorry," she said, with a sweet smile. "I'm worried, that's all. Could we try again tonight?"

"I'll think about it." Only two days until the wedding. If Rune was on the way here, it might be better to wait until he arrived before taking such a risk. Maybe Laerke would uncover the truth, whatever it was. Maybe she would cause a disaster with her meddling. "Hadn't you better go and do your cleaning, so nobody gets suspicious?"

When she came back later, she had her little bag with her. I was on the floor playing with my kitten, but when she took out a snow-white puppy and made him run and jump and let out little wuffing sounds, I could not wait to play with him.

"Oh, how precious! What wonderful things you have!"

"For you, if you would like it. It's a gift, yours even if you say no to my request. We are friends, aren't we?" She put her hand on my shoulder. It was an offence that would have earned her a whipping if Mother had seen, but it filled me with warmth.

"We're friends," I said. "Try again tonight if you wish."

"Could you . . . is there a way to find out about the sleeping draught? Perhaps to be sure he does not take it?"

"Without alerting my mother? Almost impossible. I've already been down to the guard room once, asking questions about who was in that chamber. I don't see how I can do it."

She turned her eyes on me; laid both hands on mine. It was like a picture in a book of tales: *Faithful Laerke pleads with the Queen's Daughter.* "Please, Hulde."

"Why is it so important that you speak to him?" I made myself ask, though I was not sure I wanted an answer.

"I cannot tell you. I promised. If I tell, I will bring down a curse."

A curse! This really was like a tale of wonder and magic. And I was part of it. I must not be the part that prevented the happy ending. "I will try to find out about the sleeping draught," I said. "But I can't promise anything. This is very dangerous, Laerke. I don't think you can understand how dangerous."

I meant to do as I'd promised. I meant to go down to the cellars and find out if anyone was drugging the prince's wine. But my mother called me to her quarters and made me spend all day there learning a dance she said everyone would be performing at the wedding, a swaying, turning, tripping thing that made me dizzy. When I said I felt unwell, she made me lie down on her bed to rest. When I said I was hungry, she had her servants bring a tray of delicacies. By the time I escaped, it was dark outside and Laerke was nowhere to be seen.

I was tired and sad. I felt defeated. I had tried to be a hero, like Laerke, but I was no hero. I was clumsy and stupid. I had thought there might be friends for me. But Rune was gone, and Laerke would go, and I would be all alone again. Except for a prince who, I suspected, did not really want to marry me. And my mother.

I tucked my kitten and my little dog in my bed, as if they were real. I did not feel like playing with them. I took out the mirror. I did not feel like looking in it, but something in me, a spark that was not quite extinguished, made me look anyway.

The storeroom was almost in darkness. One lamp burned in a corner, throwing soft light over the sleeping form of the most beautiful man in the world, and the figure of Laerke bending over him, just as she had before when she had held out a candle to illuminate his face, and had startled him with drops of hot wax.

But it was not the same. Then, she had been trying not to wake him. Now she was pleading for him to wake. But the drug held him immobile, his chest barely rising and falling. Oh, he was indeed a beautiful man. Noble, strong and good. I need not hear him speak to know that. I need not look in his eyes. I knew it in my heart. Such a man would never, ever have chosen to marry me.

I watched a long time as Laerke wept and begged, and the prince lay deathly still. Finally, exhausted, she laid her head down on the bed and fell asleep. That was when I saw the shirt. It was draped over a chest, and even in the deceptive surface of the mirror I could tell it was the same one he had been wearing before. I knew that somewhere on that shirt there would be a mark from hot wax. I thought I remembered, in one of Rune's tales, that hot wax could be used in a magical charm. Laerke had said the prince was under a curse. And as soon as the wax drops had touched his clothing, he had told her he must leave her. Why would he bring that stained shirt all the way to the glass mountain, when he was wealthy enough to own as many shirts as he wanted?

I was afraid Laerke might sleep late and be discovered when the servant took in the prince's breakfast, but when I looked out my window in the morning there was no sign of a disturbance in the walled garden. The guards stood at the gate as usual; otherwise the place looked deserted.

One day until my wedding. One day and one night to shape the story the way I wanted. But what did I want? I did not want to be married on the strength of a lie or a curse, even if the bridegroom was beautiful and rich and my mother's choice. If I refused to marry him, Mother would be so furious she would probably kill me before she realised what she was doing. If I told her he was already married, she would hunt out Laerke and kill her. That was my mother's way.

Laerke came to my chamber in mid-morning, carrying her mop and bucket. She was sickly pale and her eyes looked bruised. She didn't say anything, only shook her head.

"I've made a plan," I said when we were both safely inside with the door bolted. "I couldn't do what you wanted yesterday, but I may have better luck tonight."

"Really, Hulde?" Her voice was trembling.

I wanted her to be brave. I needed her to be brave. Today, I had to lie to my mother. "I'll do my best," I said. "Be ready at nightfall, and don't alert the guards."

My plan depended on three things. Firstly, that my mother did not think it odd that I sought out her company for the day. Secondly, that I had guessed right about the sleeping draught—where it came from, and how it was being used. Lastly, that I could steal a small bottle from my mother's chamber and get it down to the guard room. *It's a quest*, I told myself. *An adventure*. I had not realised how terrifying a real adventure could be.

"Mother?"

"What do you want, Hulde? Can't you see how busy I am?"

"I was hoping . . . I need to practise the dance again. And walking up and down in my wedding gown. Could I do that here? I will keep out of your way. If you happened to have a moment or two free you could help me to get it right. To tell you the truth, I am a little nervous about being married. I would be happier if I could spend some time with you."

She hardly listened; she was sorting out the contents of a jewel box, perhaps deciding which of her adornments she would wear tomorrow. "Of course, if you wish," she said without bothering to look at me.

I had brought the gown, the silver shoes, the veil. I changed in and out of them. I practised dancing. I practised walking like a princess. I perfected my curtsy. I spent a great deal of time brushing my hair. When a maidservant brought refreshments on a tray I sat down with my mother to share them. The day passed, and I waited for my opportunity.

It came when a serving man knocked on the door, and told my mother the banqueting table was set up and ready for her to check. She rose with a sigh.

"How tiresome! These folk cannot be trusted to get anything right. I won't be long, Hulde. Perhaps you should come with me. One day, this sort of thing will be your responsibility."

"My feet are hurting." This was true. "I'd best go back to my own quarters. Thank you for helping with my dancing." She had been almost kind; the kindest I had ever seen her. If she knew what I was planning her mood would change in a flash.

"Very well. Make sure your maid irons that gown again and steams out the veil—there must be not the slightest crease. I can hardly believe it: my little Hulde, about to wed the most beautiful man in the whole world. Our lives will be transformed."

She swept out of the chamber, leaving me alone. I moved fast, bolting the door, then going to the special cupboard where she kept her draughts and potions. She used the sleeping draught every night. It did not fell her as it had the prince. I had seen that in order to sleep, she needed more of it now than she once had. She had the household apothecary make it up in small bottles, each a single dose. There were ten of them lined up on the shelf. I hoped she had not counted them.

With one bottle tucked under my sash, I closed the cupboard, collected my belongings, unbolted the door and returned to my own chamber. I tipped the sleeping draught out the window and refilled the bottle from my water jug. So far, so good.

Something flew past, whistling, and I ducked in fright. It flew by again, then landed on the window sill. A bird. A golden bird. Laerke had left me another gift. It was curiously made, its many interlocking parts fashioned of fine metal, though the feathers were soft to the touch. Its voice was high and clear. I could not hear it without imagining an open sky. "Oh, you are beautiful," I said, holding out my finger for the little one to perch on. It tilted its head to the side and examined me with eyes so bright and clever that I wondered if there was magic in the making of it. Over on the bed, the black kitten and the white puppy were sitting up, aquiver with excitement as they watched the newcomer. I did not remember turning any handles or pushing any buttons.

However this works out, I thought, *when it is all over at least I will have them. No matter that they are not truly alive. They are almost as good as real ones. And I will still have more friends than I had before.*

Later, I sent Marit with a message to my mother saying I would have my supper on a tray in my bedchamber. That seemed not unreasonable on my wedding eve. The kinsfolk from the Realm Beneath were celebrating for me, with a lot of shouting. There were flaming torches and folk running about outside. That scared me. What if Laerke was caught as she climbed through the garden wall?

I sent Marit early for the tray, then dismissed her. Most of the household was heading in for supper. I waited in a shadowy corner until no more guards came up from the cellars, then I went down. If I was wrong about the sleeping draught, this would be useless.

There was only one man in the guard room. When I came in he leapt to his feet.

"Only one?" I bellowed in my best imitation of Mother.

"Supper time—change of shift —"

The guard had turned grey with terror. It disgusted me that I could do this so easily. "Has the tray come down for the prince yet?"

"No, my lady. Should be here any moment."

"Go and check. Now. And keep your mouth shut, you understand, or you will pay for it."

"Yes, my lady." He fled, leaving the storeroom door unguarded. This was not as lax as it seemed, since heavy iron bolts were drawn across it. If I had so chosen, I could have pulled them open and marched right in. I could have confronted my future husband and made him tell me the truth. But that was not what I had promised Laerke; Laerke who had brought me my three little friends; Laerke who had crossed a wilderness and forded a river and climbed a mountain to get here. Laerke who stuck to her mission even when she was sad and lonely and scared half out of her wits.

That's what being brave is, Hulde, I told myself. *Not doing great deeds. Just keeping on going, whatever happens.*

No time to waste. I searched the cluttered table, hoping I was right about what I'd seen there the first time. Where was it? Ah! Here in a clutter of wine bottles. I snatched it and slipped it into my pocket, then brought out the other, identical container I had taken from my mother's cupboard. Provided this was where the prince's nightly wine was doctored, my plan would work. If the sleeping potion was already in the cup when the tray left the kitchen, Laerke would have another wasted night, and the wedding would go ahead as planned. I might be a little brave, but I was not brave enough to tell my mother outright that I refused to marry the prince. If I did, she would force the reason from me, and Laerke would die. I knew it in my bones.

The manservant was back. He set the laden tray down on the table, then stood waiting. Waiting for me to leave.

"Go ahead, take his supper in," I said. "Don't mind me."

Still he stood there, awkward, not quite prepared to speak.

"Shall I help you with that?" It was foolish, perhaps; but it would protect me from Mother's wrath if she found out. I stepped forward, picked up the little bottle, took out the cork and poured the contents into the goblet that stood on the tray beside the prince's covered platter. "There."

"You know about this, my lady?"

"Did I ask you to comment?"

"No, my lady."

"Then hold your tongue. Take the prince's supper in and, if you know what is good for you, stay silent on this matter."

There was a narrow escape on the way back to my bedchamber, as Mother came along a hallway and I was forced to shrink into an alcove, holding my breath. She passed, not seeing me. I fled. In my chamber, my three friends were waiting, the kitten and puppy now on the floor rolling about—most certainly, I had not wound them up—the golden bird perched on the peg that held my wedding gown. Curse it! I would have to call Marit or Lina to press the wretched thing.

I hid the three friends away in my storage chest, murmuring an apology. I called my maids and ordered them to take gown and veil away, get every crease out, and not bring them back until tomorrow. I closed and bolted the door after them. My supper tray was waiting on the small table, but I was not hungry. Outside, the light had faded into the long summer dusk. Soon Laerke would make her dangerous trip across the walled garden and into the storeroom. I let the little ones out, setting the kitten and puppy on the bed and letting the bird stretch its wings.

Time for the mirror. *You can do it, Laerke,* I thought. *Make the story brave and true. If he's yours, take him and be happy.* Because a good story always had a happy ending, didn't it?

In the mirror, the Prince of the Far Isles lay on his bed in the storeroom, the strong planes of his face turned to gold by the lamplight. His supper tray stood on a chest, the goblet empty. His eyes were closed, the dark lashes soft against his cheeks.

The outer door creaked open. He started, sitting up abruptly. There was Laerke on the threshold, in her serving woman's clothes, with her red hair loose over her shoulders. She closed the door and turned to face him.

"Oh, gods!" she said, her eyes alive with joy. "She did it! You're awake!"

"Laerke!" The prince was on his feet. He opened his arms wide. "My love, my dearest, you're here!"

She ran into his embrace, weeping against his shoulder. He stroked her hair; she nestled against him as if he were her home, her heart, her safety from the storm. It was just like something from a grand old story, and it made me cry, but I did not know if I shed tears of happiness that he and she had found each other, or of sorrow that nobody would ever look at me like that, hold me like that, love me like that. I was clumsy and stupid. I had achieved this for Laerke only by doing bad things: lying, stealing, frightening people.

Laerke and the prince held each other for a long time, whispering words I could not hear. They touched each other in ways that were strange and new to me. At length they sat down side by side on the bed, hand in hand.

"Tomorrow," the prince said. "After sunset, since the queen will not let me out until I am in this form again. The key is the shirt, Laerke. Wash the shirt clean and you will win me my freedom. I will be a man forever, and we can go home."

"The queen will be furious," said Laerke. "When she's angry she kills people. She rips them apart with her bare hands. One of the serving women told me."

"Nonetheless," said the prince, putting his arm around her, "a curse follows rules, like any other form of magic. Once it's lifted, it's lifted entirely and forever. I will no longer be forced to switch between human and animal form; no longer required to come here every third summer; no longer bound to this marriage. She must let us go. We will be free to live our lives and to shape our own story."

I couldn't breathe. My heart hurt. A flood of tears waited to fall, somewhere behind my eyes.

"This is all my fault," Laerke said, hanging her head. "If I had not been curious . . . if I had done as you bid me, and not tried to look at you by night . . . "

"It is not your fault."

I wondered, now, that I had not recognised his voice, so deep and soft, so gentle and sweet. How could I not have known?

"We could not have gone on that way forever. It would have destroyed us. Now we have the chance to make things right, Laerke. That is thanks to you. I don't know how you did it. How you travelled all this way to find me."

"Could you not see me in your little mirror?"

"I lost the mirror," he said. "I thought you might not come. But you're here, my brave one."

"I do not deserve you," she said. "You are too good for me, dearest Rune."

"Nonsense." He kissed her on the lips. "You are precious beyond any treasure, my love. You'd best go now. Tomorrow, perform your usual duties all day and try to avoid notice. Just make sure that when the ceremony is about to begin, you are there, concealed in the crowd. Leave the rest to me."

"Rune?"

"Yes, my dearest?"

"What about Hulde? What will happen to her?"

The most beautiful man in the world smiled as he thought of me. It was not the sort of smile he bestowed on Laerke. It was the smile of a friend; the smile a kindly man might give to a child. "I have tried to help her," he said. "To give her the means to help herself. But I cannot do more. She must make her own life."

"I am a woman," I whispered. "And I love you. You are the sun, moon and stars. Don't leave me, Rune!"

But Rune could not hear. The mirror misted over and turned to grey.

For a heartbeat I was cold stone. Then the bird flew past me, trilling merrily. I snatched her in her flight and hurled her against the wall, where she smashed into a thousand tinkling pieces.

I wept until I was sick. I wept until there was not one tear left in me. For a little, I must have fallen asleep, for I woke to find the kitten pressed against my neck and the puppy curled by my side. *They forgive everything*, I thought. *Even the most terrible of rages, the most violent of acts, they forgive.*

It was possible, then, to get up from the bed. I poured water from the jug, washed my face, cleaned up as best I could. I knelt down and gathered every fragment of the bird, every last golden cog and wheel, every last tiny glittering feather. She was broken; she would never fly again. I wrapped her pieces in a silken kerchief and held her in my hands. She weighed almost nothing.

When someone dies, there are supposed to be words spoken. I could not think what they might be. "I'm never going to do that again," I whispered. "I'm never going to let anger get the better of me. I'm not going to scare people into doing what I want. I'm not going to let people scare me into doing what I know is wrong. I'm sorry. You were so beautiful." After all, there did seem to be more tears. When I had shed them, I tucked the silken kerchief into my secret hiding place, alongside my books and my wax tablet.

Then I had to face it, the wonderful thing, the terrible thing. I could marry Rune. If I went to my mother now and told her the truth, it could still happen. I loved him. Maybe he didn't love me, not the way he loved Laerke, but he was fond of me. Mother could dispose of Laerke; nobody in the household would even know she had existed. The wedding could go ahead as planned. If I told Rune how scared I was on the glass mountain, if I begged him to take me away, surely he would do it. Hadn't he said I should make my own life? Wasn't this the life I had longed for through all those lonely years of waiting? It was within my grasp. If I wanted it, I could have it.

I lay down on the bed with my kitten on one side and my puppy on the other, and told them my plan.

Midsummer, and my sixteenth birthday. The wedding was set for dusk; if the guests thought it odd that the bridegroom did not appear earlier, they made no comment. The folk from the Realm Beneath had been quaffing ale all day and were in high spirits. When the time came to gather, the other guests clustered together at one end of the reception hall. Lamps hung from the walls; in the chamber next door, a long table was set with cups and platters I had never seen in my life before. They looked as if they were made of real gold. "My grandmother's," Mother had said. "Not used since I married your father. One day you'll be bringing them out for your own daughter's wedding, Hulde. That gives me great pride. Great pride."

Now here I was, standing beside her in my stiff wedding gown, with my feet squeezed into the too-small shoes and my face covered by the veil, waiting. I was good at waiting; I'd had a lot of practice. But this was different. It was all I could manage not to collapse from sheer terror. My heart was juddering in my chest and my body was all cold sweat. It was just as well nobody could see my face.

There were musicians. Where Mother had got them from I had no idea, but now they struck up a fanfare, and into the hall came Rune, quite alone. He was clad in snowy white, the colour of the beautiful bear he had been, the bear I had loved with all my heart. He walked the length of the hall toward us, and I saw that the man had the same blue eyes as the bear, eyes as lovely as a summer sky. I began to understand why Laerke had broken the rules and looked at him, that night of the spilled wax.

He was very solemn. He looked more like a man attending a burial than his own wedding. At the foot of the raised platform where Mother and I stood, he stopped and bowed. "My ladies."

Mother dropped into a curtsy. "My lord prince," she said.

I bobbed my own awkward curtsy, but said nothing, lest my voice come out as a squeak of terror.

"Come up beside us, Prince Rune," Mother said. "Take my daughter's hand in yours."

"Ah," said Rune.

The crowd stirred. People craned their necks to see.

"There's something I must tell you," Rune said, half-turning so everyone could hear him. "I am bound by a solemn vow; a magical vow that I cannot break for fear of my life. I can marry only the woman who can wash this shirt clean." He brought out the shirt from the pouch at his waist; though rather crumpled, it did not look soiled. "There are three drops of wax here, near the right sleeve. She who can wash them out is my true bride. She and no other."

Mother was quivering with fury. Still, she managed to keep her voice in check. There was a whole hall full of people watching and listening. "I do not understand, Prince Rune," she said. "We have an agreement. You have promised to wed my daughter, and here she is, waiting. Would you break your word?"

Rune smiled. "If your daughter can wash the shirt clean, then I will marry her."

Mother cursed under her breath. She could not defy him. A magical vow had to be respected. "Very well," she snapped, then waved a hand at the household steward. "Fetch a bowl of warm water, soft soap, a brush. Now!"

The crowd was loving this. They edged closer, not wanting to miss a moment. The hall was abuzz with excited voices, though, knowing my mother, most kept their comments to an undertone.

I stood there like a forgotten statue as the materials for washing were brought in and set on a small table, up on the raised area where folk could see. Rune had not moved; he was at the foot of the steps, grave and silent.

"Now," Mother said grandly, "let us proceed, though I do find this all rather ridiculous. Daughter, push back your veil or you'll get it wet."

I lifted the veil and threw it back over my hair. Took a long look at Rune, with his glossy black hair and his summer-blue eyes and his fine man's body. Looked back at my mother. Straight into her eyes. "I won't do it," I said.

For a moment she stood stunned, unable to believe it. Then she went white. Then an angry red appeared in her cheeks, and her veins stood out, and her eyes looked about to pop from her head. Despite myself, I took a step backward.

"*What did you say?*" She spoke so quietly most of the crowd would not have heard. Her tone turned my blood to ice.

"I said, I won't do it. I won't wash the shirt." I willed myself not to faint, not to weep, not to lose control of myself in any way at all. "If that means I can't marry the prince, then so be it." I held my back straight and my head high, as she had taught me.

She lifted her hand to strike me. I did not flinch, though I knew what damage those long nails could do. Rune took a step forward, began to say something, perhaps, *No!* And Mother, maybe deciding she did not want her daughter to be married with a set of bleeding scars across her cheek, withdrew her hand. "Give me the shirt!" she snarled.

Rune handed her the garment and she plunged it into the water. She pummelled and wrung and twisted and scrubbed. She scratched at the stain with her nails. She rubbed it against the bowl. She spat on it and cursed it and, in the end, took the sodden garment from the water and held it up. What had been a tiny blemish, a mere three drops, now spread across the entire front of the shirt. The more she had washed it, the worse the stain had become.

"Sorcery!" Mother shouted. "Evil enchantments! Foul trickery! There's no woman in the world who could get this wretched thing clean!"

Rune glanced sideways; gave the smallest nod of his head.

"I can," said Laerke, stepping out of the crowd. She was in a gown and apron of plain grey, and her red hair was demurely plaited down her back. Her eyes were all courage. *Brave Laerke confronts the Wicked Queen.*

"Fetch clean water," said Rune. "Let us make this quite fair."

Mother was seething. She was simmering like a pot on the fire. I clutched my hands together, wondering if I would see Laerke torn apart before my eyes, and perhaps Rune too. If Mother killed them it would be my fault.

The steward brought clean water. When all was ready Laerke stepped forward, rolling up her sleeves. Rune handed her the dripping shirt; they were avoiding each other's eyes. Laerke moved up to the bowl and dipped in the shirt. She soaped it gently. She swirled it around. She touched the stain with her hand, then lifted the garment out.

It was snowy white. It was as white as the most beautiful bear in all the world. It was a garment fit for a prince. "There," Laerke said, holding it up.

The folk standing close nodded and pointed and exclaimed how perfectly clean it was. There was no way Mother could pretend otherwise. There was no way out.

"This is my true bride," Rune said quietly, and he took Laerke's hand in his. "I'm sorry, Hulde. I honour and respect you, but I cannot marry you. It could never have been. A man cannot wed a troll."

A troll. I had barely time to take the word in when my mother let out an unearthly shriek. The sound made the whole hall rattle and shake. The torches flared; the benches wobbled; folk gasped and clutched on to one another.

She screamed again and the floor shuddered. There were words in her cry, ugly, terrible words, some for Rune, some for Laerke, and some for me. Things I had never thought I would hear, even from her. Things I wished I could un-hear. If I had ever thought my mother loved me, even the tiniest bit, I knew now that for her I was only a means to an end, a commodity she could use to gain herself a fortune. Vile things tumbled and gushed and spewed out of her. Even the folk from the Realm Beneath blocked their ears. Rune had his arm around Laerke; they had backed away from the platform. I wanted to run. I wanted to hide. I wanted to be anywhere but here. Instead I stood motionless as the foul wave of insults crashed over me.

The third scream was her undoing. She filled her lungs, tipped her head back and gave a mighty bellow. There was a popping sound, a change in the air, and suddenly I was teetering on the brink of a great hole in the floor, a hole so deep it seemed to have no bottom. I threw myself backwards and fell sprawling on the tiles.

She was gone. My mother, the Queen of the Mountain, was gone. Her anger had destroyed her. I sucked in a breath. Staggered to my feet. Shucked off my silver shoes. Now I was queen, and there could be no running away.

I held up my hands. The crowd fell silent.

"Please leave the hall," I said. "There will be no wedding."

Things happened. I made them happen. Rune and Laerke helped me. There was a search for what remained of my mother, conducted by the wild kinsfolk, who were good at doing things underground. They found very little. I asked them, in passing, if there were others of our kind living elsewhere, and they said there were, though they could be hard to find. Everywhere there were mountains, there were trolls, they said. Everywhere there were bridges, there were trolls. Some friendly, some not so friendly. Troll was a name other folk gave them; they preferred to be known as hill folk. It was a good idea to take gifts, they said. They drew me a map, with likely spots marked on it. Then they left.

I despatched the other guests homeward. They went all too gladly.

Rune and Laerke offered to take me with them. Or, at least, he did. I was not so sure Laerke liked the idea, though she smiled and agreed when he said it.

"Thank you, but no," I said. "I wish you a happy life."

So they left, and I watched them go from my window, with my kitten in my arms and my puppy at my feet. My friends needed no winding up now; they were just like real ones. I watched until the most beautiful man in the world and the brave girl from the story vanished down the mountain on their long journey to the Far Isles and that lovely, light-filled castle I had once dreamed might be mine. I wondered for a little if I had been stupid to say no. But not for long.

I made a count of what was in the treasure room. I gave the servants three silver pieces each and told them they could stay or go, whatever they chose. The steward said he would stay. I put him in charge of the castle.

I packed a bag with a few clothes and all my treasures: the wax tablet and stylus, the books, the silken kerchief with the remains of my bird. Maybe, somewhere in the world, there was someone clever enough to mend her. I took a small bag of silver. I took some bread and cheese wrapped up in a red and white cloth, because that was what folk did in stories. I told the steward I would be back some time.

Then I set out, with my kitten on my shoulder and my puppy at my heels, to make my own story.

DAYENU

JAMES SALLIS

Dayenu. A song that's part of the Jewish celebration of Passover:
"It would have been enough for us."

1.

At 10:36 as I'm listening to accounts on the radio of a plane lost over the Arctic Sea, the noise from within the trunk gets to be so annoying that I stop the car, open up, and whack the guy with the cut-down baseball bat I stowed under the front seat. The ride's a lot better after that. They never find the plane.

Where I've pulled off is this little rise from which you can see the highway rolling on for miles in both directions, my very own wee grassy knoll. The trees off the road are at that half-and-half stage, leaves gone brown closer to the ground, those above stubbornly hanging on. Because of Union Day there's little traffic, two semis, a couple of vans and a pickup during the time I'm there, which is the only reason I'm risking everything to be out here and on the road taking care of one last piece of business. Even the government's mostly on hold.

What they never understood, I'm thinking as I get back in the car, what it took me so long to understand, is that after rehab I became a different person. Not as in some idiotic this-changed-my-life blather, or that last two minutes of screen drama with light shining in the guy's eyes and throbs of music. *Everything* changed. How the sky looks in early morning, the taste of foods, longings you can't put a name to. Time itself, the way it comes and goes. Learning all over how to do the most basic things, walk, hold onto a glass, open doors, brush teeth, tie shoes, put your belt on from the right direction—all this reconfigures the world around you. A new person settles in. You introduce yourself to the new guy and start getting acquainted. It can take a while.

An hour later I make the delivery and go about my business, not that there is any. They'd got too close this time and I'd gone deeper to ground, pretty much as deep as one can burrow. The gig was a hold-over from before, timing rendered it possible, so I took the chance. Messages left in various dropboxes now would grow up orphans.

I was staying on the raw inner edge of the city, a gaza strip where old parts of town hang on by their fingernails to the new, in a house with rooms the size of shipping crates. Tattoo-and-piercing parlor nearby, four boarded-up houses like ghosts of mine, an art gallery through whose windows you can see paintings heavy on huge red lips, portions of iridescent automobiles, and imaginary animals.

Nostalgia, dreamland, history in a nutshell.

The house owner supposedly (this gleaned from old correspondence and visa applications) was away "hunting down his ancestry," driven by the belief that once he knows about his great-great grandfather, his own blurry life will drift into focus. So here I am, with every item on the successful lurker's shopping list in place: semi-abandoned neighborhood, evidence of high turnover, no one on the streets, irregular or nonexistent patrols, no deliveries, few signs of curiosity idle or otherwise.

A week or so in, it occurred to me that the neighborhood had this fairy tale thing going. Grumpy old man half a block south, bighead ogre seen peering out windows of the house covered with vines, guy with cornrows who resided at the covered bus stop and could pass for a genie, even a little girl who lived down the lane.

Look at the same frame sideways, of course, and it goes immediately dark: poverty, political pandering, ineptitude, dispossession. Where you watch from, and how you look, dictates what you see.

A cascade of strokes, they told me. Infarctions. Areas of tissue death brought on by interruptions in blood supply and oxygen deprivation—like half a dozen heart attacks moved far north. No problem, they said. We'll go in and fix this.

So they did.

They came for me at 4 AM. No traffic or other sounds outside; the curfews were in place. And nothing more than a promise of light in the sky. The third step of the second landing creaked. I made sure of that with a bit of creative carpentry when I moved in.

Four of them. I counted the creaks. Then was out the window and down, gone truly to ground, by the time the last one hit the landing.

We wait to be gathered, my uncle always said. Tribally, commercially, virtually, finally. Uncle Cage disappeared when I was eight, in one of the myriad foreign lands where we indulged what were then called police actions. Hard upon that, his footprints and after-image began to leak away, public records, photographs, rosters. Within a matter of weeks he no longer existed.

Nothing in this old part of town had been planned. The alleyway in which I found myself was no exception; it simply came into being as buildings grew around it. Doorways, jury-rigged gates and dog-legged side paths could lead nowhere. But exits abounded. I took one at random, looking back to where their cars (always two of them, it seemed, always dark gray) sat at curbside, still and featureless as skulls.

We wait to be gathered.

That day, days before, the wind blew hard, tunneling down through the streets of the city bearing tides of refuse. Drink containers, bits of printout, feather and bone, scraps of clothing. Birds, mostly hawks, stayed put on building tops, electing not to launch themselves into the fray as, overhead, clouds collided and the large ate the small. I was on one of those building tops too, looking down at protestors who had gathered outside People's Hall, protestors largely in their late teens or early twenties, with a sampling from the next generation up sprinkled among them. Just over a hundred, I'd say, though news reports doubled that figure.

The police had military-issue equipment: weapons, body armor, full automatics, electrics. They waded into the kids, stunned a number of them, gassed the rest, now had them facedown on the ground roughly in squares.

There are no right angles in nature.

We're never too far from the ground. My uncle again.

Watching events below so closely, I had failed to notice the drone hovering nearby, took note of it only when one of the hawks launched from a rooftop. The hawk hit hard. Its talons scrabbled for a hold but, finding no purchase, it flew on. Unable to right itself, the drone crashed into the side of a building. Though not before it had scanned me and dialed it in.

Tulips.

In 17th century Holland, Uncle Cage told me, a single bulb of the rare *Semper Augustus* sold for the price of a good house. The tulip craze geared up in November 1636, ran its course, and burned itself out by February of the next year, forever a lesson on inflated markets, fabricated desire and greed of a sort not so much unlearned as endlessly learned and forgotten.

I was seven and had no idea what he was talking about. This was a year or so before he was supposed to come back for a visit, for shore leave. Before he disappeared. Before he got gathered.

I had no idea what he was talking about, but I did have memories of earlier stories, stories that would adhere over time to experiences of my own, form a latticework upon which hung notions of life untempered by slogans, manipulation and misdirection.

I took breakfast at a Quick'n'Easy, street name Queasy, directly across from the fast rail's inner loop, watching passengers flow onto the platform then drain into the maw of the cars or out onto the streets.

An abandoned building nearby, once a pharmacy, bore an arc of spray-painted letters on its front: REBORN. Another farther along, faded red and yellow colors suggesting it had once been a bodega, read BELIEVE. Christians come into the neighborhood at night and leave their mark, evaporate like dew.

I'd barely settled in at a window seat on the 6:56 Express when the aisle seat beside me filled. We picked up speed; station, sky and buildings outside ran together in a single blurred banner. The light on the camera at the front of the car blinked steadily. I kept my face averted as though looking out the window. Not that this would help all that much, should they engage recognition software.

"Sorry to keep you waiting," I said without turning to my seat mate.

"Two hours, a smidge less. About as I expected. This was your most likely egress."

"You ran a sim?"

"No need. The dogs were closing in, I knew where, I had absolute confidence they'd fail. There was a time we thought alike."

"You might easily have called in the dogs yourself. Primed the pump."

"Ah, but that would lack subtlety. Not to mention it would leave my size ten footprints scattered about digitally. Still, there it was. And when was I likely ever to have another chance to find you?"

Security came through the car randomly checking, a young woman shiny with purpose, uniform pants pressed blade-sharp, and we stopped talking. Outwardly calm, within I was anything but. Flee if possible, fight if not. But she passed us by. Moments later the train slowed almost to a stop as we drew abreast of the war memorial. Passengers went about their business, chatting to companions, working or browsing on links. One woman's eyes never left the wall. She could not see the name, but she knew it was there. Husband? Sibling? Child? As the last row of names crawled by, the train regained speed. At the border between municipalities, guards waved us through.

We went down, temporarily, at West End Station. Sniffers had flagged probable contraband—illicit drugs or explosives, usually—so trains were held and passengers offloaded to the platform. We'd scarcely lined up behind the sensor gates when a young man near the end broke and ran, only to stop moments later as though he'd run into an invisible wall—the first time I'd seen the new electrics in action. Guards unsheathed a wafer-thin stretcher, rolled him bonelessly onto it, and bore him away. Soon we were on the move again.

Warren waited till a teenaged Asian passenger, belt and backpack straps studded with what looked to be ancient revolver casings, passed.

"Here."

I took what he held out, a shape and weight familiar to my hand. Its cover creased and worn though it had to be new.

"A new name, history, vitals, the data manipulated just enough that scans won't flag it, but it's basically you. Most anywhere in the city and surround, these will suffice. You'll want to stay away from admin buildings, information centers." He turned to the window. "This would be your stop."

The announcement came then over the speakers. All our grand technology, and station calls still sound like hamsters gargling.

"Use the papers if you wish. If not, dispose of them. On the chance that you use them, Frances looks forward to seeing you."

I turned back and motioned for him to follow.

We're sitting in a foxhole in some country with too many vowels in its name. Officially this is a TBH, Transport Battle Habitat, and doesn't have much of anything to do with foxholes, but that's what we call it. Made of some mystery plastic that goes hard when you inflate it and soft again when you go the other way. Full stealth optics: bends and reflects light to blend with the surround or disappear into it—woodland, plains, whatever. Desert's harder, of course, but you could almost feel the poor thing struggling, doing its best.

Fran is sniffing at an RP she just tore into. The pack itself looks like jerky or tree bark. A meaningless script of letters and numbers on it but no clue what waits inside. She tries to break off a piece of whatever it is and can't, pulls the knife out of her boot.

"Adventure," I say. "Suspense."

"Hey, chewing on this at least will give me something to do for half an hour." We hear the wheeze and hollow grunt of shells striking not too far off. "The boys are playing again."

"Ding dong the witch ain't dead."

"Just polishing her teeth."

"Shiny!"

Lots of time to talk out there. I know about her favorite toy when she was four or five, a plastic submarine with a compartment you filled with baking soda to make it dive and surface, dive and surface. The head made of a carved coconut with seashells for eyes and ears. Her first kiss—from a boy twice her age whose hand crawled roughly into her shorts. The twin brother who died in a bombing, in the coffeeshop across the street from the college where he taught, when she was in boot camp.

"Everybody was going," she said when she told me about that. "My cat died. My brother. Our old man. Ever feel surrounded?"

I waited for a shell to hit, said "Nah" when one did.

Timing is everything.

She looks out the gun slot of the foxhole. "Dogs'll be next," she says.

The dogs were everywhere back then. Genetically manipulated, physical and mental augmentations. Ten or twelve of them would spill up over the horizon and surge towards you. Nothing short of heavy artillery stopped them. Even then, what was left of them, half dogs, forequarters, kept coming Most of the time they couldn't see the foxholes but knew they were there—smelled them, sensed them.

These do what we hope: circle us twice, snuffle ground, sniff air, do it all again and move on.

"Damn things give me the willies every time," Fran says.

"They're supposed to. Bring you up against the elemental, the savage, within yourself."

"Deep waters, college boy. Good to see all that schooling wasn't wasted."

"Most of it was. But knowledge is like cobwebs, get close enough, some stick."

Our coms crackle. Go orders. Moments later we're over the top, on our way to finding the elemental and savage within ourselves.

At night Foragers come out, looking for food, cast-off clothing, machine parts, citizens marooned for whatever reason in their world—anything they can use. Theirs is a mission of salvage, scooping up leftovers, cast-offs, the discarded. They decline the housing, employment, health care and securities guaranteed to all, choosing to live invisibly, perilously, and when every few years the government extends offers of amnesty, those offers go ignored.

Walking away from the station into thinner ground and air, we passed a number of Foragers who looked on, even followed a bit, before concluding it unwise to approach.

Warren watched as one, a woman in her late teens or early twenties, face pale above an ankle-length dark overcoat, military issue, took a final look and withdrew. "Interesting lives," he said.

"They're a part of you, deep inside, that longs to scream *No.*"

"Perhaps not so deep as you imagine." He touched a wall, ran his hand along it. Dark grit fell from the hand when he took it away. "How did we come to live in a world where everything is something else?"

"Other than what it seems? We've always lived there."

"Then how do choices get made?"

"Faith."

"Now there's something you can hold onto." He pulled out a link, looked for a moment at the screen, and replaced it. "Our plan to protect Frances—"

"By staging her death."

"—was solid, with high probability of success."

"Not that it would ever occur to others that it was a ploy."

He met my eyes, an action intended to register sincerity and directness but in effect defensive.

"*High probability* means you ran sims," I said, "as many times as it took for someone to get onto those runs."

"Of course."

"Then you had the tag. Trawled out and put them down. It wasn't about protecting Fran."

We walked on. Pavement out here was everywhere cracked, fractured into multiple planes, grass and weeds growing from the fissures like trees on a hundred tiny hills.

"Afterwards," Warren said, "she simply chose *not to*—much as you did."

Thinking I heard footsteps, I put out an arm to halt us. We stood quietly, breathing slowly. Nothing more came. "Do you know where she is?"

"No. Nor, we trust, do those attempting to kill her."

"You've intel?"

He shook his head. "Five words to a secure address. *Introduce me to your friend?*"

"A safe word."

"And her way of asking for you. A request she would make only . . . "

Around us, like his sentence, the city trailed off, neither quite there nor absent. Heaps of refuse that looked to be undisturbed. Few sign of rats or other rodents—larger beasts who'd rarely venture closer to the city saw to that.

College days. Stray bunches of us had got our heads filled with notions of retrieving history, scrubbing away the years, getting back to common ground we'd misplaced. Music became a part of this; for about five minutes I played at being a musician. Fell in quickly with Sid Coleman, and while I wasn't ever much good and wasn't going to be, I could bite into a rhythm and never let go. We started out playing for parties, college gigs and such. Later, it was mostly protest meetings.

Sid steamed with frustration from the get-go. What he wanted to do was talk politics but what everyone else wanted was for him to bring his guitar and sing. He had started out with old-time mountain music, discovered calypso and Memphis jug bands, slid into home base with songs against what we started calling the forever wars. He sang right up to the day he got his notice. That day he put his guitar away for good.

Sid and his crew were chowing down on a breakfast of beer and RPs when mortar shells struck. Eight were killed. And while Sid escaped further injury, the blasts took his hearing. This was a couple of borders over from where we are now. It's all the same war, he used to sing, they just move it from place to place.

—Hang on, Fran said, I need to pee. She checked with the infrared scope for all clear and stepped out. Got back and said Okay . . .

That's it. There isn't any more.

Oh.

But there was.

Years later, back home, I ran into Sid on the street. I could see in his face that he didn't remember me, though he claimed to. He wore fake fatigues, the kind they sell at discount stores, and bedroom slippers. His hair was carefully combed, with a sheen of oil that smelled rank. Don't get out much, he said. One social engagement on my calendar every month. On the 15th, 0900 to the minute, the government check lands in my account. No fanfare, no fail, there it is, egg plopped in the nest. And there I am too, waiting to claim my money.

Someone hands you a gun, you don't check it out before you use it, be sure of its function, you're a fool. Same with false papers. Next morning I crossed the southeast border into Palms, a city with no industry or trade centers and of scant strategic interest, populated as it is by the aged afloat on their pensions.

Cities, like the civilizations they reflect, find their rhythm. Their surges, falls. Areas within falter, decline and bottom out, open to new strains of inhabitants and push their way back up. Palms for now was on hold, a single sustained note.

From town's center I walked out to the grand artificial lake where picnic tables, benches, and teeter-totters squatted at eight-meter intervals around clear water. Teeter-totters, one assumes, for visiting grandchildren, though that day there were none. Plenty of elderly folk at the tables or sitting with feet in the water on low-slung walls, people a generation or two younger standing by. Caretakers.

I ended up back in town at a sparsely populated outdoor café, server and barrista of an age with those around. Bob, the server, put me in mind of oldtime French waiters, professional mien and mantle donned with his apron. The barrista's demeanor came from warmer climes; she tapped on cup bottoms, swiveled about, triggered the steamer in syncopated bursts as she worked. Mildred's a peach, Bob said, directing his gaze briefly that way when I commented.

A couple I'd estimate to be in their eighties sat across from one another at a table nearby, each with a link propped before. She'd key in something on hers, he'd look at his. They'd both look up and smile. Then it was his turn.

Children? Images from long ago—a vacation on the big island before the embargos, places they'd lived, concerts and celebrations attended, their younger selves?

Even stolid Bob registered their happiness, careful not to interrupt but repeatedly locating himself close by lest they need something.

A frail-seeming man in eyeglasses sat reading an actual book whose title I eventually made out to be *A History of Radical Thought*. Interesting, that use of the indefinite article, I thought, *a* instead of *the*; one had to wonder at the content. There could be so many such histories.

When Bob set down a tea cake at another table, the woman there waited for him to walk away then quickly dipped her head and with one hand in half a moment sketched a shape in the air before her: silent prayer, and what few would recognize as the sign of the cross.

Across the street, in a park bordered on the far side by offset stands of trees, two women in sundresses, a style I recalled from childhood, were flying a kite made to look like a huge frog and awash with bright yellows, crimson, metallic blues. The runner had just let go the kite; both laughed as the frog took to sky.

Smelling of fresh earth, rich and dark, the coffee was good. I had three cups, took another walk round the lake, and remounted the train without challenge or incident. On the trip back, mechanical or guidance problems delayed us, and it grew dark as we reached the city, lights coming on about us, curfew close enough to give concern. Officials waited on the platform to issue safe passes. Elsewhere, automatic weapons cradled in their arms, soldiers who looked to be barely out of adolescence patrolled.

2.

So there I am in a room, rooting about in the few personal belongings left behind, listening for footsteps outside in the hall or coming up stairs. How did I arrive here? We wonder that all our lives, don't we?

It was as much the idea of a room as it was a room. Plato and Socrates might have stood at the door arguing for days. A single small window set high, its plastic treated so that light blossomed as it passed through, flooded the room with virtual sunshine. From one wall a lower panel let down to become a bed, another panel above to serve as table or desk.

Where a man lives and what's inside his head, they're mirrors of one another, my trainers said. In which case there shouldn't be a whole lot going on in Merrit Li's. And if I had the right person, I knew *that* wasn't true.

My inventory disclosed a packet of expired papers and passes bound together in a drawer, a thin wallet containing recent travel visas, a drawerful of clothes, some disposable, some not, all of them dark and characterless. On his link I found itineraries and receipts, forty-six emails that seemed to be business related, though what business would be impossible to discern, and a young adult novel about the Nation Wars.

Elsewhere about the room, apportioned to the innards of various appliances, a Squeeze, a cooker, a coffee maker, I found what could only be the components of a stunner, cast in a hard plastic I'd not seen before, doubtless unkennable to scanners.

Immediately I became aware of a presence in the doorway behind me. There'd been no warning sounds, no footsteps. Right. So he had to be who and what I thought.

"We have mutual friends," I said, turning.

"Else you wouldn't be here."

Older than myself by a decade and more, conceivably old enough to remember the wars he'd been reading about. No sign of recognition at the safe word. Stance and carriage, legs apart, shoulders and hips in a line, confirmed other suspicions. Military.

I glanced up from his feet at the same time he did so from mine. Anticipating attack, one sees it begin there.

"Your belongings remain as they were," I said.

He nodded. Waited.

"Three days ago you were in Lower Cam, at a train stop where an attack took place. Two citizens were injured. The target, Frances diPalma, fled."

"Leaving a body behind her. That one not a bystander."

He held out both hands to signal non-aggression and, at my nod, stepped to the console to dial open the built-in screen. Habit—and of little benefit should we be on lens, but one takes the path available.

A spirited discussion of the city's economic status bloomed onscreen: female moderator, one man in a dark suit, one in a sky blue sweater. It's really quite simple, assuming you have the facts, the suit-wearer said. The other's expression suggested that not once in his life had he encountered anything other than complexity, nor could he anticipate ever doing so.

"You believe I was there to take her down," Merrit Li said.

"Yes."

"I was there, but to a different purpose than you suppose. She is in fact a mutual friend. I know her as Molly."

Rueful Tuesday, two days before. I had the windows dialed down while watching a feed on vanishing species. I sat back, dialed the window up, the screen down, to look across at the next building. Uncle Carl used to tell me a story about how this early jazz man, Buddy Bolden, threw a baby out the window in New Orleans and a neighbor leaned out his window and caught it. That's about how close we were.

For a moment I could make out moving shapes over there, people, before they dialed down *their* window.

I had punched back in for the sad tale of vanished sea otters and was remembering how when we'd first come here to the city, half-jokingly calling ourselves settlers, jumpy with wonder, with the effort and worry of fitting in, there'd been a linkstop showing disaster movies round the clock. World after world ravaged by giant insects, tiny insects, momentous storms, awakened deep-sea creatures, carniverous plants, science, our own stupidity.

With no forewarning, otter, shore and sea contracted, siphoned down to a crawler.

Warren's face above.

"This," he said, then was gone.

Rosland, time stamp less than an hour ago. A train stop. Single tracks up- and downtown, a dozen people waiting. Strollers, shufflers. Solitary busker playing accordion, license pasted to his top hat, little movement otherwise. Then suddenly there was.

A man walked briskly towards a woman waiting by the uptown track. She turned, transformed at a breath from citizen to warrior, everything about her changing in that instant. She shifted legs and feet, leaned hard left as he fired, followed that lean into full motion.

Moments later, the man lay on the platform, face turned to the camera.

Then another face glancing back, gone as its owner sprinted up the walkway Fran had vanished into.

Merrit Li's face.

Whereupon Warren's returned.

"We think there were two other incidents, but this is the first we've had surveillance."

"Fran took one of the attackers down."

"Cleanly."

"The second attacker followed her."

"In the tunnel they're off lens. We lost them. Nothing topside, nothing on connected platforms."

"Any luck flagging her follower?"

"Check your drops. The bundle I sent should help with that."

"We fought together at Kingston," Merrit Li said. "Deep penetration. She had the squad."

Doing what Rangers do.

"Not many walked away, either side." He thumbed the sound on the room's screen up a notch. "With the years, details have taken on a life of their own. You know the song?"

Two of them, actually. The official version, Kingston as a triumph of patriotism and the human spirit; the other underscoring the battle's death toll, social cost, and ultimate pointlessness.

"Three of us came out of the fire. Two walking, one on Molly's shoulder."

Onscreen discussion of city economy had given way to the latest stats on immigration. Full-color graphs rolled across the screen. Authorities revoiced the stats and graphs: a marked uptick in Citizen Provisionals from rural regions far south, this fueled by border disputes among neighboring city-states. Graphics and voice-over were out of synch. Technician error, I thought. Then for a moment before getting shut down, voice and content changed drastically. Revisionist overdubs. Official news reestablished itself.

Li pointed to the screen, one of the southern borders. Drones from a couple generations back floated above scattered groups of ragged troops and rioters.

"I'm supposed to be there. Just about now, my CO is discovering I'm not."

Even those you never see cast shadows. What I'd had were forests of filters and firewalls, limited access to public records, and no idea at all to whom his allegiance belonged, or if he might be off the grid entirely. But I also had Li's face, by extrapolation his body volumes, and the way his body moved. It had taken me the best part of the two days since Warren dialed in with the clips, and a sum of chancy data diving, to find him.

"I assume your story varies little from my own," Li said.

"Little enough."

He waited a moment, then went on.

"One of my links stays on free scan, reach-and-grab for anything that hints of undisclosed military activity. Tagged one that felt half solid. Then another came through ringing like bells. Not much to doubt there. A takedown, and good—but it didn't work. And seeing how it unrolled, I knew why. Molly. That first time too, I figured, so now they'd come at her twice and she put them down. They'd be getting ready to kick it into overdrive."

"You have any idea why she was targeted?"

"It's not like we were sending Union Day cards to one another, with a nice write-up about our year."

"Right. Time to time, I'd hear things. She married and had a family up in Minnesota or Vancouver. She was consulting for or riding herd on private companies. She'd taken up teaching. Until last week, as far as I knew, she was dead."

"While on assignment."

"What we all heard. Turns out we weren't the only ones."

Li didn't react, didn't ask where that came from. The pieces were falling together in his mind. "A crawler," he said.

"Followed by full-frontal assault. Once that closed down, Fran elected to stay off chart."

"The moves on her could be flashback from that."

"Could be."

"And we don't know who the crawler found."

"What we know between us doesn't take up much space in the world."

Li glanced back at the screen. Forsaken drones. Ragtag troops and rioters. "Everything's like paper folded so many times you can't tell what it is anymore."

I remembered Warren's rhetorical *How did we come to live in a world where everything is something else?*

"Molly called out to you," Li said.

"Relayed a message with a trigger word." I told him much of the rest as well.

"Wanted you at her back."

"As you said, they'll be stepping it up."

"And you came to me."

Yes.

"So now she has us both."

"Or will have."

Li pulled his duffel from a shelf by the door. "Not much here I can't leave behind. Give me ten minutes. Molly, you, me. Damn near have the makings of a volunteer army here, don't we? A militia—just like that hoary old piece of 1787 paper said."

3.

What I remember is questions, questions that should have been easy enough but weren't, and I had no idea why. What is today's date? Do you know where you are? It took time before I realized the voices were speaking to me. They were voices beamed in from some far-off world that had nothing to do with me, grotesque half-faces hovering over me, random collections of features that changed and changed again.

Do you know where you are?

No—but at some point I began looking about for clues. Hospital, I said early on, but that wasn't good enough.

Gradually I came to understand that at the end of each night shift someone wrote the new day's date on a whiteboard at one side of the room along with the physician, RN and NA assigned that shift, so pretty soon (with no idea what *soon* in this circumstance might encompass) I had that much covered.

Progress.

Good boy.

They were *so* pleased.

Over time, too, I learned to fake recognition of staff members, and to look for the hospital's name, which I never could keep hold of in my mind, on nametags.

Yep, I know where I am all right.

And it's the 21st. (Though if they pushed for day of the week I foundered. That wasn't on the whiteboard.)

Seizures? I answered. Stroke?

Then the questions got harder. After which they said let's go for a walk why don't we, an absurd goal given my inability to turn unassisted in bed or move my legs, the physical therapist's verbal commands meeting with no greater success in converting directive to action than those coursing along my nervous system.

This page currently unavailable.

Please try again later.

Error.

But I needed ambulation to qualify for further rehab. So therapist Abraham sandbagged me into sitting position, hauled me to our feet and, with mine dragging and scraping at the floor, carried me the required half dozen steps, the unlikeliest dance partners ever.

We were on our fifth, maybe sixth provisional government by then. Some were ill-advised, rapidly imploding coalitions, so . . . five, six, seven, who can be sure? This one had begun to look as though it might stick, like the stray cat that follows you home and, once fed, stays.

I learned that later, of course.

Three worlds, Abraham said, coexist. There was the old world of things as they are—of acceptance, of discipline, where we take what pleasure exists in what we have and expect no more. There was the new world, in which everything, country, selves, the world's very face, becomes endlessly reinvented, remade, refurbished. And now this third world struggling to be born, where old world and new will learn to live with one another.

Like Abraham and myself scuttling across the hospital's tiled floors.

I'm not supposed to be talking like this, Abraham said.

We were on a break, and he'd pushed me outside, to a patio bordered by scrubby bushes and smelling of rosemary, where with minimal help I'd successfully tottered from the wheelchair and stumbled five terrifying steps to a bench. Applause would have been in order.

I asked if reinventing myself was not what I was doing.

More like rebuilding, he said. Refurbishing.

When I was a child, living in the first of our many homes, money was aflow, families and the neighborhood on their way up. If you tore a house down entire, you had to apply for new building permits. Leave one wall standing, it could pass as a remodel. So crews arrived in trucks and on foot to swarm over the site, piles of roofing, earth, brick and siding appeared, and within days, where the Jacobs or Shah house had been, there stood, in moonlight among hills of rubble, the ruins of a single wall.

Ready to get back to work? Abraham said. Patiently they await: Leg lifts, stationary cycling, weights, countless manifestations of pulleys and resistance. Row . . . Pull . . . Hold . . . Hold. Stepping over minefields of what look like tiny traffic cones. Balancing atop a footboard mounted on half a steel ball. Both of those last while clinging to walk bars and waiting for the state to wither away as Abraham said the old books predicted.

But five weeks further in, buckets of sweat lost to history, I've still not progressed past totter, trip and hope like hell I'll make it to the bench. A convocation gets called. The physician I've taken to thinking of as Doc Salvage is spokesperson. Here's the story, he begins. He smiles, then puts away the smile so it won't get in the way of what he has to say.

They fully appreciate the work I've done. My attitude. My doggedness. My determination. They know I've hung on like a snapping turtle and refused to let go. The consensus is that we (pronoun modulating now to first-person plural) have gone as far as might reasonably be expected. In short, I can stay as I was, with severely diminished capacities, or.

Or being that I undergo an experimental procedure.

They would reboot and reconnect synapses, restore neural pathways, rewire connections that had failed to regenerate autonomously. And while they were in there they'd go ahead and rearrange the furniture. Spruce things up here and there. New carpet, fresh paint.

You have the technology to do that? I asked.

We do.

And I'll be myself again, physically?

A better version. Though we understand (the smile is back) that sentimentally you may be attached to the present one.

And what of risks? Complications?

Oh, nothing terribly untoward. More or less the standard OR checklist: bleeds, infection, drug reactions. A long recovery.

You've all this certainty, with an experimental procedure?

Life itself is an experimental procedure. As you know.

And I've already had a long recovery.

Ah, that. Fundamentally you will have to start over, I'm afraid. Begin again.

And so I did in subsequent months as Doc Salvage and crew watched closely to assess development and as I pushed harder at my limits than I'd ever have thought possible. We were down in the swirly deep, in the sludge, as Abraham deemed. But within weeks the leg that before could scarcely clear the floor now could kick higher than my head, I could hop across the room, steady as a fence post, on a single foot, and fingers could pick bits of straw from off the table top. I could climb, crawl, swim, run, lift.

And wonder at what I'd been told, what I'd not.

You've taken note, Doc Salvage said six months later, how little resistance there is for you in physical activity.

Uncharacteristically, window shades were up behind him and light streamed in, so that he appeared to have a halo about his body, or to be going subtly out of focus.

All much as we anticipated, he said. But it is far from being the story's end.

He paused, letting the moment stretch. Something reflective passed outside, a car, a copter, a drone, tossing stabs of light against the rear wall.

Our bodies teem with censors built and inculcated into us, Doc Salvage continued, censors that create distraction, indecision, delay—drag, if you will. Morality. Cultural mores. Emotions. Most particularly the last. And we have learned how to bypass those. Eliminate the drag. We can peel away emotions, mute them, dial them down to the very threshhold.

As, he said, we've done with you.

Which explained a lot of what had been going on in body and mind, things I'd been unable to put into words.

I now fit, they believed, a container they'd made for me.

But already, even then, I was spilling from it.

They had given me something. They had taken something. On such barter is a society founded. How much control over our lives do we retain, how much cede to the state? What debts do we take on in exchange for the state's benefits? How does the state balance its responsibilities to the individual and to the collective? To what degree does it exist to serve, to what degree to oversee, its citizenry?

Theories grinding against one another in the dark.

The truth is this: Our enemies at the time were messing about with neurotoxins. It was those neurotoxins, not a CVA, not seizures as I'd been told, that came upon me in the burned-out fields of the far northwest. Those upon whose reach I was borne to the government hospital to awaken empty, blank, and helpless, isolate fragments of the world cascading around me.

The truth is this as well: I was changed. By the gas. By Doc's procedure. By the experience of reinhabiting my own body. And later, by my actions.

Only with time did I come to understand the scope and nature of the changes within. Doc was right that emotions no longer obscured my actions; about much else he was wrong.

A single image remains from before medics scooped me up. I am dragging myself across stubble. I can hear nothing, feel nothing. My legs refuse to function. And all I can see—this fills my vision—are my arms out before me. They stretch and stretch again. Each time I pull my body forward, they stretch more. My hand, my fingers, are yards away, meters, miles. And I do not advance.

But within a year of that meeting with Doc Salvage I was on the move. There was much, in this fledgling nation, to be done.

The lamentations of old men forever fall deaf on youngster's ears, my uncle said. He knew that early.

Sometimes I imagine myself an old man tied by sheets into my chair in the day room of a care center speaking—even though there is no one listening, no one there to listen—about the things I did, things I refused to do, things I never quite recovered from doing.

At a table nearby, two men and a woman play cards, some game in which single cards get dealt back onto the table. In at least ten minutes no one's put down a card. It's the woman's turn. The men sit unmoving, hands before them, cards fanned. They could be mannikins propped there. On the screen across the day room a giant face says she loves us, in the same movie that plays at this time every Tuesday, but no one cares.

How does one assay right and wrong? With change crashing down all around us, do the words even have meaning?

Is everything finally relative?

What would you give, Sid Coleman used to sing, *in exchange for your soul?* An old, old song.

I know that the world of which I speak sitting here tied into my chair would be unrecognizable to the young. Unrecognizable to most anyone, really, should they chance to be around to hear. And as I speak, I watch cockroaches scuttling on the wall, lose my thoughts, begin to wonder about the cockroach's world. They've been around forever, never changed.

All this, of course, knowing that I will never be an old man.

4.

"This is your place?"

"Borrowed. Property is theft—right?"

Out on the farthest edge of the city. Forager territory. Dog-pack-and-worse territory. I looked about at the cot, racks of storage cells, plastic units stacked variously to form furniture of a sort. All of it graceless and functional, the sole concession to domestication being a plaque hung on a side wall and jiggered to look like an old-time sampler: *Always Drink Upstream of the Herd.*

"You can't be here often, or for extended periods. What happens when you're not?"

"I have guard rats." He began pulling cubes from one of the stacks. "Joking. About theft and property, too." He reconfigured the cubes as a chair, more or less. "Those who live out here and I have an understanding. Turns out we've much in common."

"Being?"

"That you deal with an unfree world by making yourself so free that your very existence is an act of rebellion. Camus, I think."

"Yet you run with the marshals of that world."

"Their screens, drones and watchers catch most of what happens on the surface of their world. But much goes on beneath, in ours."

"Giants of the deep?"

"Minnows and small fish. Thousands upon thousands of us. Where the true history resides."

Li pulled a link from his pocket, punched in.

"The villagers want to climb the hill and storm the castle, and there is no castle. The castle is all around us. What we have to do is learn to live in it."

As he spoke, perfectly relaxed, he was sweeping and scanning at impressive speed. "Ever come across a series of children's books, *Billy's Adventures*?"

I shook my head.

"I read them when I was five, six. The first one started off: 'Two years it was that I lived among the goats. Two years that I went about on all fours, ate whatever came before me.' Like most kid's books, as much as anything else they were put out there as socializers. Teach the boys and girls how to get along with others, shore up received wisdom, hip-hurrah things-as-they-are. But scratch the surface and what was underneath gave the lie to what was on top. The books weren't about joining the march, they were about staying apart while appearing to fit in. They were profoundly subversive."

Back when this area was a functioning part of the city, Li's squat had been a service facility, a utilities satellite maybe, a goods depot. Layers of steel shelving six- and eight-units deep sat against the rear wall. Stained and worn cement floors, splayed heads of ancient cables jutting from the wall. Steel everywhere, of a grade not seen for better than half a century, including the door that now rang open to admit an elderly man in clothing at once suggestive of tie-dye and camouflage. Balding, I saw as he slipped off his cloth cap.

"And so here you are back with us," the man said. Trace of a far-northern accent in his voice. "And not alone."

Li introduced us. "Thank you for minding the burrow, Daniel—as ever."

"Well then, we can't have just anyone moving in here, can we? We do have standards." Then to me: "Welcome to the junkyard."

Li had continued to monitor his link as we spoke. Now he beckoned me. The screen showed a street in the central city, masses of people moving along, dodges, feints, near-collisons.

"There," Li said. The cursor became an arrow, touched on one individual moving at a good clip close to storefronts and walls. "And there." Two larger figures, perhaps six meters back, matching speed with the first. "I'm piggy-backed on security feeds. Seconds ago, sniffers at the corner dinged."

"Those two are armed."

We watched as the lone figure turned into a narrow side street or entryway. Both pursuers hesitated at the mouth, then stepped in, first one, then, on a six count, the other. People streamed by on the sidewalk. We waited. Moving at an easy pace, the single, smaller figure emerged. Patently she'd taken note where the cameras were and kept her face averted, but size and carriage were unmistakeable.

Fran.

Molly.

"By now she's in the wind and the area's spilling over with police."

"And those hunting her will have new dogs in the area along with them," Li said. "Unless, of course, they're the same." He thumbed over to news feeds. No mention of the incident. Then to the city's official feeds, where delays from technical problems had been reported in the area and citizens were advised to consider alternate routes. "So many multiple realities," Li said. "Is it any wonder we're unable to see the world straight on?"

Time passed, as it will, however hard one holds on.

Li told me about religious practices among the Melanese who during old wars and due to the island's tactical location, grew accustomed to airplanes arriving almost daily filled with goods, some of which got shared, much of which got cast off and reclaimed. For many years after, with that war over, the islanders carved long clearings like runways in the forest, built small fires along them to either side, constructed a wooden hut for a man to sit in with wooden disks on his ears as headphones and bamboo shoots jutting out like antennae. They waited for the airplanes to return with goods. Everything was in place. Everything was just as before. But no airplanes came.

It began to feel as though what we were doing in our approach to the whole Fran-Molly affair wasn't far removed.

Why would Fran signal for backup then fail to make contact, even to make herself visible? Leapfrog, maybe? Assuming we'd move in and her pursuers's focus would shift to us, leaving her free to . . . what?

Look again.

There had been urgency, power, in that attack. The air crackled with it. Fran knew where cameras were placed, carefully kept her face averted. From visual evidence her pursuers also knew, yet took little effort to skirt the cameras. (1) They were protected or (2) They didn't exist.

And just what did we hope to learn by endlessly reviewing the incident? "One works with what one has," Li said every time we thumbed up the file.

What we had was next to nothing.

And hellhounds on our trails. We could all but hear them snuffling around out there in the dark.

5.

Government after government fell, each trailing in its wake the exhausted spume of grand theories. Anomie had come piecemeal over so long a time that we were hard pressed to remember or imagine another way. Platitudes, slogans and homilies had supplanted thought. That, or unfocused, unbridled hatred.

Was the government at which we arrived a better one, or were we simply too exhausted to go on? The bigfish capitalism we fled and the overseer government we embraced had much the same disregard for bedrock democratic principles. But each individual was housed, educated to the extent he or she elected, provided sustenance and medical care, state-sponsored burial.

Border disputes, blockades, financial sloughs, outright attacks, the collapse of alliances. Those early years thrummed with dangers to which our nascent union, fussily jamming the day, often reacted with little regard for long-term consequence.

Ever on the go, the world's contours shifting and reshaping themselves even as I passed among them, I grew accustomed to media and official reports of a world far removed from that I witnessed. Which among these gaping disparities were sinister, which utilitarian? And just what was it I was doing out there? The people's work? The government's? That of a handful of wizards behind the curtain? One of Sid Coleman's songs comes to mind again, "Which Side Are You On," not all that much of a song really, but a damned good question. I wonder every day.

I was a good soldier, as soldiers go. One would expect years of such service to fix in place conventional, conservative beliefs. Instead, they honed within me an innate aversion to authority and to organizations in general. When

I rummage in the attics of my mind, what I come up with is an immiscible regard for personal and civil liberty.

Claeton, pronounced Claytown by locals, mid-January and so cold that when your nose dripped, icicles formed. A thick white mist rose permanently from the ground. Bare trees loomed in the distance, looking as though someone had strung together a display of the hairless legs and knobby knees of old men. We inhabited a ghostly sea bottom.

Hansard and I were squirreled down in a scatter of boulders where a mountain range ran out into flatlands. There was one pass through the range and a patrol from Revisionist forces was on it. We were waiting for them.

Everyone knew the satellites were up there, circling tirelessly, bloated with information. And if satellites monitored even this afterbirth of a landscape, I told Hansard, they had to be watching us as well—not us here, us everywhere. Hansard shrugged and squeezed a nutrient pack to start it warming.

Drones might have dealt with the patrol, of course. Quickly. Efficiently. But drones hadn't the dramatic effect of a couple of warriors suddenly appearing at the mouth of the cave. Something in our blood and ancestral memory—others of our kind come for us.

Hansard finished drinking his nutrient, rolled the pack into a compact ball and stuffed it in a cargo pocket. The wind rose then, mist swirling like huge capes, cold biting into bones. Go codes buzzed in the bones behind our ears.

We couldn't pronounce the name of the place but were told it translated as Daredevil or Devil-May-Care. Biting cold had turned stewpot hot, barren landscape to cramped and crowded city. The stench of used-up air was everywhere. You could smell bodies and what they left behind. Sweat mixed with fine grit, pollen and laden gases and never went away. It coated your body, a hard film, a second skin that cracked when you moved. Hansard, rumors said, had gone down up here near the Canadian border some weeks before.

That time, we almost failed to make it out, beating a retreat through disruptions turning ever more chaotic (dodging raindrops, an old Marxist might have said) hours before the region tore itself apart, this being what happens when a government eloquently tottering on two legs gets one of them kicked out from under.

They came for us on the bullet train in Oregon. I turned from the window where sunlight shone blindingly on water, blinked, and there they were. Boots, jeans, Union jackets with the patches torn off. I've a brief memory of Tomas aloft, zigzagging towards the car's rear on the backs of the seats, right foot, left, starboard, port, before I turned to confront the others. All became in that instant clear and distinct. I could see the tiniest bunching of a muscle in the shoulder of one before that arm moved, see another's eyes tip to the left before head and body followed, sense the one about to bound directly toward me from all but imperceptible shifts in footing and posture.

I remember condensation on windows from the chill inside the car, the wide staring eyes of a child.

Afterwards, we liberated a pickup from a parking lot nearby and rode that pale horse into Keizer to be about our business.

Years after that day in Oregon, and as many after what I'm recounting here, Fran and I stand where Merritt Li died. In those years, wildness has reclaimed that edge of the city. Sunlight spins toward us off the lake to our left as though in wafer-thin sheets. Spanish moss beards the branches of water oaks populated by dove and by dun colored pigeons that were once city birds. Fran touches another oak near us; scaly ridges of its bark break off in her hand.

We're the only ones, she says.

Who will remember, I say.

It's become rote now.

No memorials for such as Merritt Li.

Only memory.

For another who has been erased. Who has been gathered. And for a time before Fran speaks again, we are quiet. Our voices drift away into the call of birds, the sough of wind.

Our kind were redundant before and will be again.

As the successful revolutionary must always be, right?

Okay. She laughs. *They can be redundant too.*

A heron floats in over the trees and lands at water's edge. A heron! Who would have believed there were herons left? I see the same light in Fran's eyes as in mine. Still, after all that has happened in our lives, we have the capacity for surprise, for wonder.

6.

When I was eleven, a contrarian even then, I made a list of all the stuff I never wanted to see again on TV and in movies. Wrote it out on a sheet of ruled paper, signed and dated the document, and submitted it to my parents.

People jumping just ahead of flames as house, car, pier, ship or what-have-you explodes.

The disarming of bombs with everyone else sent away as our hero or heroine sweatily decides which wire to cut.

Police or soldiers putting down their guns in hostage situations.

Hostage situations.

The cop, finally pushed to his/her limit, tossing badge or detective's shield onto his/her CO's desk.

The cast, be they doctors, lawyers, or cops, all striding side by side, often in slow motion, along a corridor on their way to another fine yet difficult day as credits roll.

"I wanted to give back."

"This is your chance to do the right thing."

"You're not going to die on me!"

How with two minutes left in the show the bad guy tells us why he's done all he has, that it's all justified.

The original screed ran two pages. In following years, amendments—additions, truthfully—added another fourteen, growing ever more prolix until attentions strayed elsewhere. From time to time as I submitted new editions, I requested progress reports from my parents. Could he have been so innocent, that fledgling contrarian, as to believe some channel existed whereby they might actually deal with these issues? Was he attempting to bend the world to some latent image he had in mind? Just to shout out to the world: *I am here?* Whatever else it may have presaged, the project attests that at least, even then, I was paying attention.

By this time I'd got heavily into reading and may have had at the back of my mind, like that movement in the room's corner you can't locate when looking straight on, intimations of how powerfully words affect—how they give form to—the world about us.

I became aware that my greatest pleasure lay not in what was happening within the confines of the narrative but in its textures: the surround, the moods and rhythms, the shifting colors. And that it was auxiliary characters I found most interesting. A quiet rejection of celebrity, maybe—this sense that those spun out to screen's edge, the postmen, foils, second bananas, loyal companions and walk-ons, are the ones who matter? History with its drums and wagons and wars marches past, and we go on scrabbling to stay in place, huddled with our families and tribes, setting tables, trying to find enough to eat.

Sheer plod makes plow down sillion shine, Gerard Manley Hopkins wrote. Not that, when you come down to it, we do a hell of a lot of shining. At best we give off just enough light to hold away the dark for an hour or two. That's all the fire Prometheus had to give us.

Light was failing, if never the fire, as Merritt Li and I made our way on glistening streets, cleaving insofar as we could to shadow and walls. Rain had begun hours earlier. Streetlights shimmered with halos, windows wore jackets of glaze—as would lens. That gave small comfort at the same time that the fact of fewer bodies abroad gave caution.

We weren't following leads so much as what someone once called wandering to find direction and someone else called searching for a black hat in a pitch-black room.

Rain made a rich stew of a hundred smells. Took away edges and corners and the hard surface of things. The city was feeling its way towards beauty.

There did seem to be a rudimentary pattern, the attacks moving outward from city's center, but patterns, what's there, what's not, can't be trusted. Apophenia. The perception of order in random data. See three dots on an otherwise blank page, right away you're trying to fit them together. Nonetheless, we were trolling in rude circles towards the outer banks, touching down at rail stations, pedestrian nodes, crossroads and terminals of every sort. That amounted to a lot of being out there in the open, exposed, and as chancy for Li as for me at this point, but (returning to a prior observation) what else did we have?

In such situations, while outwardly you're alert to every small shift or turn, changes in light, in movements around you, your own heartbeat or breathing, inwardly you're floating free, allowing your mind to do what it does best unpinned. Thoughts skitter, burn, and flare out, some shapeless, others barbed. As I scurried from sillion to sillion, bench to stairway to arcade, thoughts of childhood, books, folk songs, populism and political exhaustion accompanied me.

All I wanted was for my life, when you picked it up in your hands, to have some weight to it, Fran once told me. Rain coming down then outside our TBH as it was now on city streets, the two of us waiting for nightfall and go codes, foxhole reeking of processed food, stale air, unwashed bodies.

Within months of that, the GK virus had carved away fully a sixth of our population, especially among the elderly, infants and the chronically ill, all those with compromised immune systems, poor general health, low physical reserves.

Explanations for the virus? Natural selection at work in an overpopulated world, willful thinning of the herd by intellectual or financial elitists, Biblical cleansing, our own current government's research gone amiss, biologic agents introduced by any of a dozen or more current enemies.

Or that old friend happenstance.

Substantive as they were, Li's and my excursions had yielded little more than an anecdotal accounting of the city as it stood, along with instances of kindness, cruelty, anxiety and insouciance in fairly equal measure, in every conceivable shape or form.

Crews were busily tearing out the forest of digital billboards at city center, these having recently been judged (depending on the assessor) unaesthetic or ineffective.

The dry riverbed, cemented over years ago, was now being uncemented on its way to becoming a canal complete with boats and waterside city parks. Government-stamped posters with artists' renditions of the final result hung everywhere. Those of a cynical disposition well might wonder where funds for this massive project originated. More positive souls might choose not to take note of the disrepair in surrounding streets.

Repeatedly as we moved through the city we encountered flash-mob protests. Participants assembled without preamble at rail stations, on street corners, in the city's open spaces. Most protestors were young, some looked as though they'd awakened earlier in the day from Rip Van Winkle naps. They'd demonstrate, sometimes with silence and dialogue cards, other times with chants or improvised songs, and within minutes fade back into the crowd, before authorities showed up.

"We're chasing shadows at midnight," Merritt Li says one day.

And I hear Fran, another day, another time, saying "We're the shadow of shadows."

We'd come in country under cover of night, the two of us, and trekked on foot miles inland. The sky was starting to lighten and birds to sing when we reached the extraction point. Joon Kaas had not spoken a word the whole time, from the moment we breached his room. He had looked up and nodded, risen and gone ahead of us when signalled to do so. Now at the clearing he lowered his head, to pray I think, before meeting Fran's eyes (instinctively aware she was prime) and nodding again, whether in surrender or some fashion of absolution I can't say.

"He knew," she said after.

That we were coming. Of course he did. And how it had to end.

Later I would understand that for most of his countrymen, thousands of them cast onto the streets and huddled together in houses, the eternally poor and forgotten, those without influence who went on scratching out a bare subsistence as terrible engines fell to earth all around them, Joon Kaas was a savior. With his passing, much of what he had worked to put in place, his challenges to privilege and to authority, new laws and mandates, new protections, began one by one to disappear.

Perhaps more than anything else, we've enslaved ourselves to the grand notion of progress. In our minds we've left behind yesterday's errors, last year's lack of knowledge and crude half measures. Now we're headed straight up the slope, getting better and better, getting it right. But really we go on hauling along these sacks of goods we can't let go of, can't get rid of, tearing apart our world only to rebuild it to the old image.

In 1656 Spinoza was excommunicated from Amsterdam's Portuguese-Jewish congregation for inveighing against those who promoted ignorance and irrational beliefs in order to lead citizens to act against their own best interests, to embrace conformism and orthodoxy, to surrender freedom for security. This, even though Dutch society had long agreed upon liberty, individual rights and freedom of thought. Four hundred years down the road, not much has changed. Same hazard signs at the roadside. Same crooked roads.

It was in the last months of the struggle, while I was over the border in Free Alaska commandeering armaments, that I first felt the gears slipping. Four degrees coldly Fahrenheit outside. With a wind that felt to be removing skin slice by micrometric slice. Fortunately I was inside, and alone, when it happened, having just entered a safe house there. I remembered walking in and stepping towards the bathroom. Now I was on the floor, with urine puddled about me. How long? Five, six minutes by my timer. Vision blurred—a consequence of the fall? Taste of metal, copper, in the back of my throat. And I couldn't move.

That was far too familiar, a replay of week after week in rehab, frantically sending messages to legs, arms and hands that refused to comply, Abraham urging me on.

I doubt the immobility lasted more than a minute, but hours of panic got packed into it. I began to remember other stutters and misfires, each gone unremarked at the time. Now they took on weight, bore down.

"What are you thinking?" Fran will ask not long after, on our visit to Merritt Li's final foothold.

"An old sea diver's creed," I tell her, unsure myself of the connection, thinking of the fighters we took down there, of Merritt Li going down, of my own fall and my jacked-up system, "the one thing a diver forgets at great peril: If it moves, it wants to kill you."

Then I tell her what happened at the safe house, what it means. Simple physics, really. Put more current in the wire, it burns out faster.

"When did you know?"

"From the first, at some level—wordlessly. One sleepless morning in Toledo I got up, tapped in, and pulled the records. I wasn't supposed to be able to do that. They had little idea what I could do."

I, the soft machinery that was me, was failing. Sparks failed to catch, messages misfired, data was corrupted.

I had, I supposed, a few months left.

• • •

7.

We never knew how Merritt Li came to be there.

His and my courses were set so as to bring the two of us together, close enough to rendezvous anyway, every three hours. When he didn't show at the old waterworks, I went looking. We both carried ancient low-frequency 'sponders we thought wouldn't be tapped. Guess we were wrong. They knew I was coming.

He had two of them back against a wall of stacked, partly crushed vehicles, tanklike cruisers from the last century. Two others, halfway across a bare dirt clearing hard as steel, had turned away to intercept me. Where numbers five and six came from I have no idea, they dropped out of nowhere like Dorothy.

A couple of them had weapons we'd never seen, the kind that, if you go looking, don't exist. Focused toxin's my guess. Or some fry-brain electronic equivalent. I saw nothing, no muzzle flash, no recoil, no exhaust, when one of those locked on Li lifted his handgun, but I saw the result. Li went down convulsing, limbs thrashing independently as though they belonged to different bodies.

Three of the four coming for me fell almost at the same time, one down, two down, three, without sound or obvious reason. Once I'd dealt with the fourth and looked again, the two by Li were on the ground and still. The whole sequence in just under sixteen seconds.

Movement atop a battered steel shed to the right took my attention, as it was meant to do.

Never show yourself against the sky.

Unless you're purposefully announcing yourself, of course.

She came down in three stages, over the side and catch with the left, swing to the right, drop and turn. Faultless as ever. No sign of what weapon she'd used. I recalled her late interest in antiquities, blowpipes and the like. One violinist wants shiny new and perfectly functional, another's always looking for old and funky, an instrument that makes you work to get the music out.

Her hair was cropped short and had tight curls of gray like steel filings in it. The row of geometrical earrings, circle, square, triangle, cross, was gone from the left ear. Otherwise not much had changed. Musculature stood out in the glisten of sweat on her skin. Yellow T-shirt, green pants.

"Interesting choice of clothing for someone doing her best to be invisible."

"Figured if it came to it and I stood dead still, they might take me for a vegetable."

Blood had pooled in Li's face, turning it purple, then burst in a scatter of darker splotches across it. Limbs were rigid. No respiration, no pulse. A pandemic of that: No pulse or respiration in the ones she'd put down either.

"Here we go leaving a mess behind us," I said.

"Ah, well."

"With a bigger mess waiting ahead."

"Ah, well again." She snatched the mystery weapons from those by Li. "We hit the floor with whoever shows up on our dance card." Then looked around. "No eyes out here. No trackers."

"Chosen for it. So they're not government."

"Who can say?" At the time we believed them to be a single team, didn't understand there were three factions at work, a tangle of forces.

Fran had dropped to a squat and was breaking down one of the weapons. "Indications are, they think of themselves as freedom fighters. Then again, who doesn't? Freedom from taxes, bureaucracy, using the wrong texts at school? Or maybe they just want to tear the house down. Maybe we should have asked them."

She stood and brought over the gutted weapon. "Ever seen a power source like that?" A bright blue marble with no apparent harness or connection, spinning gyroscopically in a chamber not much larger than itself. "Have to wonder what else they have."

"Six less footmen, for a start."

"There'll be backup. We should be missing."

"Missing, we're good at."

"Have been till now."

She retrieved the second weapon and we started away. Darkness had begun unfurling from the ground and the air smelled of rain. Insects called to one another from trees and high grass, invisibly.

"When I was a child," Fran said, "no more than four or five, there was a cricket that sang outside my window every night. I'd go to bed, lie there in the dark and listen to it sing, night after night. Then one night it didn't. I knew it was dead, whatever dead was, and I cried."

Fran as a child, crying, I could scarcely picture. "Why were these six, and the others, on you?"

She pulled the power source from the first weapon, discarded its carcass. "They weren't."

She'd been working a private job much like that of mine back before the team in dark gray cars came for me, and stumbled onto something that wasn't right. She finished the job and took to side roads, kicking over traces till she realized that both job and not-rightness were come-ons. Hand-tied lures, she said, designed to bring her out. So out she came. They were stalking her. She was stalking them, coming in and out of sight. Getting a fix on them. Who they might be, how many.

"They were moving around in teams, randomly, and about where you'd expect, train stations, transfer points. They'd see me, hang back, never close. Which was how I knew it went deeper. So I stepped it up."

"And they stepped in."

"Maybe they got impatient. Maybe like me they decided to push to see what pushed back. And I sent a message up the line to you—which is what they anticipated."

By this time we were moving towards the central city but on back streets long forsaken, block after block of abandoned warehouses and storage facilities from a past in which people were driven to accumulate so much that it spilled over. We'd spotted a few stragglers of the kind that, once seen, quickly vanish. Tree dwellers brought to earth, I think of them, on the ground but never quite of this world.

8.

A razor-cold January morning. Snow falling past the windows—silently, but you can't help looking that way again and again, listening. How could something take over the world to such degree and make no sound? The room's warmth moved in slow tides toward the windows, tugging at our skin as it passed by. Even the machines were silent as I did my best to become one with them.

Abraham watched and paced me, speaking in low tones about Ethical Suicides back during our string of interim governments.

"Not much there when you go looking. . . . Loosen up, I can see your shoulders knotting. . . . Barely enough information to chew on. . . . Breathe. Everything comes from the breathing. . . . "

I'd often wondered how a man with such leanings could possibly wind up working where he did. Were his intimations a furtive challenge, a testing?

"This is difficult for us to grasp, but you have to look back, to the sense of powerlessness that got tapped into. People were convinced that government, that the country itself, was broken and couldn't be repaired. They saw an endless cycle of paralysis and decay about which they could do nothing. ES's were not about themselves, they were about something much larger."

I stopped to catch breath and shake muscles loose. Took the water bottle from Abraham. Eager electrolytes swarmed within. "Absolute altruism? In addition to which, they acted knowing their actions would come to nothing?"

"That's how it looks to us. To them, who can say? Can we ever appraise the time in which we act?" Abraham stacked virtual weights on the upper-body pulleys, thought a moment and dialed it down a notch. "You're skeptical."

"Of more and more every day."

"With good reason." He reached for the water bottle at the very moment I held it out. *Another dead soldier* had become a joke between us.

Shortly thereafter, as had become our custom, sheathed in featherweight warmsuits, we were walking the grounds. Snow still fell, but lightly, haltingly. "When I first came, not so many years ago," Abraham said, "there were still dove in the trees, calling to one another. It was the loneliest sound I'd ever heard."

The rehab facility had originated at city's edge, adjacent to a cemetery with old religious and older racial divisions, then, as the city burgeoned, found itself ever closer to center. The cemetery was gone, doves too, but bordering stands of trees and dense growth remained.

Further in towards the heart of the complex sat the original building about which all else had accrued, three storeys of rust-colored brick facade and clear plastic windows that on late evenings caught up the sun's light to transform it into swirling, ungraspable, ghostlike figures. Other times, passing by, I'd look up to see those within, on the second floor, peering out, and feel a pull at something deep inside myself, an uneasiness for which I had neither word nor explanation.

It was Abraham who took me there late one night. *The colony*, as he put it, *is sleeping, nessun dorma.* Entering, we passed up narrow stairs and along a corridor with indirect lighting set low in the walls, then to a single door among dozens. There was a scarred window in the door and in the window, still as a portrait in its frame, a face.

"This is Julie," Abraham said.

The woman's face turned slightly as though to locate the sound of his voice. Her eyes behind the glass were cloudy and unfocused. They didn't move, didn't see. After a moment she shuffled back away from the door, obviously in pain, perhaps remembering what had happened other times when voices came and the door opened.

"Surely you must have known," Abraham said. "You had to suspect."

That scientific advances do not happen without experimentation, and that experimentation walks hand in hand with failure?

So much gone deeply wrong with this woman, so many failures in the world that put her there.

9.

Most of the rest you know, or a version of it. You live in a world formed by the rest. You also believe you had some say in the making of that world, I suspect, and I suppose you did, but it was a small say, three or four words lost to a crowded page. There's a long line of wizards behind the curtain vying for their turn at the wheel. When Fran and I floated to the top one more time before sinking out of sight for good, whatever grand intentions might have been packed away in our luggage, truthfully we were doing little more than the wizards's work. Can we ever appraise the time in which we act? Probably not. How do we decide? With a wary smile and fingers crossed.

It was Abraham who called out to me, and to others like me with whom he had worked over the years. Abraham, who once carried me across the room as though I could walk, to qualify me for rehab. Abraham who never hesitates to remind us that we stagger from place to place, day to day, beneath the moral weight of acts we didn't commit but for which we are responsible. That in allowing ourselves collectively to think certain thoughts we risk damaging, even destroying, the lives of millions, yet surely, if any of this means anything at all, we must be free to think those thoughts, to think *all* thoughts.

Never forget it's because of such men as Abraham and Merritt Li that you have the life you do, with its fundamental rights and fail-safes.

Try always to remember the responsibility that comes with those freedoms.

The easy part of government? Ideals. Rational benevolence.

The hardest? Avoiding the terrible gravity of bureaucracy, the pull away from service towards self-survival.

Max Weber had it right over a century ago.

Not much time left for me now. What came to the fore in that Alaska safe house has run its course. I can feel systems shutting down one by one, like lights going off sequentially from room to room, hallway to hallway. The overloaded wire burning down. I'm intrigued by how familiar it feels, how welcome, a visit from an old friend.

Fran is here waiting with me.

Opposite my bed there's a window that for a long while I took to be a link screen as in it I watched people come and go, out in the world, I thought. Couples strolling, crowds flowing off platforms and onto trains, scenes of towns like Claeton, like those in Oregon. Children playing. But that couldn't be right, could it?

I am 8. I have no idea as yet how much heartache is in the world, how much pain, how it goes on building, day by day. I have a new toy, a two-tier garage made of tin, with ramps and tiny pumps and service pits, and I'm running my truck from one to another, making engine sounds, brake sounds, happy driver sounds. On a TV against the wall at room's end, videos of war machines flanked by infantry unspool as a government official inset upper left reads from a prompter saying that high-level talks are underway and that we expect—

And that can't be right either. I'm imagining this, surely, not the garage, the garage was real, but the crash of that newscast into my revery . . . Am I dreaming? It's harder and harder to tell memory from dream, imaginings from hallucination. Harder and harder, too, to summon much concern which is which, to believe it matters.

All in a moment I am that child with his garage, I am pulling myself along with impossible arms after the toxins take over, I am struggling to stand and stay upright in rehab once brought home from the battlefield and yet again after the surgery, I am driving deserted highways at 10:36 on Union Day.

Fran leans close, her hand on mine. I see but cannot feel it. As she will not hear the last thing I tell her. That we go on and on and, all the time, terrible engines whirl and crash about us, in the great empty spaces that surround our lives.

FIRELIGHT

URSULA K. LE GUIN

He was thinking of *Lookfar*, abandoned long ago, beached on the sands of Selidor. Little of her would be left by now, a plank or two down in the sand maybe, a bit of driftwood on the western sea. As he drifted near sleep he began to remember sailing that little boat with Vetch, not on the western sea but eastward, past Far Toly, right out of the Archipelago. It was not a clear memory, because his mind had not been clear when he made that voyage, possessed by fear and blind determination, seeing nothing ahead of him but the shadow that had hunted him and that he pursued, the empty sea over which it had fled. Yet now he heard the hiss and slap of waves on the prow. Mast and sail rose above him when he glanced up, and looking astern he saw the dark hand on the tiller, the face gazing steadily forward past him. High cheekbones, Vetch had, his dark skin stretched smooth on them. He would be an old man now, if he were still alive. Once I could have sent to know. But I don't need a sending to see him, there in the East Reach on his little island, in his house with his sister, the girl who wore a tiny dragon for a bracelet. It hissed at me, she laughed . . . He was in the boat, and the water slapped her wood as she went east and east, and Vetch looked forward, and he looked forward over the unending water. He had raised the magewind but *Lookfar* scarcely needed it. She had her own way with the wind, that boat. She knew where she was going.

Until she could not go anymore. Until the deep sea went shoal beneath her, ran shallow, ran dry, and her bottom grated over rock, and she was aground, unmoving, in the darkness that had come on all round them.

He had stepped out of the boat there in the deep sea, over the abyss, and walked forward on dry land. In the Dry Land.

That was gone now. The thought came to him slowly. The land across the wall of stones. He saw that wall—the first time he saw it, saw the child running silently down the dark slope beyond it. He saw all the dead land, the shadow-cities, the shadow-people who passed one another in silence, indifferent, under stars that did not move. It was all gone. They had harrowed it, broken it, opened it—the king and the humble sorcerer and the dragon who soared over them, lighting the dead skies with her living fire . . . The wall was down. It had never been. It was a spell, a seeming, a mistake. It was gone.

Were the mountains gone then, too, that other boundary, the Mountains of Pain? They stood far across the desert from the wall, black, small, sharp against the dull stars. The young king had walked with him across the Dry Land to the mountains. It seemed west but it was not westward they walked; there was no direction there. It was forward, onward, the way they had to go. You go where you must go, and so they had come to the dry streambed, the darkest place. And then on even beyond that. He had walked forward, leaving behind him in the waterless ravine, in the rocks he had sealed shut and healed, all his treasure, his gift, his strength. Walked on, lame, always lamer. There was no water, no sound of water ever. They were climbing those cruel slopes. There was a path, a way, though it was all sharp stones, and upward, upward, always steeper. After a while, his legs would not hold him, and he tried to crawl, hands and knees on the stones, he remembered that. After that, the rest was gone. There had been the dragon, old Kalessin, the color of rusted iron, and the heat of the dragon's body, the huge wings lifting and beating down. And fog, and islands beneath them in the fog. But those black mountains were not gone, vanished with the dark land. They were not part of the spell-dream, the afterlife, the mistake. They were there.

Not here, he thought. You can't see them from here, in this house. The window in the alcove looks west, but not to that west. Those mountains are where west is east and there is no sea. There's only land sloping up forever into the long night. But westward, true west, there's only the sea and the sea wind.

It was like a vision, but felt more than seen: he knew the deep earth beneath him, the deep sea before. It was a strange knowledge, but there was joy in knowing it.

Firelight played with shadow up in the rafters. Night was coming on. It would be good to sit at the hearth and watch the fire a while, but he'd have to get up to do that, and he didn't want to get up yet. The pleasant warmth was all around him. He heard Tenar now and then behind him: kitchen noises, chopping, settling a knot into the fire under the kettle. Wood from the old live oak in the pasture that had fallen and he'd split winter before last. Once she hummed some tune under her breath for a minute, once she muttered to her work, encouraging it to do what she wanted, "Come on there now . . . "

The cat sauntered round the foot of the low bed and elevated himself weightlessly onto it. He had been fed. He sat down and washed his face and ears, wetting one paw patiently over and over, and then undertook extensive cleansing of his hind parts, sometimes holding a back paw up with a front paw so that he could clean the claws, or holding down his tail as if expecting it to try to get away. Now and then he looked up for a minute, immobile, with a strange absent gaze, as if listening for instructions. At last he gave a little belch and settled down beside Ged's ankles, arranging himself to sleep. He had sauntered down the path from Re Albi one morning last year, a small gray tom, and moved in. Tenar thought he came from Fan's daughter's house, where they kept two cows and where cats and kittens were always underfoot. She gave him milk, a bit of porridge, scraps of meat when they had it, otherwise he provided for himself; the crew of little brown rats that holed up in the pasture never invaded the house anymore. Sometimes, nights, they heard him caterwauling in the throes of impassioned lust. In the morning he would be flat out on the hearthstone where the warmth still was, and would sleep all day. Tenar called him Baroon—"cat" in Kargish. Sometimes Ged thought of him as Baroon, sometimes in Hardic as Miru, sometimes by his name in the Old Speech. For after all, Ged had not forgotten what he knew. Only it was no good to him, after the time in the dry ravine, where a fool had made a hole in the world, and he had to seal it with the fool's death and his own life. He could still say the cat's true name, but the cat would not wake and look at him. He murmured the name of the cat under his breath. Baroon slept on.

So he had given his life, there in the unreal land. And yet he was here. His life was here, back near its beginning, rooted in this earth. They had left the dark ravine where west is east and there is no sea, going the way they had to go, through black pain and shame. But not on his own legs or by his own strength at last. Carried by his young king, carried by the old dragon. Borne helpless into another life, the other life that had always been there near him, mute, obedient, waiting for him. The shadow, was it, or the reality? The life with no gift, no power, but with Tenar, and with Tehanu. With the beloved woman and the beloved child, the dragon's child, the cripple, daughter of Segoy.

He thought about how it was that when he was not a man of power he had received his inheritance as a man.

His thoughts ran back along a course they had often taken over the years: how strange it was that every wizard was aware of that balance or interchange between the powers, the sexual and the magical, and everyone who dealt with wizardry was aware of it, but it was not spoken of. It was not called an exchange or a bargain. It was not even called a choice. It was called nothing. It was taken for granted.

Village sorcerers and witchwives married and had children—evidence of their inferiority. Sterility was the price a wizard paid, paid willingly, for his greater powers. But the nature of the price, the unnaturalness of it—did that not taint the powers so gained?

Everyone knew that witches dealt with the unclean, the Old Powers of the earth. They made base spells to bring man and woman together, to fulfill lust, to take vengeance, or used their gift on trivial things, healing slight ills, mending, finding. Sorcerers did much the same, but the saying was always *Weak as woman's magic, wicked as woman's magic*. How much of that was truth, how much was fear?

His first master, Ogion, who learned his craft from a wizard who'd learned his from a witch, had taught him none of that rancorous contempt. Yet Ged had learned it from the beginning, and still more deeply on Roke. He'd had to unlearn it, and the unlearning was not easy.

But after all, it was a woman who first taught me, too, he thought, and the thought had a little gleam of revelation in it. Back long ago, in the village, Ten Alders. Over on the other side of the mountain. When I was Duny. I listened to my mother's sister Raki call the goats, and I called them the way she did, with her words, and they all came. And then I couldn't break the spell, but Raki saw I had the gift. Was that when she saw it first? No, she was watching me when I was a tiny child, still in her care. She watched me, and she knew. *Mage knows mage* . . . How silly she'd have thought me, to call her a mage! Ignorant she was, superstitious, half fraud, making her poor living in that poor place on a few scraps of lore, a few words of the true speech, a stew of garbled spells and false knowledge she half knew to be false. She was everything they meant on Roke when they sneered at village witches. But she knew her craft. She knew the gift. She knew the jewel.

He lost the thread of his thoughts in a surge of slow, bodily memories of his childhood in that steep village, the dank bedding, the smell of woodsmoke in the dark house in the bitter winter cold. Winter, when a day he had enough to eat was a wondrous day to think about long after, and half his life was spent in dodging his father's heavy hand in the smithy, at the forge where he had to keep the long bellow pumping and pumping till his back and arms were afire with pain and his arms and face burning with the sparks he could not dodge, and still his father would shout at him, strike him, knock him aside in rage, *Can't you keep the fire steady, you useless fool?*

But he would not weep. He would beat his father. He would bear it and be silent until he could beat him, kill him. When he was big enough, when he was old enough. When he knew enough.

And of course by the time he knew enough he knew what a waste of time all that anger was. That wasn't the door to his freedom. The words were: the words Raki taught him, one at a time, miserly, grudging, doling them out, hard-earned and few and far between. The name of the water that rose up from the earth as a spring when you spoke its name along with one other word. The name of the hawk and the otter and the acorn. The name of the wind.

Oh the joy, the pride of knowing the name of the wind! The pure delight of power, to know he had the power! He had run out, clear over to the High Fall, to be alone there, rejoicing in the wind that blew strong, westward, from far across the Kargish sea, and he knew its name, he commanded the wind . . .

Well, that was gone. Long gone. The names he still had. All the names, all the words he'd learned from Kurremkarmerruk in the Isolate Tower and since then. But if you did not have the gift in you, the words of the Old Speech were no more than any words, Hardic or Kargish, or birdsong, or Baroon's anguished yowlings of desire.

He sat up partway and stretched his arms. "What are you laughing at?" Tenar asked him, passing the bed with an armload of kindling, and he said, a little bewildered, "I don't know. I was thinking of Ten Alders."

She gave him her searching look but smiled and went on to the hearth to feed the fire. He wanted to get up and go sit at the hearth with her, but he would lie here a while longer. He disliked the way his legs would not hold steady when he got up, and how soon he tired and wanted only to lie quiet again, looking up into the firelight and the friendly shadows. He had known this house since he was thirteen, just named. Ogion named him in the springs of the Ar and brought him on around the mountain. They went slowly, welcomed into the poor villages like Ten Alders or sleeping out in the forest, in the silence, in the rain. And they came here. He slept for the first time in the little alcove and saw the stars in the window above him and watched the firelight dancing with the shadows in the rafters. He did not know that Ogion was Elehal then. He had had a lot to learn.

Ogion had the patience to teach him, if only he'd had the patience to be taught . . . Well, never mind. One way or another he'd blundered his way through, from mistake to mistake. Even a very great mistake, the wrong, the evil done with the spell they taught him on Roke. But before he knew the spell, he'd found the words, in Ogion's book, here, in this house, his home. In his ignorant arrogance he had summoned it, the darkness behind the door, the faceless being that reached out to him, whispered to him. He had brought the evil here, under this roof. As this was his home . . . His thoughts blurred again. He drifted. It was like sailing in *Lookfar*, alone, in cloudy night, in the great darkness on the dark sea. Only the way the wind blew to tell him where he went. He went the wind's way.

"Will you have a bowl of soup?" Tenar asked him, and he roused. But he was still very tired. "Not very hungry," he said.

He didn't think she'd be satisfied by that. And indeed after a while she came back round the half wall that divided the front part of the house, the hearth and the kitchen and the alcove, from this darker back part. It was bedroom and workroom now but once had been the winter byre for the cow or the pig or the goats and the poultry. This was an old house. A few people in Re Albi knew it had once been called the House of the Sorceress, but they did not know why. He knew. He and Tenar had the house from Elehal, who had it from his teacher, Heleth, who had it from his teacher, the witch Ard. It was the kind of house a witch would live in, by itself and apart from the village, not so near anyone had to call her neighbor, but not so far as to be out of reach in need. Ard had put up houses for her beasts nearby and made her bed against that half wall, where the manger had been. And Heleth, and then Elehal, and now Ged and Tenar slept where she had slept.

Most people called it the Old Mage's House. Some of the villagers would tell a stranger, "He that was the Archmage, away off there in Roke, he lives there," when city folk and foreigners from Havnor came seeking him; but they said it distrustfully and with some disapproval. They liked Tenar better than they liked him. Even though she was white skinned and a real foreigner, a Karg, they knew she was their kind, a thrifty housewife, a tough bargainer, nobody's fool, more canny than uncanny.

A girl, white face, dark hair, sudden, startled, stared at him across a cavern of dazzling crystal and water-carved stone, topaz and amethyst, in the trembling radiance of werelight from his staff.

There, even there in their greatest temple, the Old Powers of the earth were feared, wrongly worshipped, offered the cruel deaths and mutilations of slaves, the stunted lives of girls and women imprisoned there. He and Arha had committed no sacrilege. They had released the long hunger and anger of the earth itself to break forth, bring down the domes and caverns, throw open the prison doors.

But her people, who tried to appease the Old Powers, and his people, who held witchery in contempt, made the same mistake, moved by fear, always fear, of what was hidden in the earth, hidden in women's bodies, the knowledge without words that trees and women knew untaught and men were slow to learn. He had only glimpsed it, that great quiet knowledge, the mysteries of the roots of the forest, the roots of the grasses, the silence of stones, the unspeaking communion of the animals. The waters underground, the rising of the springs. All he knew of it he had learned from her, Arha, Tenar, who never spoke of it. From her, from the dragons, from a thistle. A little colorless thistle struggling in the sea wind between stones, on the path over the High Fall . . .

She came round the divider with a bowl, as he knew she would, and sat down on the milking stool beside the bed. "Sit up and have a spoonful or two," she said. "It's the last of Quacker."

"No more ducks," he said. The ducks had been an experiment.

"No," she agreed. "We'll stick to chickens. But it's a good broth."

He sat up and she pushed the pillow behind him and set the bowl on his lap. It smelled good, and yet he did not want it. "Ah, I don't know, I'm just not hungry," he said. They both knew. She did not coax him. After a while he swallowed a few spoonfuls, and then put the spoon into the bowl and laid his head back against the pillow. She took the bowl away. She came back and stooped to brush the hair back from his forehead with her hand. "You're a bit feverish," she said.

"My hands are cold."

She sat down on the stool again and took his hands. Hers were warm and firm. She bowed her head down to their clasped hands and sat that way a long time. He loosened one hand and stroked her hair. A piece of wood in the fire snapped. An owl hunting out in the pastures in the last of the twilight gave its deep, soft double call.

The aching was in his chest again. He thought of it not so much as an ache as an architecture, an arch in there at the top of his lungs, a dark arch a little too large for his ribs to hold. After a while it eased, and then was gone. He breathed easily. He was sleepy. He thought of saying to her, I used to think I'd want to go into the woods, like Elehal, to die, he meant, but there'd be no need to say it. The forest was always where he wanted to be. Where he was whenever he could be. The trees around him, over him. His house. His roof. I thought I'd want to do the same. But I don't. There's nowhere I want to go. I couldn't wait to leave this house when I was a boy, I couldn't wait to see all the isles, all the seas. And then I came back with nothing, with nothing left at all. And it was the same as it had been. It was everything. It's enough.

Had he spoken? He did not know. It was silent in the house, the silence of the great slope of mountainside all round the house and the twilight above the sea. The stars would be coming out. Tenar was no longer beside him. She was in the other room, slight noises told him she was setting things straight, making up the fire.

He drifted, drifted on.

He was in darkness in a maze of vaulted tunnels like the Labyrinth of the Tombs where he had crawled, trapped, blind, craving water. These arched ribs of rock lowered and narrowed as he went on, but he had to go on. Closed in by rock, hands and knees on the black, sharp stones of the mountain way, he struggled to move, to breathe, could not breathe. He could not wake.

It was bright morning. He was in *Lookfar*. A bit cramped and stiff and cold as always when he woke from the broken sleep and half sleep and quick, quick-vanishing dreams of nights in the boat alone. Last night there had been no need to summon the magewind; the world's wind was easy and steady from the east. He had merely whispered to his boat, "Go on as you go, *Lookfar*," and stretched out with his head against the sternpost and gazed up at the stars or the sail against the stars until his eyes closed. All that fiery deep-strewn host was gone now but the one great eastern star, already melting like a water drop in the rising day. The wind was keen and chill. He sat up. His head spun a little when he looked back at the eastern sky and then forward again at the blue shadow of the earth sinking into the ocean. He saw the first daylight strike fire from the tops of the waves.

Before bright Éa was, before Segoy Bade the islands be,
The wind of morning on the sea . . .

He did not sing the song aloud, it sang itself to him. Then came a queer thrumming in his ears. He turned his head, seeking the sound, and again the dizziness passed through it. He stood up, holding to the mast as the boat leapt on the lively sea, and scanned the ocean to the western horizon, and saw the dragon come.

O my joy! be free.

Fierce, with the forge smell of hot iron, the smoke plume trailing on the wind of its flight, the mailed head and flanks bright in the new light, the vast beat of the wings, it came at him like a hawk at a field mouse, swift, unappeasable. It swept down on the little boat that leapt and rocked wildly under the sweep of the wing, and as it passed, in its hissing, ringing voice, in the true speech, it cried to him, *There is nothing to fear.*

He looked straight into the long golden eye and laughed. He called back to the dragon as it flew on to the east, "Oh, but there is, there is!" And indeed there was. The black mountains were there. But he had no fear in this bright moment, welcoming what would come, impatient to meet it. He spoke the joyous wind into the sail. Foam whitened along *Lookfar*'s sides as the boat ran west, far out past all the islands. He would go on, this time, until he sailed into the other wind. If there were other shores he would come to them. Or if sea and shore were all the same at last, then the dragon spoke the truth, and there was nothing to fear.

ABOUT THE AUTHORS

A former academic and adjunct, **Alix E. Harrow** is now a full-time writer living in Kentucky with her husband and their semi-feral children. Her short fiction has been nominated for the Nebula and Hugo awards, and her first novel—*The Ten Thousand Doors of January*—is forthcoming from Orbit Books. Find her at @AlixEHarrow on Twitter.

Kelly Robson is an award-winning short fiction writer. In 2018, her story "A Human Stain" won the Nebula Award for Best Novelette, and in 2016, her novella "Waters of Versailles" won the Prix Aurora Award. She has also been a finalist for the Hugo, Nebula, World Fantasy, Theodore Sturgeon, John W. Campbell, and Sunburst awards. In 2018, her time travel adventure *Gods, Monsters and the Lucky Peach* debuted to high critical praise. After twenty-two years in Vancouver, she and her wife, fellow SF writer A.M. Dellamonica, now live in downtown Toronto.

Dale Bailey is the author of eight books, including *In the Night Wood, The End of the End of Everything,* and *The Subterranean Season.* His short fiction has won the Shirley Jackson Award and the International Horror Guild Award, and has been nominated for the Nebula and Bram Stoker awards. He lives in North Carolina with his family.

Beth Goder works as an archivist, processing the papers of economists, scientists, and other interesting folks. Her fiction has appeared in venues such as *Escape Pod, Fireside*, and an anthology from Flame Tree Press. You can find her online at www.bethgoder.com.

Alex Jeffers has been publishing various flavors of fiction off and on since 1976. His latest book is a massive collection, *Not Here. Not Now* (Lethe Press, 2018). Forthcoming from Less Than Three Press is a sword-&-sorcery romance, *The Reach of Their Blades*, under the byline Jack Lusignan. He lives in Oregon with a cantankerous, elderly cat and performs tricks for generous supporters at patreon.com/Alex_Jeffers.

Rich Larson (patreon.com/richlarson) was born in Galmi, Niger, has studied in Rhode Island and worked in the south of Spain, and now lives in Ottawa, Canada. He is the author of *Annex* and *Cypher*, as well as over a hundred short stories—some of the best of which can be found in his collection *Tomorrow Factory*. His work has been translated into Polish, Czech, French, Italian, Vietnamese and Chinese.

Yoon Ha Lee's debut novel, *Ninefox Gambit*, won the Locus Award for best first novel and was a finalist for the Hugo, Nebula, and Clarke Awards. Its sequels, *Raven Stratagem* and *Revenant Gun*, were both Hugo finalists. Lee's short fiction has appeared in *Tor.com*, *Lightspeed Magazine*, *Clarkesworld Magazine*, *Beneath Ceaseless Skies*, *F&SF*, and other venues. He lives in Louisiana with his family and an extremely lazy cat, and has not yet been eaten by gators.

James Patrick Kelly has won the Hugo, Nebula and Locus awards. His most recent books are a collection, *The Promise of Space* (2018), from Prime Books, and a novel, *Mother Go* (2017), an audiobook original from Audible. In 2016 Centipede Press published a career retrospective *Masters of Science Fiction: James Patrick Kelly*. Coming in January 2020, *King Of The Dogs, Queen Of The Cats*, a novella from Subterranean Press. Jim's fiction has been translated into eighteen languages. With John Kessel, he has co-edited five anthologies. He writes a column on the internet for *Asimov's*. Find him on the web at www.jimkelly.net.

Sarah Pinsker's fiction has won the Nebula & Sturgeon Awards, and she has been a finalist for the Hugo and other awards. Her stories have been translated into Spanish, French, Italian, and Chinese, among other languages. Her first collection, *Sooner or Later Everything Falls Into the Sea* (Small Beer Press), was published in March 2019, and her first novel, *Song For A New Day* (Berkley), in September 2019. She is also a singer/songwriter with three albums and another forthcoming. She lives in Baltimore, Maryland.

Juliette Wade never outgrew of the habit of asking "why" about everything. This path led her to study foreign languages and to complete degrees in both anthropology and linguistics. Combining these with a fascination for worldbuilding and psychology, she creates multifaceted science fiction that holds a mirror to our own society. The author of short fiction in magazines including *Analog*, *Clarkesworld*, and *F&SF*, she lives in the San Francisco Bay Area with her Aussie husband and her two sons, who support and inspire her. Her debut novel, *Mazes of Power*, will come out from DAW in 2020.

S. Woodson lives in Virginia and is a graduate of the Hollins University M.A. in Children's Literature program. She's written a handful of Twine games, but this was her first story in print. You can find her on Twitter @Citrushistrix.

David Gerrold & **Ctein** are the proverbial twin brothers from different mothers. Both are obsessive-compulsive control freaks who fight ferociously with each other about getting the details right. Ctein is the author of *Saturn Run* (with John Sandford) and *Digital Restoration*, the definitive guide to digital restoration of old photos. David Gerrold wrote a script for Star Trek once, and some other stuff too. He is also the author (and the father) of "The Martian Child."

Erin Roberts' short fiction has appeared in publications including *Asimov's*, *Clarkesworld*, *PodCastle*, and *The Dark*. She has an MFA from the Stonecoast program at University of Southern Maine, is a graduate of the Odyssey Writers Workshop and was the winner of the Speculative Literature Foundation's 2017 Diverse Worlds and Diverse Writers awards and a 2019 Maryland Individual Artist Award. To learn more about her work or read her musings on writing and life, follow her on Twitter at @nirele or visit her website at writingwonder.com.

Adam-Troy Castro made his first non-fiction sale to Spy in 1987. His twenty-six books to date include four Spider-Man novels, three novels about his profoundly damaged far-future murder investigator Andrea Cort, and six middle-grade novels about the dimension-spanning adventures of young Gustav Gloom. His many works have won the Philip K. Dick Award and the Seiun (Japan), and have been nominated for eight Nebulas, three Stokers, two Hugos, and, internationally, the Ignotus (Spain), the Grand Prix de l'Imaginaire (France), and the Kurd-Laßwitz Preis (Germany). Adam lives in Florida with his wife Judi and a trio of revolutionary cats.

Octavia Cade is a New Zealand writer. Her short stories have appeared in markets such as *Clarkesworld*, *Strange Horizons*, and *Asimov's*, and there is a poetry collection, *Mary Shelley Makes A Monster*, forthcoming from Aqueduct Press. She attended Clarion West 2016, and will be the 2020 writer-in-residence at Massey University.

Julie Nováková is a Czech author and translator of SF, fantasy and detective stories. She has published short fiction in *Clarkesworld*, *Asimov's*, *Analog* and elsewhere. Her work in Czech includes eight novels, one anthology and over thirty short pieces. She has been translated into Chinese, Romanian, Estonian,

German, Filipino and Portuguese. Julie received the Encouragement Award of the European SF and fantasy society in 2013, the Aeronautilus award for the best Czech short story of 2014 and 2015, and the best novel of 2015. Her translations appeared in *Strange Horizons*, *Tor.com* and *F&SF*. More at www.julienovakova.com, Twitter @Julianne_SF or patreon.com/julienovakova.

Lavie Tidhar is the author of the Jerwood Fiction Uncovered Prize winning and Premio Roma nominee *A Man Lies Dreaming* (2014), the World Fantasy Award winning *Osama* (2011) and of the Campbell Award winning and Locus and Clarke Award nominated *Central Station* (2016). His latest novels are *Unholy Land* (2018) and first children's novel *Candy* (2018). He is the author of many other novels, novellas and short stories.

Cadwell Turnbull is the author of the science fiction novel *The Lesson*. He is a graduate from the North Carolina State University's Creative Writing MFA in Fiction and English MA in Linguistics. He attended Clarion West 2016. Turnbull's short fiction has appeared in *The Verge*, *Lightspeed*, *Nightmare*, and *Asimov's*. His short story "Loneliness is in Your Blood" was selected for *The Best American Science Fiction and Fantasy 2018*. His novelette "Other Worlds and This One" was also selected as notable story for the anthology.

Carolyn Ives Gilman is a Hugo and Nebula Award nominated author of science fiction and fantasy. Her books include *Dark Orbit*, a space exploration adventure; *Isles of the Forsaken* and *Ison of the Isles*, a two-book fantasy about culture clash and revolution; and *Halfway Human*, a novel about gender and oppression. Her short fiction has appeared in *Lightspeed*, *Clarkesworld*, *F&SF*, *The Year's Best Science Fiction*, *Interzone*, *Realms of Fantasy*, and others. Her work has been translated into a dozen languages. Gilman lives in Washington, D.C., and works as a freelance writer and museum consultant.

Rick Wilber has published several novels and collections and more than fifty short stories in the usual markets. His novel, *Alien Morning* (Tor, 2016), was a finalist for the John W. Campbell Award for Best Science Fiction Novel of 2016. The sequel, *Alien Day: Notes from Holmanville*, will be out in 2020. He is a visiting assistant professor in the low-residency MFA genre-fiction program at Western Colorado University and is administrator of the Dell Magazines Award for Undergraduate Excellence in Science Fiction and Fantasy Writing. His remarkable Down syndrome son has heavily influenced the story in this collection and many others.

Kathleen Jennings is a Ditmar Award winning writer and World Fantasy and Hugo nominated illustrator in Brisbane, Australia. She has recently completed a Master of Philosophy in Creative Writing (Australian Gothic Literature) at the University of Queensland. Her short stories have appeared on *Tor.com*, in *Lady Churchill's Rosebud Wristlet*, in anthologies from Candlewick, Ticonderoga and Fablecroft Publishing, and elsewhere, and her novella *Flyaway* has been acquired by Tor.com, to be published in 2020. She can be found online at tanaudel.wordpress.com.

Alec Nevala-Lee is a Hugo Award finalist for the group biography *Astounding: John W. Campbell, Isaac Asimov, Robert A. Heinlein, L. Ron Hubbard, and the Golden Age of Science Fiction* (Dey Street Books / HarperCollins), which was named one of the best books of 2018 by The Economist. He is the author of three suspense novels published by Penguin, and his stories have appeared in *Analog*, *Lightspeed*, and two editions of *The Year's Best Science Fiction*. His nonfiction has been featured in the New York Times. He is currently at work on a biography of the architectural designer Buckminster Fuller.

P H Lee's fiction has appeared in *Uncanny Magazine* and *Worlds Without Master*. In addition to their writing, P H Lee has worked as a game developer, tutor, graphic designer, and administrative assistant. Their hobbies include translating the Chinese classics and reading Wikipedia. They live together with several other people, far from the bells of the city.

Justina Robson (www.justinarobson.co.uk) was born in Yorkshire, England, in 1968. She sold her first novel in 1999, which also won the 2000 amazon.co.uk Writers' Bursary Award. Her eleven books have been variously shortlisted for most of the major genre awards, including her latest novel *Glorious Angels*. A collection of her short fiction, *Heliotrope*, was published in 2012. Her novels and stories range widely over SF and fantasy, often in combination and often featuring AIs and machines who aren't exactly what they seem. She is also the proud author of *The Covenant of Primus* (2013)—the Hasbro-authorised history and 'bible' of The Transformers. She lives in t'North of England with her partner, three children, a cat and a dog.

New Zealand born, Australian resident **Juliet Marillier** is the author of twenty-one novels, including the Sevenwaters and Blackthorn & Grim series, plus assorted short fiction. Juliet is a member of OBOD (the Order of Bards, Ovates and Druids.) Her lifelong love of mythology and folklore is a major influence on her writing. Juliet's new novel, *The Harp of Kings*, first book in the Warrior Bards series, comes out in September 2019. When not writing, Juliet tends to a small crew of rescue dogs. More at www.julietmarillier.com

Jim Sallis has published seventeen novels, multiple collections of stories, poems and essays, three books of musicology, a biography of Chester Himes, and a translation of Raymond Queneau's novel Saint Glinglin. "As a child" he helped edit *New Worlds,* and for many years has contributed a books column to *F&SF.* Shorter work appears regularly in literary journals, *Asimov's*, *F&SF*, *Interzone*, and many others. Jim has received a lifetime achievement award from Bouchercon, the Hammett Award for literary excellence in crime writing, and the Grand Prix de Littérature policière.

Ursula K. Le Guin (1929-2018) was a celebrated and beloved author of twenty-one novels, eleven volumes of short stories, four collections of essays, twelve children's books, six volumes of poetry and four of translation. The breadth and imagination of her work earned her six Nebulas, seven Hugos, and SFWA's Grand Master, along with the PEN/Malamud and many other awards. In 2014 she was awarded the National Book Foundation Medal for Distinguished Contribution to American Letters, and in 2016 joined the short list of authors to be published in their lifetimes by the Library of America.

RECOMMENDED READING

G. V. Anderson, "Down Where Sound Goes Blunt", (*F&SF*, 3-4/18)
Madeline Ashby, "Work Shadow/Shadow Work", (**Robots vs Fairies**)
Bo Balder, "A Cigarette Burn in Your Memory", (*Clarkesworld*, 1/18)
L. X. Beckett, "Freezing Rain, a Chance of Falling", (*F&SF*, 7-8/18)
Gregory Benford, "A Waltz in Eternity", (*Galaxy's Edge*, 11/18)
Simon Bestwich, "Breakwater", (*Tor.com*, 2/28/19)
Aliette de Bodard, **The Tea Master and the Detective** (Subterranean Press)
Gregory Norman Bossert, "The Empyrean Light", (*Conjunctions*, Fall/18)
Joseph Bruchac, "The Next to Last of the Mohegans", (*F&SF*, 3-4/18)
Bryan Camp, "The Independence Path", (*Lightspeed*, 3/18)
Siobhan Carroll, "The War of Light and Shadow in Five Dishes",
(*Beneath Ceaseless Skies*, 3/15/18)
Michael Cassutt, "Unter", (*Asimov's*, 7-8/18)
Adam-Troy Castro, "The Unnecessary Parts of the Story", (*Analog*, 9-10/18)
P. Djeli Clark, "The Secret Lives of the Nine Negro Teeth of
George Washington", *Fireside Quarterly*, 2/18)
P. Djeli Clark, **The Black God's Drums**, (Tor.com Publishing)
Pip Coen, "Inquisitive", (*F&SF*, 5-6/18)
F. Brett Cox, "The End of All Our Exploring",
(**The End of All Our Exploring**)
Tina Connolly, "The Last Banquet of Temporal Confections",
(*Tor.com*, 7/11/18)
C.S.E. Cooney, "As for Peace, Call it Murder", (**Sword and Sonnet**)
John Crowley, "Flint and Mirror", (**The Book of Magic**)
Leah Cypess, "Attachment Unavailable", (*Asimov's*, 7-8/18)
Andy Duncan, "Joe Diabo's Farewell", (**An Agent of Utopia**)
Andy Duncan, "An Agent of Utopia", (**An Agent of Utopia**)
Andy Duncan, "New Frontiers of the Mind", (*Analog*, 7-8/18)
Greg Egan, "3-adica", (*Asimov's*, 9-10/18)
Susan Emshwiller, "Suicide Watch", (*F&SF*, 9-10/18)
AJ Fitzwater, "Through the Eye of the Needle", (*Giganotosaurus*, 2/18)

Gwynne Garfinkle, "The Paper Doll Golems", (**People Change**)
Carolyn Ives Gilman, "We Will Be All Right", (*Lightspeed*, 5/18)
Beth Goder, "How to Identify an Alien Shark", (*Fireside Quarterly*, 7/18)
Theodora Goss, "Queen Lily", (*Lightspeed*, 11/18)
Daryl Gregory, "Nine Last Days on Planet Earth", (*Tor.com*, 9/19/18)
Sally Gwylan, "Fleeing Oslyge", (*Clarkesworld*, 5/18)
Kate Heartfield, **Alice Payne Arrives** (Tor.com Publishing)
Azuma Hiroki, "A Fish in Chryse", (**Speculative Japan 4**)
Kameron Hurley, "Sister Solveig and Mr. Denial", (*Amazing*, Fall/18)
Ruth Joffre, "Nitrate Nocturnes", (*Lightspeed*, 4/18)
Bill Johnson, "Go Random My Love", (*Analog*, 9-10/18)
Clifford V. Johnson, "Resolution", (**Twelve Tomorrows**)
Rahul Kanakia, "The Coward's Path", (*Lightspeed*, 2/18)
Rahul Kanakia, "Weft", (*Beneath Ceaseless Skies*, 4/12/18)
T. Kingfisher, "The Rose MacGregor Drinking and Admiration Society", (*Uncanny*, 11-12/18)
Naomi Kritzer, "The Thing About Ghost Stories", (*Uncanny*, 11-12/18)
Rich Larson, "Meat and Salt and Sparks", (*Tor.com*, 6/6/18)
J. M. Ledgard, "Vespers", (**Twelve Tomorrows**)
Yoon Ha Lee, "The Starship and the Temple Cat", (*Beneath Ceaseless Skies*, 2/1/18)
Tonya Liburd, "Superfreak", (**Shades Within Us**)
Jane Lindskold, "A Green Moon Problem", (*Lightspeed*, 5/18)
Marissa Lingen, "Left to Take the Lead", (*Analog*, 7-8/18)
Arkady Martine, "*The Hydraulic Emperor*", (*Uncanny*, 1-2/18)
Ian McDonald, **Time Was**, (Tor.com Publishing)
Sandra McDonald and Stephen B. Covey, "Time Enough to Say Goodbye", (*Asimov's*, 5-6/18)
Sandra McDonald, "Sexy Robot Heroes", (**Mothers of Invention**)
Seanan McGuire, **Beneath the Sugar Sky**, (Tor.com Publishing)
Sean McMullen, "Extreme", (*F&SF*, 11-12/18)
Will McIntosh, "What is Eve?", (*Lightspeed*, 4/18)
Christopher McKitterick, "Ashes of Exploding Suns, Monuments to Dust", (*Analog*, 11-12/18)
Maria Romasco Moore, "Dying Light", (*LCRW*, Spring/18)
Heather Morris, "A Slip in the Slice", (*Kaleidotrope*, Winter/18)
Samantha Murray, "Singles' Day", (*Interzone*, 9-10/18)
Ray Nayler, "Incident at San Juan Bautista", (*Asimov's*, 11-12/18)
Mari Ness, "The Ceremony", (*Fireside Quarterly*, 7/18)
Annalee Newitz, "The Blue Fairy's Manifesto", (**Robots vs Fairies**)
Garth Nix, "The Staff in the Stone", (**The Book of Magic**)

Julie Novakova, "Reset in Peace", (*Amazing*, Winter/18)
Sandra M. Odell, "The Home for Broken", (**Godfall**)
Paul Park "Creative Nonfiction", (*Asimov's*, 5-6/18)
K. J. Parker, "The Thought That Counts", (*Beneath Ceaseless Skies*, 4/26/18)
Josh Pearce, "Sensorium", (*Bourbon Penn*, 3/18)
Josh Pearce, "Such Were the Faces of the Living Creatures",
(*Beneath Ceaseless Skies*, 2/15/18)
Sarah Pinsker, "Do As I Do, Sing As I Sing", (*Beneath Ceaseless Skies*, 3/1/18)
Hannu Rajaniemi, "A Portrait of Salai", (**Infinity's End**)
Robert Reed, "Love Songs for the Very Awful", (*Asimov's*, 3-4/18)
Robert Reed, "Obliteration", (*Clarkesworld*, 2/18)
Justina Robson, "S'elfie", (**Mothers of Invention**)
Kelly Robson, **Gods, Monsters, and the Lucky Peach**, (Tor.com Publishing)
Margaret Ronald, "Silence in Blue Glass", (*Beneath Ceaseless Skies*, 4/26/18)
Jess Row, "Radical Sufficiency", (*Granta*, Autumn/18)
Ryan Row, "Superbright", (*Interzone*, 7-8/18)
Joanna Ruocco, "Stone Paper Stone", (*LCRW*, 7/18)
Karen Russell, "Orange World", (*The New Yorker*, 6/4-11/18)
Geoff Ryman, "This Constant Narrowing", (*F&SF*, 11-12/18)
Karl Schroeder, **The Million** (Tor.com Publishing)
Jack Skillingstead, "Straconia", (*Asimov's*, 7-8/18)
Amanda Sun, "The Travellers", (**Shades Within Us**)
Lavie Tidhar, "Yiwu", (*Tor.com*, 5/18)
Brian Trent, "An Incident on Ishtar", (*Analog*, 3-4/18)
Brian Trent, "Crash-Site", (*F&SF*, 5-6/18)
Brian Trent, "The Memorybox Vultures", (*F&SF*, 9-10/18)
Carrie Vaughn, "The Huntsman and the Beast", (*Asimov's*, 9-10/18)
Cynthia Ward, **The Adventure of the Dux Bellorum**, (Aqueduct Press)
Peter Watts, "Kindred", (**Infinity's End**)
Peter Watts, **The Freeze Frame Revolution**, (Tachyon)
Martha Wells, **Artificial Condition**, (Tor.com Books)
Fran Wilde, "The Synchronist", (**Infinity's End**)
Liz Williams, "Sungrazer", (**The Book of Magic**)
M. C. Williams, "The Ghost of Zefort", (*Bourbon Penn*, 11/18)

PUBLICATION HISTORY

"A Witch's Guide to Escape: A Practical Compendium of Portal Fantasies" by Alix E. Harrow. © by Alix E. Harrow. Originally published in *Apex*, February 2018. Reprinted by permission of the author.

"Intervention" by Kelly Robson. © by Kelly Robson. Originally published in *Infinity's End*, edited by Jonathan Strahan. Reprinted by permission of the author.

"The Donner Party" by Dale Bailey. © by Dale Bailey. Originally published in *F&SF*, January/February 2018. Reprinted by permission of the author.

"How to Identify an Alien Shark" by Beth Goder. © by Beth Goder. Originally published in *Fireside Quarterly*, July 2018. Reprinted by permission of the author.

"The Tale of the Ive-ojan-akhar's Death" by Alex Jeffers. © by Alex Jeffers. Originally published in *Giganotosaurus*, April 2018. Reprinted by permission of the author.

"Carouseling" by Rich Larson. © by Rich Larson. Originally published in *Clarkesworld*, April 2018. Reprinted by permission of the author.

"The Starship and the Temple Cat" by Yoon Ha Lee. © by Yoon Ha Lee. Originally published in *Beneath Ceaseless Skies*, 1 February 2018. Reprinted by permission of the author.

"Grace's Family" by James Patrick Kelly. © by James Patrick Kelly. Originally published in *Tor.com*, May 2018. Reprinted by permission of the author.

"The Court Magician" by Sarah Pinsker. © by Sarah Pinsker. Originally published in *Lightspeed*, January 2018. Reprinted by permission of the author.

"The Persistence of Blood" by Juliette Wade. © by Juliette Wade. Originally published in *Clarkesworld*, March 2018. Reprinted by permission of the author.

"Lime and the One Human" by S. Woodson. © by S. Woodson. Originally published in *LCRW*, July 2018. Reprinted by permission of the author.

"Bubble and Squeak" by David Gerrold & Ctein. © by David Gerrold & Ctein. Originally published in *Asimov's*, May/June 2018. Reprinted by permission of the author.

"Sour Milk Girls" by Erin Roberts. © by Erin Roberts. Originally published in *Clarkesworld*, January 2018. Reprinted by permission of the author.

"The Unnecessary Parts of the Story" by Adam-Troy Castro. © by Adam-Troy Castro. Originally published in *Analog*, September/October 2018. Reprinted by permission of the author.

"The Temporary Suicides of Goldfish" by Octavia Cade. © by Octavia Cade. Originally published in *Kaleidotrope*, Winter 2018. Reprinted by permission of the author.

"The Gift" by Julia Nováková. © by Julia Nováková. Originally published in *Asimov's*, November/December 2018. Reprinted by permission of the author.

"The Buried Giant" by Lavie Tidhar. © by Lavie Tidhar. Originally published in *Robots vs Fairies*, edited by Dominik Parisien and Navah Wolfe. Reprinted by permission of the author.

"Jump" by Cadwell Turnbull. © by Cadwell Turnbull. Originally published in *Lightspeed*, October 2018. Reprinted by permission of the author.

"Umbernight" by Carolyn Ives Gilman. © by Carolyn Ives Gilman. Originally published in *Clarkesworld*, February 2018. Reprinted by permission of the author.

"Today is Today" by Rick Wilber. © by Rick Wilber. Originally published in *Stonecoast Review*, Summer 2018. Reprinted by permission of the author.

"The Heart of Owl Abbas" by Kathleen Jennings. © by Kathleen Jennings. Originally published in *Tor.com*, 11 April 2018. Reprinted by permission of the author.

"The Spires" by Alec Nevala-Lee. © by Alec Nevala-Lee. Originally published in *Analog*, March/April 2018. Reprinted by permission of the author.

"The House by the Sea" by P H Lee. © by P H Lee. Originally published in *Uncanny*, September/October 2018. Reprinted by permission of the author.

"Foxy and Tiggs" by Justina Robson. © by Justina Robson. Originally published in *Infinity's End*, edited by Jonathan Strahan. Reprinted by permission of the author.

"Beautiful" by Juliet Marillier. © by Juliet Marillier. Originally published in *Aurum*, edited by Russell B. Farr. Reprinted by permission of the author.

"Dayenu" by James Sallis. © by James Sallis. Originally published in *LCRW*, Spring 2018. Reprinted by permission of the author.

"Firelight" by Ursula K. Le Guin. © by Ursula K. Le Guin. Originally published in *Paris Review*, Summer 2018. Reprinted by permission of Curtis Brown, Ltd.

ABOUT THE EDITOR

Rich Horton is an associate technical fellow in software for a major aerospace corporation and the reprint editor for the Hugo Award-winning semiprozine *Lightspeed*. He is also a columnist for *Locus* and for *Black Gate*. He edits a series of best of the year anthologies for Prime Books, and also for Prime Books he has co-edited *Robots: The Recent A.I.* and *War & Space: Recent Combat*.